PENGUIN BOOKS
AMERICAN LAKE ☆

Peter Hayes is a consultant to many international organizations on security, energy and developmental affairs in the Asia-Pacific region.

Lyuba Zarsky edited *Economic Report of the People* and has written articles on international economic and strategic affairs.

Walden Bello, author of *Development Debacle – The World Bank in the Philippines*, has been widely published in *The Nation*, *Le Monde Diplomatique* and *World Policy Journal*.

All are research principals for Nautilus Pacific Research, a public-interest organization which focuses on strategic, political and nuclear issues in Asia and the Pacific.

American Lake is the first title in The Penguin Asia–Pacific Series, published under the general editorship of Alfred W. McCoy.

"Tomcats" fly over USS *Nimitz* in the Indian Ocean, May 1980 (U.S. Navy)

Peter Hayes
Lyuba Zarsky Walden Bello

AMERICAN LAKE ☆

Nuclear Peril in the Pacific

PENGUIN BOOKS ☆

Penguin Books Ltd, Harmondsworth, Middlesex, England
Viking Penguin Inc., 40 West 23rd Street, New York, New York 10010, U.S.A.
Penguin Books Australia Ltd, Ringwood, Victoria, Australia
Penguin Books Canada Limited, 2801 John Street, Markham, Ontario, Canada L3R 1B4
Penguin Books (N.Z.) Ltd, 182–190 Wairau Road, Auckland 10, New Zealand

First published by Penguin Books, Australia, 1986
Published in Penguin Books in Great Britain 1987

Printed and bound in Great Britain by
Cox & Wyman Ltd, Reading
Typeset in Baskerville and Avant-Garde

CONTENTS

AMERICAN LAKE ☆

A fortified position on Quemoy Island.
In the distance is the China mainland. 1955
(Pentagon Archives)

PREFACE

There are some roads not to follow; some troops not to strike; some cities not to assault; and some ground which should not be contested.

– Sun Tzu, *The Art of War*, 400 BC

The superpowers are on the road toward nuclear war. While everyone's future is at stake, few people know the full extent of the nuclear peril. Even fewer have any say in military strategy. In the nuclear era, the art of war must become the subject of urgent public enquiry, education and discussion.

This book tells the story of American and Soviet plans for nuclear war in the Pacific. It reveals that the superpowers are locked in a nuclear arms race in the region – a race which could trigger a global nuclear war. Indeed, recent changes in superpower military strategy and force deployments have made it as likely that World War III could break out in the Pacific as in Europe or the Middle East.

Written for the novice, this is a big book – because it has to be. The key arguments, however, are summarized in the Introduction and the more technical material has been relegated to appendices.

The United States was the first to use and deploy nuclear weapons in the Pacific. Part I, "Manifest Destiny," describes U.S. nuclear strategy in the Pacific from the administration of Harry Truman in the late 1940s to that of Ronald Reagan in the 1980s. We demonstrate that nuclear weapons were rapidly integrated into the new "forward-based" U.S.

military strategy in the Pacific after World War II, in part to compensate for overextended conventional forces (Chapters 2, 3).

Part I also discloses that the United States came perilously close – much closer than is commonly known – to launching nuclear attacks on Korea and China in the 1950s (Chapters 3, 4, 5). After a short period of American military withdrawal from the region following defeat in Vietnam (Chapter 6), the Pentagon reasserted and upgraded the strategic role of the Pacific (Chapter 7). Centered primarily on the Navy, the renewed U.S. regional build-up relies heavily on nuclear weapons. In the 1980s as in the 1950s, nuclear war in the Pacific has again become "thinkable" – at least in the minds of American nuclear warplanners (Chapter 8).

The second part of the book surveys American and Soviet forces, nuclear and "conventional", in the Pacific. While nuclear and non-nuclear forces can be distinguished for the sake of analysis, they are deeply integrated at the level of hardware, deployment and strategy. This "deadly connection" must be understood to comprehend the nuclear peril in the Pacific (Chapter 9).

American nuclear-capable naval, air, and land forces span the vast Pacific Command from Hawaii to the African seaboard (Chapter 10). These forces are supported by an "invisible arsenal" of communication and intelligence facilities (Chapter 11).

Despite the recent build-up, U.S. forces remain overextended in the volatile Asian region – their potential interventionary tasks far exceeding their capabilities. As a result, the U.S. military leans more and more heavily on nuclear weapons to project power in the region in order to contain social revolution and to intimidate the Soviet Union (Chapter 12). The MX, Trident and anti-ballistic missile tests over the ever-expanding Pacific Missile Range (Chapter 13) and the dangerous new Tomahawk cruise missile are central components of American striving for nuclear superiority (Chapter 14).

The exercise of American power in the Pacific rests largely on the support of regional allies. Allies not only host forward-deployed American forces; they also provide political legitimacy for the U.S. military role in the region. Pacific Command sponsors dozens of joint military exercises with Pacific allies and relies heavily on allied airfields and ports for transiting warplanes and warships (Chapter 15).

The nuclear peril in the Pacific cannot be understood by ignoring the Soviet Union. Soviet non-nuclear forces in the Pacific cannot match those of the U.S. (Chapter 16). But the Soviet Union compensates for its relative political, economic and military weakness by deploying a huge nuclear arsenal in its Far East. The core of this force is the expanding force of Asian-based SS-20 missiles (Chapter 17). When threatened, the Soviets point to this sledgehammer and emphasize that they will use nuclear weapons to respond to any American attack on their homeland.

Lodged between these nuclear giants, the Pacific is trapped in a "state of terror". It would certainly be crushed in any nuclear war between the superpowers (Chapter 18). Under what conditions might American and Soviet fingers pull their nuclear hair-triggers in the Pacific and ignite a global nuclear war?

We present such a scenario in Chapter 19, centered on the tense Korean peninsula. Although it is fictional, the scenario combines actual events with current doctrines and deployments, weaving together information presented in preceding chapters. Like good science fiction, it carries current trends in the Pacific to their logical conclusion – from the preparation for to the actuality of nuclear war.

The logic of the day, however, is not irreversible. Nuclear war in the Pacific can be averted. In Part III, "Charting a New Pacific", we argue that the most promising path to peace is to physically disengage U.S. and Soviet nuclear forces from the region. This approach grows out of initiatives already taken in New Zealand and other nations who have closed their lands and waters to nuclear forces. Most urgent in Korea, such nuclear-free zones could eventually encompass the entire Pacific.

We have taken great care throughout the book to document our arguments. Many of our sources were provided by various offices and branches of the U.S. military. An enormous amount of information is available in the public domain to those willing to dig for it.

In its raw form, such information is often incomprehensible to the uninitiated. Indeed, this book is in large part a translation of military jargon into plain English. Take, for example, a recently released document which states that Pacific Command's Nuclear Operations and Safety Division:*

---

* This and subsequent quotations are from Commander-in-Chief Pacific, *Organization and Functions Manual, FY 1984*, CINCPAC instruction 5400.6K, December 5, 1985, p. 75 and *passim*; released under the Freedom of Information Act to Peter Wills.

Develops J3 inputs for updating nuclear annexes of USCINCPAC OPLANS and CONPLANS; reviews and prepares comments and component and subordinate unified command nuclear annexes and strike plans.

This terse sentence reveals that Pacific Command is planning and preparing to fight a nuclear war in the Pacific.

We could not have written this book without the uniquely democratic U.S. Freedom of Information Act, which allowed us to pry loose many important documents. Even after security deletions, these documents provided crucial insights into American nuclear warplanning in the Pacific. As the book went to press, for example, we discovered that Pacific Command maintains an astonishing array of organizations devoted solely to nuclear war activity at its headquarters in Hawaii. Particularly important is the Nuclear Operations Team, which works out of the Nuclear Operations Center.* This Center apparently coordinates all of Pacific Command's nuclear warplanning activities.

The document also revealed that Pacific Command maintains a newly created Cruise Missile Branch, which plans attacks for the newly deployed Tomahawk cruise missiles. The Branch also runs the Nuclear Contingency Planning System, which provides "preplanned and adaptively planned theatre nuclear options."

While such organizations are not new to Pacific Command, the bureaucracy of nuclear warfighting has proliferated since Reagan came to power. One example is the office devoted to nuclear war communications in the Pacific, known as the Strategic Systems Branch. This Branch aims to construct a "survivable" system to enable Pacific Command to communicate reliably "to its nuclear forces during a protracted nuclear conflict".

While such disclosures help to fill in the information gaps, we continue to know little about the inner sanctums of American nuclear warplanners in the Pacific. We know even less about their Soviet (or Chinese) counterparts. Much more research is needed before we will fully understand the nuclear peril in the Pacific.

---

* Known members of the Nuclear Operations Team at Pacific Command are: Nuclear Operations and Safety Division, SSBN (Ballistic Missile Submarines) Operations Branch, Nuclear Safety/Security Branch, Permissive Action Link Management Control Branch, Nuclear Operations Procedures Branch, and the Automatic Data Processing Support Branch.

We regret that the Soviet Union hampers this effort at public education and official accountability by denying access to information on its nuclear and military affairs. The information access policies of U.S. allies in the Pacific are typically not much better than those of the Soviets, with controls ranging from anti-democratic to totalitarian.

Many people helped with the information and analysis contained in *American Lake*. Crucial to Parts I and II were the prior work and generous provision of extensive data from the Stockholm International Peace Research Institute's files on foreign military bases, compiled by Owen Wilkes.

Naka Ishii competently managed the production of the manuscript with cheerful determination. Glenn Ruga artfully produced the maps and graphics. Angela Siscamanis and David Lawrence supplied early research assistance. The Nautilus Board of Directors, Harriet Barlow, David Chatfield, Lenny Siegal, John Steiner, and Isabel Wade, encouraged us to persevere at difficult times.

A project of this type and scale incurs many debts to many people, not all of whom can be named. We would especially like to thank: Gordon Adams, Alan Adler, Glen Alcalay, Bob Aldridge, Jim Albertini, Jim Anthony, Bill Arkin, Tom Athanasiou, Desmond Ball, Neil Barrett, Michael Bedford, Roman Bedor, Ian Bell, Bruce Blair, Elizabeth Bounds, Bob Brower, Jo Camilleri, James Castro, Carl Connetta and South End Press, Wendy Carlin, Peter Chapman, Noam Chomsky, Helen Clark, Bruce Cumings, Christine Dann, David Easter, Maud Easter, Jim Falk, Richard Falk, Tom Fenton, Randall Forsberg, Nelson Foster, Greg Fry, Sandy Galazin, Gary Gamer, Angela Genino, Andrew Glyn, Linda Golley, Stephen Goose, Fay Graef, Eric Guyot, Nicky Hager, Michael Hamel-Green, Pharis Harvey, Robert Hayes, Paul Hutchcroft, Giff Johnson, Aroldo Kaplan, Tetsugi Kawamura, John Kelly, Ingrid Kircher, Michael Klare, Ian Krass, Ed Luidens, Andrew Mack, Arjun Makhijani, Nic McClellan, David Morrison, Frank Muller, Ched Myers, Warren Nelson, Seiko Ohashi, John Pike, Susan Quass, Joel Rocamora, Jeffrey Richelson, Mavis Robertson, Sue Roff, David Rosenberg, Douglas Smith, Bob Steiner, Masafumi Takubo, Richard Tanter, Gordon Thompson, Marian Wilkinson, Peter Wills, Martha Winnaker, John Wiseman, and various Filipino friends who must remain anonymous.

Many civilian and uniformed officials in the various branches of the U.S. military, especially those who staff those in the Freedom of Information and Public Affairs Offices, replied to our enquiries with promptness and courtesy.

Writing this book cost a lot. We are grateful for the financial support of Carol and Ping Ferry; the Fund for Tomorrow; Jay Harris; George Jay; Richard Parker and the Sunflower Fund; J. Steiner; the United Methodist Church; United Methodist Women; the United Presbyterian Church; and other donors who wish to remain anonymous.

American Lake originated with the new Asia-Pacific series of Penguin Books, Australia. We benefited greatly from the labors of Al McCoy, who edited the manuscript for style, made suggestions for changes in structure, and helped refine some of the concepts in the book. Brian Johns and John Curtain also loaned a patient hand at crucial times, ensuring that the book did not run aground.

Finally, this book owes an incalculable debt and is dedicated to the thousands of people on many continents who are working toward a peaceful, nuclear-free and independent Pacific.

U.S. President Ronald Reagan at the DMZ, Korea, 1984
(Pentagon)

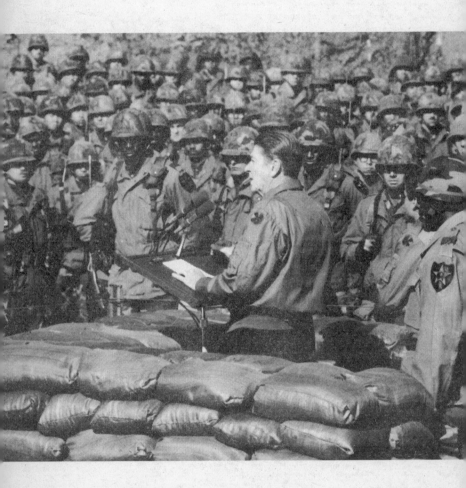

INTRODUCTION ☆
NUCLEAR PERIL IN THE PACIFIC

You cannot help but feel that the great Pacific Basin – with all its nations and all its potential for growth and development – that is the future.

—President Ronald Reagan, August 1984[1]

The United States has made a fundamental decision that we are a Pacific nation, and that we will remain a Pacific power and a force for peace and stability in the region. Our nation's future does indeed lie in the Pacific . . . Let no one misread the past or misjudge our resolve.

—Secretary of Defense Caspar Weinberger, June 1985[2]

For much of the postwar period, the risk of nuclear war in the Pacific has been eclipsed by the nuclear threat in Europe. There the superpowers directly confront each other in a region where both have vital strategic and economic interests. Echoing and reinforcing the general public perception, most analysts and fictional accounts have projected that the spark to ignite nuclear conflagration will be struck in Europe.

But it is just as – perhaps more – likely in coming years that it will be in the Pacific that global nuclear war is triggered. As in Europe, the superpowers confront each other "eyeball-to-eyeball" with nuclear weapons in the Far East. Here, as in Europe, both the United States and the Soviet Union have vital political, economic, and strategic interests. Indeed, it was in the Pacific, not in Europe, that the first atomic bomb was exploded in war.

This book demonstrates that the threat of nuclear war in the Pacific is great and growing. Many sources – political and institutional, as well as technological, doctrinal, and geographical – pose the peril. First and foremost is the build-up of large, increasingly lethal and accurate Soviet and American nuclear forces in a politically volatile area. While Cold War blocs have remained steady in Europe, they have shifted dramatically in the Pacific. Two major land wars and a host of bloody insurrections and heavily armed repressive governments have erupted in less than half a century. Communist, democratic, and nationalist insurgencies, as well as continuing conflicts between nations, will continue to make the region politically turbulent into the foreseeable future, heightening the possibility of superpower interventions. Should their interventions overlap, the superpowers could clash and escalate to nuclear war.

The U.S. faces fewer constraints on the use of its nuclear weapons in the Pacific than in Europe, where it must consult with a host of allies in the multilateral framework of NATO. In contrast, the U.S. is linked to its Pacific allies via a network of bilateral treaties. It need not seek broad consultation on local deployments and strategy in the Pacific. Furthermore, the opinions of European elites are weighted by deep historical and cultural ties to the U.S., ties which Asian elites lack. And at sea or in the U.S.-controlled Demilitarized Zone in Korea, American actions are wholly unilateral.

Soviet posture and policy in the Pacific also enhance the nuclear peril. Ironically, the danger stems from Soviet weakness in conventional force in the region, which prompts it to rely heavily on nuclear weapons. The Soviet Union uses its huge, primarily land-based nuclear arsenal in the Far East to confront the forward-deployed naval, aerial and land-based nuclear and conventional forces of the U.S.

The Pacific, in short, is deeply and dangerously engulfed in the superpower nuclear arms race. Recent shifts in American warfighting strategy and foreign policy have heightened the nuclear danger in the Pacific.

American Lake

The vast Pacific is an American lake. From Northeast Asia to the South Pacific and the Indian Ocean, American military bases and political alliances assert the regional power of the United States. A huge arsenal of integrated U.S. conventional and nuclear forces confronts the Soviet Union on its very doorstep in the Far East.

With the "New Militarists" at the helm of state in the U.S., the superpowers are moving closer to the brink of nuclear war in the Pacific. They are closer now than they have been at any time since the 1950s, when the United States nearly launched a nuclear attack on Korea and China.

Who are the "New Militarists"? They are the Cold Warriors who swept into Washington, D.C., in 1981 on the coattails of Ronald Reagan's presidential election. Seeking nuclear superiority, they have chilled relations with the Soviet Union and upgraded the role of nuclear weapons in American military strategy. Many of them are old Cold Warriors, architects of U.S. foreign policy and strategy in Asia in the 1950s, when the U.S. enjoyed nuclear superiority.

Other Cold Warriors such as John Lehman, Reagan's Secretary of the Navy, also seek to restimulate America's appetite for intervention, which waned after U.S. defeat in Vietnam. "For a long while," explained Lehman in 1982, "Americans have been embarrassed rather than excited by the prospect of exerting power abroad. In such exertion we saw entanglement, not a sense of mission; we discerned risk, not opportunity."[3]

In their belligerent thrust into the Pacific, the New Militarists have deployed new nuclear weapons, such as the Tomahawk sea-launched cruise missiles and long-range, submarine-based Trident I missiles. They have also expanded conventional forces and revised U.S. warfighting strategy and doctrine in ways which enhance the role of the Pacific-based nuclear Navy. In response, the Soviets have further increased their already huge Far Eastern arsenal of medium-range missiles.

Pacific Century

The vigor of the American military push into the Pacific reflects the growing political and economic importance of the Pacific Basin, as well as its strategic role. The world's fastest-growing economies are in East Asia, and by 1983, U.S. trade with Pacific nations outstripped its trade with Europe by a third.[4] Important U.S. corporations such as IBM and Westinghouse find their fastest-growing markets in Asia–Pacific.[5]

American alignment with China as it undertakes "socialist moderniz-ation" not only strengthens the U.S. military against the Soviet Union; it also cements Sino–American political relations, potentially opening the door to an economic bonanza.[6]

Some American strategists, especially those close to the Navy, have declared that the U.S is already entering a "Pacific century."[7] Business and military analysts have even suggested that U.S. forces in Europe be redeployed to the Pacific in light of the growing importance of the region.[8] "When we measure the near-unoptimized markets of Europe and its 250 million persons against the 1.5 to 2 billion people of the Pacific Basin alone," argued a 1981 article in the *Wall Street Journal*, "Europe seems a puny affair."[9]

Aware that where there is new wealth, there is rising power, the U.S. State Department takes the view, as one spokesperson put it, that American "economic success in East Asia is a projection of American influence. Consequently, any sign of weakness or lack of competitive-ness or incompetence has an important political dimension."[10] To ensure that U.S. foreign policy boosts American economic perfor-mance, Reagan has appointed a special roving Ambassador in the Pacific who works closely with the newly formed private U.S. National Committee for Pacific Economic Cooperation.[11]

According to the New Militarists, American diplomacy and econ-omic influence rest on military muscle. "We have *stability*," former Commander-in-Chief Pacific Admiral William Crowe often em-phasized, "and one of the prime reasons that stability – and affluence – have been allowed to develop in an uninterrupted fashion is American military strength."[12]

Indeed, the Pentagon's largest multi-service, unified region of mili-tary operations is in the Pacific. Stretching from the Aleutian Islands off the coast of Alaska to China and the Soviet Far East, and encompassing all of the Pacific and Indian Oceans, Pacific Command covers nearly half the surface of the earth. In 1984, the Commander-in-Chief Pacific (CINCPAC) commanded over 320,000 U.S. Army, Navy, Marine and Air Force troops assigned to the Pacific.[13] Since the Pacific is primarily a maritime theater, CINCPAC is by tradition a Navy admiral and the Pacific a Navy precinct.

While they are unlikely to abandon Europe, the New Militarists view the Pacific as a zone of increasing American strategic interests. Richard

Armitage, U.S. Assistant Secretary of Defense and Reagan's "Pacific Architect" in the Pentagon, explained why in 1985:

The strategic importance of the Pacific to the United States is attested by the fact that five of our eight mutual security treaties are with nations of the region. The world's six largest armed forces are in the area of responsibility of the United States Pacific Command: those of the Soviet Union, China, Vietnam, India, North Korea, and the United States. Five of these six have been at war within the past 11 years and the sixth is North Korea who, some have said, is at war all the time.[14]

In 1985, the New Militarists spent $47 billion to keep American forces in the West Pacific.*[15] While this represented only about 20 per cent of total U.S. spending on General Purpose Forces, it exceeded the GNP of most countries in East Asia.† It was also two hundred times greater than U.S. economic assistance to East Asia in 1983.[17]

The appointment of Admiral William Crowe, CINCPAC from 1983 to 1985, as Chairman of the Joint Chiefs of Staff in June of 1985, made it clear that the new emphasis on the Pacific is no passing fad.‡[18] "My trips to Washington", cabled Admiral Crowe from Hawaii in 1984, "have left me with a strong feeling that there is a growing awareness of this region's importance by our National Command Authority as well as service headquarters."[19]

New Militarism in the Pacific

The central aim of the New Militarists is to reassert nuclear and conventional military superiority over the Soviet Union. They can achieve this, they believe, by demonstrating beyond doubt American capability

---

* Excluding the cost of long-range nuclear forces and communications and intelligence infrastructure.

† The only countries with a GNP larger than U.S. military spending in the region in 1983 or 1984 were China, Japan, south Korea, Indonesia, and Taiwan.[16]

‡ His replacement as CINCPAC was Admiral Ronald Hayes.

and will to fight – and win – a war with the Soviets. To this end, the New Militarists have thrust the Pacific onto the frontlines of nuclear war in two ways.

First, their strategy calls for a *global* war in which the U.S. surrounds the Soviet Union on all sides. In the past, U.S. doctrine rested on the notion that Europe would be the primary war theater. Now, U.S. war-fighting plans are as firmly anchored in the Pacific as in Europe. In wartime, it is just as possible that U.S. forces would swing from Europe to the Pacific as in the opposite direction. Furthermore, if war breaks out in Europe, the Navy may attack the Soviets in the Pacific and *vice versa*. American attacks in the Far East would focus on Vladivostok, home of the Soviet Pacific Fleet.

Second, the New Militarists are equipped and ready to fight a "theater" nuclear war in the Pacific. If war breaks out in volatile Korea, they envisage a nuclear attack limited to the Peninsula. If a naval shoot-out takes place in the North Pacific, they think that they can keep it from spreading from sea to land. This shift toward "limited nuclear war" began well before Reagan's New Militarists took over. But they have refined the doctrine and deployed weapons such as the Toma-hawk cruise missile to make it more feasible.

To bolster the overall U.S. military posture, the New Militarists have reinvigorated American forces in the Pacific. In Korea, they have increased Army personnel, and transferred the very latest in aircraft and artillery to U.S. occupation forces. They have revived the Special Forces in Okinawa, beefed up the Marines throughout the region, and expanded bases and stockpiles of the weaponry necessary for punitive strikes. They also undertook a crash build-up of the island base at Diego Garcia to permit the Rapid Deployment Force to focus its firepower on the Indian Ocean region.

Underlying these doctrines and deployments is a geopolitical ideology deeply engrained in the U.S. Navy. In this view, control of the seas – especially the Pacific and the Indian Oceans – is the key to matching Soviet land-based power on the great Eurasian continent. Seapower and the quest for global maritime supremacy have become the keynote of the Reagan military build-up. As Navy Secretary Lehman declared brashly in 1981, "Nothing below clear superiority will suffice." [20]

In the Pacific, the Navy's strategy rests on "offensive defense", that is, projecting its power to the shores of the Soviet Union. Drawing on refurbished battleships and new aircraft carriers, the Pacific armada of forward-deployed surface warships almost doubled between 1980 and 1983, from twenty-one to forty.*

The biggest increase in American nuclear firepower lies with the Trident I missile aboard Ohio-class submarines. Each submarine can fire twenty-four missiles over 7,700 km to rain 240 warheads within 500 m of targets in the Soviet Union. Trident II, with even greater lethality, will arrive in 1989, threatening Soviet land-based missiles and worsening what Theodore Postol, a former advisor to the U.S. Navy's Nuclear Warfare Division, has called a "pathological instability."[21]

Deployment of the Tomahawk cruise missile is another menacing development in the Pacific. No larger than a sea gull to Soviet radars, the Tomahawk can travel 2,500 km over the sea before exploding a nuclear bomb above Soviet airfields or ports. These targets were formerly inaccessible to American aircraft carriers and warships. By disarming Soviet coastal defenses, the Tomahawk would allow the big U.S. carriers to steam into waters adjacent to the Soviet Far East for subsequent attacks on Soviet land forces or Soviet nuclear missile submarines at sea.

To back up these weapon systems and plans for regional or global war, the U.S. is also "hardening" Pacific-based command, control, and communication posts. If Soviet nuclear weapons rendered these sites inoperative, nuclear commanders and forces would be left deaf, blind and mute. With either or both sides "decapitated", uncontrolled escalation is nearly certain. This gruesome possibility may prompt one side to strike first to "limit" its own damage.

Exercise of Power

Tomahawk and Trident missiles are merely the latest addition to a vast American arsenal comprised of inextricably integrated nuclear and non-nuclear military forces in the Pacific. Nuclear and conventional forces are interlinked not only at the level of technology but of strategy and doctrine as well. "When you go out there and sail your ships and run your tanks and drive your airplanes," emphasized General John Vessey, former Chairman of the Joint Chiefs of Staff, in 1984, "you have

---

* Including nuclear submarines, the total in the West Pacific rose from thirty-seven in 1980 to fifty-two in 1983.

to recognize that there are nuclear weapons out there. There is no such thing as non-nuclear strategy."[22]

Although the U.S. has not launched a nuclear attack since 1945, it has constantly threatened China, north Korea, Vietnam, and the Soviet Union with nuclear weapons, a practice known as "coercive diplomacy." Naval nuclear weapons are particularly well suited to coercive diplomacy because warships are a very flexible way to establish "presence" and convey "interest", all the while signifying the inconceivable power of the Bomb – the teeth, as the Chinese say, behind the lips.

The allies provide crucial stepping stones for the New Militarists to project power to every corner of Pacific Command's vast domain.* The great naval bases in Japan and the Philippines allow the Navy to wrap a chain of steel around the globe from Hawaii to the Indian Ocean. The bases in Korea, Okinawa, and the Japanese mainland place an iron triangle of U.S. military power on the Soviet doorstep in the North Pacific. Australia, New Zealand, and France, America's junior partners in the Pacific, relieve the U.S of security burdens south of the equator. And virtually every U.S. ally hosts an invisible arsenal of communications and intelligence systems supporting the nuclear arsenal.

Lubricated with military aid and training, warship visits, and joint exercises – all of which have expanded since 1979 – the allies have become more important than ever to the New Militarists. With its commitments and priorities expanding around the globe, the U.S. is pressing its allies to "share the burden." Japan especially is the target of intense American pressure to "remilitarize." Military aid to the "front-line states" – south Korea, Thailand, and the Philippines – has been increased and the U.S. is nudging Southeast Asian nations toward establishing their own mutual defense commitment.

Soviet Lake?

According to the New Militarists, the American build-up in the Pacific merely balances a recent Soviet naval thrust into the region. Indeed, the Navy's rhetoric often borders on the hysterical. "The Pacific moat's integrity", railed a 1985 editorial in *Proceedings*, a prestigious U.S. Navy

---

* See W. Bello, P. Hayes, and L. Zarsky, *Bases of Power, The Politics of Nuclear Alliance in the Pacific*, forthcoming.

journal, "is being challenged by the Soviet Union and, today, it is a waterway over which the Soviet Pacific Fleet is probing, prowling, and testing."[23] Admiral Sylvester Foley, Commander-in-Chief of the U.S. Pacific Fleet, warned in 1985 that "it could turn into a Soviet lake out there."[24]

In reality, the Soviet strategic position in Asia is bleak, as even senior American commanders admit. The major portion of the Soviet Union's Far East military effort is directed at China, which shares a 7,500 km border with the Soviets. With the U.S. and Western Europe on one side and the U.S., China, and Japan on the other, the Soviet Union is surrounded by hostile powers.

Conventional Soviet military power in the Pacific, as well as Soviet economic and political strength in Asia, pales beside that of the United States and its Pacific allies. The Soviets do not have a single aircraft carrier to match the six U.S. carrier battle groups in the Pacific. Most of its bombers and fighter planes are capable only of territorial defense. Even its air defenses are suspect after their incompetent chase of a lumbering, intruding Korean Airlines jetliner in 1983.

With few forward bases and little forward capability, Soviet military strategy can be summed up as "defensive defense." It is a strategy aimed primarily at facing and countering the "American threat" in the West Pacific. Even Francis J. West, one of the Navy's top analysts, was forced to conclude that the Soviet Navy could not "perform adequately any but its primary mission of homeland defense."[25]

Nonetheless, the Soviets also stand at the nuclear brink in the Pacific, casting a long shadow. To compensate for its weakness in conventional force, the Soviet Union has built a huge, primarily home-based nuclear arsenal which hangs over the region like a giant sledgehammer. While the New Militarists in the White House plan for "limited war", the Soviets repeatedly point to their sledgehammer and emphasize the certainty that it will crush the region in any nuclear war.

While the New Militarists' global strategy, as Admiral James Watkins put it in 1983, keeps the Soviet Union on edge, it also leaves American forces grossly overextended.[26] Simply put, there is a gap between the ever-expanding strategic goals of the U.S. and the means to carry them out. With military commitments and forces strewn from Hawaii all around the globe to Africa, the U.S. may lean over the nuclear brink at the outset of a crisis, whether in Korea, at sea in the North Pacific, or elsewhere. Nuclear war could erupt in a few minutes on the divided

Korean Peninsula, where two heavily armed and hostile states confront each other – and where the U.S. keeps its finger on a nuclear hair trigger.

The gap between the means and ends is the source of the renewed American strategic bias toward nuclear weapons, a posture which increases the risk of superpower combat and a global nuclear war.[27] As the U.S. ups the ante with its naval nuclear deployments, the Soviet Union calls the bet by piling up its home-based arsenal.

These overlapping and interacting nuclear arsenals are the twin sources of nuclear peril in the Pacific. Either side could push the other over the brink into the nuclear abyss.

Charting a New Pacific

The United States and the Soviet Union do not dance on an empty stage in the Pacific. The peoples and nations of the Pacific are deeply entangled in superpower strategy, hosting forward-deployed military forces and receiving visiting warships.

But nuclear deployments, especially the American forces, have evoked far-reaching national and popular opposition in the midst of the American Lake. "The aggressive promotion of nuclear weapons within alliances", declared Helen Clark, Chair of New Zealand's Foreign Affairs and Defence Select Committee, in 1985, "now stands to destroy the alliances themselves."[28]

While Korea smolders, a full-scale insurrection threatens to evict the U.S. from its bases at Subic Bay and Clark Airfield. Further south, fires are also breaking out in what used to be a quiet strategic backwater of Pacific Command. New Zealand has rejected nuclear alliance with the U.S., breaking up the ANZUS pact, while anti-nuclear microstates such as Vanuatu lead the battle to evict French nuclear colonialism from Kanaky (New Caledonia) and French Polynesia. North in Micronesia, the U.S. has been unable to quell anti-nuclear sentiment in Belau. Even in Hawaii, Pacific Command's bastion, native Hawaiians and disarmament activists have fanned the flames by prompting the declaration of whole islands as nuclear-free zones.

Reducing the nuclear threat in the Pacific will require the separating and disengaging of superpower nuclear forces. Since conventional and nuclear forces are deeply integrated, disengagement means withdrawing from the region all offensive superpower forces. To achieve this, the nations of the Pacific will have to enhance their role in Pacific political and military affairs. Nations which serve as platforms for the nuclear arsenals of either superpower can force the superpowers to disengage by posting "Not Welcome" signs to all nuclear forces and creating nuclear-free and non-intervention zones.

The most promising path to reducing the risk of nuclear war, while preserving regional peace, independence and security, is collective action by Pacific nations, especially American allies. Popular movements and some Pacific states have already taken important steps toward disarmament and demilitarization in the Pacific and Indian Oceans. Some states have already closed their ports to nuclear warships, and established national and local nuclear-free zones. Transnational networks have campaigned against regional deployment of weapons such as the Trident and Tomahawk missiles, and proposed zones of neutrality in Southeast Asia and the Indian Ocean and a nuclear-free zone in the South Pacific.

The creation of a nuclear-free zone is most urgent in Korea and the Northwest Pacific, where American and Soviet nuclear forces directly confront each other. China and states throughout the region, most likely in response to popular agitation, could initiate a political and military settlement on the Korean Peninsula, prompting the U.S. to withdraw its nuclear weapons.

Acting in concert, typically in response to popular pressure, Pacific nations can defuse the nuclear time-bomb in the Pacific. Regional initiatives would also help to create a political climate conducive to pressuring the superpowers to first freeze, and then cut deeply their long-range nuclear stockpiles. As the superpowers disengaged, strong regional concert would allow Pacific nations to curtail the emergence of new nuclear-armed regional powers.

The alternatives are stark. One future is a Pacific of heightened tension and risk, ending with visions of scorched, radiating islands and poisoned waters. Or a new Pacific may be forged as people reach across the ocean, from Manila to Suva, from Sydney to Seoul, to form a regional community founded on cooperation, free of the threat of nuclear war.

PART ONE ☆
MANIFEST DESTINY

Atomic bomb victim, Hiroshima, 1947
(Pentagon Archives)

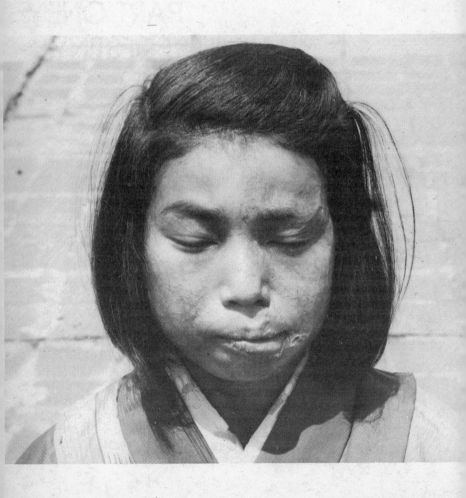

ONE ☆
THE NEW ORDER IN
THE PACIFIC

We are now in a favorable position . . . We should get our bases now and plan not for 10 years but for 50–100 years ahead.

> —General Leslie Groves,
> head of Manhattan Project, 1945[1]

If America wills it so, and constructs several systems of overseas bases, the next war can be broken down into localized conflicts locally dealt with before they spread all over the world . . . Where is the American frontier now? There is no frontier. America fights around the globe.

> —George Weller, 1944[2]

America's decisive victory over Japan in World War II ushered in the modern order in the Pacific. For most of the preceding century, the great European powers – Britain, France, Holland, Portugal, Russia – had battled for colonial dominance in the new frontier. Japan had joined their ranks by the turn of the century, the first time the Europeans faced a "great power" challenge from a non-white nation.

The United States had struggled for a toehold in the region since the mid-nineteenth century, when the Navy forcibly "opened" Japan, Okinawa and Korea to commercial trade. With its fabled market and its huge land-mass and population, China was the plum of the would-be conquerors. By 1898 the U.S. had established beachheads in its colonies in Hawaii, Guam, and the Philippines. But until the 1930s and 1940s, American strength rested primarily in its great economic power, and

15

demands for "open markets" characterized U.S. policy toward the region.[3]

By the 1920s, European control in the Pacific was crumbling in the face of nationalist movements and Japanese militarism. To boost the imperial order, the U.S. undertook a massive program of shipbuilding and naval deployment. Meant to block Japan, the naval race in the Pacific in the late 1930s sparked domestic controversy, since isolationism still dominated American public opinion. As the U.S. was drawn into the Pacific vortex, the Navy wondered if the American people were "ready for the burdens which inevitably would be thrust on them if this nation is to take on the responsibilities for the maintenance of order in the Far East?" Raising a familiar rallying point for America's global "entanglements", the Navy challenged: "Is the United States prepared for a new Manifest Destiny?"[4]

Japan's attack on Pearl Harbor in December 1941 brought forth a resounding "yes" to the Navy's challenge. It was a military disaster: the Japanese bombs missed the new aircraft carriers and struck obsolete battleships. Even worse, the attack shattered the isolationist pressure which had kept the U.S. out of the spiralling war.[5]

By the end of the war, Japan was in ruins and Europe's colonial hold in the Pacific was mortally wounded. Furthermore, the U.S. had maneuvered to deny the Soviet Union, its ally in the Pacific as in Europe, any role in the post-war occupation of Japan. American military power had triumphed and pervaded the region. Via a frenzy of destruction, the age of imperial rivalry was gone forever. When the new order was constructed after the War, the Pacific would be an American lake.

Frenzy of Destruction

World War II was the greatest naval war in history. To dismember the Japanese empire which extended into the Pacific islands and Southeast Asia, the U.S. adopted an island-hopping strategy which relied on fast-moving carriers and amphibious forces.[6] Born of necessity after the battleships were lost at Pearl Harbor, the strategy called for the U.S. to surround Japan by wresting control of its islands in the west, central and southwest Pacific. U.S. victory in the bloody island battles assured Japanese defeat (see Map 1.1).

Obsessed with the Pacific after the stinging defeat at Pearl Harbor,

Map 1.1:
U.S. Island-hopping Strategy

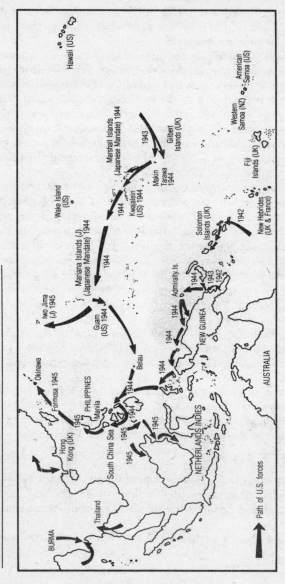

the U.S. Navy viewed it as the primary front of World War II.[7] Indeed, until 1943 more Americans fought in the Pacific than in the Atlantic theater and 53 per cent of Americans polled in that year thought that Japan was their primary enemy.[8]

World War II was stunning not only for its global scale, but also for its unprecedented brutality and indiscriminate terror against civilians involving nuclear, biological, and chemical warfare. Many millions died under Japanese military rule in the vast concentration camp that was China. In an orgy of violence, Japanese forces slaughtered 250,000 civilians after they captured Nanking in 1938. In another apocalypse, over 160,000 Okinawan civilians who served and shielded Japanese troops were killed by U.S. fire or were forced to commit suicide by their Japanese masters.*

American saturation bombing of Japanese cities matched the Japanese military in ferocity. In a massive raid on Tokyo on March 10, 1945, U.S. bombers directed by General Le May ringed the densely populated Shitamachi District with incendiary bombs. More than 80,000 civilians trapped inside the firestorm burned to death that night.[10] Over 140,000 civilians died in America's nuclear attacks at Hiroshima and Nagasaki on August 6th and 8th, 1945, acts of such brutality that the neutral Swiss Legation in Tokyo protested to the U.S. State Department that the bomb "constitutes a new crime against humanity and civilization." [11]

Unlike Claude Eatherly, the pilot of the lead plane in the Hiroshima attack who was later consumed by guilt and remorse,[12] General Le May remained unrepentant. Thirty-three years later, he reminisced:

Killing Japanese didn't bother me very much at that time. It was getting the war over with that bothered me. So I wasn't particularly worried about how many people we killed in getting the job done. I suppose if I had lost the war, I would have been tried as a war criminal. Fortunately we were on the winning side . . .[13]

A frenzy of military base construction, often on the ruins of previous battles, provided the infrastructure for the carnage. The U.S. assault on Guam, for example, reduced the principal cities of Agana, Piti, and

---

* U.S. and Japanese military casualties in the battle for Okinawa were 50,000 and 110,000 respectively.[9]

Sumay to utter ruins. All dock facilities, the entire water system, and the road system had been destroyed by bombing in July 1944.[14] Within a year, 37,000 U.S. construction troops had erected thirty-six docking piers, numerous bomber hangers and airfields, a 103-mile road network, a vast fuel depot, and over 700 buildings for supply depots.[15]

The Navy's advance bases – airfields in the Southwest Pacific, naval staging areas, and the huge repair and logistics bases – were springboards for the attack on Japan. The bomber which dropped the nuclear bomb on Hiroshima, for example, took off from Tinian in the Marianas Islands, which the U.S. had captured from the Japanese in 1944. Such advance bases were backed by hundreds of other Navy bases. Indeed, Pacific bases accounted for over 90 per cent of all Naval base construction expenditures in World War II. Of the Navy's eighteen "major" bases in 1945, fifteen were in the Pacific.[16]

The abrupt victory over Japan left the U.S. occupying bases in every corner of the Pacific. Planning for post-war bases began in 1942, barely a year into the Pacific War, when Franklin D. Roosevelt requested the Joint Chiefs of Staff to prepare a global study of bases for an "International Police Force."[17] The military complied by presenting JCS (Joint Chiefs of Staff) 570/2 to the President in the autumn of 1943. Reluctant to assume the mantle of a dominant world military and economic power in the pre-war world of the 1930s, the U.S. began planning for its new international posture even before the conflict was over.

"The Base Bible"

Prepared by the Joint Strategic Survey Committee, JCS 570/2 divided the world into three areas: a green-bordered area showing bases in Canada, Greenland, Iceland and other Atlantic locations where the U.S. would have "participating or reciprocal military rights"; a blue-ringed area comprising bases in Alaska, the Philippines, Micronesia, Central America, and the Caribbean, where the U.S. would have "exclusive military rights"; and a black-bordered region including bases in the far Southwest Pacific, Indochina, eastern China, Korea, and Japan, where the U.S. would have "participating rights" as one of the "Great Powers enforcing peace."[18]

JCS 570/2 became the "base bible" which guided the services' thinking about post-war deployments. Its adoption marked a definitive break with pre-war isolationism and the acceptance of a global perspective best expressed by General George Marshall, the Army Chief of Staff: "It no longer appears practical to continue what we once conceived as hemispheric defense as a satisfactory basis for our security. We are now concerned with the peace of the entire world. And peace can be maintained only by the strong." [19] Marshall's high-minded argument for a posture of "forward defense" was put in a different light by Secretary of State James Byrnes: "What we must do now is not make the world safe for democracy, but make the world safe for the U.S.A." [20]

Base planning, however, did not stem from military motivation alone. Hand in hand with military requirements in the minds of strategists were the post-war opportunities for U.S. commercial aviation. Post-war basing plans were characterized by the interweaving of military and economic considerations. "The drives for overseas military bases and commercial air facilities reinforced one another," asserts Air Force historian Elliott Converse:

Open Door economic expansion which had always had a global reach was now joined by a search for physical security not bound by geographical limits . . . Transit rights in North Africa, the Middle East, and South Asia would connect the eastern and western borders of the defense system; they would also promote maintenance of airfields that someday might be used against the Soviet Union. The same air facilities might contribute to achieving economic goals . . . Commercial air rights at Cairo, Karachi, Rangoon, and Bangkok were seen as important links in an air transport route between Europe and the Far East . . . The impetus provided by military and civil aviation thus helps to explain America's outward surge after World War II. [21]

Congressional supporters of maritime interests were also enthusiastic about post-war economic prospects in the Pacific:

Trade with China and other parts of the Orient, Australia, New Zealand, the Dutch East Indies, and with many islands of the Pacific will unquestionably develop and expand during the postwar era. These areas not only offer many markets for American products but are substantial producers of raw materials useful to our economy . . . Our merchant marine and commercial firms should be given the opportunity to take over a large portion of that trade formerly handled by the Japanese and their vessels.[22]

One of the most important military offspring of JCS 570/2 was the Navy's "Basic Post War Plan No. 1." Reflecting the re-emergence of the "Asia First" orientation of the admirals, it proposed seventy-five foreign bases, fifty-three in the Pacific and the remainder in the Atlantic. As Converse explains:

Unlike in the Atlantic, where the most important bases would lie close to home, the pattern of Pacific bases showed that the Navy intended to wield a very big stick in the Far East. In addition to the Philippines, the Navy targeted Guam-Saipan (the Marianas), the Bonin-Volcano, and Ryukyu Islands [Okinawa] for regular operating bases – in other words almost half of the most important Pacific bases . . . Furthermore, the Navy planned to acquire base rights at twenty places in the Black Area ["Required by the U.S. as one of the Great Powers enforcing peace . . ."] – about half in the Southwest Pacific with the remainder in the Far East (e.g., parts of the Netherlands' colonial empire; Bangkok, Thailand; Hainan Island; Formosa; Japan proper; Korea; the Kurile Islands and North China).[23]

In justifying the size of the Navy wish-list, Admiral Horne told Secretary of the Navy James Forrestal: "I wish to point out that we do not necessarily need to have naval shore bases at *all* the sites listed . . . However, for international political and negotiating reasons, we would *ostensibly* plan to establish bases at every island and location that has any real value as a base in our defense concept." [24]

The strategy guiding the U.S. command's proposed basing complex would later be known as forward deployment. Defended by an "outer perimeter" of bases designed to reconnoiter enemy actions and intercept attacks, the "primary bases" would be the fulcrum of American response, supported by "connecting secondary bases" serving as "stepping-stones" between the outer-perimeter and primary bases. This network would provide "security in depth, protection to lines of communication and logistic support of operations." [25] The practical effect of this arrangement was "to extend the United States strategic frontier outward to the fringes of Europe, Africa, and Asia." [26]

The Nuclear Imperative

The atomic bomb introduced a new imperative for the acquisition of military bases. As the Joint Strategic Survey Committee (JSSC) of the Joint Chiefs of Staff explained in an October 1945 memorandum:

[T]he importance of adequate bases, particularly in advanced areas, is enhanced by the advent of the new weapons, in that defensively they keep the enemy at a distance, and offensively they project our operations, with new weapons or otherwise, nearer the enemy. The necessity for wide dispersion of naval forces in port as well as at sea, will tend to increase the number and extent of anchorage areas required in our system of bases.[27]

The Committee's report on January 12, 1946, was even more emphatic on the importance of overseas bases "to keep any enemy at a distance":

Since the only known means of defense against the bomb, other than action against its sources, is the interception of its carrier in flight, our national security demands that our defensive frontiers be well advanced in the Atlantic, Pacific, and Arctic regions, and to the southward through a hemispheric defensive structure with our Latin American neighbors, in order to keep any enemy at a distance and to afford every possible opportunity to intercept any hostile move.[28]

Overseas bases, moreover, would draw fire away from the United States. Describing the Navy's thinking on forward bases, *The Bulletin of Atomic Scientists* stated in July 1947:

These bases may themselves be vulnerable to atomic bomb attack, but so long as they are there, they are not likely to be by-passed. In this respect the advanced base may be likened to pawns in front of the king on a chess-board; meager though their power may be individually, so long as they exist and the king stays severely [sic] behind them, he is safe.[29]

At a press conference shortly after the nuclear attack on Nagasaki in August 1945, General Hap Arnold, Chief of the Army Air Corps, explained the value of Pacific bases in post-war nuclear warfare. American super-bombers, he claimed, could soon drop nuclear bombs anywhere on the globe. To illustrate his point, Arnold displayed a map of the world showing five circles each of 8,000 km radius (within the projected range of the new bombers). Except for small parts of the Arctic and Antarctic, the bombers could hit the whole earth. Existing U.S. bases near Manila could support such nuclear operations in China and the West Pacific.[30] The Air Force quickly moved beyond speculation. By early 1947, assembly and loading facilities were in place to support nuclear attack in the Far East.[31]

Nine Points of the Law

By late 1945, the military high command had come to the consensus, reflected in the Joint Chiefs of Staff document 570/40, that bases in the Philippines, Marianas, and the Ryukyus would be the most vital in the Pacific. The Joint Chiefs were not particular about the methods of acquiring the bases. While negotiation with other governments was seen as necessary in areas not traditionally under U.S. influence, military occupation was the final arbiter in the Pacific. By the end of World War II, the U.S. military had occupied or built several thousand bases in the Pacific and as the victor, expected to maintain permanent control over many (see Map 1.2). Having defeated or subordinated its former imperial rivals in the Pacific, the U.S. military was in no mood to hand back occupied real estate.

As a Joint Chiefs of Staff Committee put it in 1944: "In many cases, possession will be nine points of the law and present United States occupancy or control of any required base or facility should not be relinquished so long as negotiations for its future use . . . are pending or in process."[32] Operating under this principle, the Navy urged Washington to annex the Marianas and the rest of the Japanese-mandated islands which had been wrested in its bloody wartime approach to the Japanese mainland. However, the Truman administration, sensitive to charges of being branded colonialist at the very time that it was trying to break up the French and British empires, instructed the military to halt further study of annexation in May 1946 and settled for a United Nations-mandated "trusteeship" over the Marianas, the Carolines, and the Marshalls.[33] To all intents and purposes, this trust was annexation, since the United Nations – then controlled by the United States – pro-

Map 1.2:
Post-war Pacific Bases Proposal, 1945

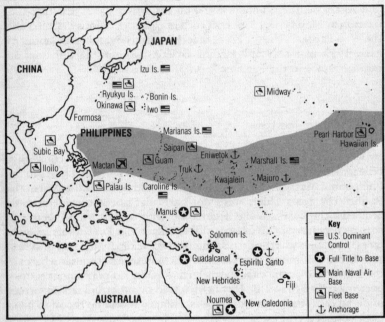

Source: U.S. House of Representatives, Committee on Naval Affairs, Subcommittee on Pacific Bases, *Study of Pacific Bases*, U.S. GPO, Washington, D.C., 1945, p. 102.

vided a mandate which allowed the U.S. unrestricted authority to fortify the "Strategic Trust Territory of the Pacific Islands."

In a speech after his return from the Potsdam Conference in 1945, President Truman made it clear that the mandate system was a cloak for annexation:

Though the United States wants no territory or profit or selfish advantage out of this war, we are going to maintain the military bases necessary for the complete protection of our interests and of world peace. Bases which our military experts deem to be essential for our protection, we will acquire. We will acquire them by arrangements consistent with the United Nations charter.[34]

Although the U.S. had pledged to give the Philippines independence by 1946, U.S. strategists unanimously agreed on the necessity of keeping bases there. The importance of Philippine bases was underlined in June 1944, four months before General MacArthur's liberation of the Philippines, when the U.S. Congress passed a joint resolution "reserving" air and naval bases after independence from the U.S. in July 1946. The base bible (JCS 570/2) described the role of the Philippines in terms which revealed the global security stance of the U.S.:

This boundary [the outermost defense line] treats the Philippines as an area from which our Pacific interests may be defended rather than United States territory against which attacks from any direction (except the northern) can be interdicted.[35]

The U.S. threat to withhold post-war reconstruction aid forced the new Philippine Republic to make major military and economic concessions. Faced with the terrible destruction wrought by the war, the Filipino elite had no choice but to give what the U.S. wanted: a rent-free lease for ninety-nine years to twenty-three bases and installations. The most important of these were Subic Naval Base, which became the forward base of the Seventh Fleet, and Clark Air Base, home of the 13th Air Force.

As for Japan, there was no question of the vanquished resisting the demands of the victors for base rights to Okinawa and other Ryukyu islands, as well as the establishment of strategic bases on Japan itself.

The reconstruction of Japan included the establishment of hundreds of U.S. bases and facilities, some of which were expected to have a long-term presence. A precondition for later normalization of diplomatic relations with Japan was the "presumption that the defeated enemy would 'invite' the United States to station troops on Japanese territory after restoration of sovereignty and that those troops, supported by air and naval power, would have all the facilities and rights of movement they might require to carry out their defensive tasks." [36] The American military presence, including the massive naval complexes at Sasebo and Yokosuka, was legitimized by the U.S.-Japan Peace Treaty of 1951, which also provided for continued U.S. administration of the Bonin (Volcano) Islands and Ryukyu Islands (Okinawa).

From Alliance to Confrontation

As the U.S. moved to impose the post-war *Pax Americana* on the Asia–Pacific region, it found much of the region in a state of civil war and was drawn into intervention on the side of embattled, conservative elites. After using communist Huk guerillas to liberate Manila in 1945, the U.S. Army sided with Philippine conservatives and supported the repression of the armed peasantry.

The Philippine experience was repeated in China. U.S. troops were sent to North China, ostensibly to disarm the Japanese occupation forces, but actually to assist the Nationalist troops of Chiang Kai-shek against the Communist forces led by Mao Tse-tung. The scope of this intervention was revealed by General Albert Wedemeyer, Commander of the China Theater:

Whole armies, spearheading the reoccupation, were airlifted in American planes to Shanghai, Nanking, and Peiping. From the Pacific came part of the U.S. Seventh Fleet, which later assisted in carrying Chinese troops into northern China, and 53,000 marines who occupied the Peiping–Tientsin area. The air redeployment of the Chinese occupational forces, which was undertaken by the 10th and 14th Air Forces, was unquestionably the largest troop movement by air in the world's history. [37]

When American troops moved in to accept the surrender of Japanese troops in Korea south of the 38th Parallel, they entered a fluid political situation. At the initiative of the leftist Committee for the Preparation of Korean Independence (CPKI), a Korean People's Republic (KPR) had been founded. The Republic, notes Asia scholar Bruce Cumings,

did far better than any other Koreans in the south in laying the groundwork for sovereignty in terms of organization, mobilization, and the delineation of national goals . . . All this proceeded in spite of the opposition of Japanese, and subsequently American, central authorities.[38]

Aware of its revolutionary identity, the Americans dismantled the new republic in the South, harassed the left, and erected a governing bureaucracy around conservative politician Syngman Rhee.

American backing of right-wing forces reflected a transition in foreign policy from the "internationalism" of President Roosevelt to the hardline "containment" of Harry Truman. For Roosevelt, revolutionary anti-colonial movements were not anathema, but they had to be channelled in "responsible" directions through "multilateral trusteeships" dominated by the great powers, including the Soviet Union. Roosevelt anticipated that the partnership with the Soviet Union would outlast the war and was the best way of making the Soviets "responsible members of a new international system." As Cumings points out, this was a variety of containment – "but instead of drawing the lines in the dirt, this sort of containment policy embraced and enrolled the adversary in mutually beneficial relationships."[39] With Roosevelt dead and his vision gone, U.S. foreign policy began a troubled journey toward a hardline confrontational crusade against communism which would come to be called the Cold War.

George Kennan, an expert on Soviet affairs who headed the Policy Planning Staff at the State Department, was a key figure in transforming U.S. foreign policy in the years after Roosevelt's death. He articulated his rationale for confrontational globalism in the famous "Mr. X" article he wrote for *Foreign Affairs* in July 1947: "[T]he main element of any United States policy toward the Soviet Union must be that of a long-term, patient but firm and vigilant containment of Russian expansive tendencies."[40]

In moving containment from ideology to policy, Truman, Kennan, and the post-war U.S. leadership confronted strong domestic opposition. With the coming of the peace, the isolationists renewed their bitter opposition to international commitments, especially to the large-scale

aid which would be needed to "contain" the Soviets. Equally threatening to the advocates of this new policy were pressures for demobilization which had led to riots and demonstrations, from London to
Manila, by ordinary GIs resentful of an officer corps that wanted "to
keep playing war." [41]

In short, the Truman administration faced the same dilemma that
had stymied Roosevelt on the eve of World War II: with limited troops
and finances, it had to order its priorities. And the choice was the same
as that made by Roosevelt: "Europe First", a strategic decision that the
Truman Administration set forth in National Security Council Memorandum 48/1:

Since . . . the primary strategic interests and war objectives of the United States
consistent with the destruction of the enemy's means to wage war are not now
in Asia, the current basic concept of strategy in the event of war with the USSR
is to conduct a strategic offense in the "West" and a strategic defense in the
"East" . . . As a primary matter in the event of war, it is essential that a successful strategic defense in the "East" be assured with a minimum expenditure
of military manpower and material in order that the major effort may be
expended in the "West." In order to gain freedom of access to the Asian continent within these limitations, the United States must now concentrate its
efforts on bringing to bear such power as can be made available, short of the
commitment of United States military forces, in those areas which will show the
most results in return for the United States effort expended. [42]

The Offshore Island Strategy

Where were these areas of concentration? General Douglas Mac-
Arthur, described as "probably the most important individual for-
mulator of American ideas concerning strategy in the Far East," [43]
defined the first significant approach to the problem. Then serving as
Supreme Commander of Allied Forces in Japan, MacArthur advanced
the concept of an "offshore island perimeter": "Our line of defense
runs through the chain of islands fringing the coast of Asia. It starts
from the Philippines and continues through the Ryukyu Archipelago,
which includes its main bastion, Okinawa. Then it bends back through
Japan and the Aleutian Island chain, to Alaska." [44] Deployed along this

island chain, "air striking power" would be able to effectively cover the whole East Asian mainland.[45]

George Kennan, the State Department's Euro-centric proponent of containment, agreed with the Asia-oriented MacArthur. After a meeting between them in early 1948, Kennan wrote:

We should recognize that our influence in the Far Eastern area in the coming period is going to be primarily military and economic . . . We should make a careful study to see what parts of the Pacific and Far Eastern world are absolutely vital to our security, and we should concentrate our policy on seeing to it that those areas remain in hands which we can control or rely on. It is my own guess, on the basis of such study as we have given the problem so far, that Japan and the Philippines will be found to be the cornerstones of such a Pacific security system and that if we can continue to retain effective control over these areas there can be no serious threat to our security from the East within our lifetime.[46]

Kennan and MacArthur's strategy came to be known as the "minimum position." By relying on the island-chain strategy, the United States would be "able to apply pressure on fronts at times of its own choosing rather than spreading itself thin in reacting to every threat posed by the Soviets." The "Asian offshore island chain," asserted the National Security Council, would be "our first line of offense from which we may seek to reduce the area of Communist control, using whatever means we can develop, without, however, using sizable United States armed forces."[47]

Air power was seen to be the key to controlling the mainland. American strategists saw the atomic bomb as a key weapon to contain the Chinese Communists without necessitating "sizable United States armed forces." This faith in the bomb was reflected by General Omar Bradley, chairman of the Joint Chiefs of Staff, who stated in 1949: "I am wondering whether we shall ever have another amphibious operation. Frankly, the atomic bomb, properly delivered, precludes such a possibility."[48]

The political correlates of this military posture were laid out by Kennan in a February 1948 policy review. His first recommendation was that the U.S. "liquidate as rapidly as possible our unsound commitments in China and . . . recover, vis à vis that country, a position of detachment and freedom of action."[49] This was quite clearly a prescription for unloading Chiang Kai-shek and the Nationalist Chinese, then on the verge of defeat. He also suggested that the U.S. "devise policies with respect to Japan which assure the security of those islands . . . and which will permit the economic potential of that country to become again an important force in the Far East." His final recommendation was "to shape our relationship to the Philippines in such a way as to permit to the Philippine Government a continued independence in all internal affairs but to preserve the archipelago as a bulwark of U.S. security in the area." [50]

Barely a year after it was adopted as policy, the offshore island strategy was effectively abandoned, torpedoed by three momentous developments: the elevation of containment from strategy to ideology, the backlash from the "loss of China", and the Korean War.

Nuclear-capable B-36 bomber landing at Yokota, Japan,
for Operation Big Stick, August 26, 1953
(Strategic Air Command)

TWO ☆
THE KOREAN WATERSHED

[The]cold war is in fact a real war in which the survival of the free world is at stake.
—NSC-68, April 1950[1]

These two nations [U.S. and U.S.S.R] are now, to all intents and purposes, engaged in war – except for armed conflict.
—Joint Strategic Survey Committee, June 1950[2]

American strategists viewed the Pacific apprehensively as 1950 began. Nuclear weapons had proven to be less useful than anticipated in shaping Soviet behavior in Europe, while the prospect of a united Sino-Soviet bloc in Asia–Pacific was ominous. The military services were squabbling over a shrinking military budget, while vying for the leading role in nuclear war. The U.S. had still not settled on a clear strategy to link its forward position in the Pacific with its military power, especially its nuclear weapons. Events in Korea soon forced the U.S. to decide its priorities. The services and their civilian commanders hammered out a new global strategic and military policy on the anvil of the Korean War. But even before the war, American strategists were skirmishing over U.S. military policy in the Pacific.

Drawing the Lines

As initially formulated by George Kennan, the State Department's leading strategic planner, containment was a sophisticated strategy consisting of adroit and vigilant application of counter-force at a series of constantly shifting geographical and political points, corresponding to the shifts and maneuvers of Soviet policy.[3] Kennan felt it was impossible to confront the Soviet Union and revolution everywhere, a stance reinforced by his view that U.S. relations with the Soviet Union should be based on *realpolitik*:

We should stop putting ourselves in the position of being our brothers' keeper and refrain from offering moral and ideological advice. We should cease to talk about vague – and for the Far East – unreal objectives such as human rights, the raising of living standards, and democratization. The day is not far off when we are going to have to deal in straight power concepts. The less we are then hampered by idealistic slogans, the better.[4]

Kennan's doctrine clearly singled out the Soviet Union as the enemy, a view which was emerging even as Roosevelt embraced Stalin in the "grand strategy" to defeat the Nazis at the end of World War II. While Roosevelt was trying to involve the Soviets in a post-war great power scheme for the defeated Axis powers and the Third World,[5] the U.S. Navy began contingency planning in 1943 for post-war confrontation with its ally. To keep the Army–Air Force in the dark, these plans were developed in utmost secrecy.[6] While the Soviet Union loomed large as a candidate for "enemy", Navy strategists faced a double dilemma: the Soviets were an ally, and a landpower to boot.[7] Suffering from acute career anxiety, the Navy was traumatized by its wartime battle against the Army for survival, and perplexed by the lack of a plausible enemy.[8] In an attempt to construct an ideological base for naval resurgence, Secretary of the Navy James Forrestal commissioned an official study in 1945 on "Dialectical Materialism and Russian Objectives." The study concluded:

Capitalist Democracies can expect no mercy if Communist philosophy prevails; it is equally clear that under these circumstances it is tantamount to suicide to strengthen the power of Communism or to weaken our powers to withstand it.[9]

After the war, Forrestal became the Secretary of Defense and led the anti-Soviet hardliners against the holdover appointees from the Roosevelt era,[10] his alarmism fuelling Truman's anti-Soviet instincts.* [12] In July 1946, only eleven months after the end of the war, the Joint Chiefs of Staff had appraised the Soviet threat in the Far East, and concluded that the Soviets aimed to erect a perimeter of client states in the Far East, evict the U.S. bases, and threaten Alaska.[13] The consensus for confrontation was building by the time Kennan focused on the Far East.

Viewing developments in Asia, especially the probable triumph of the Red Army in China, Kennan warned: "It is urgently necessary that we recognize our limitations as a moral and ideological force among the Asiatic peoples." [14] Less ready to bend to the winds of revolution, the Joint Chiefs of Staff complained that: "Everywhere is weakness – weakness varying greatly in kind and degree from country to country; administrative and technical weakness; military weakness; economic weakness and, most seriously of all from our point of view, ideological weakness." [15]

From *Realpolitik* to Ideological Crusade

In the celebrated National Security Council Memorandum 68 (NSC 68) drafted by Kennan's successor Paul Nitze in April 1950, containment was transformed from *realpolitik* to an ideology of anticommunist militance. While Kennan saw containment as a process of selective engagement with the Soviet Union to avoid an overextension of U.S. resources, NSC 68 made an open-ended commitment against "Soviet aggression." Kennan saw in Third World nationalism openings for exploitation of differences between the Soviet Union and national liberation movements. NSC 68, by contrast, saw only a unified, global communist movement controlled by the Kremlin. Kennan preferred a U.S. foreign policy with no idealistic pretensions, whereas NSC 68 pro-

---

* Convinced that communists were in control of the White House and the Pentagon, that the American people had been duped by communists, and that he was their number-one target for liquidation, Forrestal jumped out of a sixteenth floor window in 1948, a few weeks after vacating the Office of the Secretary of Defense. Walking along a beach one afternoon shortly before his death, he pointed to a row of beach umbrella metal sockets in the sand and told his companion, "We had better not discuss anything here. Those things are wired, and everything we say is being recorded." [11]

posed a policy which "must light the path to peace and order among nations in a system based on freedom and justice." "The only sure victory," claimed NSC 68, "lies in the frustration of the Kremlin design by the steady development of the moral and material strength of the free world and its projection into the Soviet world in such a way as to bring about an internal change in the Soviet system." [16]

Kennan and Nitze also differed over the place of military power as a means of effecting strategy. Whereas Kennan aimed to counter the Soviets primarily with diplomatic and economic influence aimed at the psychology of U.S. allies and the U.S.S.R. itself, the hardliners saw military force as the ultimate backstop of global power. Kennan advised Secretary of State Dean Acheson that the U.S. was at a crossroads in January 1950 with respect to nuclear weapons. "We may regard them as something vital to our conduct of a future war," wrote Kennan, "as something without which our war plans would be emasculated and ineffective – as something which we have resolved, in the face of all the moral and other factors concerned, to employ forthwith and unhesitatingly at the outset of any great military conflict." "Or we may regard them as something superfluous to our basic military posture," he continued, "as something which we are compelled to hold against the possibility that they might be used by our opponents. In this case, of course, we take care not to build up a reliance on them in our military planning." [17] Kennan recommended the latter but Acheson ignored him. In contrast his successor, the author of NSC 68, Paul Nitze, saw the "powerful atomic blow" as integral to the U.S. capability "to conduct offensive operations to destroy vital elements of the Soviet war-making capacity, and to keep the enemy off balance until the full offensive strength of the United States and its allies can be brought to bear." [18]

The transformation of containment from selective engagement to a sweeping crusade was spurred by the "fall" of China in 1949. In his introduction to the controversial State Department "White Paper", Secretary of State Dean Acheson stated that China went Communist mainly because the people had lost confidence in the corrupt regime of Chiang Kai-shek. The Democratic administration, he claimed, had followed an overly complicated China policy after World War II. While trying to mediate between Chiang's forces and Mao's Communists, the U.S. had tilted toward Chiang by helping him to regain territory previously under Japanese control, and providing massive military aid –

some $2 billion since September 1945. Since the American people would not have countenanced either outright withdrawal or commitment of ground troops, this policy was, he argued, the only viable choice. Acheson concluded that the "ominous result of the civil war in China was beyond the control of the ... United States ... It was the product of internal Chinese forces, forces which this country tried to influence but could not." [19]

Acheson and Truman had wanted to focus on commitments in Europe. But Republicans, the powerful China lobby, and "Asia Firsters" succeeded in making China a bitter national issue, giving Secretary of State Acheson very little maneuvering space to implement a strategy of weaning Mao away from Stalin. And even that little space, the last remnant of Roosevelt's foreign policy, vanished with the outbreak of the Korean War in June 1950.

From Periphery to Pivot

The Korean War became a pivotal point in the Cold War. Ironically, prior to the onset of war, Korea had been excluded from the area considered vital for United States security. Right after Truman's famous containment speech in March 1947, when he promised aid to a conservative Greek government to crush a Communist-led revolution, the Joint Chiefs of Staff stated that if "the present diplomatic ideological warfare [in Korea] should become armed warfare, Korea could offer little or no assistance in the maintenance of our national security." [20] Thus, "the United States has little strategic interest in maintaining the present troops and bases in Korea." [21] Given the role MacArthur would later play in Korea, it was indeed ironic that in 1948 his island defense perimeter in Asia excluded Korea.

Acheson was simply following MacArthur when he stated, in his controversial National Press Club speech of January 1950, that America's line of defense in Asia "runs along the Aleutians to Japan and then goes to the Ryukyus [mainly Okinawa] ... [and] from the Ryukyus to the Philippine Islands." As for places like Taiwan and south Korea, Acheson said that "it must be clear that no person can guarantee these areas against military attack. Should such an attack occur ... the initial reliance must be on the people attacked." [22] The right wing never forgave Acheson for airing this consensus among military and State

Department pragmatists, and accused him of giving north Korea the "green light" to invade the south.*

Although the U.S. excluded Korea from its strategic defense zone, the Truman Administration used limited political and military measures to convert the peninsula's southern half into a bastion of anti-communism. As historian Bruce Cumings explains in his seminal study of post-war Korea, General John Hodge, head of the U.S. military government, "sought to make the south a bulwark against communism in the north and revolution at home . . . a policy . . . [which] took precedence over the desires of Koreans." [23] When U.S. troops left the south in August 1948, they left behind 400 military advisers for Syngman Rhee's armed forces.

The Korean War, then, can be seen as one phase of a civil war that began with the defeat of the Japanese occupation government in 1945. The U.S. had intervened on one side of that war and added to the polarization by encouraging the permanent partition of the peninsula.

Whatever its origins, the Korean War rushed the decline of Roosevelt's internationalism and the parallel rise of "containment militarism" within the U.S. leadership. NSC 68 represented the views of those Cold War Democrats who would use the Korean War to batter down public opposition to the new militarism. "A large measure of sacrifice and discipline will be demanded of the American people," warned NSC 68. "They will be asked to give up some of the benefits which they have come to associate with their freedoms." [24]

Korea, in short, solved the contradiction between the vast global commitments demanded by NSC 68 and limited American military resources and political will. The Korean War became one means of channelling some "benefits of freedom" toward military expansion.

Containment Versus Rollback

Domestic opposition to large increases in defense spending and new international commitments was not the only obstacle that the Cold

---

* As north and south Korea are not recognized as legitimate states by the United Nations and as there remains only one Korean people despite the political division, we refer throughout this book to the Republic of Korea as south Korea and the Democratic People's Republic of Korea as north Korea.

Warriors had to surmount. During the Blair House conference called in response to the outbreak of conflict in Korea, General Bradley, Chairman of the Joint Chiefs of Staff, declared that the "Korean situation offered as good an occasion for action in drawing the line as anywhere else . . ." [25] While Bradley's metaphor reflected the dominant view, others approached containment from different perspectives. Indeed, the emerging containment policy represented a compromise among New Deal internationalists, proponents of "realism" in dealing with Soviets, and advocates of "rolling back" Communism. It was not the question of ends but means which separated these three schools. As Cumings notes, containment "was a low-risk strategy which left open the possibility either of accommodating communism in a new global order or pushing it back." [26] NSC 68 itself combined rollback rhetoric with the realists' more limited goals:

The mischief may be a global war or it may be a Soviet campaign for limited objectives. In either case we should take no avoidable initiative which would cause it to become a war of annihilation, and if we have the forces to defeat a Soviet drive for limited objectives it may well be to our interest not to let it become a global war. Our aim in applying force must be to compel the acceptance of terms consistent with our objectives, and our capabilities for the application of force should, therefore, within the limits of what we can sustain over the long pull, be congruent to the range of tasks which we may encounter. [27]

The Korean War consolidated containment as America's basic foreign policy, but not before the proponents of containment successfully blunted a strong challenge from the rollback school. Its advocates had scored a major victory when Truman allowed General Douglas MacArthur, the commander of U.S. forces in Korea, to cross the 38th Parallel and "reunify" the peninsula. When MacArthur's forces reached the Yalu River and provoked China's entry into the war, however, the fragile consensus began to collapse. Instead of withdrawing, the imperious commander proposed bringing the war to China itself by blockading its coast, bombing its industries, and sponsoring a "counter-invasion against vulnerable areas of the Chinese mainland" [28] by Chiang's nationalist troops in Taiwan. His cable to the Joint Chiefs of Staff on December 30, 1950 revealed MacArthur's agenda. Attacking China via Korea and Taiwan, he claimed, "could severely cripple and largely neutralize China's capability to wage aggressive war and thus save Asia from the engulfment otherwise facing it." [29]

MacArthur's scheme rested upon nuclear and radiological warfare. In his biography of MacArthur, William Manchester sketches out the general's nuclear strategy:

The enemy's air would first have been "taken out" by nuclear attacks on Manchurian air bases. Then he would have enveloped the enemy with "500,000 of Chiang Kai-shek's troops, sweetened by two United States Marine divisions" and landed behind Chinese lines . . . In little more than a week, he said, the starving Chinese and North Koreans would have sued for peace. Sowing a belt of radioactive cobalt from the Sea of Japan to the Yellow Sea, he would have prevented another land invasion of Korea from the north for at least sixty years.[30]

The radioactive cobalt belt was pure fantasy since the U.S. had no such weapons. But MacArthur's vision of destroying the "Asiatic hordes" with nuclear warfare would inspire the imaginations of many U.S. military men over the next two decades.

In 1950, MacArthur's call to "roll back" Communism above the 38th Parallel and aim for "total victory" unified conservative forces opposed to almost twenty years of Democratic control of foreign policy – the old isolationists and Asia-Firsters, an alliance that Arthur Schlesinger called the "Asialationists." Their main aims were reduction of military commitments to Europe, the use of unilateral military action unrestrained by allies, and a focus on Asia as the principal field of U.S. expansion. MacArthur stirred these passions in 1952: "The communist conspirators," he wrote, "have elected to make their play for global conquest in Asia – here we fight Europe's war with arms while the diplomats there still fight with words." [31]

With its appeal to bold and sweeping action, the rollback rhetoric was far more attractive to conservatives than a "long-term, patient, but firm and vigilant containment of Russian expansive tendencies." [32] Townsend Hoopes, former Under-Secretary of the Air Force, explains the psychological appeal of the rollback formula:

[A] potential difficulty was that the strategy [of containment] required endurance, steadiness, patience, and resistance to the temptation of "all-out" response, qualities that tended to run against American temperament in war.

Moreover, it showed itself, both as formulated by Kennan and as orchestrated by Truman and Acheson, to be a doctrine oriented primarily toward Europe and lacking the same confident clarity when applied to the less familiar terrain and conditions of Asia. As the profound dislocations in China produced the traumatic collapse of Chiang's armies and brought to power a regime that many thought was a direct agent of the Kremlin, the cold war seemed to spread relentlessly despite effective containment in Europe. Troubled, impatient Americans began to view it as a negative, overly defensive policy, a treadmill going nowhere, yet at the same time absorbing vast amounts of national attention, energy, and resources.[33]

MacArthur was eventually sacked for his defiance of President Truman in April 1951, and the policy current he represented was soundly defeated as a solution to the Korean question. Rollback did not vanish, however, as an alternative to liberal containment policy. Always strident, its supporters would shout from the sidelines until 1981, when they rode into power with Ronald Reagan.

Global Military Buildup

Although they prevented the Korean conflict from sparking a global war, the containment liberals still used it as a lever to reshape the global political order. Indeed, the Korean War gave the U.S. the opportunity to rearm Germany, commit a huge permanent garrison of troops in Europe, and impose the creation of SHAPE*, the integrated military command of the North Atlantic Treaty Organization. Moreover, it allowed the containment liberals to reverse demobilization, triple defense spending, and create a global military machine. In just two years, 1950 to 1952, annual U.S. military expenditures increased four-fold from $13 billion to $50 billion. Simultaneously, personnel in the armed forces doubled to almost three million, naval ships increased from 671 to over 1,100, and Air Force wings rose from 48 to 108.[34]

The Korean War enabled the political and military components of the containment strategy in Asia to fall into place. The U.S. returned in force to the peninsula itself, with its troop strength topping 225,000 by the time the armistice was signed in 1953. While U.S. troops were scaled

---

* Supreme Headquarters, Allied Powers Europe.

down after 1953, two army divisions remained to garrison the 38th Parallel until 1972, when President Richard Nixon withdrew one.

The war did more than bring Korea into the American "defense perimeter." Beleaguered in Taiwan, Chiang Kai-shek's forces were taken under U.S. military protection. In 1954, the 7th Fleet was sent to the South China Sea to block the Red Army from invading the nation- alist-held islands. A spurt of treaty-making formalized U.S. political and military influence in other strategic areas. The U.S. concluded a peace treaty with Japan, which gave it almost unrestricted military rights in. Japan proper and continued U.S. administration of Okinawa. "Mutual defense" pacts were signed with the Philippines, Australia, and New Zealand.

Korea also allowed the United States to experiment with "collective effort" to promote its national interests behind a facade of inter- nationalism. From among the Asian and Pacific countries, Australia, Thailand, the Philippines, and New Zealand contributed contingents to the war effort in Korea, under the convenient flag of a "United Nations" command.

The Korean War sparked the remilitarization of Japan. Soon after the outbreak of hostilities, General MacArthur ordered the formation of the "Self Defense Forces" to take over security duties from American troops being assigned to Korea. Former Japanese troops were used as military engineers in Korea, and Japanese ships were used in combat operations, such as minesweeping Wonsan Harbor.[35] As Japanese his- torian Seizaburo Shinobu has stated, the Korean War "made Japan into a counterrevolutionary base in all senses of that expression."[36]

The Korean War also allowed the U.S. to cement Japan into place as the cornerstone of its strategic program for the Pacific region. As the heart of the U.S. military presence in the Far East and the only available potential balance to Soviet and Chinese economic and military influence in the Pacific, U.S. strategists decided to revive Japan as the industrial "workshop" of Asia.[37] This vision entailed separating Japan from its "natural" raw material suppliers and markets in Communist China, and integrating Southeast Asia into Japan's economic sphere.[38] Military procurement of Japanese goods and services to support U.S. forces based in Japan and to fuel the Korean War effort were key ingredients in the success of this strategy.

The U.S. spent $6.8 billion in aid, special procurement, and troop expenditures in Japan between 1947–1958, equal to nearly 50 per cent of Japan's exports over the same period. Indeed, the Korean War put Asia on the global map as far as U.S. security aid is concerned. Military and economic aid to Asia jumped from less than 10 per cent of the U.S. total before the War to above 60 per cent in 1955.[39] In 1953 alone, the U.S. pumped $825 million into the Japanese economy for textiles, metal products, fuels, and munitions for the war effort.[40] Military orders in 1952 alone provided foreign exchange earnings equal to 64 per cent of Japan's pre-Korea War exports and 37 per cent of all foreign exchange receipts.[41] As Japanese economist Takafusa Nakamura concludes, the "prodigious impact" of the Korean War boom freed the Japanese economy from its crippling balance-of-payments deficit. By driving up international prices and demand for Japanese exports due to war-engendered shortages, and by direct procurements in Japan, Takafusa estimates that "war dollars" rose to 60–70 per cent of Japan's exports, enabling key sectors to import technology and raw materials, and embark on rapid economic growth.[42]

The Korean War and the post-war procurement program also transferred advanced U.S. technology to Japan by co-financing Japanese production of aircraft, missiles, jet engines, and communications equipment. Produced under license from U.S. firms, these products were procured by the U.S. military. Out of the many aircraft-related agreements, a key deal struck in 1954 between Kawasaki and Lockheed for jet engine and air frame overhaul led to the assembly of advanced jet aircraft in 1955. Transfer of technical information, tools, jigs and other components of modern industrial techniques followed soon after.[43] In a report to the Pentagon, Daniel Spencer estimated that Japanese firms thereby obtained access to 50–60 per cent of the latest U.S. research and development capability in these sectors.[44] The resulting web of relationships between Japanese and U.S. aircraft firms is shown in Figure 2.1. "These procurements," stated Spencer, "laid the technical groundwork for the modern growth miracle of Japan. At minimum, they opened Japan to contact with American companies with whom they served to initiate or renew commercial tie-ups." [45]

The short- and long-run effects of the military bases in Japan were thus immense. In addition to strategic and economic reverberations regionally and in the U.S., the American military presence had profound social impacts inside Japan itself. Military procurement helped to resuscitate the big *zaibatsu* firms which had profited from World War II. Under the benign guidance of the Ministry of International Trade and

Figure 2.1:
Principal Japanese–United States Aircraft License Relationships, 1956

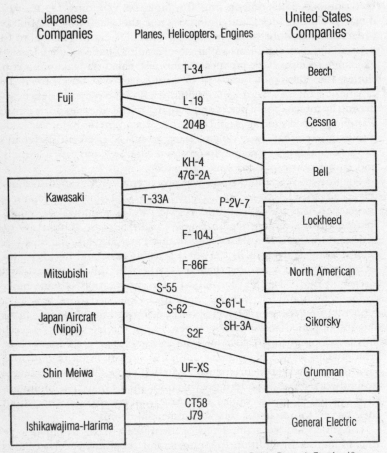

Source: D. Spencer, "Military Transfer of Technology, International Techno-Economic Transfers Via Military By-Products & Initiative Based on Cases from Japan & Other Countries," (Mimeo report to US Department of Defense), Howard University, Washington DC, March 1967, p. 96.

Industry[46] and with the blessing of American Occupation officials, the *zaibatsu* teamed up with U.S. firms, stomped on small Japanese firms competing for military procurements[47] and bulldozed textile merchants seeking trade with China. The *zaibatsu* and their political allies also circumvented a wave of popular opposition to the U.S. bases themselves in the 1950s.[48] The way was cleared for Japan to serve on the frontline of nuclear war in the 1950s (see Chapter 5).

Pacific Garrison

The Korean War had a major impact on the U.S. military posture in the Pacific, fostering what was, in effect, a transnational garrison state of U.S. bases beyond the control of their host countries. Scores of bases in Japan served as the springboard for the American war effort in Korea. U.S. planes, for example, took off directly from Japan on bombing missions in Korea, while a fleet of over 400 warships of the U.S. naval forces, Far East, operated out of Yokosuka and Sasebo.

Okinawa, the central "island bastion" in MacArthur's "offshore island chain" became the base for B-29 bombing runs over Korea.[49] In only five years, a vast military expansion program converted 40,000 acres, or 13 per cent of the total land area of the island, into interlocking Army, Navy, Marine and Air Force bases, including storage areas for nuclear and chemical weapons.[50] It was the strategic value of Okinawa, apparent in the Korean War, which made the Americans insist on retaining administrative control of the island during the Japanese peace treaty negotiations.

The Korean conflict also led to a major new base in the Philippines, Cubi Point, to support naval air operations in the Asian mainland. The two vast bases in the country, Subic and Clark, became logistical centers for Filipino troops and military supplies headed for Korea, as well as stop-over points for troops from Australia and Singapore *en route* to Korea.[51]

The Rise of the Regional Policeman

Of all the armed services, it was the Navy which reaped the benefits of the Korean War. With its destruction of the Imperial Japanese Navy during the Battle of Leyte Gulf in October 1944, the U.S. fleet achieved maritime supremacy, a cherished goal of the Navy's foremost strategist, Alfred Mahan, a half century earlier. The Navy thus emerged from World War II as a service in search of a mission. The immediate post-war years were a time of discontent for the admirals, who had to fight off the Air Force's drive to reduce the Navy to a minor service in a nuclear strategy that relied on long-range bombers and missiles.

Seventh Fleet aircraft carriers were among the first combat units to respond to the outbreak of war in Korea, as military historian David Rosenberg notes, thereby "vindicating the Navy's claims about the value of mobile, flexible carrier striking forces." [52] Thus, only a year after he had cancelled the order for the super-carrier u.s.s. *United States*, Defense Secretary Louis Johnson told Admiral Forrest Sherman, Chief of Naval Operations: "I will give you another carrier when you want it." [53] By the end of the war, the fleet had grown from seven to twelve attack carriers, and from eight to fifteen light and escort carriers. Beginning with the *Forrestal* in 1952, a new super aircraft carrier was included in each annual defense budget. [54]

The build-up was just one of the Navy's gains. Korea proved that not all conflicts would escalate to global nuclear war as the Air Force had anticipated. The bloody stalemate on the ground between the north Korean-Chinese and U.S. infantry neutralized U.S. superiority in naval, air, and amphibious forces, and made the Navy wary of any future support role in another of the Army's land wars. Admiral Sherman, then Navy member of the Joint Chiefs of Staff, wrote that he had been uneasy about the Korean War from its inception. "It was unavoidable," he said, "but I was fully aware of the hazards involved in fighting Asiatics on the Asiatic mainland, which is something that, as a naval officer, I have grown up to believe should be avoided if possible." [55] Such distaste for protracted land warfare would re-emerge fifteen years later in the battle over strategy in the Vietnam War.

Meanwhile, the Navy moved quickly to stake out a key role in the "limited war" situations favored by containment strategists. During Korea and later Pacific crises, notes U.S. naval analyst Francis West, the Navy "demonstrated its 'new' concept of warfare, the use of carrier-based air to project power over the land on the enemy's homeland." [56] In other words, the Navy's fast-carrier task forces lent themselves to quick intervention in local conflicts. The aircraft carrier mission was particularly apt for the Asia–Pacific region, where revolutionary movements threatened pro-American elites. As West states:

Though there were U.S. ground and air forces in various countries of the region, the primary burden fell on naval forces both as the unifying link between all the bilateral agreements and because the carrier's air power provided a rapid means of responding to conflict or crisis with significant potential to persuade or punish.[57]

The 7th Fleet as the regional police force, the Navy as a rapid intervention force – this was a face of American power which would become familiar to peoples in Asia–Pacific for the next thirty years.

U.S. Secretary of State John Foster Dulles (center) at his arrival in
Taipei, October 1958
(Pentagon Archives)

THREE ☆
NEW LOOK AT THE
NUCLEAR BRINK

You seldom see a cowboy, even in the movies, wearing three guns. Two is
enough.

—Admiral Arleigh Burke,
Chief of Naval Operations, 1960[1]

General Dwight D. Eisenhower's presidential candidacy in 1952 was a
compromise between the Europe-centered, eastern wing of the Republican Party and its "Asialationist" wing based in the West and mid-
West. Unsympathetic to alliances with Europe, the "Asialationists"
championed the unrestrained use of U.S. power in the Far East. The
compromise, however, was built on the false assumption that Eisenhower would adopt a "rollback" posture against Communism. The
Republican right, headed by Senator Robert Taft of Ohio, pinned its
hopes on John Foster Dulles, who was expected to be named Secretary
of State in an Eisenhower administration. Before the election Dulles
had proclaimed his belief in rollback, which he styled "a liberation
policy which will try to give hope and a resistance mood inside the
Soviet Empire."[2]

While the new administration retained the Truman–Acheson
emphasis on a defensive alliance in Europe, the right was not totally
disappointed. Eisenhower combined rollback rhetoric with a strong
military and political offensive in the Asia–Pacific region. "Brinkman-
ship" aptly captured the stance of the new administration, particularly

its dealings with the People's Republic of China, which competed with the Soviet Union for primacy in U.S. policymakers' demonology.

Close examination, in this and succeeding chapters, of Eisenhower's military posture and new reliance on nuclear weapons will make clear just how close the United States came to launching a nuclear war in the 1950s. More important than the incendiary rhetoric, a bitter inter-service rivalry over control of nuclear weapons nearly pushed the U.S. military over the brink of the nuclear precipice.

Brinkmanship in Korea

In 1953, President Dwight D. Eisenhower threatened China and north Korea with the use of atomic weapons to force an armistice in Korea. In his memoirs, Eisenhower revealed that "One possibility [to bring about an agreement] was to let the Communist authorities understand that, in the absence of satisfactory progress, we intended to move decisively without inhibition in our use of weapons, and would no longer be responsible for confining hostilities to the Korean peninsula." [3]

This was not idle talk. Advised by the U.S. Joint Strategic Planning Committee, the Joint Chiefs of Staff had already considered numerous proposals to attack Korea and China with nuclear weapons during the early 1950s. The Committee had proposed, the Joint Chiefs of Staff had recommended, and President Truman had approved the establishment of U.S. nuclear delivery capability.

In March 1951, a Johns Hopkins University research group, under contract to the Far East Command in Tokyo, submitted an immense report to General MacArthur entitled *Tactical Employment of Atomic Weapons*. [4] The newly declassified study noted that:

The Korean War has offered an excellent opportunity for the study of the tactical employment of atomic bombs in support of ground forces. It has been possible to consider the war a kind of laboratory within which everything was at hand in the most realistic proportions, except the bomb itself and the means to deliver it. [5]

A covering memorandum from the Far East Command in July 1951 reveals that the study, while not yet adopted as Army policy, was far from academic. "This headquarters," stated General Doyle Hickey, "is continuing study of [the] report with a view to taking any actions that may be indicated to prepare the Far East Command offensively and defensively for possible employment of nuclear weapons." [6]

The report revealed, however, that Far East Command faced major obstacles to conducting nuclear war in Korea. Applying the "Hiroshima Death Function" * to a variety of actual battle situations in the Korean War, the study demonstrated that there were many "lucrative" military targets for nuclear attack. One such attack would have employed ten 40 kiloton nuclear bombs dropped just 6.5 km apart to "neutralize" the "Pyongyang-Chorwon-Kumhwa Triangle" [7] – that is, to destroy the north Korean capital city and surrounds. The authors noted that such nuclear attacks would kill many civilians, which they termed a "distorting consideration". They suggested that destroying 10,000 enemy troops with a nuclear attack was worth killing 500 "friendly civilians", although they were "reluctant" to recommend killing 50,000 civilians for the same gain. [8]

Aside from relatively immobile targets such as cities and towns occupied by Chinese forces, the report considered the possibility that problems might arise from the Chinese tactic of dispersing their troops to counter American mechanized columns: [9]

The heavy padded cotton uniform of the Chinese soldier would offer him substantial protection from thermal radiation. In a dry condition, this uniform would require for ignition about 10 to 12 calories per square centimeter. His fur cap would be more readily ignited, but it could be discarded readily. His uncovered face, neck, and ears would be subject to serious burns at about 5 calories per square centimeter. His feet in canvas shoes with padded soles would have been subject to injury at about 15 calories per square centimeter. The overall effect of thermal radiation on a Chinese soldier in the open can thus be seen to depend a great deal upon his posture with respect to the bomb as well as his distance from ground zero. [10]

The report also found that U.S. forces in Korea were ill equipped for

---

* The "Hiroshima Death Function" was an algorithm developed in the report to calculate mortality as a function of distance from ground zero of an airburst nuclear explosion; the function is:

$$D(r) = 0.93 \, Exp \, \{-0.693 \, [(r-800)/850]^2\}$$

where D = Deaths and r = slant distance in yards from point of burst for r greater than 800.

nuclear warfare. Few American soldiers and practically no allied forces had received "atomic indoctrination" in safety and radiological protection, and by January 1951, only two radiological defense officers had been trained.[11] Furthermore, the lack of adequate roads and bridges precluded the use in Korea of Army nuclear artillery which moved on cumbersome, heavy equipment.[12]

Nuclear-capable aircraft carriers, moreover, had not yet arrived off the Korean coast. Only the 70 B-29s in the Far East Air Force – flying from Yokota in Japan and Kadena in Okinawa – could deliver nuclear bombs.[13] And the estimated time between target identification and B-29 nuclear bomb drop was 12 hours[14] – far too long in the rapidly shifting frontlines of the Korean War.* This delay was primarily attributable to poor intelligence capability, indicating that it was "probably the least prepared of any branch of the U.S. Army to cope with the problems of atomic warfare."[16] Effective nuclear bombing was also hampered by poor ground-air coordination in the final approach of the B-29 bombers to the target.[17]

Deterred by these obstacles from actually using nuclear weapons in the ground war in Korea, the report recommended staff training to "perform all the *real* staff work required to plan and execute *simulated* atomic attacks on targets as they develop."[18] The staff training was to be matched with combat training for B-29 delivery of nuclear bombs, "to fly simulated atomic sorties against real enemy targets . . . as a part of an actual bomber or fighter strike with conventional weapons or immediately after such a strike." The report recommended: "These test sorties should be made as realistic as possible in all details except that conventional rather than atomic explosions would be used."[19]

Accordingly, from late September to October 15, 1951, several simulated nuclear strikes were conducted as *Exercise Hudson Harbor* in Korea.†[20] These exercises laid the groundwork for the May 15, 1953 National Security Council meeting where Eisenhower argued that nuclear weapons were cheaper in Korea than conventional weapons.

---

* While the B-29s in the Far East were not then nuclear-capable, the report notes that one week sufficed to deploy into the Far East Command an especially trained crew capable of nuclear bomb assembly, backed by complete, assembled sets of ground equipment for advance base operations to support the B-29s.[15]

† Whether these nuclear mock attacks were conducted as part of actual conventional bombing attacks is unknown.

To make the threat clear, the 92nd B-36 Bomb Wing flew to Japan, Okinawa, and Guam for a month-long exercise, *Operation Big Stick* in August–September 1953. The official Strategic Air Command history states that *Big Stick* "demonstrated the U.S. determination to use every means possible to maintain peace in the Far East." [21] Not to be outdone, the aircraft carrier u.s.s. *Champlain* with four nuclear bombers aboard cruised off the Korean coast, waiting for the attack order. [22]

The threats continued even after the Armistice was signed in July 1953. The Joint Chiefs of Staff and the Department of State recommended in January 1954 that if hostilities were renewed in Korea, the U.S. should employ "atomic weapons . . . against military targets in Korea and against those military targets in Manchuria and China which are being used by the Communists in direct support of these operations in Korea, or which threaten the security of U.S./U.N. forces in the Korean area." [23]

President Eisenhower's threat was not too different from the advice General MacArthur gave him soon after his election as President. The rollback advocate had urged Eisenhower to inform the Soviet Union that "should an agreement not be reached, it would be our intention to clear North Korea of enemy troops . . . through the atomic bombing of enemy military concentrations and installations . . . and the sowing of fields of suitable radio-active materials . . . to close major lines of enemy supply and communication." [24]

Nuclear weapons were not used during the Truman–MacArthur phase of the Korean War (June 1950 to January 1953) because American leaders were dismayed by the universal outcry after Truman off-handedly referred to using nuclear weapons in Korea at a press conference in November 1950. [25] And as the Johns Hopkins study demonstrated, the military was unprepared for such escalation.

The reasons for American restraint later in the war are less clear. The fact that Eisenhower finally withheld approval for nuclear attacks in 1953 may have been due to the opposition of U.S. allies, alarmed by U.S. nuclear threats; the lack of suitable urban–industrial targets (which were already destroyed by conventional bombing); and/or the continuing inability of the U.S. to obtain necessary intelligence and targeting capability for a nuclear attack on Chinese and north Korean troops.

Just how close Eisenhower came to using his nuclear option is revealed in the record of a National Security Council meeting on May 20, 1953. Eisenhower's "only real worry" about the Joint Chiefs' view that "more positive action" would entail nuclear attack on China was the possibility of Soviet intervention. "He feared the Chinese much less," stated the record, "since the blow would fall so swiftly and with such force as to eliminate Chinese Communist intervention." [26]

Eisenhower's nuclear threats in Korea were part and parcel of "massive retaliation" – the defense doctrine of his administration. This meant, as Dulles put it, that the U.S. would "depend primarily upon a great capacity to retaliate, instantly, by means and at places of our choosing." [27] Retaliatory capacity meant, in the first instance, that the Strategic Air Command would be able to deliver an overwhelming hail of nuclear bombs.

The "New Look" Strategy

Limited war, nonetheless, had its place in the Eisenhower-Dulles strategy. Learning from Korea, a meatgrinder for conventional forces, the administration felt that limited war required the liberal use of tactical nuclear weapons. Atomic weapons, insisted Dulles, were "becoming more and more conventional." Eisenhower himself argued: "Where these things are used on strictly military targets and for strictly military purposes, I see no reason why they shouldn't be used just exactly as you would use a bullet or anything else." [28] The "bullets" Eisenhower had in mind were about as powerful as the bombs used against Hiroshima and Nagasaki. [29]

In limited war conditions, ground forces could not be totally dispensed with. But in the view of Admiral Arthur Radford, Chairman of the Joint Chiefs of Staff, the U.S. ground commitment would be restricted to Marine units and "small atomic task forces" from the Army. [30] The bulk of the ground fighting would be done by U.S.-equipped and trained "indigenous troops." [31] Conceived as a way to avoid the massive defense spending of Korea in future conflicts, the "New Look" strategy was "intervention on the cheap." As American strategist Townsend Hoopes wrote, it was essentially "an approach to warfare based on an acceptance of greater destructiveness in war in return for a lower cost in the preparation for war." [32]

Asian Contingencies and Nuclear Threats

In the eyes of Eisenhower's strategists, Asia was the arena where tactical nuclear weapons and surrogate troops – the New Look's strategy for Third World intervention – could be most effectively applied to meet "localized Communist aggression." Indeed, it was here that Eisenhower, Dulles, and the Joint Chiefs of Staff went to the brink of nuclear war.

In the spring of 1954, French forces at Dien Bien Phu were entrapped by nationalist guerillas as the first Indochina War moved to a climax. Abandoning the post-war U.S. policy of anti-colonialism, the administration and the Joint Chiefs proposed to help the French by blasting the Vietnamese guerillas with tactical atomic bombs. *Operation Vulture*, the American plan to save the French, involved delivery of nuclear bombs either by B-29 Superfortresses flying out of Clark Air Field in the Philippines, or by Navy fighter-bombers launched from Seventh Fleet carriers. Indeed, two carriers were cruising offshore, ready to intervene on behalf of the French.*[33]

Freeing the French garrison, however, was not the only American aim. As JCS Chairman Arthur Radford later admitted, the "real purpose was to provoke a military reaction from Peking, bringing the United States and China to war before China had a chance to become strong enough to threaten U.S. interests in the future." [34] According to one account, *Operation Vulture* was approved by "President Eisenhower, the Secretary of State, and four of the five members of the Joint Chiefs of Staff." The plan was aborted only by British opposition and French fears that their forces would be annihilated along with the Vietnamese.†[35]

The Dien Bien Phu nuclear scenario was not an aberration. It flowed from an official posture of limited war in Asia – nuclear attack on liberation forces to avoid what would be a domestically unpopular alternative of committing ground troops. In 1954, Admiral Radford summarized the "New Look" thinking on Southeast Asia in a Joint Chiefs Memorandum: "Committing to the Indochina conflict naval forces in excess of a fast carrier task force and supporting forces as necessary in accordance with developments in the situation . . . will

---

* There is, however, no evidence that preparatory deployments of nuclear weapons occurred to support *Operation Vulture*.

† In 1971, the *Washington Post* reported that the French Premier accepted a U.S. offer to sell the French four nuclear bombs for the last-ditch defense of Dien Bien Phu, but that the commander rejected the nuclear tactic for fear of frying his own forces.

involve maldeployment of forces and reduce readiness to meet probable Chinese Communist reaction elsewhere in the Far East." However, these constraints did not bar offensive operations "employing atomic weapons, whenever advantageous . . . against selected military targets in China, Hainan, and other Communist-held offshore islands which are being used by the Communists in direct support of their operations, or which threaten the security of U.S. allied forces in the area." These tactical nuclear strikes would be supported by "French Union Forces augmented by such armed forces of the Philippines and Thailand as may be committed." [36]

After Dien Bien Phu, the next opportunity for the United States to flex its nuclear muscles against China appeared in May 1954, when crisis erupted near Taiwan over the Tachen and Kinmen (Quemoy) Islands. When the People's Republic asserted its sovereignty over the Nationalist-occupied islands, the U.S. Navy sent five 7th Fleet carriers to the area.[37] The U.S. quickly deployed fighter-bombers from Japan and the Philippines to cover the Nationalist evacuation of the Tachen Islands, 475 km north of Taiwan. To block any future moves against the Nationalists, the U.S. began a massive build-up of conventional and nuclear weaponry on Taiwan itself.[38]

In March 1955, Admiral Robert Carney, U.S. Chief of Naval Operations, revealed that the Eisenhower administration was seriously considering taking advantage of the crisis to solve "the Communist Chinese problem." He told the press that the administration was discussing a plan of action "to destroy Red China's military potential and thus end its expansionist tendencies." [39] Moving towards the brink, the Strategic Air Command subsequently increased the strength of its "ground alert" forces in Guam and readied several bomber wings "for possible contingency operations in the Pacific." [40]

A recently released study shows that after the 1954 crisis, the Air Force ordered the Tactical Air Command to develop a "Mobile Composite Air Strike Force with an atomic capability, to be used in small localized wars." [41] Codenamed *Double Trouble*, this unit drew on fighters, bombers, reconnaissance planes, troop carriers, communication and supply units – in short, the full paraphernalia required to launch a nuclear strike.[42] Although assigned to a U.S.-based wing, the Strike Force was available "on loan" to Pacific Command, and, in the *Mobile Zebra* exercise of November 1957, it practised deploying to the Far East.[43] The Strike Force reinforced Pacific Air Force fighter-bombers which had been "organized, trained, equipped, and positioned for the primary mission of nuclear strikes in general war."[44]

In August 1958, regional tensions increased rapidly as Chinese fighters appeared on mainland airfields in Fukien Province opposite Taiwan. Although on alert in Europe over the Lebanon crisis, the Air Force diverted advanced F-100D fighters from NATO to reinforce the Taiwan garrison. On August 6th, General Kuter, Commander-in-Chief of the Pacific Air Force, distributed to his staff his portion of CINCPAC's May 1958 three-phase war plan, known as *Ops Plan 25–58*.* The first phase, already under way, required U.S. patrol and reconnaissance of the Taiwan Straits and the China mainland. The second phase called for defeat of a Chinese offensive with nuclear strikes by the Pacific Air Force – amended shortly after to include six Guam-based Strategic Air Command B-47 bombers with Mark 6 nuclear weapons to give SAC a role in "limited nuclear war." Phase III involved SAC nuclear strikes against China's urban–industrial areas to destroy the Chinese Communist capability to make war.[45] "Initial atomic strikes," reports the official history, "would be launched from Clark Air Base in the Philippines and Kadena Air Base in Okinawa"[46] (see Map 3.1).

U.S. war planners in the Pacific, in short, assumed they would drop nuclear bombs from the very beginning of a war with China. As then U.S. Commander-in-Chief Pacific Harry Felt recalled in 1974: "It is true that at that time [in the 1958 crisis] we had plans for use of tactical nuclear weapons. Most of us believed in those days that the use of tactical nuclear weapons wouldn't key off the big war, and *we didn't have any plan to do it any other way*."[47] General Kuter of the Pacific Air Force argued vehemently for the use of nuclear weapons. In 1957, the Air Force had ordered him to give first priority to improving "capability to deliver conventional [sic] atomic weapons," and last priority to "development of the capability to develop obsolete [non-nuclear] weapons."[48]

On August 23, 1958, mainland Chinese forces began intense shelling of Quemoy (Kinmen) Island, 113 km to the west of Taiwan. In response, General Kuter requested deployment of the nuclear- armed Composite Air Strike Force. The Air Force supplied the so-called X-Ray Tango units by September 12, giving the Pacific Air Force 183 nuclear-capable strike aircraft. The Air Force was so anxious to demonstrate nuclear

---

* Prepared by then CINCPAC, Admiral Felix Stump.

Map 3.1:
Taiwan Straits Crisis, August 1958

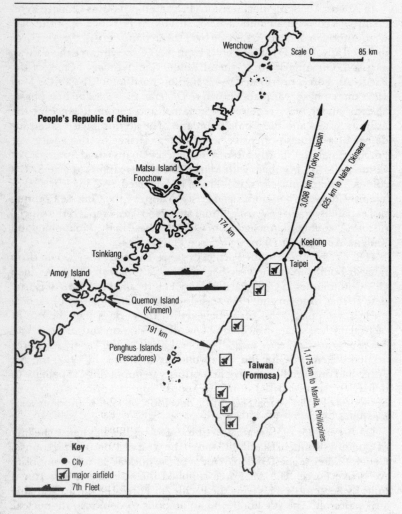

prowess that it took the wings off California-based F-104 fighter-bombers lacking trans-Pacific range, and flew them to Taiwan in giant air transports.[49] In September, the Navy's attack carriers arrived with another 66 nuclear-capable strike planes, and in mid-September, a Nike-Hercules nuclear missile unit was on duty in Taiwan.[50]

The U.S. Army, according to Commander-in-Chief-Pacific Admiral Harry Felt, also transferred nuclear-capable 8-inch howitzers to Taiwan in late August.* Felt explained in 1974: "We provided [them] to our friends in Taiwan and they managed to get them over onto Quemoy. It seems kind of a silly exercise when you think back on it, but there we were thinking perhaps we might be authorized to use these kinds of weapons." [51]

That Washington commanders might block the use of nuclear weapons in August 1954 caused Admiral Felt "much anxiety", according to an Air Force history. On August 25, Felt told his subordinates "that his original plan envisaged the employment of nuclear weapons and that the *accompanying logistical systems would be inadequate for non-nuclear operations.*" [52] Felt later recollected that when "the Joint Chiefs [realized], 'Gee, this might break out into a full-scale war here, with the United States right in the middle of it, we can't use those weapons,' . . . they directed me to draw up a plan for use of conventional ones. And that took some doing." [53] Only on September 11, after soliciting appraisal of his conventional capabilities for the first time, did Felt issue a non-nuclear "Annex H" to the war plan. If full-scale war with China had broken out between August and early September 1954 – and Chiang Kai-shek was straining to draw the U.S. into such a war[54] – Pacific Command's war plans and forces to defend Taiwan were designed *solely* for nuclear strikes in China.

On the command side in Washington, D.C., the Pentagon and the State Department were pressuring Eisenhower to clarify his role in commanding nuclear forces and to authorize Pacific Command's nuclear warplans to defend the islands.[55] On August 25, the President approved an order to CINCPAC and the U.S. Taiwan Defense Command which approved the general nuclear thrust against China, but reined in the military. While the military were told to "*prepare to use atomic weapons* to extend deeper into Chinese Communist territory if necessary," they were first to try a non-nuclear defense.[56] It was still

---

* Felt replaced Stump in July 1958.

unclear on September 3 if Eisenhower would approve a general escalation to nuclear weapons, and how tightly he would control their battlefield use.[57] Three days later, he finally ordered that only he could authorize specific nuclear attacks in a war with China. At the same time, he delegated authority to the Joint Chiefs of Staff to use nuclear weapons when time did not permit securing his specific approval.[58]

Even after U.S. forces in the Taiwan area had adopted conventional strategies by mid-September, the Pacific Air Force commanders estimated that they had less than fifteen days supply of bombs and fuel. Local commanders believed that the Air Force and the Navy could have sustained no more than three days of operations. After only three days of conventional warfare, the U.S. would either have to withdraw or escalate to nuclear war.[59] The U.S. thus came perilously close to *obliging* itself to fight a nuclear war against China, whether the national command willed it or not. Furthermore, high-level military commanders in the Pacific viewed the order to defend Taiwan with conventional weapons, issued by the Joint Chiefs on August 29, to be a backward step in the art of warfare.[60]

The non-nuclear presidential/JCS directive aimed to keep the Soviets out of the conflict. Secretary of State Dulles on the other hand, later claimed that he flexed American nuclear muscle to force China "to demand more from Russia . . . thereby placing additional stress on Russian-Chinese relations."[61] This effort to split the Communist alliance bore fruit after 1958, when Soviet failure to counter renewed American nuclear threats against China soon alienated the Chinese and may have contributed to the Sino-Soviet split.[62]

It is significant that all these nuclear threats were aimed at exploiting political and military advantage, not the defense of U.S. territorial integrity. The potential for inadvertent nuclear war at this time was great. If the Chinese had misjudged American resolve in 1958, or if the Americans had misinterpreted Chinese action – or both – it is likely that the U.S. would have used nuclear weapons. Indeed, the U.S. took the world to the nuclear brink to thwart what even some senior administration officers considered the legitimate right of China to self-defense. As the crisis erupted, Secretary of State Dulles wrote to his staff:

I do not feel that we have a case which is altogether defensible. It is one thing to contend that the CHICOMS [Chinese Communists] should keep their hands off the present territorial and political status of Taiwan, the Penghus, Quemoy, and

Matsu, and not attempt to change this by violence which might precipitate general war in the area. It is another thing to contend that they should be quiescent while this area is used by the CHINATS [Chinese Nationalists] as an active base for attempting to foment civil strife and to carry out widespread propaganda through leaflets, etc., against the CHICOMS regime. We are, in effect, demanding that these Islands be a "privileged sanctuary" from which the CHINATS can wage at least political and subversive warfare against the CHICOMS but against which the CHICOMS cannot retaliate.[63]

Racism and Restraint

A deep racism underlies these nuclear threats against China and Korea. The 1951 Johns Hopkins study provides a particularly telling example in its analysis of the psychological impacts of U.S. nuclear attack in Korea. The report first notes that many of the civilian casualties from U.S. nuclear attacks would be "friendly" rather than the "enemy" civilians who were the casualties in past wars, posing special problems for U.S. relations with the "friendly" government. The study then reviews the effects of nuclear attack on enemy troops: "Given the general disregard of death among Asiatics compared with Americans, it [nuclear attack] might come to be accepted as a normal hazard of war." The analysts quickly add that "Before such acceptance, however, there might be local or temporary fear reactions that would pay off largely in terms of the ratio of defeated to destroyed."*

The authors felt, however, that intimidating Asian communists would not be so easy:

The impact on the enemy's leading cadres of political type, that is, government and party, would be one of embitterment. The cadres of world Communism have now had three decades in which to adjust themselves to fighting against superior materiel. They have what amounts to preconditioned reactions to such events as a defeat imposed through superior enemy material, mixed reaction of masochistic pride in their own suffering and magnified hatred of their enemy ... Such reactions do not make them incapable of calculation or

---

* That is, U.S. nuclear attack might increase the ratio of psychologically defeated enemy troops to those physically destroyed, relative to the same ratio achievable with conventional attack.

caution. They are quite capable, of course, of adopting the tactics of a general political retreat, or an intensified offensive, on the cold-war front. The world communist system of which they are a part has many means and methods ready for either line.[64]

Accustomed to losing, Communists were as likely to advance as to retreat in the face of nuclear attack, according to these eminent American scholars. With academics feeding military commanders such pseudo-scientific nonsense, it is remarkable that the U.S. did *not* use nuclear weapons in Korea.

Indeed, the primary restraints on escalation in each of these near-nuclear wars were not moral or military qualms, nor even the prospect of domestic or international popular revulsion, but the reaction of America's allies. The threats against China in 1958, for example, led to the almost total diplomatic isolation of the United States. One can only imagine the reaction of a British diplomat, assigned to protect his country's commercial interests in Hong Kong, when Dulles told him that a U.S. nuclear attack on China would be "no more than small airbursts without fallout. That is of course an unpleasant prospect, but one I think we must face up to." [65]

Similarly, the U.S. Ambassador in Japan had cabled to Washington in 1958 that the Japanese government might object to the use of American bases in Japan in a war against China.[66] The air build-up in Taiwan had drawn on the 5th Air Force units from Japan for the Composite Nuclear Strike Force, including airlift C-130s from Ashiya.[67] The U.S. kept the Japanese government well enough informed about its use of the bases to avoid the need to request permission. But the uncertainty over Japan's response – already embroiled in a domestic debate over the renewal of the U.S.–Japan security treaty – cast doubt over the feasibility of implementing the nuclear attack plan in 1958.[68] Such uncertainty may have played a crucial role in the plan's ultimate abandonment.[69] As Edwin Reischauer, U.S. Ambassador to Japan from 1961 to 1966, commented recently, "We were walking along a dangerous precipice the whole time." [70]

Matador nuclear cruise missile being prepared for launch, Andersen
Air Force Base, Guam, January 1961
(Pentagon Archives)

FOUR ☆
NUCLEAR OVERKILL

To my mind, the question to be decided is not whether we should or should not use atomic weapons . . . the question is rather when and how such weapons should be used. Should we, for example, in the event of war, begin by bombing major centers of population in enemy territory or start with smaller centers important for transportation or specific industries? This question should be answered not so much on the basis of humanitarian principles as from a practical weighing of the long-run advantage to this country.

    —W. Walton Butterworth, Director of the Office of Far Eastern Affairs, September 15, 1948[1]

To make credible its nuclear threats against China and other "Soviet surrogates", the Eisenhower administration accelerated the deployment of nuclear-delivery systems surrounding mainland Asia. The real estate was ready throughout the Pacific since, as a 1951 Joint Chiefs of Staff memo put it: "[A]cquisition by the United States of its foreign bases has been dictated largely by atomic weapons considerations."[2] These considerations were not, however, the result of rational preparation for nuclear war. U.S. bases and nuclear delivery systems in the Pacific were the legacy of positions won in World War II and vicious infighting over the shrinking post-war military budget. As historian Roger Dingman explains, strategists primarily wrote warplans which inflated the nuclear role and basing requirements of each service:

Concerns of this sort helped make revised plans for war in East Asia more offensive, if not pre-emptive. Indeed, they transformed the East Asian main-land into a tempting target of opportunity whose very existence could help validate individual service claims for exclusive possession or priority perfor-mance of a particular function.[3]

While Eisenhower projected an image of national unity and deter-mined anti-Communist resolve, the story of nuclear war in the Pacific during the 1950s was less heroic. Battling over division of the defense budget, U.S. military services competed for pre-eminence in nuclear offensive capability and squabbled over nuclear targets. The main con-tenders in this inter-service nuclear rivalry were the Navy and the Strategic Air Command.

SAC's Pacific Spearhead

In the years after World War II, the Strategic Air Command (SAC), the heavy bomber division of the newly independent Air Force, moved quickly to take control of all aspects of nuclear war against the Soviet Union. As the admirals were well aware, SAC was about to challenge the Navy's dominion over its "own" ocean. SAC's General Whitehead wrote to the Commander of his Pacific Air Command in May 1947: "Can you imagine the consternation at Navy headquarters when you make the announcement of a mass move of a VHB [Very Heavy Bomber] Group, complete with its personnel from the Z.I. [Zone of Interior, that is, the U.S.] to Guam or Okinawa?"[4]

SAC did not delay pressing for advantage over the Navy in the Pacific. In April 1947, it began to rotate a bomber squadron from the U.S. to Japan for month-long tours in *Operation Finback*. In July, SAC highlighted its nuclear capability by flying B-29 bombers from Yokota, Japan to Washington, D.C. in thirty-one hours, stopping only at Alaska.[5] In July, 1948, SAC staged an even more spectacular demon-stration of its nuclear reach by flying two B-29s on an inaugural, globe-girdling trip via the Middle East, the Indian Ocean, and thence on to the Philippines and Okinawa.[*7]

---

* The planes flew from the U.S. to Azores Island, Libya, Aden, Ceylon, Philippines, Oki-nawa, Hawaii, and back to the U.S. SAC planes deploying to the Far East thereafter often flew the Indian Ocean route to keep their hand in for an all-out attack on the U.S.S.R.[6]

For all its publicity-generating activity, SAC had only twenty-seven B-29 bombers in 1948 fitted out and trained to drop nuclear bombs.[8] Codenamed Silver Plate, these aircraft were deployed to the Far East in 1948, the first time that they had flown outside the U.S. since the nuclear attack on Japan.[9] In the month-long tour in the Far East, the unit flew six "maximum effort" training missions in which the planes dropped bombs on Micronesian or Japanese islands, and simulated attacks on air bases in Guam, Korea, and Japan.[10] The Silver Plate bombers also flew a series of nine "Top Secret" missions.

Whether these flights were dry-runs of the March 1948 emergency plan for nuclear war with the U.S.S.R. – code-named *Grabber* – is unknown. Under *Grabber*, SAC bombers were to begin the "air-atomic" offensive from bases in Britain, Pakistan, India, and Okinawa within a fortnight of the outbreak of a war.* The Navy, then conducting the *Operation Sandstone* nuclear tests in the West Pacific to prove its viability in the nuclear age, also objected vociferously to *Grabber*, which denied it a significant role in war with the U.S.S.R.[12] The need to demonstrate conclusively its superior offensive capability *vis-à-vis* the Navy may have impelled SAC to send the Silver Plate bombers to the Pacific in the first place.

It was not until the Korean War, however, that SAC developed an effective nuclear warfare capability in the northern Pacific. On paper, early plans such as the 1947 *Plan Earshot* assigned nuclear-armed SAC bombers to targets in the Soviet Union and China in the event of war.[13] In reality, SAC bombers in the Pacific were not fully nuclear-capable until the early 1950s. At the height of the Korean War in 1951, SAC's Emergency War Plan allocated fifteen nuclear bombs to its wing on Guam for attacks on Vladivostok and Irkutsk.†[15]

Loaded with bombs – labelled "Look out Commies!" – the SAC B-29 bombers carried out their primary mission during the Korean War with devastating efficiency.[16] In just two months, from mid-July to late September 1950, they "destroyed all significant strategic targets and enemy airfields in Korea," according to the official SAC history, and the

---

* The July 1948 joint emergency warplan described Okinawa as the *only* site from which the U.S. could launch a nuclear attack without worrying about allied consent.[11]

† The military wrested possession of nuclear weapons back from the civilian Atomic Energy Commission in 1950, and received permission to store them outside of the United States in 1952.[14]

22nd and 92nd bomb groups returned to the U.S.*[17] General Emmett O'Donnell, head of SAC's Far Eastern Bomber Command, described the results graphically in 1951: "Everything is destroyed . . . There is nothing standing worthy of the name." [18]

SAC's Japanese bases at Kadena and Yokota remained springboards for attacks on Soviet and Chinese targets after the Korean War. Since the early SAC bombers (the B-29, B-50 and B-36) were handicapped by a relatively short range, SAC was forced to rely on the forward bases close to potential targets. The advent of the B-47 in 1953, the first strategic jet bomber, did not substantially alter the situation. Although the plane could accelerate to 980 km per hour, it lacked the range to reach the Soviet Union from bases in the United States.[19] Existing facilities were consequently expanded for B-47 use in Guam, Japan, and Okinawa.[20]

In 1954, Guam became SAC's chief base in the Pacific, the keystone of its arc of forward support bases stretching to Okinawa and Japan. One of thirty-eight overseas SAC bases which encircled the Soviet Union and China from all points in the compass,[21] Guam aimed its attacks primarily on airfields and nuclear bombers in the Soviet Far East.[22]

Aside from the SAC bomber wing on Guam, the Air Force deployed nuclear-tipped cruise missiles in Taiwan, South Korea, and Okinawa to threaten China and the Soviet Far East. With a range of 960 km, the Matador missile was based in Taiwan in 1957 (under the overall command of the Navy),[23] while the Mace, with a range of 1,900 km, was deployed in 1961 in Okinawa and South Korea.[24] Though both of these cruise missiles were limited in range, they could nevertheless reach targets deep inside China. The Mace could even reach Vladivostok – the Soviet Union's primary naval base – and other targets in the Soviet Far East.[25]

The Navy's Fight for a Nuclear Role

In the race for the lucrative budgetary link with nuclear warfare, the Army lost out to the Air Force and the Navy. The Army did manage to persuade Eisenhower to send its Long Tom 280 mm nuclear artillery to

---

* The 98th and 307th bomb groups remained in Yokota and Kadena, respectively.

Korea in 1953,[26] and Honest John short-range missiles followed between 1954 and 1956.[27] But the Army's nuclear programs were swamped by the Navy's nuclear fleet.

Nuclear weapons had threatened the independent existence of the Navy in the 1940s. With the Air Force positioned as the premier nuclear attack force, the Navy was forced into a painful examination of its role. In a famous memo written in December 1947, Rear Admiral Daniel Gallery argued:

The Navy will soon be obsolete. The next war will be different from any previous one. It seems obvious that the next time our Sunday punch will be an Atom Bomb aimed at the enemy capitols and industrial centers and that the outcome of the war will be determined by strategic bombing . . . I think the time is right now for the Navy to start an aggressive campaign aimed at proving that the Navy can deliver the Atom Bomb more effectively than the Air Force can.[28]

While such a statement was heresy in the tradition-bound Navy of 1947, the Navy was fighting desperately with the Air Force for a nuclear role by the early 1950s. The two services first skirmished in 1948–1949 over planning for nuclear offensives against the Soviet Union in the Mediterranean. But the main battle for control over nuclear warfare capability unfolded in the Pacific.

The Navy's first maneuver to counter SAC's emerging control of all aspects of nuclear war was a defensive one: prove that the fleet could survive a nuclear attack. Staged in 1946, *Operation Crossroads* involved a full-blown atomic attack on an unmanned fleet off Bikini Atoll in the U.S. Trust Territory of the Marshall Islands. In the Navy's opinion, the fleet "survived." [29]

Moving to the offensive, the Navy developed a "carrier-based nuclear option" to match the Air Force challenge. By February 1951, it had forged a rudimentary nuclear attack capability for carriers, with the deployment of nuclear-capable AJ-1 Savage and P2V-3C Neptune bombers.[30]

The Navy demonstrated its readiness for a possible nuclear war by deploying the nuclear-armed carriers *Oriskany* and *Kearsage* off Korea in 1952.[31] At the Navy's urging, the Atomic Energy Commission dramatically reduced the size and weight of nuclear weapons, permitting small aircraft to carry atomic bombs from carriers.[32] Thus, by the late 1950s, most of the fighters and all attack aircraft on Navy carriers could deliver light-weight nuclear ordnance, while selected fighter-bombers, the A3J Vigilante and the A6 Intruder, were assigned the city-busting, strategic bombing mission.[33] From 1960 until 1964, when Polaris missile submarines were deployed in the Pacific, two nuclear-strike carriers were on constant patrol off the Soviet Far East to defend the Navy's role in the SAC-dominated *Single Integrated Operational Plan* for nuclear war.[34] The Navy often flew fighter-bombers armed with nuclear weapons from its carriers toward China, ordering them to veer away just before crossing the coastline so that Navy intelligence planes could monitor Chinese radar defenses.[35]

The Marines in the Pacific further enhanced the Navy's nuclear delivery capability. Former nuclear A-4 Skyhawk Marine pilot Lieutenant John Buchanan recently recalled:

My job on my primary mission days was to take off from Iwakuni, Japan, proceed across the China Sea, let down at low-level just before I reached the coast of China, and proceed inland at 100 feet off the ground and 350 knots or so until I came closer to my target. Then I was to accelerate to 500 knots and as I came over the target, to do a loop and toss my nuclear bomb in the air, continue the loop and proceed back to base . . . Later we were told that the purpose [of these SIOP missions] was to blow corridors through for the B-52s to make their way deeper into Russia . . . I was the Cold Warrior, very mechanical. I was gonna go over and bomb the military airfield in Peking and do a good job at it.[36]

Although it conceded targets to the carriers, the Air Force was not enamored of the Navy's plan to hit coastal targets in Asia and Europe, seeing it as a "poorly camouflaged intrusion into the responsibilities of the newly autonomous service [i.e., the Air Force]." [37] This inter-service conflict was so fierce that it often resulted in duplication of targeting plans.

Even *after* an inter-service conference in 1954, which had been convened expressly to address this problem, U.S. nuclear war planners still found that the Air Force and Navy had "duplicate" attacks on 115 airfields and forty industrial complexes in the Far East. There were even "triplicate" attacks on thirty-seven airfields and seven industrial complexes[38] – a phenomenon called "overbombing." Indeed, some Asian cities and bases were targeted by up to twenty-five nuclear warheads each! The 1958 nuclear war plan for the Pacific, in fact, specifically assigned the high priority ("enemy atomic delivery") targets to both the Navy and the Air Force.* SAC planners, however, refused to attach any significance to the Navy's nuclear attack forces, regarding them as too slow, unreliable, and small to bother adjusting the Air Force's Pacific strike strategy.†

In May 1954, the bitter Air Force–Navy conflict was played out in the proposed bombing of Dien Bien Phu (see Chapter 3). Aside from bombing the Viet Minh and provoking China, Admiral Arthur Radford, chairman of the Joint Chiefs, apparently had another motive – proving the effectiveness of nuclear-bomb delivery by the Navy's carrier-based planes. In Pentagon planning conferences, the Air Force argued for a tactical nuclear strike by its B-29 bombers operating out of Clark Air Force Base in the Philippines. However, Admiral Radford, a leading advocate of naval air power, later stated that the attack, if carried out, would have relied on the Navy's carriers.[42]

In an effort to match the Air Force's deployment of Matador and Mace cruise missiles in Taiwan and Okinawa, the Navy developed a carrier-based nuclear option, and, in 1955, introduced a sea-fired cruise missile – the Regulus I – in the Pacific. The Regulus cruise missile, which could deliver a nuclear warhead 640 km to Soviet ports and cities, was carried by submarines like the *Grayback* and *Growler*, operating from Yokosuka Naval Base in Japan.[43]

The Polaris missile-firing submarine was the Navy's answer to Air Force dominance over strategic nuclear weapons. Developed under the leadership of Admiral Arleigh Burke, Chief of Naval Operations during the Eisenhower administration, "the Polaris program [was] a specifi-

---

* SAC targets after 1955 were primarily inland Soviet airfields, while Navy targets were primarily Soviet airfields on the coastal periphery which would launch attacks on aircraft carriers and naval targets, especially pens which housed submarines which might threaten U.S. aircraft carriers. By 1956, however, naval nuclear-strike bombers could strike up to 2,700 km inland, competing with and greatly distressing SAC.[39]

† The situation in 1954 continued. The 1958 nuclear appendix to the General Emergency Operational Plan called on SAC and CINCPAC to minimize the use of ground bursts which would increase fallout in order "to avoid alienation of potentially friendly populations in satellites and fringe areas (and allies)."[40] Indeed, then-CINCPAC Admiral Felt worried that he might have to be "more concerned about residual radiation resulting from our own weapons than from the enemy."[41]

cally dedicated naval contribution to the strategic mission which, when fully implemented would allow the general purpose forces to remain dedicated to their limited war mission." [44] Deployed in 1964, the new submarines operated in the Western Pacific using Apra Harbor in Guam as their forward base and carried Polaris missiles with a range of 2,000 km.

The Navy, in short, had more than caught up with SAC. It had become the cutting edge of the U.S. capacity to wage limited war, *and* was fast becoming a pillar of nuclear strategy.

Nuclear Lake

By the end of the Eisenhower administration in 1960, the Pacific had become a nuclear lake. After expelling the indigenous population, the U.S. used Bikini and Eniwetok atolls in the central Pacific for at least sixty-six nuclear tests between 1946 and 1958. These included the *Bravo* hydrogen bomb explosion of 1954, the largest and dirtiest ever detonated by the U.S. Patrolling the Western Pacific were two 7th Fleet carriers which had a primary role under the new strategic targeting program, adopted in 1961.[45] Roaming the Pacific's depth were five submarines capable of attacking the Soviet Far East and China with nuclear-armed Regulus cruise missiles. Ground-launched cruise missiles were stationed in Okinawa, Taiwan, and South Korea. The Marines and Army had small nuclear weapons ready for use in ground wars. And in Guam a SAC wing was prepared to spearhead a nuclear offensive.

On offshore islands, on surface vessels, underwater, and in the air over the Pacific, U.S. forces were ready to rain nuclear ruin on the Soviet Union, China, or any other enemy. One U.S. Senator called this awesome nuclear strike capacity "a perfectly fabulous capability of delivering nuclear weapons in the Communist countries." [46]

Well-wishers wave at B-47 nuclear-capable bomber departing Yokota, Japan, 1954
(Strategic Air Command)

FIVE ☆
NUCLEAR WAR BY
THE BOOK

We have the ability now, right now, to destroy any enemy that wants to attack us or does attack us, regardless of what it [the enemy] does, or when it does it, or how it does it, or anything else.

—Admiral Arleigh Burke, 1960[1]

Limited nuclear war represents our most effective strategy against nuclear powers or against a major power which is capable of substituting manpower for technology.

—Henry Kissinger, 1957[2]

American nuclear threats in the 1950s were matched by a frenzy of nuclear war preparation and planning. These preparations pivoted on the string of forward bases in Japan and the Western Pacific, which were fashioned into a bastion for U.S. nuclear forces. While Asia–Pacific host countries became involved in every aspect of nuclear war – command and control of nuclear weapons, communications and intelligence for "target nomination", and execution of atomic attack – the U.S. sought neither their advice nor approval of the nuclear build-up.

U.S. plans for nuclear war were complex, confusing, and contradictory. Other than the bombing of Hiroshima and Nagasaki, the U.S. had no real experience in nuclear war. Although the atomic tests in the Marshall Islands simulated nuclear war operations in remote areas,[3]

U.S. military leaders were simply shadow-boxing with their own imaginations. As pioneers of a whole new concept of warfare, they were forced to invent bureaucratic rules and procedures for nuclear operations.

In 1955 and 1956, the Far East Command formalized these new rules as the *Standard Operating Procedure for Atomic Operation in the Far East* (hereafter, *SOP*).[4] These recently discovered documents provide a rare glimpse of the surreal character of nuclear war planning in the Pacific in the mid-1950s. Most importantly, they reveal that the all-important problem of control over the use of nuclear weapons – who can give the order to fire and under what circumstances – was far from resolved. Indeed, the *SOP* demonstrates no less than four ways in which the use of nuclear weapons could escape the control of the responsible military commanders.

Furthermore, the documents demonstrate conclusively that the United States, despite repeated refusals to confirm or deny the presence of nuclear weapons, routinely stored nuclear weapons in Japan and the Far East in the 1950s. They also show that Japan was the hub for nuclear command and communications and that nuclear bombers intended for attack on China and Korea were to have been launched from and "recovered" to Japan.

The U.S. Navy's Commander-in-Chief, Pacific (CINCPAC) developed an *Operational Plan* in 1958 that offers another view inside the bizarre world of nuclear war planning of the 1950s. As the 1958 *Operational Plan* explains in great detail, U.S. Navy commanders expected to lose communication with each other and with Washington, D.C., in a nuclear war. Once communications collapsed, local commanders were still expected to use nuclear weapons.

The *Operational Plan* reveals remarkable discrepancies between the intent and probable outcomes of U.S. plans in the event of an actual nuclear war. The inability of CINCPAC to separate China from Russia, the possibility of inadvertent nuclear war due to loose control procedures, and CINCPAC's expectation that nuclear weapons would be used at the outset of a general war, all highlight how little the U.S. military had learned after a decade of deploying nuclear weapons in the Pacific. Indicative of their remarkable ignorance of the consequences of nuclear war, U.S. commanders prepared Asian and American Special Forces for combat inside the Soviet Union and China *after* the advent of nuclear war.

Competing Nuclear Commanders

The fragmentation of command among competing services made control of nuclear weapons in the Pacific especially complex. Headquartered in Tokyo, the Far East Command was an Army fiefdom from 1946 to 1957. Created to accommodate General MacArthur's ego and the ferocious inter-service rivalry over spheres of command in the wartime Pacific, the Far East Command was a unified inter-service command (Army, Navy, Air Force) covering Japan, Korea, Taiwan, Okinawa,* the Philippines, and the Bonin Islands. Reflecting MacArthur's enormous personal prestige, the Commander-in-Chief Far East (CINCFE) answered directly to the Army representative on the Joint Chiefs of Staff.

The rest of the Pacific, China, and Micronesia fell under the Navy's Pacific Command, reflecting the role of carrier airpower and the Marine amphibious forces in World War II.[6] In 1947, the Commander-in-Chief of the Pacific Fleet, accountable to the Chief of Naval Operations in Washington D.C., donned a second hat as Commander-in-Chief Pacific (CINCPAC). Although he supplied naval forces to the Army's Far East Command, CINCPAC retained operational control of the 7th Fleet in the West Pacific.[7]

Overlapping these boundaries in 1947, the Strategic Air Command (SAC) kept command posts in Japan and Alaska to coordinate with theater commanders. Senior SAC staff were at home in the Pacific. Indeed, the Chief Commander of SAC in the late 1940s, General Curtis Le May, had directed the World War II bombing of Japan and his three top staff had served with him in the Marianas.[8]

In 1954, Guam became the command post for Far Eastern operations by SAC's Third Air Division,[9] and in October, the first B-36 wing to be deployed outside the U.S. arrived on ninety-day rotation.[10] SAC regarded training deployments in the Pacific as more convenient than Europe because U.S. allies did not constrain SAC's overflights.

This division of commands by area and function continued until 1952, when the Joint Chiefs shifted Taiwan from the Far East to Pacific Command after rejecting MacArthur's request to stock nuclear weapons there at the height of the Korean War.[11] In 1957, the Navy – by allying itself with the Air Force – scored a final victory in the bureau-

---

* Okinawa was added October 4, 1950 after the outbreak of war in Korea.[5]

cratic battles for the Pacific when its Pacific Command swallowed the Army's Far East Command.[12]

Fragmentation of U.S. military commands meant that the Far East Command's *Standard Operating Procedure for Atomic Operations* (*SOP*) formed only part of Pacific nuclear war planning. It did not control SAC's operational procedures (which remain classified) or CINCPAC's, which are available only for 1958. During its brief ascendancy during the Korean War and its aftermath, the Far East Command's *SOP* clearly attempted to impose some order on the decentralized chaos of nuclear operations. The *SOP* refers obliquely to this imperative by stating that its rationale was to ensure that the Far East Commander employed his allocation of nuclear weapons "efficiently and effectively."[13]

The 1951 Johns Hopkins University report to the Far East Command on nuclear warfare in Korea had concluded: "[I]t generally will not be feasible to set up new separate procedures and doctrines for the tactical use of nuclear weapons except to the extent that these new procedures and doctrines can be integrated into and coordinated with, procedure and doctrine applicable to the tactical use of *all* weapons."[14] Like the 1955 *SOP*, the study recognized that nuclear weapons were unprecedented and their use would compress the normal time for military organization from years and months to weeks and days. The 1955 *SOP* tried to resolve the key organizational problems identified in the 1951 report – maintenance of central control, effective integration of ground–air intelligence and operations, and target identification.[15]

Rules of the Game

After the Korean War, General John Hull, former head of the 1948 U.S. nuclear tests in the West Pacific, was appointed Commander-in-Chief, Far East, over the heads of senior Army officers. Drawing on his experience with the testing program which, he wrote in 1948, "simulates actual [nuclear] wartime operations", Hull brought considerable nuclear enthusiasm and expertise to Tokyo.[16]

General Maxwell Taylor took over in April 1955, and issued the Command's first *SOP* in June 1955. The *SOP* was revamped in 1956 by Taylor's replacement, General Lyman Lemnitzer.

In 1955, General Taylor was responsible for waging nuclear war in the Far East. Denied prior authority to use nuclear weapons, he had to get the nod from the President via the Joint Chiefs of Staff (JCS) when hostilities broke out or were imminent. The General assumed that receipt of such a go-ahead would be problem-free: "Upon initiation of hostilities, on a scale warranting the use of atomic weapons," he stated, "it is expected that CINCFE [Commander-in-Chief, Far East] will be authorized to expend atomic weapons, in support of combat operations, in accordance with current JCS policy and operation plans."[17] Although this authorization would have activated the entire structure of command and control over atomic warfare in the Far East, the General offered absolutely no operational procedures if he were to lose contact with Washington.*

Unlike the nuclear weapons authority structure of the 1980s, this arrangement did not require Taylor to seek approval for each atomic strike. Instead, he apparently received a general authorization to use nuclear weapons as he saw fit, and even had the discretion to further delegate nuclear authority† to subordinate commanders.

General Taylor appointed a Deputy for Atomic Operations (hereafter the Deputy) who acted as his representative at the Theater Joint Operations Center (hereafter the Center). The brain of atomic warfare in the Far East, the Center acted as his "joint agency for the planning and coordination of atomic operations."[18] Besides his Deputy, the General selected the Center's administrative/executive director. General Lemnitzer instructed the center's director to keep "a current display of all Far East Command Atomic Operations and those operations of other commanders which may affect the Far East Command effort."‡[20] The three component commands – Army, Navy, Air Force§ – were also represented at the Center, which was based at Taylor's headquarters in Tokyo.‖

---

* It is possible, of course, that he received orders on this matter which were regarded as so sensitive that they were not incorporated in the top secret *SOP*.

† By which we (following the *SOP*) mean authority to expend nuclear weapons as specified.

‡ The Center was initially run by the Far East Air Force, which appointed the director and operated "in coordination" with two assistant directors from the other two services. In 1956, General Lemnitzer took back the power to appoint the Center's director.[19]

§ The component commands were: Army Forces, Far East/8th U.S. Army; Navy Forces, Far East; Far East Air Force.[21]

‖ Emergency alternate sites were located at Fuchu Air Station and Yokosuka in Japan.[22]

At the most general level, the Far East Commander's responsibilities were exercised through the Center "by acting on component commanders' proposed atomic strike plans, by allocating weapons, and by delegating to component commanders authority to expend weapons." [23] Taylor or his Deputy was also responsible for approving targets and resolving local inter-service rivalries. [24] In 1956, General Lemnitzer for the first time dealt with emergency destruction of nuclear weapons, claiming that he controlled such activity. [25]

Once granted nuclear authority, Taylor had two options: he could retain all authority to use nuclear weapons; or he could order his commanders to expend specific warheads. These standing orders detailed further procedures for either a planned or emergency war situation. Significantly, General Lemnitzer defined an "emergency" in 1956 to be "a situation which gravely affects a commander's forces and requires immediate usage of any weapons at his command *without regard to Standing Procedures*." [26] In other words, the appropriate procedure for emergency situations was to abandon all the control and coordination structures set up by the *SOP*!

General Taylor could also authorize his commanders to nominate targets for atomic destruction. "Analyzing a specific target and determining that it warrants atomic attack," he directed, "is the responsibility of the nominating commander." [27] If General Taylor elected to retain expenditure authority either before or during an actual war, his commanders would submit Atomic Strike Nomination Messages to the Center which maintained the current list of targets, updated with the latest information for the first day of nuclear war. [28] In an emergency, when conditions changed and new situations emerged rapidly, the Center switched to a Prenominating Intelligence Reporting System. The System then used intelligence information to classify a nominated target as a "scheduled target", a potential "target of opportunity", or a "contingent target" (needing more intelligence to qualify for the nuclear hit-list). [29]

The primary role of the Center was to ensure that targeting was coordinated – and correct. Anticipating problems of duplication, both Generals ordered the Center "to include all target conflicts which have not been resolved" in the presentation to the Commander-in-Chief Far East at the daily meeting on the Atomic Operations Plan. [30] Inter-service conflicts and competitive targeting, in other words, had remained a problem despite the creation of two major multi-service boards, the

Joint Coordination Center at Hawaii, and the Joint Coordination Center Far East of the Joint Chiefs of Staff.* [32] Indeed, General Taylor may have initiated the *SOP* for presentation to the annual Worldwide Coordination Conferences held in Washington, D.C., to mediate interservice squabbles over nuclear targets. [33]

While targeting procedures were the same whether the Far East Commander retained or delegated nuclear strike authority, the procedures for executing the attack differed. If he retained authority, his officers developed the strike plan and he approved all strikes. In a nuclear war, he was to have sent out Atomic Strike Execute Messages to his commanders from the Center, giving the signal to bomb nominated targets. If he chose to delegate his authority, his commanders were required only to notify the Center of their intended targets. The Center, in turn, was to coordinate these intention-to-strike messages at a daily planning conference to ensure that nuclear weapons were used efficiently. Once the nominated target was checked, the Center would then reply to the commanders with Atomic Strike Execute Messages, [34] and nuclear warheads, in theory, would start flying.

Whichever option the Far East Commander chose, nuclear strikes were supposed to require receipt of the execute message. When he retained authority to expend nuclear weapons, his execute message to commanders ordered them to implement *his* warplan. Conversely, if he delegated his authority to component commanders, the execute message merely rationalized the nuclear attacks, weeding out duplication and error. As we shall see, this distinction was central to the loopholes in the system that could allow the whole procedure to go haywire.

In either case, the Far East Commander was to compile an Atomic Strike Plan Summary Message for dispatch to the Joint Chiefs' representative at the Joint Coordination Center in Tokyo and to his own commanders. To transfer these messages, General Taylor set up a communication system over eleven teletype, telephone, and radio channels which connected the Center with subordinate commanders, the Joint Chiefs of Staff representative in Japan, and the region's other nuclear command posts (most importantly, the Strategic Air Command). Each, in turn, "patched" messages through to their own senior commanders in the U.S. [35] The General ordered that "instantaneous

---

* Which included the Far East Command, Strategic Air Command, Alaskan Command, and Pacific Command. [31]

communications" were "mandatory" in nuclear operations and warned commanders that "delays inherent in normal command and administrative networks cannot be tolerated."[36] Although consistent with the imperatives of controlling nuclear weapons, this order defied the reality of unreliable communications across the vastness of the Pacific. Loss of communications, as we shall see, was a key pathway to loss of control over nuclear weapons. The dilemma continues to haunt nuclear war planners four decades later.

Loss of Control

Although control over its own nuclear arsenal was a top priority of the Far East Command during the 1950s, the actual control over atomic weapons remained highly decentralized and was weakened by four crucial loopholes in the standard operating procedures. The first loophole concerned exceptions to the requirement that the Center issue an execute message before an atomic strike could be carried out. "Failure to receive such an execute message . . . from the TJOC [Theater Joint Operations Center]," declared General Lemnitzer, "will *not* preclude such a strike from being executed as scheduled in the atomic intentions message . . ."* In plain English, a commander with delegated authority to use nuclear weapons did not require approval from the Center to carry out an atomic strike. This leeway was granted despite explicit assertion elsewhere that the Atomic Strike Execute Message was crucial in avoiding unauthorized, incorrect, or improper targeting.†[38]

Since this reversal of standard procedure might encourage a cavalier attitude toward atomic strikes among field commanders, General Lemnitzer warned:

This is not to be construed that the coordination machinery of the TJOC [Theater Joint Operations Center] be ignored but rather that *the tactical com-*

---

* The issue was simply neglected in the first *SOP*.

† General Lemnitzer noted that if the Execute Message did not include the identifying numbers attached to nominated targets by the originating command in his message to the Center, then those targets "either were *not approved by the CINCFE* (Commander-in-Chief, Far East) *or were in conflict with another commander* and are being held pending the results of that commander's strike."[37]

mander is free to exercise his command prerogatives, if for some reason (i.e. loss of communications, mission or forces are in jeopardy) such coordination machinery is not available. Notwithstanding, it is the responsibility of the individual commander to insure that all precautions have been taken to prevent the inadvertent destruction of friendly forces. Under these circumstances, it would be incumbent on the commander having so exercised his command prerogative to inform this command of his action as soon as the tactical situation permits.[39]

By admitting that an Execute Message aimed only to coordinate but not control nuclear strikes, this *SOP* directive contained immense room for nuclear mistakes.

A second potential loss of centralized control arose from General Lemnitzer's order to the head of Far East Air Force about the conduct of close air support strikes. If the commander "desires to assign an alternate target," he instructed, "*the plan will not be delayed for inclusion of this alternate target* if such delay could prevent meeting the [bomb delivery] time on target."[40] That is, if the original target could not be located, and if an air commander in close enemy range spotted a suitable substitute, the attack could proceed without prior approval from either the Center or Far East Command.

This blanket approval for atomic air strikes clearly allowed for enormous error on the part of a combat commander. Aside from the directive's obvious potential for poor coordination, bombardiers were notorious for misidentifying targets from the air.*

Another potentially disastrous source of confusion arose from the possibility of naval nuclear strikes outside of the Far East Command's control system. General Taylor ordered that "when conditions require that carrier task forces maintain radio silence, Naval commanders to

---

* Because pilots and aircrews were untrained in air observation and interpretation of ground targets, flew over unfamiliar territory, and moved at high speeds at low altitude, the 1951 report on use of nuclear weapons in Korea concluded that "Visual observation, particularly by bombers and fighters, has low credibility."[41] Identifying nuclear targets added special intelligence requirements, viz. estimation of the point location of the target center; the size of the target and the numbers and distribution of equipment and personnel within the area target; and distinguishing friend from foe.[42] In a training bombing run in 1948, for example, B-29 bombers hit the inhabited island of Kuma-shima rather than the target island range on Tori-shima, despite the lead bombardier's clear view of the target.[43]

whom authority to expend [nuclear] weapons has been delegated *may accomplish planning and execution of strikes with these weapons within the Navy structure.*" Thus, all the Navy had to do to launch a nuclear attack was submit its Strike Intention Messages to the Center "as far in advance of execution as possible."[44] This discretion simply recognized the *de facto* autonomy of the Navy's Pacific Command and its extreme reluctance to subordinate naval nuclear forces to the Army's Far East Command. These decentralized procedures allowed for overlapping and potentially disastrous nuclear strikes by the Army's Far East Command in competition with the Navy's Pacific Command headquarters.

The instructions to the emergency disposal units are the fourth and most remarkable route to a potential loss of control over nuclear weapons. "In the event that capture of atomic weapons is imminent and communications have been disrupted or time *does not permit the request for and receipt of authority to dispose of atomic weapons,*" directed General Lemnitzer, "all concerned" were, in order of priority, to:

(1) Evacuate all material.
(2) Evacuate nuclear components and utilize non-nuclear components [presumably the high explosive detonators] . . . against known or suspected targets.
(3) Evacuate nuclear components and destroy non-nuclear components.
(4) *Utilize weapons as atomic weapons against known or suspected targets.*
(5) Destroy nuclear and non-nuclear components.[45]

The General ordered, in short, that nuclear weapons should be used – without further approval – if the warheads could not be evacuated during a crisis. That is, he preferred the risks of nuclear explosions to the risks of simply rendering the weapons inoperable.

Japan, Nuclear Pivot of the 1950s

Military strategists of the 1950s imagined nuclear war to be a more relaxed activity than the apocalypse envisaged in the 1980s. Instead of minutes and hours, nuclear war planners thought in terms of months and even years. As Albert Wohlstetter wrote in a 1954 Rand Corporation report: "The job of Strategic Air Command is not likely to be accomplished by the first strike, and repeated strikes against the enemy will be required."[46] In establishing its procedures for *daily* wartime planning conferences at the Center, General Taylor anticipated that nuclear warfare would be a protracted affair.[47] CINCPAC's nuclear annex to the Joint Chiefs' *General Emergency Operational Plan** likewise assumed that the first phase of a nuclear war would last a month.[48] Logistical planning for nuclear war reflected the military's conception of a leisurely pace.

Some time between 1952, when nuclear weapons were released to the military for overseas deployment,[49] and 1955, when General Taylor issued the first *SOP*, the Far East Command set up a fullblown nuclear weapons storage and logistics system in the Pacific. While nuclear command and control were superficially centralized at Taylor's Center in Tokyo, nuclear weapons delivery, storage, recovery, and disposal units were dispersed throughout the Far East. Due to the limited facilities available to the Far East Command when General Lemnitzer issued the second *SOP* in November 1956, even the forward-deployed portion had to be kept at the SAC-controlled storage site in Guam. "In the event of a global war or contingency operations in the Far East," explained Lemnitzer, "that portion of CINCFE's [Commander-in-Chief, Far East's] allocation of atomic weapons remaining in CONUS [Continental United States] on D-Day will be airlifted to the Far East Command."[50]

The *SOP*, moreover, reveals what the U.S. military has never admitted publicly: "In addition to those [nuclear weapons] stored in the CINCSAC [Commander-in-Chief, Strategic Air Command] sites referred to above,† *CINCFE's atomic weapons and components are stored in storage sites under the operational control of the component commands of the FEC* [Far East Command]."[51] This statement provides the first official documentary evidence that the U.S. stored nuclear weapons in Japan and elsewhere in East Asia in the 1950s.

Under Lemnitzer's *SOP*, either he or his Deputy for Atomic Operations coordinated supply and resupply of nuclear weapons (except for naval forces which were to normally rely on CINCPAC for nuclear weapons support). Moving downward on the chain of command, twenty-three officers at thirteen sites held nuclear weapon "accounts"

---

* This is not the *Oplan 25–58* used in the Taiwan Straits crisis.

† Earlier, the *SOP* refers to a singular SAC site being used for CINCFE nuclear storage. As SAC forces based at Yokota shifted to Guam between June 1954 and April 1955, this SAC site must have been Guam, as must have been those referred to as CINCSAC "sites."

Table 5.1:
Nuclear Weapon "Accounts and Disposal Units", Far East Command, 1956–1957

Country	Command	Site
A. Sites of Far East Command Nuclear Weapon Accounts (1957)[a]		
Japan	Army Forces, Far East	Ikego AD, Zuchi (2)
	Air Forces, Far East	Hazuke Air Field, 80th Fighter Bomber Squadron (1)
		Johnson AB (1)
		Misawa AB (2)
		Komaki AB (1)
	Navy Forces, Far East	Sasebo NOF (1)
		Yokosuka NOF (1)
		Iwakuni NAS (2)
		Atsugi NAS (1)
Okinawa	Army Forces, Far East	Sobe, RYCOM AD (2)
	Air Forces, Far East	Kadena, 7th Tactical Depot Squadron (5)[b]
		Kadena, 12th Fighter Bomber Squadron (1)
	Navy Forces, Far East	Naha NAF (1)
Iwo Jima	Air Forces, Far East	Central Air Base, 7th Tactical Air Squadron (2)
B. Far East Command Sites with Nuclear Weapon Disposal Capability, (1956)[c]		
Japan	Army Forces, Far East	7th OD, Ikego AD, Zuchi
		17th OD, Funaoka AD, Funaoka
		Hozono AD, Kamada
	Air Forces, Far East	2715th ASSD, Tachikawa AB

Table 5.1: (cont)

	Naval Forces, Far East	2716th ASSD, Yamode AP, Kokura 2718th ASSD, Kozojo NOF, Yokosuka NOF, Sasebo
Okinawa	Army Forces, Far East Air Forces, Far East	5th OD, Machinato 546th ASSD, Kadena AB
Guam	Air Forces, Far East	Anderson AB
Philippines	Air Forces, Far East	Clark AB
South Korea	Army Forces, Far East	8th OD, Uijongbu

Key: ( ) = Number of nuclear weapon accounts; AB = Air Base; AD = Ammunition Depot; AP = Ammunition Park; ASSD = Ammunition Supply Squadron Depot; NAS = Naval Air Station; NOF = Naval Ordnance Facility; OD = Ordnance Detachment; RYCOM = Ryukyus Command.

Notes: a. From Far East Command, *Standard Operating Procedure for Atomic Operations* (mimeo), 1956, Appendix 11, p. D–11–1.

b. Three of these officers were in receipt of "Nuclear items only". The remainder could also receive non-nuclear parts of nuclear weapons.

c. From *ibid.*, Appendix 1 to Annex D, revised January 1957.

and were responsible to Lemnitzer for receipt, custody, and tracking of nuclear weapons (see Table 5.1). In 1957, these officers were located in Japan, Okinawa, and Iwo Jima.

In addition, fourteen nuclear weapon disposal units were active in the Far East Command in 1956. The Far Eastern Army and Air Forces had six units each, and the Navy had two units. Since emergency disposal was integral to nuclear warfighting orders, the presence of disposal capability identified a fighting unit as nuclear-capable. Although concentrated in Japan, the disposal units were more widespread than nuclear weapon accounts, and were found in Okinawa, Iwo Jima, south Korea, Guam, and the Philippines.

The presence of a disposal unit, however, did not demonstrate that nuclear weapons were stored at a particular site; for that, munition storage units were undoubtedly required. It seems logical that only the six sites with both nuclear accounts *and* storage depots listed in Table 5.1 could have served as nuclear weapons storage sites.* Nuclear weapons were probably just transshipped through the nine account sites without munitions storage† in peacetime; in wartime, nuclear weapons would have been shipped to nuclear-capable forces at these sites without interim storage. Overall, Japan was clearly the logistical center for Far Eastern nuclear operations.

It is possible that the U.S. stored the actual nuclear fissile material of the bombs – known as the "core" – only in U.S.-controlled Okinawa, and not at Ikego, Sasebo, or Yokosuka in mainland Japan. However, we can infer from the *SOP* statement that, at the very least, the "non-nuclear" mechanical assemblies for nuclear weapons were stored at one of the mainland sites in Japan in the late 1950s.‡ Indeed, a 1958 CINCPAC message to the U.S. Joint Chiefs of Staff confirms that this was probably the arrangement.§ "With the advent of sealed pit

---

* That is, at Ikego, Sasebo, and Yokosuka in Japan; Sobe/Machinado and Kadena in Okinawa; and Anderson in Guam (where SAC stored Far East Command's weapons).
† That is, Hazuke, Johnson, Misawa, Komaki, Iwakuni, Atsugi, Sobe, Naha, and Iwo Jima.
‡ The *SOP* states that "atomic weapons and components are stored in [Far East Command-controlled] storage *sites*", that is, not just at Okinawa.
§ Because the heat released from fissile materials could distort sensitive components, the nuclear cores were stored separately from the rest of the bomb in the first designs. In about 1958, advanced designs known as "sealed pit" allowed the core to be stored in the

weapons," cabled Admiral Harry Felt, "the need for complete weapons at aircraft sites will become immeasurably greater."[52] The introduction of nuclear weapons into Japan, Felt stated, had "no solution which will meet fully Jap [sic] and U.S. desires." He then outlined U.S. nuclear weapon options in Japan:

(1) To maintain the status quo with respect to weapons in Japan even though other stocks are converted to sealed pit weapons.
(2) To remove non-nuclear components from Japan when they become obsolete, without replacement.
(3) Secretly to replace non-nuclear components with sealed pit weapons when the former become obsolete.[53]

The "status quo" may therefore have been the storage of nuclear weapons components in Japan without the cores. While the third option – secretly introducing weapons with cores into Japan – was the "most desirable militarily", Felt recommended maintaining the status quo because it was "the most practicable at this time." The third option was adopted – as far as is known – only at one, and possibly two sites after 1960.

General Lemnitzer's *SOP* also reveals some of the potential U.S. nuclear targets in Asia. In explaining how to transmit Atomic Strike Execute messages, he cites the example of a one-megaton attack by a bomber from Kadena Air Base in Okinawa on a Chinese airfield about 95 km from the Soviet border.[54] A typical Atomic Strike Intention message ordered a F-100 plane from Misawa Air Base in Japan to launch a nuclear strike on a target in Korea just north of the Demilitarized Zone.[55]

In cases where Far East Command's forces could not deliver the nuclear strike, the Center was to request support from Strategic Air Command (SAC).[56] In one example, Far East Command requests a SAC bomber to deliver a 1 megaton Mark 6 bomb on an airfield in northwest Korea close to the Chinese border, to explode at 1,000 m altitude over a large concentration of aircraft.[57] Another model message calls for an Honest John missile to explode 300 m above the "target of

---

assembly, simplifying logistical arrangements, but complicating the political aspects of overseas storage. Before sealed pit weapons were deployed, the U.S. could claim that nuclear weapons minus the core were not nuclear weapons.

opportunity", a concentration of troops north of the Demilitarized Zone, just 6 km from U.S. forces.[58]

Op Plan 58: Quick Strike and Preemptive Strike

The *SOP* was not the only attempt to rationalize and control nuclear warfare in the Pacific. Admiral Harry Felt, the Commander-in-Chief Pacific (CINCPAC), compiled the Pacific portion of the Joint Chiefs' *General Emergency Operational Plan* for his Command in 1958, one year after it absorbed the Far East Command.* Reviewing the nuclear near-misses in Korea, Vietnam, and the Taiwan Straits, he also ordered his subordinates to amend all his contingency warplans to include non-nuclear options.[59] Despite this development, his warplan continued to assume that nuclear weapons would be used at the *outset* of general war between the "Sino-Soviet bloc" and the U.S.[60]

Codenamed *Normal*, the basic CINCPAC nuclear warplan contained options ranging from *Quick Strike* mobilization to counter a Soviet attack-without-warning, to a carefully planned U.S. preemptive strike against the Sino-Soviet bloc.†[64] In contrast to the 1958 Taiwan crisis, CINCPAC's 1958 *Operational Plan* relied on nuclear forces already based in the Far East. The plans called for SAC KC-97 tankers loaded with nuclear weapons in Guam and Okinawa to fly to Japan in an all-out war. There the nuclear weapons were to be shifted to nuclear aircraft for strikes on China and the Soviet Union.[65]

These CINCPAC arrangements may have supplanted the nuclear storage system maintained by the Far East Command until its absorp-

---

* Hereafter called CINCPAC's 1958 *Operational Plan*.

† To implement *Normal* in 1958, Felt had 48 B-57s bombers from Johnson Air Base in Japan, and 225 F-100 fighter-bombers based in Itazuki and Misawa in Japan, Kadena Air Base in Okinawa, and Clark Air Base in the Philippines,[61] as well as numerous carrier-based strike aircraft and missiles in Taiwan and south Korea. The *Plan* orders that a preemptive strike "will be directed to the elimination of Soviet long-range nuclear weapon delivery capability, attainment of air superiority, containment of Soviet air-ground offensives, destruction of Soviet war sustaining facilities, and isolation and elimination of deployed Soviet and Satellite [that is, Chinese, north Korean, and possibly north Vietnamese] military forces."[62] In the *Quick Strike* option for nuclear attack, on the other hand, U.S. bombers were to attack Soviet and Chinese cities and military targets for instant retaliation to "cause maximum disruption."[63]

tion by CINCPAC in 1957. Reflecting the changes in command, the 1958 *Operational Plan* ordered the 315th Air Division in Okinawa to "maintain sufficient aircraft on a continuous 30-minute departure alert at Kadena and Central Air Base, loaded with weapons and/or nuclear capsules for delivery of first wave requirements to bases in Japan."[66] The 5th Air Force in Japan in turn was ordered to "maintain capability to commence launch of atomic forces in Japan within one hour of receipt of complete nuclear weapons."[67]

Japan's role as the key nuclear attack platform was spelled out with absolute clarity in the 1958 *Operational Plan*. Similarly, in 1960, the Defense Department informed the U.S. President of a top secret plan for SAC aircraft to use two U.S. bases in Japan for recovery of Guam-based nuclear bombers and SAC "post-strike operations."[68] Not even U.S. Ambassador to Japan Edwin Reischauer was apprised of these plans. He later noted of the Japanese that "They wouldn't [have known] if I didn't."[69]

Unconventional Nuclear Warfare

Air-delivered nuclear bombs evidently did not satisfy CINCPAC. The 1958 *Operational Plan* reveals that Admiral Felt intended to use trained Asian* and U.S. "unconventional warfare" forces in a nuclear attack in China or the Soviet Far East "to exploit the chaotic conditions resulting from the atomic attacks." These forces were to infiltrate "*indigenous* special forces into areas which have been attacked with atomic bombs and disorganized", and "rally indigenous elements opposed to Communist regime before enemy security control could be reestablished."[70] The U.S. personnel, furthermore, could back-pack atomic demolition munitions, and were assigned the dangerous mission of pinpointing "targets such as bridges, tunnels, power plants, difficult to attack by conventional means." The *Operational Plan* noted that "Unconventional Warfare use of Atomic Demolition Munitions allows precise placement and limits excessive destruction . . . Initial strikes against psychological-political forces [later defined as "fixed military installations adjacent to population centers"] may provide necessary

---

* Presumably the Nationalist Chinese, possibly trained at the CIA Station at Saipan in the Marianas Islands in the 1950s.

show of intent and strength to dissuade the enemy from further aggression."[71]

Nuclear Dilemmas

Like the Far East Command's *SOP*, CINCPAC's 1958 *Operational Plan* contained many loopholes through which an over-zealous field commander could easily run amok with nuclear weapons. Admiral Felt had already experienced the problems of unreliable communications and unwieldy nuclear command structures in the 1958 Taiwan crisis. Poor communications, in the words of an official historian, were CINCPAC's "most critical deficiency." Classified messages for nuclear strike aircraft piled up or were simply lost altogether.[72]

Admiral Felt's alarm grew in 1958 when *Hard Tack* nuclear tests over Johnston Island produced a dramatic black-out of all communications across the Pacific.[73] He was also worried about the organization of nuclear command and control. In the Taiwan Straits Crisis, he had discovered the incompatibility of the *highly centralized* command organization required for effective nuclear war with the *highly decentralized* command needed for effective conventional war by the same forces in Taiwan.[74] All in all, Felt knew his nuclear forces were a mess, and he called on Washington for help. In 1959, Washington sent to Hawaii an eager strategic analyst from the Rand Corporation named Daniel Ellsberg.[75]

Poring over the 1958 *Operational Plan* in CINCPAC's top secret "cage" at Camp Smith in Hawaii, Ellsberg was amazed and alarmed. He quickly discerned that the problems in the *Operational Plan* were far worse than Admiral Felt had imagined. As nuclear command and control messages cascaded down the partly automated and bureaucratic communications of Pacific Command, clarity faded and confusion grew within the vast, multi-layered hierarchy.

The biggest flaw in the *Operational Plan*, Ellsberg later recalled, was the widespread belief that authority to use nuclear weapons had been delegated from Washington to CINCPAC and from CINCPAC to his senior commanders. This belief rested on the assumption that communications would probably be lost at the outset of nuclear war. While Ellsberg initially feared that erroneous *beliefs* were the problem, he soon found that reality was even worse: nuclear weapons in the Pacific were *in fact* beyond centralized control.

The *Operational Plan* stated unambiguously that: "In the early stages of general war, atomic coordination procedures may fail because of disrupted communications."* The *Plan* continued: "The Fleet Commander who has access to atomic weapons suballocated to him will destroy targets as required by this Plan *despite the lack of communications and subject to the receipt of authentic indication that the President has authorized the employment of atomic weapons.*"[76]

The contradiction built into this directive left the field commander in an ambiguous position, recognized by the *Plan* itself:

It is recognized that a disaster could occur which would disrupt normal operational and command channels . . . thus precluding the transmission of notification and weapon release instructions to effect implementation of emergency war plans . . . Should the time come when it is apparent to a commander that he must proceed on his own initiative, he must take such courses of action, based on the information at his disposal, as appears to best suit the national interest. Prior planning, a complete understanding of his mission, and common sense are the considerations that a commander must consider in reaching his decision.[77]

Since the *Operational Plan* had been designed to *provide* commanders with just this sort of prior understanding of their missions, Admiral Felt was simply throwing up his hands in despair, and informing his subordinates that they were on their own.

Ellsberg immediately saw through this transparent contradiction, and began to poke further into the "common sense" beliefs about the use of nuclear weapons under loss-of-communications conditions at various levels in Pacific Command. As he travelled around the Pacific talking to senior and junior officers with nuclear responsibilities, he became aware of the widespread attitude that the President had "predelegated" authority to the Pacific Commander to launch his nuclear forces if he believed that a nuclear attack was imminent:[78]

This was a belief, in the Pacific, that clearly contradicted the principle that

---

* This assumption was realistic as communications between Hawaii, Washington, and Tokyo were usually broken at least once every day.

everyone seemed to believe in Washington, that only the President could launch or execute nuclear weapons, that nothing has been delegated . . . In the case of this belief in Pacific Command, I found that the psychological effects of the belief were extremely widespread, because it was applied at each level of command *by analogy* to themselves. Since they were all "aware" that the unified commander had this alleged authorization from the President, they believed that in logical terms it should also apply to them, if *they* were out of touch with their next higher level of command.[79]

Ellsberg also learned that senior civilians in Washington's national security elite had views about nuclear controls which clearly contradicted those of many senior commanders in the Pacific. Washington civilians did not think they had pre-delegated nuclear strike authority to the Navy's Pacific Command, but the Admirals were, in fact, operating as if they received those very orders. The confusion continued until July 1961, when civilian security officials in Washington finally located a looseleaf "blackbook" containing letters issued by President Eisenhower in 1957 to delegate advance authority to commanders such as CINCPAC in case of communications breakdown or emergency.[80] Ironically, for the first six months of the Kennedy administration, junior officers in the Pacific appear to have been better informed than the President's own advisors on this crucial issue.

Ellsberg tried to identify how the confusion might have allowed inadvertent nuclear war to start at lower levels of Pacific Command. Early in 1960, Ellsberg flew without notice to Kunsan Airfield in Korea, then the closest U.S. air base to the Soviet Union with about a dozen nuclear-armed aircraft on alert. Ellsberg remembers that the airfield was "like a little western town with a dusty airstrip". He asked the major in command what he would do if a nuclear explosion occurred at Osan, the main communications center in south Korea, or if he lost communications with the rest of the world in the midst of a crisis.*

---

* In time of war, a communications loss could indicate that the next higher level of command had been destroyed by nuclear war. Ellsberg had earlier discovered that nuclear armed fighters at Kadena were loaded with obsolete 1.1 megaton bombs without redundant safety pins. He had realized that in a real alert in which the planes were actually flown into a holding pattern rather than merely revved up as in practice alerts, the probability of accidental nuclear explosion and a nuclear false alarm at a base such as Osan were real and would increase in times of tension.

The Major replied that he would launch his planes in self-defense, despite specific orders that only the President could authorize such action. Ellsberg then asked what the pilots would do if they did not receive an order to execute their nuclear attack. Ellsberg recollects the Major's response vividly:

He paused for a moment and then said, reflectively, "I think they'd come back. I think most of them would come back." I will always remember, at that moment, a voice inside my head crying out, "Think?!" This was a man who was entirely in charge of the training, disciplining and control of these planes, and he was telling me, who had been sent from CINCPAC headquarters, that he thought that *most* of them would carry out their orders to return if they did not get an execute order. He then went on to say, "Of course if *one* of them were to break out of that circle and go for his target, I think that the rest would follow." "And they might as well," he added, "since, of course, if one was going to go, they might as well all go." He was quite philosophical about this possibility, although as he said, "I tell them not to do it."[81]

Despite the elaborate system of "positive control" requiring authenticated messages from the Joint Chiefs of the President to attack,* a single wing commander on the strategic frontier could still defeat the best-laid plans and start an inadvertent nuclear war.[82]

Continuing his enquiries, Ellsberg found that low-level officers with access to authenticating codes were often left alone at night in the

---

* The *Spark Plug* system of positive control of nuclear attack relied on a message sent first to duty officers at forward bases, and then communicated via UHF radio to attack units. The message contained only *authenticating* codes which had to match series of numbers in a special envelope, unlike the *enabling* codes for some modern nuclear weapons which cannot be armed without the right code series. Authenticating codes cannot stop the arming of the weapons, but only authorize their use. The *Spark Plug* system used a double envelope. If the series in the message matched that on the outside of the envelope, the envelope was to be opened, and the second envelope withdrawn. If the first two letters in the message matched with the first two phonetic code letters on the face of the inner envelope, the message ordered the units to launch. If the message contained four letters and the first two letters in the series matched those on the outside of the inner envelope (or if such a four letter code was received later), the inner envelope was to be opened. If the card inside listed all four letters in the same order, the order was to "expend" weapons on the assigned target.[83]

communications rooms of Pacific Command. Moreover, there were absolutely no procedures to send a STOP message to units winging their way toward their targets – even if the strike message proved inauthentic, a false alarm, or if the foe had already capitulated![84] As the *Operational Plan* put it, albeit rather cryptically: "Once the undertaking [the target] is specified, there will be no subsequent change."[85]

The *Operational Plan* foresaw that in "limited" nuclear war, CINCPAC might decentralize control of nuclear strikes, "subject to specific restrictions."[86] How CINCPAC hoped to "control" the back-pack nuclear commandos operating behind enemy lines was beyond Ellsberg.[87] Admiral Felt's *Operational Plan* was so seriously flawed that a host of unplanned, uncontrolled nuclear strikes was possible in any serious military crisis.

Nuclear Follies

The worst was yet to come. The *Operational Plan* assumed that nuclear weapons would be used from the very start of a general war with the "Sino-Soviet bloc." CINCPAC believed in June 1958 that nuclear weapons could substitute for U.S. conventional power in the Far East:

If U.S. forces in Far East were committed to defense of Taiwan or Southeast Asia, U.S. capability to resist Communist aggression in either Japan or Korea would be considerably reduced . . . Neither ROK [south Korean] or GRC [Taiwanese] forces could halt unaided a determined Chinese Communist [Chicom] invasion. Nor Japan and Ryukyus . . . Chicoms will probably remain capable of overrunning all of Southeast Asia if opposed only by indigenous forces.[88]

Complementing this pessimistic military evaluation was the crude assumption that the U.S. objective in a general war was "the defeat of the Sino-Soviet bloc."[89] Since the Soviet Far East offered more conventional military targets for SAC's long-range bombers (thirty-four bomber bases to China's eighteen[90]) the Navy concentrated its short-range nuclear weapons on China. "Once you destroyed Vladivostok, war with Russia was no longer 'interesting' to the CINCPAC forces," recollects Ellsberg, "whereas China, although offering few really 'lucrative' industrial targets, loomed as a large land mass suitable for attack and largely within reach, with the additional feature that the *population* was heavily concentrated in the seaboard area close to the Seventh Fleet carriers."[91]

Unlike the Joint Chiefs of Staff, CINCPAC assumed that general war with the Soviet Union would automatically involve China as part of a monolithic "Sino-Soviet" bloc. Training and attitudes at all levels of Pacific Command reflected this belief. Indeed, officers responded to Ellsberg's questions about fighting only the Soviet Union with "bafflement, horror, almost physical nausea at the thought."[92] The CINCPAC *Operational Plan* therefore did not provide for separating an attack on the Soviet Union from an attack on China.[93]

The automated targeting of CINCPAC aircraft, moreover, printed out only target coordinates, and did not distinguish between Chinese and Soviet targets. Adding to the confusion, CINCPAC commanders' top secret target maps did not show the Chinese–Soviet border even if the specific target coordinates had been laboriously entered! Under the time pressure of an actual nuclear crisis, it was simply impossible to separate the planes on the runway, deciding which were to fly to China and which were to hit the Soviet Union. Since virtually no CINCPAC bases had planes aimed only at the Soviet Union, the only way to avoid attacking China was to eliminate all CINCPAC's forces from a nuclear war. Ellsberg concluded: "Of course, you would do that only if it occurred to you that this might be a problem. I never found anyone in Washington who had any idea that there was this kind of problem."[94] Thus, even if the *national* command had issued an order to hit only Russia, "one could show that it would almost surely be aborted by the execute orders and responses at lower levels."*[95]

CINCPAC's response to an order for an attack only on Russia could thus be a nuclear-sized mistake – "the destruction of all cities in China."[96] And since north Korea was assumed to be a pawn of the Sino-Soviet bloc,[97] CINCPAC's nuclear strikes under the *Operational Plan* would probably have extended to Korea.

To his amazement, Ellsberg also discovered that CINCPAC could not

---

* As most of Pacific Command's forces were aimed against China, nuclear war with China without attack on the U.S.S.R. would have been more easily arranged by Pacific Command by simply grounding Pacific Air Force bombers in Japan and south Korea and ordering nuclear-armed warships to hold their fire. But as no one was aware that the problem existed, this feasible order would probably not have been issued.

even control nuclear weapons properly in peacetime, let alone in the midst of nuclear war. While travelling in Japan for Admiral Felt, he ascertained that the u.s.s. *San Joaquin County*, a Marine vessel, was loaded with nuclear weapons stationed off the beach at Iwakuni.* This local storage enabled the Marines to beat the Air Force to the nuclear draw by many hours. Although its presence transgressed the 1960 security treaty between the U.S. and Japan, the vessel was homeported in Okinawa, and anchored at Iwakuni with an electronic repair cover mission for convenience.[98] Despite Ellsberg's protests to Washington, the vessel remained in Japan because of the Navy's objection to civilian interference.[99]

Under the revised 1960 Security Treaty, according to former U.S. Ambassador to Japan Edwin Reischauer, "America was giving up on storage."[100] While unobstructed transit was tacitly accepted by the Japanese government as part of the 1960 compromise, the Navy kept the nuclear barge at Iwakuni at least until 1966 when Reischauer demanded its removal.[101] Says Reischauer, "I was furious because that was not according to the treaty at all. They were fudging it as the barge was not in transit."[102]

Nuclear Heyday

The mid-1950s were the heyday of U.S. nuclear offensive operations in the Pacific. From its nuclear springboards in Japan and the Far East, the U.S. threatened Asia with nuclear annihilation on numerous occasions. During this fleeting era of absolute U.S. nuclear supremacy, CINCPAC's nuclear forces were only a hair-trigger away from inadvertent or intended nuclear war in the Far East. If such a war had occurred, CINCPAC's arsenal would have destroyed most of East Asia, whether or not Washington ordered it.

During the 1960s, the increasing range of Soviet nuclear missiles and the new American communication systems transformed these U.S. bases from springboards of U.S. nuclear attack to lightning rods for Soviet and Chinese nuclear retaliation. America's Asia–Pacific allies were now cooperating not only in nuclear offensives, but – for the most part unwittingly – in their own potential annihilation.

---

* Although undocumented, confidential sources informed the authors that the Navy also kept anti-submarine depth bombs offshore Japan's coast for aircraft at Atsugi after 1960.

U.S. Military advisor in south Vietnam, 1962
(Pentagon Archives)

SIX

LOSING THE WAR,
WINNING THE PEACE

Henry viewed the world as a chessboard with black and white Soviet and U.S. pieces.

—U.S. Foreign Service officer, 1982[1]

Henry, you tell those sons of bitches [the Vietnamese] that the President is a madman and you don't know how to deal with him. Once re-elected I'll be a mad bomber.

—Richard Nixon, 1972[2]

We have sought to rely on a balance of mutual interest rather than on Soviet intentions as expressed by ideological dogmas. In dealing with the Soviets, we have, in a sense, appealed to the spirit of Pavlov rather than Hegel.

—Henry Kissinger, 1974[3]

A decade of military doctrine which placed nuclear weapons at the forefront of strategy ended abruptly when the U.S. embarked on a full-scale ground war in Indochina. For the next decade, the Pentagon focused less on nuclear weapons in the Pacific and more on conventional and covert means of warfare. Propagated by Robert McNamara, President Lyndon Johnson's Secretary of Defense, his strategy became known as Flexible Response, and self-consciously supplanted the Massive Retaliation strategy of the 1950s. A key proponent, General Maxwell Taylor, claimed that Flexible Response would enable the U.S. "to respond anywhere, anytime, with weapons and forces appropriate to the situation."[4]

The first "situation" which prompted American response under the new doctrine was the demise of French colonialism in Indochina. After the French eviction, the U.S. undertook to suppress the exploding social and political revolutions long contained by French and Japanese colonial occupation. Instead of protecting colonialism or keeping Indochina within the Western orbit politically and economically, the U.S. ended up defending little more than its reputation as a superpower capable of dealing with an upstart challenger.

To implement Flexible Response in Indochina, the U.S. drew on a three-pronged strategy. First, it took a leaf from the CIA's book on successful counterinsurgency against the Huk rebels in the Philippines.[5] This campaign combined elements of psychological warfare with repressive paramilitary operations against the insurgents, as well as political opponents of south Vietnamese strongman Ngo Dinh Diem. Diem, however, stymied efforts at land reform and political liberalization and the U.S. supported his assassination in 1963. Under Diem's successor, Marshall Thieu, U.S. policy fared little better.

Second, bombers rained devastation onto Indochina. American airpower bombarded much of the population of north Vietnam, Laos, and Cambodia into caves or refugee camps. Third, U.S. ground forces and their allies herded much of the south Vietnamese population into strategic hamlets and conducted "search and destroy" missions in the countryside.

Vietnam became the arena for a replay of the Truman–MacArthur policy struggle between proponents of rollback versus containment. The Air Force and the Navy strained to hit the vitals of north Vietnam and juicier targets in China with bombs dropped by B-52s or from aircraft carriers. Containment liberals, on the other hand, sought to stabilize the political situation by imposing changes on the south Vietnamese regime and by restraining the air war.[6] Amidst the increasingly acrimonious debate, the Johnson White House took direct control of U.S. ground troops after detaching them from the operational control of Pacific Command. The air war, however, remained under the control of CINCPAC Admiral Ulysses Grant Sharp, an adherent of the rollback current.

Transnational Garrison

U.S. bases in the West Pacific were ideally placed to prosecute the Indochina War. Nevertheless, the military acquired new bases throughout Indochina and expanded existing offshore bases in the Philippines, Okinawa, Guam, and Micronesia. At the peak of base construction in 1966, U.S. forces operated from seventy-three major air bases and airfields in south Vietnam, as well as four major and ten smaller military ports. Army garrisons and encampments dotted the whole country. This infrastructure supported over 500,000 U.S. troops, 1.2 million South Vietnamese troops, about 50,000 south Koreans, and contingents sent by Australia, New Zealand, Thailand and the Philippines.[7]

The military also constructed eight major bases in Thailand. The largest, U Tapao Air Base, hosted seventy B-52 bombers which carried out tactical bombing missions, and KC-135 refuelling planes. Subic Bay in the Philippines, together with Marine bases in Japan and Okinawa, served as a huge training ground and rear area for U.S. Marine Corps units deployed to Vietnam. Clark Air Base served as the main logistical staging area for the mainland war effort, with traffic reaching as high as fifty transports a day bound for Vietnam, while Subic Bay served as the "essential fulcrum for projecting naval and naval air power into the Tonkin Gulf."[8] Yokusuka Naval Base in Japan functioned as a rear base and maintenance center for the Seventh Fleet's four aircraft carriers operating in the South China Sea and the Gulf of Tonkin. The U.S. network of bases in the West Pacific, in short, was akin to a transnational garrison.

At the zenith of the war, the U.S. activated its maximum non-nuclear firepower – a complete inversion of its strategy in Taiwan fifteen years earlier. The B-52 bombing runs from Guam and Thailand climaxed in the "Linebacker II" attack in December 1972. Ordered by President Richard Nixon, the attack rained 20,370 tons of high explosive for over eleven days on Hanoi and Haiphong.[9] Equivalent to the explosive power of one small nuclear bomb, the air attacks did not reverse U.S. losses in the ground war where the insurgent forces retained the initiative. Indeed, the Vietnamese had already defeated the U.S. politically by forcing a withdrawal of U.S. troops from south Vietnam without a reciprocal pullout of north Vietnamese forces.

Frustrated by these failures, Nixon and Secretary of State Henry

Kissinger commissioned studies of nuclear attack on north Vietnam to interdict the Ho Chi Minh supply trail and the railway from China. But at this time, in contrast to the 1950s, the potential of domestic political fallout from even the mention of nuclear threats rendered Nixon and Kissinger unable seriously to consider nuclear attacks. Only once, when B-52 bombers were placed on maximum nuclear alert for twenty-nine days in October 1969, were nuclear forces mobilized during the war – and even that instance remained a secret between the U.S. and the Soviet commands.[10]

By the end of the Indochina War in 1975, all three prongs of the U.S. military strategy in Vietnam were badly bent. Instead of showing that conventional weapons could relieve nuclear weapons of the burden of winning "low intensity" wars, the defeat exposed the limits of U.S. military power, nuclear or non-nuclear.

The U.S. in Retreat

The U.S. defeat in Vietnam had immense geopolitical consequences. Except for its toehold in Korea, American forces were expelled from the Asian mainland and thrown back to its fortified offshore island chain. The defeat pushed Thailand, America's key remaining mainland ally in Southeast Asia, toward neutrality – a change underlined by its pressure to close U.S. bases. Neutralism swept both mainland and island Southeast Asia, with the newly formed Association of Southeast Asian Nations (ASEAN) timidly advancing a proposal that the region be converted into a "zone of peace, freedom and neutrality."

Not even the island chain escaped the impact of the debacle. Philippine President Ferdinand Marcos, a longtime ally, distanced himself from the U.S. by issuing a joint communique with the newly established Socialist Republic of Vietnam promising "not to allow any foreign country to use their respective territories as a base for direct or indirect aggression against each other."[11] And in Okinawa, protests against the use of local bases as a staging area for the Vietnam war pressured the U.S. into returning Okinawa to Japan in 1972.

Pressures for disengagement came not only from Asia but from influential elements within the United States. Key policymakers in the Democratic Party favored a withdrawal of U.S. forces from Korea. The author of the containment policy himself, George Kennan, came out in favor of abandoning American bases in the Philippines. "The original justification for the maintenance of those bases has now been extensively undermined," wrote the dean of American diplomacy. "The American response to the situation that now exists should be, surely, the immediate, complete, resolute, and wordless withdrawal of the the facilities and equipment they contain, leaving to the Philippine government the real estate, and only that." [12]

The Rise of Strategic Diplomacy

To arrest this unravelling of U.S. power in Asia-Pacific, President Richard Nixon revived a policy in 1969 which the Truman administration had seriously considered adopting before the Korean War eliminated it as an option – the encouragement and exploitation of differences among Communist powers. Nixon's Secretary of State, Henry Kissinger, began to implement *rapprochement* between Washington and Beijing in 1971.[13] The new relationship was too late to save the U.S. position in Vietnam, but apparently not for want of trying on the part of the Chinese. According to the Vietnamese, China had repeatedly urged them to accept a Taiwan-style solution for south Vietnam, with the rationale that they could win by diplomacy later what they now failed to get by force.

Both the "China Card"* and detente with the Soviet Union were elements of a new U.S. policy of "strategic diplomacy", an approach which succeeded the reliance on unilateral American force which had failed so miserably in Vietnam. In his memoirs, Kissinger explained the political and strategic assumptions which underpinned his approach:

The late 1960s had marked the end of the period of American dominance based on overwhelming nuclear and economic supremacy. The Soviet nuclear stockpile was inevitably approaching parity. The economic strength of Europe and Japan was bound to lead them to seek larger political influence. The new, developing nations pressed their claims to greater power and participation. The United States would have to learn to base its foreign policy on premises analogous to those on which other nations conducted theirs. The percentage of

---

* That is, the "normalizing" of U.S.-Chinese relations and discussion of U.S.-China diplomatic recognition, finally concluded in 1978.

the world's Gross National Product represented by our economy was sinking by 10 per cent with every decade: from 52 per cent in 1950 to . . . some 30 per cent in 1970. . . . This meant that if all the rest of the world united against us, if some hostile power or group of powers achieved . . . hegemony . . . America's resources would be dwarfed by its adversaries. Still the strongest nation in the world but no longer preeminent, we would have to take seriously the world balance of power, for it tilted against us and might prove irreversible. No longer able to wait for threats to become overwhelming before dealing with them, we would have to substitute concept for resource. We needed the inward strength to act on the force of assessments unprovable when they were made.[14]

Kissinger's program for arresting America's decline relied on manipulating conflicts in a "pentagonal" world where Western Europe, Japan, China, the Soviet Union, and the United States were the principal actors. In his scheme, detente was a carrot-and-stick policy aimed at denying the Soviets nuclear superiority while simultaneously enrolling them in a tacit alliance to contain the spread of national liberation movements in the Third World. Playing the China card would both check the Soviets and moderate the victorious Vietnamese. Inspired by both conservatism and *realpolitik*, Kissinger's diplomacy bore a striking resemblance to George Kennan's original containment policy.

Containment by diplomatic pirouettes, however, failed to appease either American liberals whose experience in Vietnam led them to desert the containment framework altogether, or the rollback advocates who saw the Indochina debacle as a failure of American resolve. Just as Kennan's earlier vision of containment as the "adroit and vigilant application of counter-force" had failed to appeal to the ideological temperament of the American foreign policy establishment, Kissinger's strategic diplomacy did not spark a consensus, especially in the volatile aftermath of defeat. As political scientist Jerry Sanders argues in his seminal study of U.S. policymaking in the Vietnam era:

Such *realpolitik* satisfied very few, however, and became a subject of bitter debate almost from the start. Conservatives, who supported the renewal of bombing and the Cambodian incursion made possible by detente, nevertheless held a visceral contempt for negotiated deals with the USSR and the People's Republic of China. Liberals, who applauded the easing of Cold War tensions, were to the same degree appalled at the cynical application of detente in re-escalating the level of destruction in Southeast Asia.[15]

Detente through strategic diplomacy was only one side of the "Grand Design" Nixon announced at Guam in 1969. The other was retrenchment and revitalization of U.S. military power to match Soviet conventional forces, then seen to be probing for advantage in the Third World.[16] The Sino-Soviet shooting war which erupted in March 1969 was a vital factor in Nixon's strategy. If Soviet and Chinese Communists were killing each other instead of presenting a monolithic threat to the West, reasoned Nixon, then the way was clear to enlist China in the containment of the Soviet Union and to reassert U.S. centrality in the global balance of power. The Sino-Soviet split also implied that less overall military power was needed to sustain "containment".[17]

Far from the withdrawal perceived by some, Nixon aimed to compensate for reduced U.S. military disengagement with increased allied power. Most importantly, indigenous troops rather than Americans were to fight ground wars. The U.S. would continue, however, to provide training, war materiel, and airpower backing. The first test of this aspect of the doctrine was Vietnamization, which promptly proved a massive failure. Even as the south Vietnamese Army collapsed, the U.S. Army fell back to island bases or to the continental United States. The Air Force, especially the Strategic Air Command, stayed on in Guam and trained its sights back to its traditional enemy, the Soviet Union. And the Navy simply sailed away to implement the military side of the Guam Doctrine, known in naval circles as the "offshore strategy".

The surface fleet faction of the Navy, led by Admiral Elmo Zumwalt, the new Chief of Naval Operations, launched a radical reform of his tradition-bound service and its fixed ideas – faith in big carriers, an almost obsessive focus on East Asia, and avoidance of land-intervention. Recognizing the failure of carrier-based bombing in guerilla wars like Vietnam and under pressure to cut costs as the war wound down, Zumwalt stopped big-carrier construction in 1974 and opted for smaller mid-sized carriers. He also established new naval priorities: control of the seas; protection of U.S. access to sea lanes and Third World resources; and, reversing established naval doctrine, intervention on land. Even these land operations, however, were seen only as brief attacks to initiate political changes. The new naval doctrine still required island bases in the Pacific for anti-submarine warfare. Professor Franz Schurmann has explained the key features of this naval modernization program:

While the U.S. would have to retrench militarily, it still had to maintain a "presence" throughout the world. The military instrument of that presence would be primarily the Navy, not the old Navy obsessed by East Asia but a new Navy with truly global awareness, strategies and capabilities.[18]

This military-reform counterpart to Kissinger's strategic diplomacy collapsed in 1974, however, when the Watergate scandal forced Nixon's ignominious departure from the Presidency. Successfully exploiting tensions between the hardliners and the diplomats in the national security elite, Nixon had won room to maneuver in withdrawing from Vietnam. With Nixon gone, Kissinger made peace with the old Navy, dropped the redeployment of carriers to the Indian Ocean ordered in 1974, and restored three of the Navy's big carrier forces in the West Pacific. Accommodating the rollback conservatives was not so easy, however, for its leaders believed that the way forward was not to avoid commitments such as Vietnam but to fight them differently. In the rightist resurgence that followed Nixon's resignation, Kissinger's strategic diplomacy was unceremoniously dumped. Throughout the debates, the Navy's Pacific fleet remained centered on big carriers, and had only begun the painful process of shifting from an anti-Chinese to an anti-Soviet posture. The philosophy of the incoming Carter administration only increased the right's restlessness and alienation, and after 1976, they moved rapidly to ally with anti-Soviet hardliners in Congress dedicated to sabotaging arms control and detente with the Soviet Union.

While Kissinger's strategic diplomacy had lowered East-West tensions in the mid-1970s, the relative peace it bought was an unstable one – a lull between leftist advance and right-wing counter-attack. While it successfully maintained nuclear parity with the Soviet Union through SALT I,* detente did not discourage Soviet aid to national liberation movements, particularly in southern Africa and the continent's north-west Horn. Kissinger's status in conservative circles fell to the point where Senator Henry Jackson, a leading Cold Warrior, accused him of "having been beguiled by the Soviets", and columnist Joseph Kraft charged that he had been "taken in".[19]

The Asia–Pacific region was the one area where strategic diplomacy was an unqualified success. But not even this achievement was his

---

* The first U.S.–U.S.S.R. Strategic Arms Limitation Treaty, signed in 1972.

alone. Continuing Kissinger's policies, the Carter administration's skilful Asia team completed the process of pro-American strategic stabilization in the Asia–Pacific region.

Trilateralism in Power

President Jimmy Carter took office in 1977 with a policy of "constructive engagement" that was supposed to depart, as he put it in his celebrated Notre Dame speech, from "our inordinate fear of Communism." As it emerged over the next four years, Carter's foreign policy encompassed aspects of the traditional containment approach, Kissinger-style strategic diplomacy (the China Card and detente), and what Jerry Sanders has aptly described as "trilateral managerialism".

Carter's policy was strongly influenced by his experience on the Trilateral Commission, a forum of prominent public figures drawn from the industrial Western countries. Responding to the defeat of containment and to increasing dissatisfaction with Kissinger's "balance of power" politics, the Commission sought a new model for world order that could mediate the growing contradiction between the military and economic requirements for the maintenance of American power. The Commission's solution to this dilemma tried, as Sanders puts it, "to shift emphasis to the economic pillar of containment but without disavowing the military pillar." [20]

The strategy's success rested on the "management of interdependence" through a reinvigorated system of world trade and refurbished financial institutions to replace the defunct international financial order which had been one of the casualties of Vietnam. For selected Third World countries, the Trilateralists "envisioned a role . . . in a rationalized world economy that offered them greater promise of economic gain through interdependence than by striking out on an independent course." [21]

It was an approach reminiscent of Woodrow Wilson's prescription for a new world order following World War I and Franklin Delano Roosevelt's vision of multilateral "internationalism" following World War II. Like its predecessors, Trilateralism was never given a chance. By the end of the Carter administration in 1980, U.S. foreign policy, after floundering for three years, had returned to hard-line containment.

Economic Unravelling

The decline in American economic power was one of the main factors that encouraged the Trilateral search for a new world order. The Vietnam War over-heated the American economy, and President Johnson, insisting on both "guns and butter", refused to raise taxes to finance an increasingly unpopular war. The result was a war-induced inflation that contributed to a domestic economic crisis.[22] Domestic contraction and dollar inflation also sparked crises in the world economy when the U.S. abandoned dollar-gold convertibility and fixed exchange rates, the bedrock of the post-war financial order, and slashed the value of the dollar – to the dismay of foreigners holding millions of Eurodollars.

The huge military effort in Indochina also reduced American economic power by stimulating the economies of south Korea, Taiwan, and Thailand. Just as the Korean War boosted Japan's industrial capability, the Asian equivalent of the Marshall Plan in Europe, so the Vietnam War propelled these second-tier Asian countries toward an export capability which would undermine U.S. economic power. All the large south Korean construction firms, for example, which outcompeted U.S. contractors in the Mid-East during the 1970s, started by building U.S. bases in Vietnam.[23] Other Asian electronic and clothing companies that later became major exporters to the U.S. traced their origins to the Vietnam War.[24] As one U.S. military officer put it: "Ten years ago, the Koreans couldn't use a can-opener, but since 1962–63, they have been underbidding the Japanese in equal quality work on overhaul of U.S. aircraft."[*][27]

The emergence of Japan as a powerful engine of export-led growth in the early 1970s further eroded U.S. economic power. After following the American lead by investing in Southeast Asia during the 1960s, Japan now considered joint development of Siberia with the Soviet government. American strategists viewed with trepidation the possibility of Japanese *rapprochement* with both China and the Soviet Union. Furthermore, the U.S. and Japan were fighting a "textile war" between 1969–71, and embarked on a trade war to export their way out of oil-related trade deficits after 1973.[28]

---

[*] Korean troops also earned $928 million in wages for fighting the Vietnam War.[25] Thailand and the Philippines received windfalls of foreign exchange from U.S. procurement and war-related business.[26]

U.S. strategists were clearly aware that a decline in economic strength reduced American strategic options in the Pacific. In the post-Vietnam crisis of retrenchment, even the military recognized the new power realities. As former CINCPAC Admiral Robert Long testified in 1982:

In my area of responsibility [the Pacific] all of our chiefs of mission are very sensitive to any political or economic action that goes on in their own host country. They insure that CINCPAC is kept fully apprised of that because those actions so closely interrelate with military action that anyone who looks at a situation from a purely military point of view is going to have a myopic view of the situation.[29]

After the military failure in Indochina, the economic basis of strategic diplomacy in the Pacific, codenamed "interdependence", became paramount for a brief period. The most radical expressions of Pacific "interdependence" were the various proposals for a U.S.–Japanese economic condominium in the Pacific, quaintly called the Pacific Basin Economic Community.[30] As Carter's Secretary of State Cyrus Vance stated in 1980: "Pacific economic integration would be best managed by a 'Pacific Roundtable' – composed of leaders and experts from the private sector across the entire Pacific (primarily the business communities and the academic world.)"[31] After a flurry of conferences, papers, and press statements, the idea faded quietly and soon disappeared from policy discussions.

Playing the China Card

East Asia was the one area of stunning success for Carter's foreign policy. But even here, it was *realpolitik* rather than the Trilateralist approach that worked effectively.

The new administration adopted the Ford–Kissinger policy of refusing to normalize relations with Vietnam, thus continuing to play the China Card to the detriment of detente in East Asia. In contrast to his early policy of accommodation with the Soviets and Third World liberation movements, Carter's policy in Asia was based on backing one side in local conflicts. In support of China's strident criticism of Vietnam as a nation "seeking regional hegemony", the U.S. toughened its economic blockade of Vietnam.

By 1978, China was openly encouraging a continued U.S. military presence in the Pacific, and its deputy prime minister told the Western press that "there were practical reasons for the stationing of U.S. troops in both Japan and the Philippines." After briefly flirting with the idea of "neutralizing" the area, the ASEAN* countries swung strongly in support of the U.S. military presence when the Vietnamese invaded Kampuchea in late 1978.

The "Vietnamese threat" was not, however, the only factor. Traditionally anti-Chinese, the ASEAN dictatorships also sought the U.S. presence as a counter-balance to the diplomatic drive of the People's Republic. By the end of the decade, the diplomatic maneuvering of Carter's Asia-Pacific team had brought the United States into a position of being courted to *stay* in Asia by both the Chinese and the ASEAN countries.

Indeed, what Malaysia's U.N. ambassador described as "the coincidence of strategic interests" had been translated into an active political and military alliance. The three allies – China, America, and ASEAN – spearheaded the effort to retain the notorious Pol Pot regime as the official representative of Kampuchea in the U.N. Simultaneously, China and some ASEAN states armed the Khmer Rouge to carry out guerrilla warfare against the Vietnam-backed Heng Samrin Government.

To carry off its diplomatic triumph in Asia, Carter's foreign policy team sacrificed a key feature of his administration – the promise to make "human rights" a major consideration in American relations with its Third World allies. Since the end of World War II, encouragement of human rights and democracy had been the idealistic side of the containment policy. When the consensus around containment shattered over Vietnam, McGovernite liberals appropriated containment's democratic mission while rejecting its *realpolitik* methods, particularly counterinsurgency.

Once in office, however, Carter could not escape the insoluble contradiction between containment and democracy. In the case of the Shah of Iran, human rights policy retreated rapidly in the face of "strategic" considerations – oil and Middle Eastern stability. And in East Asia, repressive but "strategic" allies such as Marcos in the Philippines and Park Chung Hee in South Korea, escaped the aid cuts and arms

---

* Association of Southeast Asian Nations, including Thailand, Malaysia, Indonesia, Singapore and the Philippines. Brunei joined in 1984.

embargoes applied to military dictatorships in Latin America. Indeed, Carter backed down from his campaign pledge to withdraw U.S. troops from south Korea, and negotiated a new military base agreement with the Philippines which gave President Marcos $500 million in aid.

By 1980, with Vietnam pinned down in a two-front war against China and the Khmer Rouge, and left-wing movements throughout Southeast Asia split by the Vietnam–China conflict, the U.S. had won the peace after losing the war. As Richard Holbrooke, Assistant Secretary of State for East Asia, explained:

If we had predicted in 1975 that less than 5 years after the end of our long and traumatic involvement in the Indochina wars our position in the Pacific would be as strong as it is today, almost no one – optimist or pessimist – would have found the prediction credible . . . The basic cause of tension in the region [has] become the rivalries among Communists. The non-Communist countries of Asia, relieved of many of the pressures caused by old Cold War divisions, are experiencing unprecedented economic and political development.[32]

Carter's Defense Secretary Harold Brown, a person not given to hyperbole, went even further: "Nearly thirty years after the end of the [Korean War], and a decade after the end of the [Vietnam War], the political–military balance in 1980 in the Pacific appeared more favorable to U.S. security interests than at any time since the Communist revolution in China in 1949."[33] It was a considerable accomplishment, and the U.S. had achieved it without firing a shot.

U.S. helicopters exercise in Indian Ocean before attempting to rescue
American hostages in Iran, February 1980
(U.S. Department of Defense)

SEVEN ☆
RESURGENT ROLLBACK

In a world which is becoming smaller every day, the United States cannot protect its interests by drawing an arbitrary line around certain areas and ignoring the rest of the world. That approach was tried once. It resulted in the Korean War . . . No region of the world can be excluded in advance from the agenda of our concern, for each may be used as an instrument of expanding the means of control as Soviet campaigns advance.

—Committee on the Present Danger, January 1980[1]

The emphasis on strategic diplomacy during the Nixon, Ford and Carter presidencies disturbed the military. The tension surfaced openly in 1978 when Carter ousted Major General John Singlaub, Chief of Staff of the U.S. forces in south Korea, for publicly disagreeing with the proposed troop withdrawal from the peninsula. But something deeper, more profound than the dominance of diplomacy over warfare troubled the military in the Pacific – they no longer had a clearly defined adversary.

In Search of Enemies

The U.S.–China *rapprochement* had removed the rationale which had justified military expenditure and adventure for thirty years. As Rand Corporation analyst Richard Solomon put it:

Since the disintegration of the Sino–Soviet alliance, and with the more recent normalization of U.S.–PRC relations, the sources of threat to American interests in Asia have diffused. Whereas the sharp political–military demarcation between NATO and Warsaw Pact states in Europe has been blurred only slightly by detente and American diplomacy in Eastern Europe, the one clear line of military confrontation in Asia toward which defense planning can be oriented is the heavily armed boundary between North and South Korea. The main lines of conflict in the region are now between the Communist states – disputes such as the Sino–Vietnamese rivalry, in which Americans have little incentive to become involved.[2]

One army colonel was candid in his assessment of the malaise gnawing at the military in the Pacific:

One cannot cite the Soviet airborne divisions as a threat to our interests in the Pacific, nor can one count the dozens of Soviet divisions deployed along the Chinese border. Both forces certainly exist, but they do not directly threaten our interests . . . Therein lies the difficulty for the Army in the Pacific. The threat that the U.S. Army is needed to counter is an ill-defined insidious one that comes and goes and manifests itself in the form of perceptions in the minds of our Pacific allies.[3]

The coming of peace and the loss of a clearly defined enemy was most distressing for the Navy, since "Pacific defense" had been its traditional justification for a large, modern fleet. The loss of an Asian enemy reinforced the Carter administration's Europe-first, "Central Front Strategy" which, the Navy brass feared, "would result in reduced funding for Navy and Marine Corps units around the world in order to build up and modernize US air and ground units assigned to the Central Front in Europe."[4]

The Navy watched apprehensively as the Pacific Command shrank and scarce budgetary resources were shifted to Europe. By 1977, the number of service forces in the Western Pacific area was down to 140,000 – the lowest level since 1941. The number of ships in the Navy's global fleet dropped from nearly one thousand at the height of the Vietnam War to less than 500 under Carter. Aircraft carriers, the most prized naval weapon, declined dramatically from twenty-five to twelve. Disregarding the greater efficiency of the new ships that replaced those which had been decommissioned, the Deputy Chief of Naval Operations complained: "The Navy's share of the cost of the Vietnam War was the loss of a generation of new ships." Since the U.S. Navy was replacing the British fleet as the "guardian" of the Indian Ocean, Admiral James Watkins complained that "a one-and-a-half ocean Navy" had to face the contingency of a "three-ocean war." The Navy was not appeased in 1978 when the Carter administration announced that it was abandoning the Nixon administration's "swing strategy", which would have shifted Pacific naval forces to Europe in the event of a crisis in the North Atlantic.

"The Great Soviet Bugaboo"

As it groped for a mission in the era of air power and atomic bombs in the immediate aftermath of World War II, the Navy had raised what one Air Force general once disdainfully referred to as "the great Soviet bugaboo" – a mythical Russian submarine fleet – to justify more naval defense expenditures.[5] Searching for an enemy in the Pacific in the era of detente, the U.S. naval command rediscovered the Soviet menace. Admiral Sergei Gorshkov, chief of the Soviet Navy, provided the rallying point for the Navy's counterattack. Under Gorshkov, warned the U.S. Navy brass, the Soviet Navy had outstripped the U.S. fleet. They cited the numerical build-up of the Soviet Navy and its "warm water" port at Cam Ranh Bay in Vietnam. More ominously, Gorshkov had upgraded the Soviet Navy from mere coastal patrol to a "blue water" navy capable of deep water sailing. The Russian bear, they complained, had learnt to swim. Ignored in these Cassandra-like warnings was the simple fact that the Soviets did not have even one real aircraft carrier, the essential component of effective power projection.

With the loss of the massive bases in Vietnam and Thailand, the threat to the U.S. base system in the Asia–Pacific region worried resurgent militarists. Proposals to close down bases, such as those in the Philippines, alarmed the navalists:

Given the current size of the forces allotted to the Pacific Fleet and the vast ocean areas of the Pacific Command, the loss of bases, especially in the Philippines or Japan, would make it impossible for CINCPAC to carry out his mission throughout the entire region . . . [It] would mean giving up the concept of a forward strategy in the Pacific.[6]

By the end of the Carter administration, there was a virtual schism among Asia-Pacific policymakers between (mostly civilian) proponents of containment through diplomacy, and advocates of an increased American military presence. Nowhere was the debate more bitter than over the question of the balance of power in Northeast Asia. Military analysts accused the Carter administration of running down U.S. military "raw power" and credibility in East Asia. No symbol of this decline was more potent than the absence of even a single aircraft carrier in the Pacific Far East after Carter deployed 7th Fleet vessels to the Indian Ocean.[7]

The Unraveling of Strategic Diplomacy

By 1980, Carter's Trilateralist foreign policy was floundering badly, ravaged by external failures which fed its domestic enemies. As the Ayatollah Khomeini held Americans hostage in Iran, SALT II, which limited new strategic weapons, was held captive in the U.S. Senate. Conservative think tanks like the Committee on the Present Danger and the Heritage Foundation rattled off the "losses" of the detente period: Vietnam, Kampuchea, Laos, Angola, Guinea–Bissau, Mozambique, Nicaragua, Iran, Grenada. The one bright spot in Carter's "watch", the Asia–Pacific region, could not, to the angry right wing, make up for losses elsewhere. Retired Admiral Elmo Zumwalt, former Chief of Naval Operations, reflected on the militarist challenge to the complexities of strategic diplomacy:

Increasingly, we will find ourselves outgunned everywhere, unless something is done. The present trend seems, however, to have a negative effect on the determination of our political leaders to use our remaining power. In the absence of courageous leadership to alert and rally, the prophets of doom have created a self-fulfilling prophecy.[8]

To appease the right and to break its ideological momentum, the President proclaimed his "Carter Doctrine" in February 1980 following the Soviet intervention in Afghanistan. Warning that the U.S. would repel a threat to the Persian Gulf "by any means necessary", the Carter Doctrine marked a return to containment militarism. The effort, however, did not placate the right. In their eyes, the doctrine was correct but its exponent was badly miscast. As Republican pundits put it, "Carter speaks stickly but carries a big soft."

The right's anger was not only confined to Carter and his band of "McGovernite Democrats." They also attacked Kissinger and the moderate, Eastern wing of the Republican Party which had "acquiesced" to his detente diplomacy. Kissinger, asserted one prominent conservative thinker, deserved as much blame for the demise of American power as Carter:

It was not the Carter administration that concluded the first SALT agreements within the terms of which the Soviet Union was able by 1977 to develop a clearly superior counterforce capability. Nor was it the Carter administration that inaugurated detente in 1972 and claimed that in doing so it had laid the foundations of a stable and lasting structure of peace . . . There were the actions of the predecessors of the present administration. In their effects, they compromised American interests and power to an extent we can only now fully appreciate.[9]

By the time of the Republican national convention in August 1980, Kissinger himself had adopted the right's militant rhetoric and joined the Reagan forces in attacking Carter's foreign policy – conveniently forgetting that Carter had, in fact, continued his own policies on detente, defense, and China.

The liberal consensus for containment had been shattered by Vietnam. Under attack from the resurgent right, Kissinger and Carter distanced themselves from detente diplomacy. The way was clear for a militant revival of rollback ideology.

Soviet ship cuts across bow of USS *Sterrett* during nighttime search for downed
KAL 007 jetliner, September 1984
(U.S. Navy)

EIGHT ☆
NEW MILITARISM

We're not General Motors; we don't have a profit and loss column every month. The only way we can tell whether we're doing a good job is to go to war and see if you win or lose, and wars don't come along that often. That's a hell of a handicap to work under.

> —Admiral W. Crowe,
> Commander-in-Chief, Pacific, 1984[1]

Simply stated, the concept is to get the archer before he releases his arrow.
> —Admiral S. Foley,
> Commander-in-Chief, U.S. Pacific Fleet, 1983[2]

"The United States has made a fundamental decision," exclaimed Assistant Secretary of Defense Richard Armitage in February 1985. "We are a Pacific nation and a force for peace and stability in the region. The future lies in the Pacific." [3] Billed as Reagan's Pacific architect, Armitage addressed the Pacific Symposium, an annual military bash sponsored by the U.S. National Defense University. Just in from Manila, the former Marine stood in civilian garb, a gray suit draping his double-barreled chest, his gravelly voice stabbing the air like a machine gun, his raised finger punctuating his points.

Swept into power in January 1981, the new hardliners lost no time in remilitarizing U.S. foreign policy. Following three administrations which buttressed America's declining power through detente and diplomacy, Reagan's strategists adhere to the rollback posture eclipsed since the late 1940s. In a throwback to Truman's NSC 68 in 1950, Richard Pipes, member of Reagan's first term National Security Council, succinctly expressed the old-new hard line: "Rather than seek to modify Soviet *behavior*, the West should assist those forces within the Communist bloc which are working for a change of the *system*." [4]

While the Reagan administration has been preoccupied with bellicose thrusts into the Middle East, the Caribbean, and Central America, it has not forgotten Asia-Pacific. The strategy is global in scope and it is only by examining the grand geopolitical design, the encirclement of the Soviet Union, that the importance of the Pacific becomes clear.

The new strategy is an extreme version of the globalist posture adopted during the late 1940s. Embracing a stance of global readiness, the Pentagon has abandoned the "swing" strategy whereby troops based in the Pacific could be transferred to Europe in a time of crisis. [5] Instead, forces will be built up in each theater to fight a two-front, global war. In the Pacific, according to Navy officials, the new policy permits the Navy "to originate new plans for the Far East, such as using carrier aircraft for offensive missions against the Soviet port of Vladivostok." [6]

Global Aura of Power

The new stance reveals a profound schism within the Defense establishment about U.S. strategic goals and military capabilities. Incoming Pentagon officials attacked the procurement policy called "concretism", based on a cost-benefit calculus which relates particular military capabilities to vital U.S. interests. Instead, they prefer "holism". Holists like Francis West, a former Assistant Secretary of Defense, believe that U.S. goals are best realized by pursuing global military policies which preserve an "aura of power". Adopted by Reagan's civilian defense experts, this perspective rejects the idea that U.S. commitments be ranked – *all* interests are vital. [7]

The Reagan strategy is clearly designed to recapture America's "warfighting" supremacy. There are three aspects to the new strategy: attaining nuclear superiority over the Soviet Union; upgrading U.S.

capacity to intervene against Third World forces which challenge the balance-of-power status quo; and preparing U.S. forces to wage a "protracted" war against the Soviets.

To attain nuclear superiority, the administration is developing the MX, Trident I, and Trident II ballistic missiles, the "theater-nuclear" Pershing II and ground-launched cruise missiles in Europe, and sea-launched "Tomahawk" cruise missiles in the Pacific. To beef up U.S. capacity to intervene against "Soviet proxies", there is the 300,000-man Rapid Deployment Force which covers twenty countries in the Persian Gulf area, Southwest Asia, and East Africa.[8]

The third pillar involves preparing U.S. forces to fight a "protracted conventional–nuclear war" against the Soviets. By linking nuclear superiority to interventionary capability, this aspect of Reagan's policy carries unique risks of escalation to nuclear war.

Limited War

American military strategists are actively preparing for "limited war" with the Soviet Union – that is, a nuclear war confined to one theatre or region, or a world war fought without nuclear weapons. During his 1980 campaign, Reagan confidently proclaimed: "I can see a situation where you can have a nuclear exchange without it necessarily turning into a bigger war."[9] Alarmed American allies in Europe and the Pacific restrained Reagan from making more explicit statements. Nonetheless, administration spokesmen have indicated that limited war, either the "theater nuclear" or conventional variety, remains a serious policy option.

Naval analyst Francis West, for example, told Congress in 1982: "A limited clash with the Soviet Union, quickly followed by a ceasefire, is a possibility." He elaborated:

A strategy of global flexibility does not necessarily mean simultaneous, intense conflict worldwide. Quite the opposite. It means assessing the opponent's strength on the entire global chessboard, assessing the capabilities of theater criticalities [sic], and assigning moves and countermoves designed to terminate the conflict speedily and with minimum escalation, while protecting the interests of the United States and its allies.[10]

West's scenario was recently affirmed by Lieutenant General Bernard Trainor, Deputy Chief of Staff at the Pentagon, who asserted that a limited war with the Soviet Union is an "almost inevitable probability." He hastened to add, however, that the war would be a "non-atomic, conventional, regional conflict . . . which would not result in World War III." [11]

"Global War Games" played at the Naval War College in 1983 confirmed the Navy's belief in the likelihood of protracted war with the Soviets. Captain Marshall Brisbois, Director of the Center that hosts the Games, asserted: "Global conflict will not necessarily lead immediately to the use of nuclear weapons, if at all. The United States must be prepared to fight and win a conventional war." [12] This policy is a radical shift from U.S. naval planning before 1975, which assumed that general war with the Soviets would *automatically* activate nuclear weapons. [13] Since Secretary of Defense Caspar Weinberger promulgated his Defense Guidance in 1982, the capacity to fight a protracted war with the Soviets, conventional or nuclear, has been U.S. military policy. [14]

The U.S. military puts a premium on firing first in either a nuclear or a conventional war. As Navy Secretary John Lehman put it, "Who gets to shoot first will have more to do with who wins than any [other] factor." [15]

Horizontal Escalation and Multifront War

Defense Secretary Weinberger has emphasized that the U.S. must be capable of pressing the Soviet Union simultaneously on several fronts. As he put it before the Senate Armed Services Committee: "Our long-term goal is to be able to meet the demands of a worldwide war, including concurrent reinforcement of Europe, deployment to Southeast Asia and the Pacific and to support other areas." [16]

Pentagon strategists have therefore revived the option of extending "limited war" with the Soviets from the region where it starts to other fronts. "We might choose not to restrict ourselves to meeting aggression on its own immediate front," Weinberger explained. For instance, the U.S. might choose to respond to a conflict in Europe by "horizontally escalating", that is, attacking perceived points of Soviet vulnerability like Cuba or the Soviet Far East. [17] Vietnam and north Korea are also included in the Defense Guidance as potential "horizontal" targets.[18] While navalists continue to debate whether the Soviet Far East is more or less "vital", the thrust of the strategy is clear. As John Hessman, editor of *Sea Power* magazine, wrote in 1983: "It's the Navy's way of saying a Central Front [European] war would be confined to the Central Front for only as long as it takes the Pacific Fleet to get under way."[19] An important new front is the Indian Ocean, which falls under the operational control of Pacific Command. While the U.S. moved into the Indian Ocean in 1971 to fill the "vacuum" left by the British, a major military build-up began only after 1980. Under the new strategy, the Indian Ocean represents a third major front, deserving of the same commitment as Europe and the Pacific.

The multifront strategy is trumpeted as a significant departure from the conventional war strategy of the Nixon, Ford, and Carter administrations based on a Europe-first posture. This so-called "Central Front" policy sought to endow U.S. forces with the capacity to fight a "one-and-a-half war" – that is, a major war in Europe and a smaller war in Asia or elsewhere. To replace what the Navy's Lehman has characterized as a "bankrupt and discredited view",[20] the Pentagon has advanced instead a globalist strategy akin, in the world of Admiral James Watkins, to a basketball zone defense of "going where the ball is."[21]

This strategy is reminiscent of former Secretary of State Dulles's 1954 pronouncement that the U.S. was "willing and able to respond vigorously and at places and with means of its own choosing."[22] As the Chief of Naval Operations, Admiral Watkins, testified in 1984: "It is the Soviets who must be prepared to defend their territory 'anywhere' on their perimeter."[23]

"Horizontal escalation", however, differs in one vital respect from the "massive retaliation" posture of the 1950s. Administration officials take pains to distinguish "horizontal" from "vertical" escalation, the move to all-out nuclear war. In other words, the existing "equivalence" in Soviet and American nuclear capability will not deter U.S. conventional interventions, nor preclude even theater nuclear or global conventional war with the Soviet Union.

Why does the White House adhere to this view despite Soviet warnings that theater nuclear wars would quickly escalate to all-out nuclear war? To Congressional probes on this issue, Francis West asserted simply that the Soviet Union is a "mature global superpower." [24] While administration propagandists portray the Soviets as reckless adventurers, key military theorists appraise them as cautious actors who would make – in the heat of battle – a rational decision to keep a war limited, conventional, and theater-nuclear in scope.

Maritime Supremacy

Despite Weinberger's directive, neither the Army nor the Air Force were planning or preparing for global, multifront war as late as 1984.[25] The Navy, however, soon pressed forward, reflecting its central role in formulating and implementing the new strategy.

The key to building a global "aura of power" is "maritime supremacy", a policy of securing dominion over the world's oceans. The idea has been around since World War I, when navalists argued that to expand commercially and politically, the U.S. must attain the "command of the seas" much as the British Navy enjoyed at the zenith of its imperial power. Formulated anew by the administration's leading military strategists, the global strategy relies heavily on the Navy, which views the Pacific as its special preserve. Pentagon strategists feel that the Navy has the flexibility to wage a protracted multifront war with conventional or theater-nuclear weapons.

In explaining his view of the Navy's key role, Weinberger relies on the venerable notion of sealane defense in the context of multi-theater war: "Our naval force requirements are potentially worldwide, because . . . we must be able to defend sea lines of communication along which critical U.S. reinforcements and resupply travel to forward theaters." [26] Even more important than sealane defense in the eyes of Reaganauts is the Navy's capacity "to conduct offensive operations against enemy naval forces and facilities." [27]

Geopolitical Foundations

The new emphasis on the Navy stems from what defense analysts of the "maritime school" regard as a Soviet edge on the Eurasian land mass, coupled with Soviet nuclear "parity." This "unfavorable" balance can be redressed only by assigning the primary role in conventional warfare to a superior U.S. Navy.

Navy Secretary John Lehman and other "navalists" draw their inspiration from the English thinker Halford Mackinder and the American strategist Admiral Alfred Mahan. From Mackinder, the founder of the "geopolitical school" of strategic thinking, the navalists have drawn their strategic map of the globe as a duality – a "world-island", the Eurasian land mass, and its surrounding "world-ocean." It was Mackinder's axiom that the centrally located land powers dominate the world-island – yesterday Germany, today the Soviet Union.[28]

To counter Mackinder's pessimistic dictum, "Who rules the Heartland commands the World-Island," the navalists refer to Mahan, leading propagandist of U.S. naval and imperial expansion at the turn of the century. In his view, control of the "world-ocean" is the key to nullifying the landpower of the "Heartland". Great Britain, runs his argument, effectively used control of the seas to neutralize various land powers throughout the eighteenth and nineteenth centuries. The U.S., say the navalists, finds itself with a similar option today: as a "bastion-redoubt" in the world-ocean, America can use its seapower to neutralize Soviet superiority on the Eurasian land mass at a time of overall nuclear parity, by controlling the "rimlands". As naval analyst James Roherty puts it:

The central role of sea power in American force structure rests on the overriding need to control and to exploit the oceans in the critical relationship with the World-Island . . . The oceans permit the United States to project, relatively unimpeded, immense power to points of its choosing along the "rim" of the World-Island. The projection of power by air is an important complement to the ocean medium but cannot be regarded as a substitute. The oceans provide not just the primary mode of transit but a congenial ground for engagement.[29]

Doctrinal War in Washington

To translate theory into policy, the navalists had to outmaneuver competing interest groups within the defense establishment. In addition to Reagan's sympathetic ear, the navalists had an effective warrior in Navy Secretary John Lehman. Before becoming Navy Secretary, Lehman held a string of government positions, including National Security Assistant to Henry Kissinger in the Nixon administration. As a partner of Abington Corporation – consultant to major defense contractors such as Northrop, Boeing, and TRW Corporation – Lehman has close ties with the defense industry. A member of the U.S. Navy Reserve, Lehman enjoys a strong base within the Republican Party,[30] an asset which has served him well in the bureaucratic wars.

The first major battle pitted navalists against adherents of the old Eurocentric "Central Front" strategy. Within the cabinet, the most serious obstacle was Secretary of State Alexander Haig, former Supreme Commander of NATO. Despite the tough anti-Soviet rhetoric he shared with the navalists and their ally Weinberger, Haig played the traditional strong suits of U.S. defense policy – Europe, Israel, and South Korea – adding only the "China card" that had been dealt by his mentor, Henry Kissinger. This strategy relied heavily on the Army, Air Force and allies – a "coalition defense", as one proponent put it.[31] By contrast, Lehman argued that "every strategy must be based on the use of the sea."[32]

The navalists exploited the strains which developed between Haig and White House insiders like Edward Meese, then Reagan's prime counselor, who distrusted Haig's ambitions.* Thus, when Haig was sacked by Reagan in the Fall of 1982, the Navy was well positioned to seize the initiative.

After sinking the "Eurocentrists", the navalists turned their guns on a different set of adversaries – "military reformers" in Congress and their supporters in the Pentagon. Led by Senator Gary Hart and others, the reformers pushed for a Navy of smaller ships armed with high technology weapons like surface-to-air cruise missiles to guard the sealanes. A key target of the reformers was the large aircraft carrier which they regarded as a sitting duck for precision-guided weapons. Mobilizing a pork-barrel coalition of Congress members who had ship-building and Navy homeports in their districts,[33] Navy Secretary Lehman won this battle in 1982 when Congress agreed to appropriate funds for two more super-carriers.

Finally, Lehman won the inter-service battle for budgetary appropriations within the Defense Department. Here he clashed with pro-Army advocates like Deputy Secretary of Defense Paul Thayer, who tried to transfer funds earmarked for naval modernization to the Army

---

* Reagan and his closest advisors may have been particularly put off by Haig's televised exclamation, "I'm in control here!" shortly after a presidential assassination attempt in 1982.

budget.[34] What appeared a mere budget battle was in fact a conflict over military strategy. Advocates of increased Army spending also tend to be adherents of the "Central Front" strategy, since the Army will play a key role in any European land war with the Soviet Red Army. When Thayer resigned in early 1984 to face charges of stock fraud while chairman of a defense firm, the Navy apparently had repulsed the Army assault.

Not one Navy program, boasts Lehman, has been cut back by Congress: "If you study and understand Washington, well, you can play it like a Stradivarius." [35] According to one bitter critic of the maritime strategy, the staggering $62 billion allocated to shipbuilding meant that "the Navy is the only service that is getting substantial force structure; most increases requested by the other services have been deferred." [36]

The "Lehman Doctrine"

By 1984, Secretary Lehman's effort to make the Navy the cutting edge of conventional and "limited" nuclear warfare had overwhelmed all opposition. Dubbed the "Lehman Doctrine", its main points are:

● *Maritime Supremacy*: The doctrine's objective is "outright maritime superiority over any power or powers which might attempt to prevent our use of the seas and the maintenance of our vital interests worldwide." [37] In short: "If challenged, we will be capable of sending any opponent to the bottom." [38]

● *Offensive Forward Deployment*: The Navy should abandon its sealane defense for one "visibly offensive in orientation, [with] offensive power . . . widely distributed throughout the fleet." [39] Such an aggressive posture "would prevent Warsaw Pact concentration of forces in Central Europe by forcing them to defend and distribute their forces against maritime vulnerabilities around the entire periphery of Warsaw Pact territory." [40]

Furthermore, according to navalist Francis West, keeping the Soviet Pacific Fleet "in a defensive posture and boxed up in the Northwest Pacific assures the maintenance of certain policy goals elsewhere in the region. It does not, however, contribute to its defeat, which would assure U.S. dominance throughout the region, including the vital Northeast Asia area, which is a broader post-[U.S.–Soviet]war goal. To do this requires the use of naval forces to defeat them in their home waters." [41] West concludes that the U.S. can "bottle up the Soviet Navy or . . . defeat it. The strategy for defeating the Soviet Navy is the one for which the U.S. Navy should plan." [42]

● *Targeting the Soviets*: An offensive posture requires the capacity for simultaneous attack on the Soviet fleet, its coastal installations and targets further inland. Says one Navy spokesman: "We must be able to threaten the potential adversary in his most secure areas." [43] Candidates for U.S. naval attack include Soviet shore facilities in the Barents Sea and the Soviet Far East.

● *Expansion*: According to the doctrine, the minimum number of warships necessary for command of the seas is 600. Reaganites criticize previous administrations for allowing the number of active U.S. warships to decline to 479 in 1980. With a program to build 133 new ships and refit sixteen, the Navy hopes to reach its magic number by 1988.

The expansion centers on:

● *Aircraft Carriers*: The large aircraft carrier, supported by the rest of the surface fleet, is the centerpiece of the navalists' strategy. The number of carriers will increase from twelve in 1980 to fifteen by the end of the decade.* Dismissing the criticisms of military reformers who claim that $17 billion is too much for a battle group easily targeted by Soviet cruise missiles, Lehman and his allies have convinced Congress that the big carrier is the best weapon for both offensive operations against the Soviets and intervention in the Third World. Navalist James Roherty extolls the virtues of aircraft carriers:

The supreme exploitation of oceanic opportunities is achieved in the air–sea striking power of fast carrier forces. The versatility if not the mobility of the fast carrier force exceeds that of the fleet ballistic missile submarine, making it the premier ocean system. Participating in joint operations or acting alone, the fast carrier force lends itself to innumerable tactical scenarios . . . It is in the highly mobile and flexible capabilities of fast carrier forces that we confront the "continental" threat with a dimension that is unfamiliar to the enemy. [44]

Lehman believes that big carriers can survive all but direct nuclear hits and are less vulnerable than U.S. land-based forces to attack by Soviet

---

* Six carriers were deployed in the Pacific in 1985.

missiles and aircraft. He also argues that carriers suffer fewer political constraints from U.S. allies:[45]

The carrier provides the most secure nuclear storage site possible in politically volatile areas in the Far East and Europe where tactical nuclear weapons have been the central element of the U.S. guarantee. The rear-deployed carriers are the least vulnerable basing mode against pre-emptive attack.[46]

Lehman also believes: "It's a matter of physics that ships are the best possible kind of bomb shelter there is . . . [if] anything is going to survive an all-out nuclear war, it's going to be naval ships, much more than land-fixed assets." [47]

● *Battleships*: To strengthen the conventional war capability of the fleet, the navalists have resurrected the battleship. Known for its deployments in Lebanon and Central America, the *New Jersey* has already been recommissioned, while three more Iowa-class veterans of World War II will soon be refitted. "The battleship," boasts Weinberger, "can . . . absolutely devastate and level whole areas, if that is indeed the mission." [48] One battleship is already attached to the Pacific Fleet.

● *Attack Submarines*: To sharpen the offensive edge, the administration is also raising the number of nuclear-powered attack submarines from seventy-four in 1981 to 117 by 1989. The Navy has deployed conventional and nuclear-armed Tomahawk cruise missiles, and has stepped up the arming of ships and aircraft with the Harpoon anti-ship missile.

Flex Ops

To maximize combat readiness and American military visibility, the Lehman doctrine calls for a greater pace of military activity. Exemplified by a series of multi-carrier, inter-service *Flex Ops* exercises, the operating tempo of the Navy in the Pacific increased in 1983–1984.[49] These exercises involved sailing two carrier task forces off the Kuriles and Aleutians. In an effort to make the training more realistic, the *Fleetex* exercise also called on the Air Force to support the carriers, and involved Canadian forces.

By expanding the mobility of U.S. forces and reducing the predictability of their location,[50] the operations aim to increase Soviet uncertainty about American intentions. A portent of what the Navy would do in a war off the Soviet Far East, *Fleetex* demonstrated the *offensive* nature of U.S. maritime strategy. When the two carriers *Carl Vinson* and *Midway* threw down the gauntlet in the Sea of Japan by conducting exercises off the Soviet bases at Vladivostok after the *Fleetex* exercise, more than 100 Soviet aircraft scrambled over the U.S. fleet.[51]

Pacific Commander Admiral Crowe described *Fleetex 85* – a barely disguised dry-run for an attack on the Soviet Far East – in a cable to Defense Secretary Caspar Weinberger:

A. [security deletion] Fleetex 85. One of the largest and most extensive exercises ever conducted in the USPACOM [Pacific Command]. Fleetex 85 took place 18 Oct-1 Dec 84. The CINCPACFLT [Commander-in-Chief, U.S. Pacific Fleet] directed. COMSEVENTHFLT [Commander 7th Fleet] sponsored exercise involved the *Vinson*, *Constellation*, *Midway*, *Enterprise*, and *Independence* battle-groups in operations conducted off the California coast, in the vicinity of Hawaii, in the mid and northwest Pacific, and the Indian Ocean. Exercise activity gradually increased in intensity until, on 22 November 1984, the *Carl Vinson*, *Midway*, and *Enterprise* CVBGs [aircraft carrier battle groups] joined forces in the Philippine Sea, commencing a northerly transit. The battleforce engaged in concentrated air operations near Okinawa, supported by USAF [Air Force] tactical and tanker aircraft. Continuing north, the battleforce dispersed its assets and successfully countered an extensive sub-surface threat. The exercise terminated with a large number of U.S. power projection strikes flown against land and maritime targets on and near the island of Hokkaido in northern Japan. [security deletion].

B. [security deletion] During the period of Fleetex, the Japanese Maritime Self Defense Force (JMSDF) (13 ships and 17 aircraft) participated with U.S. units in a separate and distinct exercise, ASWEX 85-1. [security deletion]

C. [security deletion] Sea of Japan (SOJ) operations. Following Fleetex the *Midway/Vinson* battle force (BF) transited Tsugaru Strait and entered the SOJ on 1 Dec.[52]

This massive exercise skirting the Soviet Far East Naval Command Center took place just six weeks after regional tensions were inflamed by the shooting down of Korean Airlines Flight 007, a commercial flight which strayed into Soviet airspace.

Activating Pacific Allies

The unprecedented level of U.S. exercises in the Pacific since 1980 is symptomatic of the increasing militarization of U.S. alliances in the Pacific. Japan, for example, has agreed to "take responsibility" for "defense of the sealanes" 1,600 km to its east and south – thus bringing both the Philippines and Vietnam within its sphere of influence. Japan has also agreed to export defense-related civilian technology, a move critics claim is a violation of Japan's pacifist constitution. But despite Prime Minister Yasuhiro Nakasone's promise to make Japan "an unsinkable aircraft carrier", the Reagan administration has not yet been able to convince the Japanese Diet (Parliament) to make major increases in military expenditures.

Besides pressuring Japan, the Reagan administration has followed what his former Secretary of State described as "the strategic imperative of strengthening our relations with the People's Republic of China." [53] In marked contrast to the caution of previous administrations, the Reagan White House is now openly promoting a U.S.–China military alliance against the Soviet Union. While differences over the future of Taiwan continue to block fuller cooperation, the Reagan administration is providing incentives to the Chinese by selling weapons like anti-tank guns and anti-aircraft missiles. The U.S. and China have also discussed the possibility that a Tomahawk-capable destroyer visit a Chinese port, the first such contact with the mainland since 1948.

Without waiting for a formal military alliance, Pentagon mandarins have integrated China into their strategic planning against the Soviet Union. "The PRC," says the Joint Chiefs' *Posture Statement* of 1984, "indirectly contributes to U.S. global and regional security as a counterweight to Soviet land power in Asia." [54] The most recent Pentagon *Defense Guidance* is quite specific about China's role in the event of war: "[T]he U.S. will encourage PRC military initiatives that fix Soviet forces in the USSR's Far Eastern territories and will be prepared, if necessary, to provide logistics and other support for those initiatives." [55]

Pacific Command is playing an increasing role in the emerging de facto alliance. In December 1984, a Chinese naval delegation visited

Pacific Command headquarters in Hawaii for discussions of the proposed U.S. ship visit. Cabled Admiral Crowe to the Secretary of Defense in January 1985, "I see these events as signalling U.S. PACOM's involvement in the growing U.S.-China relationship." [56]

The third thrust of Reagan's Asia policy is arming south Korea to place north Korea on the defensive. The Pentagon has upgraded south Korea from "a significant interest area" to a "vital interest area" and given it equal billing with Western Europe as a "first line of defense." [57] To make sure that north Korea and the Soviet Union understood this change, U.S. and south Korean units in the peninsula, backed by U.S. forces from all over the Pacific, held *Operation Team Spirit '84*. Involving 207,000 troops, this was the biggest ever held in the series, and dwarfed the more publicized *Big Pine* exercises in Honduras.

The Pentagon is also considering the deployment of neutron bombs to Korea, adding to its already massive stockpile of tactical atomic weapons. [58] A closer, multilateral military alliance among the U.S., Japan, and south Korea is being explored to facilitate operations currently impossible under the separate bilateral defense pacts.

In Southeast Asia, the centerpiece of the Reagan's policy is to "bleed Vietnam white" by supporting the Khmer Rouge and other guerilla forces inside Kampuchea (Cambodia). By cultivating fears of "Vietnamese expansionism", the U.S. hopes to speed up the militarization of the Association of Southeast Asian Nations (ASEAN) to replace the defunct Southeast Asia Treaty Organization (SEATO), which fell apart during the Vietnam War. Military aid to Thailand and Indonesia has been increased, and high levels maintained to the Philippines. A spate of visits by Pentagon officials, including Weinberger, has stressed the standardization of ASEAN's weaponry, creation of a common arms depot, and the prospect of sales of advanced weapons like the F-16 fighter-bomber.

The U.S. is also nudging the allies toward closer, preferably multilateral defense planning – a move that comes on top of existing intelligence exchanges, combined training exercises, military staff meetings, and joint naval patrols. [59] To implement this policy, CINCPAC instructed his staff in May 1982 that:

Special emphasis should be placed by planning agencies in the development of facilities for joint use by U.S. and host countries [listed are strategic roads, railways, airfields, ports, harbors, pipelines, munitions depots, communications, etc.] . . . Insofar as possible, equipment to be sold or provided to allies should be similar to or compatible with that used by U.S. forces in order to facilitate combined operations and logistic support.[60]

In the light of their increasing reliance on Pacific allies, the severe American reaction against the one that baulked, New Zealand, becomes understandable. Linked to the U.S. and Australia via a mutual defense pact (ANZUS), New Zealand in July 1984 elected a Labor government committed to keeping nuclear warships out of its ports. The Reagan administration's reaction bordered on hysteria. High-level U.S. diplomats made stern threats about "punishing" New Zealand economically, especially after the U.S. warship *Buchanan* was denied entry in February 1985. While New Zealand has little direct strategic value to the U.S., the unravelling of the region's alliance system would undermine the entire U.S. posture in the Pacific.

Upgrading Pacific Command

Even as it activates U.S. military alliances, the Pentagon argues that the U.S. should have the strength for unilateral action.[61] To this end, it is swiftly building up Pacific Command. The Seventh Fleet's forward-deployed surface ships increased by almost 100 per cent between 1980 and 1983, from twenty-one to forty. Including missile and attack submarines, U.S. warship strength in the Western Pacific rose from thirty-seven to fifty-two in just three years.* Naval personnel afloat in the Pacific more than doubled, from 15,000 to 34,000.[62]

As Admiral Crowe, Commander-in-Chief of the Pacific (CINCPAC) testified in 1984: "In terms of weapon systems, we've added the Carl Vinson-class carrier; Ohio SSBNs [nuclear ballistic missile submarines]; Los Angeles SSNs [nuclear attack submarines]; *New Jersey* battleship, Spruance destroyers, and Perry frigates, F-14s, F-15s, F-16s, and now F-18s [fighter/bomber aircraft] . . ."[63] Crowe stated that his "highest priority is strategic nuclear modernization", particularly "upgrading our theater nuclear posture combined with the supporting survivable and enduring C3 [command, control and communications] systems." The admiral emphasized that: "*All* of our military efforts in the PACOM

---

* Not all are sailing at any point in time.

[Pacific Command] area must rest on the foundation of a viable and credible nuclear deterrent." [64]

The Contest for Control

Although the new militarists are united on the need for a build-up of American military power, political battles continue for control over how this ever-swelling force should be used. Because nuclear weapons are the core of American military force, the political infighting is most pronounced over nuclear arms control, the classic diplomatic means of striving for advantage under conditions of mutual nuclear deterrence.

Even before coming to power, the ultra-hardliners took aim at the Strategic Arms Limitation treaties (SALT) as a sellout of U.S. nuclear superiority. Lehman called the professional "community" of arms control diplomats "unfit to serve" and called for their replacement by people "chosen for intelligence and toughness" – that is, himself and his friends. [65] Led by Richard Perle in Defense Secretary Caspar Weinberger's office, a network of anti-SALT advocates have campaigned for withdrawal from arms control agreements with the U.S.S.R. [66] They are pitted against an array of entrenched diplomats who concur on the need for nuclear superiority, but anticipate political and military advantages from engaging in arms control negotiations with the Soviets.

The effects of their unremitting hostility quickly sabotaged U.S.–U.S.S.R. arms control talks, which ended in a Soviet walkout in 1983. Lehman is well placed to assault existing arms control agreements. When the seventh Ohio-class submarine was launched in June 1985, he refused to "begin dismantling perfectly good Poseidon submarines" to comply with SALT II [67] until ordered by President Reagan. The previous year, the Navy also deployed a nuclear land-attack version of the sea-launched cruise missile. Indistinguishable from the non-nuclear model, it cannot be easily included in future arms control agreements contingent upon reliable verification of deployment limits, thus making arms control *per se* more difficult to implement.

The Pentagon and the State Department also wrangle over how the enlarged military force should be applied for purposes of routine coercive diplomacy. The Pentagon first waged an unrelenting campaign to root out any residual notions that force is the option of last resort. That approach "is a prescription for disaster," argued Major General Bernard Trainor in June 1984, "because diplomacy without the implicit existence, capability, and willingness to use force is totally ineffective."[68] In 1984, Secretary of Defense Caspar Weinberger and Secretary of State George Schultz openly clashed on whether force should be applied with an eye to outright military victory or subordinated to broader diplomatic imperatives in crises such as that of Lebanon.[69]

Constantly contending for pre-eminence, the militarists and the hardline diplomats never definitively resolved this dispute. Nevertheless, it is clear that the Pentagon has now won greater control over the conduct of military interventions, in effect, shutting the diplomats out of military decision making. No abstract debate, the new approach is embodied in U.S. military doctrine. Determined to avoid the diplomatic restraints such as those on the bombing of Vietnam, the Air Force's new Basic Aerospace Doctrine, for example, speaks candidly of "decisive defeat" of the enemy.[70]

The American Threat

While the maritime supremacists have won control of U.S. foreign policy, their military strategy remains contentious, even within the national security elite. In 1984, for example, prestigious thinkers such as John Gaddis, the doyen of conservative defense intellectuals,[71] and the Cold Warrior George Kennan criticized the policy of horizontal escalation. Military analysts such as Robert Komer[72] and Jeffrey Record at the Institute for Foreign Policy Analysis have also indicted the Reagan posture for its poor priorities – ignoring the importance of Europe, dispersing U.S. forces, confusing naval victory with defeat of Soviet landpower, assuming that nuclear escalation would not occur and incurring unaffordable costs. "In sum," says Jeffrey Record, "the Reagan administration's declared military strategy is not only militarily defective. It is also foolishly ambitious, betraying an unbridgeable abyss between aspirations and resources. Indeed, if strategy is the calculated relationship of ends and means, the strategy of worldwide war is not a strategy at all."[73]

More embarrassing is the near-mutiny of top Navy brass against the civilian Lehman's anti-Soviet belligerence. When Lehman announced in May 1983 that aircraft carriers would sail close to attack the heavily defended Soviet shoreline in war, Admiral Watkins challenged his superior by telling the press that "aircraft carriers should not go charging into waters near the Soviet Union in wartime." [74] The Navy fended off their zealous Secretary again in 1984 by giving a prestigious essay award to Captain L. F. Brooks, a critic of the Lehman Doctrine who believes that the Soviets are likely to pre-empt a carrier attack by escalating directly to nuclear weapons. Captain Brooks noted dryly: "The danger . . . is that the U.S. Navy will become a victim of its own rhetoric." [75]

These critics are not strong enough, however, to challenge the alliance of anti-Soviet hardliners in the Pentagon, State Department, and White House. Rearguard action by the Army and Air Force in the budgetary battles may slow but apparently cannot stop the maritime supremacists. As long as the domestic landscape is tranquil and America's allies remain compliant, the military build-up will continue.

Under Reagan's leadership, U.S. military leaders feel they have finally overcome the "Vietnam syndrome", the American public's strong antipathy to U.S. military interventions following defeat in Indochina. As Lieutenant General Bernard Trainor said in June 1984 to the Current Strategy Forum: "If we *talk* about doing it, you are not going to get support. If you *do* it, if it's quick, if it's successful, and if it's bloodless, people will applaud it." [76] Potential candidates for such "surgical strikes" are Korea, the Philippines, Pakistan, the Gulf area in the Middle East, and Central America.

Nevertheless, there are signs that the new military net cast over the Pacific is already fraying. In the decades after World War II, the system of bilateral alliances in the Pacific allowed the U.S. great freedom in the use of military power. But the United States is now losing control over allies. Rising public concern about the growing militarism and the danger of nuclear war threatens the ideological consensus among Pacific allies. Throughout the region – Japan, Australia, New Zealand, the Philippines and Micronesia – growing popular opposition to the U.S. presence represents a major challenge to America's forward deployment in the Pacific.

Over-extension and Nuclear Escalation

"We have plenty of forces," asserted Lieutenant General Trainor of the Marines in 1984, "for force projection into the third world, the developing, the non-industrial world." Since three billion people will live in Third World cities by 2000, concluded the General: "We are going to get more and more involved in urban scenes." [77] Reformers such as Admiral Stansfield Turner have made a similar case for a new Navy: "Our most urgent need is to be better prepared in the area where we are most likely to be challenged – namely, in intervention around the world." [78] With one loss (China), one draw (Korea), and one defeat (Vietnam) on its scoreboard, the U.S. has discovered that simply rounding up an international posse will not necessarily defeat a Third World liberation movement. A fundamental dilemma remains – the U.S. does not have the resources to field sufficient troops for multiple, simultaneous interventions. As General Trainor admits, the problem is "strategic mobility", that is, "getting those forces there, heavy enough to fight, and light enough to get there." [79] The Vietnam War, for example, was – in terms of American military planning – only a "half-war", even though over 40 per cent of U.S. forces were involved.[80]

Pressure Point, a Joint Chiefs of Staff exercise in 1984, revealed that in an imaginary north-south Korean War, the U.S. would run out of ammunition in less than a month, and would be forced to either accept a stalemate *or escalate*. If a crisis in Korea occurred simultaneously with one in Egypt or Central America, troops could not be sustained in the extra interventions.[81] This exercise confirmed a major Congressional study which concluded that "United States forces in Korea will have to sink or swim on their own." [82]

At the other end of Pacific Command's domain, the Indian Ocean, U.S. forces face even more severe logistical constraints (see Chapter 10). Although 111,000 tonnes of war materials are already pre-positioned on ships at the U.S. base on Diego Garcia island, 1,600 km south of India,[83] a "surge" operation in Southwest Asia would require about 2.3 million tonnes of additional cargo and ammunition.[84] Strategist Thomas Etzold has characterized Pacific Command's Indian Ocean build-up as a "serious error" for the U.S. – "the dissipation of American power and the scattering of American military resources." [85] Supporting "vital interests" in the Middle East or the Far East, he argues, has little to do with the Navy's primary mission in the region – the Soviet Union and the military balance in the Pacific. The conflict between strategic missions arises, as conservative critic Jeffrey Record puts it, because: "America's unlimited global military objectives render almost any conceivable U.S. military means inadequate." [86]

Over-extension leaves two options, both unsavory to the Pentagon. The U.S. can scale its strategy to realistic military goals. While this route risks destabilizing U.S. military alliances, it emphasizes diplomatic and economic components of U.S. foreign policy. The alternative is business-as-usual, sending in the Marines and then retreating in disorder, earning a reputation for unreliability. Faced with the ever-accelerating pace of social and political transformation in the Third World,[87] the U.S. faces an inevitable decline in its power to intervene militarily. Whether or not the U.S. engages in a massive "hot war" in the Third World or the Soviet Union, the domestic economic costs of the Reagan rearmament are likely to impose some political restraint on the rollback strategy.*

The growing gap between America's infinite global commitments and finite resources means that U.S. allies will likely be pressed into a future war. Under crossfire in Congress, Admiral Watkins admitted that over-extension means: "All tasks cannot be accomplished simultaneously without considerable risk. Thus, our current maritime strategy emphasizes maximum use of the other services and our allies in coalition warfare." To drive the point home, he added, *"We know that any major war conflict will involve our allies."* [88]

More importantly, the U.S. military's over-extension pushes it to escalate conflict to nuclear war. As its conventional resources are strained, the U.S. will therefore lean more heavily on the nuclear crutch in a conflict with a non-nuclear adversary.[89] When the U.S. prepared to withdraw half its ground forces from Korea in 1975, for example, Secretary of Defense Schlesinger publicly announced for the first time that the U.S. would not foreclose the option of using nuclear weapons in the peninsula.[90] In a similar vein, Admiral Miller testified in Congress in 1976 that nuclear weapons could compensate for conventional force in "situations that are far from our shores, where we would have difficulty, from a logistics point of view, at least, in reaching the areas in which we would have considerable U.S. interests." [91]

"All of a sudden," notes Joseph Addabbo, a Congressional critic of the Pentagon, "nuclear is a new synonym for strategic. If we cannot get the men and weapons there, we are forced to go strategic or nuclear."

---

* Or prompt a major restructuring of the domestic political process, closing opportunities for Congressional and popular input into the making of foreign policy.

Frustrated by the military, Addabbo warned: "There is no such thing as a graduated nuclear war. Nuclear is nuclear." [92]

Adding to the risk of nuclear war, Reagan's strategists attribute all Third World revolutions to the long hand of the Soviet Union, a perception which links a peasant revolt in Asia to a superpower confrontation in the Pacific. Even conservatives committed to preserving U.S. power object to this linkage. As American strategists have warned, the strategy of maritime supremacy "is based on war-widening initiatives that elevate secondary regional objectives into nothing less than determination to defeat the Soviet Union." [93]

Major General Bernard Trainor sums up the views of those who advocate maritime supremacy in the Pacific:

Given what's happening with the Soviets in their force projection, we probably in some point in our lifetime will clash with them. Now, there's enormous dangers involved with that. The dangers of escalation. Both sides know it. It'll probably be an unintended clash and when it happens, there will be a rush on the part of both sides and the rest of the world who are so nervous about the two elephants bumping and getting stamped. The odds are that any such clash would be short-lived. If it is short-lived, somebody's going to come away with the perception that one side bested the other. The world better get the perception that we bested them, because the fight will be on "our turf." In our role as world leader, if in the outbacks of the world the Soviets are perceived to have bested the United States, then we have invited a great deal of international trouble for ourselves." [94]

The following chapters look more closely at how the two elephants might bump in a conventional war or crush the Pacific – and likely the world – in a nuclear war. The possibility offers cause for great concern, since, as an old Malaysian proverb says, "When the elephants fight, the grass gets trampled."

PART TWO ☆
PACIFIC ARSENALS

Dual-capable B-52 bomber landing in Guam, 1972
(U.S. Air Force)

I'll tell you how the war in Korea was ended. We got in there and had this war on our hands. Eisenhower let the word go out . . . to the Chinese and the North Koreans that we would not tolerate this continual ground war of attrition. And within a matter of months, they negotiated. Well, as far as negotiation [in Vietnam] is concerned, that should be our position . . . I'll tell you one thing. I played a little poker when I was in the Navy. I learned this – when a guy didn't have the cards, he talked awfully big. But when he had the cards, he just sat there – had that cold look in his eyes. Now we've got the cards. What we've got to do is walk softly and carry a big stick.

—President Richard Nixon, 1969[1]

The function of Pacific Command is to project American military power beyond the territory of the United States into Asia and the southern flank of the Middle East. There are two dimensions to power projection: "coercive diplomacy", that is, the use of the means of war to influence adversaries and allies; and "warfighting", the actual engagement of military forces in combat. Pacific Command relies on nuclear and non-nuclear forces to project power. For coercive diplomacy, both means are used routinely. Warship visits, naval shows-of-force, military exercises, and military alerts to back up direct or indirect military threats are examples of coercive diplomacy.

Before a war erupts, warfighting and coercive diplomacy are conceptually and practically distinct. Once combat begins, however, they are usually merged so that the threat of escalation to even greater violence is used to coerce the opponent into accepting defeat.

While nuclear weapons* have not been used in warfighting since 1945, both superpowers rely on nuclear forces to conduct coercive diplomacy in the Pacific. The U.S. especially has tried to extract political and military advantage from nuclear threats. Indeed, some U.S. planners feel that the outcome of *non-nuclear* conflicts is dependent on the capacity to threaten the use of *nuclear* weapons. Paul Nitze, one of the most influential leaders of the defense establishment, put it this way:

It is a copybook principle in strategy that, in actual war, advantage tends to go to the side in a better position to raise the stakes by expanding the scope, duration or destructive intensity of the conflict. By the same token, at junctures of high contention short of war, the side better able to cope with the potential consequences of raising the stakes has the advantage. The other side is the one under greater pressure to scramble for a peaceful way out. To have the advantage at the utmost level of violence helps at every lesser level. In the Korean War, the Berlin blockades, and the Cuban missile crisis the United States had the ultimate edge because of our superiority at the strategic nuclear level.[3]

Despite their proclivity to inject nuclear elements into coercive diplomacy, American leaders have often found themselves confronted by the inherent difficulty of moving from symbolic threats to nuclear warfighting. Even Henry Kissinger, the high priest of coercive diplomacy, discovered in 1974 that the vast destructive potential of nuclear weapons made it impossible to use them to communicate an unambiguous threat to the Soviets. Defense analyst Fred Kaplan reports that Kissinger ordered the Pentagon to prepare a limited nuclear war contingency plan for trading blows with the Soviets over Iran. The generals presented Kissinger with a plan to blast the southern Soviet Union with two hundred nuclear weapons. Aghast, he threw them out. Chastened, they returned with a new plan: two nuclear weapons. Kissinger rolled his

---

* Long-range nuclear weapons are often called "strategic" and are distinguished from "tactical" nuclear weapons. As every war is strategic, and all means of war are tactical,[2] we simply refer to wars in which nuclear weapons are exploded as nuclear war, stating if we mean that the war is limited or all-out, and if the nuclear weapons are long- or short-range.

eyes and gave up since the puny size of this "limited" nuclear attack would have revealed nervousness rather than resolve.[4]

Incorporating nuclear blackmail into the toolkit of U.S. diplomacy, in short, has not been easy. Nuclear weapons remain essentially a-strategic, or unusable, and some senior commanders in the Pacific know it.[5] In addition to the politically cumbersome nature of nuclear weapons, U.S. strategists have not solved the technical problems in managing the battlefield on which many "small" nuclear weapons are exploding, especially if both sides are nuclear-armed.*

In fact, projecting power with conventional weapons – which requires flexibility in the application of force – has been cramped at times by the technology required to threaten nuclear attack. During the 1958 Taiwan Straits crisis for example, the Joint Chiefs of Staff had to issue a special instruction *not* to use nuclear weapons during the initial stage of conflict. Since air units were "operationally and logistically tailored primarily for nuclear warfare", the instruction disrupted basic planning assumptions (see Chapter 3).[7] In the 1968 *Pueblo* incident in Korea, U.S. policymakers were alarmed to discover that F-4 fighter-bombers based in south Korea were still so nuclear-laden that they could not be used in time to retaliate against north Korea.[8]

Although the a-strategic nature of nuclear weapons has blocked their use in warfighting, the United States and the Soviet Union have designed and deployed an incredible array of nuclear weapons for every conceivable wartime mission. Because the nuclear and non-

---

* Nuclear weapons are seen by military planners as appropriate for destroying massed adversarial forces concentrating to attack with conventional weapons. An army under nuclear attack will therefore disperse and move around quickly to avoid offering "lucrative" nuclear targets. But countering such tactics will stretch resupply and support capabilities beyond breaking point, and logistical beachheads (ports, airfields) are also highly vulnerable to nuclear counter-attack. Vigorous attacks would be necessary to achieve rapid victory under these conditions, but the dispersed frenzy of mobile forces, already difficult to command or communicate with, cannot be coalesced to impose "victory" without providing tempting nuclear targets. Alternatively, in a conflict in which only one side uses nuclear weapons, the non-nuclear party's troops can disperse, and then gather quickly around the opposition's concentrated forces. This "hugging" tactic effectively blocks use of nuclear weapons to achieve battlefield victory. Except as a desperation measure, some U.S. military analysts have concluded that the nuclear battlefield is untenable.[6]

nuclear forces are inextricably connected at all levels of technology, doctrine, and practice, the threat of nuclear war is always latent in any crisis involving the military forces of the superpowers. It is this deadly connection between the nuclear and non-nuclear means of war which is central to fully comprehending the nuclear peril in the Pacific.

First, American conventional and nuclear forces are technologically inseparable. Most U.S. military units are now structured to fight a nuclear war, even if their primary mission is non-nuclear coercive diplomacy. As Paul Wolfowitz, senior State Department official for Asia and Pacific Affairs emphasized in 1985: "We have only one Navy, not one conventionally-capable Navy and one nuclear-capable Navy." [9]

The degree of integration of nuclear and non-nuclear forces varies. The Ohio-class submarines which carry Trident ballistic missiles are dedicated wholly to projecting nuclear power against nuclear-armed enemies. Communications and intelligence facilities, on the other hand, can switch easily to support nuclear or non-nuclear military force.

Most of the important weapons systems are designed to support both nuclear and non-nuclear power projection. Moreover, the distinction between nuclear and non-nuclear firepower is eroding rapidly. The "firebreak" – the dividing line between conventional and nuclear weapons – is rapidly disappearing as low-yield nuclear and high-yield conventional weapons are deployed, more weapons deliver nuclear *or* conventional warheads, and military planners integrate nuclear *and* conventional tactics. [10] Through the convergence of military doctrine and *technical* capability, the "firebreak" is now primarily a *political* concept, composed of what Michael Klare calls "moral and psychological" elements. [11]

The "firebreak", in other words, is nothing more than the *political* constraints imposed on America's nuclear decision-making by its allies, the Soviets, and domestic political forces. Technically and militarily, American conventional posture is now indistinguishable from its nuclear posture.

Second, at the level of *doctrine*, the distinction between "nuclear" and "conventional" war planning disappeared decades ago. Within five years after the bombing of Hiroshima and Nagasaki, the Air Force had completely reorganized itself around the delivery of nuclear weapons. The Army and the Navy were not far behind, integrating nuclear weapons during the postwar decade. With nuclear weapons fully deployed by 1953, President Eisenhower proclaimed that: "Atomic weapons have virtually achieved conventional status within our armed forces." [12] In 1956, the U.S. Army instructed war colleges to "depict atomic warfare as the typical and to treat non-atomic warfare as a modification of the typical." [13] Admiral William Crowe, Commander-in-Chief of the Pacific from 1983 to 1985, stated the obvious in 1985: "U.S. forces, nuclear and non-nuclear, are indivisible. When someone says that they are anti-nuclear and not anti-American, that is an intellectual distinction that is not meaningful." [14]

Third, in *practice*, both superpowers have used nuclear coercive diplomacy to seek the upper hand in conflicts in the Asia-Pacific. The Soviet Union, for example, rattled its rockets against the U.S. in the Korean War and during the Taiwan Straits crises in 1954 and 1958, against China in 1969, and against Japan in the 1950s and 1980s. While the Soviet threats remain verbal, the U.S. style has been to couple verbal threats with the mobilization of nuclear-capable units, as against China in 1953, 1954, 1958; in Korea during 1951, 1953, and 1968; and in Vietnam during 1954 and 1968.* [16] The actual use of U.S. nuclear weapons was blocked by the response of America's European or Pacific allies, or by the popular revulsion which would have erupted at home and abroad. As Admiral Noel Gayler, former Commander-in- Chief Pacific, points out: "*Any* use of nuclear weapons against any Asian people for any reason whatever would undoubtedly be regarded as a racist act and would polarize all Asia against us." [17]

American strategists have also attempted to gain political advantage by manipulating the risk of nuclear war with the Soviet Union, which is capable of massive nuclear retaliation. In 1973, for example, Secretary of State Henry Kissinger ordered U.S. bases on a global nuclear alert (Defense Condition 3) to warn the Soviets against increasing their involvement in the Arab–Israeli war. Some U.S. military commanders, such as former CINCPAC Admiral Noel Gayler, disapproved of this ambiguous political use of nuclear weapons. As he pointed out in a 1984 interview:

---

* This list does not include the events involving U.S. Pacific- based nuclear forces in global alerts; for example, in the Cuban Missile Crisis in 1962, the 1968 B-52 month-long alert aimed at bringing pressure on Vietnam via the Soviet Union, [15] or the use of nuclear-armed or nuclear-capable weapon systems such as B-52 bombers or aircraft carriers in non-nuclear attacks or threat displays which always connote the ultimate threat.

I think that a lack of proportion between diplomatic gains and the risk of nuclear war has been manifest. I was extremely unhappy in Henry Kissinger's going to Condition 3 during the Arab–Israeli War. I thought he used that as a "signal" to the Soviets, and actually put all our forces in a higher state of readiness. In my experience, to use military states of readiness as a signal to the opposition is a profoundly mistaken thing to do. In the first place, the signal is always, not even sometimes, but always misread. What we think is a prudent show of resolve or a prudent buildup in order to be able to negotiate is regarded by the other side as getting ready to attack, as attempting to impose our will on them, or attempting to get a strategic advantage which permits coercion of the other side. They are always, not just usually, bad signals . . . It is that lack of proportion in the nuclear field which is the most dangerous situation which we can have.[18]

In addition to their technological and doctrinal integration, nuclear and non-nuclear means of war are intertwined in buttressing the forward deployment of the superpowers in the Pacific. Conventional forces, for example, obtain and secure forward bases such as communications and intelligence facilities which support long-range nuclear weapons. In an all-out nuclear war, non-nuclear and short-range nuclear forces would be mobilized to protect and to deliver nuclear weapons. Indeed, in 1981 the U.S. Pacific Command issued a comprehensive order that "contingency war plans will consider maintenance of a logistic posture necessary to support a general war."[19] Few analysts believe general war can be maintained against the Soviet Union without the use of nuclear weapons.

Even the Green Berets, the archetype of non-nuclear forces trained for counterinsurgency and unconventional warfare, are intimately involved in nuclear war plans. In a nuclear war, Green Berets such as the newly revived contingent in Okinawa, will parachute behind the lines with back-pack guidance devices for nuclear missiles or nuclear bombs to attack "choke points" such as bridges or narrow valleys.[20]

While U.S. forces and weapons in the Pacific can be separated analytically into nuclear and non-nuclear components, the deadly connection must always be kept in mind: the interlocking of conventional and nuclear capability is at the very heart of U.S. military strategy. Conventional forces support the nuclear and the nuclear reinforce the conventional, in projecting American power through coercive diplomacy and fighting wars. American forces in the Pacific comprise a single arsenal – nuclear weapons are at its core.

USS *America* underway with her Battle Group in the Indian Ocean, April 1983
(U.S. Navy)

TEN ☆
PACIFIC COMMAND

Sea power equals surface ships *plus* submarines *plus* Naval bases *plus* trained personnel *plus* the productive capacity to equip, operate and fight them.
—Admiral King, 1945[1]

Deterrence is less effective than destruction in that it permits the enemy to retain a threatening force in being.
—U.S. Navy Doctrine, 1978[2]

The United States projects power in the Pacific through its massive arsenal encompassing Navy, Air Force, Marine and Army forces. Each type of force – naval, airborne, amphibious, and ground, as well as counterinsurgency and "irregular" combat units – contributes to American coercive diplomacy and warfighting capabilities in the Pacific.

Pacific Command

The vast, multi-service U.S. arsenal is welded together into a unified structure – the Pacific Command. The largest of all U.S. unified commands, the Pacific is the responsibility of a Navy admiral who bears the title, Commander-in-Chief Pacific or CINCPAC (see Table 10.1). From his headquarters at Camp Smith in Hawaii, CINCPAC commands 320,000 troops of the Army, Navy, Marine Corps, and Air Force over a region encompassing the Aleutian Islands, the Pacific and Indian Oceans, China and the Soviet Far East – half the earth's surface*[3] (see Map 10.1).

Reflecting the Navy's de facto dominance in the Pacific, CINCPAC is by tradition a Navy Admiral. Admiral William J. Crowe, CINCPAC from 1983 to 1985, is typical of the senior stature of the post. Crowe is an expansive and witty Naval Academy and Princeton University graduate, whose experience includes tours in Vietnam (Naval Riverine Force); the Office of Micronesian Status Negotiations (Department of the Interior); the Defense Department (Director, East Asia and Pacific Region); and the United Nations (Senior U.S. Military Representative). Immediately prior to his appointment as CINCPAC in July 1983, Crowe served concurrently as Commander-in-Chief Allied Forces Southern Europe and Commander-in-Chief U.S. Naval Forces Europe.[4] From CINCPAC, Crowe moved into the Pentagon's top military position, Chairman of the Joint Chiefs of Staff.

More than just a military commander, CINCPAC plays a pivotal role in U.S. diplomacy. "The State Department ought to pay half his salary," claims Crowe's former executive assistant, "as he really is an ambassador."[5] Indeed, so prominent is CINCPAC's foreign policy role that, since 1957, the State Department has assigned an advisor to travel and consult with him.[6] One scholar of American bureaucratic politics describes CINCPAC as "one of the most important centers of political as well as military power in America."[7] In addition to appointing his own representatives to U.S. missions and embassies within his Command (see Appendix A1), CINCPAC undertakes "grand state visits" and receives visiting dignitaries.[8] As the head of a de facto diplomatic service, CINCPAC operates, in the words of General T. R. Milton, as "the powerful proconsul of a powerful nation."[9]

Command Structure

Branching out from CINCPAC are long, multi-tiered chains of command. In addition to commanding each service, CINCPAC heads

---

* The ocean adjacent to South America is excluded from Pacific Command, as are Africa, the Middle East, Pakistan, or Afghanistan. How far west into the Soviet Union or China the Command extends in peace or wartime is classified.

Table 10.1:
U.S. Military Forces Assigned to U.S. CINCPAC,[a] 1984

Army

1 Infantry Division (south Korea)
1 Infantry Division (Hawaii)

Marine Corps

1 Marine Division (Okinawa)
1 Marine Division (Hawaii)
1 Marine Division (California)

RDF Forces [b,c]

Air Force

1 Strategic Bomber Squadron
10 Tactical Fighter Squadrons
5 Tactical Support Squadrons

Navy

6 Carriers with Air Wings
89 Surface Combatants
32 Amphibious Ships
40 Attack Submarines
12 Maritime Patrol Aircraft Squadrons

Special Operations Forces [c]

1 Army Battalion (Okinawa)

Notes: a. U.S. Commander-in-Chief, Pacific; b. Rapid deployment forces, now under Central Command; c. Forces assigned by Joint Chiefs of Staff on *ad hoc* basis.
Source: C. Weinberger, *Annual Report to Congress, Fiscal Year 1985*, Department of Defense, Washington, D.C., 1984, p. 203; D. Meyer, 'Does the U.S. Need to Modernize its Army in the Pacific?' *Armed Forces Journal International*, May 1985, p. 100.

Map 10.1:
CINCPAC Area of Responsibility

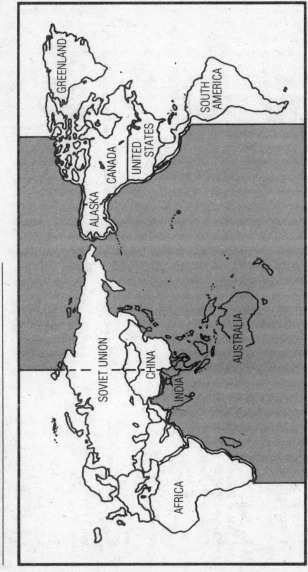

Note: Whether PACOM area of operational control envisaged in war plans extends to an undefined line across central China and Siberia is unknown.

multi-service, unified commands in particular geographic areas (such as U.S. Forces Japan and U.S. Forces Korea); and elements of single service commands (such as the Military Aircraft Command), when they are deployed in his region.* The Guam-based forces of the global Strategic Air Command, however, maintain complete operational independence from CINCPAC.

The immediate subordinates of CINCPAC are the regional heads of the Navy, Army, and Air Force. The Navy Commander (CINC-PACFLT), based at Pearl Harbor, directs the 7th (West Pacific) and 3rd (East Pacific) Fleets; seven functional commands based in Hawaii or San Diego; and four sub-regional commands (see Appendix A2 and B).

Although they are part of the Department of the Navy, the Marines have their own command structure, with overall headquarters in Hawaii and a regional command post in Okinawa.† The Air Force Pacific Commander-in-Chief is based in Hawaii, and directs subordinates in Japan, south Korea, Okinawa, and the Philippines.

Army Commands in the region are more fragmented than those of the other services, with authority split between Army Western Command in Hawaii,‡ 8th Army Command in south Korea, and Commander U.S. Army Japan. Complicating the situation further, when the Commander of the 8th Army in Korea puts on his hats as the U.S. Commander in Korea and Combined Forces Commander for the

---

* A unified command is composed of forces from two or more services. A single service or specified command on the other hand is a "top echelon U.S. combatant organization with regional or functional responsibilities, which normally is composed of forces from one military service." The Army and the Navy command are thus specified commands.[10] Military Airlift Command (MAC) is another specified command run by the Air Force. MAC's transport planes fall under CINCPAC's operational control when they reside in rather than merely transit through Pacific Command. In contrast, ships of Military Sealift Command in the Pacific fall wholly under CINCPAC.[11] Specified Commands such as the U.S. Army or Air Force retain *administrative* responsibility for their Pacific forces, while CINCPAC is their *operational* Commander.

† The Commander, Fleet Marine Force Pacific reports to CINCPAC through CINCPACFLT, who is the senior naval officer under CINCPAC.[12]

‡ Western Command controls the rapidly deployable 25th Infantry Division in Hawaii, and in peacetime, the 2nd Infantry Division in south Korea. In wartime the latter passes to the Commander U.S. Forces Korea, who also has operational control over Air Force but not over naval U.S. forces in his theater.

peninsula, he is responsible to the Joint Chiefs of Staff rather than CINCPAC.[13]

Born of inter-service jealousies, this complex of overlapping, contradictory military capabilities has often complicated the implementation of CINCPAC's strategy. In an actual war situation, CINCPAC could lose effective control over the massive U.S. nuclear arsenal in the Pacific because of confusion in the command structure (see Chapters 5 and 12).

The Pacific Fleet

The Navy is the cutting edge of American power in the Pacific, a role it has played since the U.S. became a world power at the turn of the century. In 1908, the Great White Fleet sailed around the world to signal the emergence of the United States as a global naval power.[14] To counter the rise of Japanese naval power, a Pacific-wide fleet was first established in 1919.[15]

Today the U.S. Navy's Pacific Fleet is divided into two major flotillas: the 7th Fleet, which cruises the West Pacific and Indian Oceans; and the 3rd Fleet, which operates in the East Pacific along the broad littoral of North and South America. The 7th Fleet deployed on average about twenty-three major warships at sea in 1984*, available for grouping into two carrier battlegroups or surface action groups centered on rejuvenated battleships. These task forces operate mostly in the northwest Pacific or the Indian Ocean, with visits to intermediate areas such as the South China Sea. A large number of assigned and active vessels back up these warships (see Table 10.2).†

Between 1968 and 1978, the number of general purpose‡ ships in the

---

* Average 7th Fleet West Pacific/Indian Ocean at-sea surface warship deployments in 1983 were two aircraft carriers, nine escort cruisers and destroyers, and twelve frigates.[16]

† The 3rd Fleet in the East Pacific is oriented toward training and is not considered deployed. Overall, the average 3rd Fleet vessel is at sea only 28 per cent of the time, while the average 7th Fleet vessel is at sea – actively engaged in exercises, diplomacy, or war – 60 per cent of the time.[17]

‡ Excluding ballistic missile launching submarines.

Table 10.2:
Overall Pacific Naval Forces, January 1, 1982

Vessel Type	Western Pacific	Active Fleet Operating Days, 1982	Eastern Pacific	Active Fleet Operating Days, 1982	Totals
General Purpose Vessels					
Attack Carriers	3		3		6
Helicopter Carriers	1		5		6
Cruisers	5		9		14
Destroyers	13		18		31
Frigates	17		24		41
Subtotals	39	—	59	—	98
Amphibious Units	7		24		31
Submarines	13		34		47
Totals	59	216	117	101	176

Note: Active Fleet Operating Days are at sea, and do not include days spent in foreign ports. Foreign port visits would add about 25 per cent to fleet operating days. General Purpose Units: aircraft carriers, destroyers, cruisers, frigates. Not inclusive of logistic support vessels.

Sources: C. Wright, "U.S. Naval Operations in 1982." *Proceedings/Naval Review*, May 1983, p. 53; J. Collins, *U.S./Soviet Military Balance, Statistical Trends, 1970–1982.* Congressional Research Service Report 83–153S, Washington, D.C., August 1, 1983, p. 128.

Map 10.2:
Military Forces, Weapons Systems and Bases in Pacific Command

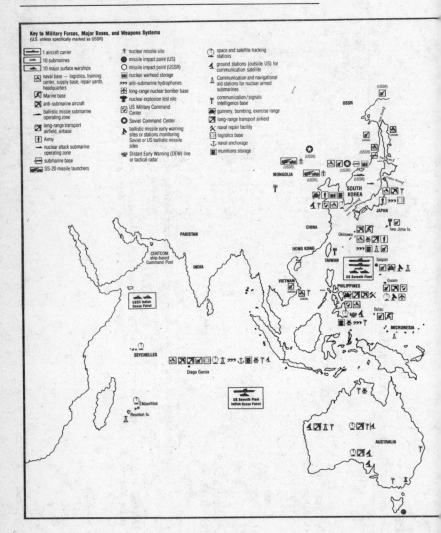

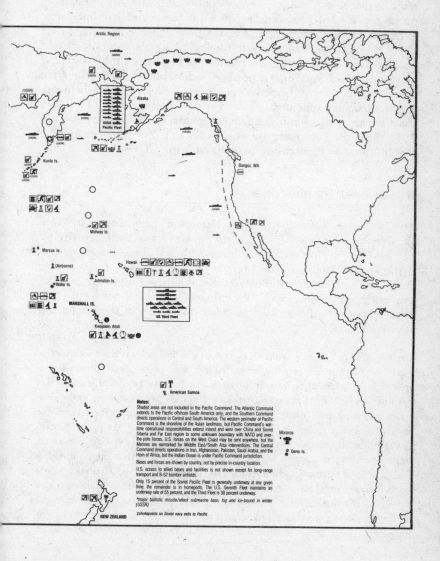

Notes:

Shaded areas are not included in the Pacific Command. The Atlantic Command extends to the Pacific offshore South America only, and the Southern Command directs operations in Central and South America. The western perimeter of Pacific Command is the shoreline of the Asian landmass, but Pacific Command's wartime operational responsibilities extend inland and west over China and Soviet Siberia and Far East region to some unknown boundary with NATO and over-the-pole forces. U.S. forces on the West Coast may be sent anywhere, but the Marines are earmarked for Middle East/South Asia interventions. The Central Command directs operations in Iran, Afghanistan, Pakistan, Saudi Arabia, and the Horn of Africa, but the Indian Ocean is under Pacific Command jurisdiction.

Bases and forces are shown by country, not by precise in-country location.

U.S. access to allied bases and facilities is not shown except for long-range transport and B-52 bomber airfields.

Only 15 percent of the Soviet Pacific Fleet is generally underway at any given time; the remainder is in homeports. The U.S. Seventh Fleet maintains an underway rate of 55 percent, and the Third Fleet is 30 percent underway.

*major ballistic missile/attack submarine base, fog and ice-bound in winter (USSR)

‡chokepoints on Soviet navy exits to Pacific

Pacific Fleet fell from 503 to 206 as the Navy opted for a "hi-tech" strategy of ship modernization and the U.S. retreated from intervention after its defeat in Vietnam (see Appendix A3).[18] The loss in numbers prompted a vociferous outcry from the Navy and its supporters, although the Fleet's tonnage declined by only 20 per cent between 1965 and 1981, and ship range and technological sophistication increased dramatically. Furthermore, the number of key capital ships – such as carriers, frigates, and nuclear-powered submarines – stayed the same or even increased.[19] Nonetheless, Navy Secretary John Lehman, Ronald Reagan's appointee, pledged in 1981 to increase the Fleet by a third as part of an overall campaign to build a 600-ship Navy. By early 1984, the Pacific Fleet had grown to 231 warships and will swell to some 300 by the time the Reagan build-up ends in 1988.

The 7th Fleet: Premier Force

The 7th Fleet is a World War II veteran which never came home from the Western Pacific. With air striking power based on three aircraft carriers, the 7th Fleet is the most formidable and versatile fighting arm in the Western Pacific. It is the premier force for asserting "presence" in the practice of coercive diplomacy, and comprises immense punitive power for warfighting. Vice Admiral George Steele's ode to this U.S. armada captures the breadth of Navy operations in the Pacific and Indian Oceans:

On a given day in the Seventh Fleet, one might find several ships well east of Japan entering or leaving the Seventh Fleet area of responsibility. An anti-submarine warfare exercise is in progress on Tokyo Bay. An aircraft carrier with her cruiser-destroyer screen and a submarine are exercising in the Okinawa operating area, while another carrier task force group is in port in Subic for maintenance. A third carrier task force group is visiting Mombasa, Kenya. An amphibious exercise involving ships and marines of Ready Group Bravo is in progress on the coast of Korea . . . and ship visits are in progress in Hong Kong; Beppu; Japan; Kaohsiung; Taiwan; Manila; Sattahip; Thailand; Singapore; Penang; Malaysia . . . Patrol planes of Task Force 72 are conducting ocean surveillance in the Indian Ocean in support of the carrier task force group there and range along the Asian mainland at a respectful distance on the lookout for unusual happenings . . . British and Australian destroyers are engaged in an anti-submarine warfare exercise with U.S. destroyers and a submarine in the Subic operating area. Several cruisers and destroyers are making preparations for a missile shoot on the Poro Point Range nearby.[20]

The centerpiece of the 7th Fleet is the gigantic aircraft carrier. In 1984, there were six carriers assigned to the Pacific; on average, three in the Western Pacific, though more are deployed in times of crisis or to conduct exercises. One carrier, currently the *Midway*, is permanently based in the Western Pacific and homeported at Yokosuka, Japan. Task Force 77, which patrols the South China Sea and Indian Ocean, is spearheaded by carriers like the new *Carl Vinson* from the 3rd Fleet.

The 7th Fleet's contemporary carrier task group is a far cry from the weapon system which fought and won in the Pacific in World War II. Instead of the 100 ships, 400 attack aircraft, and heavy anti-aircraft artillery typical of a 1940s carrier task force, the 1980s task group has trimmed down to nine vessels, thirty-six to forty-eight attack aircraft, and sleek missile defenses[21] (see Figure 10.1).

Punitive Power

The aircraft carrier task group is the most flexible and fluid offensive force in the Pacific Fleet. It can be internally reconstituted, temporarily divided, and rapidly shifted. In combat, the group's forces aim to carry out three military missions. First, their fighter planes seek air superiority in the vicinity of the task force itself, extending out to the range of the carrier's aircraft and missiles.* These fighters aim to intercept medium-range bombers, such as Soviet Backfires, which are armed with anti-ship missiles.

The carrier also uses its A6/7 aircraft armed with Harpoon anti-ship missiles to destroy any surface vessels within reach. One Navy report proclaimed of this newest anti-ship missile, "It's simple and reliable, yet versatile and lethal." [23] Third, the carriers seek to eliminate submarines capable of launching cruise missile or torpedo attacks, using an anti-submarine screen of aircraft and ship escorts (see Figure 10.2).

---

* These are typically F-14 and F-15 fighters, armed with air-to-air missiles. The first operational F-18 wing was deployed on the carrier *Constellation* in the Pacific in 1984.[22]

The carriers have demonstrated the capability to attack targets 2,400 km from the carrier with the A-6 fighter-bomber.[24]

As a massive target continuously advertising itself by electro-magnetic emissions, the carrier group must devote much of its power to controlling its own operating environs. Once the task force is secure, the carrier can launch its offensive forces, supplemented by land-based P3C Orion or B-52 aircraft, in tasks such as anti-submarine warfare or mining operations. Alternatively, the carrier delivers aerial strikes to cover amphibious forces landing in foreign territory, or simply pulver-izes land targets to display its "punitive power."

These floating, mobile airbases can launch up to three waves of seventeen to twenty-one bombers per day. At this rate, the attack car-rier can deliver up to 360 tonnes of high explosives daily.[25] Large carriers such as the U.S.S. *Enterprise* in the Pacific Fleet store 1,800 to 2,300 tonnes of bombs – enough for at least a five-day continuous, all-out attack.[26]

Diesel-powered carriers, such as the Forrestal-class, can cruise only 22,000 km without refueling, at a cruising speed of 37 km per hour (a minimum endurance of twenty-five days; longer if they slow down). Nuclear-powered carriers, by contrast, have practically unlimited en-durance and high speed. Depending on the endurance of their escorts, nuclear carriers can hit 61 km per hour for short periods and can reach any part of the Pacific in a matter of days.

Aircraft carriers are floating nuclear weapons storage depots. Carrier strike aircraft are also nuclear capable. An important new complement to carrier airpower is the power-projection capability of the "Surface Action Group" (SAG), recently formed around the recommissioned battleship *New Jersey*.* Armed with Tomahawk cruise missiles, this World War II veteran "can take under attack . . . most of the MIG bases in places like North Korea" according to Navy Secretary Lehman, "and punch right through the hangarettes, bunkers, and caves where the real high-priority targets are."†[27]

---

* The SAG aims to "show the flag" off Third World shores, although it lacks the range, versatility, and sheer power of the aircraft carrier. The *New Jersey* is the first of two battleships assigned to Pacific Fleet. The second will be the *Missouri*.

† These MIGs are supplied by the Soviets, although they are mostly obsolete models.

Figure 10.1:
Hypothetical U.S. Carrier Task Group, 1980s

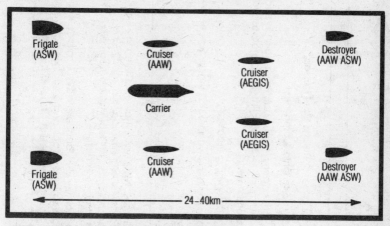

AAW: Anti-Air Warfare, by short- & medium-range anti-aircraft SAMs and guns
AEGIS: Advanced gun & missile fire control system for wide-area SAMs
ASW: Anti-submarine warfare systems

NOTE: The US Navy began experimenting with combined carrier task groups in the 1980s, combining and extending the escort screen.
Source: S. Deitchman, "Designing the Fleet and its Air Arm," *Astronautics and Aeronautics*, Volume 16, no. 1, November 1978, p. 19.

Table 10.3:
Major U.S. Naval Bases in the Pacific

Country/Site	Main Function
United States	
San Diego/Alameda, California	Homeport and rear base for Pacific Fleet vessels.
Bangor, Washington	Homeport, Trident missile Ohio submarines.
Pearl Harbor, Hawaii	Homeport for 40–60 surface vessels, logistics, repair, drydocking capability, POL and munition storage, intermediate base for nuclear attack submarines.
Kaho'olawe Island, Hawaii	Naval gunnery and bombing practice.
Barking Sands, California	Torpedo and anti-submarine warfare training, practice.
Midway Island	Limited naval facilities.
Wake Island	Port facilities, POL.
Japan	
Yokosuka	Major U.S. naval base, NW Pacific. Homeports ten 7th Fleet vessels, including carrier *Midway*. Logistics, repair, and drydocking capabilities for 7th Fleet including carriers. Forward port for nuclear attack submarines.
Sasebo	Naval base used jointly with Japanese Navy. Logistics, huge POL and munitions storage, repair and drydocking capabilities. Home and forward port for nuclear attack submarines.

Table 10.3: (cont)

Philippines
Subic Bay

Operational base for 7th Fleet in SW Pacific, Indian Ocean. Logistics, repair and drydocking capabilities, POL and munitions storage. Forward port for nuclear attack submarines.

Subic Bay/Zambales and Tambones Training Ground

Marine training; 7th Fleet and allied bombing and gunnery practice.

Guam
Apra Harbor

Naval base for logistics and repairs, forward port for nuclear attack submarines.

Okinawa
White Beach

7th Fleet forward port.

South Korea
Chinhae

Navy facilities at Korean naval base.

Diego Garcia

Logistics and forward base.

Key: POL = Petroleum, oil and lubricant storage.
Note: Pacific Fleet vessels have access to facilities in many other points in allied territory such as Australia, Singapore, Alaska, Somalia, etc., for logistics, repair, and rest and recreation, but these are not under CINCPAC control. CINCPAC does not control the bases on the U.S. West Coast. U.S. ''use rights'' in the North Mariana Islands and possibly Belau are not listed: nor are Naval Air Stations.
Source: O. Wilkes, Foreign Military Bases Project, SIPRI, 1983.

Figure 10.2:
Air Defense of U.S. Carrier Task Group

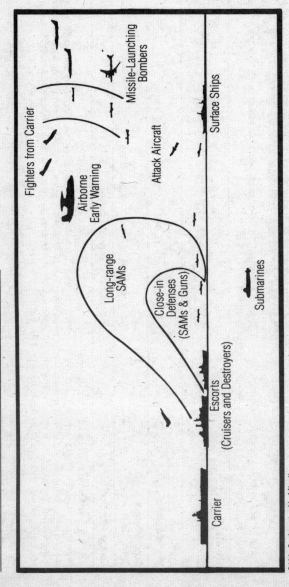

SAM: Surface-to-Air Missile.
Source: S. Deitchman, as in Figure 10.1 p. 22.

Bases and Naval Power

Bases are essential to the quick deployment of naval power. Whether forward, intermediate or rear area facilities, all bases in the Pacific and Indian Oceans are components of a tightly integrated naval defense system. The island of Diego Garcia, for example, is regarded as an advance base for the 7th Fleet's high-risk operations in the Indian Ocean and Southwest Asia. Eight thousand km away in the Philippines, Subic Bay provides supply and maintenance services for Carrier Task Force 77, the 7th Fleet's Indian Ocean operation. Subic, in other words, is the intermediate base which links naval operations on the advance base at Diego Garcia with the rear bases at Yokosuka in Japan and CINCPAC headquarters in Honolulu (see Table 10.3).*

Serving as mobile forward bases, aircraft carriers can eliminate the Navy's *logistical* need for bases on foreign soil.† Indeed, when supplied by intermediate bases, carriers are capable of operating from Hawaii or mainland U.S.[28] But the bases in the Pacific and Indian Oceans are convenient and cheap, and they enhance the Navy's overall capability by providing supplementary land-based support for escort vessels.

Marines: The Amphibious Threat

While the Navy rules the seas, Marines are the spearhead of U.S. intervention in Asia–Pacific. Indeed, the region has loomed so large in Marine Corps history that their unofficial slogan is: "We train for the Atlantic but we fight for the Pacific." [29] Immediately after World War II, 53,000 Marines were deployed in north China for nearly two years in an attempt to prevent the Red Army from controlling the area. Marine divisions were the cutting edge of U.S. interventions in Korea in 1950–1953 and Vietnam from 1965 to 1973.

---

* To support operations in the Indian Ocean, carrier aircraft also fly out of airfields in Atsugi (Japan) and Cubi Pt. (Philippines), and receive mid-air refuelling *en route* to Diego Garcia.

† Because bases also serve important political functions in maintaining U.S. military alliances, they are not disposed of when they become technologically obsolescent.

In the late 1970s, the Marines suffered acute career anxiety when the U.S. pulled back from an interventionist posture under President Carter (see Chapter 7). Their traditional role restored under the Reagan administrations's aggressive foreign policy, the Marines are again in the forefront of a reinvigorated U.S. rapid response force. Beyond intervention, they are also ready, according to Admiral Watkins, to "conduct credible offensive operations against territory on the perimeter of the U.S.S.R., especially in the Far East." * [30]

The 32,000 Marines currently in the Pacific [31] serve as shock troops for the carrier task forces. The main technique of marine fighting is the amphibious attack.† After offloading from a Navy carrier task force onto landing craft, Marines storm the shore under naval air cover. The III Marine Amphibious Force (MAF) (see Appendix A4) at Okinawa prepares for such amphibious assaults in the Far East (especially Korea) and reinforces U.S. forces in Southwest Asia. One unit of the III MAF, consisting of 800 Marines, is kept afloat in the Indian Ocean with the 7th Fleet, and a Brigade of Marines operates from Hawaii.‡ [35] Marines are also moved into the West Pacific and Indian Ocean from the U.S. mainland via a regular series of exercises in Hawaii, Guam, and Okinawa. [36]

Deployment of a Marine Amphibious Unit is no small affair, and usually requires five to seven amphibious warships, two to three helicopter-capable amphibious assault ships, up to two dock landing craft, one to two tank landing craft, and perhaps one amphibious cargo ship [37] to lift troops, landing craft, tanks and vehicles, and helicopters to the shores of intervention. While the Pacific Fleet has thirty-one amphibious warfare ships, only five are devoted to non-amphibious warfare

---

* These operations would likely aim to wrest control of the Kurile Islands from the Soviets, a move which would allow U.S. attack submarines to enter the sea of Okhotsk or to interdict supply of the crucial Soviet base at Petropavlosk.

† The technique was refined in the assault on Tarawa in 1943, and perfected in the 1945 attack which epitomizes Marine operations, Iwo Jima. [32]

‡ The 7th Marine Amphibious Brigade based in California is intended to join up with pre-positioned equipment at Diego Garcia for military expeditions in South Asia. [33] As of February 1985, a second Marine Amphibious Unit was deployed into the West Pacific from California to support the Marine Amphibious Force in Okinawa. [34]

tasks, and only six are amphibious lift vessels[38] – shortcomings that might delay the arrival of *all* marine forces up to a month.*[39]

With about 60 fighter aircraft and helicopters stationed at Okinawa and Iwakuni in Japan, and an Air Wing at Hawaii, the Marines maintain sufficient airpower for their own close, land-based support operations.[40] Unless an airfield is available close to the site of the attack, however, the Marines in the Pacific are dependent on the good graces of the Navy to support the Marine's carrier-launch vertical take-off strike.

Faced with the spectre of obsolescence after the atomic attacks at the end of World War II, the Marines quickly developed helicopters to outflank a hypothetical nuclear assault on an amphibious invasion force by whisking the Marines to the shore over the waves.[41] Heavy-lift and close-support helicopter gunships are now integral weapons in the Marine arsenal. Once the Marines in the Pacific obtain vertical lift aircraft and new air-capable amphibious assault ships,† they will finally have wrested control of their close air-support mission from the Navy.

Combined with the mobile amphibious assault fleet and carrier operations, Marine bases provide flexible staging points for land assaults throughout the Pacific (see Appendix A4). Marine offensive capability on the Asian periphery would be greatly reduced without these forward bases. Operating together, the Navy's carrier and the Marines' amphibious assault task forces project formidable military power against a land-based opponent.

The Navy often displays these two forces to communicate the threat of intervention. On twenty-six separate occasions between 1955 and 1975, the Navy sent warships to protect U.S. interests in East Asia and the Indian Ocean.[42] Naval supremacists, such as Reagan's former Assistant Defense Secretary Bing West, extol the flexibility of naval power in serving a trinity of strategic goals – deterrence, alliance building, and intervention. While surface escorts are most effective in "peacetime" and in a superpower confrontation, amphibious forces are deemed useful for intervention and showing the flag. Like the aircraft carriers, however, Marines project the threat of nuclear war. They fly

---

* Unless an aerial beachhead war was already in hand, so that an airlift could fly in the Marines.

† Currently in the Atlantic Fleet only.

nuclear-capable aircraft and are equipped to fire nuclear artillery and atomic demolition mines.

Air Force: Threat from the Sky

The independent Air Force was born in the Pacific Theatre during World War II. Precursor of the post-war service, the U.S. Army's 20th Air Force was created "to transcend theater air operations" and carry out the strategic bombing of Japan. According to military historian John Schlight:

A more descriptive name of this unusual organization – a name that had, in fact been suggested for it at one point – would have been the Joint Chiefs of Staff Air Force. Based first in Washington and later moved to Guam as the Pacific war progressed, it was run by the Joint Chiefs through their agent, General [Hap] Arnold. The Twentieth Air Force directed the strategic air war against Japan over the heads of Nimitz, MacArthur, and Stilwell. For the first time in American aviation history, the terms airpower and Air Force had become synonymous and the post-war air leaders meant to keep it that way.[43]

Following the war, the new Air Force moved quickly to consolidate its position as the main American strike force. Believing that the next war would be nuclear, the Air Force "essentially deprived itself of a conventional capability" during the 1950s, removing "the bomb shackles for carrying conventional bombs."[44] During the Vietnam War, they were again installed when Presidents Johnson and Nixon ordered the Air Force to carry out massive conventional bombing.

Today land-based aircraft in the Western Pacific provide tactical support for Army and Marine Infantry, the Navy offshore, and strategic bombing of land targets. To these ends, the Pacific Air Force currently fields 216 fighters in the Western Pacific (excluding Alaska) from airfields in Korea, Japan, the Philippines, and Okinawa (see Table 10.4). Two squadrons of F-16 fighters at Misawa, Japan, will be deployed early in 1985, increasing U.S. tactical airpower in the West Pacific to 264 fighters. With refuelling, the Pacific Air Force is able to reach the whole of Pacific Command's region (see Map 10.3). Virtually all these strike aircraft can be quickly equipped to drop nuclear bombs stored in Guam, Alaska, or Hawaii.

While the Marines and Navy operate to *extend* the boundaries of the U.S. sphere of influence, the Pacific Air Force acts to *consolidate* it. After the Marines or Army have occupied a nation, Air Force fighters are designed to attack targets such as tanks in the immediate battle zone close to U.S. forces. Striking deep into rear areas against transport chokepoints or massed reinforcements, F-14 and F-16 fighters may break up an attack or buy time for U.S. reinforcements to arrive from aircraft carriers, intermediate bases, or the U.S. In intensely defended sites, the U.S. may use air or sea-launched conventional land-attack cruise missiles to destroy valuable immobile targets.[45]

The second major Air Force role in support of U.S. forward deployment is long-range bombing. The 3rd Air Division keeps twenty Strategic Air Command* B-52G bombers at Anderson Air Force Base in Guam. In the Korean War, SAC strategic B-29 bombers dropped 151,000 tonnes of bombs on Korea.[47] They were finally grounded for lack of suitable standing targets anywhere in north Korea! SAC B-52s, deployed at Guam in 1965 and later at U Tapao AFB in Thailand, bombed Vietnam with similar ferocity.†[49]

After concentrating on nuclear capability in the 1950s, SAC was ill prepared for a conventional mission, especially one involving jungle warfare, and its first B-52 bombing raid over Vietnam in 1965 was a fiasco. There was no evidence of a single Vietnamese casualty and two B-52s were destroyed in a mid-air collision. The press likened the use of the mammoth, nuclear-capable B-52s against the Vietnamese to "swatting flies with a sledgehammer."[50] Despite these early failures, more than 3,000 B-52 bombing missions were flown over Vietnam in 1968.[51] During the Christmas bombings of December 1972, B-52s delivered nearly 14,000 tonnes of bombs in only eleven days.

---

* Strategic Air Command forces deployed in the Pacific fall under the operational authority of the Air Force representative to the Joint Chiefs of Staff and the Secretary of the Air Force at all times. They do not fall under the authority of the Pacific Air Force, which is subordinate to CINCPAC, even when engaged on crucial missions requested by CINCPAC. SAC also provides aerial refuelling support to CINCPAC and SAC aircraft in Pacific Command from KC-135 Stratotankers and KC-10A Extender aircraft.[46]

† B-52s also deploy widely via allied airfields or direct to Diego Garcia. As of 1982, Diego Garcia could only accommodate B-52s landing without bombloads.[48] Bombs could be loaded onto the planes, however, for missions over the littoral area of the Indian Ocean.

Table 10.4:
U.S. Tactical Land-based Airpower in the West Pacific

Forces	Air Bases (AB)
Korea	
2 squadrons/48 F-16	Osan AB [a]
2 squadrons/24 F-4	Kunsan AB [a]
1 squadron /24 A-10	Taegu AB [a]
Total: 5 squadrons, 96 fighters	Suwon AB
51st Tactical Airwing, 314th Air Division	+ 16 airfields, 2 gunnery ranges
8th AF Tactical Fighter Wing	
497th Tactical Fighter Squadron	
25th Tactical Fighter Squadron	
Japan	
2 squadrons/48 F-16	Misawa AB
6112th Air Base Wing[b]	Yokota AB
HQ USAF 5th AF,[c] 475th Air Base Wing	Kwang Ju Air Base
6171st Air Base Squadron	Use of or use rights at 3 airfields
Okinawa	
18th Tactical Fighter Wing	Kadena AB
313th Air Division	
3 squadrons/72 F-15	
1 R-F4 tactical reconnaissance	

Table 10.4: (cont)

Philippines

3rd Tactical Fighter Wing
2 squadrons/48 F-4   Clark AB
1 squadron/10 F-5, 4 T-38   Crow Valley Gunnery Range

Alaska[d]

Tactical Fighter Squadron   Elmendorf AB
Tactical Fighter Squadron   Eielson AB

Notes: a. Planes rotate to Osan, Kunsan, and Taegu from Kadena in Okinawa in Japan.

b. Deployment of 48 F-16s projected for early 1985.

c. The Japanese Air Self-Defense Force has primary responsibility for air defense of Japan. USAF Japan-based fighters were withdrawn to Okinawa.

d. Not under CINCPAC's operational control.

Sources: J. Collins, *U.S./Soviet Military Balance, Statistical Trends, 1970–1982*, Congressional Research Service Report 83–153S, Washington, D.C., August 1, 1983, pp. 128–130; O. Wilkes, Foreign Military Bases Project, SIPRI, 1983; *New Straits Times*, August 24, 1983, p. 15; *Air Force Magazine*, May 1983, pp. 94–95; U.S. Air Force, Office of Public Affairs, January 15, 1985.

The dominant role of the Air Force in the Vietnam War disturbed the Navy, which feared an erosion of its traditional dominance in the Pacific. With the ascendancy of a strong supporter to the White House in 1981, however, the Navy regained its confidence and signed an official truce ("cooperation agreement") with the Air Force in October 1982 which approved a limited role in maritime operations.*[53] This new integration of land and sea airpower in the West Pacific partly overcomes the traditional rivalry which has characterized Navy–Air Force relations in the past.

As the backbone of Strategic Air Command's nuclear bombing mission against the U.S.S.R., the B-52G planes in Guam are a perfect example of the capability of American weapon systems to fight nuclear and conventional wars. Each plane can deliver up to 27 tonnes of high explosive bombs to saturate an area. The Air Force extolls the giant B-52 as "capable of delivering more concentrated firepower on the battlefield than any other weapon system." [54] But it is primarily dedicated to nuclear attack against the Soviet Union, and Strategic Air Command can "yank" the B-52s from supporting Pacific Command at its own discretion.

Occupation Force: The U.S. Army

While the Navy and Air Force provide the U.S. with a quick response to crisis, the commitment of ground troops remains the most telling sign of U.S. resolve to impose its will. American policymakers have learned repeatedly that without a massive occupation force, naval and air power are limited in what they can achieve.

The Army's role as a combat and occupation force in the Pacific originated at the turn of the century, when over 50,000 troops were committed to crushing a struggle for independence in the Philippines. This was followed in 1900 by the landing of 6500 troops in Beijing to put down the Boxer Rebellion. Beginning in 1912, the 15th Infantry

---

* Pacific Air Force KC-135 and KC-10 aerial refuelling tankers have also joined naval exercises. SAC B-52s and the Navy's land-based P3C Orion reconnaissance aircraft have practiced mining straits in the West Pacific since 1982, and four SAC B52s at Guam, along with P3Cs, are armed with Harpoon anti-ship missiles.[52]

Map 10.3:
Pacific Air Force Fighter Range with
Aerial Refuelling

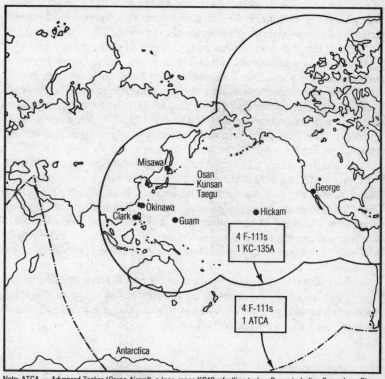

Note: ATCA = Advanced Tanker/Cargo Aircraft, a long-range KC10 refuelling tanker. Range in Indian Ocean from Diego Garcia not shown.

Source: U.S. Congress, House of Representatives, *Hearings on Military Posture and H.R. 11500*, Part 2 (procurement), Washington, D.C., 1976, p. 242.

Regiment garrisoned Tientsin for twenty-five years as a symbol of U.S. determination to "protect" its interests in China.

After World War II, U.S. Army occupation forces were the pillars of military governments in Japan under General Douglas MacArthur and in Korea under John Hodge. As in the Philippines in the early 1900s, Army-based governments in these two countries shaped local power structures, imposed democratic reforms, repressed nationalistic opposition, and left the government in the hands of conservative elites.[55]

Today approximately 33,000 U.S. 8th Army 2nd Infantry Division forces remain in south Korea's Demilitarized Zone (DMZ) (see Appendix A5).* This garrison grew out of the crushing defeat of the Korean People's Republic between 1945 and 1947 and the footslogging stalemate in the Korean War between 1950 and 1953.[59] Reflecting the high level of tension along this "trip wire", the Army units at the DMZ are on 24-hour war-status.

With south Korean and U.S. Army troops facing hostile north Koreans, the DMZ is a powderkeg. Local incidents in the area, such as a Soviet tourist guide's run across the zone in late 1984, spark lethal firefights which could easily escalate. In this incident, north Korean guards, in violation of the rules, chased the defector into the south Korean area, some firing automatic rifles. Four soldiers, three north and one south Korean, were killed, and one American soldier was wounded.[60]

Such incidents could easily spark a wider conflict in a site where the U.S. Army maintains nuclear artillery, and can call upon air-dropped nuclear weapons, atomic demolition mines, and a panoply of naval nuclear weapons (see Chapter 12).

Irregular Warfare

A new form of power projection – irregular warfare – has become part of the American arsenal in the last four decades. Irregular warfare takes many forms: covert operations to destabilize a weak, unfriendly gov-

---

* Backed up by the 19,000-strong "Tropic Lightning" Division in Hawaii which forms a "vital part of all the Pacific OPLANS [Operational Plans]", according to a 1984 Congressional Staff report.[56] It is ready for action anywhere in Pacific Command,[57] and is earmarked to become a rapidly deployable, light infantry division by 1986.[58]

ernment; psychological warfare against revolutionary states to sap their morale; and counterinsurgency designed to strengthen local armed forces against revolutionary insurgents.

The Central Intelligence Agency (CIA) is the practitioner *par excellence* of irregular warfare with decades of experience throughout the Asia-Pacific region*. To support its operations on the Asian mainland in the 1950s and 1960s, the Agency maintained a number of facilities in the offshore island chain. A secret memo by CIA operative Edward Lansdale in 1961 details some of these. In Manila, jointly with the Philippine government, the CIA ran the Security Training Center – a "countersubversion, counterguerilla, and psychological warfare school." [63] Other Western Pacific CIA bases† were located in Okinawa and in Saipan, where a training center for CIA operatives and their recruits functioned under the cover of the "Naval Technical Training Unit." In Taiwan, the CIA maintained the headquarters and maintenance facilities of Civil Air Transport, a body which "provides air logistical support under commercial cover to most CIA and other U.S. Government Agencies' requirements." [65]

With its close ties to the United States, the Philippines is the favorite rear base for CIA operatives throughout Southeast Asia and is rumored to be its regional communications headquarters. Honolulu is another hub of agency activity directed at Asia and the Pacific, as revealed in a recent case involving a corporate executive named Ron Rewald. In sensational revelations in mid-1984, a CIA-front company called BBRDW Inc. was exposed in bankruptcy proceedings as a conduit for

---

* The CIA found it difficult to "break into" the Korean War due to MacArthur's dislike of clandestine military operatives.[61] In 1953, the Central Intelligence Group attached to U.S. forces during the 1950–1953 war period was assigned to the U.S. 8th Army, whereupon it trained commandos to infiltrate and sabotage north Korea on a small island southwest of Seoul. Shortly after the 1953 ceasefire, guards at the CIA site mistakenly opened fire on south Korean President Rhee, out for a boating trip. Rhee expelled the CIA, who kept only a covert presence in south Korea until the CIA station was formally reopened in 1959.[62] It finally came into its own in Korea when the Korean CIA was established in 1961.

† A CIA base such as that at Okinawa is defined in the *Pentagon Papers* as "a self-contained base under Army cover with facilities of all types necessary to the storage, testing, packaging, procurement and delivery of supplies – ranging from weapons and explosives to medical goods and clothing." [64]

CIA funds and a shelter for the finances of foreign politicians and businessmen from whom the CIA wished to obtain favors. BBRDW Inc. operated in the territory of all U.S. Third World allies in Pacific Command and set up a subsidiary trust company in Guam as an offshore tax haven. The CIA also used it to arrange the supply of military hardware to India with liberal allowance for kickbacks and bribes. In a press interview, Rewald, the firm's executive officer, explained the rationale for the operation:

Q. Why would the CIA want to get involved with something like that, Ron – just to make the contacts with these people?
RR. Oh. To put someone like that in a position where we could be dealing with him on that level. Are you kidding? You don't know the answer to that?
Q. No. What is that? What is the answer to that? You were going to blackmail him then?
RR. Oh, not blackmail him. But, certainly, we'd be in a position to know everything that's happening. To ask a favor. To do a lot of things. Not the least of which is to gain his confidence. You never know when you might need that card down the road.[66]

The CIA also gathers crucial intelligence information on the weak points of Soviet weapon systems, air defenses and the like, and provides pinpoint location of prospective nuclear targets from such Satellite Ground Stations as Pine Gap in Australia.

Counterinsurgency

Honed to a scientific "calculus" in the Vietnam War by Rand analysts,[67] counterinsurgency never caught on in the U.S. Army, since it involved significant non-military actions as well as unconventional warfare. By contrast, the CIA's General Lansdale was one of the earliest, most creative practitioners of the art. In the early 1950s, Lansdale orchestrated an elaborate operation against Communist Huk rebels in the Philippines. Here Lansdale describes a typical tactic:

A combat psywar [psychological warfare] squad . . . planted stories among the town residents of an *asuang* [vampire spirit] living on the hill where the Huks were based. Two nights later . . . the psywar squad set up an ambush along the trail used by the Huks. When a Huk patrol came along the trail, the ambushers silently snatched the last man of the patrol, their moves unseen in the dark night. They punctured his neck with two holes, vampire-fashion, held the body up by the heels, drained it of blood, and put the corpse back on the trail. When the Huks returned to look for the missing man and found their bloodless comrade, every member of the patrol believed that the *asuang* had got him and that one of them would be next if they remained on that hill. When daylight came, the whole Huk squadron moved out of the vicinity.[68]

Irregular warfare in the Pacific is not a CIA monopoly. In the early 1970s U.S. Army Special Action Forces, Asia, operated out of Okinawa and worked in isolated conditions on missions ordered by CINCPAC in Hawaii until the Vietnam pullback.[69] CINCPAC currently is represented on the inter-service Joint Special Operations Agency established in early 1984 to provide unconventional forces upon request.[*][72] "The PACOM [Pacific Command] region," cabled CINCPAC Admiral William Crowe to U.S. Defense Secretary Caspar Weinberger in October 1983, "includes many potential hotspots which could require selective employment of SOF [Special Operations Forces]."[73] In March 1984, an airborne company of the Army's Special Forces 1st Battalion reappeared at Torii Station in Okinawa under Western Command.[74] Gary Turner, Western Command's Brigadier-General, bragged, "this unit has been able to open doors with countries that we haven't had relations with in a long time."[75]

The Navy also gets into the counterinsurgency act with its SEAL teams, developed originally for riverine warfare operations in Vietnam.[76] Today, SEAL teams exercise regularly in the Philippines and even had two midget submarines of their own based inside a larger submarine, the u.s.s. *Grayback*. They also train Filipino counterinsurgency forces in mobile operations against the New People's Army.

---

* The 1st Special Operations Squadron moved from Okinawa to Clark Air Force Base in the Philippines in 1981, probably after participating in the disastrous Iranian hostage rescue operation.[70] Their missions include "day/night infiltration and exfiltration, resupply of Special Operations ground forces, psychological warfare missions, aerial reconnaissance, and air-dropping and surface-to-air retrieval of personnel."[71] As noted in Chapter 9, the Special Forces also play a "behind-the-lines" warfighting role.

Psychological Operations

Psychological Operations (PSYOPs) in the Pacific are a little-known but significant variant of irregular warfare operations. A form of ideological warfare, PSYOPs were "discovered" by a Congressional Committee in 1970 when it was revealed that the Army's 7th PSYOP Group was operating at Okinawa under CINCPAC control. A typical PSYOP involves the broadcast over the Voice of U.N. Command in south Korea of a strident anti-north Korea line "harder" than the State Department's Voice of America.[77]

The U.S. Navy also maintains a PSYOPs presence in the Pacific. Naval PSYOPs attempt to sway attitudes through a variety of media and intelligence systems. The Navy classifies sources in PSYOPs as White (acknowledged, overt source), Grey (indeterminate source), or Black (false, attributed source). A Navy manual notes that "Demonstrations of power by naval forces may be considered an implicit means of delivering a PSYOP message." "Strategically," states the Navy, "PSYOP may be appropriate to increase the willingness of foreign nations to provide facilities which support U.S. naval operations, to reduce their willingness to support the naval operations of potentially hostile powers, and to retaliate for foreign actions that adversely affect or interface with naval operations."[78]

As a Congressional investigator discovered, balloons and bombs full of pamphlets, radio broadcasts, even secret soap are enlisted in Pacific PSYOPs:

Mr. Pincus: We were discussing the 7th Psyops program in Thailand. One of the programs we were told about was a Thai soap which was brought into Thailand that was made in Taiwan, and apparently as you wash yourself with it at each level there is a new message. They pass it out in the hinterlands. We were told that the 7th Psyops had provided about 10,000 bars of this soap in Thailand.

Senator Symington: What does this soap do?

Mr. Pincus: As the soap washes down there is a new message with each layer of soap.

Senator Symington: I see.

Mr. Pincus: And apparently they are made on Taiwan and very successful. I do not know what the message is. It is probably a secret message.[79]

Of course, the presence of nuclear weapons in Pacific Command is a continuous PSYOP aimed at American enemies and allies (see Chapter 18). On occasion, the U.S. may broadcast the presence of nuclear weapons to immediately affect a local conflict involving U.S. forces. In 1958, for example, the U.S. introduced nuclear-capable missiles in Taiwan to intimidate China. But nuclear weapons are so widespread in the Pacific arsenal as to introduce an element of nuclear threat wherever U.S. forces are found. The latest additions to the ever-growing nuclear arsenal, such as the Tomahawk, underscore this omnipresent, latent nuclear component of Pacific Command's power projection.

Hit-and-run Force

Each of the regular and irregular forces in the Pacific arsenal has been developed for specialized missions. As U.S. strength in the Middle East crumbled in 1978 with the fall of the Shah, the U.S. drew on its combined military capabilities to form a unified Rapid Deployment Force (RDF).[80] Initially subordinate to the Readiness Command, the unique, mobile multi-service force was upgraded and renamed Central Command or CENTCOM in 1983, reporting directly to the Secretary of Defense through the Joint Chiefs of Staff (see Map 10.4).[81]

Although the Marines are CINCPAC's traditional "brush-fire" brigade, they are not effective in the Middle East. To intervene on land in such a distant area where the U.S. has few local support bases requires a special combination of air and sea-lift, army-air and marine beachstorming forces, and heavy and light armor.[82] Drawn from existing units, especially from the California-based Marine Amphibious Force I, the RDF *increases* Pacific Command forces only when it is assigned to CINCPAC (see Appendix A6). On the other hand, CENTCOM action outside the Pacific may call on and draw down Pacific Command forces in a crisis, as happened when Air Force Special Forces from Okinawa were used to rescue American hostages in Iran in 1979. The new approach, in short, may have sharpened the U.S. spear at the point of intervention, but it has also dramatically increased CINCPAC's range of potential interventions and thereby contributed to the over-extension of Pacific Command forces.

Map 10.4:
CENTCOM Area of Responsibility

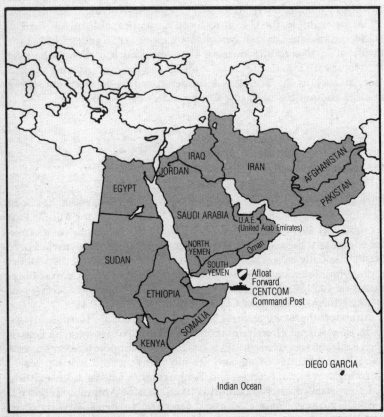

Source: U.S. House of Representatives, Committee on Armed Services, *Department of Defense Authorization for Fiscal Year 1985* (Hearings), Washington, D.C., 1984, Part 2, p. 1217.

Nuts and Bolts of War

In nuclear as in conventional war, logistics – the science of supply – dictates the choice of tactics and strategy to combat commanders. The Pacific Command's forces demand goods and supporting services such as logistics, storage, repairs, weapons testing, and environmental research.* "Logisticians" provide the nuts and bolts of war, organizing the massive supply flows to sustain forward deployed forces. As an invisible hand behind the exercise of military power, logisticians provide the sinews of war and determine the limits of military operations.

Logisticians from the Military Airlift Command and Military Sealift Command face a daunting task. They have to cover 14,000–17,000 km of sea and airlift supply pipelines in the Pacific,† a task further complicated by the unconventional nature of Asian wars. The Vietnam War typifies the problems with modern interventions. Small, isolated combat units were spread over a constantly changing war zone with no secure ports or depots available to military suppliers.[83] Moreover, the fantastic array and complexity of U.S. weapon systems strained the supply systems to the point of collapse.[84]

At the U.S. logistic frontier in Diego Garcia, a pre-positioned fleet of ships full of tanks, water and ammunition awaits a war to erupt in the Indian Ocean region.[85] Working from Guam and Okinawa, the fulcrum of Pacific logistics, the Military Sealift Command (MSC) and Military Airlift Command (MAC) will maintain the flow of supplies to forward bases in any future intervention zone (see Appendix A7). In a war involving Diego Garcia, U.S. bases in the Philippines, rather than those

---

* For reasons of space, we have not detailed environmental research conducted by or for the military in the Pacific. Such research, including climatic, meteorological conditions, disease vectors, wear and tear, atmospheric conditions, geographical data, space observation, anthropological and socio-cultural research, etc., is crucial to warplanning, equipment design, and training. In Antarctica, for example, the U.S. conducts research into the effects of auroras on the ionosphere directly relevant to the study of disruption of communications in nuclear war. Much environmental research is conducted by apparently non-military scientific bodies such as the Smithsonian Institution in Washington, D.C. Omission here is not intended to slight the importance of these support activities.

† Logistic pipelines are measured to *and* from the war zone.

on the U.S. West Coast, will serve as the key logistics depot for supply of the warzone.

Naval warfare in Pacific Command uses two pipelines to maintain ships in the combat zone. Operating from a shore base to supply a carrier task group, the Underway Replenishment Group (URG) remains at sea for up to ninety days. The second system inserts a floating naval base called a Mobile Support Group (MSG), between the shore base and the URG, thereby lengthening the supply pipeline.[86]

A "half" war like Vietnam consumed huge quantities of supplies. In 1968, U.S. forces used 44 million barrels of oil and over 1 million tonnes of ammunition alone.[87] Whether U.S. Pacific logisticians can supply similar volumes over greater distances without collapsing into chaos is doubtful. As late as 1984, CINCPAC strategists had reportedly not even calculated the basic lift requirements for supply across Pacific Command's vast distances.[88]

To sustain a carrier task force at war in the Indian Ocean will be quite difficult, requiring two URGs resupplied at Subic Bay.*[89] Three carrier task groups fighting in the Western Pacific and Indian Ocean would require up to nine URGs to support the 7,600 km pipeline. If, as proposed by Navy Secretary John Lehman, *fifteen* carrier task groups fight a long-distance, global war simultaneously with the Soviet Union, they will wallow helplessly in the ocean since there are simply not enough URGs to supply them. Faced with the prospect of their carriers floating for days and perhaps weeks without supplies, they might be forced to escalate rapidly to nuclear warfare to end the war quickly.

---

* At a modest four days operations between replenishment visits.

The Joint Defence Facility, Pine Gap, Northern Territory, Australia
(Department of Defence, Canberra)

ELEVEN ☆
THE INVISIBLE ARSENAL

If you want to screw up the other fellow, find out how he functions and focus on the weaknesses.

—Former Vice-Admiral David Richardson, 1981[1]

The vast intelligence and communications network which spans the Pacific is the brain and nervous system of America's nuclear and conventional arsenal. Without command/control and communications/intelligence facilities (C³I) U.S. forces would be deaf, mute, and blind. By keeping commanders well informed and reliably coupling their decisions to military hardware, communications and intelligence improve the destructive performance of weapons systems. "Responsive and reliable command, control, communications and intelligence as a force multiplier," stated General Joseph Palastra in 1982, "is not a buzzword for us – it is a fact of life." [2]

Communications Architecture

Whether in nuclear or conventional warfare, combat forces must exchange information with CINCPAC (Commander-in-Chief Pacific) in Honolulu, as well as communicate with each other to coordinate battlefield movements. Once issued, commands have to reach the fighting forces secure and ungarbled. To facilitate these needs, Pentagon wizards have erected an invisible architecture of communications which stretches across the Pacific. Transiting on earth-orbit satellites, the information infrastructure bounces its messages around the earth off the upper atmosphere and beyond like an inverted ping pong table.

Pacific Command's invisible microwave architecture serves the most dispersed and diverse set of forces in the history of warfare. Information specialists have to maintain connections across the vastness of the Pacific; keep occupying forces in touch with each other; and direct the tactical operations of the Pacific-based fleet and aircraft. All this military chatter generates gigantic mountains of information, moved via Automatic Data Processing Centers.[3] In addition to the enormous routine flows, specialized networks have sprung up to serve senior military like the Commander-in-Chief Pacific, or to control important weapons like nuclear bombs.

The basic building blocks of the communication system are radio waves and submarine cables. Each contributes to the communications arsenal by complementing or substituting for an option which faces severe obstacles. Submarine cables, for example, are highly reliable but immobile. Radio waves vary widely in capability depending on time, frequency and power of radiation, but offer unique capabilities for broadcast to diffuse, multiple receivers. Lower frequency radio waves can penetrate air and water over great ranges, but have very low transmission rates. Higher frequency radio waves typically trade range for transmission rate, a shortcoming which has been overcome by the use of satellites. Typically, both media are used to transmit information: automatic and manual switching devices aboard earth- or satellite-based relay points convert the transiting message from one to another.

The great distances involved make the possibility of communication across the Pacific an art as well as a science. For example, in the 14,000 km stretch between Diego Garcia in the Indian Ocean to CINCPAC in Hawaii, signals officers have to probe the atmosphere or plumb the oceans to lodge the home message to its intended receiver – without losing it in the vastness of atmosphere, ocean, or space. In ordinary circumstances, that is, when sunspots or nuclear war do not interfere with the atmosphere, a determined specialist working with receivers, relay sites or ground stations can usually connect headquarters to scattered field forces (see Appendixes A8 and D).

The Defense Communications Agency (DCA), a global functional command headquartered in Washington, D.C., coordinates all information systems in the Pacific Command. From its Area Communication Operation Center in Hawaii and from field offices across the Pacific, the DCA provides centralized control to ensure that the services' separate systems interface and operate jointly. In addition to providing regional centralization, DCA integrates Pacific Command communications systems into the global Defense Communications System.[4]

For all its efforts, centralized integration under DCA auspices is still feeble.[5] The services jealously guard their communications autonomy, resulting in fragmented and often incompatible hardware. In the early 1970s, Pacific Command and each of the services maintained thirty-three telecommunications sites on the Hawaiian island of Oahu.[6] Although that number shrank to eleven by 1984, the system remains diffuse and fragmented across Pacific Command.

Evolution or Involution?

As with all aspects of the Pacific Command, the existing communication architecture is as much the accumulated baggage of the past as a rational plan for the present. Up to 1964, pan-Pacific and tactical communications were wholly dependent on high frequency radio and submarine cables[7] (see Map 11.1). While the low frequency radio infrastructure in Northeast Asia was established in the Korean War,[8] the real innovations came during the Vietnam War when field forces were connected to commanders in Hawaii and Washington, D.C. In 1964, the first trans-Pacific commercial cable reached the Philippines and the military leased a piggyback ride. In 1965, a submarine cable snaked along the coast of Vietnam and Thailand, and military microwave and troposcatter radio infrastructure soon covered Southeast Asia.[9] Communication satellites appeared next, beginning with the first satellite receiver on the u.s.s. *Canberra* in 1967 in the Western Pacific,[10] followed by limited service on leased satellite channels between Washington, Hawaii, and the forward bases, reaching the newly acquired Diego Garcia in the Indian Ocean in 1969.[11]

Satellite service expanded gradually after 1969, and today, virtually every point in CINCPAC's domain is accessible by satellite[12] (see Maps 11.2 and 11.3). At an altitude of about 35,900 km, satellites in the

Map 11.1:
Defense Communications System in PACOM, 1964

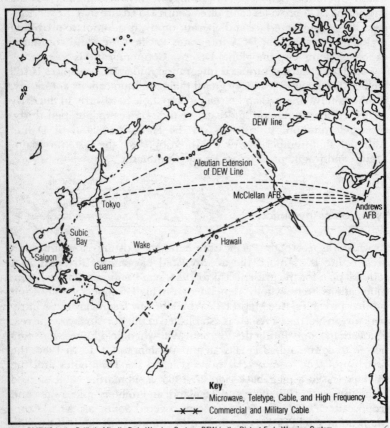

Key
- - - - - Microwave, Teletype, Cable, and High Frequency
-✕-✕- Commercial and Military Cable

Note: BMEWS is the Ballistic Missile Early Warning System. DEW is the Distant Early Warning System.
Source: From *Electronics*, October 19, 1964.

equatorial plane* are in geosynchronous orbit, that is, they stay above the same earth-point (see Figure 11.1). From such a position, each communication satellite covers 34 per cent of the earth's surface area and can instantly relay messages between two earth terminals.

Satellites orbiting in the equatorial plane, however, are not suitable for transmitting directly to earth receivers located above 70° north and south latitude. Since the angle between satellite-and-receiver and horizon-and-receiver becomes very acute because of the curvature of the earth, interference occurs at these high latitudes. For these areas, satellites adopt an elliptical orbit in order to maximize the time spent over the northern-polar regions (see Figure 11.2). Satellites in a north–south orbit operate at lower altitudes and require on-board recorders to store incoming information for replay later when they arrive in line-of-sight of a receiver or a relay ground station. These satellites are especially convenient for Arctic operations where high frequency radio works poorly.[13] In 1989, the new MILSTAR system will combine both orbits in a truly global, continuous coverage.[14]

Satellites are uniquely proficient in reaching mobile transmitters. Indeed, no other long-distance communication system can pass such large amounts of information so rapidly. Their only limits are determined by the size of the antennae on the earth-based sending and receiving transmitters, and the amount of transmission power to and from the satellite.

Overall, the Pacific Command communications systems can muster over 250 cable or satellite links to support 1200 trunklines and over 8,000 circuits at once. The long-haul system reaches to over 330 force commanders and to 450 branch exchanges,[15] fanning out from there to deployed forces (See Appendix D). CINCPAC also emphasizes compatibility with allied communications infrastructures within the Pacific Command system,[16] making allies dependent on the U.S. for vital transmissions.[17]

The Navy uses all possible media to connect its various forces to their commanders. Submerged submarines, for example, rely on lower frequency systems, although they can draw on all radio frequencies with a buoyed or surfaced antenna. High frequency (HF) radio is the

---

* The equatorial plane is that plane transecting the earth at the equator. Many U.S. communication, meteorological, and early warning satellites are placed in orbit above the earth in the equatorial plane.

Map 11.2:
Defense Communication Satellite System in PACOM, 1984

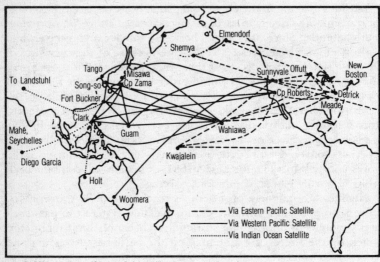

Note: PACOM also leases 181 commercial satellite channels not shown here.
Source: *Signal,* February 1984, p.,36.

Map 11.3:
Submarine Cables in PACOM, 1984

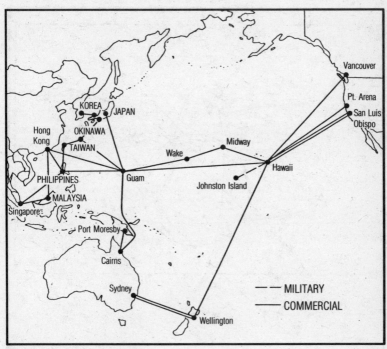

Note: No cables transit the Indian Ocean yet.
Source: *Signal*, February 1984, p. 25.

Figure 11.1
Communication and Intelligence Satellite Orbits

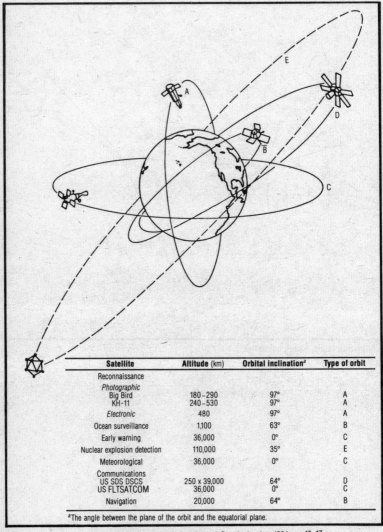

Satellite	Altitude (km)	Orbital inclination[a]	Type of orbit
Reconnaissance			
Photographic			
Big Bird	180–290	97°	A
KH-11	240–530	97°	A
Electronic	480	97°	A
Ocean surveillance	1,100	63°	B
Early warning	36,000	0°	C
Nuclear explosion detection	110,000	35°	E
Meteorological	36,000	0°	C
Communications			
US SDS DSCS	250 x 39,000	64°	D
US FLTSATCOM	36,000	0°	C
Navigation	20,000	64°	B

[a]The angle between the plane of the orbit and the equatorial plane.

Source: After B. Jasani & C. Lee, *Countdown To Space War,* Taylor & Francis, London, 1984, pp. 16–17.

Figure 11.2:
Satellite Earth-view over PACOM

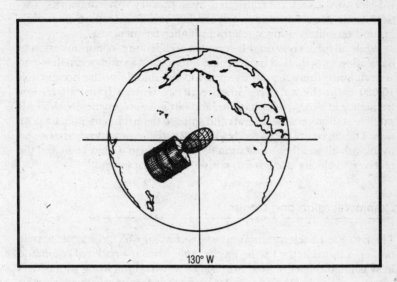

130° W

Source: E. Fthenakis, *Manual of Satellite Communications*, McGraw-Hill, New York, 1984, p. 19.

mainstay of surface fleet and naval air communications, as well as for the Air Force's land-based aircraft in the Pacific Command. On land, U.S. forward bases are connected by in-country relay networks. Tactical Army communications rely on HF back-pack radios, or mobile ground terminals using satellites in higher frequencies.

While all forces rely on this complex architecture, communication of navigation information is particularly important to mid-ocean fleet and aircraft since there are no signposts in the middle of the ocean or at 10,000 m in the air. Very low frequency Omega transmitters, low frequency LORAN radio stations, and ultra-high frequency NAVSTAR satellite stations enable aircraft and ships to determine their exact position. The currently deployed NAVSTAR satellite provides earth-bound users with all-weather navigation fixes accurate to within 16 m and the receiver's velocity accurate to within 0.7 m per second.[18]

Communication and Control

The first use of telecommunications technology to facilitate U.S. military operations in the Pacific was in 1898, when the national command in Washington telegraphed Admiral Dewey in Hong Kong with orders to occupy Manila.*[19] Although Dewey waited for the go-ahead from his superiors, the relatively crude character of the communications system meant that field commanders were able to operate with a high degree of autonomy. During the Korean War, for example, delayed communications made it impossible for the Pentagon or President Truman to fully control General MacArthur's provocative strategy. The communications system in Northeast Asia was often overloaded, and MacArthur's superiors often received word of his initiatives after the fact.†[20] Between 1950 and 1970, however, the increasing sophistication of the military's communications network allowed the Pentagon to centralize command of operations in the Pacific. In Vietnam, instant satellite communications allowed the White House to virtually by-pass CINCPAC and direct combat operations from Washington.

---

* Thereafter, high frequency radio became the mainstay of military communications until the 1960s.

† MacArthur was also adept at exploiting the weaknesses of the system for his own ends.

An incident on the Demilitarized Zone in Korea in 1976 provides a clear example of the trend toward centralized command. Two American GIs were shot by north Korean troops while pruning a poplar tree in the Zone. In response, the U.S. undertook *Operation Paul Bunyan* – an armed tree-cutting expedition backed up with F-111s flown in especially from Idaho and a carrier task group offshore.[21] The chain-saw operators were in direct contact with the Pentagon via helicopter to the command in Seoul, by-passing the Korean Command and CINCPAC altogether. Since the dividing strip is one of the most tense spots in the world, Washington was determined to exercise complete control over the field situation. Moreover, the attitude of the U.S. Commander in Korea, General Stilwell, probably did not inspire the Pentagon's confidence in local military leadership. Later Stilwell revealed his game-plan: "We hoped that they [the north Koreans] might meet us around the base of the tree and we would perhaps bash in a few skulls with karate chops, clubs, and what not."[22]

Centralization of command, however, is a two-edged sword. While communications systems shorten commanders' response time to events halfway around the world, reliable control of war, especially nuclear war, remains elusive due to automated and increasingly faster delivery systems which accelerate the pace of war. While technological improvements, in short, have speeded up communications, the time required for delivery of nuclear weapons is decreasing faster than that needed to control the hardware. The quality of decisions made by commanders in Washington moreover, is inevitably reduced by their distance from the site of conflict.

Military Intelligence

The complexity of Pacific Command's communications architecture is nearly matched by its intelligence system. The U.S. intelligence system in the Pacific works like a voracious vacuum cleaner, sucking up heaps of information and dumping it on the desks of analysts. But it can also be used like a stethoscope when CINCPAC wants to listen closely to the pulse of American enemies and friends in the Pacific.

The heart of the Pacific intelligence system is the Intelligence Center Pacific (IPAC) based in Hawaii, a joint, subordinate operational command of CINCPAC. IPAC draws on all sources of intelligence in and out of the Pacific to maintain background files or warn of impending adverse developments. To these ends, IPAC monitors all intelligence sources and assesses each country's military, political, and economic affairs. It also analyzes air defenses and keeps target plans up-to-date.[23]

Information sources include communications, electronic and photographic intelligence from spy satellites, planes, and stations on U.S. bases throughout the Pacific Command, as well as reports from the more traditional double agents.* IPAC is also the Pacific contact point for the Pentagon's Worldwide Indications and Warning System which tracks political and military events.[26]

Intelligence systems, especially communication and electronic intelligence, rely heavily on U.S. foreign bases (see Appendixes A9 and C). Ground bases for spying on communications or electronic activity (especially radars), for example, are best located close to the source. Where range reduces the efficiency of eavesdropping, mobile collection bases are used, usually on ships and aircraft.

Spy satellites, such as the Central Intelligence Agency's KH-11 and the Air Force's Big Bird,† also require ground control stations to obtain global coverage, especially in Australia, Guam, Alaska, Hawaii, and the Seychelle Islands in the Indian Ocean. These stations send commands to the satellite to shift orbit or activate or deactivate the satellite electronic systems. Ground receiving stations are also needed to collect data recorded in orbit while out of reach from ground stations, which is then communicated via satellite to the Intelligence Center, Pacific. Photographic intelligence satellites also drop capsules of film back to earth which are caught mid-air by aircraft or helicopters out of Hawaii, Alaska, or Okinawa (see Appendix C2).

In the past, many spy satellites have been launched into orbit from Vandenberg Air Force Base in California over the South Polar region. The manned Space Shuttle provides unique surveillance and satellite launching capabilities for the Air Force. Ship or air-based systems are

---

* This information is assembled into summaries of military capability in each country in the region, detailed studies to support the various warplans, and target lists for attack should war erupt.[24] These reports are passed on to the relevant commands via the office of Pacific Command.[25]

† "Close look," low-altitude ferret satellites back up these spy satellites by collecting electronic and photographic intelligence.[27]

used where more prolonged, closer collection is required, especially for photographic or electronic intelligence.* These systems cluster around active U.S. interventions, and continuously monitor the Alaska–Northeast Asia zone for Soviet missile test telemetry and air defense radar emissions.

The U.S. is not averse to "tickling" Soviet radar systems to assist the design of U.S. counter-measures and attack routes. In 1978, for example, the U.S. sent several spyplanes and six ships, including destroyers, into the Sea of Okhotsk, the "inner sanctum" of Soviet submarine operations in the Pacific. The Soviets either failed to observe their presence, or refused to turn on their radar, and the U.S. spies retired empty-handed.[30] In September 1983, a Korean Airlines plane was shot down in the same vicinity, causing the deaths of 269 passengers and crew.[31] The Soviets claimed that they had confused the commercial flight with a U.S. military plane, an RC-135, which was also in the area. Amid the acrimony and accusations, two former RC-135 pilots confirmed previous U.S. intelligence missions: "It has been our experience that, on occasion, NSA [National Security Agency] adjusts the orbits of RC-135s so that they will intentionally penetrate the air space of a target nation."[32] Whatever the commercial airliner was doing in Soviet airspace, its demise provided an enormous U.S. intelligence *coup* – the configuration of many Soviet air defense radars activated during the plane's tragic incursion.

Early Warning

The Pacific serves as a platform for early warning of nuclear attack on the U.S. itself or its bases, and for monitoring a nuclear war (see Table 11.1). Whether it is fixed or mobile, each forward base must also be

---

* The most important systems are the continuous electronic intelligence monitoring by RC-135 aircraft off the Soviet Far East, and the Blackbird SR-71 reconnaissance aircraft which monitors electronic (ELINT) and photographic intelligence until a satellite arrives overhead.[28] The Pacific Command ELINT Center is located at Hospital Point, Honolulu; the Air Force's 548th Reconnaissance Technical Group is supervised by Intelligence Center-Pacific, and is located at Hickam Air Force Base in Hawaii with a subordinate squadron at Yokota Air Base in Japan and possibly at Yongsan Air Base in south Korea. The 548th mostly conducts imagery analysis.[29]

Table 11.1:
Nuclear Detonation Detection and Missile Early Warning Systems in Pacific Command

A. *Satellite NUDET and EW Systems:* orbit in geosynchronous equatorial orbit to provide infrared sensor area coverage. DSP Satellite EW System, Code 647 Satellites, two satellites in geosynchronous orbit over Pacific (135° W) and Indian Ocean (70° E) with infrared sensors. Integrated Operational Nuclear Detection System, infrared sensors on Navstar GPS Satellites, also on 647 EW satellites (see below).

B. *Ground Stations:*

Guam:	Ritidian Pt., Station for monitoring effects atmospheric NUDETs.
Kwajalein:	Pacific Barrier ASAT radar.
Australia:	Nurrungar, non-U.S. ground terminal for Program 647 missile EW satellite system (also known as Defense Support Program – DSP).
Alaska:	Shemya, Cobra Dane ground-based, Cobra Ball airborne, and Cobra Judy ship-based missile tracking radar. Clear, Ballistic Missile Early Warning Missile sites; EW radar system. Alaskan Air Command Air Surveillance, 13 missile EW sites. DEW line, seven sites, missile EW radar system. Pacific Barrier ASAT radar.
Philippines:	Cagayan de Oro, John Hay Camp; sites for remote detection atmospheric NUDETs. San Miguel, Pacific Barrier ASAT radar.
Canada:	DEW line sites continuing Alaskan system along edge of Arctic Ocean; tactical SIGINT/PHOTINT intelligence assets.

Table 11.1: (cont)

Key: NUDET = Nuclear detonation; EW = Early warning; DEW = Distant early warning; SIGINT = Signals intelligence; PHOTINT = Photographic intelligence.
Source: O. Wilkes, Foreign Military Bases Project, SIPRI, 1983.

defended. To this end, radars survey the airspace around each of the major U.S. bases in Pacific Command, forming an almost continuous early-warning belt in the Western Pacific, Alaska, and Canada. These are supplemented by readings from long-range radar early warning systems in the northwest Pacific, especially off Alaska, and by Airborne Warning and Control planes above war-prone areas such as Korea (see Appendix C4).

As a primarily naval theater, Pacific Command constantly tracks thousands of ships on a computerized system operated by the Pacific Fleet's Intelligence Directorate.[33] U.S. warships keep tabs on potential target vessels such as Soviet warships, merchant vessels, or fishing trawlers using high frequency radio direction-finding equipment. This information is supplemented by fixes from the network of land-based stations with the same function,* by reports from visual encounters on the high seas, and by sightings by U.S. and allied P3C Orion ocean reconnaissance aircraft. Merchant vessels and friendly warships are called OSIS (for Ocean Surveillance Information System) WHITE, and communist vessels are called OSIS RED.[34] The Classic Wizard naval surveillance system supplements these terrestrial systems with eyes-in-the-sky satellite collection of radar and radio emissions from vessels 1,100 km below. In Pacific Command, Classic Wizard relies on the ground station at Diego Garcia, Guam and Adak.[35]

The computer identifies each vessel by name, type, and radio call-sign. The Fleet Intelligence Center at Pearl Harbor issues two reports based on this information system.[36] The first, called DEPLOC for Daily Estimated Position Locator, provides routine information on a regular basis as to vessel positions. The second, named CASPER for Contact Area Summary Position Report, can inform a commander of the vessels in a requested area at a specific time. In as little as ten minutes, the CASPER can supply a U.S. warship with complete, up-to-date target information needed to fire a Harpoon or Tomahawk anti-ship missile at a distant naval target.[37]

---

* In Japan, Guam, Canada, New Zealand, Australia, Hong Kong, and Diego Garcia.

Calibrating the Oceans

A system of top-secret underwater hydrophones (the Sound Surveillance System or SOSUS) and Anti-Submarine Warfare Centers in the Pacific sift recordings of Soviet submarine "noise prints" echoing through the ocean (see Appendix C5). Soviet submarine departures and movements are monitored continuously. By the mid-1970s, the Soviets reported that two U.S. SOSUS systems snared the sound signatures of Soviet submarines in the Pacific: *Colossus*, installed in the late 1960s to cover the approaches to the U.S. West Coast; and *Sea Spider*, in the mid-Pacific north of Hawaii.

These arrays were supplemented by SOSUS nets along the Aleutian chain;* by offshore systems around Okinawa, Korea, Taiwan, and the Philippines;[38] and by rapidly deployable "barriers" of long-lived sonar buoys. Proximity of the processing base to the submarine hydrophone nets is important since the gigantic volume of recorded information must be "massaged" immediately by computers to provide up-to-date, "tactical" intelligence. Additional intelligence comes from SONAR arrays towed by submarines or surface vessels, and disposable sonar buoys dropped by Viking E2C and P3C Orion aircraft which pin-point Soviet submarines in the zone predicted by the Ocean Surveillance Information System (OSIS) (see Appendix C5 and C6).

OSIS is the overall intelligence system which supports the Anti-Submarine Warfare Command and Control System in the Pacific.[39] OSIS gathers the SOSUS data and adds it to the intelligence on submarine communications from the network of high frequency radio stations across Pacific Command. All this information, in turn, is communicated instantly by satellite to a bank of computers, which sifts out the submarine signatures from the background of oceanic noises. The computers also constantly update a giant computer model of the ocean's vertical temperature profile,† information gathered since 1957 by a global system of thermometers at various depths[40] and more recently supplemented by infra-red satellite

---

* And, according to the Soviets, in the Kuriles-Kamchatka Trench, which seems technically difficult and is denied by informed sources in Pacific Command.

† The velocity of sound through water depends on the water's temperature and pressure which does not change uniformly with depth. The temperature profile is therefore required to predict the refraction paths of sound through the ocean.

Figure 11.3:
Operating Radius of P-3 Aircraft Using Current Bases

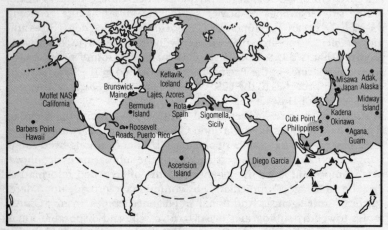

Note: Shaded areas indicate airfields from which US P-3 Orions operate. Orion P-3 flying capability is 2,660 km range from airfield, with 4 hours "on station." Dotted lines indicate P-3 coverage if no time spent "on station." P-3s for ASW have no refueling capability as yet. Additional coverage is available from allied ASW planes or airfields marked ▲.

Source: B. Cooper, *Maritime Roles for Land-Based Aviation*, Congressional Research Service report 83-151.F, Washington, DC, 1983, p. 23; US Air Force, Office of Public Information, October 1984; O. Wilkes, SIPRI Foreign Military Bases Project files, 1983 and "Strategic Anti-Submarine Warfare," *SIPRI Yearbook, 1979*, Taylor and Francis, London, 1979, p. 434.

imagery.[41] The model then interprets the SOSUS recordings in light of the sound velocity structure of the deep ocean layer (between 1,200 and 1,400 m), which transmits submarine noise over thousands of kilometres. This model thereby predicts how submarine sounds will bend and reconstructs the location of the Soviet submarines – critical intelligence for U.S. anti-submarine forces in the event of war.

To operate this vast acoustic and thermal monitoring system spanning the globe requires many forward bases in the Pacific. Since anti-submarine intelligence enables the superpowers to threaten the least vulnerable nuclear weapons, viz. those aboard submarines, it can be argued that these capabilities increase the risk of nuclear war by inducing one side to pre-empt the other.[42] To block a first strike from U.S. submarines, these apparently innocuous communication bases are prime Soviet targets in a nuclear war.

Busy Observers

Land-based aircraft provide crucial reconnaissance over the oceans, seeking indications of submarines or surface ships. P3C Orion and more recently B-52 aircraft under the Air Force Busy Observer program are primarily responsible for this task. As revealed in the structure of back-up airfields (see Appendix C6 and C7), this system focuses on the major sealanes.

Aircraft carriers supplement this strategic reconnaissance with their own Hawkeye E2C reconnaissance aircraft. With this system, when combined with P3C Orions, the U.S. can reconnoitre virtually any area at short notice (see Figure 11.3). Since 1976 the earliest ocean intelligence has been provided by Classic Wizard surveillance satellites which use radar and electronic intelligence to locate surface ships.[43]

While U.S. intelligence capabilities are almost omnipresent in the Pacific, they are also unreliable. Indeed, U.S. intelligence systems in the Pacific may be so vast as to be unmanageable, and the intelligence itself so voluminous as to be incomprehensible. "Intelligence" may become assured ignorance. Automated and bureaucratic systems are notoriously fallible, and Pacific Command intelligence is both highly automated and highly bureaucratic. Nonetheless, when the U.S. turns on the spotlight, a great deal of landscape is illuminated and information is acquired. Whether commanders have much idea what to do with it all is another matter.

USS *Ohio*, Trident missile-firing submarine in dry-dock,
Bangor, Washington state, U.S., 1983
(Pentagon)

TWELVE ☆
THE MEANS OF ANNIHILATION

I can go into my office and pick up the telephone and in twenty-five minutes seventy million people will be dead.

—President Richard Nixon, November 1973[1]

The ultimate threat in the global military arsenal of the United States is nuclear annihilation. Based primarily on submarines, surface warships, and bombers, Pacific Command's ever-ready nuclear forces are found everywhere in the region.*

Planning and preparing for nuclear war has preoccupied the Pentagon and Pacific Command since the 1950s. Under Reagan's pronavalist, global military doctrine, however, preparing for nuclear war has acquired new momentum in the Pacific. The Pacific Commander-in-Chief is pushing hard to "modernize" his nuclear forces by introducing increasingly lethal nuclear missiles such as the Tomahawk and the Trident I and II. Nuclear war support functions, especially the vulnerable – and crucial – communications facilities, are being hardened to "endure" nuclear war. The concept of fighting a protracted or "limited" nuclear war, such as a nuclear exchange in Korea or at sea, has reappeared in military discourse.

As the hardware piles up and the anti-Soviet rhetoric becomes more

---

* While we describe in this chapter the major nuclear weapon systems in the Pacific, we do not dwell on technical details available elsewhere.[2] Furthermore, we do not deal with biological, chemical, or climatic means of warfare.

strident, the nuclear arms race in the Pacific imposes an ever-increasing nuclear threat.

Nuclear Vortex

Nuclear weapons work by releasing huge quantities of energy from fissioning or fusing atoms, an energy which differs in quantity and quality from that of conventional weapons. The energy released in the heat, blast, and radiation of a nuclear bomb can incinerate, vaporize, explode or otherwise destroy whatever is in the radius of 30 to 40 km of the explosion. Rather than the *block*-buster bombs and military occupation of past wars, nuclear strategists talk of *city*-buster weapons and country-killing warfare.

The development of nuclear weapons inverted the traditional relationship between means and ends of weapon systems. Formerly, states armed partly to deter attack but mainly to fight for victory, a strategy which produced periodic stretches of war and peace. Since nuclear weapons are so powerful as to be virtually useless for warfighting, nuclear weapons can be "used" only to avoid or deter nuclear war. In effect, nuclear weapons have transformed "peacetime" from a state of non-war to one of feverish preparation for nuclear war, a state of permanent nuclear stalemate which could culminate in one final cataclysm.

A succession of doctrines has attempted to transform nuclear weapons into manageable tools of war and diplomacy. In the 1940s and 1950s, coined the "Age of Assured Ascendancy" by defense analyst John Collins, U.S. warplans called for immediate escalation to all-out nuclear war, with attacks aimed principally at cities and military bases in China and the Soviet Union.[3] In the 1960s, the "Age of Assured Destruction", the U.S. adjusted to the certainty of Soviet retaliation in the event of a nuclear attack. Nuclear war became "unthinkable" and nuclear weapons became the backdrop instead of the centerpiece of superpower rivalry. U.S. nuclear targeting "packages" were broken into discrete sets of cities and military targets, which allowed war planners to escalate "less rapidly" to the final cataclysm.

In the 1970s and 1980s, the "Age of Assured Anxiety", American strategists rethought the "unthinkable." They refined their techniques of nuclear warfighting and resuscitated the notions of nuclear "victory", limited nuclear war, and gradual escalation. The doctrine of "counterforce" – attacking Soviet nuclear forces first, and then urban–industrial targets, thus avoiding the city populations *per se* – was openly declared for the first time. While counterforce *targeting* had been part of every nuclear warplan since the 1940s, its formal adoption signalled a move away from deterrence and proclaimed the Pentagon's belief in the possibility of victory in a protracted nuclear war. It also underscored the utility of an all-out, pre-emptive first-strike (see Chapter 18).[4]

Since the Korean War, the size of the global nuclear stockpile has constantly increased. In an effort to keep ahead of the Soviet Union, the U.S. arsenal reached about 25,000 nuclear warheads by the 1980s. These nuclear warheads have been deployed in the Pacific in virtually all their bewildering variety (see Table 12.1).

The ultimate threat, nuclear weapons embody so much potential power – including self-destructive power – that they undermine their own credibility. Yet the Pentagon continues to rely on them heavily in its warfighting plans. It *has* to behave as if nuclear weapons can be used strategically – that is, to some rational, military end – if the threat of deterrence is to work and the blackmail potential of nuclear weapons is to be exploited for coercive diplomacy. But the likely effects of a nuclear attack undermine the very concept of employing weapons strategically.

Nuclear warplans involve targeting military forces, both nuclear and non-nuclear, and urban-industrial areas. While the warplans neatly distinguish between these "hard" and "soft" targets on paper, an actual nuclear attack would be blind to the distinction.* Unless genocidal revenge against civilians becomes the military's goal – which can hardly be deemed "rational" – this inability to discriminate military targets from civilian populations makes the strategic use of nuclear weapons impossible.[5] Furthermore, an initial use of nuclear weapons crosses a psychological "firebreak" and contains the risk of rapid escalation. The risk stems, in part, from the fact that both American and Soviet forces bristle with massive nuclear arsenals at the ready. Command and con-

---

* This is as true of Soviet as of U.S. nuclear attacks. An attack on the U.S. naval nuclear weapons ammunition depot in Concord, California, for example, would annihilate the San Francisco metropolitan area to the west. The affected civilian populations do not have to be co-located with military targets – just downwind.

Table 12.1:
U.S. Nuclear Weapons Forward-deployed in the Pacific

Type	Range	Launch Platform	Dual Capable	Firepower
Missiles				
ASROC	2–11 km	surface, submarine fleet	yes	1 kt
SUBROC	56 km	submarine	no	1–5 kt
Terrier SAM	34 km	surface fleet	no[a]	1 kt
ALCM	2,500 km[b]	B-52s	no	200–250 kt
SLCM	2,500 km	surface, submarine fleet	yes	200–250 kt
Trident I	7,700 km	submarine	no	100 kt
SRAM	56–220 km[c]	bombers	no	170–200 kt
Bombs				
Air-dropped gravity bombs	short and long range bombers	aircraft	yes	5–9000 kt
Artillery				
155 mm shells	30 km	artillery gun	yes	0.1 kt
203 mm shells	29 km	artillery gun	yes	less than 12 kt
Atomic Demolition Mines				
Medium ADM	n/a	vehicle, helicopter, tunnel	no	1–15 kt
Special ADM	n/a	backpack portable	no	less than 1 kt
Anti-Submarine Warfare Depth Charges				
B-57	n/a	helicopter, aircraft, surface fleet	yes	less than 20 kt

Table 12.1: (cont)

Coming Soon?			
Standard Missile	surface fleet	yes	low kt
Neutron bomb	artillery	no	1–10 kt
ASW Standoff weapon	more than 56 km	yes	?
Trident II	surface, submarine fleet submarine 7600–11,400 km	no	150–600 kt

Key: ASROC = Anti-submarine Rocket; SUBROC = Submarine-Launched Rocket; SAM = Surface-Air Missile; ALCM = Air-Launched Cruise Missile; SLCM = Sea-Launched Cruise Missile; SRAM = Short-Range Attack Missile; ADM = Atomic Demolition Mine; ASW = Anti-Submarine Warfare.

Notes: In a nuclear war, both powers will use home-based ballistic missiles against each other in the Pacific; a. Originally dual-capable, the remaining Terriers are nuclear-armed; b. Nuclear land-attack version; ALCM on B-52H bombers on U.S. West Coast only; c. Depending on altitude. SRAMs are stockpiled at Guam for B-52G delivery.

Sources: T. Cochran, *et al.*, *U.S. Nuclear Forces and Capabilities*, Ballinger, 1984; Nautilus Pacific Research, *Warships and Warheads, U.S.–Pacific Connections*, Leverett, Massachusetts, 1984.

trol systems, relying on an unlikely combination of technological controls and level-headed, quick-thinking decision-makers, are vulnerable to serious error.

Despite the a-strategic nature of nuclear weapons, each military service has developed specialized means of annihilation to enhance its mission – and thereby increase its slice of the U.S. military budget. Of the nuclear forces in the Pacific, only the missile submarines are dedicated *solely* to nuclear war. If the superpowers wage nuclear war, *all* the nuclear and non-nuclear weapons described in Chapters 10 and 11 – the fleet, the bombers, the communications and intelligence systems – will be mobilized to amplify the annihilation.

Trident: The Ultimate Weapon System

The first nuclear weapons to be fired in an all-out nuclear war will probably be land-based intercontinental ballistic missiles (ICBMs). Based in the continental U.S., these highly accurate missiles are immobile and vulnerable to preemptive attack. Not wishing to lose them, the U.S. would probably fire them immediately in an all-out nuclear war.

Submarine-launched ballistic missiles back up the ICBMs. The fraction of the U.S. nuclear arsenal based on submarines has increased as nuclear bombers, intermediate-range ballistic missiles, and land-based intercontinental ballistic missiles have become vulnerable to Soviet attack. In December 1964, the first submarine capable of firing long-range Polaris ballistic missiles to prowl the Pacific was the u.s.s. *Daniel Boone*.[6] Ten missile submarines eventually joined the Pacific Fleet, each capable of launching 16 Polaris missiles with three 200 kiloton warheads each. With a 4,750 km range, these submarines operated in the West Pacific in order to be capable of hitting urban-industrial targets deep in Central Siberia (see Figure 12.1).[7]

Today the most important nuclear weapons in the Pacific are the Trident I ballistic missiles aboard the Ohio-class submarines – commonly called Trident submarines*. On their seventy-day prowl through

---

* While submarines carrying nuclear missiles are often named after their missile, more than one class of submarine may carry the same missile. The point is not merely semantic: besides the Ohio, the Benjamin Franklin and Lafayette classes currently carry Trident I missiles, although only the Ohio currently operates in the Pacific.

Figure 12.1:
U.S. Ballistic Missile Submarine Operating Areas
Before and After Trident Missile Deployment

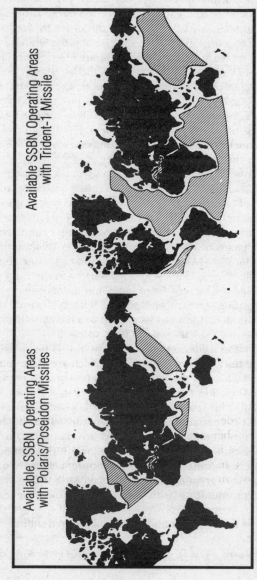

Available SSBN Operating Areas
with Polaris/Poseidon Missiles

Available SSBN Operating Areas
with Trident-1 Missile

Source: S. Catola, *Strategic Nuclear Policies, Weapons, and the C³ Connection*, MITRE Corp. Document
#M83-30, Bedford, Massachusetts, p. 69.

the Pacific at a cruising speed of about 25 km per hour, an Ohio submarine can reach the mid-Pacific in about ten days.[8] It then has about
seven weeks to wait at its "station" for the order to fire its missiles.

Judged by cost, range, firepower, or accuracy, the Ohio is a leviathan.
Costing about a billion dollars, each submarine weighs 15,000 tonnes
and stretches 171 m from bow to stern – the length of two-and-a-half
747 jumbo jets.[9] Capable of cruising at a depth up to 300 m, the Ohio is
superquiet, reportedly emitting less sound at low speeds than an auto-
mobile on a highway.[10] Nevertheless, the Ohio can hit a submerged
speed in excess of 56 km per hour. Inside, the hull is so crowded with
electronics, a nuclear reactor, and weapons that some of the crew must
sleep between the Trident missiles![11]

The Ohio submarine is the ultimate land-attack weapon. Packing a
payload of 192 nuclear warheads on 24 Trident I missiles, an Ohio can
deliver a total of 19 megatons within 500 m of its target – the equivalent
of 1,500 Hiroshimas. With a firing range over 7,700 km, nearly twice as
far as the Polaris missile, the Ohio system enlarges submarine operating areas by a factor of 10 to 20. (see Figure 12.1). Its future armament
may feature MK 500 MARV* warheads which can maneuver to evade
Soviet anti-ballistic missile interception. Starting in the early 1990s, the
Trident II missile will be retrofitted into Ohio submarines in the Pacific.
Without losing range or explosive power, Trident II is even more accurate than the Trident I, due to its capacity to navigate from the stars
before the re-entry vehicles plunge back to earth.

Protected by the wilderness of opaque water, Ohio submarines are
the long-range nuclear launch platforms which are least vulnerable to
preemptive attack, and the most likely survivors in a nuclear war.
However, the Ohio has two disadvantages. First, it cannot be used to
"show the flag" to threaten a non-nuclear adversary in coercive diplomacy since it is kept submerged and invisible when deployed. It is
dedicated to threatening nuclear-armed adversaries with a nuclear
reprisal capability. Second, the deep water which protects submarines
so well is also a poor transmitter of radio communication (see Appendix
D). For this reason, great emphasis is placed on building systems that
can reliably communicate with submarines without revealing their
position.

Since there is a strong probability that submerged submarines will be

---

* Maneuverable Re-entry Vehicle, designed to confuse and evade Soviet defenses.

incommunicado during war, commanders of the Ohio submarines are not constrained by technology from firing the nuclear warheads. The command from above to fire merely authenticates codes kept aboard rather than unlocking them, thereby authorizing the submarine commander to launch the missiles.* Since the consequences of error or misjudgement are so grave, the command to fire must be verified by four or more officers. To protect the world against inadvertent or insane use of the awesome power of the Ohio's Trident missiles, these officers are authorized to mutiny against their captain should the worst occur.[12] There is no authorization, however, for the crew to mutiny against the collective insanity of all the officers.

The first Ohio submarine (the U.S.S. *Ohio*) cruised the Pacific in late 1983, replacing the last of the ten Polaris missile-firing submarines.[13] Each year, one Ohio submarine will join the Pacific Fleet until no less than ten are based at Bangor, Washington, on the Northwest coast of the U.S.[14]

Whether U.S. missile-firing submarines have been or will be deployed in the Indian Ocean is hotly disputed. Some analysts point to the Very Low Frequency (VLF) communications station at NW Cape in Australia and the early research at Karachi, Pakistan as proof that the Pentagon deploys these weapons in the Indian Ocean.[15] Since NW Cape was also needed to complement other VLF signals in the Pacific, this argument is unpersuasive.[16] Others have pointed to vague references that the Ohio-class submarines are *capable* of operating in the Indian Ocean as evidence.[17]

There is no doubt that the Ohio submarine *could* reach all the way to the Indian Ocean and back without refuelling, and still have a month to threaten the Soviet Union from a southern launching site against urban or industrial targets (see Figure 12.2). However, the submarine would also be out of target range and vulnerable to Soviet attack during its long travel time to and from the Pacific through the straits of Southeast Asia. Regular Indian Ocean deployment appears a relatively risky and "inefficient" use of the threat-power of a multi-billion dollar submarine. An occasional training visit to the Indian Ocean or low-cost strategic deception at Diego Garcia to make it appear that Ohio submarines

---

* Most other nuclear weapons are designed so that a communicated code *enables* the weapon to be armed, physically precluding unauthorized or inadvertent use.

are present might be undertaken to force the Soviets to spread out their anti-submarine forces.

The eventual deployment of Ohio submarines under the Arctic ice like their Soviet counterparts is much more likely.* Strengthened external hulls to smash through the ice would enable its Trident missiles to be launched only minutes away from Soviet targets.[19]

Manned Penetrators

Almost relics compared with Trident missiles, twenty B-52G nuclear bombers of the 43rd Strategic Wing are based at Anderson Air Force Base in Guam.[20] Currently, the B-52Gs are armed with four to eight short-range nuclear attack missiles† and four big gravity nuclear bombs. Grim Strategic Air Command generals refer to the bombers as "manned penetrators" aimed at "soft" targets.[21]

While communications with B-52Gs are more reliable than those with the Ohio submarines (see Appendix D), the bombers are vulnerable to attack when concentrated on the ground. A fraction of them are always ready to take off, therefore, within minutes of early warning of attack. Once airborne, they are slow compared to ballistic missiles. Whereas missiles cannot be stopped once the fatal launch takes place, the bombers may be recalled by radio.[22] After take-off, in other words, the bombers offer commanders time to reconsider the attack – up until the moment that the nuclear weapons are dropped. Commanders cannot be too leisurely about issuing the final word, however: flying from Guam at 800 km per hour,[23] a B-52G can reach the Soviet Far East coastline within three to four hours.

The B-52s are the most suited of all the long-range nuclear weapons for communicating nuclear threats. They are often the first nuclear weapon system to be mobilized in nuclear alerts used in the course of coercive diplomacy against nuclear-armed adversaries.

---

* In December 1984, satellite photographs reportedly showed evidence of a Soviet submarine ice-boring test slightly northwest of Wrangel Island in the Arctic north of the Soviet Far East.[18]

† To suppress Soviet coastal or target defenses.

Figure 12.2:
Range of Trident I Missile Fired from Mid-Pacific

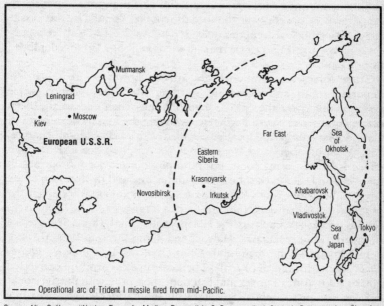

- - - Operational arc of Trident I missile fired from mid-Pacific.

Source: After G. Kemp, "Nuclear Forces for Medium Powers," in C. Bertram edited, *Strategic Deterrence in a Changing Environment,* Gower & Allenheld, Osmun, London, 1981, p. 121.

Hunter-killers

As ballistic missiles and bombers unleash an atomic cataclysm, all short- and medium-range nuclear weapons will also mobilize. These short-range delivery systems will "bounce the rubble" created by the missile attack, using nuclear weapons delivered by A6E and A7E strike bombers launched from aircraft carriers, or medium-range fighters deployed from Guam.

These forces for additional land-attacks, however, are much less important than anti-submarine warfare. Maritime reconnaissance systems, especially the SOSUS hydrophones anchored to the deep ocean floor in the North Pacific, will provide the initial coordinates of likely Soviet submarine locations. Laden with nuclear depth charges, P3C Orion bombers and any spare B-52s will then head for the predicted locations, using sonar buoys to pinpoint Soviet submarines. If there are no U.S. attack submarines in the area and the location of the Soviet submarines is not known exactly, the bombers will pepper the ocean with nuclear depth charges over a large area.* The likely areas for this undersea assault are the North Pacific, South China Sea, the Sea of Japan, Guam, Okinawa, Hawaii, and along the U.S. West Coast.

In addition to the mammoth Ohio class, the U.S. deploys *nuclear attack* submarines in the Pacific. The Los Angeles-class and converted Polaris submarines[25] hover and listen for their prey with passive sonar devices, waiting to ambush Soviet missile submarines which are exiting into the ocean or heading for protected bastions, such as the Sea of Okhotsk. In 1983, for example, as part of U.S.–Japanese straits blockage exercises following the Korean Airlines 007 incident, the attack submarines u.s.s. *Watchdog* and *Tomcat* were sent into the Sea of Okhotsk. In the event of war, these attack submarines, two of thirty-eight in the Pacific, would have launched four salvos of nuclear SUBROC missiles or torpedoes to destroy the Soviet missile submarines at a range less than 60 km.[26] This hunter-killer version of hide and seek is played at close quarters – so close that the U.S. attack submarine u.s.s.

---

* A megaton of nuclear depth charge will "kill" a submarine within a 6 km radius, or over a 115 square km circle of ocean.[24] Location to within 25 km requires peppering 2000 square km of ocean, or twenty to twenty-five nuclear weapons worth. With location of the target submarine known to within a 10 km radius, only three to five weapons are needed for a high probability of submarine destruction.

Pintado collided underwater with a Soviet Yankee-class missile submarine off Petropavlosk in 1974.[27]

U.S. forces directed against Soviet *attack* submarines are almost as important as those which attack Soviet *missile-carrying* submarines. Soviet attack submarines aim to defend the Soviet surface fleet and missile submarines and potentially, to cut U.S. supply lines across the Pacific to the Far East. The U.S. Navy plans to divert Soviet submarine attack on U.S. supply vessels by attacking Soviet missile and attack submarines at the outset of a war, forcing them back into the seas adjacent to the U.S.S.R.[28] This strategy is provocative in the extreme. While intended to avoid nuclear war, it could also trigger it, making U.S. anti-submarine weapons as dangerous as land-based intercontinental missiles to the Soviets in a crisis.

The American attack on the Soviet submarines would be led by anti-submarine escort ships, which fire ASROC nuclear missiles; carrier-launched helicopters and aircraft which drop nuclear depth charges; and land-based aircraft. The weapons are all key elements of the nuclear warfighting mission and are generally not used to menace non-nuclear adversaries.

Nuclear Napoleons

Unlike the highly decentralized command over conventional weapons, nuclear forces are commanded directly by the U.S. President and his immediate advisors from the National Security Council and the Joint Chiefs of Staff. To prevent unauthorized use, Presidential command is ostensibly guaranteed by a system of organizational controls, authenticating codes and equipment arming codes. Thus, the normal nuclear weapons command chain for the Pacific runs from the President, to the Joint Chiefs of Staff, and then to the Commander-in-Chief of the Pacific (CINCPAC).[29] In principle, only CINCPAC can release nuclear weapons from storage to field commanders and only he can order the commanders to use them.*

---

* For the Trident I missiles, the Emergency Action Message ordering use of nuclear weapons would flow from CINCPAC to CINCPACFLT to Commander Submarines, Pacific Fleet, and then on through the communications system to the Ohio submarine. Under U.S. law, only the wholly U.S.-owned and controlled portions of Pacific Command's communications arsenal may be used to transmit Emergency Action Messages.[30]

Unlike NATO, where at least the rituals of joint U.S.-allied control over nuclear weapons are maintained, the U.S. does not – with one exception – share command of the ultimate weapon with its Pacific allies.* When U.S. warships and aircraft move into the Northeast Pacific sector off Canada's coast to hunt Soviet submarines, nuclear weapon delivery systems fall under Canadian operational control.† Otherwise, nuclear weapons are the exclusive preserve of the U.S.

The President may exercise sufficient authority in conventional wars to control American forces – although General Jack Lavelle's resumption of the bombing of north Vietnam in 1971 directly contravened Presidential orders.[33] Whether or not Presidential control would be an effective safety catch on the trigger of a nuclear war is unknown. But the technology of nuclear annihilation moves at supersonic speeds, compressing decision-making time into minutes and seconds. The tempo of nuclear battle may surpass the time needed to make command decisions, forcing the national or unified commanders to release their nuclear weapons quickly. Top Navy officers admit openly that the time required for the President or Pentagon to release nuclear weapons is so short as to be "unrealistic." Furthermore, the proliferation of anti-ship cruise missiles with extremely rapid delivery times has increased pressure to revise the "rules of engagement" in order to allow U.S. ships to strike first. Navy Secretary John Lehman considers that the revision of these rules is "the most critical national security nexus that I can think of."[34]

These pressures may result in the pre-delegation of authority to expend nuclear weapons in emergencies. It is certain that such a pre-

---

* The Army's Western Command safeguards the *Single Integrated Operational Plan* (SIOP) at Fort Shafter with extremely stringent controls on distributing SIOP information to foreign governments. In general, orders WESTCOM, "SIOP briefings will not be given to foreign nationals."[31]

† The same applies in reverse to Canadian warships in the Pacific outside this sector when they pass into the Western Operation Area and fall under the U.S. Pacific Fleet's control. This area extends from the southern tip of the Kamchatka Peninsula to a line about 4,000 km east of New Zealand. West of this line, U.S. vessels are on their own or join West Pacific allies, who fall under U.S. control in joint operations.[32] Note that operational control means tactical coordination. Considerations of sovereignty and different organization preclude passing over command of allied forces to the U.S. or vice versa.

delegated system existed in the Pacific in the mid-1950s. Whether such authority is pre-delegated today is a matter of conjecture. According to a senior officer of the Defense Communications Agency Pacific: "CINCPAC expects to lose most of its communications at the outset of a nuclear war." [35] Loss of two-way communication between the national command in Washington and the Pacific would be even more de-stabilizing than in the 1950s, a contingency which may prompt prior or immediate pre-delegation of authority to expend nuclear weapons at the start of a nuclear war. Alternatively, if Washington believes that Pacific Command may have been hit by Soviet nuclear weapons or may already have fired off its own nuclear weapons, it may try to preempt a Soviet retaliation with other U.S. nuclear forces still in contact. Either way, the U.S. – or the Soviet Union – may start a nuclear war out of fear of the worst because of a communication breakdown.

The biggest command and control problem springs, however, from the intangible factor of bureaucratic rigidity and confusion. As command systems and their controls increase in number and complexity, the number of possible technical and human errors increases. Redundancy in the communications systems may then amplify the confusion and the errors into an uncontrollable spiral of nuclear annihilation.

On June 3, 1980, for example, the Pacific Command airborne nuclear command post took off from Hawaii *after* a false alarm of impending Soviet missile attack was *terminated* by NORAD. While the faulty computer chip which caused the false alarm was quickly identified and replaced, mystery remains as to why the command response went awry. Since the activation of an airborne command post is regarded as a key indicator to the Soviets that a U.S. nuclear attack may be imminent, this was no small incident. [36] Demonstrating some basic problems in the nuclear command, the event involved no less than four separate Commands, resulting in what two U.S. senators euphemistically described as "an air of confusion." *[38]

There are also major problems in the implementation of nuclear "standard operating procedures" at lower levels in the forces, remi-

---

* The June 3rd event was repeated on June 6th. These alarming events followed a series of earlier incidents, including a nuclear "threat assessment conference", convened by NORAD on March 15, 1980 to determine the appropriate U.S. response to the submarine launch of four SS N-6 ballistic missiles from the Kurile Islands north of Japan. These turned out to be part of a Soviet exercise. [37]

niscent of the confusion discovered by Rand analyst Daniel Ellsberg in 1959 (see Chapter 5). A 1970 Congressional investigation, for example, discovered nuclear-laden F-4 aircraft on full alert in two Far East countries (probably Taiwan and south Korea):

Against whom? we asked. At a secret Pentagon briefing we were told the host countries initially had permitted us to station F-4 squadrons; the F-4s could carry both conventional and nuclear weapons; that [sic] F-4s were most cost effective when nuclear armed and the most efficient manner to be so armed was on 15-minute alert.[39]

If CINCPAC loses communications with Washington, he will likely board one of three EC 135J airborne command posts which sit in Hawaii. These flying command centers are alerted whenever U.S. forces reach Defense Condition (DEFCON) 2 or above (DEFCON 1 signifies preparation for all-out nuclear war; DEFCON 5 is peacetime).[40] At the best of times, reports former Presidential Security Assistant William Odom, the National Command will be dealing with strong-minded unified commanders who "are all going to be posing as the Napoleons of the modern age."[41] Faced with silence from Washington, the nuclear Napoleon in his underground bunker at Camp Smith in Hawaii or in an airborne command post would have to judge from isolated scraps of information whether to ride out the storm without firing his nuclear weapons or to head straight into the hurricane with an all-out attack.[42]

Supporting the Means of Annihilation

Specialized supply and storage arrangements are required to support the means of annihilation.* Throughout the 1960s, nuclear weapons were secretly stored ready for use throughout the Pacific. In one case, the "President of a Far East ally" did not know that the U.S. had nuclear weapons stored on its soil.[43] A 1970 Congressional investigation found that the chief U.S. military officer and the American ambassador did not know whether or not nuclear weapons were stored in Taiwan. And

---

* The other major nuclear support function in the Pacific is missile testing. See Chapter 13 for description of the Pacific Missile Range.

the Japanese leadership has feigned ignorance over the years of the stationing and transiting of nuclear weapons.

Today, nuclear weapons are stored only in Guam, Hawaii, Alaska (the Aleutians), south Korea, possibly Diego Garcia, and aboard nuclear-certified ships and aircraft. In major forward bases such as the Philippines and Yokosuka (as well as at sea), nuclear weapons may be routinely transferred between launch platforms ("cross-decked"). So prominent are nuclear supply, transfer, and replenishment operations in the Pacific that more than 2,000 Navy and Marine personnel are assigned full-time to nuclear weapons security.*[44]

Nuclear weapons are transported to U.S. bases by the Military Airlift Command, or delivered in parts or assembled to underway ships from shore by aircraft, munitions supply ships, and helicopters.[45] Although south Korea offered Cheju Island as a major storage site when Okinawa reverted to Japanese control, modern airlift for nuclear weapons combined with aerial refuelling enables Guam, Alaska, or Hawaii to serve as convenient rear bases for nuclear weapons.

Nuclear deployments are also supported by intelligence systems. These systems allow the U.S. to monitor Soviet weapons development, note changes in the alert status of the forces, and identify new and confirm old targets. Some systems will serve nuclear warfighting forces until the sensors and supporting communications infrastructure are consumed by nuclear war.

CINCPAC's Intelligence Center, Pacific (IPAC) manages the Pacific Command Targeting Program. This program provides commanders with detailed target information and matches nuclear weapons to designated targets. The Target Action Group of IPAC coordinates all the information processing, and maintains the Pacific portion of the global Automated Installation Intelligence File and Target Data Inventory.† The Navy's Fleet Intelligence Center Pacific at Pearl Harbor also provides "direct support and assistance to CINCPACFLT [Commander-in-Chief, U.S. Pacific Fleet] which will enable him to fulfill his requirements for nuclear weapons employment and planning." [47] Once early warning satellites and radars independently confirm that the nuclear

---

* Many of these personnel may be assigned to guard nuclear weapons on ships.

† The latter is presumably a central repository for updating the overall target plans for U.S. global nuclear forces.[46]

missiles are flying, only "real-time" intelligence flows to warfighting forces will be relevant, and these will last only until shortly after the first missiles arrive.

CINCPAC's command post operates the Nuclear, Biological and Chemical Warning and Reporting System (NBCWRS) to detect attack throughout Pacific Command. During and after a nuclear war, central collection centers at the surviving commands or CINCPAC-designated Defense Representatives in allied countries are to locate any reporters still capable of reporting from U.S. command posts, bases or units (see Table 12.2). These observers are instructed to send reports of nuclear events by any means possible to CINCPAC. The system is activated and tested without notice every three months.*[49]

CINCPAC has special codewords for nuclear intelligence reports (shown in Table 12.3). Combined with the geographical range of the Warning and Reporting System, the events signified by these code-words indicate the scope of nuclear war planning in the Pacific. In the mind of no less than the Commander-in-Chief, Pacific, *all* countries with U.S. bases or stations providing substantial support for U.S. forces are evidently potential victims of the full range of nuclear attacks and accidents.

Communicating Nuclear Commands and Intelligence

As with all modern war, nuclear annihilation is a communications-intensive activity. In a nuclear war, intelligence from early warning satellites, early warning radars, conferences between commanders, and attack, targeting and re-targeting orders will crowd the military airwaves. Nonetheless, according to defense analyst Desmond Ball, the U.S. national command can transmit the fire order to CINCPAC or directly to nuclear forces over no less than forty-three communications routes, in most cases via radio. Even if substantial portions of the communications architecture are inoperable at the outset of a nuclear war,

---

* CINCPAC also operates the Pacific Command Airborne Reconnaissance for Damage Assessment (PARDA) system which can direct any available military or civilian aircraft to investigate a nuclear explosion.[48]

the Minimum Essential Emergency Communications Network* is designed to provide redundant "bare-bones" communications between the national command and CINCPAC.[50] At least some of the nuclear Emergency Action Messages are therefore almost certain to arrive.

It is equally certain that most Pacific communications will collapse immediately after nuclear war starts. Command, intelligence, and communication bases will be high priority targets as both sides strive to decapitate their enemy, thereby destroying their nuclear targeting, damage assessment, and retaliation capabilities. This vulnerability ensures that it is highly unlikely that a protracted or even a limited nuclear war could be reliably commanded or controlled, although the nuclear bugle call would almost certainly activate a major retaliatory strike under any circumstances.

Specific anti-communications weapons are being developed over the Pacific Missile Range to knock out Soviet satellites with F-15-launched non-nuclear missiles.[51] Such pre-emptive attacks would give the U.S. a short extra period to transmit nuclear fire orders and collect intelligence before the Soviets attacked U.S. communications satellites in low-altitude orbit.[52] With support from its space tracking facilities, U.S. anti-satellite attacks could be launched from a southern hemisphere airfield to catch the Soviet satellites when they swing close to earth.[53]

Nuclear Tripwire in Korea

In addition to scenarios for an all-out nuclear war, American strategists also prepare for lesser nuclear contingencies. They view all-out nuclear war as the top rung of a ladder which starts with limited (non-nuclear) war, moves to limited and then theater nuclear war. These rungs, in their eyes, are clearly defined and one can choose to climb up or descend the escalation ladder.

---

* VLF/LF radio to submarines, and HF/VHF/UHF/SHF radio to the bombers, fleet, and anti-submarine aircraft. The Network's elements in Pacific Command are the CINCPAC airborne command post, the Navy (VLF/LF) and Air Force (HF/UHF) radio systems backed up by naval (VLF) airborne transmitters, and Air Force missile-borne (UHF) communications.

Table 12.2:
Nuclear Biological Chemical Warning and Reporting System in Pacific Command

Responsible Commander	Primary/Alternative Command Centers	Geographic Area of Responsibility
Commander-in-Chief, Pacific Fleet	Commander, U.S. Navy Marianas/ Strategic Air Command 3rd Air Defense	Guam, Wake Is., Trust Terr. of the Pacific Islands (Caroline, Marshall, Gilbert, Mariana Islands) and U.S. Navy afloat
Commander-in-Chief, Pacific Air Forces	13th Air Force/Commander, Subic Bay Naval Base	Philippines
Commander, Western Command	Western Command/Hawaii Command	Hawaiian chain, Johnston, Midway Islands
Commander U.S. Forces, Japan	Commander U.S. Forces, Japan/ Commander, Naval Forces, Japan	Japan, Okinawa, Taiwan
Commander U.S. Forces, Korea	Commander U.S. Forces, Korea/ 314th Air Defense	Korea
Commander-in-Chief, Pacific	CINCPAC Command/Alternate Command/Airborne Command Post	Australia, New Zealand, Diego Garcia, Antarctica, through American embassies, Military Attaches, Military Assistance Groups, CINCPAC representatives[a]

Table 12.2: (cont)

Note: a. CINCPAC's Defense Representatives in Australia (U.S. Air Force Liaison Officer), New Zealand (U.S. Defense Attache), and Southwest Pacific Islands (U.S. CINCPAC Representative, Southwest Pacific) may serve as Reporting Activities for the System.

Sources: CINCPAC, "Visits by Senior U.S. Military and Civilian Personnel to U.S. Military Installations and Activities in PACOM", Effective Instruction 5050.2F, June 25, 1982; and "Pacific Command Nuclear Biological Chemical Warning and Reporting System (Short Title: PACOM NBCWRS)", Effective Instruction 3401.3J, February 6, 1981, p. I-1,2.

Nuclear weapons for "limited" war are part of the daily practice of every service in Pacific Command and could be used in at least two contexts – Korea and a naval war.

The Demilitarized Zone (DMZ) of the Korean Peninsula is the most militarized place on earth. On each side of the DMZ are nearly a million heavily armed troops. Since only a truce was negotiated in 1953, north and south Korea are still technically at war and tensions remain high. Korea is the volatile powderkeg of the Pacific, the place where war may break out with only minutes notice – and the most likely site for the use of nuclear weapons.

The Army keeps nuclear weapons on hand in Korea to stun or stop an attack from the north. Under heavy attack, states the U.S. Army *Field Manual*, "nuclear weapons provide the urgently needed tactical edge in combat power that is required for a successful defense." [54] In a nuclear war, U.S. forces could use Atomic Demolition Mines and nuclear artillery[55] in approved "packages" over a specified area and period. A hypothetical nuclear "package" in south Korea might include two atomic demolition mines, thirty artillery, and five or ten aircraft-delivered nuclear weapons.[56]

Atomic Demolition Mines (ADMs) are the centerpiece of the "limited" nuclear arsenal in south Korea. Up to twenty-one ADMs are reportedly stored in south Korea, ready to be placed in underground tunnels near or under the Demilitarized Zone.* These small nuclear weapons are intended, according to the Army, to "block avenues of approach by cratering defiles [narrow valleys] or creating rubble; sever routes of communication by destroying tunnels, bridges, roads, and canal locks; create areas of tree blowdown and forest fires; crater areas including frozen bodies of water subject to landings by hostile airmobile units, [and] create water barriers by the destruction of dams and reservoirs." [59]

Specially trained Marines or Army Special Forces can explode ADMs with a timer or by remote control to halt advancing tanks with impass-

---

* According to defense analysts Richard Fieldhouse and William Arkin, in early 1985, the U.S. Army had sixty gravity nuclear bombs, forty 203 mm and thirty 155 mm nuclear artillery shells, and twenty-one atomic demolition mines stockpiled at Kunsan Air Base in south Korea.[57] Elsewhere, Western Command has referred to "deletion of mission requirements ... to maintain ... 8 inch (203 mm) weapon systems" in nuclear-capable units, indicating that the 203 mm shells may have been retired in mid-1984.[58]

able craters. Along the way, notes an Army writer, considerable damage will be inflicted on villages in valleys where ADMs are used.[60] U.S. F-4 and F-16 fighter jets in south Korea are also nuclear-capable, and their gravity bombs are stored at Osan and Kunsan airfields.

The U.S. Army is prepared for nuclear war in the Pacific. All Army units – including those in south Korea – have set up an "NBC [Nuclear Biological Chemical] Control Party", which aims to achieve "a high degree of NBC readiness" and during combat, to "coordinate the NBC defense efforts." Each company in Korea also maintains an "NBC Defense Team", "for detection, monitoring, and decontamination." [61] NBC training exercises are held under "realistic battlefield conditions," including "simulated friendly employment of nuclear/chemical weapons and enemy employment of NBC weapons." [62] Since north Korea does not have nuclear weapons, the Army evidently anticipates Soviet or Chinese entry into a war in north Korea, or a spillover into Korea of a battle in the North Pacific.

In addition to its general forces, the Army's units responsible for delivering nuclear warheads also train constantly for nuclear war in south Korea. The nuclear-capable artillery battalion at Uijongbu, for example, conducts quarterly exercises and training "to emphasize tactical realism to the maximum extent possible." [63] "Nuclear training," states the Army's Western Command, "must be integrated into the total training program without detracting from either the [unit's] nuclear or conventional capabilities" and should cover tactical movement, nuclear assembly, and control.*[64]

The Army can refer openly to the idea of waging a limited nuclear war in Korea because it faces far fewer political constraints than in Europe. In January 1983, U.S. Army Chief of Staff in Korea General Edward Mayer discussed the use of nuclear weapons. The general blurted out, "It's far simpler here than in Europe where consultations have to be made with fifteen different sovereign nations." [65]

For the U.S. military, nuclear weapons on the DMZ deter the north Koreans from "invading" the south. As former U.S. Commander in Korea, General Richard Stilwell, wrote in 1977: "Encamped between the demilitarized zone and any logical military objectives, he [the U.S.

---

* The directive that the nuclear training should not detract from conventional capability underscores the reality of "deadly connection": virtually all offensive units in the U.S. military are *dual* capable.

Table 12.3:
Codewords for Reporting Nuclear Attack and Events in Pacific Command

Codeword	Signifies
PINNACLE NUCFLASH	Nuclear event affecting U.S. national interest with a risk of nuclear war such as accidental, unauthorized launch of nuclear-armed/nuclear-capable missile in direction of Soviet Union or China°; unauthorized flight or deviation from flight plans of nuclear-armed/nuclear capable aircraft with capability to fly to Soviet Union or China; early warning system detection of threatening unidentified object or interference.
PINNACLE FRONT BURNER	Any attack, harassment of U.S. forces.
PINNACLE BROKEN ARROW	Nuclear weapons event without risk of nuclear war, but with nuclear explosion, non-nuclear destruction, radioactive contamination, seizure, theft, or loss of nuclear weapon.
PINNACLE EMERGENCY DESTRUCTION/DISABLEMENT	Report on nuclear weapon destruction/disablement operation
PINNACLE EMERGENCY EVACUATION	Report on emergency evacuation of nuclear weapon.
PINNACLE COMMAND ASSESSMENT	CINCPAC assessment of actual or developing crisis.
OPREP-3 BENT SPEAR	Operational report of a nuclear weapon incident not covered by NUCFLASH or BROKEN ARROW.

Table 12.3: (cont)

OPREP-3 FADED GIANT   Reactor or radiological accident.

Note: a. As occurred in 1960 when an aberrant Matador nuclear missile headed for China from the Taiwan Straits.
Sources: CINCPAC, "Pacific Command Nuclear Biological Chemical Warning and Reporting System", Effective Instruction 3480.6F, April 14, 1982, p. I-1–3; U.S. House of Representatives, Committee on International Relations, Subcommittee on International Security and Scientific Affairs, *First Use of Nuclear Weapons: Preserving Responsible Control* (Hearings), U.S. GPO, Washington, D.C., 1976, p. 202.

ground soldier] constitutes the real earnest of U.S. investment in deterrence." [66] The military believe that if a north-south war erupts, nuclear weapons would be used immediately on the "use them or lose them" imperative. In this logic, the question of escalation simply does not arise since the nuclear weapons should deter war from breaking out. If, in fact, a war does embroil Korea again – and it well might – nuclear weapons would pose a dilemma for the U.S.,* since their use would run a high risk of escalation. As strategic analyst William Overholt notes:

The choice would be between [politically] unacceptable use of the weapons and the unacceptability of withdrawal under fire. This dilemma would be greatly enhanced if the weapons were stationed relatively far forward and therefore the decision became necessary almost immediately after the initiation of what would likely be a surprise attack. [68]

While U.S. military leaders believe that limited nuclear war can be controlled by using "small", short-range nuclear weapons that do not threaten the Soviet Union directly, experienced commanders are less sanguine. Former CINCPAC Admiral Noel Gayler warned:

It is very difficult to think of using nuclear weapons [in Korea] in a way which doesn't contain the seeds of escalation. There will be backers [the superpowers] again in a war on the Korean Peninsula and a strong political temptation to raise the ante when either side are involved. The step from a nuclear war involving our proteges, as it were, and nuclear war between ourselves [the superpowers] is a very narrow one, a very dangerous one. [69]

---

* If nuclear weapons in south Korea were about to be lost to the Korean rebels or northern forces, current commanders have apparently been ordered to destroy the nuclear weapons without nuclear yield if the weapon cannot be evacuated. [67] This is a change from the situation in the 1950s, when commanders were ordered to first evacuate, *then* *use*, and only if use was impossible, destroy the weapon (see Chapter 5). This apparent change in procedure does not change the withdrawal/use choices confronting the President under the pressure of time and the heat of battle.

Naval Shootout

A naval war between U.S. and Soviet Pacific Fleets is a second situation which nuclear strategists think is suitable for a "limited" nuclear war. In a major study of naval strategy for the ascending U.S. navalists in 1977, Paul Nitze referred to the "growing and inevitable linkage" between conventional and nuclear weapons in naval war: "The restricted use of nuclear weapons at sea carries neither the degree of moral stigma nor the threat of further escalation that applies to their use against land targets." [70]

Since nuclear weapons have never actually been used in naval war, Nitze's perceptions of social morality and escalation risks are little more than his own opinion. Nonetheless, Nitze's assessment that nuclear war at sea will not destroy cities or civilians and will not escalate to land attacks became the basis for maritime policy. To implement the idea that nuclear war can be fought – and contained – at sea, the Navy has begun to "harden" its ships and aircraft for nuclear war. [71]

When naval strategists talk about limited nuclear naval war, they usually have the Northwest Pacific in mind. U.S. naval planners are, in fact, nearly obssessed with the "Vladivostok strike scenario" – an assault on the homeport of the Soviet Pacific Fleet. According to the Joint Chiefs of Staff 1983 *Posture Statement*, in the event of war, a major U.S. advantage is the ability of American forces – including those in Japan and Korea – to bottle up the Soviets' Pacific Fleet at Vladivostok. [72] To get from Vladivostok to the open Pacific, the Soviets must pass through one of three straits, the widest of which is only 160 km across. Under U.S. naval doctrine, this American advantage would be translated into concentrated attacks by the U.S. Fleet, "which would try to outmaneuver the opponent and to overwhelm him in one location rather than fighting all across the vast expanses of the Pacific Ocean." [73]

A holdover from World War II, the concept of a stand-off naval battle in the nuclear age is incredible and contradictory. The Soviets have emphasized repeatedly that, under conditions of local inferiority, they would have no choice but to escalate to all-out nuclear war.

"Limited" war, in short, undermines the logic of deterrence, as Richard Perle, the Pentagon's key nuclear hawk, found in 1983. "We would not permit the Soviet Union to confine a nuclear war to the sea," Perle told Congress, since that would mean abandoning the policy of escalated retaliation and allowing Soviet land-based bombers to freely attack U.S. forces.*[75] Despite the contradictions, the Navy is proceeding with its plans for nuclear war at sea.

Modernizing the Means of Annihilation

CINCPAC is modernizing the nuclear forces in the Pacific.[76] This nuclear upgrade includes the Tomahawk nuclear cruise missile, 155 mm artillery shells for the Army and the Marines, and Trident I ballistic missiles. Ground and air-launched cruise missiles remain under active consideration and in 1991, the first Ohio submarines in the Pacific Fleet will be retrofitted with Trident II missiles. According to Admiral Clark, Trident II missiles are designed to give U.S. submarines "a hard target kill capability which we do not now have." [77]

The U.S. Defense Nuclear Agency is also studying how to "enhance" the survivability, security, employment, and modernization of the Pacific Command's "theatre" nuclear weapons for naval or land-attack nuclear war.[78] This study will provide "automated nuclear weapon planning tools" (presumably computerized warning, targeting, and damage assessment) to CINCPAC's nuclear war planners. Another Pentagon office is studying Soviet views on nuclear war in the Pacific to develop operational concepts, which in turn will allow U.S. forces to shadow-box with Soviet forces in the Pacific.[79] Recognizing the vulnerability of the Pacific's communications architecture, the Pentagon is "upgrading" the system to ensure its survivability during a nuclear war.† The Pentagon has discussed these programs in jargon-laden Congressional testimony:

---

* Perle stated that the policy rests on three principles: "First, the essence of deterrence is that our retaliatory capability must raise incalculable risks to any potential aggressor; in this regard, we have never [security deletion] confine[d] our retaliation within the boundaries of any particular theater . . . Secondly, it is a fact that we and our allies are far more dependent on using the sea than our potential adversaries . . . [Thirdly, agreeing] to confine a nuclear war to the sea would in essence allow the Soviets to operate nuclear strikes against our naval forces from a sanctuary of land-based airfields, and this would undercut both deterrence and defense." [74]

† Including numerous mobile satellites, ground terminals and new, state-of-the-art HF radio stations (for example, in Hawaii).

U.S. Pacific Command as part of its program directed toward modernization of Non-Strategic Nuclear Forces . . . has requested DNA [Defense Nuclear Agency] to conduct research that would lead to insuring that nuclear C^3 systems are responsive to needs of those forces. *This DNA research has identified future C^3 system requirements that will insure survivable and endurable C^3 in a nuclear environment.* A complementary Defense Communications Agency program, the Non-Strategic Nuclear Forces System Program Plan, identifies the specific system hardware capabilities need to support the nuclear C^3 systems requirements.[80]

Given the crucial role of communications and directing the U.S. nuclear arsenal, such programs amount to an admission that the Pentagon is planning for a protracted nuclear war.

Moreover, in 1982, Pacific Command proposed the redeployment of U.S.-based "existing assets" to the Pacific, military jargon for moving stockpiled nuclear weapons from the continental U.S. to Pacific Command. Dr. Richard Wagner, a nuclear specialist from the Pentagon, described this action as a "very nice step." [81]

But the most dangerous additions to the Pacific nuclear arsenal in the near future are already on the visible horizon. These are the refinement of missile capability at the Pacific Missile Range, and the deployment of Tomahawk cruise missiles.

Re-entry vehicles from Minuteman missile-test plunge into the
atmosphere over Kwajalein Atoll, 1979
(Pentagon)

THIRTEEN ☆
PACIFIC MISSILE
TEST LABORATORY

Yesterday evening my husband Ataji Balos was arrested while peacefully leading Marshallese people living on their own land on Kwajalein Atoll. At this
moment, hundreds of Marshallese people are peacefully living on their own
islands at Kwajalein, Roi-Namur and several small islands within the mid-atoll
corridor missile hazard area. These people include women and very small
children. Tomorrow the Air Force has scheduled an operation which en-
dangers these people.

—Alice Balos, June 21 1982[1]

If we didn't have Kwajalein, we wouldn't be able to test such long-range stuff
over open, largely uninhabited areas of the earth's surface. So it's important to
have a place like this in the middle of the Pacific Ocean.

—Pentagon official, 1985[2]

The Pacific has served as America's major site for testing and modernizing nuclear weapons and delivery systems since the dawn of the
atomic age. In addition to the valuable information gained from the
annihilation of Hiroshima and Nagasaki, the U.S. obtained data after
the war by dropping bombs on its new Trust Territory in the North
Pacific. Between 1946 and 1958, sixty-six nuclear tests were conducted
in the Marshall Islands in Micronesia.[3]

To conduct these tests, the U.S. military relocated some of the Islanders from their ancestral homes and exposed others – along with

American servicemen and Japanese fishermen – to high levels of radiation. Whole islands were vaporized or made forever uninhabitable.

Christmas Island in the mid-Pacific was also used for U.S. nuclear tests, as new missile technology became available. Beginning with *Operation Dominic* in 1962, there were some forty tests,[4] including one with a Polaris missile fired from a submarine off the coast of California, which exploded a half-megaton bomb over the island.[5] The U.S. also launched five missiles from Johnston Island straight up to a high altitude where the warheads exploded in the atmosphere. During one of these *Bluegill Prime* tests, the Thor rocket misfired and was blown up before lift-off, scattering plutonium over the island.[6]

The most remarkable test was *Starfish*, a 1.4 megaton explosion* at an altitude of 400 km over the mid-Pacific on July 9th, 1962. The explosion "lit the sky all the way to Hawaii and Australia", destroyed satellite equipment, blacked out radio communications, and popped streetlights in Hawaii. It also modified the immense Van Allen radiation belt† around the earth itself.[7]

By the time the Atmospheric Test Ban Treaty was ratified in 1963, the U.S. was ready to switch the emphasis of its test program from perfecting nuclear explosions to refining nuclear delivery systems.

Pacific Missile Range

The first long-range U.S. nuclear missiles were tested over the Pacific in 1959 when an Atlas D missile blasted off from Vandenberg Air Force Base in California.[8] Today, the Pacific Missile Range‡ (PMR) extends 7,200 km from the California coast to Kwajalein Atoll in the Marshall Islands, located in the central Pacific just north of the equator. Missiles

---

* The Hiroshima bomb was 12.5 kilotons.

† The belt is an immense cluster of charged particles held in space by the earth's magnetic field in two belts extending from 800 km to 32,000 km altitude.

‡ PMR is an amalgam of the Navy's PMR, extending only a short distance off the California coast, the Air Force's Western Test Range, which stretches all the way from Vandenberg to Kwajalein, and the Army's Kwajalein Missile Range, at Kwajalein itself. In addition to testing missile delivery systems, PMR in California is also ideally located for launching U.S. satellites into polar orbits without endangering land areas with a rain of burnt-out booster rockets or debris in the case of failure.

are fired from Vandenberg and Point Mugu Naval Base in California, tracked in flight by stations on Johnston and other islands, and splash down in the lagoon of Kwajalein Atoll (see Map 13.1).

One of the few major Marshall Islands spared during the post-war testing program, Kwajalein is covered with camera, radar, and sonar equipment to determine the precise re-entry point of the missiles plunging into the lagoon (see Map 13.2). Besides accuracy, the range and payload of missiles are attributes which make nuclear weapons increasingly lethal. It is precisely these characteristics which are tested over the Pacific Missile Range. According to New Zealand defense analyst Owen Wilkes, Kwajalein has contributed more to the arms race than any other place on earth.*

To gain maximum maneuverability along a 60 km-wide overflight corridor, the U.S. relocated 328 Kwajalein Islanders to Ebeye Island. With no high school, hospital or sewage system, and such a severe housing shortage that people live thirteen to a room, Ebeye has been dubbed the "slum of the Pacific." [10]

In March 1970, 200 islanders conducted a "sail-in" in the face of a series of missile tests. Although Army Security suppressed news coverage, the occupation won an initial financial settlement from the military.[11] During the late 1970s, the Kwajalein land-owners again organized protests to win control of their islands and increase the low rents the U.S. paid for use of Kwajalein. In 1982, they occupied islands used for testing for over three months in an action they called "Operation Homecoming".

Coinciding with pending changes in the political status of Micronesia, still a U.S. Trust Territory, the protests created a climate of political uncertainty. As early as 1975, the military considered defusing the problem by relocating the Islanders from Ebeye to the far northern atoll of Bigej.[12] The study was updated in 1978 and 1981 but the marginally changed missile course would have been even more dangerous than the one currently in use. As a 1981 military study noted: "Even with the *existing* corridor, certain target points may be unacceptable from a safety viewpoint." [13]

---

* The Pacific range offers much better instrumentation and less risk to populations in case the missile goes awry than the Atlantic Missile Range,[9] which fires in a southeasterly direction from Cape Canaveral in Florida.

Map 13.1:
Pacific Missile Test Ranges

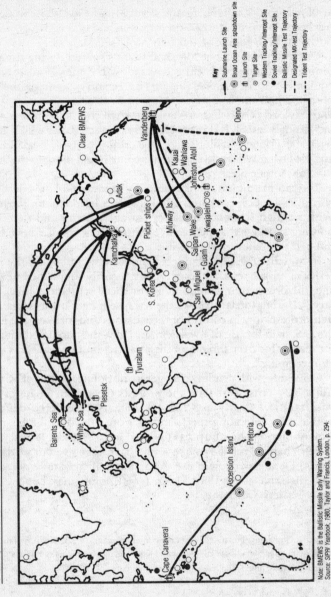

Note: BMEWS is the Ballistic Missile Early Warning System.
Source: SIPRI Yearbook 1980, Taylor and Francis, London, p. 294.

Map 13.2:
Kwajalein Missile Range

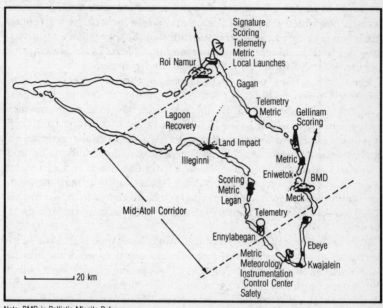

Note: BMD is Ballistic Missile Defense.
Source: Stanford Research Institute International, *Strategic Systems Tests Support Study* (SSTSS), report to U.S. Ballistic Missile Defense Systems Command, Alabama, 1981.

Given the enormous cost and effort involved, relocation of the U.S. military from Kwajalein and the other islands currently used for missile tests seems highly unlikely. Furthermore, in 1983 the Marshall Islanders voted to accept a Compact of Free Association with the U.S. which permits continued testing in Kwajalein. While bickering over rentals and terms is likely to persist, the resolution of the sovereignty issue may have defused the independence movement, at least in the short term. Nonetheless, the future of Kwajalein is far from clear.

Even more than political problems, technical necessities have prompted American military planners to expand their testing horizons. Kwajalein is too close to California to test the new long-range missiles such as the MX, which has a 13,000 km range. According to a Congressional expert on strategic affairs, the Kwajalein site also generates a phony sense of accuracy: "If first you send weather balloons up and radio back what the wind is at 10 and 25 thousand feet, and you make [trajectory] corrections before you fire – based on information which you wouldn't have in an operating [i.e. warfare] environment – it means you have created a laboratory and not a realistic testing environment." [14]

Another technical limitation of the Kwajalein Range is that the missiles fly on an East-West trajectory, while in a war they would be fired at the Soviet Union over the North Pole.* The varying gravitational pull of the earth's crust and the angle at which the missile is fired across the earth's spin significantly affect the missile's accuracy. "If you're going to use [missiles] in a real environment, you've got to judge them in that real environment," emphasizes the Congressional expert. "That's a North-South, polar direction, not East-West." [16] To rectify these deficiencies, U.S. military planners have extended the testing range into the expanse of the Southwest Pacific.

---

* As a Pentagon official testified in 1978, "We have fired nearly all our missiles at Kwajalein with the exception of a few at Eniwetok, Canton, and Oeno. Supposedly, if we fought a war with Kwajalein, we would win hands down. On the other hand, we have not shot a missile at Russia, nor do we expect to, and the question is, is there some kind of effect which we don't know about?" [15]

State-of-the-Art

The state-of-the-art testing procedure is to shoot the new long-range missiles such as Trident and MX into an open ocean with a shallow bottom (less than 1,000 m deep). Months or even years earlier, a survey ship positioned instruments called transponders on the seabed, which receive and send sound signals to sonar equipment on the surface. On the day of the test, P3C Orions and EC-135 ARIAs (Advanced Range Instrumentation Aircraft) fly above the missile impact point. The ARIAs collect radio transmissions from the re-entry vehicles as they plummet toward the sea. The Orions drop sonar buoys, which float on the surface like ears listening for the sound of the re-entry vehicles crashing into the ocean. The sonar buoys "interrogate" the transponders on the ocean floor with loud pinging sounds to set up a reference grid for the sonar sound patterns. The sonar buoys, in turn, listen for the splash of the re-entry vehicle and transmit this noise to the aircraft by UHF radio. The military claims that the impact point can be measured to within 15 m of its true "geodetic" splashdown position[17] (see Figure 13.1).

This new technique is already in practice. At least two of the six MX tests to date splashed into Broad Ocean Areas (BOA) in 1983, one of them 586 km northwest of Guam, well to the west of Kwajalein. In July 1984, a Trident I missile test hit a similar area, probably near Wake Island (see Table 13.1). Relying on U.S.-controlled islands for staging airfields, these tests went largely unnoticed. But U.S. plans to test MX and Trident missiles in the South Pacific have been delayed by local protests.

In November 1984, the authors revealed[18] that a recently declassified report on the future of the Pacific Missile Range indicated that the Pentagon was looking for new test sites in the West and the South Pacific. Specifically, the 1981 inter-service study had called for Trident I missiles "to be launched from the California waters into three different BOAs [Broad Ocean Areas], located near Wake, Chatham, and Oeno Islands."[19] Chatham Island is New Zealand territory and lies only 500 km east of its main islands. The Pentagon report also disclosed that the Navy's site for fixed Trident open-ocean tests is somewhere near Oeno Island, west of Pitcairn Island, which served as refuge for the *Bounty*'s mutineers, and is still a British possession. The Navy has officially stated that "Oeno" is a designated site for future Trident tests.[20] Oeno had

Figure 13.1:
Broad Ocean Area Splashdown Monitoring System

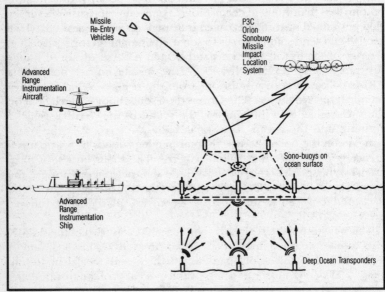

Source: SRI International, *Strategic Systems Test Support Study*, report to Ballistic Missile Defense Systems Command, Volume II, 1981, p. 80.

been used previously in past U.S. ballistic missile tests, at least for Trident I missile tests in the 1976–1977 period.[21]

The report also noted that the Pentagon had briefed the State Department in April 1981 on the need to secure staging airfields from South Pacific governments for Orion and ARIA aircraft. With a limited operating radius of only 2,500 km, the Orion needs nearby staging airfields. Military sources confirm that the U.S. State Department is currently negotiating with the French Government for transit rights through Tahiti airport, 2,500 km from Oeno.[22]

When New Zealand's Prime Minister David Lange got wind of the new U.S. approach, he declared: "If the United States sought New Zealand's agreement to firing such missiles into the Chatham Area, it would not be given." [23]

The report's most explosive revelation was that Sydney was also being considered as a possible staging area. In February 1985, the Australian *National Times* reported that the U.S. had set in motion plans for MX tests in the Tasman Sea between Australia and New Zealand.[24] The Liberal government of Malcolm Fraser had secretly approved the plan in 1981 and Labor's Robert Hawke had confirmed it – without informing members of his own cabinet and party – when he came to power in 1983.[25] The resulting outcry by the Labor Party and the public forced Prime Minister Hawke to suffer the embarrassment of reneging on the agreement while on a high-profile diplomatic visit to Washington.[*][27] Amidst charges of incompetence and inconsistency, the pro-U.S. Prime Minister suffered a major foreign policy defeat which severely undercut his domestic political position.[28] In November 1985, the authors revealed that the Australian government was misinformed as to the relationship between satellite measurements by the U.S. Navy over the Tasman Sea and increasing American missile accuracy. In the

---

[*] The U.S. may substitute Advanced Range Instrumentation Ships for the ARIA aircraft, and sea-based sonar-equipped aircraft for land-based P3C Orions to conduct the Tasman MX tests, a precursor to the greater siting flexibility in the technology pipeline. The U.S. might also fall back on a system called "SADOTS", which relies on a seabed system of hydrophones which records the splashdown noise of the re-entry vehicles at a site off the coast of South Africa, which also limited the staging of P3C Orion aircraft. A ship would arrive prior to the test, activate SADOTS, and synchronize self-contained clocks on the seabed devices via noise signals. After the test, the ship would return and read out the recordings via its acoustic link.[26]

Table 13.1:
MX and Trident I Missile Tests into the Pacific, 1983–84

Missile	Date	Impact Area
MX	June 17, 1983	6 RVs into BOA north of Kwajalein
MX	Oct. 4, 1983	same
Trident I	Dec. 6, 1983	Wake Island
MX	Dec. 20, 1983	8 RVs in BOA 600 km northwest of Guam
MX	Mar. 30, 1984	10 RVs into Kwajalein Missile Test Range
Trident I	June 3, 1984	Wake Island
MX	June 15, 1984	6 RVs to Kwajalein Atoll
Trident I	July 2, 1984	BOA-1ᵃ
MX	Oct. 1, 1984	Kwajalein Missile Test Range

Key: RV = Re-entry Vehicles; BOA = Broad Ocean Area.
Notes: a. Likely near Wake Island.
Sources: Navy Office of Public Information, October 29, 1984; Air Force Office of Public Affairs, October 5, 1984.

resulting hubbub, the Australian government revealed that the U.S. had postponed the MX tests, presumably due to lack of staging facilities. If this is the case, it is the first time a major U.S. missile test has been abandoned due to opposition, representing a stunning victory for the peace movement in Australia.

The Tasman MX tests are likely to be aimed at showing that the new inertial guidance systems and the Mark 21 re-entry vehicle for the MX are accurate enough over the full MX range of 13,000 km to destroy hardened Soviet missile silos.[29] As such performance claims can never be proven, the tests will mostly reinforce the Air Force's "first strike" mentality. As one senior official in the MX-test program said, "While we can simulate the long-range capabilities of MX by varying the angle of re-entry over Kwajalein, we are curious to see whether all the models and engineering assumptions are correct, just to prove over the maximum range that we haven't overlooked some crucial error."[30]

The MX controversy also complicated Prime Minister Hawke's proposal for a Nuclear Free Zone in the South Pacific. Under his proposal, French nuclear tests would be banned, but nuclear warships, nuclear communications bases, and nuclear missile tests would not. To maintain his credibility, Hawke faced the very difficult task of persuading his South Pacific neighbors that French nuclear bomb tests are objectionable while U.S. nuclear missile tests are not.

Range Expansion

The new approach to missile testing has major political implications for the nations of the South Pacific. By placing temporary instrumentation in shallow ocean areas and recording the acoustics of missile splashdown with aircraft, the U.S. has dramatically expanded its Pacific Missile Range. In so doing, the U.S. may be in violation of international law. The Seabed Treaty prohibits placing weapons of mass destruction on the ocean floor and expressly forbids use of the seabed for any "facilities specifically designed for storing, testing, or using such weapons."[31]

Kwajalein offers cheap, highly instrumented testing and still serves as the base for the Army's Anti-Ballistic Missile test program.* The string

---

* Kwajalein also plays a role in Star Wars.

of radar tracking stations along the PMR cannot be easily replicated elsewhere (see Appendix A10). Rather than displacing the range at Kwajalein, the ocean area approach in fact expands it. As a 1982 review for the Space and Missile Test Organization concludes, the Western Missile Test Center at Vandenberg "will continue to support ICBM operational testing, advanced strategic missile systems, cruise missiles, and aircraft tests." [32]

In the late 1980s, the NAVSTAR navigation satellites will enable the U.S. to drop sonar buoys anywhere in the Pacific to determine the precise splashdown point of incoming re-entry vehicles.[*][34] When that happens, the whole Pacific will become a U.S. missile test range.

* The sonar buoys will then communicate their information back to the U.S. via "satellite data relay systems" and communication satellites rather than by P3C aircraft.[33] At this time, communication satellite ground stations in allied nations will become heavily involved in tests of missiles such as the Trident II, especially in the Southern Hemisphere.

The first test-launch of the Tomahawk cruise missile, off the
California coast, March 1980
(Pentagon)

FOURTEEN ☆
MISSILE IN SEARCH
OF A MISSION

Why does the Navy need TOMAHAWK? It is the most cost-effective way of maximizing our fleet's capabilities to deter war, or force its earliest termination on terms favorable to the United States, if deterrence fails. In essence, TOMAHAWK will conserve valuable resources and save lives.
—Rear Admiral Stephen Hostettler, 1984[1]

It's always better to have bigger bullets, holding everything else constant.
—J. F. Lehman, U.S. Secretary of the Navy, 1984[2]

More than just another weapon system in America's nuclear arsenal, the cruise missile changes the capabilities of U.S. forces in ways that are new and fraught with hazard. With deployment of the sea-launched Tomahawk cruise missile,* the number of ships in the Pacific Fleet which can launch a nuclear land-attack strike will increase from five in 1984 to about fifty by 1990, perhaps raising the potential for nuclear war by the same ratio.

This escalation in nuclear firepower began in June 1984, when Sturgeon- and Los Angeles-class nuclear submarines in the Pacific were

---

* A cruise missile is categorized by three characteristics: how it is launched (by sea, air, or land); what kind of warhead it carries (nuclear or conventional); and what its target is (anti-ship or land-attack).

armed with the sea-launched version of the Tomahawk.*[5] To test the political acceptability of the cruise build-up, the U.S. sent the *Tunny*, a Sturgeon-class submarine known to be Tomahawk-capable, to Japan as part of a 7th Fleet visit. In response, five thousand people filled a park facing the naval base at Yokosuka to protest at the Tomahawk deployment.[6]

Origins of the Cruise Missile

Deployment of the cruise missile in the Pacific was the result of superpower politics, rather than the usual U.S. domestic pressures in weapons procurement – intra-service rivalry, Congressional porkbarrel politics, and competition among defense contractors.[7] Indeed, a 1984 Congressional study reveals that the military services, each with their own plans for new weapons, were far from enamoured with the new missile:

The services opposed cruise missiles for a variety of specific reasons, the common thread of which was fear that the cruise missile would threaten and/or compete for scarce funds and weapons systems they preferred. The Air Force was concerned that development of a long-range air-launched cruise missile (ALCM) would undermine its rationale for a new manned penetrating bomber (the B-1); the Navy feared that SLCMs [Sea-Launched Cruise Missile] would compete with big aircraft carriers, since they could be placed on any ship and be used against targets at sea or on land; and the Army worried that ground-launched cruise missiles (GLCMs) would compete with artillery on the battle-field and with the other services' existing "tactical" and "strategic" weaponry, thus draining resources from desired improvements in conventional forces.[8]

Furthermore, deployment of the cruise missile in Western Europe and the Pacific was not, as is sometimes claimed, an answer to Soviet

---

* This was the nuclear, sea-launched, land-attack version of Tomahawk. The sea-launched, conventionally armed anti-ship version appeared on four Pacific Fleet vessels a year earlier.[3] Currently there are no ground- or air-launched cruise missiles in the Pacific. However, armed with air-launched cruise missiles, B-52s from SAC's Fairchild Air Force Base in the state of Washington can fly quickly to the Soviet Far East to supplement the B-52Gs from Guam, which are armed with nuclear gravity bombs.[4]

deployment of either intermediate ballistic or cruise missiles. Rather, the cruise missile grew out of political maneuvering between the U.S., the Soviet Union, and Western Europe.

The initial development contracts sprang from Henry Kissinger's need for another bargaining chip in arms control negotiations in 1972.[9] Later in the decade, right-wing American strategists undermined the Strategic Arms Limitation Talks (SALT II) by skillfully exploiting West European fears about the reliability of the Atlantic alliance. The West European leadership argued that the U.S. was "giving away" a weapon – the cruise missile – that the Europeans wanted. As a *quid pro quo* for support for the SALT Treaty, the U.S. provided the ground-launched cruise missile to the Europeans. Additionally, the air-launched cruise found an advocate in Jimmy Carter, who used it to beat back an Air Force campaign to fund the B-1 bomber. The U.S. military was thus armed with cruise missiles, unsure of exactly what to do with them.

Cruising with the Cruise

The cruise missile is a pilotless, self-guiding jet bomber. The version currently deployed in the Pacific, the sea-launched Tomahawk, comes in three models – nuclear-armed for land attack, conventionally armed for land-attack, and conventionally armed for anti-ship strikes.

The missile flight begins with launch, followed by a relatively high cruise towards the target, and finally a low altitude search and attack phase (see Figure 14.1). While nuclear Tomahawks are relatively fast compared to aircraft, they still take two to three hours to cover their maximum range – a long time in a nuclear war. Ballistic missiles, by comparison, require only thirty minutes to travel 12,000 km – about twenty times as fast as the cruise. Since conventional warheads are so heavy, the non-nuclear Tomahawk can cover only half the distance of its nuclear sibling.

Tomahawk missiles are very "smart". The land-attack models use inertial guidance systems to pilot them to a pre-designated stretch of coast. There, the downward-looking altimeter radar measures the terrain contours, and checks it with the 10 km-wide landfall terrain contour map stored in its memory. If it has strayed, the computer corrects the course to the next checkpoint, perhaps 200 km away.[10] To conceal its approach from air defense radars with high terrain, it zig-zags towards the target. As it reaches home, the computer compares digital video pictures of the target with its computer-stored image to provide last-minute guidance, theoretically delivering the missile to within an average 91 m of the target.[11]

The Tomahawk is hard to detect, presenting only one-thousandth of the radar signature of the B-52.[12] Depending on the missile's altitude, radars do not notice the Tomahawk until it is 15–50 km or one to four minutes away.[13] The nuclear firepower and accuracy of the Tomahawk equals that predicted for each warhead on the Trident II ballistic missile.[14] Like the Tridents, nuclear cruise missiles can "kill" hard targets with a high probability of accuracy.

Unlike in Western Europe, there has been little demand for cruise missiles by Pacific elites. Indeed, their deployment may encounter stiff resistance in some Pacific nations. In Japan, for example, deployment of the ground-launched cruise would be illegal under the peace constitution. Indeed, Pacific Command is aware that even deployment out-of-sight at sea is embroiling it in political controversy.[15] Since the ship-based Tomahawk obviates the need for ground deployment, it is unlikely that land-based models will appear in the Pacific in the foreseeable future.*

Slick 'ems

Sea-launched cruise missiles, or Tomahawks, are known in the Navy as "Slick'ems" (SLCMs). Both the conventionally armed anti-ship SLCM (destined for surface ships) and the nuclear land-attack SLCM (mostly for submarines at first) are already at sea. The conventional land-attack SLCM is still under development.[18]

Unlike air-launched cruise missiles (ALCMs), the Slick'ems are not coordinated by the Pentagon's Single Integrated Operational Plan for fighting nuclear war. Instead, the Navy will set up a ground station for command and targeting analysis, most likely at its Intelligence Center, Pacific, in Hawaii. The Center will generate cassette tapes of pre-deter-

---

* However, a communications base for the mobile ground-launched missiles is reportedly under consideration at an unannounced site;[16] and the military initiated a study of the possibility of basing ground-launched cruise missiles in south Korea.[17]

Figure 14.1:
Tomahawk Land-attack Flight Path

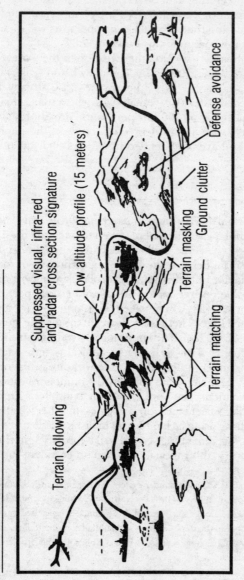

mined missions by integrating data on terrain, air defense, and missile capabilities. In the event of war, CINCPAC will communicate only the mission selection code and time of attack. The operators will then plug in the cassettes and the computers will take over.*[22]

The U.S. military boasts that "No other weapon in the world today can fly at the distance demonstrated by Tomahawk and strike targets with their degree of accuracy." [23] Nonetheless, the U.S. is already developing new air-launched "stealth" Tomahawks with radar signatures the size of a sea gull flying at 800 km per hour. Already capable of hitting "hard" targets with a high degree of accuracy, the improved Tomahawk could also have an extended range of 4,000–5,000 km.[24]

Strategic Rationale

Since the missile's origins were political, its military role and rationale remained obscure until the services were forced to integrate the Tomahawk into their forces. As the political debate raged, the nuclear Tomahawk lurched from being a "desirable augmentation of capability, a unique potential for unambiguous, controlled single-weapon response and invulnerable reserve force," (1976) to a crucial part of the "strategic reserve force" (1984). In between, it disappeared for a while as the military claimed that "There is no strategic submarine-launched cruise missile planned" (1978).[25] The contradictory statements indicate that the nuclear Tomahawk is – despite its technical virtues – actually an aimless missile, blundering into the Pacific without a mission.

Nonetheless, the U.S. military has concocted a number of rationales for Tomahawk deployment. The Tomahawk, for example, is supposed to deter a second strike Soviet attack on U.S. cities. In other words, they deter a Soviet first-strike using its land-based ballistic missiles by ensuring the destruction of its remaining second-strike forces.[26] Ignoring the reality of Soviet strategy, this rationale is based on President Reagan's

---

* ALCMS flown in the Pacific will use a similar system incorporated into the Offensive Avionics System of the B-52 computer.[19] The Navy is also developing equipment for rapid retargeting and rapid strike planning, suggesting that the launch delay caused by aligning inertial guidance gyroscopes to the ship's location and landfall coordinates may still be a problem.[20] The NAVSTAR navigation satellites will probably solve this problem in the late 1980s.[21]

concept of a "window of vulnerability." Under this theory, the Soviets are supposed to launch a disarming first strike against U.S. land-based missiles and then hold its cities hostage until the United States capitulates.

Numerous strategic analysts of the left and right, however, have criticized this nightmare scenario as implausible. It is simply not possible for the Soviet Union to achieve such a well-coordinated first strike – scoring the simultaneous destruction of U.S. missile silos, bombers and submarine bases. The problem of timing is pointed out by military analysts Sverre Lodgaard and Frank Blackaby:

[T]he Soviet Union would have to use different weapon systems to attack the bombers and the ICBMs. To attack the bombers, they would have to use the system which arrives promptly – submarine-launched missiles from submarines close offshore. However, these missiles are not accurate enough to destroy U.S. ICBMs [which have] a 30-minute flight time. If the Soviet Union tried a simultaneous *launch* of submarine-launched ballistic missiles (SLBMs) and ICBMs, the detonation of the SLBM warheads would precede the arrival of the Soviet ICBMs by 15 minutes – and U.S. ICBMs could be launched before they were destroyed . . . If on the other hand the Soviet Union fired its missiles in such a way that the SLBMs and ICBMs would *arrive* together, the early warning of the firing of the Soviet ICBMs would give time for the bombers to take off before they were destroyed.[27]

The notion that Tomahawks would be useful in fighting protracted nuclear wars also flies in the face of a simple reality – protracted, "limited" nuclear wars are simply not possible. The sudden collapse of command and control capabilities would force a rapid escalation to total nuclear war.[28] Even if such a war were possible, Tomahawk attacks – intended to demonstrate the war's limited nature – would quickly generate all-out war. Since the cruise flies both low and fast, Soviet air defense teams along the missile's route would report the overflight of the same missile many times before the Tomahawk would arrive at its target. Not *knowing* exactly how many missiles are attacking, the Soviets would almost certainly perceive an all-out attack.[29] Instead of a controlled climb up the ladder of nuclear escalation, the U.S. would soon plunge over the nuclear precipice.*

---

* Another red herring is that cruise missiles are intended to blunt a Soviet offensive against Japan. The Soviets, however, do not have the necessary amphibious forces and air cover to attack Japan successfully.

The idea that the purpose of Tomahawks is not to *deter* but to *launch* a disarming or preemptive first strike against the Soviet nuclear arsenal in the Far East is equally erroneous.[30] Tomahawk missiles are simply too slow for first-strike attacks. Only covertly deployed attack submarines would be close enough to launch Tomahawks that could hit Soviet first-strike command centers, communications, missile targets, or submarine pens. Such use would make a tiny contribution to a first strike, and would expose the location of valuable submarines while diverting them from their primary, anti-submarine warfare mission. Even this marginal contribution to a first strike, therefore, seems militarily illogical, although not unfeasible.[31]

A variation of this theme is that Tomahawks may fly in low and slow through the nuclear war environment to deliver the tail end of a first strike.[32] It is an incredible notion, however, that a cruise missile can pick its way around firestorms, absorb radiation, pass over massive modifications of the terrain on which its navigation relies, survive the electromagnetic pulse effects of an all-out nuclear first-strike – and arrive unscathed to demolish its target.

Another first-strike claim for Tomahawk is that it frees a large fraction of the Trident and land-based ballistic missiles from second-strike duty. These larger missiles can then participate in a first-strike, carrying a maximum load of warheads to destroy the Soviet Union.[33] This is probably the most serious of the Tomahawk's destabilizing effects, but it also requires that the vast, dispersed U.S. nuclear-capable fleet be located within striking distance of coastal entry points of the guidance systems, an unlikely notion.*

Strategic Thrust: Distributed Offense

All these rationales divert attention from what the services are really doing with cruise missiles. Forced by the White House and Congress to accept the cruise missile, the services have adapted them to their existing strategic plans. For the Navy, this means using Tomahawk to

---

* Some analysts have claimed that conventional land-attack cruise missiles are potentially important for suppressing shore defenses preceding an amphibious intervention in the Third World.[34] Given the cost – one million dollars per 400 kg of high explosive – this is not a likely role for the cruise missile.

defend the darling of the surface fleet, the aircraft carrier. For the Air Force, cruise missiles keep Soviet air defenses constantly off-balance, unable to predict whether the versatile B-52 bombers are carrying cruise missiles, short-range attack missiles, or gravity bombs.

While the Navy deployed the Tomahawk in the Pacific without an operational concept of how to use it in combat,[35] it now contends that the missile has ushered in a new type of naval warfare, dubbed *distributed offense.* The nuclear land-attack Tomahawk enables the Navy to deflect any Soviet attempt to launch a saturation missile assault on an aircraft carrier. Furthermore, to stop a nuclear land attack, the Soviets must now target dozens of ships instead of just the aircraft carriers (see Appendix A11). Attack submarines are far harder to trace than an aircraft carrier, the electronic emanations of which make it a convenient target. Sinking this new, dispersed nuclear-armed fleet far surpasses Soviet capability.[36]

The anti-ship Tomahawk also allows the U.S. fleet to take pot shots at Soviet surface ships even when they are in home waters under land-based air cover. Furthermore, the anti-ship Tomahawk would be useful if the U.S.-Soviet regattas in the Sea of Japan turned into a shoot-out.[37] Deployment of the Tomahawk in the Pacific adds a flexible, unpredictable offensive weapon to the U.S. arsenal, which, in the event of war, will accelerate escalation to total war.

Going for the Jugular

The conventional land-attack Tomahawk is particularly destabilizing because its use may precede a U.S. carrier attack on either north Korea or the Soviet Far East. Under current plans for its use in warfare, the U.S. Navy would bottle up the Soviet fleet in port and then destroy it in a protracted, *conventional* war, or a "limited" theater *nuclear* war. The conventional land-attack Tomahawk is supposed to disable Soviet air defenses and airfields so that U.S. carriers can fight their way close enough to launch their aircraft against targets in the Soviet Far East. The command and control required by the Soviet fleet for anti-carrier strikes would also be hit by Tomahawk.

Navy Secretary John Lehman promotes this concept at every opportunity. In 1984, Lehman testified that the Navy plans to rollback the Soviet submarines in the Sea of Okhotsk and off Petropavlosk to allow

U.S. carrier task groups to approach striking distance from the Soviet mainland.[38] He showed an astonished Congressional Committee a graphic presentation of combined carrier strike aircraft and Tomahawk missile attacks on the U.S.S.R. (see Figure 14.2). He explicitly referred to Navy war games using this tactic to catch the Soviet Backfire bombers "on the ground." [39] Backing up Lehman was Chief of Naval Operations Admiral James Watkins who noted that the Far East is the Soviets' geographic area "most vulnerable to attack." [40] "We understand their weaknesses," noted the Admiral. "We know what they are. We go for the jugular on those weaknesses."[41]

One Senator responded skeptically to the Lehman strategy. Senator Sam Nunn declared that "the very tactics you are describing will lower the nuclear threshold and make it much more likely that that nuclear threshold will be crossed." Added the Senator, a "huge, lucrative target" such as an attack aircraft carrier, will "pose such a threat to them [the Soviets] that I think it will be almost irresistible." [42] Indeed, Pacific Command may order American warships protecting the aircraft carriers to fire their Tomahawk missiles at the outset of war in the expectation that they will be disabled by Soviet anti-carrier forces.[43]

Another problem with the Navy's cruise missile doctrine is that the Soviets would have no way to determine if the incoming Tomahawks are nuclear or conventional until they explode. This uncertainty provides a strong incentive for the Soviets to fire a pre-emptive first strike. Far from playing a role in deterrence, the Tomahawks may help to trigger a nuclear war.

Since the Tomahawk has no other military rationale, this carrier-related mission *is* the main strategic thrust of its deployment in the Pacific. Vice-Admiral Ralph Weymouth (Ret.), former Director of Navy Program Planning at the Pentagon, was on target in 1984 when he said, "I don't see how the long-range Tomahawk with a nuclear warhead is going to be part of deterrence. It's going to be part of war-fighting."[44]

Floating Political Time Bomb

Deployment of the ground-launched cruise missiles in Europe nearly destroyed the political unity of NATO. SLCMs were initially viewed as being less visible, less constrained by collective control, and less likely

Figure 14.2:
Aircraft Carrier and Tomahawk Attack on Soviet Union

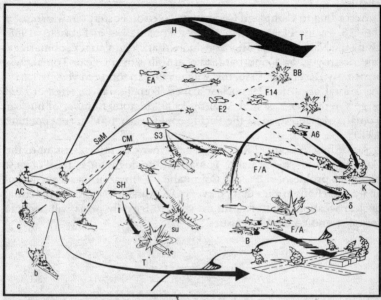

Source: U.S. Senate, Committee on Armed Services, *Department of Defense Authorization for Appropriations for Fiscal Year 1985*, Part 8, Washington, D.C., 1985, p. 3858.

H	Harpoon Anti-ship Missile	K	Kiev
T	Tomahawk Cruise Missile	δ	Destroyer
BB	Backfire Bomber	B	A-6 and F/A-18 Strike Bombers
F14	F14s	su	Submarines
EA	EA-6B Jammers	L	LAMPS Helicopter Torpedoes
SaM	Surface-Air Missiles	t	Torpedoes
CM	Cruise Missile	SH	SH-3 Helicopter
S3	S3 Anti-Submarine Torpedoes	b	battleship
E2	E2 Early Warning and Surveillance	A6	A-6
f	Fighters	F/A	F/A-18
c	Cruiser	AC	Aircraft Carrier

to evoke political opposition.[45] In the Pacific, however, Tomahawk deployment may severely strain U.S. alliances. On March 1, 1985 the anniversary of the Bikini H-bomb explosion, peace organizers in Honolulu announced a Pan-Pacific Campaign Against Sea-Launched Cruise Missiles.

According to Campaign Coordinator Nelson Foster, ten warships in the U.S. Pacific Fleet carried nuclear Tomahawks in February 1985. Using the Navy's data, Foster concludes that: "Eight attack submarines, one destroyer, and one battleship are already nuclear Tomahawk-armed. By December 1986, this will increase to fourteen vessels, carrying a total of up to 216 nuclear-armed Tomahawks directed at land targets in the Far East and Asia. By 1990, the total number of nuclear Tomahawks deployed in the Pacific could reach 400." (See Appendix A11.)[46]

According to Colonel Ralph Cossa, former executive assistant to the Commander-in-Chief Pacific, Tomahawk deployment is the "biggest potential problem in Pacific Command." [47] In a similar vein Naval analyst R. Hibbs argues that "if every U.S. warship becomes a potential nuclear weapons platform, future visits to friendly ports will become complex and contentious issues." [48]

Marine landing vehicles come ashore in south Korea for *Team Spirit*
exercise, March 1984
(Pentagon)

FIFTEEN ☆
EXERCISE OF POWER

Our entire politico-military philosophy today is based on the concept of collective security, which [is comprised of] overseas alliances, overseas bases, and U.S. military forces deployed overseas.

—Admiral Robert Carney
Chief of Naval Operations, 1953[1]

Conventional and nuclear deterrence are not separable in U.S. forces, and the nature of U.S. deterrence responsibilities requires that they not be separated.

—James Kelly, Deputy Assistant Secretary of Defense
for East Asia and Pacific Affairs, March 1985[2]

American global military strategy rests on a system of collective security based on overseas alliances. In the Pacific as in Europe, allies provide the real estate and ports which make possible U.S. forward deployment, as well as the political and ideological support upon which U.S. global leadership depends. Covered by the American nuclear umbrella, the allies in turn host the U.S. military machine – nuclear and non-nuclear – and would inevitably be drawn into a superpower war. Without their active support, U.S. capacity to fight an offensive nuclear war, to project power and especially to achieve "maritime supremacy", would be severely constrained. Plied with military and economic aid, the Pacific allies enable the U.S. to refine its warfighting plans by receiving visiting Navy warships and joining in military exercises with the

U.S. Making clear U.S. expectations, Secretary of State George Shultz declared in 1985: "It is not enough for allies to agree that when war starts they will come to each other's aid . . . Allies must work together to ensure that we have the capability to fight and win such a war[.]" [3]

While joint exercises and ship visits have long cemented U.S. ties with Pacific allies, their pace and scale have jumped under the "new militarism" of the 1980s. Navy Secretary John Lehman boasted to Congress in 1985 that the Navy is "at a higher OPTEMPO [operating tempo] than we were at the height of the Vietnam War." Indeed, Lehman added that the global fleet "was spending more time at sea than it had even averaged in the Second World War." [4]

The intensification of war preparations, including increased military assistance to "frontline states", has enhanced the military dimension of U.S. relations with its Pacific allies. By exposing allies to the risk of nuclear war or nuclear accidents, it has also fuelled popular, and to a lesser extent, governmental protest throughout the region, particularly in Japan, Australia, New Zealand, some South Pacific islands and the Philippines.* Unsurprisingly, these protests often focus on the Navy, the most visible of American forces, and call for the closure of ports to nuclear-armed or nuclear-powered warships. Aimed at reducing the danger of nuclear war by "denuclearizing" the alliance, the Pacific movement challenges the entire alliance system which supports U.S. military strategy in the region and which, in turn, rests squarely on nuclear weapons.

Intimate Relations

Erected in the 1950s, the Pacific alliance structure† is composed of a

---

* And in the mid-1970s, in Thailand.

† U.S. security relations in the Pacific include three types of "alliances". These are: formal alliance, which is defined by treaty and often involves mutual commitment of troops or combined military commands; semiformal alliance, which is defined by bilateral agreements or unilateral statements of intent, supported by defense cooperation and military sales; and informal alliance, which entails U.S. military and economic assistance, and sometimes an executive branch assertion of U.S. "interest" in the security of the informal ally. Most of the U.S. alliances in the Pacific are formal, including ties with Japan, Australia, New Zealand, south Korea and the Philippines. The current trend, however, is toward more flexible, informal ties, especially in the Indian Ocean. [5]

series of mostly bilateral treaties which fan out across the Pacific (see Figure 15.1). These treaties entangle the U.S. and its allies in a web of commitments and dependencies. Japan, the most important ally in the Pacific, is bound to the U.S. via the Mutual Security Treaty (1951; revised formally in 1960, and informally in 1978). Alliance with Japan is the linchpin of U.S. strategy in Northeast Asia, closely linked to that with south Korea (1954). Australia and New Zealand are junior partners in the South Pacific (ANZUS, 1952), while treaties with the Philippines (1952) and other ASEAN nations, (the Manila Pact, 1955),* tie the U.S. to Southeast Asia.

Western allies also support the Pacific system. Canada plays an important role in the North Central and Northeast Pacific. Alliance with the U.K.-facilitated U.S. occupation of Diego Garcia in the Indian Ocean, while ties with France provide the U.S. with access to military facilities on the French island colonies of the South Pacific.

In addition to formal treaties, the Pacific alliance system includes informal ties with many Pacific islands, most notably with Fiji, and with China. The newfound friendship with China, in which U.S. anti-Soviet strategy plays a crucial role, reflects the region's turbulence and fluidity. The metamorphosis of America's primary Pacific enemy into a friend colored all U.S. relationships in the region and ruptured the formal U.S. alliance with Taiwan. When relations were normalized with the People's Republic of China in January 1979, the U.S. broke off diplomatic relations with the Taipei regime and terminated the U.S.– Republic of China Mutual Defense Treaty (1954).[7]

The clearest evidence of alliance with the U.S. is military assistance, which includes arms transfers and military training. Often justified as necessary to an ally's peace and security, military assistance lightens the U.S. military burden by arming and training allies to act as local or regional gendarmes. Because allies often become dependent on U.S. aid to contain domestic insurgencies, military assistance enhances their support for American global and regional objectives.[8]

---

* The Manila Pact, also known as the Southeast Asia Collective Defense Treaty, is still technically in force although not operational. It includes Australia, France, Great Britain, New Zealand, Pakistan, the Philippines, Thailand, and the United States. The Pact established the Southeast Asia Treaty Organization (SEATO), which was formally dissolved in 1977 at the request of the Asian members.[6]

Figure 15.1:
The Pacific Alliance System

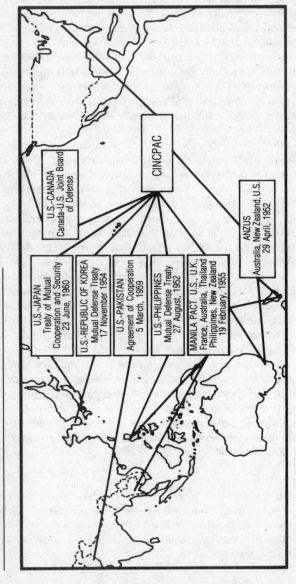

In (fiscal year) 1984, the U.S. supplied nearly half a billion dollars in military assistance to its Pacific allies. Credits through the Foreign Military Sales Financing Program – grants or loans to purchase U.S. weapons – accounted for nearly 85 per cent of the total. South Korea got the lion's share, followed by Thailand and the Philippines. After declining during the Carter years, military assistance to these "front-line" states has been on the rise since 1981 (see Table 15.1).*

In addition to military aid, the U.S. also arms its allies via Foreign Military Sales Agreements. Approved by the State Department, these agreements entitle allies to purchase arms from the U.S. government arsenal on a pay-as-you-go basis. In 1984, Pacific allies purchased over a billion dollars worth of U.S. arms through this program. While no subsidy is involved, such purchases nonetheless enhance technological – and thus political – dependence on the U.S. As the Vice President of Lockheed Aerospace explained: "When you buy an airplane, . . . you also buy a political partner." [9]

To bolster its partnerships in Asia–Pacific, the U.S. competes vigorously for the arms trade with the Soviet Union, as well as with Western Europe.† Marketed in close assistance with the Military Assistance Advisory Groups,‡ the U.S. won nearly 40 per cent of the region's in-the-pipeline arms sales agreements between 1980 and 1983, compared to 25 per cent for the Soviet Union and 15 per cent for Western Europe. The entire communist bloc won a meager 28 per cent, compared with the West's 72 per cent. [10]

The value of arms actually delivered reflects the fulfillment of past sales agreements, plus current levels of arms subsidy or aid. Between 1980 and 1983, the U.S. delivered weapons to Asia–Pacific worth $4.4

---

* Levels of military assistance to the Philippines proposed by the Defense Department were pared or held up by Congressional concern over human rights and the incompetence of Ferdinand Marcos before his fall in 1986.

† Primarily France, United Kingdom, West Germany, and Italy.

‡ The MAAGs were first set up in the early 1950s in an arc stretching from Japan to Pakistan as part of the security assistance arrangement spearheaded by John Foster Dulles. The MAAGs evolved into Joint U.S. Military Advisory Groups (JUSMAGs) and today five of these (in south Korea, the Philippines, Thailand, Malaysia, and Indonesia) provide training and advice to the host nations, as well as guiding arms suppliers and consumers toward each other.

Table 15.1:
U.S. Military Assistance to Allies in East Asia/Pacific, FY 1976–1984 (millions current $US)

	1976	1977	1978	1979	1980	1981	1982	1983	1984
Indonesia	44.8	39.4	56.4	35.9	33.3	32.4	41.3	27.3	47.3
South Korea	319.6	154.6	276.6	237.8	252.0	162.6	167.4	187.7	231.8
Malaysia	17.3	36.3	17.1	8.0	7.3	10.3	10.5	4.7	10.9
Philippines	37.0	36.4	36.5	32.2	76.7	75.6	51.9	52.0	51.8
Singapore	—	—	—	—	—	—	0.05	0.05	0.06
Thailand	54.9	47.0	37.8	32.3	48.4	54.5	76.2	78.6	95.7

Note: Levels of aid in real terms (adjusted for inflation) declined in the 1970s. The trend was reversed in 1981 for Indonesia, in 1982 for south Korea, and in 1980 for Thailand. See "Rivalry and Reconstruction: Security Implications of Pacific Economic Dynamism," (mimeo) Nautilus Pacific Research, April 1986.

Includes Foreign Military Sales Financing Program, Military Assistance Program, and International Military Education and Training Program. Australia, Japan, and New Zealand do not receive direct military assistance. Taiwan has not received military assistance since 1978.

Source: Department of Defense Security Assistance Agency, *Foreign Military Sales, Foreign Military Construction Sales and Military Assistance Facts*, September 30, 1984.

billion, up from $2.6 billion between 1976 and 1979.*[12] The U.S. share equalled that of the Soviets, each taking about 35 per cent of the total. If the allies of both blocs are added in, however, the West emerges as the dominant supplier, with 61 per cent of the total.[13]

Armed to the teeth with U.S. weapons, the military establishments of Pacific allies are carefully cultivated by CINCPAC. To promote cohesion among the allies, the Army's Expanded Relations Program has held an annual Pacific Armies Management Seminar since 1978 to establish a "working relationship" with mid-level officers who will be the future leaders in their countries.[14] According to General Eugene Forrester, head of the first seminar, the greatest advantage of the gathering – aside from displaying the latest U.S. weaponry and striving for regional "interoperability" between equipment and practice – is creating a "reservoir of people who know one another." [15] Backing up the seminar is military education and training: in 1984, the U.S. spent $9 million on such training for Pacific Command allies, up from $4.6 million in 1981.

Besides military aid, trade, and training, the Pacific alliance system is kept shipshape by joint military exercises and visits by U.S. warships. Involving hundreds of thousands of U.S. and allied forces, the exercises are a clear signal that the U.S. intends, as Secretary of Defense Caspar Weinberger emphasized in 1984, "to remain a Pacific power." [16]

Shoulder to Shoulder

To maximize U.S. military visibility and to prepare for active combat, U.S. forces in the Pacific spend most of their time practicing for war.† Exercises intimidate adversaries, keep the military machinery well-oiled, and remind U.S. allies that the American military is their senior

---

* There are also purely commercial (non-FMS) arms transfers. Data for these shipments, however, are unreliable and difficult to obtain. Commercial sales account for only a small fraction of the total.[11]

† There were nearly 100 exercises in 1984: 18 in south Korea; 17 in Japan; 28 in Southeast Asia; 8 in Australia and New Zealand, 2 in the Indian Ocean; 18 in the mid and east Pacific (including Hawaii); and 2 "other" (JCS and command post exercises), totalling 93 exercises.[17]

partner. According to the Commander-in-Chief of the Pacific (CINCPAC), the exercises aim to:

a. Enhance joint readiness and combined force interoperability.
b. Exercise, test, and evaluate certain aspects of war plans.
c. Fulfill international defense agreements and obligations.
d. Demonstrate U.S. capability and resolve.
e. Enhance collective defense and coalition strategy.
f. Assist in the exercise of allied and friendly nation forces.
g. Develop, test, and evaluate joint tactics, techniques, and procedures.[18]

"The value of these exercises cannot be overemphasized," exclaimed former CINCPAC Admiral W. Crowe in February 1984.[19] As the goals demonstrate, exercises aim to impress allies as much as the Soviet Union. Even the names of the exercises – *Welcome Guest*, *Team Spirit*, *Forward Thrust* – are selected carefully. Exercises are to be named, instructed CINCPAC in 1983, so that they do not "convey connotations offensive to our allies or other Free World nations", nor "express a degree of bellicosity inconsistent with traditional American ideals and current foreign policy." [20]

CINCPAC-sponsored exercises fall into at least eight categories covering every aspect of war preparation: land, naval, marine, aerial, command and control, counterinsurgency, crisis, battle, diplomatic, and nuclear war.

Every U.S. ally in the Pacific participates in joint exercises on land. The annual *Team Spirit* exercise in Korea, however, tops them all as the "free world's largest exercise." [21] A practice run for a war against north Korea, the exercise has swelled dramatically since it was initiated in 1976. Involving a "tidal wave" of 188,000 U.S. and south Korean Navy, Air Force, and Army forces, *Team Spirit '83* was more than four times larger than in 1976* and included thirty-one Navy surface warships, among them two aircraft carriers. At the climax of the exercise, 30,000 sailors and Marines stormed the shore and crossed frozen rice fields while U.S. and Soviet naval units shadow-boxed offshore. In the naval activity surrounding *Team Spirit '84*, a U.S. aircraft carrier and a Soviet attack submarine collided by mistake. Comprising a whopping 207,000 forces, *Team Spirit '84* aimed, according to CINCPAC's office, to

---

* *Team Spirit '76* involved 46,000 forces.

"demonstrate the President of the United States's pledge to strengthen U.S. forces in Korea." [22]

The Navy's version of all-out allied mobilization is the Rim-of-the-Pacific exercise, or RIMPAC. Begun in 1971, RIMPAC is held every two years at the Hawaiian island of Kaho'olawe, San Diego and Pearl Harbor and involves Australia, Canada, New Zealand, and the U.S. Reflecting American and internal pressure to remilitarize, Japan joined the exercise for the first time in 1980,*

Like *Team Spirit*, RIMPAC is growing. The May 1984 exercise was the largest to date and assembled 80 ships and submarines and 250 aircraft, manned by 50,000 sailors and Marines from the five nations.[23] As part of the exercise, the forces bomb the island of Kaho'olawe for target practice. Since the island is filled with important archaelogical sites, the bombing has sparked stiff opposition by native Hawaiians and generated international controversy.

The Marines have their own show in the Pacific. Marine exercises usually commence from San Diego in California, staging via Pearl Harbor. In 1983 they stormed the beaches in exercises in Oman (*Jade Tiger*), Australia (*Valiant Usher*), Philippines (*Tangent Flash*), and Okinawa (*Valiant Blitz*), as well as south Korea (*Team Spirit*).† Reflecting the strategic importance and growing domestic turmoil of the Philippines, the 1983 *Tangent Flash* exercise was the largest to date. The Philippines houses Subic Bay Naval Base, the Seventh Fleet's primary support and logistics base for operations in the Indian Ocean. To counter popular dissatisfaction with the U.S.-backed government, civic action projects such as installing water works and providing medical care were major features of the exercise.[24]

Not to be outdone, the Pacific Air Force (PACAF) participates in about fifty readiness and command post exercises each year. Because the West Pacific, unlike Europe, offers an uncongested and unregulated airspace, Air Force commanders claim it is the best place to train for air combat. According to *Aviation Week and Space Technology*, "several joint-use, Pacific-area ranges have been developed, complete with electronic

---

* Although Japan's Navy had previously participated in bilateral exercises in Hawaii, this was the first time Japan's military participated in *multilateral* exercises.

† The Marines also practiced joining their prepositioned equipment at Diego Garcia in *Stratmobex*.

warfare and simulated surface-to-air threats guarding realistic tactical targets representing enemy airfields, truck convoys, tanks and anti-aircraft artillery emplacements." [25]

PACAF stresses multinational air exercises. [26] *Cope Thunder*, held seven times a year at Clark Air Force Base in the Philippines, brings together Australian, New Zealand and Philippine aircraft for a fortnight of bombing of mock targets, including evasion of Soviet-style SA-7 surface-to-air missiles. [27] A similar range is now active in south Korea for the *Cope Strike* U.S.–south Korean joint bombing exercises. [28] The U.S. also operates a gunnery and bombing range known as Nightmare at Chorwon, only 20 km from the Demilitarized Zone. [29]

Pacific Command tries to keep its command and control organization primed for war. *Beach Crest*, a typical command and control exercise held in Japan in 1984, involved eight hundred U.S. Marines, Air Force personnel, and Japanese Self Defense Forces who played a joint command post exercise on maps of Japan. These exercises are politically delicate in Japan due to the unconstitutional nature of the Japan Self Defense Force. This problem, according to a U.S. military analyst, challenges the U.S. to create U.S.–Japanese coordinated command and control "while not creating the perception among the Japanese of a collective defense arrangement." [30]

A sixth type of exercise tests counterinsurgency forces in Pacific Command. In the 1960s, such exercises included *Forward Thrust* on Taiwan, which practiced Chinese Nationalist attack on the mainland, and *Jungle Drum* in Thailand, which trained SEATO* forces for action against Thai insurgents. [31] In October 1982, Australian and Japanese forces participated in *Thermal Gale*, a U.S.-sponsored special warfare excercise in Hawaii which prepared allies for U.S.-led regional interventions. [32]

A step closer to superpower war are the "crisis" exercises. In the largest joint maneuvers since World War II, the U.S. and Japan conducted naval exercises in the Sea of Japan shortly after KAL 007 was shot down in 1983. The exercise involved 150 Japanese ships, and

---

* Southeast Asia Treaty Organization.

30,000 Japanese military personnel along with two U.S. aircraft carriers and escorts. Planned long before the tragedy, the exercise nonetheless exacerbated Soviet tension. In what the U.S. press described as "highly provocative" maneuvers,[33] the forces practiced blockading the Tsugaru and Tsushima Straits against Soviet ships leaving their headquarters at Vladivostok. Signalling the upgrade of Japan's military posture, the exercise was important symbolically. As an American journalist observed: "Never has Japan thrown itself so wholeheartedly into military exercises with the U.S. so close to U.S. territory." [34]

A related "battle" exercise in 1983 was *Fleetex*, a north Pacific "armada" of three aircraft carriers and forty-one escorts plus land-based naval and Air Force planes from Guam, Adak, Japan, and the U.S. West Coast. Held back-to-back with *Team Spirit* in 1983, *Fleetex* reasserted U.S. presence in the northwest Pacific up to a few hundred kilometres off the Soviet Far East – less than twenty minutes flight time for carrier strike aircraft. This exercise in the Soviet Union's backyard was aimed, as Commander of the Pacific Fleet Admiral Foley put it, at "taunting the Soviet Pacific Fleet." [35]

Because these exercises usually elicit Soviet response such as mock Backfire nuclear bomber attacks,[36] the U.S. Navy is able to monitor the latest Soviet tactics. As Admiral Watkins, Chief of Naval Operations, testified in 1984, "We are shoulder to shoulder with them in all dimensions – air, surface, subsurface – all the time, as we have been for twenty years." Added the Admiral, the exercises allow the U.S. Navy to "see how tall they [the Soviets] are; certainly not ten feet, but there are a lot of them about six feet tall." [37]

Apart from demonstrating "resolve" to the Soviet Union, Pacific Command exercises are timed to influence the domestic political affairs of U.S. allies. Exercises with New Zealand, for example, were designed to strengthen the hand of the conservative National Party government until it lost power in 1984.[38] Stage-managed by U.S. Ambassador Monroe Browne, these exercises involved timing the arrival of U.S. warships to highlight the Labor Party's anti-nuclear stance, thereby undercutting Labor's support with the pro-American electorate. This strategem backfired, however, by fuelling Labor Party opposition to nuclear alliance with the U.S. Much to the chagrin of Pacific Command, the Labor Party ended up in government in July 1984. *Triad*, an October 1984 exercise of U.S. Air Force planes with the New Zealand Air Force, only worsened the situation.[39]

Nuclear War Games

Unlike in U.S.-led conventional exercises, allies participate only in-directly in U.S. war nuclear exercises in the Pacific. Begun in 1979, the annual *Global Shield* exercise is perhaps the most important. Run by the Strategic Air Command, this exercise involves a global alert, simulated escalation of the Cold War, and finally a mock nuclear attack on the Soviet Union. The B-52s in Guam disperse to pre-selected bases sup-ported by ground teams, and fly sorties over practice targets. To add to the realism of the *Global Shield* exercise in 1979, the Air Force fired two Minutemen missiles over the Pacific Missile Range.

B-52s which are transiting or overflying foreign territory at this time – as in Australia in 1981 – may be involved in *Global Shield*. SAC-related communications and intelligence bases in the territory of Pacific allies would certainly be active in the exercise.[40] While little is known about exercises of nuclear ballistic missile submarines, Trident missiles are probably fired from submarines as a nuclear war exercise.

Pacific Command also plays nuclear war games. Unlike the exercises, which mobilize forces and materiel, war games require participants merely to play-act their parts. Aimed at flexing the ability of Pacific forces to "think on their feet" – to make decisions under various war-time conditions and scenarios – players are given a script by CINCPAC setting out the conditions and rules of the game. In one game, a "Nuclear Radiation Casualty Play", the script states that the crews of aircraft "who meet or exceed a dose of 400 rad [of radiation] during the course of a flight, will be declared dead." The manual notes laconically that this "will also cause the loss of the aircraft." [41] Another game cul-minates with Nuclear Detonation Scenario 16, a nuclear attack which pulverizes a U.S. base. The players are instructed to assume that "All facilities are destroyed or damaged and beyond repair. All personnel are dead or dying. All exercise participants should simulate loss of communications and refuse to accept any further exercise traffic." [42]

Warship Visits

Pacific Fleet warships typically make an annual training cruise through-out the Pacific and Indian Oceans. Engaging in exercises with allies along the way, the cruises make port visits, often giving little public warning or explanation. Behind these visits lies more than "goodwill" in the host port and rest and recreation for crews. Before and after a warship visits a port, it is invariably "exercising" for war or pursuing a strategic goal of U.S. foreign policy, such as "showing the flag" in a trouble spot. But the warship visit is itself a diplomatic intervention, signalling U.S. friendship and military support for particular allies or even particular political groups within allied nations.*

According to CINCPAC, port visits aim to:

a. Protect U.S. interests and support U.S. policies in foreign countries.
b. Assist U.S. representatives abroad in the discharge of their responsibilities.
c. Obtain logistic support.
d. Liberty and recreation.
e. Area familiarization.[43]

In 1983, U.S. warships in the Pacific Fleet spent about 20 per cent of their forward-deployed time in ports, mostly in Hawaii, Japan, and the Philippines†. Up by 20 per cent from 1976,‡ the overwhelming number of the visits – 91 per cent excluding Hawaii – were to Pacific ports, while Indian Ocean visits accounted for the rest. (See Appendix A8.)

The number and type of warships§ to visit a particular country or region reflect two political considerations: its current importance in U.S. foreign policy, and the temperature of its relations with the U.S. Classified as routine, informal, and formal, all visits must be approved by CINCPAC, who reviews them for "unusual politico-military considerations." [44] Such considerations are evident in the three major shifts in the regional distribution of warship visits between 1976 and 1983. In response to the build-up at Diego Garcia and the Carter Doctrine, ship-days‖ in Indian Ocean ports increased from 4 to 611 between 1976 and

---

* While often less visible, U.S. aircraft also engage in jet-set diplomacy, especially the versatile Airborne Warning and Control Aircraft (AWAC) now stationed at Okinawa.
† Followed by Hong Kong, south Korea, Guam, Australia, Diego Garcia, Singapore, Thailand, and Bahrain.
‡ There were 5,728 ship-days in 1976; this increased to 6,936 in 1981 and fell to 6,879 in 1983.
§ Aircraft carriers, surface carrier escorts, attack submarines, or amphibious vessels.
‖ Ship-days in port are not the same as numbers of port visits, as many ships may visit and accumulate the same time as one ship. Cross-country analysis, however, shows that the two indexes largely move together, although only forward port ship-days are considered here.

1983, peaking at 860 in 1980. In Taiwan they fell to zero after 1980 due to the U.S. embrace of China. And in Australia, ship-days increased from 17 in 1976, when a newly elected conservative government revived ship visits, to 310 in 1982.[45]

Social and Political Effects

Ship and air visits are a two-edged sword for the U.S. A viable symbol of U.S. power, visits encourage pro-U.S. political forces in an allied country, or intimidate those with cold feet. On the other hand, the visits fuel opposition to the U.S. by a diverse coalition: anti-nuclear or disarmament forces; opponents of U.S. allies; and/or those adversely affected by local health, social, and economic effects of the visits. While New Zealand's ban on all warship visits is the most explosive action taken to date, major protests have erupted in Japan, Australia, Fiji, Hawaii, and San Francisco. The newly independent island republic of Vanuatu even passed a Constitutional amendment making itself a nuclear-free zone.

Warships create problems for port communities whether they are homeported, as in Japan, Hawaii, and the U.S. West Coast, or are merely "visiting" as in most Pacific Command ports. Direct risks include exposure to radiological accidents or even accidental detonation of nuclear weapons, as well as the possibility of becoming a Soviet nuclear target. Moreover, with an average visit involving the sudden influx of up to 10,000 sailors and officers for two to five days, the social and economic fallout can be severe.

While warship visits stimulate some economic sectors such as rental housing, recreation, prostitution, and drug-running, they generally undermine the local economy. In typical boomtown fashion, warship visits generate price inflation in local food and housing markets by introducing an abrupt increase in demand. Locked into union contracts or employer agreements, local workers must then spend a larger part of their income on basics, such as food. The visits may also draw in skilled or unskilled labor from around the country, bypassing the local workforce and even displacing it if newly arrived laborers stay on during the "bust" period after the warship leaves. The boom-bust cycle, in short, makes economic development unstable.

Furthermore, with the structure of the economy skewed toward satisfying the particular demands of U.S. sailors, the economic and social needs of local people may go unsatisfied. Host governments often invest substantially to make their ports more attractive to the Navy, without examining economic alternatives such as job creation and community programs. Naval monopoly over port-rights may even block commercial development of the port resource, as is starkly evident at Subic Bay in the Philippines.

The social effects of ship visits and homeporting are also invidious. Prostitution, to take the most glaring example, proliferates everywhere the U.S. Navy sails or makes its home. The entire economy of the city of Olongapo, which surrounds the Subic Bay Naval Base, for example, is based on prostitution. While women are the primary providers of sexual services, child prostitution is also rampant and even a few men are involved.[46] Distorting the social and economic life of Asian-Pacific societies, prostitution also affects the social fabric of the U.S. by engendering sexist and racist attitudes in American sailors.

The sailor at sea dreams of the "kinky and oriental" sex awaiting in Asian port visits – at Pattaya in Thailand, at Subic Bay in the Philippines, at Hong Kong or south Korea, or at Okinawa, where Filipinas are imported by entrepreneurs for sex with sailors. The military's official *Stars and Stripes*, for example, advertises the sexual delights of *kisaeng* (prostitute) parties in south Korea:

The ultimate experience is a *kisaeng* party. Picture having three or four of the loveliest creatures God ever created hovering around you, singing, dancing, feeding you, washing what they feed you down with rice wine or beer, all saying at once, "You are the greatest." This is the Orient you heard about and came to find . . . but probably haven't, yet . . . Japanese tourists – who are mostly male – say the intriguing thing about a *kisaeng* party is that the guest never has to use his hands. That's true . . . but there's more. The royal treatment really can't be described adequately. Give it a try. It's a memorable experience.[47]

While Asian ports are particularly well known in the Navy as prostitution centers, Australian ports are becoming increasingly popular as well. Reuters reported in 1984 that the Australian government officially requested that U.S. sailors desist from "lusting after" Australian schoolgirls.[48] The protest was prompted by publicity surrounding *Perth Good Times*, a magazine circulated by U.S. sailors. The controversial issue read:

All day long secretaries, shop assistants and lady shoppers cute enough to make your head bend, parade up and down the mall . . . Most of them are on business, but when the Americans are in town lots of schoolgirls and other girls hang around in anticipation.[49]

While prostitution in Australian ports is on the rise, women are also increasingly visible in protests against the ship visits. In October 1984, four women in two dinghies battled high pressure hoses to paint "No Death Ships" on the hull of the visiting U.S. destroyer *Cushing*.[50]

Nuclear Leviathans

One of the most controversial aspects of U.S. warships is the potential health hazard from their nuclear reactors and weapons. In 1983, over a third of the visits to Pacific forward ports were by nuclear-powered vessels, mostly attack submarines.[51] While routine U.S. policy is to deny the possibility of nuclear reactor accidents, the fact remains that many nuclear warships *have* experienced mishaps.[52]

Such accidents may pose significant hazards to port communities. To alleviate popular concern, CINCPAC is prepared to extend radiological assistance and even accept liability for nuclear accidents in foreign ports.* Nonetheless, port cities or national authorities in Japan, Australia, New Zealand, Fiji, Vanuatu, Belau, Mauritius, the Seychelles and even Hawaii have at various times all found the risks imposed by warship nuclear reactors to be unacceptable. Since many U.S. aircraft carriers, cruisers, and submarines are nuclear-powered, these protests raise major obstacles to U.S. port visits.

Even more sensitive than reactors are the nuclear weapons carried by U.S. warships. While CINCPAC's routine policy is "to neither confirm nor deny the presence of nuclear weapons or components on board any ship, station or aircraft," even if the weapon system has "been properly identified as having nuclear capability," virtually *all* classes of U.S. warships visiting forward ports have units which are

---

* The U.S. 1974 Public Law 93–513 states that "it is the policy of the United States that it will pay claims or judgements for bodily injury, death or damage to or loss of real or personal property proven to have resulted from a nuclear incident involving the nuclear reactor of a United States warship."

certified* to carry particular nuclear weapons.[53] Any Pacific Fleet vessel of a class so certified may actually carry those nuclear weapons into port.[54]

A U.S. Navy manual describes the handling of nuclear weapons at sea as "one of the most hazardous of all shipboard operations." According to the Navy, such handling "contains all the dangers found in conventional ammunition transfer plus the grave consequence of accidental loss or contamination."[55] The risk of accident is even greater in congested ports, especially for nuclear submarines, which are more vulnerable to collisions in port than at sea. While ships at sea can simply sail away from any radiological mess they may produce, the immobile, dense populations near ports are directly vulnerable to radiological hazards. In the long run, of course, radiological contamination of the seas could pose hazards far afield through the food chain.

"Worst Case" Accidents

Most U.S. allies are aware of the risks of *reactor* accidents. Only a few defense officials in each country know, however, about the risks of nuclear *weapon* accidents. American officials downplay the risks and consequences of such accidents. They claim that the probability of accidents involving the release of fission products approaches zero. Nonetheless, major accidents involving nuclear weapons have occurred. The best-known involved the crash of two B-52 bombers, one in Palomares, Spain, in 1966 and the other in Thule, Greenland, in 1968, which caused severe plutonium contamination within the local communities. Another accident, this one in 1960 at McGuire Air Force Base in New Jersey, involved a nuclear missile which caught fire and melted after a helium bottle aboard the missile exploded. The fire burned for forty-five minutes, spreading plutonium over an "undetermined number of acres."[56]

These and more recent accidents involving nuclear weapons on land, in the air, and in the sea[57] prompted the Pentagon to initiate a series of

---

* A "certified" vessel is one which has qualified to carry nuclear weapons by meeting rigid training requirements and by passing a Nuclear Weapons Acceptance Inspection.

accident exercises.* Codenamed *Nuwax*, the exercises are currently guided by the Defense Nuclear Agency's *Nuclear Weapon Accident Response Procedures Manual*, which distills U.S. military thinking on the subject. Released to the authors under the Freedom of Information Act, the *Manual* reveals a different attitude towards the hazard of nuclear accidents than that expressed overseas. According to the *Manual*, there is a "very real possibility of radioactive contamination at the accident scene, and extending many miles downwind." [58] Other documents reveal that the U.S. military held week-long *Nuwax* exercises in 1979 (Nevada test site), 1981 (Nevada test site), and 1983 (Virginia). These exercises involved 700–1,000 personnel whose mission was to recover mock nuclear weapons damaged by impact, fire, and high explosive detonations. To enhance the "realism" of the exercises, radioactive radium 223 was sprinkled in the area to simulate weapons-grade plutonium.

The exercises revealed that the response to nuclear accidents is problematic, due in part to the lack of interest and inexperience of U.S. officials responsible for the operations.[59] Additionally, *Nuwax* uncovered defects in response capability which appear to be inherent in the nuclear events themselves. These deficiencies include unreliable communications capability, grossly delayed warning messages, and undefined levels of acceptable radiation exposure and site restoration levels, termed a "monumental problem" in the official report.[60]

Difficult enough under test conditions within the U.S., these problems would be compounded in a nuclear weapon accident overseas. U.S. plans for such an event call for rushing rapidly deployable satellite and sideband radio communication units to the site, probably from the Naval Communications Station in the Philippines, where a mobile unit stands on alert for such contingencies.† [62] According to a high-level

---

* Another factor motivating the exercises was the dispersion of experienced U.S. officials into other military and non-military careers in the 1960s. The example of the U.K., which started nuclear weapons accident exercises in 1976, also inspired Pentagon officials to take up the issue actively.

† This Pacific Fleet unit is called an Ashore Mobile Contingency Communications system and provides HF radio, teletype and voice circuits, UHF satellite secure voice circuits. It is transported in a C-130 aircraft or a CH-53 helicopter.[61]

Pentagon official involved in accident response, Pacific Command's nuclear accident teams "are really hot on this." Navy Nuclear Accident Response Crisis Actions Teams (CATs) are "all over the place," he adds, at overseas bases and travelling aboard warships in the Pacific.[63] CINC-PAC's Nuclear Safety/Security Branch, known as Office J322 has "primary cognizance of nuclear weapons accidents/significant incidents and nuclear reactor accidents in USPACOM [Pacific Command]."[64]

While *Nuwax* exercises responded to U.S.-based accidents, the official report for *Nuwax-81* specifically addressed the problems of overseas nuclear weapon accidents. "Extensive consultation with the Department of State and local U.S. embassies," states the report, "is required to coordinate U.S. efforts overseas." Noting that *mutual* training is "essential", the report adds that "U.S. and host capabilities need to be *blended* for a coherent plan and a capable response force." The report recommends joint exercises and the development of overseas versions of the *Response Manual* tailored to each country.[65]

"Blending", however, has a rather specific meaning in a Pacific "host" nation. Since the U.S. military is determined to defend its nuclear secrets, it insists that only U.S. personnel cleared for "Critical Nuclear Weapon Design Information" will have access to the damaged weapons themselves.*[67] As the "shape, form, or outline" of nuclear weapon components may also reveal these secrets, the site must be "protected" against visual access and overhead photography.[68] And because "unfriendly elements" or "enemy or dissident elements" may listen in to site radio communications, thereby obtaining classified "compilations of individually unclassified material", the *Manual* instructs the use of equipment which scrambles voice into unrecognizable garble "to defeat this threat."[69]

Even in an accident, the U.S. may stick to its "neither-confirm-nor-deny" policy about the presence of nuclear weapons. Indeed, U.S. officials may even purposely issue *false* public information to divert attention away from the shipment of damaged nuclear components – a practice for which the participants in the 1983 *Nuwax* exercise were criticized.[70]

Requirements to keep accident sites off-limits to all except U.S. per-

---

* These conditions apply in domestic nuclear accidents, and it is logical to assume that they will be applied even more stringently in overseas accidents. Such has also been the historical experience.[66]

sonnel imply that host nations will be obliged to relinquish sovereignty over the site for the duration. To add insult to injury, the U.S. will probably call on host nation security forces to guard the site. In the 1981 *Nuwax* exercises, several demonstrators at the site broke through the security cordon and, as the report put it, "It was simulated that one demonstrator was shot." [71]

The Pentagon has already drafted soothing but bizarre press statements for release in the event of nuclear weapon accidents. "Contingency Release Number 3, When Public is Probably in Danger," instructs residents that:

The most appropriate initial action is to remain calm and inside homes or office buildings. Turn off fans, air conditioners, and forced air heating units. Drink and eat only canned or packaged food that have been inside. Trained monitoring teams wearing special protective clothing and equipment will be moving through the area to determine the extent of any possible contamination. The dress of these teams should not be interpreted as indicating any special risk to those indoors. [72]

Current response planning for nuclear accidents bases its worst case scenario on the most dangerous, factual accidents.* The *Manual* also refers to the contamination problems arising from nuclear fission products such as strontium 90 and iodine 131 which would be produced in either a sub-critical or full-scale nuclear chain reaction.† [74] While U.S. officials insist that such events are highly unlikely, their statements are meaningless since it is impossible to predict either the origin or the precise sequence of events in a real accident.‡

---

* Defined in the *Manual* as "off a military installation with a spread of contamination, difficult weapon recovery problems, public involvement, extensive logistic support requirements, the need for extensive deployed communications support, and site restoration problems." [73] This scenario is the same as occurred in the 1966 and 1968 accidents.

† A sub-critical event occurs when a chain reaction begins in a mass of fissionable metal, but blows itself apart, thereby halting the reaction and scattering radioactive material. A chain reaction occurs when the chain reaction becomes self-sustaining, generating a full-scale nuclear explosion.

‡ In "host nations", the following events seem likely to generate accident conditions: "cross-decking" nuclear weapons between ships near or in ports, for example, between

All that can be said is that the likelihood of nuclear weapon accidents may decline with improved designs, may increase as thousands of new weapons are deployed, and probably increases in times of rising international tension as the frequency of weapons handling increases. It can be said with certainty that accidents which exceeded the worst nightmares of U.S. nuclear planners have already occurred, and U.S. officials take them seriously enough to create a response capability in the U.S. and the Pacific, albeit one that is seriously flawed.

Kiwi Disease

While concerns about health and safety run deep throughout the Pacific, the fundamental objection to U.S. Navy warship visits is opposition to the growing militarism in the Pacific and to the use of nuclear weapons as a means of war. The 1984 election of a New Zealand government opposed to visits of nuclear-powered or nuclear-armed warships – dubbed the "Kiwi Disease" in Washington – is but the latest in a long history of hot/cold welcomes to U.S. warships from Pacific allies. In an era of high-speed nuclear-powered ships and long-range nuclear weapons, New Zealand's stance is *militarily* irrelevant – unless the Soviets or the U.S. decided to invade Antarctica. New Zealand is not at the crossroads to any conceivable war, unless the U.S. loses access to the direct route through Southeast Asia to the Indian Ocean and is obliged to sail south of Australia.

---

aircraft carriers; helicopter airlift between storage depot and port or airfield; the "bouncing missile" syndrome, in which a missile/bomb or its warhead is dropped by mistake; and an aircraft shipping nuclear weapons back to U.S. repair depots or dispersing just before a nuclear war. The U.S. Navy reports that 381 naval-nuclear accidents and incidents occurred between 1965 and 1977 on all types of vessels, especially involving anti-submarine and air-defense nuclear rockets. A Pacific Fleet instruction in November 1981 notes another route to a nuclear accident: "Detonation of high explosive components of a nuclear weapon, in addition to exposing personnel to blast, thermal, and toxic gas effects, may spread radioactive material, thereby contaminating casualties and the incident/accident area." Each nuclear-armed vessel has established a nuclear casualty medical team to respond to such events. "Human remains," it orders, "which after decontamination show considerable contamination, will be wrapped and sealed in sheet polyethylene and stored in a properly labeled human remains case" – that is, a coffin.[75]

Although New Zealand's decision is of no military significance, it threatens U.S. forward deployment and collective security strategy. U.S. strategists ask themselves: "Is New Zealand the first in a line of dominoes that, once toppled, could confine the U.S. Pacific Fleet to a corridor between Pearl Harbor and Guam?" [76] The U.S. has not hesitated to reject New Zealand's stance as incompatible with its alliance with the U.S. "The United States," emphasized a State Department official, "attaches critical importance to the opportunity to use Australian and New Zealand ports that provide ready access to the South Pacific and Indian Ocean." [77] CINCPAC took an especially hard line against New Zealand, calling the New Zealand decision "an unprecedented move". "As the theater commander," he cabled U.S. Defense Secretary Caspar Weinberger, "it is difficult to see how my forces could seriously and realistically cooperate with the New Zealand military under those conditions." [78]

Beyond concern that military maneuverability may be curtailed, the U.S. is worried about the unravelling of the alliance system upon which its strategic power pivots. "Unless we hold our allies' feet to the fire over ship visits and nuclear deployments," a senior Administration official insisted, "one will run away and then the next." [79]

Vladivostok, homeport of the Soviet Pacific fleet, 1985
(TASS)

SIXTEEN ☆
THE SOVIET "THREAT"

There is good reason to believe that we normally overestimate Communist capabilities in almost every respect. That statement I base on my own experience in war. In general in the intelligence field they tend to err on the safe side ... I think we are in a dangerous position vis-à-vis the Communists in that respect [overestimating Soviet capabilities] today, because there has been an almost hysterical assumption of great capabilities on the part of the Communists, some of which, in my opinion, actually do not exist.

—Admiral Arthur Radford, Chair,
U.S. Joint Chiefs of Staff, 1956[1]

In the Pacific as in all other areas of the world, our greatest threat remains the Soviet Union.

—Admiral William Crowe,
Commander-in-Chief Pacific, 1985[2]

Few Americans have ever met a Soviet citizen. Almost none have ever fought against a Soviet soldier – the last U.S.–Soviet combat was in 1919–1921 when the Marines intervened at Vladivostok. Indeed, the superpowers were allies, not enemies, in World War II, the last major war involving both U.S. and Soviet soldiers.* Yet the image of an in-

---

* Soviet and U.S. pilots did meet in head-on aerial combat a few times in the Korean War, but this was not publicized at the time.

nately diabolical Soviet Union is deeply engrained in American popular culture.

While President Reagan's proclamations about the "evil empire" might stem from politicking or sheer ignorance,* U.S. diplomats deliberately beat the drum of the Soviet threat at home and abroad. Secretary of State George Shultz's remarks to the 1984 ANZUS (Australia, New Zealand, U.S.) conference are typical: "Soviet naval activity in the Pacific, supported by the growing Soviet air and naval presences on the Pacific Rim, continues to increase, probing for weak or vulnerable areas into which it can expand." [4] Strong on ideology and weak on evidence, such rhetoric aims to bind Pacific allies more tightly to the U.S.

A dispassionate evaluation of the "correlation of forces" – the U.S.–Soviet strategic balance – in the Far East reveals a different picture. Far from its purported invincibility, the Soviet military machine in the Pacific is homebound and vulnerable. Vastly inferior to the U.S. in every dimension, the Soviets rely for their defense on their huge, home-based nuclear arsenal. Ironically, it is precisely Soviet weakness rather than strength which increases the risk of nuclear war in the Pacific.

Unnatural Acts

Pentagon intellectuals view the world through a peculiar prism, the geopolitical outlook. According to Reagan administration strategist Colin Gray, "the world, reduced to its power-related essentials, consists of a Heartland superpower [the Soviet Union] that is locked in a permanent struggle with the offshore, insular continental superpower, the United States, for effective control of the Rimlands and the marginal seas of the World-Island (the dual continent of Eurasia–Africa) that sweep in a great arc from Norway's North Cape to South Korea and Japan." [5]

Any relevance of this theory was swept away long ago by China's defection from the Soviet bloc as well as the rise of non-aligned movements. Nonetheless, U.S. military analysts still sport geopolitical lenses. In June 1984, for example, General Bernard Trainor of the Marines told American midshipmen at the Naval War College: "We

---

* For example, Reagan claimed that the Soviet Navy "is aimed at intercepting the some sixteen choke points [of maritime trade] in the world." [3]

have a legitimate right, a legitimate interest to operate on the seas of the world and touch the continents of the world . . . That's our lifeblood, our economic blood. This is not true for the Soviet Union." The General added, "But the Soviet Union is doing an unnatural act, it is leaping the barriers, it is going into our turf." War with the Soviets, he concluded, is therefore "inevitable." [6]

Status Quo

Via forward deployment, the U.S. has delivered the threat of U.S. attack to the very doorstep of the Soviet Far East. To assess the superpower military balance, it is therefore necessary to take into account forces which are "homebased" within the Soviet Union. For analytical symmetry, we might also examine U.S. forces in the Western United States. But the situation is not symmetrical: the Soviets do not and cannot project conventional military power eastwards against the U.S. mainland. The West Coast-based U.S. forces, therefore, bear on the "Pacific" balance only as back-up forces in a U.S. attack on the Soviets. The military *status quo*, in short, is premised on the assumption that it is legitimate for the U.S. to defend itself by attacking the Soviets from foreign forward positions in the Pacific, and not vice versa.*

The major military mission of Soviet forces in the Far East is to deter China from opening a second front in the event of war with the U.S.† The Soviets keep fifty-three divisions of ground troops in the Transbaikal and Far East military districts, fifty of which are deployed along the Soviet and Mongolian borders with China (see Appendix E).‡ [9] In a global superpower war including China, these forces would try to wrest Manchuria from China to block a U.S. attack on Mongolia and Central Russia over the north China plain. [10]

---

* U.S. forces in Alaska are relevant, however.

† Soviet forces were first deployed to counter the threat of a war with China. In light of the U.S.–China alliance, the current mission of Soviet forces arrayed against China is *primarily* to avoid war on the China front in the case of war with the U.S., and secondarily, to deter a war with China alone. In this secondary mission, military analysts agree that Chinese forces are no match for the Soviets. [7]

‡ Eighteen of these are motorized rifle divisions, and only two are tank divisions, which are more typical in Eastern Europe. [8]

To defend the Far East from coastal attack, the Soviets have erected a "hedgehog" defense. Because Soviet MiG fighter planes are "short-legged", fighter interceptors flying from fourteen coastal airfields can reach out to a combat radius of only 390 km (see Map 16.1). The fighters' short range means that the spines on the hedgehog are quite short.[11]

Some 100 SA-4 and SA-6 surface-to-air missiles along Sakhalin and Kamchatka defend valuable Soviet Far Eastern military and urban–industrial targets. These missiles can hit targets up to 24 km altitude and out to a range of 70 km.[12] Although a system of coastal, over-the-horizon, and long-range radar ostensibly warns of incoming threats, the KAL 007 incident in September 1983 revealed that the Soviet hedgehog in the Far East has many bare patches. Most of the interceptors failed to find the plane as it blundered through porous Soviet airspace. According to a Soviet official, not the least of their problems was the fact that "it took us too long to sober up the pilots enough to get them to take off."[13] The airliner flew through highly defended Soviet airspace for more than two hours before it was shot down south of Sakhalin Island.[14]

CINCPAC refers often to the "menacing" number of Soviet military aircraft in the Far East – over 1,600 fighter and interceptor aircraft and 435 bombers in the region in 1983 (see Appendix E). The bulk of these planes, however, are capable only of territorial defense of the Soviet Union, and are stationed primarily along the Soviet–China border. Furthermore, many of the models in the Soviet Air Force are obsolete.[15] According to former Secretary General of the Japanese military's Joint Chiefs of Staff, Naotoshi Sakonjo: "It is . . . doubtful whether they have the capacity to conduct air-to-air fighting or mount air-to-air ground assaults following flights across the sea. Even if they had the capacity to perform such missions, they naturally would have to be accompanied by AWACs [Airborne Warning and Control aircraft]. But the Soviet AWACs . . . lag far behind their American counterparts."[16]

Red Flag Afloat

Besides airpower, the Soviet Union's strategic posture in the Far East depends on its Pacific Fleet. In 1983, American intelligence counted 84 general purpose surface vessels, 122 submarines, and 12 amphibious vessels in the Soviet Pacific Fleet (see Appendix E). The Fleet is broken into two parts, each based primarily in a distinct maritime theater.* The 5th Fleet, based at and controlled from Vladivostok, covers the Seas of Japan and Okhotsk out to the defensive barrier of the Kurile Islands. The second, the Soviet 7th Fleet, is controlled from Petropavlovsk (see Map 16.1)[18] and covers the oceanic approaches to the Kuriles, the Kamchatka Peninsula, and the Bering Strait route to the Arctic sea lanes.[19]

American naval propagandists consistently point to the Soviet threat to U.S. and allied "sea lanes of communication" (SLOCs). U.S. Secretary of the Navy John Lehman, for example, argued in April 1984 that: "A primary Soviet objective is naval interdiction of the lifelines connecting the United States, its allies, and the West's sources of vital fuel and minerals – 95 per cent of which move by sea." [20]

Yet in their private writings, key supporters of maritime supremacy tell a different story. According to naval analyst Bing West, SLOC interdiction has the lowest priority on the Soviet Pacific Fleet's wartime hitlist (see Table 16.1). Since the Soviets will be so busy fending off the U.S. fleet in the Pacific, an attempt to interdict U.S. and allied commerce and supply lines would divert Soviet forces from more important missions – protecting the Soviet mainland and its nuclear forces. The U.S. itself rates this "threat" so low that it has turned protection of northwest Pacific SLOCs over to the Japanese Maritime Defense Force, even though the U.S. Pacific Commander believes the Japanese Force to be currently incapable of achieving this goal.[21]

Writing in 1977, Paul Nitze, former U.S. Secretary of the Navy and key strategist in the Reagan administration, concluded that Soviet submarines and aircraft are not "cause for serious speculation that the Pacific sea lanes could be severed for any extended period by Soviet naval activities." [22] Informed Japanese analysts such as Admiral Naotoshi Sakonjo concur. "It is totally inconceivable," stated the Admiral in December 1982, "that the Soviet Union's major surface ships will move into the Pacific and attack Japanese and American warships or cargo ships or sea lanes." [23]

---

* Naval analyst Norman Polmar states – without documentation – that these fleets were divided in 1947 and reunited in 1953.[17]

Map 16.1:
Soviet Military Bases in the Far East

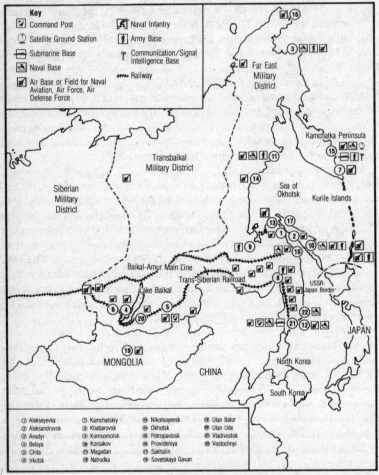

Key

☑ Command Post

◔ Satellite Ground Station

⊟ Submarine Base

◪ Naval Base

◪ Air Base or Field for Naval Aviation, Air Force, Air Defense Force

◪ Naval Infantry

⚑ Army Base

☂ Communication/Signal Intelligence Base

✜✜✜✜ Railway

① Alekseyevka	⑦ Kamchatskiy	⑬ Nikolsoyevsk	⑲ Ulan Bator
② Aleksandrovsk	⑧ Khabarovsk	⑭ Okhotsk	⑳ Ulan Ude
③ Anadyr	⑨ Komsomolsk	⑮ Petropavlosk	㉑ Vladivostok
④ Belaya	⑩ Korsakov	⑯ Provideniya	㉒ Vostochnyi
⑤ Chita	⑪ Magadan	⑰ Sakhalin	
⑥ Irkutsk	⑫ Nahodka	⑱ Sovetskaya Gavan	

Note: Army bases are not shown. U.S. 1984 estimates showed 2 Divisions on Sakhalin, 1 Division at Petropavlosvk, 19 Divisions in region of Vladivistok to Komsomolsk, 4 Divisions in Mongolia, 9 Divisions in the Southwestern Transbaikal, and 5 Divisions in the Siberia Military District. Exact sites often unknown in sources.

Sources: W. Feeney, "The Pacific Basing System and U.S. Security," in edited, W. Tow and W. Feeney, *U.S. Foreign Policy and Asian-Pacific Security, A Transregional Approach*, Westview, Colorado, 1982, p. 193; U.S. Department of Defense, *Soviet Military Power*, U.S. GPO, Washington, D.C., 1985, p. 26; W. Simons, "Command and Control in the Pacific," *Journal of Defense and Diplomacy*, Volume 3, no. 1, January 1985, p. 20. Anon. "Soviet Far East Bases," *Jane's Defence Weekly*, April 14, 1984, pp. 560-562.

Map 16.2:
Soviet Long-range Siberian/Far Eastern Nuclear Sites

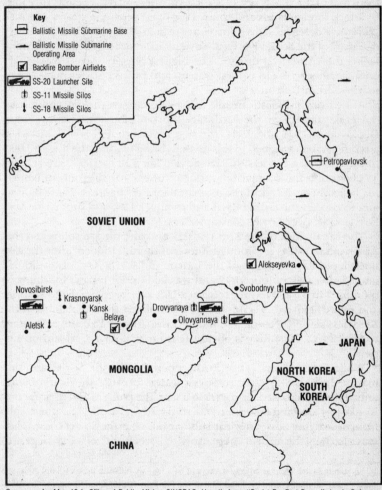

Key
- Ballistic Missile Submarine Base
- Ballistic Missile Submarine Operating Area
- Backfire Bomber Airfields
- SS-20 Launcher Site
- SS-11 Missile Silos
- SS-18 Missile Silos

Petropavlovsk

SOVIET UNION

Alekseyevka

Novosibirsk
Krasnoyarsk
Svobodnyy
Kansk
Drovyanaya
Aletsk
Belaya
Olovyannaya

JAPAN

MONGOLIA

NORTH KOREA
SOUTH KOREA

CHINA

Source: as for Map 16.1; Office of Public Affairs, CINCPAC, Hawaii; Anon "Soviet Far East Bases," *Jane's Defense Weekly,* April 14, 1984, pp. 561-62.

Slamming the Back Door

The mission of the Soviet Navy in the Pacific is fundamentally different from that of the U.S. Navy. U.S. forces are designed to occupy, threaten, or attack foreign lands and control the open oceans, a strategy termed "offensive defense." Soviet forces are primarily devoted to a "defensive defense" of the Soviet Far East. Soviet Pacific strategy revolves around facing the "American threat." The highest priority is to deny U.S. aircraft carriers access to coastal waters, and protect Soviet nuclear submarines from U.S. attack.*

Aside from its ballistic missile-firing submarines, the most important Soviet naval forces in the Pacific are the anti-submarine warfare units. Deployed in 1979 and 1984, the two much-vaunted Soviet Kiev-class aircraft carriers assigned to this mission bring to mind the huge 80,000-tonne American carriers. In fact, Soviet "aircraft carriers" are actually 34,000-tonne anti-submarine warfare cruisers, capable only of launching helicopters and short-range vertical take-off fighters. These fighters aim to protect the cruiser itself and to attack U.S. anti-submarine warfare aircraft over Soviet coastal waters.[24]

The capabilities of the Kiev cruisers and aircraft are so limited that American navalists are contemptuous of them.[25] Indeed, after the *Kiev* floundered its way through the Indian and Pacific Oceans, it limped into Vladivostok in June 1979 and was laid up for repairs for fourteen months.[26] In a 1983 naval exercise, a U.S. carrier managed to surprise and overwhelm a U.S. cruiser which simulated the capabilities of the Kiev-class ship.[27] According to Ralph Cossa, former Executive Assistant to CINCPAC: "The Kiev is obviously no match for a Carl Vinson carrier."[28]

While U.S. carriers range in the open Pacific, the Soviet anti-submarine cruisers stay close to Soviet waters because they can operate only under land-based air cover. In a war, the cruisers and their escorts would rely on land-based aircraft to try to ward off U.S. attack subs from destroying Soviet nuclear submarines near the Soviet coast. They may also help the nuclear submarines to "break out" of a U.S. siege into

---

* The Soviet Pacific Fleet is largely irrelevant in a war with China on mainland Asia, the Soviet's second major strategic headache in the Far East. Minor Soviet amphibious flanking actions would not have much impact on a ground war and cutting off U.S. supply runs to China would risk drawing U.S. firepower into the war.

open ocean. Limited by range, size, and number, Soviet anti-submarine forces in the Pacific, according to American military analysts, are hardly adequate to counter U.S. submarine forces in the Seas of Japan and Okhotsk, let alone in the Pacific.[29]

The Soviets plan to launch a much bigger carrier in the early 1990s. This new class, however, is decades behind American naval technology. Given the low performance of Soviet carrier aircraft, the new carrier will be vulnerable to land-based missile attack if it were used to intimidate a Third World country in the American style.[30] Today's American carriers are superior to future Soviet carriers in every critical dimension of warfare, most importantly, in carrier-borne long-range anti-submarine warfare and aerial early warning aircraft to defend the carrier.[31] Since the Soviets also lack substantial long-range amphibious land-attack forces, the new carrier is simply not comparable to its U.S. counterpart.[32]

The new carrier's central mission will probably be to ward off attacks by U.S. aircraft carriers against the Soviet Far East and its coastal fleets.[33] Before the U.S. put new long-range Polaris missiles aboard its submarines, U.S. 7th Fleet aircraft carriers were the main Pacific-based nuclear threat to the Soviet Far East. To counter the U.S. carriers, the Soviets built dozens of cheap diesel-powered submarines armed with conventional and nuclear-tipped anti-ship cruise missiles. The current Soviet tactic is to surround the U.S. carrier task group with cruise missile submarines and surface vessels, and then launch a simultaneous "saturation" strike to overwhelm the carrier's defenses.

This tactic severely strains Soviet centralized command and control resources. More importantly, it is rigid and inflexible. To achieve saturation, the 360° attack must be timed precisely. American naval analyst Norman Friedman explains: "Anything which upsets the timing destroys the concentration [of missiles] and permits the [U.S.] battlefleet to survive the attack and reply effectively."[34] U.S. F-14 fighters have demonstrated in mock attacks that they can shoot down 85 per cent of U.S. cruise missiles, which are even harder to detect than those of the Soviets.[35] In theory the surviving missiles can be decoyed away from the carrier with chaff radar reflectors, or shot down at close range.[36]

Since their capability to attack U.S. carriers is already limited, the Soviets will require a Herculean effort to simply maintain the *status quo* against new U.S. deployments. By 1990, U.S. deployment of Toma-

Table 16.1:
Missions of the Soviet Pacific Fleet

Mission[a]	Tasks	Forces
Strategic Offense	1. SLBM Launch	SSBN, SSB
	2. SSBN Protection	SSN, CVSG
Defense of the Homeland[b]	1. Anti-Submarine Warfare	SSN, SNA, CG, DDG, DD, SOSS
	2. Anti-Carrier Warfare	SSGN, SSG, SNA, SOSS
	3. Anti-Amphibious Warfare	SS, SNA, Coastal Defense Forces
	4. Protection of SLOC	GP Surface Defense Forces
	5. Interdiction of SLOC	SS, GP Surface Forces
	6. Defensive Mining	Mining Forces
Support of Land Forces	1. Amphibious Assault	SNI, Amphibious, Merchant
	2. Blockade	GP Surface Forces, Mining Forces
Presence	1. Peacetime employment of selected forces with minor regard to mix.	
	2. Presence forces available for interposition if political or military interests demonstrate need.	
	3. Gorshkov's "Instrument of state policy overseas".	

Notes: a. Listed in priority order.
b. Tasks listed in order of priority if concurrent accomplishment infeasible.

Table 16.1: (cont)

Key: SLBM = Sea-launched Ballistic Missile; SSBN = Ballistic Missile Nuclear Submarine; SSB = Ballistic Missile Submarine; SSN = Nuclear Attack Submarine; CVSG = Anti-Submarine Warfare and Guided Missile Carrier Task Group; SNI = Soviet Naval Infantry; SNA = Soviet Naval Aviation; CG = Guided Missile Cruiser; DDG = Guided Missile Destroyer; DD = Destroyer; SOSS = Soviet Ocean Surveillance System; SSGN = Guided Missile Nuclear Submarine; SSG = Guided Missile Submarine; SS = Diesel-powered Attack Submarine SLOC = Sea Lanes of Communication; GP = General Purpose Surface Forces.

Source: F. West *et al.*, "Toward the Year 1985: The Relationship Between U.S. Policy and Naval Forces in the Pacific", Appendix C, in Institute for Foreign Policy Analysis, *Environments for U.S. Naval Strategy in the Pacific Ocean–Indian Ocean Area, 1985–1995* (mimeo), Conference Report for Center for Advanced Research, U.S. Naval War College, Cambridge, Massachusetts, June 1977, p. 369.

hawk cruise missiles will multiply Soviet targets in an anti-carrier attack tenfold (see Chapter 14). Simply tracking all these American warships may well defeat Soviet efforts to credibly deter U.S. naval offensives in the Northwest Pacific.* Furthermore, Soviet cruise missiles are so cumbersome that they cannot be reloaded at sea on most vessels. The Soviet Fleet in the Pacific will therefore disarm itself the first time it employs the tactic.[38]

Supporting the Soviet Pacific fleet are land-based fighters and bombers, including forty naval Backfire bombers.†[39] A high-performance attack aircraft, the Backfire carries one or two anti-ship missiles armed with a nuclear or conventional warhead. With an unrefuelled combat radius of 5,400 km, Backfires can strike at U.S. carriers as far away as the Philippines or Hawaii.[40] But the Backfire lacks self-defense weapons and can be countered by U.S. carrier-launched F-14 aircraft at a range well beyond the Backfire's anti-ship missiles. American naval analysts conclude that all forty of the naval Backfires in the Far East would have to attack together to overwhelm and disable even one carrier operating close to the Soviet Union.[41]

The Soviet Union also maintains 8,000 naval infantry or Marines in the Far East, primarily to defend the Kurile Islands or to counter a U.S. or Japanese blockade of the Straits into the Sea of Japan.[42] The notion that these and other Soviet Far Eastern forces threaten Japan or the United States with a land invasion is sheer fantasy. As Japan's Research Institute for Peace and Security noted in 1981, the Soviet's weak sealift, relatively few naval infantry, and air inferiority preclude an offensive operation against Japan.[43] Indeed, the most likely "forward" use of Soviet Marines is to extricate Soviet advisors from fluid political situations like Somalia in 1977, or to counter U.S. Marine attacks on the Soviet Union itself.

Overall, it is difficult to disagree with U.S. naval analyst Bing West, who concludes that the Soviet Pacific Fleet's "overwhelming emphasis is on defense." In dense military jargon, West advised that in the Pacific, "The Soviet Navy is not projected to enjoy an excess of forces in terms

---

* As defense analyst Seymour Deitchman notes, Soviet cruise missiles rely upon long-range, subsonic Bear turboprop aircraft for targeting and guidance. Vulnerable to U.S. attack, these aircraft are yet another weak link in the Soviet cruise missile saturation attack strategy.[37]

† Based at Belaya west of Lake Baikal since 1978, and Alekseyevka since 1980.

of requirements which would enable it to perform adequately any but its primary mission of homeland defense." [44]

Far East Nervous System

Like Pacific Command, the Soviet military in the Far East is animated by an electronic nervous system which enables commanders to make decisions, communicate with forces, and receive intelligence from the field. CINCPAC's counterpart in the Far East is a Marshal of the Soviet Army, who operates from Chita.* [46] Although we can glean only an impression of the Soviet command and control system from public sources, it appears even more centralized, bureaucratic, and rigid than that of Pacific Command. In general, concludes the U.S. Defense Nuclear Agency, "the impression is gained that the whole [C³I] system depends on everything going just as prescribed, that the loss of a communication link or a command echelon would be more than disruptive, perhaps even catastrophic." [47]

Like the U.S. system, the Soviet Far Eastern Command system magnifies errors. Undoubtedly jittery since the KAL 007 overflight, the Soviet Far East Army Command in Vladivostok overreacted in August 1984 when President Reagan joked that he had outlawed Russia and "we begin bombing in five minutes." Vladivostok issued an alert stating that the two superpowers were in a "state of war." In response, U.S. and Japanese forces went onto high alert until the Soviet order was rescinded. [48]

In the Soviet Far East, the Soviets have erected some 500–600 tactical early warning and control radars. Due to the high latitudes, most Soviet satellites seeking communications or intelligence rotate in a near polar or Molniya orbit.† These satellites are especially crucial for long-haul and secure communications with Moscow. [50] In the Far East itself, Soviet communication networks are both ground and air-based, multiple and redundant, and are not designed to endure nuclear war. [51] Aircraft and naval forces rely mostly on high frequency radio communication. Only one communications and intelligence land-based facility is forward-

---

* Forces operating outside the two Far Eastern maritime theaters, for example, in the Indian Ocean, are likely to be commanded direct from Moscow. [45]

† The main satellite ground station in the Far East is located at Petropavlovsk. [49]

based in the Pacific, reportedly a high frequency direction-finding station in Vietnam.[52]

The Soviet Fleet also provides intelligence and communications, fielding tattle-tale vessels which trail U.S. carriers, spyships which sit off U.S. bases such as Guam, and fishing trawlers which gather intelligence wherever the tuna swim. Long-range turboprop maritime reconnaissance aircraft supplement ocean reconnaissance satellites in peacetime.[53]

Achilles Heel

There are many weak points in the Soviet Pacific's defense system. Their biggest problem is having to cross the 15,000 km southern supply route from the Mediterranean through the Indian Ocean and Southeast Asia to the Far East. This west–east sea route is the equivalent of the Panama Canal, except that the Soviet Far East is more dependent on maritime supply and more vulnerable to the effects of interdiction than either coast of the U.S.

The Far East regional distribution system is undeveloped,[54] and there is no high-volume, overland east-west transport system across the Soviet Union. While unclassified figures are incomplete, U.S. naval analysts estimate that the Far East is 80–90 per cent dependent on sealift for cargo imports from the Soviet industrial West and from foreign suppliers. To free themselves from dependence on imports of strategic minerals and raw materials,* the Soviets launched a massive development program in the Far East. Sea transport is undoubtedly still the most efficient link between the resources and consumers in the Far East and the factories of the Soviet West.

---

* We estimate that the supply of Far Eastern regional imports by sealift is five times greater than imports by the overland railroad, which could conceivably supply 2,000 tonnes of war materiel per day in an eastward direction.[55] The major war materiel stocks in the Far East of about 2.2 million tonnes are kept inland in the Komsomolsk region. They are shipped to the coast by rail and river.[56] The Soviet Pacific Fleet underway would use about 7,000–14,000 tonnes of fuel oil each day.[57] Coastal fuel oil storage is not publicly known, but once it was exhausted, daily usage would exceed rail and river resupply from the inland stocks – if the inland stocks, railroad, and river barges survived the outbreak of war. Soviet aircraft also guzzle gas, but even less is known publicly about Soviet jet fuel stocks in the Far East.

While such development may have improved the Soviet economy, it has weakened its strategic position. Economic autarchy does not matter in peace and sealift is vulnerable in war. The Soviet cargo fleet (including jointly owned foreign shipping firms), for example, is the biggest single user of the Suez Canal, which would be vulnerable to supply interruptions in war. Much of the Soviet naval effort, particularly beyond the coast of the Far East, aims to protect cargo ships. U.S. Naval analyst James Westwood underscores the point in his analysis of the Soviet Indian Ocean Squadron in the Gulf of Aden:

Most observers see this as being aimed at harming Western shipping. Few discern it as being aimed at protecting Soviet shipping. Nevertheless, over more than a dozen years, the composition of the Soviet Indian Ocean naval squadron signifies its primary mission. It is consistently composed of ships and aircraft primarily suitable for reconnaissance, surveillance, logistical support, and anti-surface warfare; in short, the naval functions necessary to protect shipping from interference by a hostile navy. This distinction is important because of other possible uses of a forward-deployed naval squadron, but for which its ships and aircraft, in this case, are not suited. These have not been the types and numbers of ships and aircraft useful for attacking Western shipping, antisubmarine warfare, or coercive naval "diplomacy" but, rather, those suited for the mission stated by Yuri Valikenov, Soviet representative to the Seychelles, "to secure our own maritime areas." [58]

Even within the Far East, the U.S. Navy has long recognized that transport to facilities is undeveloped. One Navy analyst concluded in 1956 that "the entire position of the Russians in the eastern Arctic is dependent upon control of the sea lanes along the maritime coast of Far Eastern USSR." He added that unless the Soviets controlled sea lanes in the Pacific, they "not only cannot think realistically of offensive military thrusts in the Far East, they cannot even be certain of being able to supply their own outlying areas." [59]

Admiral Noel Gayler, former Pacific Commander, admitted that "A special case arises in the logistic resupply of the Soviet Far East. Much tonnage traverses the Indian Ocean, and a limited amount crosses the Northern sea route." He hastened to add, however, that "this is not a vital interest for the Soviet Union, in the same sense as sea communications are to the alliance." [60] But the Admiral's comments ignored the Soviet dependence on sealift to supply its armed forces in the event of war. There is simply no denying that sealift is vulnerable – and vital – to the Soviet Far East. As Admiral James Watkins testified in 1984: "Kamchatka is a difficult peninsula. They have no railroads to it. They have to re-supply it by air. It is a very important spot for them, and they are as naked as a jaybird there, and they know it." [61]

The world's "great landpower", in other words, is possibly more dependent on sealift in the Far East than the U.S. and most of its allies. As one U.S. naval analyst told us, the U.S. can simply cut the Soviet Union in half. Since Soviet war materials stockpiled in the Far East are relatively small, the U.S. has only to provoke the Soviet Air Force and Navy into using up its fuel and then blockade resupply. In such conditions, the Soviet armed forces in the Far East might collapse in less than thirty days.

Pacific Command is assuredly aware of this acute Soviet weakness. Indeed, in 1978 the Intelligence Center-Pacific produced a report, *Soviet Far East Logistics*, although it refuses to divulge any of the contents. The U.S. Navy does not like talking about Soviet dependence on sea transport and its vulnerability to a simple blockade, lest it undermine the rationale for a strategy based on ever more sophisticated, high-technology weapon systems.

Bottled Up

Before they can even put to sea in the Pacific, the Soviets must overcome a host of geographical obstacles. Their Far Eastern ports and airfields are fogbound or battered by storms over the summer, and icebound and frozen in the winter. Worst of all, the Soviets lack direct access to the Pacific Ocean from Vladivostok and the Sea of Japan (see Map 16.3). American strategist Anthony Cordesman describes this Achilles heel:

The Pacific fleet is concentrated at Vladivostok, on the Sea of Japan, and Petropavlovsk, in the northwest Pacific Ocean. Forces at Vladivostok have access to the Sea of Japan, which icebreakers can keep open in the winter, but to reach the Pacific Ocean they must pass through one of five straits close to Japan and South Korea – the widest of these is 110 miles wide, and these are waters readily accessible to U.S.–allied forces. Although the fleet at Petropavlovsk has easy

Map 16.3:
Key Choke Points of the Soviet Pacific Fleet

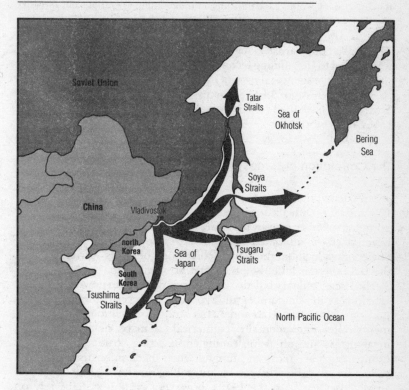

access to the Pacific Ocean, Petropavlovsk is located on the Kamchatka Peninsula, which is remote from the Soviet heartland and not easily resupplied. Thus, the Soviet navy would have difficulty in maintaining operations out of Petropavlovsk unless major sea lines of resupply could be sustained.[62]

The choke points are also highly susceptible to sonar and aerial monitoring* and to U.S. mining technology.[64] If the Soviet Fleet tried to enter the Pacific to wage war, it would have to get past what one analyst calls a "surly lynch mob" of U.S. forces waiting to pounce.[65] Indeed, the Soviets may have to mine the straits and blockade them to keep *out* the U.S. Pacific Fleet![66]

The Correlation of Forces

As an enemy, the Soviet Far East forces have always disappointed the U.S. military. Difficult to provoke into combat and huddling in their homeports 95 per cent of the time, the Soviet Far Eastern forces have never faced the ultimate test of power – war with the U.S. In spite of Soviet bravado about the world "correlation of forces" turning against the U.S., there is little doubt about who would win.

The "true" military balance is a difficult ratio to pin down. Soviet and U.S. forces differ in number and type, and have very different military missions. Moreover, U.S. and Soviet strategic intentions and requirements differ fundamentally. Numerical comparisons are, therefore, meaningless and often misleading in assessing "true" power ratios. Comparisons are more meaningful when made in terms of countervailing forces: submarines *versus* anti-submarine forces, bombers *versus* air defenses, etc.[67] In the 1980s, however, weapon systems rely on immense support infrastructure – such as communications and logistics – which are as important as weapons systems in determining military power balances.

The U.S. Navy appears almost schizophrenic in its public assessments of relative strength, alternately strutting its might and bemoaning its impotence. Testifying before the Senate in 1984, Secretary of the Navy

---

* From SOSUS and rapidly deployable sonar buoys; C-130, B-52, and P-3C aircraft and submarines.[63]

John Lehman exclaimed: "I believe that our margin of [maritime] superiority disappeared at some point in the seventies. Not until we have achieved our force structure and readiness increases by the end of the decade will we regain it." [68]

Yet Lehman himself has pointed to America's forty-year lead in aircraft carrier technology.[69] As for anti-submarine forces, the Soviets not only lack the territory and the technology for long-range underwater hydrophone nets to snare U.S. nuclear submarines, but U.S. attack submarines are far superior to Soviet models. As Pentagon Anti-Submarine Warfare specialist Gerald Cann explains: "The position our submarine force has enjoyed for the last twenty years is that they were able to detect the other guy so far away that if we were to engage him and actually shoot, there is a high probability that he never would have known what was happening until the torpedo hit him." [70]

The schizophrenia may stem from the changing political objectives which underlie particular military assessments. After extolling the virtues of the U.S. Navy before Congress in 1984, Admiral Watkins, Chief of Naval Operations, was asked about Lehman's insistence that the Navy was inferior to the Soviets. Watkins replied: "In comparing our major warfare areas versus the missions required in the execution of the Navy's maritime strategy, I would say our strengths ... would include *all* major naval warfare areas." [71] The U.S. Navy, in other words, is simply superior to the Soviet fleet. Only two years before, Watkins – then Pacific Fleet Commander – played the dubious numbers game of "net assessment" when he reported to Congress that while the U.S. would win a head-on naval confrontation with the Soviet Fleet in the Pacific, the outcome is only a "toss-up" when respective readiness and logistical capabilities were factored in.[72] The Admiral then followed through with a predictable pitch for funds: "I cannot yet assure you of victory in the Pacific against our most likely opponent. I need several more battle groups to assure victory and clearly establish Pacific maritime superiority." [73] The Admiral's plea recalls a warning by Peter Karsten, author of a classic study of the U.S. naval aristocracy: "We must always be suspicious of men in blue double-breasted suits with gold on their sleeves who want us to buy them big boats and things that go bang to save us all from evil." [74]

In introspective moments, the U.S. Navy acknowledges its own self-confidence. In an official *Naval Operational Planning* manual, for example, the Navy provided its officers with a model calculation for planning a campaign strategy. The example in the current manual* – a protracted, global war with the U.S.S.R. with "limited" use of nuclear weapons, a favorite nightmare of naval strategists – is described in detail:

GREEN [Soviet Union] and WHITE [U.S.] have been at war for eighteen months. GREEN, an Asiatic–European coalition, has occupied the entire mainland of Asia and has overrun Europe, excluding France, Portugal, Spain, and Great Britain. Africa, the Middle East, and Pacific Islands of strategic importance are still held or controlled by WHITE. At present both sides are executing major efforts in France and at the Turkish–European border ... During the first month of war, WHITE Aleutian Island and Alaskan bases were destroyed by nuclear attack. Kodiak Island, with the only remaining major WHITE naval base in the Alaskan area, was left undamaged. Efforts in other areas have prevented WHITE from rebuilding the destroyed advanced bases. GREEN has occupied [the Alaskan island of] Attu without opposition but has not exploited this acquisition. Until now WHITE has considered GREEN occupation of Attu to be of minor significance ... Recent intelligence indicates that GREEN plans to establish advanced air and naval bases on Attu Island. It has been reliably reported that GREEN is assembling advanced base construction units in the Petropavlovsk area for this purpose. It is believed that these units will be transported to Attu by a strongly protected convoy ...[75]

The manual calculates that the U.S. Pacific Fleet, operating only from Kodiak Island in the Aleutians and the U.S. mainland, is still able to mount an effective counterattack with an aircraft carrier group supported by attack submarines. The sample calculation shows that the U.S. battlegroup can be supplied in the North Pacific for three months. Despite the great distance and proximity to the U.S.S.R., the Navy estimates that it can prevent the GREEN (Soviet) forces from operating – even close to their own coastal waters. Even *without forward bases*, the Navy projects that it can suppress Soviet land-based air cover for naval forces at Komandorski Island and the Kamchatka Peninsula, halt the hypothetical Soviet expedition to reinforce Attu Island as an advance base, and take Attu Island back for itself![76] (See Table 16.2.)

Overall, it is difficult to disagree with defense analyst Anthony Cordesman that "There is no doubt that the West must falter as a result

---

* The manual was issued in 1978 and is still current in 1985.

of its own contradictions if the Soviet Navy is to overcome the present obstacles to launching any successful conflict against the United States." [77]

Allied Power

The relative weakness of the Soviet Union becomes stark when the naval and air forces of allies are added to the superpower lineup in the Pacific. In a 1978 comparison, Barry Blechman and Robert Berman demonstrate that the U.S. and its East Asian allies: (1) outnumber the Soviet Pacific Fleet and its single ally in East Asia (north Korea) by a 5:1 ratio; (2) displace nearly twice as many tonnes; and (3) outgun the Soviet bloc in virtually every naval armament.* [79] In air capabilities as well, the U.S. clearly outguns the Soviet Union. In addition to its own impressive airpower in the West Pacific, the U.S. can also call on its allies. Japan alone can scramble more tactical air power, especially F-15s, than all the U.S. fighters in Japan, Korea, and the Philippines combined.† [81]

The one deficiency of the U.S. in the Pacific is landpower – the ground troops needed for a land war. While the U.S. cannot hope to match the Soviet Union in landpower, the alliance with China has

---

* Adding Australian, New Zealand, and Southeast Asian navies on the U.S. side and those of Vietnam on the Soviet side to the comparison cited only further favors the U.S. All those ratios would worsen dramatically for the Soviets if the U.S. blockaded the Straits out of the Sea of Japan. [78]

† It is ironic that the U.S. analysts often cite the arrival in 1976 of a defecting Soviet Foxbat MiG-25 high-speed fighter aircraft at a Japanese airfield without interception as evidence of Soviet offensive capabilities. Aside from the fact that the pilot was *fleeing* from the Soviet Union, hardly a terrifying image, they fail to mention that the Foxbat, the *enfant terrible* of the Soviet Air Force, had nearly crashed from fuel shortage. U.S. research on the plane revealed that the Pentagon had overestimated its combat radius sevenfold, that its engines melted at high speed, that it lacked low-altitude, look-down radar, and high-altitude missiles, and that it was crudely constructed from what a U.S. Air Force General called "ancient" technology. Like the Kiev "aircraft carrier", the *bête noire* of the Soviet Air Force turned out to be much less fearsome than depicted. As a U.S. Congressperson concluded: "No U.S. F-15 or F-16 pilot need fear the Foxbat unless he is asleep, radically out-numbered, or an utter boob." [80]

Table 16.2:
U.S./Soviet Comparative Strength in "Sample Operation Problem": Protracted Nuclear War in Pacific

A. Strength Factors

WHITE (U.S.)

1. Freedom of action afforded by carrier mobility and mobile support.

2. Numerical air superiority in the objective area.

3. Ability to move to areas of favorable weather for conduct of air operations.

4. Surprise in timing of air strikes

5. Numerical superiority in all-weather aircraft.

6. Superiority in missile anti-aircraft defense.

B. Weakness Factors

1. The greatest distance of the objective area from supporting bases makes operation dependent upon underway replenishment.

2. Limited air reconnaissance capability in the Kamchatka area.

GREEN (Soviet Union)

1. Superiority in number of ships and firepower.

2. Adequate shore-based logistic support.

3. Can move towards Attu under protection of advancing weather front.

4. Submarine superiority.

1. Lack of continuous air defense aircraft over convoys and covering force.

2. Reliance on Komandorski based aircraft for defense of Attu area.

Table 16.2: (cont)

3. Lack of carriers.

Notes: Assumes U.S. lost forward bases in Northeast Asia. A current comparison would add superiority of Tomahawk cruise missiles to overwhelm air defenses to U.S. side.

Source: Chief of Naval Operations, "Sample Solution of an Operation Problem", *Naval Operational Planning*, NWP 11 (Rev. C), Appendix F, Washington, D.C., 1978.

largely rectified the imbalance. The U.S. embrace of China, however, has distressed some of America's Southeast Asian allies. Ultimately the U.S.–Sino marriage of convenience may end in divorce over disagreements on Taiwan, Korea, and South Asia.[82] Nonetheless, the U.S. seems confident that the Chinese will remain antagonistic to the Soviets.[83] While Soviet ground forces are better armed and organized than the Chinese, a Sino–Soviet war could embroil the Soviets in an endless landwar. The U.S., as Pentagon analysts put it, is like a lamb sitting in a tree watching two lions tear each other apart.

What strategic value the Soviet Union gains from its East Asian allies, north Korea and Vietnam, is a matter for debate – and public posturing – within Pacific Command. Even its former Commander, Admiral Crowe, cannot seem to make up his mind. While he claimed in November 1983 that "North Korea is a relatively independent entity," [84] he referred to it three months later as Moscow's "surrogate." [85] In an interview in 1984, he claimed that north Korea is an unreliable and ungrateful Soviet "ally", but added that Kim Il Sung is "a very independent type – and consequently very dangerous, because he's so independent and uncontrollable." [86]

In addition to a paucity of reliable allies in the Pacific, the Soviets have no economic influence.[87] The U.S. is a major trading partner of ten states that collectively account for almost 90 per cent of the Asian GNP. The Soviet Union, by contrast, accounted for a much smaller fraction of Asia's trade.* While the Soviets receive the bulk of Vietnamese and north Korean foreign trade, their major trading partner in Asia, Japan, has tilted economically toward their enemy, China.[89]

The U.S. and its allied elites in the Pacific often claim that alignment with the West is required for protection from the Soviets. Soviet economic and military weakness, however, betrays the claim. Indeed, if Pacific states could muster the strength to resist alignment with the U.S., they would be more than capable of resisting the symmetric pressure from a militarily and economically weaker Soviet Union.

---

* The U.S. accounted for between 5 and 24 per cent of the imports of fourteen Asian countries in 1979, and 3–36 per cent of the same countries' exports. The Soviets accounted for 0–6 per cent of the imports and 0–11 per cent of the exports of the same countries.[88]

Base Race?

Although the Soviet Union cannot directly "threaten" the Pacific, it does not follow that it is always a "good neighbor." The Soviet Union deploys forces in the Pacific, the character of which reflects competing domestic foreign policy lines as well as service interests.[90]

Like the U.S. Navy, the Soviet Navy seeks foreign bases and access to forward ports. To demonstrate Soviet power, its fleet conducts war games in the Pacific and Indian Oceans. Former Pacific Commander Admiral Crowe has argued that this forward naval deployment is a Soviet strategy of substituting military power and intimidation for political and economic influence.[91] As Ralph Cossa, his former Executive Assistant, argues: "It is not so much what they can do in wartime, but the peacetime impact of these aircraft and vessels" which worries the U.S.[92]

Probably the most important bases under Soviet control are those on the disputed Kurile Islands just north of Japan. Acquired as booty from World War II, the islands enable the Soviets to control the area north of the Kuriles Strait into the Pacific. Since the beginning of the new Cold War in 1978, the Soviets have refurbished airfields, deployed forty MiG fighters, and stationed naval infantry in the Kuriles. In light of the U.S. offensive in the Northwest Pacific, this forward deployment appears to be permanent.[93]

Another key aspect of Soviet forward deployment is its access to naval, air, and communication facilities in Vietnam. Through these bases, the Soviet Union can open a southern front from Vietnam against China, and protect the supply route via the Indian Ocean. Since 1978, the Soviets have maintained an impressive arsenal in Vietnam: a signals intelligence station; military aircraft at Da Nang and Cam Ranh Bay;[94] up to twenty submarine and surface warships and a floating dry dock; and two squadrons of MiG fighters at Kep Air Base north of Hanoi.[95]

The Soviets also rotate long-range bombers through Vietnam.* But as Lieutenant-Colonel Ralph Cossa admits, "We are still talking about a handful of aircraft, a dozen TU-16s." While the bombers *could* mine Southeast Asian waters, so *could* American bombers.† Given the mutual

---

* No Backfire bombers have flown to Vietnam as of mid-1985.[96]
† U.S. B-52s have even practiced such mining.

need of both superpowers for transit between the Pacific and Indian Oceans, *why* either superpower would conduct this operation remains obscure. As Cossa notes of the Soviet aircraft in Vietnam, "Once a protracted war starts, they are vulnerable." [97] They represent only a very marginal *military* threat to either U.S. or Chinese forces in the region.

Soviet forces in Vietnam are vulnerable to the U.S. Navy's 7th Fleet and to airpower from Guam, Okinawa, and the Philippines, as well as to the powerful Southern Chinese coastal navy.[98] While they appear to be entrenched in Vietnam, the Soviets' forward position may be as tenuous as their access to Egypt or Somalia turned out to be.* If Sino–Soviet tensions ease, the Soviets may rethink spending a billion dollars a year to maintain a second front of limited military value. While the China–Vietnam antagonism is complex, the Chinese might soften their anti-Vietnam stance to encourage Vietnam to evict the Soviets. The independent Vietnamese, anxious to cultivate better relations with ASEAN states and China, might well oblige. The Soviets would then find themselves unceremoniously deported from Vietnam like a guest worker with an expired visa.[100]

Access to Vietnamese bases drains as well as amplifies Soviet military power. Each year, the access reportedly costs the Soviet Union about one billion dollars in economic and military aid to Vietnam – nearly as much as they provided in ten years of the Vietnam War. Added to this is the political cost of alienating other Southeast Asian states.

In addition to Vietnam, the Soviets also attempted to rent a "fishing" base on Addu Atoll in the Maldive Islands in 1979. Only 570 km from the U.S. base at Diego Garcia, Addu Atoll sports a 2,500 m British-built airfield. Failing in this maneuver, Soviet warships in the Indian Ocean spend a good deal of time anchored at mid-ocean buoys to conserve fuel,† and occasionally visit neutral or accessible ports in India, Ethiopia, and South Yemen. The Commander-in-Chief of the Soviet Navy, Admiral Gorshkov, likes to explain to his party comrades that visiting Soviet warships "are clearly and convincingly spreading the ideas of the

---

* After two decades of Soviet support and presence in Egypt, Sadat summarily expelled the Soviets from all facilities in 1972.[99]

† Carefully listed by U.S. intelligence statistics as Soviet active shipdays in the Indian Ocean.

Leninist peace-loving policy of the Communist Party and the Soviet government through many countries of the world." [101] Most Third World elites, however, probably look upon the visiting rust-buckets with skepticism, and are well aware that they are ill suited for combat.[102]

Although the Soviet Pacific Fleet operates at a much lower tempo than the U.S. Navy, it nonetheless conducts exercises. The most memorable, the global *Okean* exercise, was held in 1975 and involved four Soviet anti-submarine and anti-carrier task forces in the Pacific, as well as similar activity in the Indian Ocean.[103] It has also engaged in coercive naval diplomacy with the Chinese Navy in the Pacific, most importantly when the Soviet Pacific Fleet sent twenty surface warships and some submarines off the Chinese coast in 1978–79 to warn China to limit its invasion of Vietnam.[104] That the Chinese might have provoked the Soviets into attacking seems unlikely – but the prospect of the two premier Communist navies sinking each other can hardly have frightened the U.S. 7th Fleet or its allies.

American military analysts have carefully analyzed Soviet naval forward activity for evidence of the aggressive intent ascribed to them by navalists such as Admiral Crowe and Navy Secretary Lehman. They concluded that the Soviet Fleet has not and cannot project power similar to U.S. interventions in Korea and Indochina. The Soviet Fleet has never been used to support a Third World ally's offensive warfare or to prop up a beleaguered ally. Rear Admiral John Butts, director of Naval Intelligence, has stated that "[T]he Soviet Navy still lacks the extensive logistics chain necessary to support and supply the equipment requirement for sustained, distant operations." [105] The Soviet Navy is irrelevant,[106] even in Afghanistan where the Soviets have trapped themselves in a Vietnam-like quagmire.[107]

While a navy is the main force for an aspiring superpower, army and air forces are also tools of coercive diplomacy and occupation. The Soviets have used conventional ground forces to repel Chinese challenges to their borders. During the 1970s, the Soviets airlifted Cuban troops to support allies in Angola and Ethiopia. Nonetheless, the Soviets have been sparing in their use of combat personnel outside of areas immediately adjacent to their borders.* [110]

---

* Besides its role in Eastern Europe, direct Soviet military involvement has been limited to its role in advising or manning air defenses in Korea, Manchuria, Vietnam, Egypt, Sudan,

As many communist parties have discovered, Soviet military and economic aid to its allies has been slow and its political support unreliable. When Soviet support is available, it is usually rather small compared to U.S. aid,* and aims to bolster the *status quo* rather than promote social and political revolution.[112]

Far Eastern Nightmare

For American strategists used to relying on forward bases in the Pacific, it seems obvious, indeed inevitable, that the Soviets *must* do likewise – that is, they must seek to enhance their influence through military expansion. This assumption, however, is not borne out by Soviet capability or behaviour. In a study for the U.S. Congress, Michael MccGwire of the Brookings Institution concluded that Soviet activity outside its national security zone (Soviet territory and immediately adjacent territory) "does not support the hypothesis of imperial colonialism based on military force."[113] A Rand Corporation study on Soviet Pacific strategy concurs: "A Soviet Grand Design for Asia is almost certainly illusory."[114]

Indeed, far from power growing out of the gun barrels of the Soviet military complex in the Pacific, the Far East has taken on a nightmarish quality for the Soviets.[115] By 1954, the Soviets lost their only forward naval base, at Port Arthur and Darien in China.[116] In 1966, Soviet influence dissipated in Indonesia with the massacre of hundreds of thousands of Indonesian leftists in a U.S.-supported coup. In 1977, the Soviets were evicted from their Indian Ocean facilities in Somalia with less than a week's notice.

By the early 1970s, the Soviet position in the Far East looked more favorable. The U.S. appeared to be disengaging from the Asian mainland, Japan was not actively anti-Soviet, and China was consumed by internal political divisions.[117] The Soviets did not consolidate any

---

Iraq, and airlifting supplies to Vietnam, Laos, India, Ethiopia.[108] In all cases (except Egypt in 1973), this presence served to defend the sovereignty and territorial integrity of a Soviet ally rather than to support offensives against a third party. Often, this Soviet support ended up supporting the same party as the U.S. in the local conflict.[109]

* Soviet expenditure on the Vietnam War totalled about $1.7 billion versus U.S. costs of $112 billion.[111]

advantage, however, nor fill the region's post-Vietnam "power vacuum". Indeed, it was a reinvigorated U.S., in alliance with China, which was the ultimate beneficiary of these changes.[118] Furthermore, rather than contemplating an invasion, Moscow was urging Japanese capitalists to invest in underdeveloped Siberia, a policy which would have *increased* Western leverage over Soviet foreign policy.[119]

Soviet forward deployment in Vietnam and its military build-up in Northeast Asia began only after 1978. By this time, a resurgent U.S. had enlisted China into an anti-Soviet alliance. Japan, too, had swung actively into the U.S.-led anti-Soviet camp and launched a military build-up of its own. Under U.S. and Chinese pressure, the Japanese withdrew from most joint projects in Siberia.

Viewed objectively, the Soviet forward deployment seems more defensive than offensive. As Michael MccGwire explains, if one looks at the world through a Soviet rather than a U.S. strategic prism, a rather different picture emerges:

The Soviets do not have the advantage of 3,000 miles of ocean on one side and 5,000 miles of ocean on the other, nor do they enjoy the luxury of overwhelming predominance in their hemisphere. Standing with their back to the Urals, facing west, they see the NATO alliance curving around their flanks, with a fully restored Germany in the center. Turning east, they see 4,500 miles of border flanking one billion Chinese, and beyond that their traditional enemy Japan. In both directions they see U.S. forces deployed forward in considerable strength. To the south, meanwhile, they have the worry of Muslim irredentism.* [121]

Former Secretary of Defense Harold Brown adds that the Soviets' situation is East Asia is weak and declining:

To the Soviets, these three nations [U.S., Japan, and China] represent the world's still leading and adversary superpower, the U.S.S.R.'s competitor for the role of second-largest industrial power, and the world's most populous state, bordering the U.S.S.R.'s own most underpopulated and resource-rich

---

* Exhibiting some rare realistic empathy, General Nathan Twining, Chief of Staff of the United States Air Force, admitted candidly in 1956, "I often think that I would hate to see our country . . . today, the United States, rimmed with three or four hundred Russian bases in Canada and New Mexico. It would be a pretty bad situation." [120]

territories. The prospect of such an alliance must be truly a nightmare for the Soviets.[122]

Thus encircled, the Soviets must find the Far East more of a defensive liability than an offensive asset. Beset by enemies on every side, the Soviets may even *prefer* a forward-deployed U.S. military – and a subordinate Japan and south Korea – to the threat of an independent, remilitarized Japan and unified Korea on its border.

What the Soviet Union probably cannot accept however, is a U.S. military poised to strike from forward bases in the Pacific. It is this *imbalance* of power among the superpowers in the Asia–Pacific region that contains the seeds of nuclear war and the true "threat" to the region.

Soviet Backfire bomber with missile
(Pentagon)

SEVENTEEN ☆
"SOCIALIST BOMB"

We will never be the first to let such weapons fly. I will still have time to respond. There will be no more United States. But we will still get it in the neck.

—President Leonid Brezhnev, 1978[1]

Use of nuclear weapons against insignificant secondary objectives contradicts the very nature of this weapon. The selection of targets should be approached with special care and nuclear weapons should not be thrown around like hand grenades.

—A. Sidorenko, 1970[2]

Inferior to the United States in conventional weapons, as well as economically and politically, the Soviet Union relies on nuclear weapons as the ultimate guarantor of its territorial integrity. Despite its relatively primitive nuclear technology, its geographical disadvantages,* and its vulnerable, land-based nuclear forces, the Soviet Union can annihilate the U.S. in any conceivable nuclear war. By calling on the simple, massive destructive *power* of its nuclear weapons, the Soviets can negate the greater accuracy and flexibility of the U.S. nuclear arsenal. Unequal in other dimensions of power, the two superpowers have nonetheless reached a nuclear standoff – a terrifying stalemate called "parity."

Largely in response to American nuclear deployment, the Soviet

---

* Such as lack of warm-water ports with direct oceanic egress for missile submarines.

Union deploys an enormous nuclear arsenal in the Far East and the Pacific, which it uses primarily but not *solely* for defensive purposes. Like the U.S., and more recently China, the Soviets bear a heavy responsibility for the risks that nuclear weapons impose upon the region.

Nuclear Sledgehammer

Confronted with forward-deployed U.S. nuclear bombs and ballistic missiles, the Soviet Union has fortified its Far Eastern region with an array of nuclear weapons. Like a mighty club, this arsenal is ready to slam down on U.S. forces in the Pacific, as well as to bludgeon China.

Like the U.S., the Soviet Union's nuclear capability is based on ballistic and cruise missiles. Normally, the Soviets keep these nuclear weapons (see Table 17.1) forward-deployed in the Pacific aboard submarines and surface warships.* Two Yankee-class submarines, carrying SS-N-6 ballistic missiles with a firing range of 3,000 km, are normally sailing in the Pacific. One is stationed off the U.S. West Coast, ready to fire away at coastal cities. A second is normally *en route* to or from this station and the Soviet Far East bases, but beyond the range where it can hit the U.S. (see Map 10.2).† [4] Twelve Delta-class submarines, which carry SS-N-8 ballistic missiles capable of hitting the U.S. from 9,000 km, stay in port or venture into the Japan or Okhotsk Seas.‡ In a nuclear war, the Soviet Fleet may try to "break out" some of its Yankee and Delta submarines past U.S. anti-submarine barriers into the mid-Pacific.

---

* We estimate that in "peacetime", the Soviets deploy in the Pacific about 115 submarine-launched ballistic missiles, 50–60 nuclear-tipped cruise missiles, and 240-odd assorted anti-submarine warfare depth charges and rockets, surface-to-air missiles, and anti-ship cruise missiles, totalling about 400 routinely forward-deployed nuclear weapons. [3]

† Of course, the Yankees are within range of Alaska and U.S. bases in the northwest Pacific as they sail to or from the East Pacific station.

‡ Before 1966, Soviet ballistic-missile submarines were mostly withheld from forward deployment. They were utilized instead as a reserve force in a nuclear war to be fought with land-based missiles by the Soviet Strategic Rocket Force (SRF). After 1966, the ballistic-missile submarines were mostly held in port as insurance against a U.S. preemptive attack on the SRF, and to reduce the risk that U.S. anti-submarine capabilities could preempt the submarines as well. [5]

In addition to the Delta and Yankee submarines, about nine old Golf II- and Hotel II-class ballistic submarines are sailing in the Pacific.* Given the short range (1,200 km) of their SS-N-5 ballistic missiles, these submarines are probably dedicated to attacking "theater" targets. Rarely sent far beyond the Seas of Japan and Okhotsk,[6] they are apparently prone to engine failure. In September 1984, for example, a stricken Golf II submarine was sighted belching smoke 200 km north of Japan, and had to be towed to Vladivostok.[7] Apparently, such incidents are not uncommon. Journalist David Kaplan has reported that the U.S. Navy maintains a classified file called "Submarine Accidents: A Continuing Problem for the Soviet Navy."[8]

In addition to ballistic missile submarines, the Soviet Union also deploys a fleet of ninety-odd diesel-powered subs which fire anti-ship nuclear cruise missiles and torpedoes. This "mosquito fleet" was developed in the 1960s, when an increase in the range of naval planes put American aircraft carriers beyond the reach of Soviet land-based and air-delivered ballistic missiles.†[9] In a war, the mosquito fleet would try to surround a U.S. aircraft carrier and launch a simultaneous 360° strike with the cruise missiles, which have a range up to 570 km.

At any given time, there may be one or two of these Soviet attack submarines prowling the Pacific, several more in the Indian Ocean, and up to seven each in the South China, Japan, and Okhotsk Seas.[10] Like their ballistic-missile counterparts, the Soviet cruise missile submarines seem to have a penchant for self-destruction at sea. In June 1983, for example, a nuclear-powered Charlie submarine sank with its crew of ninety off the Kamchatka Peninsula.[11]

The Soviet Union also sports a surface fleet, which packs a smaller nuclear punch than the submarines. Surface ships carry a small number of nuclear-armed cruise missiles, and an unknown number of nuclear anti-submarine depth bombs and torpedoes. Until October 1984, when the new SS-NX-21 cruise missile with a 2,500 km range was reportedly

---

* These are the names given by Western intelligence for the Soviet classes of weapons.

† For economic and political reasons, Soviet Premier Nikita Khruschev blocked the development of a big surface fleet in the 1950s to counter U.S. aircraft carriers ready to launch offshore nuclear attacks. Khruschev opted instead for a strategy based on air-delivered nuclear bombs and land-based ballistic missiles against U.S. aircraft carriers.

deployed, all Soviet surface- and submarine-launched nuclear cruise missiles were aimed at naval ships rather than land targets.[12]

Composed of small, lightly protected, and generally expendable warships which lack staying power, the Soviet Pacific Fleet relies on nuclear weapons to compensate for its shortcomings. Like his American counterparts, Admiral Gorshkov, head of the Soviet Navy, has repeatedly said that the "struggle for the first salvo" will determine the outcome of a superpower war at sea.[13] In an all-out nuclear attack, the forward-deployed nuclear fleet will be reinforced by land-based ballistic missiles, long distance bombers, and additional nuclear-armed ships.

The Soviets also forward-deploy a relatively minimal infrastructure for nuclear war operations in the Pacific. Deployed on ships and reconnaissance aircraft, Soviet C^3I^* systems for nuclear war rely heavily on satellites for targeting and communications.[14] It is highly doubtful, however, that the Soviet Union can conduct a naval nuclear war without inadvertently destroying its own naval communications and intelligence systems, especially if the battle is at relatively close quarters.†[15]

Another aspect of Soviet forward deployment is the use of the Pacific as a missile test range. The Soviets mostly test-fire missiles into a target site in the Kamchatka Peninsula, but on occasion, they aim them to splash down in the Pacific. The impact points since the late 1970s lie in an arc reaching from Wake Island to the Alaskan Peninsula.‡ In December 1984, for example, the Soviet Union announced two week-long exclusion zones in the central Pacific Ocean for a test of a multiple warhead missile. One zone was 190 km across, centered about 500 km northeast of Midway Island, with a similar zone centered about 500 km southeast from Midway.[18]

---

* Command/control and communications/intelligence.

† Due to the side effects of airburst nuclear weapons on fragile antennae and the destruction caused by electromagnetic pulses.

‡ The Soviets declared 3 ballistic missile test exclusion zones (in which more than one test may be conducted) in the Pacific Ocean in 1977, 3 in 1978, 5 in 1981, 3 in 1982, 4 in 1984, and 1 up to June 1985.[16] The U.S. currently launches about 20 long-range missile tests into the Pacific per year[17] (see Chapter 13).

Rocket Rattling

Most of the Soviet nuclear arsenal aimed at the Pacific is kept at home in the warheads of intermediate-range ballistic missiles. SS-4 ballistic missiles with a 2 megaton warhead were first installed along the Sino–Soviet border in 1966, and were originally aimed at China (see Map 16.2).[19] Indeed, the only known Soviet nuclear threat against a Third World state occurred in a Sino–Soviet border confrontation in 1969. A Soviet broadcast on March 8, 1969 reported that: "The rocket troops showed at the important exercises just completed that the formidable weapons entrusted to them by the motherland for defense of the Far Eastern frontiers are in strong, reliable hands. Let any provocateurs remember this."*[21] To add weight to the threats, the Soviets deployed early models of the new SS-11 missiles along the China border in 1969,[22] and reinforced and replaced them with more sophisticated, variable-range SS-11s in 1972.[23] The SS-11 initially carried a 1 megaton warhead, which it could deliver over 11,000 km with twice the accuracy of the old SS-4s.†

While these Soviet nuclear threats may have tempered Chinese border provocations, they also drove China to develop nuclear weapons, and prompted China's de facto alliance with the U.S. and Japan.[26] The use of the nuclear threat in the Far East eventually proved extremely counter-productive – a lesson not lost on the Kremlin.[27]

SS-20: "A Real Dog of a Missile"

In 1978, the Soviet Union upgraded its nuclear arsenal in the Far East with new mobile SS-20 missiles. Transported on giant trucks, the SS-20s are less vulnerable to attack than the old SS-11s and are propelled by

---

* Unlike U.S. nuclear threats,[20] this Soviet rhetoric was not accompanied by an observable state of increased alert or mobilization of actual delivery vehicles. The Soviet Strategic Rocket Forces (SRF) were created in 1959 as the premier nuclear fighting force. The SRF commander takes precedence over the other military services. SRF commands the long- and medium-range nuclear missiles in the Far East.

† SS-11 missiles were supplemented by a small training contingent of SS-14/15 missiles each of which could lob a 1 megaton warhead up to 7,600 km.[24] The SS-11s replaced seventy SS-4 and SS-5 missiles dismantled at this time.[25]

Table 17.1:
Soviet Nuclear Weapons

Type	Range (km) Delivery System	Launch Platform
Missiles		
SS-11, Mod 1,3[a]	8,800–10,500[a]	Fixed Silo
SS-20[a]	4,800	Mobile Ground
SLBM[b]	1,400–8,300[a]	Submarines
Anti-ship Cruise[c]	111–555[a]	Warships
Anti-ship Cruise[d]	250–1,000[a]	Bombers
Land-attack Cruise[e]	3,000	Warships
SAM (land-launched)[f]	34–280[a]	Ground
SAM (naval)[g]	23–67[a]	Warships
SCUD B/C	290–370	Mobile Ground
SCALEBOARD SS-12	900	Mobile Ground
SSC-1	450	Ground
Bombs		
Short-range gravity[a]	300–1,900[a]	Bombers[h]
Long-range gravity[a]	5,500–8,300[a]	Bombers[j]
Battlefield		
152, 240, 253 mm shells	18–30[a]	Mobile Ground
FROG 7/SS-21[k]	120–450	Mobile Ground
Anti-submarine Warfare		
Depth bombs	n/a	Bombers, helis
SS-N-15[l]	37–48	Submarines
SUW-N-1[m]	30	Warships
533mm Torpedoes	16	Submarines

Notes: n/a = not applicable. Not all these nuclear weapons have been confirmed as present as in Soviet Far East, especially the battlefield missiles. a. Range covers least and greatest across all delivery systems where more than one in a weapon category. b. Submarine-launched ballistic missiles, SS-N-5/6/8/17/18/20. c. SS-N-3A-B-C, 7, 9, 12, 22. d. AS-2, 3, 4, 5, 6, 11, 15 fired from Backfire, Bear, Bison bombers e. S-N-21 f. SA-1, 2, 5, 10, range is slant miles g. SA-N- 1, 2, 3, 6, 7 h. Fencers, Fitters, Fishbeds i. Estimated j. Backfires, Badgers, Blinders, Beagles, Bears, Mails, Bisons k. Artillery rocket l. Submarine-launched rocket m. Anti-submarine rocket

Sources: W. Arkin and J. Sands, "The Soviet Nuclear Stockpile," *Arms Control today*, volume 14, no 5, June 1984, p. 4; W. Arkin *et al*, "Nuclear Weapons," in *SIPRI Yearbook 1985*, Taylor and Francis, London, 1985, pp. 56–64; R. Berman and J. Baker, *Soviet Strategic Forces*, Brookings Institution, Washington DC, 1982, pp. 102–105; General Dynamics, *The World's Missile Systems*, Pomona, California, 1982; N. Polmar, *Guide to the Soviet Navy*, Naval Institute Press, Annapolis, Maryland, 1983, pp. 348–369; J. Collins, *U.S.-Soviet Military Balance, 1980- 1985*, Pergamon-Brasseys, New Jersey, 1985, pp. 171–199.

solid fuel, which is more reliable than liquid fuel. The SS-20 can carry up to three highly accurate warheads.* Unlike the "triplet" warheads of the late-model SS-11, which could only straddle a single target "shotgun-style", the SS-20 warheads can be aimed independently at up to three targets.[29]

The U.S. credits the SS-20 with an accuracy† of 750 m and a range of 7,500 km when it carries one 50 kiloton warhead. With three 600 kiloton warheads, the attributed range drops to 5,700 km – still sufficient to hit U.S. bases as far south as the Philippines.[30] The SS-20's solid propellants, however, tend to burn unevenly, and the missile is probably much less accurate than generally asserted.[31] Indeed, one U.S. Air Force officer called the SS-20 "a real dog of a missile", adding that "it was just no good." [32]

Technical problems aside, the SS-20s provide more accuracy and flexibility and less vulnerability than the SS-11s. But their deployment apparently took place as part of a "routine nuclear modernization." [33] At U.S. insistence, the 1972 Strategic Arms Limitation Treaty placed no limits on U.S. forward-deployed short- or medium-range nuclear weapons in Europe or the Far East, such as land-based F-111 bombers, aircraft carriers, or cruise missiles.[34] By the same token, SALT I did not constrain the Soviets from deploying the home-based, medium-range SS-20.[35]

In 1979, however, the SS-20 became embroiled in political conflicts between the U.S., Western Europe, and U.S.S.R. over the terms of SALT II. Fearful that U.S.–Soviet arms limitation agreements might leave them weakened *politically*, the West Europeans maneuvered to obtain fresh U.S. commitments to deploy Pershing and cruise missiles by pointing to the Soviet "build-up" of SS-20s.[36] While their primary concern was SS-20 deployment in Europe, the Western allies also pointed to the Asian-based SS-20s which, though clearly aimed at China, could be moved west via the Trans-Siberian Railway and aimed at Europe.[37]

In 1980, the Commander-in-Chief Pacific fuelled the debate when he

---

* The SS-20 can also be reloaded in principle, but as the intense heat from the launch of one missile probably precludes reloading for several hours, in wartime it is practically a single-shot launcher.[28]

† That is, a Circular Error Probable or radius around the target point within which 50 per cent of the warheads will fall, in this case, 750 m.

won permission to publicize the previously classified Asian SS-20 deployment.[38] CINCPAC used the new information to fan Japanese fears that the Soviets were building-up in the Far East as a response to SALT II. Although the SS-20s added little to the old "threat" posed by the SS-11s, for domestic political reasons Japan's resurgent right-wing politicians were only too willing to be frightened. In July 1985, Japanese officials argued that "It would be unfair for the United States to reach settlement [on SS-20s] in Europe without doing anything about those in Asia. European SS-20s are mobile and easily transportable and are a threat to us." [39]

The Soviet Union, in turn, appears to have launched a more rapid Far East build-up aimed at splitting Japan from its NATO allies. In 1983, for example, the Soviets claimed that the SS-20s were a countermeasure to *U.S.* (not Chinese) nuclear forces, and told Japanese officials that there was "nothing to fear if it avoided entanglement in United States military strategy." [40] By early 1985, 163 SS-20 launchers[41] were positioned at two sites in Western Mongolia, and at two sites on the Mongolian border east of Lake Baikal* – ready to strike a broad arc encompassing China, the Aleutians, and Southeast Asia.[44]

Nuclear Shadows

Although the U.S. has consistently led the arms race,† it is clear that the Soviet leadership, like its American counterpart, has long exceeded the force required for "minimum deterrence"‡ and has used its nuclear arsenal to assert "Great Power" status.

---

* According to the Stockholm International Peace Research Institute, the SS-20s were based near Novosibirsk, Drovyanaya, and Olovyannaya.[42] A new site is reportedly being prepared in April 1985.[43]

† The U.S. developed and used nuclear weapons in World War II in part to contain Soviet power in the Far East; quickly encircled the U.S.S.R. with bomber bases; deployed medium-range ballistic cruise missiles and bombers on the shores of the U.S.S.R. while blocking equivalent deployments by the U.S.S.R. in Cuba; deployed more intercontinental ballistic missiles in the 1960s than could be justified militarily, and then placed multiple warheads on those missiles well before the U.S.S.R.; erected a global anti-submarine capability;[45] and has recently shifted the nuclear arms race to space.

‡ "Minimum deterrence" is the notion that a ceiling may be set on the nuclear arsenal equal to the minimum number necessary to credibly threaten nuclear retaliation to a first

Just as the U.S. arsenal is justified as vital for the protection of democracy against "totalitarianism", the Soviet nuclear force is characterized as necessary to protect socialism by containing U.S. imperialism. "At the present time," Soviet analysts argue, "the *principal* means for restraining imperialist aggressors *in all regions* of the world is the ability of the U.S.S.R. to deliver nuclear missile weapons to any point on the earth's surface." [46]

In the same vein, Western analyst Fred Halliday argues that Soviet nuclear parity "reduced the ability of the USA to intervene in and manage the third world, and to contain social revolution there." [47] Other than noting that Soviet "parity" coincided with its support for Third World revolutions, however, Halliday does not demonstrate how this effect works or even that it exists.

Yet Soviet nuclear weapons *have* clearly affected U.S. behavior in the Third World. As political scientist Robert Jervis emphasized, "The United States and the Soviet Union may engage in fierce rhetorical battles and even use force in such peripheral areas as Africa and Asia, *but there are sharp limits to how far they can push each other*." [48] What *are* these limits and how have Soviet nuclear weapons imposed them?

The "socialist bomb" casts a shadow over three distinct zones: the U.S. and its key military allies-in-arms; the few Soviet allies in the Third World which host Soviet combat forces; and the rest of the Third World, which has no formal or tacit military alliance with either superpower. The shadow falls darkest on the home territories of the U.S., China, France, and Britain. Well before it reached the U.S. itself, the shadow fell over U.S. allies in Europe and the Far East, playing on their fears and motivating them to restrain the U.S. from actions which might escalate into nuclear war. This shadow has deterred any attack – conventional or nuclear – on the Soviet Union and its East European allies. By opting for a maximal deterrent and "rattling rockets" in the 1950s and early 1960s, however, the Soviets also prompted Western Europe and Japan to cling closely to the U.S. in military pacts – a counterproductive result for the U.S.S.R. In the same way, the brand-

---

strike. It is usually estimated at a couple of submarine loads or 200–400 warheads, that is, about 1–2 per cent of current stockpiles. Anything above that is argued to be militarily superfluous, merely "bouncing the rubble." Alternatively, such a "maximum deterrent" may aim to maximize the psychological component of deterrence by increasing the uncertainty as to the intentions and rationality of the possessor of the arsenal.

ishing of nuclear weapons against China in 1969 successfully forced the Chinese to moderate their behavior along the border, but hastened the development of the Chinese Bomb and moves toward the U.S.

By aiming nuclear shadows to protect their Third World military allies (the second zone), the Soviets have also attempted to act as a Great Power – with mixed results. During the Korean War, the Soviets successfully deterred U.S. nuclear attack on China, primarily by alarming U.S. allies in Europe. Soviet threats could not stop Eisenhower from directly threatening China in 1954 and 1958 with nuclear attack, forcing the Chinese to back down from their attempt to reassert their sovereignty over Taiwan. The Soviets' unwillingness to confront Eisenhower in 1958 forced a wedge in the Sino–Soviet alliance (see Chapter 3).

The best-known case of direct Soviet use of nuclear weapons in the Third World was in Cuba during the missile crisis in 1962. Obviously, the U.S. was not deterred by the home-based Soviet nuclear arsenal from launching the Bay of Pigs invasion in 1961.* The following year, the Soviets tried to gain political and military advantage by deploying nuclear missiles in Cuba,[49] ostensibly to defend their ally.† The move ended in a fiasco, with Moscow backing down in the face of overwhelming U.S. local military superiority and nuclear threats. Ironically, although their Great Power image was tarnished, the Soviets underscored their commitment to defend Cuba, which has not since suffered a direct U.S. military intervention.‡

The Soviets cast another nuclear shadow at the Third World in 1973, this time in the Middle East. At the height of the Arab–Israeli War, the Soviets sent a ship carrying radioactive materials to Egypt, and threatened to intervene militarily to stop Israel from dismembering the

---

* A CIA-led attempt to roll back the Cuban socialist revolution by arming and transporting Cuban exiles back to Cuba. The invasion collapsed quickly, and, for President Kennedy, ignominiously.

† Even at the height of the crisis, Khruschev reportedly limited the extent of Soviet defensive retaliation for a U.S. invasion to a nuclear attack on the U.S. base at Guantanamo – in Cuba![50]

‡ There have been many clandestine U.S. maneuvers against Cuba, including a stream of attempts to assassinate President Fidel Castro. Nonetheless, the nuclear scare made it virtually impossible for American hawks to gain Congressional or public approval for a military adventure.

Egyptian 3rd Army.*[53] In response, U.S. nuclear forces went onto high alert on October 24, as the U.S. counteracted with its own nuclear threat. Although the Soviets backed down from unilateral intervention, their actions are likely to have prevailed upon the U.S. to force Israel to allow a retreat by the 3rd Army. The fear that a clash of their forces could spiral into nuclear war motivated both sides to seek a satisfactory "local" settlement. The events in 1973, however, are the only case in which the Soviets could be said to have *directly* accrued political gains in the Third World from their nuclear weapons.

The "socialist bomb" casts only a dim shadow over the third zone, the countries of the Third World which are not militarily allied with either superpower. Undeniably, the U.S.S.R. supported Third World revolutions before it achieved nuclear parity. Even after the Soviets obtained nuclear parity, the U.S. intervened repeatedly in the Third World, and has not hesitated to blackmail Third World adversaries with nuclear threats. Nor was the success or failure of the numerous U.S. interventions affected by the "socialist bomb." [54]

Nonetheless, the shadow in this zone still has an important effect. The U.S. is largely already "self-deterred" from using nuclear weapons in the Third World by the inherent difficulty of bringing nuclear weapons to bear. But the political fallout at home and abroad in response to taking even the slightest risk of triggering global nuclear war has deterred the U.S. command from seriously considering using nuclear weapons in this zone ever since the shadow of the "socialist bomb" undeniably reached the U.S.†

The Soviet "style" of extending nuclear deterrence evidently differs from that of the U.S. First, Soviet nuclear deterrence of U.S. interventions in the vast bulk of the Third World is quite weak, much more so than in the few Third World states allied militarily to the U.S.S.R. This ineffectiveness may account for why – apart from lack of opportunity – the Soviets rarely deploy combat troops outside of Europe and the U.S.S.R. Second, as long as the U.S. confines itself to conventional weapons and avoids Soviet combat troops, it can intervene with

---

* There is no evidence that the U.S.S.R. alerted its nuclear forces during this period.[51] U.S. intelligence analysts speculated that the radioactive emanations may have been from nuclear warheads for SCUD air defense missiles.[52]

† Not to mention the impact on Third World allies frightened by the prospect of a nuclear version of the "we had to destroy them to save them" syndrome.

impunity in the Third World, at least with respect to fears of the "socialist bomb." Third, despite its difficulties, the U.S.S.R.'s maximum nuclear deterrent has contributed to its Great Power status in the eyes of its own and American allies. Even the greatest power on earth and the least powerful national liberation movement must bring the Soviet nuclear arsenal into its military and political calculations – even if only to discount it. Finally, the coupling of U.S. and Soviet actions in the Third World to the central balance of terror has made it less likely that the U.S. will actually use nuclear weapons in the Third World.

Conversely, the existence of nuclear parity has *not* encouraged Soviet interventions in the Third World. As defense analyst Karl F. Spielmann concluded in a 1979 report to the Pentagon, the U.S.S.R. has been militarily circumspect:

● The record does not support the idea that the Soviets have become more inclined to exhibit expansionist or risky behavior as their strategic nuclear standing *vis-à-vis* the United States has improved.

● The record does not support the idea that the Soviets have become more inclined to use the military instrument, as opposed to other means, to further their foreign policy objectives.

● The record does not indicate that in discrete incidents in which the military instrument was used for political purposes, the *strategic balance factor mattered as much as the local balance of forces* (and perceptions of that local balance).[55]

Over the Edge

When it comes to the likelihood of nuclear war, however, Soviet caution is little cause for optimism. Soviet conventional forces in the Pacific cannot match those of the U.S. and its allies, the "local balance" referred to by Spielmann. Faced with likely defeat in a protracted conventional war, the Soviets have adopted a highly escalatory nuclear doctrine which substitutes risk for capability.[56] When the Kremlin judges that all-out nuclear war is imminent, they may let fly a massive nuclear attack, raining the SS-20s and SS-11s onto U.S. forward-deployed nuclear weapons at the same time as the long-range missiles head over-the-pole to the U.S. Then the slower medium- and long-range bombers equipped with nuclear depth charges, bombs, and anti-ship cruise missiles would swarm over the Pacific from the Far East to attack remaining U.S. and allied forces.

Four additional considerations may push the Kremlin over the edge if it faces the possibility of a U.S. nuclear attack. First, the highly central-ized Soviet command system will probably unravel quickly if attacked. Second, its long-range communications networks would collapse quickly if attacked by even a small salvo of American nuclear weapons, disconnecting commanders from their nuclear arsenals and constrain-ing Soviet capacity to retaliate. Third, Soviet early warning radars and satellites cannot differentiate between a "limited" nuclear attack aimed only at Soviet command posts and missile silos, and an all-out nuclear attack.[57] Fourth, the bulk of their nuclear launchers and warheads are land-based, immobile, and vulnerable to nuclear attack.

Faced with these first-strike incentives, the Soviets may elect to cross the nuclear Rubicon first in a vain attempt to limit the damage to the U.S.S.R. from a U.S. first-strike. There is no doubt that the long shadow cast by the "socialist bomb" would then become a total, permanent eclipse.

U.S. atomic test, Eniwetok Atoll, Marshall Islands, 1948
(Pentagon)

EIGHTEEN ☆
STATES OF TERROR

The worst-case scenarios of hundreds of millions dead and widespread destruction would be an unprecedented global calamity, but not necessarily the
end of history . . . [One] of the most important continuities of the nuclear era is
that wars can still be fought, terminated, and survived. Some countries will win
a nuclear conflict and others will lose, and it is even possible that some nuclear
wars may ultimately have positive results (as World War II did). Reconstruction
will begin, life will continue, and most survivors will not envy the dead.
—Herman Kahn, 1983[1]

The destruction [by nuclear war] of hundreds of millions of people, the genetic
deformation of future generations, the destruction of cities and industry, transport, communications, agriculture, and the educational system, the outbreak of
famine and epidemics, the rise of a savage and uncontrollable hatred of scientists and 'intellectuals' on the part of civilization's surviving victims, rampant
superstition, ferocious nationalism, and the destruction of the material and
informational basis of civilization – all of this would throw humanity centuries
back, to the age of barbarism, and bring it to the brink of self- destruction.
—Andrei Sakharov, inventor of
the Soviet H-bomb, 1967[2]

Enmeshed in superpower politics, the Pacific is suspended in a state of
perpetual nuclear terror. Living in the shadow of the nuclear bomb, the
peoples of the Pacific – indeed, the world – have escaped nuclear holocaust since Hiroshima because of a paradox, recognized even by

337

nuclear advocates: the coercive power of nuclear weapons is unlimited and unusable at the same time. The paradox became apparent as early as the 1950s, when the East-West blocs were frozen into place. Political scientist John Herz warned in 1959:

There is, or will be, unlimited might, the capability to inflict absolute destruction, which will go hand in hand with absolute impotence; that is, the impossibility of defense against the same infliction on the part of others; complete lack of "security" within the most accomplished, the most powerful "security" systems ever devised; disappearance of the protective function of the state, or the bloc, despite all its might and power.[3]

Nuclear weapons wreak such *absolute* destruction that their use would eliminate any possibility of settling a war with limited "defeat" for one side. Nor can nuclear weapons discriminate between civilians and military personnel, eliminating the option of maintaining a "frontline" away from the mass of humanity.

Practically useless in waging war, nuclear weapons invert the traditional relationship between weaponry and strategy. In the past, military hardware was developed to actually wage war. In the nuclear age, it is not the actual but the *threatened* use of weapons that is central to superpower strategy. Furthermore, both superpowers explain their ever-expanding nuclear arsenals in defensive rather than offensive terms.

Because there is no effective defense against nuclear attack, deterrence has become the main strategic goal of nuclear powers. A primitive practice, *deterrence* involves precluding an adversary's attack or other action by either threatening unacceptable *punishment* or *denying* political or territorial gains.

Nuclear deterrence works both through punishment and denial by aiming weapons at an adversary's mind and body. It can be thought of as a situation in which two powerful enemies are stalemated. Imagine two big people standing on a steep slope which ends at the edge of a cliff above a deep pit. The two are tied to each other by a taut rope that cannot be undone. One can easily push the other down the slope and over the precipice. But the victim will immediately drag the aggressor into the abyss as well, plunging both to certain death.

"Peace" based on a nuclear threat is a ceaseless psychological assault on the mind of the enemy. While the military capabilities underlying nuclear deterrence can be measured in various ways, the "real" balance of terror is inherently ambiguous. Intangible factors – perceptions of intention and political will – are fundamental in defining it. Together, intention and capability create the essential effect of deterrence: intimidation. It is fear of the incalculable costs and potentially uncontrollable risks associated with nuclear war that is the core of nuclear deterrence. As the distilled expression of intent to annihilate rather than to negotiate an end to a conflict, nuclear weapons are the instruments of those who would destroy civilization to save it.

Since 1945, the Pacific has been caught up in this deadly game of threat and counter-threat. To understand what the masters of war hope to achieve with nuclear weapons, we must enter the arcane and changing world of nuclear strategy. In so doing, we discover that the impossibility of defending against the destructive power of nuclear weapons undermines the credibility of mutual nuclear deterrence.*

Nuclear Monopoly and Superiority

The world's first nuclear strategy was based on the absolute nuclear superiority of the United States. The U.S. enjoyed a four-year monopoly of nuclear weapons until 1949, when the Soviet Union conducted its first nuclear explosion. Remarkably, the U.S. proved ill-equipped to exploit its supremacy, partly because military traditionalists were unable to adjust to the new era.[4] Strategists could not devise a credible means of threatening the Soviet Union in Europe. As President Truman told U.S. Army Secretary Royall in the midst of the Berlin Crisis, "You have got to understand that this isn't a military weapon. It is used to wipe out women and children and unarmed people, and not for military purposes . . . You have got to understand that I have got to think about the effect of such a thing on international relations. This is no time to be juggling an atom bomb around." [5] The U.S. briefly flaunted its nuclear weapons in the 1948 Berlin Crisis, but found the Soviets were not susceptible to nuclear diplomacy.[6]

America's global nuclear supremacy faded fast after 1949. In response, the U.S. redesigned its defense posture, focusing its nuclear

---

* Mutual nuclear deterrence exists when more than one state is able to threaten a nuclear attack.

arsenal on those areas where it was still supreme rather than directly confronting the Soviets. Because the Soviets could not yet launch an intercontinental nuclear attack,[7] the U.S. could use nuclear threats to secure peripheral interests without fear of reprisal against U.S. cities.[8] Indeed, the Korean War was the first, though not the last, "hot war" in which the U.S. threatened first-use of nuclear weapons. With near-absolute military reliance on nuclear weapons in Asia, Eisenhower declared flatly that the U.S. would *have* to use nuclear weapons because of "the way our forces are organized in that area."[9] Few realized at the time that Eisenhower meant just what he said (see Chapter 3).

Unable or unwilling to emulate the U.S. long-range bombers, the U.S.S.R. concentrated its countervailing nuclear threat on U.S. allies in Europe and Asia. This allowed the U.S.S.R. to exploit political divisions within U.S. security alliances. At the same time, the Soviets erected a massive territorial air defense system against U.S. bombers.[10] Khrushchev also employed strategic bluff, for example, flying the same bombers past assembled foreigners many times at an air show in 1958 to great effect.[11]

MAD: Mutual Assured Destruction

The Soviets launched the world's first successful satellite, *Sputnik*, in 1957, heralding a "race for space." The rocket which launched *Sputnik* was also pregnant with meaning, announcing that the U.S. was vulnerable to Soviet nuclear attack.[12] Soviet retaliatory capability forced changes in U.S. nuclear doctrine. While the precise evolution of the new doctrine is complex, the basic ideas had settled into place by 1963.[13] Finally called Mutual Assured Destruction and quickly dubbed "MAD", it was formally defined by two proponents as the ability to:

Deter a deliberate attack upon the United States or its allies by maintaining at all times a clear and unmistakable ability to inflict an unacceptable degree of damage upon any aggressor, or combination of aggressors – even after absorbing a surprise first strike.[14]

Interpreted to mean the threat of a devastating attack on the Soviet urban population and economy, MAD was adopted as the official U.S.

policy in the 1960s. Since existing arsenals were capable of massive destruction, pursuit of more powerful nuclear weapons became meaningless. And since the destruction was inevitable once nuclear war began, slow, inaccurate warheads were judged as effective as fast, accurate weapons. Indeed, advanced weapons might encourage a preemptive attack* rather than dampen conflict in a crisis. The important thing, the MADvocates argued, was to make the nuclear weapons invulnerable to attack, thus ensuring the capability to retaliate and contributing to "crisis" stability.

MAD has been likened to an ancient institution, the exchange of hostages to keep the peace. The obvious difference is that the whole of society is kept hostage without having to leave home. To the extent that this is irrevocable, MAD as a doctrine reflects the dismal, terrifying reality which underlies the global balance of terror and is not simply an ideological lubricant of the arms race.

In the mid-1960s, the golden days of MAD, the Polaris missile-firing submarines hidden in the vast Pacific Ocean, and B-52 bombers capable of rapid dispersion from Guam bases, closely matched the MAD criteria. After the hair-raising experiences in Taiwan, Berlin, and Cuba, communications and intelligence capabilities were also upgraded to reduce the risk that control errors might trigger an inadvertent nuclear war.[15]

Whatever stability MAD imparted either to the arms race or to crisis decision-making, however, was quickly undermined by a variety of factors – service rivalries, technological momentum, the paradoxes of nuclear deterrence, and superpower rivalry. The chastening experience of the Cuban Missile Crisis in 1961 showed that leaders were not, as the MAD doctrine assumed, interested solely in ensuring national survival; they would also risk global nuclear war to protect secondary interests.†

---

* Preemption refers to striking first when one believes the opponent is about to draw, in an effort to reduce the damage from what is judged to be an imminent attack.

† Openly referring to nuclear war in 1961, President John F. Kennedy obliged the Soviet Union to back down on a demand for East German control of West Berlin; in 1962 he threatened nuclear war against the Soviet Union if it did not remove nuclear-capable missiles stationed in Cuba.

Arms Racing

The credibility of MAD and "mutual restraint" was rapidly undermined by American and Soviet development and deployment of multiple warhead missiles (multiple independently targeted re-entry vehicles or MIRV*). Vulnerable to being destroyed in their own immobile silos by a pre-emptive first-strike, these powerful missiles are useless for retaliation. They must be used in a first-strike, if they are to be used at all. Even as MADvocates articulated the doctrine of stable nuclear deterrence, the Air Force was pursuing MIRV to target Soviet missile silos and to reassert its pre-eminence among U.S. nuclear forces.[17] The Soviet command similarly sought to exploit MIRVed missiles to catch up with the U.S. warhead lead, although their testing and deployment lagged behind the U.S. by five years.†[18]

As rhetoric, the MAD doctrine allayed the public's fears of nuclear war. But MAD could not resolve the paradox inherent in nuclear weapons, viz., that their destructive power makes them useless as tools for warfighting. Just as the military ignored MAD and reached for nuclear weapons with first-strike capability in the 1960s and 1970s, so civilian strategists adopted the option of "flexible response" – attacks only on Soviet nuclear weapons rather than cities. This would allow the U.S. to respond to inadvertent attack or a relatively minor provocation with less than all-out retaliation. To the U.S.S.R., however, the option

---

* A ballistic missile is composed of the booster rocket which flings the "bus" on the tip of the missile into a ballistic trajectory. Inside the "bus" ride re-entry vehicles, each of which contains a nuclear warhead. Missiles with MIRVs work by releasing the re-entry vehicles separately at different points in the post-boost stage of the ballistic arc, climbing to about 1,000 km before falling back to earth. Each re-entry vehicle then plummets toward its target from a separate angle, making defense well-nigh impossible. A MIRVed *missile* can thus attack more than one target with one or more warheads per target over an area of 160 km by 480 km, called a "footprint." [16] The crucial new capability of a MIRVed land-based *arsenal* is that only a small fraction of the MIRVed, highly accurate missiles are needed – on paper – to destroy most of the other side's MIRVed land-based missiles.
† The U.S. deployed MIRVed missiles in 1970, the Soviet Union in 1975.

of a highly accurate "limited" nuclear attack on its arsenal was indistinguishable from a U.S. preemptive first-strike capability. Furthermore, population centers would be targeted anyway because of their proximity to urban–industrial and military targets.[19] Raymond Garthoff, a senior figure in the Kennedy administration, emphasizes that it was the U.S. that initiated the missile build-up in 1961, after U.S. intelligence analysts discovered that the "missile gap" was in favor of the U.S., not the U.S.S.R. The Soviets had already joined the race when the Cuban missile fiasco virtually compelled them to embark on a relentless missile program to preserve the security of the Soviet bloc.[20]

As the arms race escalated, the U.S. recognized the need for some restraints and in 1969, Nixon and Kissinger initiated talks with the Soviet leadership which eventually produced the Strategic Arms Limitation Treaty. Nonetheless, they were loath to concede the advantages of perceived nuclear superiority. Ignoring their arms control advisors, Nixon and Kissinger excluded MIRV from arms control talks in order to exploit immediate political gains from the perceptions of U.S. technological prowess.[21] Consequently, the U.S. deployed the MIRVed Poseidon and Minuteman missiles in 1970. Three years later, before the Soviets had even deployed MIRVs, Admiral Thomas Moorer, Chair of Nixon's Joint Chiefs of Staff, justified the U.S. escalation by declaring that "the mere *appearance* of Soviet strategic superiority could have a debilitating effect on our foreign policy and our negotiating posture . . . *even if that superiority would have no practical effect on the outcome of an all-out nuclear exchange.*" [22]

Whether the Soviets were merely pacing the U.S. by deploying MIRVed missiles, or seeking an ill-defined "superiority" as U.S. hawks claimed, will never be known. Just as in the Pentagon, there are those in the Kremlin who pursue political advantage by taking a military hardline. But there is no evidence that Soviet political leaders believed then that they could fight and win a nuclear war against the U.S.[23] It is more likely that they suffered from a strategic inferiority complex and sought nuclear parity with the U.S. to boost their political standing with the rest of the world. As Kennedy's advisors stated in 1962, the Soviets expected their nuclear forces to strengthen "their ability to influence the course of events in all areas of the world" and to demonstrate their "great power prerogatives." [24]

NUTS: Back to the Brink

Pressures for better bombs and the collapse of detente led the U.S. to abandon the MAD philosophy in the 1970s. Instead of deploying nuclear weapons for a "sudden death" holocaust, the Pentagon now openly embraces the notion that nuclear weapons can be used to fight – and win – a protracted nuclear war. These ideas and their proponents are called Nuclear Use Theories or Theorists (NUTS).[25] If a nuclear war can be stopped short of all-out retaliation, argue the NUTS, victory – as against mere survival as in MAD – may be possible. A belief in the possibility of "victory" is the foundation for planning to fight protracted nuclear wars. Colin Gray, one of Reagan's key Nuclear Use Theorists, puts the case bluntly: "If there is no theory of political victory in the U.S. SIOP [Single Integrated Operational Plan for nuclear war], then there can be little justification for nuclear planning at all."[26]

The NUTS made their initial advance when the Nixon doctrine was declared in 1969. Recognizing that absolute nuclear superiority was unobtainable, Nixon declared that the U.S. would build up its regional naval and air power. This build-up, as well as increased military reliance on allies, would also bolster the effectiveness of U.S. military interventions. Nixon announced in 1970 that the U.S. would also use nuclear weapons in Europe and Asia if threatened by a nuclear power.[27] Defense Secretary Melvin Laird emphasized that nuclear forces enabled the U.S. to "contribute significantly to deterrence of Chinese nuclear attacks or conventional attacks on our Asian allies."[28]

While backing off from massive retaliation, Nixon still sought a "sufficiency" of nuclear weapons, which he defined as a credible retaliatory nuclear force *plus* enough weapons "to prevent us or our allies from being coerced."[29] The Soviets also loaded their nuclear arsenal with more land-based nuclear launchers than were then needed simply to retaliate.[30] To offset the U.S. MIRVed ballistic missiles, the Soviets proliferated and hardened their silos, and rushed missiles onto less vulnerable submarines. These Soviet moves, however, could not be characterized as striving for a first-strike capability. Why invest in inaccurate submarine missiles, harden silos, and abandon anti-ballistic missile defenses (as they did in response to the U.S. initiative build-up) if a preemptive strike was in the works? Nonetheless, the Soviets never publicly embraced or advocated MAD.

This doctrinal ambivalence was probably due to the influence of Kremlin hardliners, eager to strengthen the Soviet arsenal. It may also be a conscious strategy to force the U.S. away from the nuclear brink by encouraging fear of a Soviet preemptive strike, whatever the composition and capability of their arsenal. In response to the build-up of Soviet MIRVed missiles in the 1970s, American NUTS publicized a nightmare scenario in which the U.S.S.R. launches an unprovoked attack on the U.S. In their view, the Soviets would either immobilize the U.S. nuclear command, or destroy U.S. missile silos and bomber bases. The Soviet commanders could then sit cool in their bunkers, holding U.S. cities hostage until American leaders capitulated. The NUTS argued that new capabilities to fight a nuclear war were needed to deter this worst case, replacing MAD's threat to retaliate with irrational and immoral total war.

Under the Schlesinger Doctrine in 1974, the NUTS' perspective became U.S. defense policy. Defense Secretary James Schlesinger announced that, in addition to urban and industrial centers, U.S. warplans now targeted Soviet political and military commanders, offensive nuclear weapons, military targets, and the economic assets most valuable in "recovering" from nuclear war.[31] President Carter's *Directive 59* and Reagan's *Defense Guidance* refined this strategy still further, providing the national command with "major nuclear attack options", "selective nuclear options", "limited nuclear options", and "regional nuclear options." Each option is further subdivided into combinations of command and control posts, populations, countries, etc., to be hit in a nuclear war.[32] The big, MIRVed, and highly accurate MX and the Trident missiles were the perfect weapons for the NUTS' strategy, and development accelerated as doctrine and employment policy converged.

Now the basis for U.S. strategic plans,[33] the NUTS scenario imagines that nuclear war will begin with a period of rising tensions which culminates in a nuclear war by stages – "initial exchange; crisis periods; conventional phase; additional exchanges",[34] followed eventually by negotiation and war termination.[35] Central to the strategy's execution, according to U.S. nuclear warplanners, is upgraded command/control, and communications/intelligence systems which will survive and function in the midst of nuclear war. According to Donald Latham, Pentagon official in charge of the nuclear communications upgrade:

The enduring systems we are developing to support the follow-on phases of a conflict must survive the initial attack and the follow-on attacks, with the sustained effects of nuclear detonations and radioactive fallout.[36]

According to Latham, the aim is "to bring the hostilities to a rapid termination *on terms favorable to the United States*."[37] In addition to "victory", the system is intended for "subsequent support of force reconstitution and recovery operations after a nuclear attack",[38] that is, to fight the next war after World War III!

As a possible theater of regional or limited nuclear war, the Pacific plays an important role in the NUTS strategy. Korea is one site for potential "horizontal escalation" in the case of superpower combat in Europe or the Middle East. Alternatively, the U.S. Pacific Fleet might engage in a nuclear shoot-out at sea, or conduct its "Vladivostok strike". To back up negotiations, B-52, Trident, and sea-launched cruise missiles would be held as a reserve force. Attack on the Pacific's command/control or intelligence sites would be extremely provocative since both superpowers' regional commands (Honolulu and Chita/Vladivostok) are close to large urban populations. "Victory" for NUTS in the Pacific might mean "trading" nuclear blows on Guam and Okinawa for Vladivostok and Belaya, or south Korea for Vietnam.

The Pacific Missile Range is also the testing ground for the Strategic Defense Initiative,* the NUTS' most extreme attempt to squirm out of the vicegrip of MAD's logic. Announced by President Reagan in 1983,[39] the initiative was quickly dubbed Star Wars. Reagan promised that Soviet nuclear weapons would be rendered "impotent and obsolete" by constructing a leakproof "astrodome" defense over cities to shoot down incoming ballistic missiles with rays of energy or high-velocity projectiles. Common sense, detailed analysis, and the first tests quickly demonstrated that the astrodome could never cope with a downpour of nuclear missiles.[40] Anti-missile weapons will require error-free computer programs – programs that will stretch to 10 million lines of code – prepared in advance to respond to an attack in a few minutes. Indeed, on the first test of a Star Wars laser's capacity to hit the Space Shuttle from atop a Hawaiian volcano, the Star Warriors fed the wrong altitude into the computer, resulting in failure.[41] The astrodome defense will more likely be used to defend missile silos and bomber bases against a drizzle of Soviet missiles fired in retaliation for a U.S. first-strike.

---

* Anti-missile systems are tested at Meck Island in Kwajalein.

The Star Warriors, however, welcome the prospect of a new arena of technological competition dominated by the U.S. As the ultimate repudiation of MAD, strategic analysts such as Lockheed Corporation's Maxwell Hunter, trumpet that "We're talking about tearing up the basic deterrence strategy we've had for twenty years."[42]

Quick to recognize these implications, high level Soviet analysts emphasized that the U.S.S.R. can overwhelm it with counter-measures. But, they add, it invites both sides to preempt – the U.S. to avoid losing its space-based anti-missile systems; and the Soviets to protect their retaliatory forces if the U.S. deploys the shield in the 1990s. Meanwhile, it virtually precludes Soviet agreements to limit new offensive nuclear weapons. Even before the first components of the shield have been designed, let alone assembled and tested, the Star Warriors have gutted the possibility of arms control.

The Credibility Gap

While MAD failed to stabilize the arms race, the NUTS posture represents no escape from MAD's military, political, and moral dilemmas.

Despite the best efforts of communications architects, command and control remain the glass jaw of both superpowers. MAD required only that commands to fire nuclear weapons arrive in time for retaliation. NUTS requires that command and control survive nuclear strikes on both sides to permit negotiation and restrain nuclear forces mobilized for attack. Such communications capability simply does not exist.[43] Moreover, even if the hardware worked, commands will go awry because of incorrect interpretation or organizational "pathologies".[44]

To achieve nuclear deterrence, MAD required only that missiles were reliable and accurate enough to commit mass murder. NUTS requires missiles that can discriminate between military targets or population centres and economic assets. Not even modern missiles can reduce "collateral damage" so precisely, making it impossible to judge in advance whether either side would perceive the nuclear blows as "limited".*

---

* The U.S. Office of Technology Assessment estimated that a U.S. strike against Soviet missile silos would kill between 4 million and 28 million people immediately, and a Soviet

The NUTS' strategy is not only technically unfeasible, but also lacks any *political* theory as to how a nuclear war, once started, could be constrained from turning into an all-out, global nuclear exchange. NUTS requires, in short, that both sides observe restraints, that the conduct of nuclear war be the subject of conventions. But the Soviets have already declared that they think NUTS is absurd. In 1981 Marshal Ustinov, Soviet Minister for Defense, declared:

Could anyone in his right mind speak seriously of limited nuclear war? It should be quite clear that the aggressor's actions will instantly and inevitably trigger a devastating counterstrike by the other side. None but completely irresponsible people could maintain that a nuclear war may be made to follow rules adopted beforehand with nuclear missiles exploding in a "gentlemanly manner" over strictly designated targets and sparing the population.[46]

Some American hawks interpret this rhetoric as the crafty Soviets playing on Western fears, rather than a realistic Soviet appraisal of the feasibility of limited nuclear war. In marked contrast, a Rand Corporation report told the Pentagon in 1977: "There has been no discernible effort [by the U.S.S.R.] to explore the advantages of flexible-options strategies. Based on what is visible to the outside observer, Soviet crisis decision-makers would appear intellectually unprepared for real-time improvisation of intra-war restraint." In short, the only Soviet response to any level of nuclear attack would be massive retaliation.[47]

Moreover, Soviet war exercises, such as those held in the Far East in 1980, reveal that their nuclear forces are far from well trained and highly disciplined, as required for "limited" nuclear warfighting. Most of the forces trained half-heartedly or not at all. The training which did occur was routine and unrealistic.[48] According to Stephen Meyer, author of a definitive paper on Soviet nuclear warplans, the Soviets do not have any measures to control escalation or to observe tacit limits in nuclear war.[49] "The only true firebreak recognized by Soviet military

---

attack on U.S. missile silos only would kill between 1 million and 20 million people. Most of those killed would be civilians. The impact of "counterforce" targeting on collateral damage was found to be "no greater than the difference made by other variables, such as the size of the weapons used, the proportion of surface bursts used, and the weather."[45]

doctrine – if one is recognized at all," concludes Meyer, "is the conventional-to-nuclear firebreak." [50]

Even if Soviet intentions and capabilities for limited nuclear war-fighting, by a heroic leap of the imagination, catch up with the NUTS, there is no *political* rationale for halting a nuclear war. The notion that a halt could be negotiated successfully under nuclear fire is naive. After all, if fear of nuclear annihilation had not deterred an initial use of nuclear weapons, why should it prompt a cease-fire under the duress of nuclear attack? [51]

NUTS, in short, is no more credible than MAD. Examined closely, it dissolves into the mire of MAD's contradictions. But there is one important difference – the NUTS justify new nuclear weapons which seriously destabilize the balance of terror at the nuclear brink.

Beyond the Brink: First Strike

Faced with the credibility gaps in the MAD and NUTS approaches to nuclear war and fearing surprise attack by these gigantic arsenals, both sides are preparing for the worst. As a result, the finger on the nuclear hair trigger is getting itchy. A U.S. nuclear war planner at the Strategic Air Command told journalist Daniel Ford in 1985:

You compare going first with not going at all. If you're going to get into a nuclear war, that's bigtime. When you go, go. Do it. Finish the job. Launching under attack just means that you've missed the moment." [52]

At the nuclear brink, the worst-case calculus of decision-making may cause one or both sides to attempt to preempt the other. This could happen if resort to nuclear attack is considered the *least bad* of many bad alternatives, that is, when the risks or potential losses of *not* fighting are believed to be greater than those incurred from the other side's retaliation to a preemptive first-strike. At the brink of such a decision, any indications that the other side is about to preempt are inordinately destabilizing. All that is left to avert a nuclear war at the brink is trust, which will be sorely tried by the time both superpowers are fully mobilized. As General John Vessey put it in 1984: "first-strike is not technology; first strike is a state of mind." The General insisted that the Soviet Union "knows that we don't have that." [53] It is doubtful that the nuclear commanders on either side will view a potential first-strike capability so blithely on the eve of nuclear war.

The new MIRVed missiles in the continental U.S. and the Pacific add up – at least on paper – to a U.S. first-strike capability in the 1990s. To a lesser extent, Soviet missiles will also be capable of carrying out a pre-emptive first-strike.* At the brink, the most destabilizing are the im-mobile MIRVed missiles in land-based silos and bombers, and nuclear submarines in port. Like sitting ducks, they almost beg preemption because each missile can theoretically destroy more than one opposing missile because of its multiple warheads. Each Soviet SS-18, for example, carries ten warheads. A single SS-18 can clobber up to ten MX missiles carrying fifty to a hundred warheads. Nuclear warplanners, therefore, can easily fall into a "use 'em or lose 'em" syndrome. Since they can be much more effective if they are fired first, MIRVed missiles increase the perceived risks of *not* firing first. As in the old cowboy showdown, the fastest draw and sharpest shot win. But in a nuclear shoot-out, the whole town blows up.

First-Strike Fears – and Fantasies

While U.S. and Soviet offensive capability against land-based targets will be roughly equal by the early 1990s, the Soviets will not be able to retaliate as effectively against U.S. nuclear forces. A source of great Soviet anxiety, this asymmetry arises primarily because the U.S. has shifted over half of its nuclear warheads to relatively invulnerable

---

* There are about 2,100 "time-urgent", "hard" targets in the Soviet nuclear forces vul-nerable to ballistic missile attack: 700 command and control posts, and 1,400 ICBM silos.[54] With 1,000 warheads on 100 planned MX missiles, 1,800 warheads on 600 mod-ernized Minuteman III missiles, and 2,100 warheads on Trident I/II missiles which will be deployed on 11 Ohio submarines by 1990, the U.S. can allocate two warheads to each of the 2,100 targets, and "keep the change." [55] Operational tests show that Trident I missiles have a better-than-expected accuracy, about the same as modernized Minuteman III missiles, placing them in the first-strike arsenal.[56] The Soviets' 3,929 highly accurate land-based SS-17/18/19 missile warheads in 1982 also exceed the force required – on paper – to destroy each of the 1,500–2,000 U.S. "time-urgent", land-based nuclear offensive targets with two warheads each (at least 300–400 U.S. command and control targets, and the 1,200 missile silos, bomber bases, and submarine sites).[57]

submarine-based Trident missiles in the Pacific. It is also based on the Soviet's inability to coordinate an attack on U.S. missile silos and bomber bases without tipping off the U.S. early warning system – a constraint under which the U.S. does not labor.

Soviet apprehension is heightened further by U.S. anti-submarine capabilities such as the SOSUS sites and P3C Orion airfields in the Pacific (see Chapter 11), which contribute to the feasibility of a U.S. first-strike. Moreover, communications sites in the Pacific have been "hardened" against nuclear attack, allowing the U.S. to regroup its forces to crush Soviet retaliation.* Along with nuclear weapon storage sites such as Guam, communications bases in Alaska, Micronesia, the Philippines and Australia would be heavily barraged early in a Soviet attack. U.S. facilities in the Pacific, in short, could support a preemptive first-strike led by U.S.-based missiles and backed by submarines and short-range, forward-deployed nuclear forces. In contrast, the Soviets have little anti-submarine capability or nuclear command/communications presence in the Pacific, and their overseas, land-based intelligence is sparse. Soviet submarine-launched ballistic missiles are too inaccurate for a first-strike and their home-based, long-range bombers are too few and too slow to affect the outcome. Even if the Soviet Union is aiming to build an intercontinental first-strike capability, its Pacific-based forces contribute little to that end.

Undoubtedly, there are powerful groups in the United States and the Soviet Union who believe that preparing for preemptive first-strike is the only credible stance in a world of highly accurate, silo-buster missiles†. Not surprisingly, the services which tend the vulnerable, land-

---

* The most important of these sites in Pacific Command are the early warning radars (in the Aleutians) and satellite launch radars (in the Philippines, Guam, and Kwajalein); early warning satellite ground stations (most crucially, Nurrungar and Pine Gap in Australia); CINCPAC's command posts (on Oahu Island in Hawaii); ground stations for real-time photographic and electronic intelligence satellites for damage assessment (especially Pine Gap in Australia); and communications stations for transmitting nuclear Emergency Action Messages (especially NW Cape in Australia, Guam, and Japan).

† The recent release of a top-level report to President Kennedy in 1962 shows that first-strike has long been considered a serious option. The report advised Kennedy that Soviet pressures against U.S. interests short of nuclear attack "could, at worst, leave open to us the *unpalatable choice of a first strike* or swallowing our losses in a series of confrontations at local pressure points around the periphery of the Soviet bloc." [58]

based missiles – the U.S. Air Force and the Soviet Strategic Rocket Forces – are the most predisposed to a first-strike mentality.[59] Whether Soviet nuclear warplanners are convinced that their missiles are reliable and accurate in a nuclear war is unknown. But the Pentagon, as one senior U.S. official has testified, has "fairly high confidence" in the operational accuracy of U.S. missiles fired at the U.S.S.R. over the North Pole.[60]

This conviction, however, is based on faulty logic. Because each new missile is tested only a few times and in "unreal" circumstances, the results have little statistical significance. As U.S. physicist Richard Garwin notes:

Every time you fire a new model missile over the same range or the same missile over a slightly different range, the bias [unaccounted for factors degrading accuracy] changes. Sometimes it is greater, sometimes it is smaller, but it never has been calculated before. So you have to go back to readjusting the gyros and so on, to try and eliminate the novel bias. But if we were firing operationally [that is, in a nuclear war], both we and the Russians would be firing over a new range in an untried direction – north . . . They might feel sure that they have eliminated the bias. But they can never be absolutely certain. We certainly cannot be . . .[61]

In other words, missiles in a nuclear war will not be fired in the neat, orderly paper calculations of first-strike feasibility, but in the real world of chaos, fear, and confusion – all compounded by contract mismanagement, faulty parts, slipshod maintenance, bureaucratic cover-ups, and accidents.* Schlesinger emphasized in 1974 that U.S. and Soviet counterforce capability "goes to the dogs very quickly" with *any* degradation in the operational accuracy attributed to Soviet missiles by U.S intelligence estimates – themselves controversial.†[64] The mental

---

* In 1985, for example, the Pentagon discovered that the electronic microchips which were installed in many U.S. weapon systems and which are crucial to the guidance systems and accuracy of the systems were not properly tested.[62]

† Physicist Kostas Tsipis has shown that a reasonable estimate of such degradation for an attack by two nuclear warheads on a missile silo falls from 86 per cent probability of destruction with zero bias, 100 per cent launch reliability, no mutual destruction of exploding warheads, and no surprises in silo hardness to between 31 and 45 per cent probability of destruction when unfavorable variations in these basic parameters are

cost-benefit analyses which inform military deliberations of the feasibility of a nuclear first-strike would have little relationship to an actual nuclear war.

Global Balance of Terror

Should push come to shove, the superpowers have built enormous nuclear arsenals for nuclear attack. By 1983, the U.S. and the U.S.S.R. had stock-piled about 18,500 *long-range* air, land, and sea-based nuclear warheads. Capable of intercontinental targeting, these long-range U.S. and Soviet arsenals are structured in different ways. The Soviet Union emphasizes its land-based missiles, which constitute about half of its total long-range launchers and 65 per cent of its long-range warheads. The U.S. relies more on submarine-launched ballistic missiles than the Soviet Union, which reflects its easy ocean access and relatively superior submarine and anti-submarine technology.*

Both sides dramatically built up their nuclear stockpiles in the 1970s. The U.S. deployed the Minuteman III, Poseidon C-3, and Trident C-4 missiles, each of which carries MIRVs. Between 1970 and 1980, total deployed U.S. long-range warheads jumped from 4,000 to 10,000. The Soviets also built up their arsenal, replacing old missiles with new SS-17,

---

assumed, a plausible bad (not worst) case. Tsipis concludes that "To achieve a 90 per cent kill probability [on U.S. silos] a Soviet two-[warheads]on-one [silo] must be performed with perfectly reliable missiles that experience zero bias, no fratricide and no unfavorable variation in any of the four important attack parameters [missile accuracy (CEP), target hardness yield, and missile launch reliability]." [63]

* U.S. land-based missiles carry 22 per cent of its long-range warheads and half of its long-range launchers. U.S. submarines carry 51 per cent of its long-range warheads, versus 32 per cent for the Soviets. Fifty to sixty per cent of U.S. submarine-based warheads are routinely at-sea versus the Soviet at-sea rate of 15–30 per cent at any time. The designs of long-range bombers on both sides are twenty to twenty-five years old, but the U.S. has reconstructed and modernized its B-52 bombers, which carry 27 per cent of its long-range warheads (versus 3 per cent on the Soviet Bear and Bison bombers). The B-52s are also kept on a high state of alert. None of the Soviet planes are on alert. The Soviets emphasize air defenses more than the U.S., in part because of the immediate proximity of U.S. forward-deployed forces, and in part because the U.S. military concluded that Soviet bombers were a relatively insignificant component of the Soviet nuclear threat to the U.S. [65]

-18, and -19 land-based missiles with multiple warheads, along with the SS-N-18 submarine-launched missile. The number of Soviet long-range warheads leapt from 1,800 to 6,000 between 1970 and 1980.[66] By the mid-1980s the two arsenals contained about 13,000 megatons of nuclear explosive power (including short-, medium-, and long-range nuclear weapons), equal to about a million Hiroshima-sized bombs.[*] As Senator Symington noted over a decade ago, "We are sort of loaded, you might say, when it comes to nuclear weapons." [69]

In an all-out nuclear war, the two superpowers would explode a large fraction of their arsenals in the Pacific. Exactly how much depends on the characteristics of the war. By calculating how many warheads *could* be delivered in a hypothetical two-day all-out war, we estimate that in all, about 5,200 U.S. and Soviet nuclear weapons would release about 1,100 megatons of nuclear explosive in the region, or the equivalent of 87,000 Hiroshima-sized bombs.[†] With only about 10 per cent of the nuclear firepower in their arsenals, in short, the superpowers would totally destroy the Far East and the Pacific.[‡]

With this immense firepower, the Pentagon has assuredly targeted every major Soviet military site in the region in its Single Integrated Operational Plan (SIOP) for global nuclear war. These probably add up

---

[*] A sophisticated measure of the capacity of the most accurate nuclear warheads in each arsenal to destroy the others' offensive missiles is Counter Military Potential (CMP). In the early 1980s, the U.S. had about the same promptly deliverable CMP in its nuclear arsenal as the U.S.S.R., and twice the total (prompt and slow) deliverable CMP.[67] This index takes into account the relative contributions of yield and accuracy of the warhead to its destructiveness to the target, and is most sensitive to the accuracy. Readers should be alert that such measures are "slippery" and easily manipulated by incompetent or partisan analysts."[68]

[†] The 5,220 estimate being 2,400 warheads and 435 megatons from the U.S. arsenal, and 2,800 warheads and 656 megatons from the Soviet arsenal.

[‡] The Soviet and U.S. arsenals are not the only nuclear weapons in the region. China now has about 225–300 nuclear weapons, including at least four 12,000 km-range intercontinental ballistic missiles which can hit all of Asia, Europe, and the Soviet Union. China test-fired one of its ICBMs into the mid-Pacific near Fiji in May 1980, and tested a 1,000 km range submarine-launched ballistic missile into the Pacific in 1982.[70] France also maintains a stockpile of nuclear weapons for testing at Moruroa Atoll in the Southeast Pacific and the French Air Force and Navy are nuclear-armed.[71] But the Chinese and French arsenals in the Pacific are tiny relative to those of the superpowers.

to 200–300 targets. Even if two warheads are delivered to each of these targets to allow for the possibility that U.S. warheads destroy each other, no more than about 500 warheads delivered by land-attack delivery systems will destroy every human artifact in Siberia and the Far East.* Yet we found that in an all-out war the U.S. could deliver over 1,600 nuclear warheads onto these targets.†

By the same token, it would take no more than 200–400 Soviet nuclear warheads to destroy all the U.S. forward bases in Pacific Command, versus the 900-odd warheads that could be used.‡

As if this degree of overkill were not enough already, we estimate that both arsenals aimed at the Pacific will increase by 50–60 per cent by the year 1990 – the result of activating stockpiled nuclear weapons, and of deploying new classes of weapons such as cruise missiles and submarine-launched ballistic missiles.

"The Battle of Perceived Capabilities"

In spite of the certainty of mutual devastation and the uncertainties which would crowd the mind of a commander bent on a first strike,§

---

* In reality, fewer warheads would be needed because many targets are co-located and will be destroyed by one warhead.

† After subtracting 800-odd naval warheads used in the scenario at sea against Soviet warships from the U.S. total of 2,400 warheads.

‡ After subtracting the 1,900 air defense and anti-warship nuclear warheads in the scenario from the Soviet total of 2,800.

§ These uncertainties include: *Adversary's Response*: Will target of pre-emptive strike launch-under-warning; only launch-under-attack; predelegate authority to the military, including "theater" commanders; retaliate against attacker's military or urban/industrial assets? *Attacker's Weapon System Uncertainties*: Will missile be available when activated and perform with test accuracy and anticipated warhead yield, reliably, at the set height, at the rate planned at launch and over targets, and will necessary command/control and communications/intelligence support survive? *Target-end Effectiveness*: How susceptible to nuclear blast and radiation are the missile silos and the missiles therein, how precisely are targets located, how vulnerable is the target's command and control system, how will blast and accuracy be affected by local geology, topography, weather, and mutual destruction of incoming warheads, etc?[72]

the U.S. and the U.S.S.R. have proceeded frantically to build big silo-busting missiles like the MX and SS-18. Originally justifying the build-up by drawing hair-raising but untenable scenarios of Soviet pre-emptive attack, sophisticated hawks on the American side are now rationalizing the first-strike components of their arsenal. The new claim is that by further increasing the uncertainties faced by a preemptively minded Soviet strategist, the new U.S. silo-busters *reduce the risk* of nuclear war by making the nuclear brink *more dangerous!*[73]

The loquacious Herman Kahn candidly spelt out this circuitous logic just before he died in 1983. *If* "both sides have a significant first-strike advantage" as well as a "sufficient" second-strike capability, and *if* both sides would rather fire first if nuclear war appears "inevitable", *then*, claimed Kahn, the threat of pre-emption "is enough to deter extreme crisis, without being very destabilizing in ordinary crises." Kahn conceded that this strategy works "by making nuclear war marginally more likely in a serious crisis." But, he argues, it thereby "makes all forms of war – including nuclear war – less likely." [74]

Kahn's judgement is purely subjective, and few observers who have ever sat in the cockpit of the nuclear war machine agree with him. But he is on the mark when he states openly that the mutual build-up increases the risk that both sides may push themselves over the brink. Increasing the incentive to preempt is like putting lead in the pockets of our two people tied together on the slope. The heavier the lead, the more likely they are to slip as they make their way along the edge. If the lead is heavy enough, the momentum of a slip may sweep both the climbers willynilly over the brink to certain death. If rational, runs Kahn's argument, they will keep away from the brink altogether.

What stakes possibly could be worth increasing the likelihood that control over the nuclear arsenals would be lost – even before a nuclear war begins? Here the hawks move back into the realm of psycho-politics. It is the "battle of perceived capabilities", as the U.S. Committee on the Present Danger put it in 1978, that comprises the crucial stakes in the first-strike race. The Committee, instigator of the onslaught against detente and arms control which swept Reagan into power, argued: "The horrors of nuclear war may continue to deter its actual occurrence. But the political effects of such a shift [to nuclear parity], and its effects on the feasibility of conventional war or proxy war, is [sic] very great." [75]

The hawks are particularly worried that the Soviets might impress

U.S. allies or neutral states simply by deploying more launchers than the U.S.* Edward Luttwak, for example, argues in a report to the Pentagon: "Objective reality, whatever that may be, is simply irrelevant [to deterrence]: only the subjective phenomena of perception and value-judgement count." Luttwak even calls for a "cosmetic approach" to enhance "the images of power" that the launchers and missiles generate.[77]

The problem with American first-strike and nuclear-use theorists, apparently, is that they suffer from a deep-seated superiority complex. The complex is rooted in their frustration at the inability of the U.S. to translate nuclear "superiority" into decisive political advantage.† Even Henry Kissinger, the high priest of coercive diplomacy in Vietnam and a reformed nuclear-use theorist from the 1950s, exclaimed in 1974:

What in the name of God is strategic superiority? What is the significance of it, politically, militarily, operationally, at these levels of numbers? What do you do with it?[78]

Whether a misguided NUT, a lunatic first-strike enthusiast, or a rabid MADvocate steers the world into a nuclear maelstrom is unimportant. Each is quite capable of starting a nuclear war. Despite the carefully crafted doctrines, intentions, and estimates, such a war will certainly burn out of control, destroying all in its path.

---

* Ironically, hawks like Arnold Horelick argued the reverse in the 1960s: *despite* U.S. numerical and qualitative nuclear superiority, the Soviets could gain political parity or even advantage from an inferior force because perceptions of this force are subjective![76]

† As evidenced by the debate over the MX, which descended to strident demands in Congress for "big" missiles, when the Pentagon was quite happy with the small version.

Soviet Bear bomber flies over U.S.S. *Midway* during North Pacific
Fleetex exercise, 1983
(Pentagon)

[Brinksmanship] means exploiting the danger that somebody may inadvertently go over the brink, dragging the other with him.

—Thomas Schelling, 1966[1]

The superpowers have devoted many years and billions of dollars to preparing for war. Having anticipated war, they are likely to end up eventually fighting a war.

The build-up of nuclear and conventional deployments in the Pacific since the end of World War II has been matched by bellicose foreign policies. Both superpowers, especially the United States, have intervened massively in Asia – in Korea, in Vietnam, in Afghanistan. Given the fluid and volatile character of social and political change in many Asian countries, the superpowers will intervene again – if their policies remain unchanged. Indeed, it is possible that the U.S. could undertake multiple interventions in East and South Asia on the periphery of the Soviet Union. These engagements would dramatically over-extend American forces – and prompt severe Soviet anxiety.

In such a context, pressures to escalate to nuclear attack could mount from many directions – another military challenge to the U.S. in Asia, domestic political pressure, provocative actions by either superpower, bureaucratic loss of control over nuclear forces, deception, breakdown of superpower communication, and in the final, fatal moments, pride, fear, anger, and hatred of an apparently diabolical enemy. It is likely that hostile blocs heavily burdened with nuclear arms will eventually confront such an explosive constellation of events: the only question is when.

We present here a scenario in which political and military tensions build until a nuclear war appears to be unavoidable. Based on actual events, technological trends, projections, and informed speculation, the scenario suggests that a nuclear war would erupt out of multiple and cumulative crises.* [2] We recreate actual war-room comments from past crises, and draw on detailed studies of how leaders react to the stress of crisis.

We portray these political, military, and technological crises sequentially, as if they are spread over time.† In reality, many of the events portrayed would occur simultaneously, because of the global nature of the superpower military stand-off and the high speed of weapons delivery. This scenario, therefore, understates the problem of controlling escalation in a nuclear war.

The scenario starts with political explosions and U.S. military interventions in Pakistan, the Philippines, and Korea. Each of these countries is important to U.S. strategic interests and each poses a political dilemma for the U.S. It is in Korea, however, that the U.S. has placed a "nuclear tripwire". Against the backdrop of growing superpower and regional tensions and massive nuclear firepower, it is possible that political upheaval – coupled with human and technological error – could trigger a nuclear war.

Although our account is fictional, it is noteworthy that the last two World Wars, each a long time in the making, were finally sparked by events that were viewed as impossible – until they happened.

The Hillsides are Blazing

November, 1990: Karachi, Pakistan
"The hillsides are just blazing!" a reporter shouts into the telephone.

---

* Throughout the text, the real-life basis for our story is noted at the bottom of the page.

† Dates and times are local. In Washington, D.C., winter times are fourteen hours, and Europe eight hours, behind the Far East on the previous day or night. Thus, noon in the Far East is 4 am in Paris the same day and 10 pm in Washington, D.C., the day before.

"All the forests are on fire, and the whole valley is filled with smoke."*

He has just come from the Kunar Valley near Afghan rebel camps on the border with Pakistan. For years, the U.S. has backed a military dictatorship in Pakistan, in part because of its support to insurgents fighting the Soviet occupation in Afghanistan. Now, the U.S.-backed dictatorship Pakistan is about to collapse and the nation of Pakistan is itself on the verge of disintegration. Baluchistani and Pathani seces-sionists have attacked the Pakistan Army and the Sind and Punjab provinces are in flames.†

While the Pakistani regime is distracted by the riots in the streets, the Indian government has bombed Pakistan's nuclear weapons factory.‡ The Soviets have consolidated their occupation of neighboring Af-ghanistan, and have placed surface-to-air missiles along the border. Exploiting the crisis in Pakistan, the Soviet Union has attacked Afghan rebel camps in Pakistan.

Washington claims that the Soviets have provoked the rebellion in order to evict the U.S. from its new Pakistani naval base at Gwadur, acquired in 1989.§ This would be a step toward direct Soviet access to the Indian Ocean, long believed by the U.S. military to be the Soviets' objective.‖ To reinforce the garrison, U.S. Marine and Army forces at Diego Garcia are airlifted to Gwadur, and an aircraft carrier battle-group blockades Pakistan.

---

* So wrote a journalist of a June 1985 Soviet attack on the Pakistani village of Sineer near the Kunar Valley.[3]

† As in the early 1970s, and late 1983.[4]

‡ Reminiscent of the Israeli strike on Iraq's reactor in 1981.[5]

§ U.S. Agency for International Development is spending $40 million to build a road along the rugged coastal Baluchistani hinterland surrounding the undeveloped Gwadur harbor. "Ever since American airmen and sailors first saw this place during World War II, it has been admired – perhaps even coveted – as potentially an ideal naval base," wrote an American journalist who visited Gwadur in 1985. As of that visit, Gwadur remains attractive to the U.S. Navy, but still unavailable.[6]

‖ In 1982, the Soviets constructed airfields in southern Afghanistan which put the Persian Gulf in range of Soviet strike aircraft. The press reported that American officials inter-preted the action as evidence of Soviet intention to turn Afghanistan into a forward base.[7]

U.S. military advisors direct the fire of the hard-pressed Pakistani army, and try to distribute war materials supplied by China.* Alarmed by a Soviet airlift of arms and munitions to India, the U.S. also stations warships off the Indian coastline. The ships track and occasionally scrape their Soviet counterparts. But so far, each superpower is saving its gunpowder for the proxy battles on land.

December, 1990: Manila, Philippines
An even bigger challenge to the U.S. comes a month later in the Philippines.

Attempts at economic reform by the Aquino government fell far short of the demands of the New People's Army and the country has seen two years of violent revolution. By December 1990, the communist insurgents hold the initiative. Only Manila and a few big cities are controlled by the government.

In late December, U.S. Marines are airlifted from Okinawa in order to secure Clark Air Field in Central Luzon and the mountains behind the Subic Bay Naval Base. The Pentagon justifies the intervention as necessary to "evacuate" Americans from Manila and to "secure American interests." U.S. counterinsurgency teams on high-speed patrol boats direct Filipino forces to stop guerrilla movement between islands, operations reminiscent of riverine and delta deployments in Vietnam two decades earlier.

Assassination and Street Battles

Morning, March 5, 1991: Seoul, south Korea
By March 1991, the U.S. is engaged heavily in Pakistan and the Philippines, where Marines patrol the countryside around U.S. bases at Subic Bay and Angeles City. In south Korea, 3,000 km from Manila, American GIs guard the increasingly tense Demilitarized Zone which divides Korea.

Since 1980, when the Korean CIA killed President Park, the U.S. has backed General Chun Doo Hwan. An inflexible military dictator, Chun has clamped the lid on Korean dissent.

---

* As occurred in 1971 during the Bangladesh war.[8]

On the morning of March 5th, however, a junior officer clutching a hand grenade throws himself at the Korean strongman. Pamphlets in the slain assassin's pocket proclaim that Chun "stole" another four years of the Presidency by refusing to stand down in 1988 as he had promised.

Chun Doo Hwan, the "butcher of Kwangju" in 1980, is dead. Joyful demonstrations turn into street battles across south Korea, as the military clashes with the democratic opposition and its supporters.

8 am, March 19: Seoul

Shortly after Chun's assassination, the American Commander in south Korea, General Michael "Iron Bar" Stigwitz, recognizes the authority of a new military strongman from a faction alienated from Chun. As supreme commander of south Korean forces, General Stigwitz releases the south Korean army at the new dictator's request to repress the strife. But after two weeks, thousands of fresh rebels replace those killed or imprisoned. Whole provinces openly revolt, and key provincial cities evict the Korean military and set up Peoples' Councils.*

The south Korean military, the Commander's main military force, is disintegrating before his eyes. The 40,000-strong U.S. force is obliged to stay on the DMZ and around U.S. bases. They can provide advice, support, and arms, but there are too few to fight the insurgents as well as guard the American sector of the DMZ.

Other U.S. troops in Asia are already over-extended. To supply more American troops would require military conscription in the U.S. – a move which not only would take too much time but is also domestically unpopular. The south Korean military is wracked by internal struggles between senior political and military figures. The U.S. is unable to pin its hopes on any contender for south Korean leadership. Meanwhile, the morale of the south Korean troops dissolves.

To deter north Korean meddling in this deteriorating situation, General Stigwitz orders a series of F-16 fighter planes to scramble along the DMZ and to skirt north Korean borders. He believes that a little tension on the DMZ may also deflect some of the anger of riotous students and striking workers onto the north. Sonic booms crack windows in Seoul as an SR-71 Blackbird spyplane flying as fast as a bullet streaks above the DMZ, photographing north Korean war preparations. The south Kor-

---

* As happened in Kwangju following the death of President Park Chung Hee in 1980.

ean press features the photographs with banner headline articles on the northern threat.

Whatever Steps are Necessary

9 am, March 19: Seoul
North Korea is indeed on a war footing. Since he assumed power two years before, Kim Chong Il – the son of Kim Il Sung – has embarked on a program of military modernization to demonstrate his control. Eager to offset Chinese influence with the new leader, the Soviets have lavished arms on north Korea. Included are a number of MiG-25 high-performance fighter planes. While north Korea has long requested the modern MiGs, the Soviets agreed to supply them for the first time only three months earlier.

The revolt in the south is spreading fast and the north Koreans feel obliged to demonstrate their leadership of the rebellion. They wait until an American fighter plane flies along the Demilitarized Zone and then fire a surface-to-air missile. The attack chases the jet back into south Korea before the missile explodes, destroying the plane. At first, north Korea denies shooting down the plane. Then they claim that the plane was attacked while over north Korean airspace. General Stigwitz immediately denounces the attack. "We intend to continue these routine flights," he asserts to the press, "and will take whatever steps are necessary to assure the future safety of our pilots and planes."*

Evening, March 18: Washington, D.C.
An hour later on late night news, the majority leader of the U.S. Senate calls for a declaration of war. Exclaims one senator, "I don't disdain the diplomatic approach, but if that fails, then we are going to have to put our foot down. What would our troops fighting in the Philippines and Pakistan think if we let these fourth, fifth, and sixth-rate Communist countries kick us around?" †

---

* In 1980, a north Korean surface-to-air missile narrowly missed shooting down a U.S. SR-71 reconnaissance plane which north Korea claimed violated its airspace over the DMZ. An official U.S. response used the words attributed to the U.S. Commander above.[9]

† These are Senator Everett Dirksen's words in 1968 in reference to north Korea's arrest of the *Pueblo* spy ship, except that he referred to Vietnam, not the Philippines and Pakistan.[10]

President William "Big Bill" Herter announces an immediate "police action" in Korea. Addressing an emergency session of Congress that night, he calls for and receives a resolution asserting "the complete support of the American people for our armed forces defending American allies from Communist aggression."

Already on Defense Condition 3, a high state of alert, the Yokosuka-based Commander of the U.S. 7th Fleet sends two aircraft carrier battle-groups into the Sea of Japan. He is not obeying orders from Honolulu but exercising his own initiative in response to news of the President's speech.* The Soviets note the move with grave concern.

10 am, March 19: Seoul
In the hour after the American F-16 was shot down, a stream of intelligence reports arrive on General Stigwitz's desk at Yong San in Seoul. Reports on north Korean radio communications from spy stations at Yonchon in south Korea and Misawa in Japan show north Korean tanks, artillery, and troops massed along the DMZ on a high state of alert.

The reports show that in the south, the U.S. gambit against north Korea has clearly failed. Korean troops led by American advisors lose control of town after town. The rebels have proclaimed a provisional government to preempt north Korean invasion and American escalation. As the revolt in the south spreads north, American troops are now confined to a central region just south of the DMZ and to American bases.

Squeezed in from the south and the north, Stigwitz examines his options. He asks his aides for his emergency warplans. Atomic mines, nuclear artillery, sea-launched nuclear-tipped cruise missiles and carrier-based nuclear strike aircraft standing offshore in the Sea of Japan figure prominently in all his options. The mines will stop southward-bound tanks. The air-delivered warheads will vaporize even bases dug into solid granite.

Stigwitz is a hard-boiled realist. He reckons that the north may attack without warning, especially since his reserve forces are already tied down in Pakistan and the Philippines. While the old ruling apparatus is

---

* As 7th Fleet Commander Admiral Thomas Moorer did in October 1962 in response to Kennedy's Cuba speech.[11]

still intact in Seoul, the General's remaining political and military control in the south may collapse completely at any moment. He ponders briefly and telephones Washington to request pre-delegated authority to use a "limited" package of nuclear weapons if required to hold his position. He is instructed not to use the weapons under any circumstance without prior approval from Washington. This move, however, releases the safety catch from the the hair trigger in south Korea.

2 pm, March 19: Seoul
Within three hours, Stigwitz decides that the time has come to either apply American firepower offensively or disengage. Believing that neither the Soviets nor the Chinese will intervene if the U.S. demonstrates sufficient "resolve", he prefers force to retreat. He also knows that his chances of moving up the Army's promotion ladder are negligible if he becomes the field commander responsible for finally "losing" Korea.

On the telephone to the President, he poses stark options: "The Korean military is falling apart.* I control only the areas immediately occupied by my troops. Unless you can reinforce me massively, we have to attack with nuclear weapons or evacuate immediately. I could try to evacuate our nuclear weapons by helicopter, and fight to the coastline to get out of Korea. The revolt in the south is sustained by infiltrators and supplies from the north," he says, his voice nearly cracking under the strain. "I can regain control here, but only by going to the source. I could block a north Korean invasion with our atomic mines and a few Tomahawks in the valleys north of the De-militarized Zone."

Choosing his words carefully, he poses his request. "My judgement is that we have to preempt the north. If we don't, we will have to evacuate our troops and nuclear weapons to keep them from falling into the hands of the enemy. Mr. President, evacuation means abandoning Korea. I may not be able to evacuate safely at this time anyway."

---

* As occurred in the twilight hours of the south Vietnamese military in 1975, and the Iranian military in 1978.[12]

A Parking Lot

Midnight, March 19: Washington, D.C.

With American troops now engaged on three fronts, President Herter and his staff are weary and mentally ill equipped for the late-night bad news from the Commander in Korea.* Herter and his advisors are also alarmed at the inability of U.S. troops to contain the revolt in the south. The possibility that north Korea might make dramatic political and military gains is the last straw. Some of the President's staff are receptive to the idea of finally solving the "north Korean problem".

"We have to deal with north Korea," states a senior diplomat from the State Department's Korea desk, "as if we are negotiating with Genghis Khan. Maybe they will finally understand we mean business if we convert Pyongyang into a parking lot."†

Most of all, by decisively defeating a recalcitrant Third World power the State Department's strategists seek to avoid the international and domestic political consequences of "losing" Korea. "Even the appearance of capitulation," reads their final recommendation, "will effectively destroy the image of invincibility and prestige enjoyed by our country."‡

The Air Force and Navy Secretaries bring in aides to brief the President and his security advisors on the capabilities. An acrimonious debate emerges as to whether gravity nuclear bombs delivered by the Air Force's F-16s are better than the Navy's sea-launched Tomahawk cruise missiles in hitting north Korean targets dug into granite mountains.

---

* Nuclear analyst D. Frei reviews stress-induced effects on the individual decision-maker. These effects include increases in dogmatic rigidity, stereotyping, ethnocentric bifurcation, group conformity, denial, pretense, abstraction, perceptual distortion, misperceptions, selective perception to match misperceptions, anxiety, and fatigue; degradation in work efficiency, analytical and creative thinking; resort to habitual solutions; tunnel vision; over- simplification; projections of hostility; and apathy, withdrawal, and/or impulsiveness.[13]

† As stated to the authors by a senior State Department official in 1980. "Parking lot" is a Pentagon term commonly used when discussing north Korea after a U.S. nuclear attack.

‡ The U.S. Congressional Investigation Committee into the impact of the successful north Korean arrest of the U.S.S. *Pueblo* in 1968 used those words.[14]

After listening in silence, the President dismisses the service representatives and gathers his advisors to make a decision.

"Our worst case," states the Defense Secretary, "is the possibility that the Chinese or Soviets will counterattack in south Korea. The Soviets are encouraging the north to attack us in the south to tie us down there. But the Chinese are telling the north that they are on their own, which presents us with a tempting nuclear target with a valuable demonstration effect on the Soviets.* We do not believe that the Chinese or the Soviets will escalate to thermonuclear war over a two-bit state like north Korea."

The President sums up: "If we back down now, the whole balance of power, ambiguous enough before this show began, will slip from perceived parity to definite Soviet superiority. I will not go down in history," he says, thumping the table, "as the President who lost Korea!"†

He approves a nuclear strike of twenty atomic mines and ten Tomahawk nuclear cruise missiles, specifying the targets and time frame of the attack. This package is considered large enough to force north Korean capitulation, but small enough to avoid Soviet intervention. No warning is to be given to the north Koreans, the Soviets, the Chinese, or other Pacific or European allies, although an explanatory message is to be sent to China, the Soviets, and the allies as the attack is executed. He orders that the enabling codes for arming the nuclear weapons be issued to their respective commanders.

At the end of the discussion, the Chief of Naval Operations suggests, almost as an afterthought, that the Navy send two U.S. aircraft carrier battlegroups toward the Kamchatka Peninsula.

"The Soviets will have to worry a lot more about looking east at

---

* These words, slightly rewritten, are those of former Undersecretary of Defense Francis West in his 1977 study of U.S. strategy in the Pacific. That the Chinese would abandon their alliance commitments to north Korea to exploit the anti-Soviet effects of a U.S. nuclear attack on north Korea is a fantastic notion – but one that evidently exists in the minds of some senior American officials today.[15]

† Political analyst Richard Lebow concluded from his study of twenty-six international crises "that the most common external catalyst of brinksmanship was the perception that decisive action was required to prevent a significant adverse shift in the strategic or political balance of power."[16]

our carriers," says the Navy Chief, "rather than south toward Korea and Japan."*

The President approves the Navy's request.

The military and political leaders in Washington and Seoul see the nuclear attack as the knock-out blow to north Korea – the settling of scores stretching back to 1950. They also view it as a decisive demonstration of U.S. power to the Soviet Union, whose arms supplies are seen as encouraging north Korean mobilization at the DMZ. Furthermore, they believe that an ignominious and disorderly retreat from Korea would destroy American morale in the Philippines and Pakistan, and embolden the Soviets in Europe.

To indicate the gravity of the Korean situation, all U.S. nuclear forces are placed on a state of high alert, Defense Condition 2. After forty-six years – years of preparing and posturing – the U.S. reaches for nuclear weapons again. To maximize surprise and accuracy, the American Commander is authorized to conduct the attack exactly at dawn Korean time the next morning, March 20th. The Captain of the Tomahawk-armed battleship *New Jersey* is alerted via Hawaii through the Navy command chain.

Evening, March 19: Seoul
Red ribbons of tracer shells drape the Demilitarized Zone as American and north Korean troops exchange fire in the dark. A north Korean counter-bluff is in full swing to divert American attention and to reduce the pressure on the southern rebels. In the south, street battles and hand-to-hand fighting ensue in downtown Seoul as military units vying for power skirmish with each other. Popular opponents are mounting an all-out drive with captured weapons to gain control of the government.

Dawn, March 20: south Korea
At 6.15 am, an elite south Korean Army fighting unit defects to the rebels. Clandestinely, they surround the American–south Korean joint command post at Yong San in Seoul. At 6.20 am, they attack the main gate to divert attention from a hole blown in the concrete wall around the post. Entering the compound, they blast the vital radio antenna and

---

* Based on Chief of Naval Operations Admiral James Watkins's words in 1983. He also noted that the 1983 *Fleetex* exercise was a dry-run of a similar maneuver.[17]

communication cable junction box with anti-tank rockets. Then they concentrate their fire on the command post, trapping the personnel inside.*

The rebel offensive of the night before culminates when the rebels overrun and occupy the Presidential Palace and the American Embassy in Seoul. Remnants of south Korean forces scatter or surrender to the rebels. A U.S. field commander sends a message to Guam and Japan describing the havoc. The message arrives garbled.† Shortly after, the rebels attack communication relay stations on the Korean south coast.

Alerted that something is terribly wrong in Korea, the President orders that the nuclear attacks be halted. The message stops the battle-ship from delivering its Tomahawk warheads onto rear-based north Korean command and control posts. But events are moving too fast in Korea. U.S. forces proceed with preparations at the DMZ, unaware that the President is trying to pull back from the nuclear brink.

6.30 am, March 20: DMZ, south Korea

As scattered gunshots and roaring crowds surge through Seoul, a special U.S. Marine unit arrives at the DMZ in the greying light. Flown in two days earlier from Okinawa, the unit jumps down from trucks and places twenty atomic mines in special tunnels stretching 100 m under the DMZ itself. They quickly punch in the electronic enabling codes which arm the weapons and retreat.

As they re-emerge from the tunnel, they discover that rebels have knocked out a communication relay post and that they cannot contact Seoul or Washington. They desperately seek radio contact with a naval unit, but find that the latest Army and Navy "secure" radios are in-

---

* In February 1978, elements of the Iranian military defected to the rebels at Doshen Tappeh Air Base, handing over arms. Shortly afterward, Iran's military high command declared that it would no longer defend the Shah.[18] The attack described above is based on a composite of Vietnamese attacks on the U.S. Embassy and the U.S. command at Tan Son Nhut Air Base in Saigon in the 1968 Tet offensive.[19] Communications and command posts were attacked at many beleaguered U.S. positions in the Tet offensive.[20]

† As did two out of three urgent messages sent to Guam by participants in the *Team Spirit* exercise, 1982.[21]

compatible.* By the time they make contact via a commandeered Marine radio, it is too late to stop the explosions at the DMZ.

At 6.50 am, the mines explode. Huge fountains of dirt and snow spurt into the atmosphere. The explosions swallow whole villages, lifting the valley floors which appear to hover before crashing back into deep craters hundreds of meters across. No tanks or troops can cross these craters.

News of the nuclear attack spreads quickly in the south. American troops aim merely to hold the bases, which store their remaining atomic weapons, and a few stretches of the DMZ.

8 am, March 20: Sea of Japan

Offshore, American and Soviet warships dodge each other in foul weather. The flagship of the Soviet Pacific fleet, the *Kiev*, keeps itself in full view in the Sea of Japan between the north Korean coastline and the U.S. fleet.†

Amidst huge street demonstrations in the U.S. against – and in some cases for – the nuclear attack in Korea, the House Republican leader asserts on the CBS evening news that the Soviets are "seeking to chal-

---

* Admiral Nagler, director of Command of Control for the U.S. Chief of Naval Operations, complained in 1982 that the four services had not agreed to implement a command message system even though agreement was reached in 1978 to set up the Tri-service Anti-Jam Airborne Voice/Data Communications System. In 1982, U.S. Navy Secretary John Lehman stated, "We can talk to other nations' navies better than we can to our own Air Force." [22] In the Grenada invasion in 1983, Army radios were found to be incompatible with the Navy's. An Army officer borrowed a Marine's radio but could not follow Navy codes and procedures. A desperate paratrooper finally used his telephone credit card to call back to the U.S. to try to get the Army to communicate with ships off Grenada. [23] When President Reagan tried to order the Pentagon to hijack the Egyptian aircraft carrying three Palestinian "ship-jackers" in 1985, he discovered that the secure radios aboard Air Force One were incompatible with those at the Pentagon. Reagan used an open radio-telephone to issue the go-ahead, which was promptly intercepted by a ham radio operator. "Astounding," one shaken Pentagon official said. [24]

† As in the May 1967 Soviet Pacific Fleet deployments prompted by Soviet sensitivity to U.S. naval operations close to its territory. [25] Soviet and U.S. destroyers then collided twice in the Sea of Japan, damaging both vessels. [26] In June 1985, the U.S.–U.S.S.R. talks to refine implementation of their 1972 Agreement on the Prevention of Incidents On and Over the High Seas collapsed. [27]

lenge the U.S.". Adds the Congressman, "This unprovoked Soviet harassment of our ships forces us to show the Soviets that the United States cannot be pushed around like some third-rate power."

He demands that President Herter give American naval commanders the authority to fire on Soviet vessels.* He does not know that the President has already issued orders to American commanders, standard since the naval intervention off Lebanon in 1983, "to challenge potential aggressors and to defend themselves as required in case of attack." †

American anti-submarine warfare vessels and planes hug close to the American fleet near the northern coast of Korea. The American sonar operators are tracking so many north Korean, Soviet, and American submarines around the American and Soviet fleet that they cannot distinguish the type and nationality of all the submarines at the same time.

The computer on a U.S. PC3 plane beeps a warning that a hostile, diesel-powered submarine has slipped behind an American aircraft carrier. Assuming the worst – a hostile north Korean adversary‡ – the commander of the task group orders a cruiser and carrier-based helicopters to destroy the submarine.

The hull of a diesel-powered Soviet attack submarine crumples from the impact of an air-launched torpedo, killing the crew instantly. Soviet sonars register an underwater attack in the vicinity of the last known position of their submarine. The news is relayed to Vladivostok, Chita, and then Moscow.

---

* Gerald R. Ford, then a member of the U.S. House of Representatives and later President, made such a demand on May 11, 1967 in response to the U.S.–U.S.S.R. warship collisions.[28]

† Admiral James Watkins testified in 1984 that "We learned a most important lesson about rules of engagement in Lebanon, and that was, get aggressive . . . [We announce] that in this region, around American ships, we have these rules, and to stand clear, to come up on guard frequency, talk to us, don't come charging at us from 2,000 feet and 5 miles away and expect not to get a bunch of tracers shot across your bow. And if you come much closer than that, you are going to be brought down." [29]

‡ North Korea has at least thirteen submarines, which are deemed by naval experts to be a potent threat in their coastal operating areas.[30]

8.15 am, March 20: Sea of Japan

Over a hundred Soviet fighter aircraft are flying above the fleets, tiny specks on an ocean flecked with whitecaps far below.* They are not alone, however; each is accompanied by U.S. or Japanese fighter aircraft guided to the Soviets by a U.S. AWAC Airborne Warning and Control plane.

One group of Soviet MiG jets flying alongside a U.S. RC-135 spyplane breaks off abruptly and heads for Vladivostok. Their American escorts stay close to the RC-135. Having detected the nuclear explosions in Korea, the Soviets recall their planes. The AWAC lies between them and the coast. As the RC-135 reports the disengagement, the crew of the AWAC report an alarming development. Twenty Soviet Backfire bombers are heading for the *Carl Vinson* off the Korean coast. Shocked by the nuclear attack in Korea and the loss of a submarine, the Soviet Command has settled on a show of force.

The Commander of the *Carl Vinson* has no way to determine if the Backfires are engaging in mock attacks to warn the Americans to keep their distance, or if the strike is for real. He orders all his fighter aircraft to pull back into a cordon around the carrier as the Backfires close in at 950 km per hour from the north.

The U.S. Commander then orders his F-14s to challenge the Backfires. But the Soviet pilots ignore the radio calls and tracer bullets fired in front of them and keep approaching the carrier. When the Backfires are 400 km from the *Carl Vinson* – the maximum range of the A-6 missiles which the bombers carry – the nearby RC-135 intelligence plane registers a Soviet satellite radio transmission giving the latest location of the aircraft carrier.

The message is the signal for the Backfires to undertake the evasive maneuver which precedes an attack. The U.S. Commander interprets the satellite message as a signal for the American fighter planes to fire their Sidewinder and Phoenix missiles or lose their targets.† He trans-

---

* As occurred in early December 1984 when "An unusually heavy reaction involving at least a hundred Soviet jet fighters, bombers, and reconnaissance planes as well as surface vessels" was seen when elements of the u.s.s. *Carl Vinson* battlegroup approached within 80 km of Vladivostok.[31]

† Based on the scenario for similar events in the Atlantic as sketched by U.S. Navy analyst William O'Neil. In 1983, Backfire bombers began to fly simulated strikes against U.S. carriers in the Western Pacific.[32]

mits the fire order and all ten of the Backfire bombers are shot down, plummeting into the ocean. These events drastically escalate Soviet involvement in the war raging on the Peninsula, and now, over the Sea of Japan.

The Saturation Strike

9 am, March 20: Vladivostok, Soviet Union

Two hours have passed since the nuclear mines exploded in north Korea and one hour since the smoke cleared from the air battle. So far, the superpowers have only tussled briefly in aerial and naval skirmishes in the Sea of Japan. But U.S. naval efforts in the North Pacific to distract the Soviets from intervening in Korea have evoked the Soviets' worst fear: that the U.S. attack in Korea was a diversionary tactic, the precursor of an attack on the Soviet Union itself. The locus of the war shifts from Korea to the North Pacific, where both superpowers are sucked into a whirlpool of events beyond their control.

The worried Commander of the Soviet Pacific Fleet in Vladivostok, Sergei Borshkov, scans the latest intelligence brief on events in Korea and the Sea of Japan. Already American jets have shot down his Backfires. One of his submarines is not communicating, presumed lost to an American depth bomb. Now, two U.S. aircraft carrier task forces are heading for Petropavlosk, the Soviets' main ballistic missile-firing submarine base in the Far East.

Borshkov reads that Soviet hydrophones have picked up U.S. attack submarines entering the Sea of Okhotsk. They may already be tailing Soviet ballistic missile submarines there, not to mention around the Aleutians and Petropavlosk. This tactic fits what he knows to be the U.S. Navy's likely first move in a superpower war.* Borshkov is also worried that the bulk of the ballistic missile submarines in his command are in port, vulnerable to U.S. ballistic missile attack. He has already withdrawn the bulk of his submarine and anti-submarine forces from the Sea of Japan into the heavily defended Sea of Okhotsk. He anxiously awaits approval to send his long-range missile-firing submarines at

---

* In 1985, U.S. Navy Secretary John Lehman revealed that once a superpower *conventional* war begins in Europe, the U.S. Navy would attack Soviet sea-based missile submarines "in the first five minutes of war." [33]

Petropavlosk into the Pacific. This step, he knows, entails being ready to attack American anti-submarine forces.

A telex from the regional commander at Chita authorizes Borshkov to proceed, and adds that he is to use the minimum force necessary to protect his ballistic missile submarines from falling prey to American forces. If necessary, he may attack U.S. aircraft carriers and submarines in the Sea of Okhotsk or obstructing passage into the Pacific. Borshkov issues the orders for his commanders to execute the plan. They are to attack U.S. warships as soon as they approach within striking distance of Soviet ballistic missile-firing submarines.

10 am, March 20: North Pacific

Carrying 100 strike aircraft, the U.S. carriers *Enterprise* and *Midway* are closing in rapidly on the Soviet coastline. The carriers are now only 1,600 km away from Petropavlosk, well within striking distance of the Soviet mainland. The escort vessels carry long-range Tomahawk missiles and guidance maps stored in computer cassettes to direct the missiles to their targets. Apparently headed for Sakhalin, U.S. F-16s based in Japan also appear on Soviet radar screens. Beyond Sakhalin lies Alekseyevka, where the remaining Soviet Backfire bombers are based.

U.S. anti-submarine vessels and aircraft are moving rapidly into the Seas of Japan and Okhotsk and the North Pacific. In Vladivostok, Commander Borshkov knows from his radar, aircraft, and sonar that his submarines in the North Pacific are vulnerable to U.S. attack. He fears that a U.S. naval "rollback" of Soviet anti-carrier submarines is the first step before the U.S. attacks Soviet ballistic missile-firing submarines and the Soviet Union itself.* After consulting again with Moscow, Borshkov orders an all-out, saturation attack against U.S. anti-submarine and carrier forces in the vicinity of the Sea of Okhotsk and Petropavlosk.

---

* U.S. Chief of Naval Operations Admiral James Watkins explained to a skeptical Senate committee in 1984: "We essentially do sequential operations to roll back the enemy's defenses. We know how to do that. We know when to make our moves up into those regions. We have to know how effective the SSN [U.S. nuclear attack submarine] surge would be against the Soviet bastion force around the SSBNs [Soviet ballistic missile-firing submarines]. It is very critical to force them back up in there . . . In the Northwest Pacific, our feeling is that at the very front end of conflict, if we are swift enough on our feet, we

10.15 am, March 20: North Pacific
Soviet submarines and Backfire bombers immediately launch cruise missiles at the aircraft carriers and their escorts. Bombers and surface vessels drop nuclear depth charges aimed at U.S. attack submarines. To make up for poor coordination and U.S. electronic counter-measures, Soviet *Golf* submarines fire ballistic missiles at the last known location of the carriers. Many of these missiles kill only fish and whales, but enough explode near the *Enterprise* to knock out its fragile communications equipment and landing equipment. Sonars all over the Pacific are "blued out" by the booming sound waves.

The *Midway* steams on toward Petropavlosk. Under the rules for engagement issued that morning, he was authorized in advance to respond immediately to attack on aircraft carriers. The new rules did not specify if his response could extend to the Soviet Union itself.*

The *Midway*'s commander believes that his F-15 aircraft must disable the airfields at Petropavlosk to protect against further attack.

Knots of War

8.30 pm, March 19: Washington, D.C.
Surrounded by his advisors, the President listens to the careful translation of Soviet Premier Dmitri Stoltov's voice over the newly activated voice Hot Line. The Soviet leader recalls the 1962 Cuban Missile Crisis, a human generation and two generations of weaponry before.

"If you have not lost your self-control," says Stoltov, "and sensibly conceive what this might lead to, then, Mr. President, you and I ought

---

would move rapidly into an attack on Alekseyevka, and we think we could get away with it, because we know what the real Soviet capability is . . . [The 1983 *Fleetex*] exercise last year was one of the best exercises that we have run with the Air Force. We had 30 F-15s, AWACs and KC-10 tankers, working together with three battle groups. The *Enterprise* battle group was returning from WESTPAC. We brought the *Midway* out of Japan. We were deploying *Coral Sea* to the Western Pacific. We rendezvoused [sic] up here [indicating on map, near Aleutians] and we tested our ability with the Air Force to coordinate strikes at Petropavlosk or Alekseyevka."[34]

* One of the tacit rules of superpower interaction in the Navy's perception is that a Soviet attack on a U.S. aircraft carrier will be answered by a U.S. attack on the Soviet homeland.[35]

not to pull the ends of the rope in which you have tied the knots of war. Because the more the two of us pull, the tighter the knot will be tied. And a moment may come when the knot will be tied so tight that not even he who tied it will have the strength to untie it. Then it will be necessary to cut the knot. What that would mean is not for me to explain to you."*

Glancing at his assembled subordinates, President Herter concentrates on the telephone loudspeaker.

"Your navy sank our submarine two hours ago," the slow translation of Premier Stoltov's voice continues, "and is now attacking our aircraft. We have stopped them for the moment, but still your forces advance against the Soviet homeland. What do you hope to achieve by this incredible action? We are ready to untie the knot. But first, you must heel your dogs of war. All we can hear is their barking and growling on our borders."

"Well," says Herter to his advisors, flicking the mute switch on the telephone, "what do I say? Tell him to put a leash on the north Koreans? And what the hell is this talk of attacking their submarines and homeland?"

After a moment's reflection, he picks up the telephone and speaks.

"Mr. Premier, we will answer your questions. We want to know why you ordered your Backfires to attack our ships. I agree we should talk. We have to find the time to talk."

"Fine," replies the translated voice of Premier Stoltov. "I trust what I hear on this telephone. I have to. But remember, I have to trust what I see and hear even more. We will talk again in a few minutes."

The President hangs up looking relieved.

A dishevelled Admiral bursts into the room, sweating profusely. Out of breath, he waves a sheet of paper at the group around the President. Finally, he addresses the President with a cracking voice.

"Sir, the *Enterprise* has been disabled with a nuclear attack. The *Midway* is proceeding to counter the attack on the *Enterprise*. The Soviets are attacking our ships in Europe with conventional weapons."

Herter is stunned. Few in the room know that the Navy routinely conducts aggressive anti-submarine operations to protect aircraft car-

---

* Based on the text of Khruschev's warning to Kennedy in 1962 over the Cuba crisis.[36]

riers.* While operations in and around Korea are directed from Washington, D.C., the naval activity in the Pacific is controlled by the Commander, U.S. Pacific Fleet. The President and top brass in Washington approved the carrier operations off the Kamchatka Peninsula. But they were too absorbed in events on the Korean Peninsula to enquire into all aspects of the maneuver. Instead of deterring the Soviets from intervening in Korea, the cumulative effects of U.S. strategy – the nuclear attack in Korea, the attacks on the Soviet Backfires and submarine, the anti-submarine hunt in operating areas of Soviet ballistic missile submarines, and the carriers closing on Petropavlosk – have evoked Soviet retaliation from an unexpected quarter.

Another message arrives with the Secretary of Defense, who reads: "The latest intelligence reports that Soviet submarines are being escorted to sea by anti-submarine surface warships. Nuclear warheads are being transferred from storage to theater delivery systems, including bombers. Intercontinental ballistic missiles appear to be on increasing levels of alert, indicated by fuelling operations."

The eyes of all the advisors are glued onto the Secretary of Defense. Glaring at them, he faces his boss.

"Mr. President," he declares, "this looks like the moment we've all been waiting for."

Flushing with anger, the apprehensive President exclaims, "The Soviets are playing games with us. It takes two to tie – and to untie – knots."

Instead of reassuring the President, Premier Stoltov's words now alarm him so much that he predelegates authority to use nuclear weapons to the NATO Commander. He also orders the commander to prepare to reply in kind to Soviet naval attacks. Under this *Operation Plan*, the U.S. envisages an attack to "liberate" East Germany and Czechoslovakia.†

---

* As occurred in the 1962 Cuban missile crisis, when Naval anti-submarine operations were by far the strongest *military* signal sent to the Soviets. Despite Kennedy's preoccupation with control over the disposition of U.S. forces, the aggressive anti-submarine operations such as depth charge attacks designed to force Soviet submarines to surface totally escaped the attention of the U.S. National Command.[37]

† This section is based on *Oplan 100-6*, a U.S. European Command plan leaked to the media in 1980. It recognized that "all of NATO may not elect to participate in these operations", but expected that Britain would stick with the U.S., even if the U.S. launched a pre-emptive nuclear strike on Eastern Europe.[38]

Beijing Provoked, Europe Afraid

10.45 am, March 20: Beijing, People's Republic of China
The American nuclear attack on north Korea aimed to deter invasion of the south and to warn off the Soviets. While the American leaders expected criticism, they believed that China and other U.S. allies would have no option but to concur in this display of American resolve. Only as the attack was launched had the State Department advised Beijing by telex of the U.S. action in Korea.

Messages are sent to other U.S. allies after the nuclear attack – without even a pretense at consultation. The pace of events on the Peninsula precluded sharing decisions with the allies, whom the Pentagon perceives as weak-kneed and vacillating. The Command in Washington assumed that the allies could not afford to jump ship – they would have no choice but to acquiesce.

But rather than watching approvingly or helplessly, the Chinese leadership decides to intervene massively to express disapproval of the U.S. attack. By this action, the Chinese seek to avoid being hit by Soviet nuclear missiles in the case of a superpower nuclear war. Ten years of Sino-American military cooperation fade against this distancing imperative. China's preoccupation with its own big-power status in the rest of the third world reinforces the decision to support their military ally in Korea. China does not yet know that the rebels have already won in the south, despite the devastation inflicted along the DMZ. They pour troops into north Korea to deter further American attack.

2 am, March 20: Europe
Events are also moving fast in Europe. At the same time as the attack is launched in the North Pacific, Soviet bombers flying through the night fire missiles at two U.S. cruisers tracking Soviet nuclear missile submarines off the far north of the Soviet Union in the Barents Sea. One cruiser is crippled, the other explodes and sinks.* Unlike in the Pacific attack, conventionally armed warheads are used in Europe.

---

* This scenario is based on the Pentagon's *Ivy League* war game played by the whole U.S. command structure in March 1982. In *Ivy League*, the war starts with attacks on U.S. forces in Korea, Europe, and Southwest Africa, and crosses the nuclear threshold in Europe when a Soviet bomber attacks an American patrol ship with nuclear weapons. The Pentagon's war game also ends in general nuclear war.[39]

No major battles have broken out on the European continent as yet, as nervous commanders stare at each other down the nightvision telescopic sights of their weapons, waiting for World War III to erupt over the Berlin Wall.

Bitter Fruit

9 pm, March 19: Washington, D.C.

A group of bleary-eyed national security operatives assemble in the White House. The Secretary of Defense scans a Chinese communique demanding a halt to superpower confrontation in the Peninsula.

"Should the imperialist aggressor superpowers dare to embark on any more nuclear war adventures," he reads, "they are bound to taste the bitter fruit of their own making, and receive even more punishment."*

"What the hell does that mean?" rasps the Chairman of the Joint Chiefs of Staff. "Those Chinese bastards – they've double-crossed us after all we've done for them! They're siding with north Korea! Mr. President," he declares tersely, "we have to take them all out. Who knows where the Chinese missiles are aimed. The State Department's responsible for this mess! The Soviets have threatened Japan and attacked our submarines and aircraft carriers with nuclear weapons. Their bombers are dispersing. Their submarines are leaving port. They sank one of our cruisers and tried to put a submarine under our carrier off the Korean coast. And it looks like they might have hit our command post in Korea, although the Korean rebels claim they did it. If they didn't do it, the Soviets are behaving as if they think that we think that they did. Our best intelligence is that they are preparing for all-out nuclear attack. To limit our damage, we've got to lauch our MX, Minuteman III, and Trident I missiles. If we wait, somewhere between four and five thousand warheads will hit us. The Chinese could add another one or two hundred warheads. An attack like that would completely destroy us. But if we attack now, they might manage to fire back only a fraction of the 200–400 warheads which may survive our attack. That gives us a chance. We have no choice but to launch an immediate

---

* Based on an official Chinese statement to the U.S. over the *Pueblo* event in 1968.[40]

NUCLEAR EPITAPH? ☆ 381

preemptive attack. We have to assume that the Chinese are involved and take them out, too. This is the united opinion of the Joint Chiefs," he concludes.

The President looks up like a trapped animal.

"What are our chances," he asks, "of executing a successful strike against the Soviet Union and China?"

The Chairman replies, "If we go all out, we have just enough warheads to take out most of their political and military command posts and ICBM silos, most of their bombers and all of their submarines in port. We'll have to use the Pershing in Europe and the cruise missiles in our submarines for some of the urgent coastal targets. The biggest risk is their ICBMs and submarines," he says. "The longer we wait, the more likely it is that we will hit empty silos, and the less likely it is that we can kill all their submarines. The bombers we can handle. We have to move *now* to get their ICBMS and subs. All of them."

"What about a limited nuclear attack?" asks Herter.

"A limited nuclear strike at this stage," replies the Chairman, "would be the worst of all worlds. The Soviets or the Chinese might respond to our limited strike by launching an all-out preemptive strike against us, leaving us sitting ducks. They may reply in kind by trying to disable our command and control, which we can't risk. Or they might attack our bases in Japan or Europe and wait for our allies to jump ship.* Furthermore, ordering a limited strike may build a momentum toward all-out attack in our own forces which we couldn't stop even if we wanted to. We recommend everything or nothing, but not in-between."

The President's National Security Advisor speaks up.

"It's too risky," he asserts. "Mr. President, you are about to start World War III. We have to start negotiating with the Russians – *now*. If even a few Soviet warheads hit the U.S., we're finished."

The Chairman of the Joint Chiefs leans over the desk, blocking the Advisor's eye contact with the President.

---

* As American strategic analyst Morton Halperin wrote in 1963, "The first time that any of these limits [on superpower action against each other] are breached or if there is some other unprecedented action . . . there will be heightened danger of explosion into central war precisely because neither side can be certain that the war can be brought to a halt without the essential use of strategic nuclear forces. How serious this is will depend on the degree to which both sides are conscious of the danger of preemption."[41]

"Mr. President," he says, "we are losing precious seconds. You have a terrible choice. You can protect your people and limit the damage as far as possible. To do that, we have to attack now. Or you can wait, and absorb the full strike from the Russians which is surely coming. We are certain that they will attack any minute now. There is no other choice."

Herter asks the Secretary of State for his position.

"I agree with the Advisor that negotiations are called for in principle. But while we may wait, the Soviets may not. And if we wait, we'll lose the military and political advantage which we have at the moment. Congress will vote to back down and appease the Soviets, the press will support the peace-wimps out there – they may even invade the White House. Very soon, we'll have to deal with our allies. The West German Chancellor is leaving for Moscow in a few minutes, and the Japanese and British Prime Ministers are about to arrive here. Mr. President, we are losing our room to maneuver. This is what the Kremlin wants. They know that the allies are our soft spot. We cannot negotiate with the Soviets now. It's too late. If we prolong the agony and are indecisive, our allies will jump ship. We have only one choice – to proceed."

With that, he clasps his hands and, slumping glassy-eyed in his chair, he withdraws from the discussion.[42]

9.30 pm, March 19: Washington, D.C.
The President deliberately picks up the Hot Line telephone and speaks into it slowly.

"Mr. Premier, we wish to negotiate. But first, in response to your attack on our forces, we are obliged to launch our B-52s and my alternate aerial command post as a precautionary measure only. The Vice President will board that plane."

The perspiring National Security Advisor looks relieved. The President is evidently riding out the storm. He will risk trusting the Soviet Premier.

As Herter pauses, another messenger arrives breathlessly, obliging the President to cover the telephone with his hand.

"The Russians have launched two new satellites over the Pacific," he blurts out. "The Pacific Barrier radar says they're for assessing the damage to the United States during and after a nuclear attack. We also have signals intelligence that a Soviet intelligence trawler reported that CINCPAC's airborne command post is flying out of Hawaii . . ."

"What?!" thunders the President, his hand over the telephone. "Who in the hell ordered them to take off?" he demands.

"Why, the Commander-in-Chief of the Pacific, sir, after the nuclear attack in Korea, sir," he stammers.* "And that's not all, sir." He hands a telex to the Chairman of the Joint Chiefs, who reads:

"This is an *Oprep-3 Pinnacle Nucflash* from u.s.s. *Picksville* in the Sea of Japan as of 0308 Zulu time. At 0305 Zulu time, the u.s.s. *Picksville* inadvertently launched a Tomahawk nuclear-capable but conventionally armed missile. The missile is capable of reaching the Soviet mainland and is pointed in the direction of Alekseyevka Backfire Base. Missile whereabouts unknown. Recovery of missile not possible. Commander's estimate: no human error, computer malfunction. Last *Oprep-3* Report this incident."†

Alarmed, the Secretary of Defense yelps hysterically, "This means war with the Soviet Union."‡

The crisis managers stare at the Defense Secretary, perplexed at his outburst. The civilian Advisor slumps into his chair. The Chairman of the Joint Chiefs stands up ramrod straight and declares:

"Mr. President, negotiations won't work. The Russians won't believe you now. We have to act!"

The President's face pales. A single bead of sweat rolls down his face toward his chin. He stares at the telephone and appeals to the Secretary

---

* The confusion due to poor coordination between multiple unified and specified command nuclear war organization is based on events in 1980 when a Pacific Command Nuclear Airborne Command Post took off *after* an attack triggered by a computer chip was declared a false alarm by NORAD.[43]

† Based on a message format for an operational report given in CINCPAC's 1983 Nuclear, Biological, Chemical Warning and Reporting System. *Pinnacle Nucflash* is a codeword to report on an event which has the risk of initiating nuclear war with the Soviet Union or China. Zulu time is Greenwich Mean Time. *Oprep* is military code for operational report.[44]

‡ As Defense Secretary Robert McNamara reportedly screeched when, at the height of the Cuban missile crisis, word came that a U.S. U-2 spyplane from Alaska had "strayed" over Soviet airspace at the Chukotski Peninsula. Soviet MiGs scrambled to intercept it, and U.S. fighters took off to escort it. The U-2 escaped with no shots fired.[45]

of Defense for a suggestion. They step aside for a private discussion.*
The President can be seen listening to the Secretary of Defense
intently.

Finally, they return to the table. "We are boxed into a corner," says
Herter. "The only way out is to fight. We will confuse and attack the
Soviets and the Chinese at the same time." The President picks up the
Hot Line telephone: "Mr. Premier," he says, "the mobilization of our
forces mentioned in my previous message was the result of a false
alarm, and they are being recalled. I repeat, we wish to negotiate
immediately. Please stand by."

He switches the telephone to mute, turns, and orders the Secretary of
Defense: "Send a message to the Chinese asking them to explain their
telex." The civilian Advisor perks up.

"But," adds the President, "first send an Emergency Action Message
to all forces to implement immediately the strategic attack option outlined earlier by the Chairman. He will attend to the details."†

It is 10 pm, March 19th, in Washington, D.C.

---

* Some Presidents, like Jimmy Carter, take an active interest in nuclear affairs; others, like
Reagan, are passive and rely on advisors to prompt decisions. According to a senior
Reagan advisor in 1985, President Reagan in a nuclear war command exercise "acted like
an automaton, like part of the set instead of the main actor. Reagan was saying things like
'What do I do now? Do I push this button?' He was not very probing. Some fresh-faced
colonel says something – 'Mr. President, you have to do such-and-such in seven minutes'
– and there are no questions from Reagan."[46]

† Journalist Robert Scheer reports the following exchange in 1980 with Presidential candidate Ronald Reagan: "SCHEER: The last time I talked to you, you said no President of
the United States should rule out the possibility of a preemptive nuclear strike . . . Now in
serving notice on a confrontation down the road – would that include the possibility of a
preemptive nuclear strike by the United States? REAGAN: What I'm saying is that the
United States should never put itself in a position, as it has many times, of guaranteeing to
an enemy or a potential enemy what it won't do . . . Suppose you're the President, and
suppose you have on unassailable authority that as of a certain hour the enemy is going to
launch those missiles at your country, you mean to tell me that a President should sit
there and let that happen without saying to the other country, I've found out what you're
planning to do and I'm going to . . ."[47]

The End Begins

9.05 pm, March 19: Kansas, U.S.A.
Deep underground in a silo in Kansas, two officers peer at the telex containing the launch codes in fear and disbelief. Then they turn their launch keys together. All across the United States, missiles hurtle towards the Soviet Union. One of them is bound for Chita, the Far Eastern Soviet command post. The missile carries a hand-painted message: "Gift of the People of the United States."

4.07 pm, March 20: North Central Pacific
The captain of an Ohio submarine in the Pacific launches half his Trident missiles in twelve minutes after a short, near-mutinous debate among the officers responsible for assessing the veracity of the order received by low-frequency radio. The missiles fan out to deliver a hail of eighty warheads in an arc between Vladivostok and Petropavlosk. The submarine hovers motionless, waiting orders to fire the remaining missiles.

12.15 pm, March 20: Chita, U.S.S.R.
In Chita, the Soviet Far Eastern commander glances at the telex printout. The Intelligence collection ship sitting off Hawaii has advised that the Pacific Command nuclear command aircraft has taken off, as have the B-52s in Guam. On top of the Backfires and the submarine, this is very bad news.

An aide pushes another incoming telex from Moscow across his desk. The telex instructs him to place all Far Eastern forces on the highest alert, to target Chinese as well as U.S. nuclear targets, to prepare for nuclear attack, and to await further orders. He issues the appropriate orders and sits at his desk. He gazes at the sunlit snow framed by the window and waits.

12.45 pm, March 20: Guam
The sailor chipping at rust aboard a marine landing vessel off Guam hears the drone of B-52s lumbering onto the runway for takeoff. Even in the midst of crisis, his orders are to chip rust, not to watch B-52s landing and taking off from Guam, so he keeps his head down.

A few seconds later, a brilliant flash of light half-blinds the sailor. He swears, but quickly recovers his training to count the Flash-to-Bang time for the SS-20 missile warheads which had just exploded above Guam.* With Flash-to-Bang time he can calculate his distance from Ground Zero. The cruiser shudders from the shock wave after twenty seconds, and the sailor knows he is no more than 7 km from Ground Zero and has probably received a fatal dose of invisible radiation.

Looking toward Guam, he watches the roiling mushroom cloud shoot skywards. He also observes a giant wave advancing toward the ship. There is nowhere to run. All he can do is watch. His eyes are fixed on the albatrosses circling overhead. Their feathers are smoking from the radiant heat of the explosion, and then they burst into flames. The smoking, twisting, and blinded birds cartwheel into the ocean.†

12.48 pm, March 20: Tokyo, Japan
A Japanese woman, walking home from her factory at lunchtime, freezes with fear: she knows what the flash from the horizon over Tokyo means – she saw it before at Hiroshima as a small child. Millions are dying in the one megaton explosion aimed at crippling U.S. nuclear war communications and intelligence in the Far East.‡ Huge liquid natural gas tankfarms feed the twisting firestorm ignited by the nuclear explosions.

4.20 pm, March 19: Oahu
A native Hawaiian farmer on the north side of Oahu carefully tills the soil around taro plants in a mountain valley recently wrested from a speculative developer. The mountainside on which he stands trembles from the surface burst of a nuclear explosion over Pearl Harbor, on the

---

* This training for Flash-to-Bang time estimation is described in CINCPAC's script for a nuclear wargame which instructs players to calmly "Determine the azimuth from True North from the installation to the NUDET [nuclear detonation]. From the graph . . . Distance from Ground Zero versus Flash-to-Bang time, determine the flash-to-bang time and prepare the sighting script using the azimuth and time calculated."[48]

† A former U.S. Navy lieutenant observed albatrosses catching fire and crashing into the Pacific during a U.S. atmospheric nuclear test near Christmas Island in the Pacific.[49]

‡ Mizoe Shogo, a Japanese physicist, has estimated that one such explosion would kill 5 million people.[50]

other side of the range. Pieces of moss-covered volcanic cinder topple off the cliffs along the skyline ridge as a mushroom cloud shoots into the sky.

In CINCPAC's Airborne Command Post, 300 km to the north, the telex officer reads an incoming message: "This is reporting activity at Echo Victor Whiskey with actual immediate NUDET report. Field Three, Wheeler Air Force Base 1930 hours airburst. Acknowledge? Out."*

Engrossed in sending fire orders to nuclear forces across the Pacific, the Airborne Command Post does not reply. The operator in Hawaii keeps on repeating the message hoping that someone responsible will hear it.

12.45 pm, March 20: Beijing
Hurrying to class, a university student bends down to gather books and papers which have been scattered from her overflowing bag. A sudden flash of light brighter than the midday sun prompts her to look up. It is the fireball of a Soviet SS-20 missile warhead. She stares directly into the flash of a second nuclear explosion from an incoming American Titan missile warhead, and sees no more.

12.55 pm, March 20: Western Australia
At the Northwest Cape station in Australia, an American officer working at the VLF transmitter building notices unusually heavy traffic on the telex monitoring the relay of messages to U.S. ballistic missile submarines. A few seconds later, three SS-11 missile nuclear warheads explode in a triangular pattern 3,000 m above the base, blinding residents at Exmouth 20 km away. The 900 kilotons of blast and radiation flatten the 387 m Tower Zero antenna array, wrecking the rest of the facility.[52] A few minutes later, warheads from another missile engulf the Early Warning satellite ground station at Nurrungar, 480 km northwest of Adelaide, and Pine Gap, 20 km southwest of Alice Springs.

At Darwin, 2500 km north, fifty demonstrators are hoarse from yelling at two B-52 bombers, idling at the end of the runway ready to take

---

* Based on reporting format for a hypothetical attack on Wheeler in CINCPAC's Nuclear, Biological, Chemical Warning and Reporting System. Translated, the message means that the observer is reporting an actual atmospheric nuclear detonation over Wheeler Air Force Base in Hawaii.[51]

off. The B-52 pilots hope to survive the first salvo of a nuclear war because they believe the Soviets will not waste warheads on Darwin.*

As the demonstrators break through the police cordon onto the runway and throw sticks and rocks at the mammoth planes, the airbase is enveloped by three nuclear explosions bursting 1,000 m above. Taking no chances, the Soviet have fired an SS-11 missile at Darwin. The B-52 crews, the demonstrators, the police and most of Darwin are vaporized, incinerated, and pulverized into the atmosphere.

All around the world, cities and peoples are blasted by one or more nuclear warheads and enveloped by radioactive mists. Of the survivors in contaminated areas, most are dying of radiation sickness in hours or days. As irradiated or safe areas have no visible boundaries, all survivors are stricken with the fear of their certain death.

The few rescue parties flung together cannot enter any of the targeted cities. The dead lie unburied and the wounded uncared for in contaminated areas where certain death lurks for days and years. Millions of refugees rush from the cities in panic, creating new hazards to life in their flight on the congested highways.†

Painful death and destruction as people and the land upon which they depend is burned, vaporized, cratered and contaminated – this is the harvest reaped from decades of planning nuclear war in the Pacific. The scene is repeated wherever the superpowers can spare a warhead to preempt a nuclear attack. The climatological and biological effects are severe even where no nuclear swords fall on the population. Smoke from the burning cities cools the upper atmosphere, and a dark pall falls over the North Pacific. Within a few weeks, the cold northern airmasses are spilling south over the equator, and summer in the south, already radioactive from the war, changes abruptly to winter. Extreme cold and

---

* The 1973 global alert centered on the dispersal of B-52 bombers from Guam,[53] as have Global Shield exercises since 1979.

† The preceding two paragraphs are based word for word on a 1946 report to the Joint Chiefs of Staff on the social and psychological impacts of nuclear attack, written after the Operation Crossroads nuclear tests.[54]

radioactive gloom grip both hemispheres. The end of the world has begun.*

The Power of Protest

How plausible – and probable – is this hypothetical chain of events which ended in global nuclear war? The conjuncture of complex, fluid, and volatile political situations and hair-trigger, genocidal arsenals already exists, especially in the Pacific.

Missing in this projection of current trends into the near future, however, is the constraining influence of opposition by European and Pacific allies, as well as popular protest in the U.S. and abroad. There were many junctures in this hypothetical nuclear war when the war could have been averted by popular protests and allied dissension. Crucial turning points in the stream of events were the initial intervention in Pakistan, the subsequent occupation of a large section of Luzon Island in the Philippines, and the escalation of civil war in south Korea to a north–south war. If U.S. nuclear weapons had been removed from Korea – as demanded by south Korean opposition forces today – and if the U.S. naval build-up had been halted, the spiral to nuclear war in the scenario could well have been avoided.

Since political control over the nuclear arsenal will collapse rapidly in the radioactive fog of nuclear war, the earlier that these protests are mounted, the more likely they are to be effective. It is quite unlikely that popular protest or allied *démarches* would have much impact on the superpowers' decisions by the time both sides were fully mobilized and trading nuclear blows. The time to avert the nuclear peril in the Pacific is now, not when a nuclear war is upon us.

---

* Based on the nuclear winter theories first developed in 1983.[55] Like warplanners, we have adopted the worst-case end of the spectrum of possible outcomes predicted by the nuclear winter studies. The possibility, however small, of such a catastrophic event must be considered in evaluating the risk of nuclear war. In 1985, the Pentagon accepted the scientific bases of the theory, although it rejected its implications for dismantling nuclear weapons and nuclear war doctrine.[56]

PART THREE ☆
CHARTING A NEW PACIFIC

The U.S.S. *Pintado* blockaded by the Peace Squadron,
Waitemata Harbor, Auckland, N.Z. 5 January 1978
(Creative Photography, Auckland)

TWENTY ☆
CHARTING A NEW PACIFIC

[The] nuclear-free Pacific concept is . . . being put forward by people who either do not understand the full implications of such a policy for American strategic interests, or who do not wish to see the United States maintain a presence.
—William Bodde, U.S. State Department, 1982[1]

The great ocean that surrounds us carries the seeds of life. We must ensure that they don't become seeds of death.
—Jean-Marie Tjibaud,
New Caledonian Government Council, 1982[2]

The nuclear peril in the Pacific is growing. Hair trigger weapons, rigid and inadequate structures of command and control, sectarian rivalries between the military services, fluid political situations – all these combine to create a superpower "peace" based on a mounting risk of nuclear war and accident.

Can the nuclear threat in the Pacific be reduced? Is it possible to chart a course to greater safety?

Arms control, as it is currently pursued, is not a promising tack to take in the Pacific. The muscular diplomacy of Washington's new Cold Warriors rests on the concept of "peace through strength" – the belief that clear-cut U.S. superiority on all fronts is the prerequisite to arms control negotiations. In this view, the U.S. must deploy Tomahawk cruise missiles in the Far East to bargain against Soviet SS-20s.[3] The

Soviets, in turn, justify their Asian-deployed SS-20 missiles as a counter to Tomahawk missiles.[4] And so on in an inevitable arms race.

Nuclear arms control discussions, furthermore, have focused primarily on long-range missiles, ignoring theater or intermediate-range nuclear forces in Asia or Europe. Indeed, there exists neither a formal nor a tacit "regime" or set of understandings governing superpower deployment of nuclear weapons in the Far East.[*]

Some security analysts argue that the best way to reduce the threat of nuclear war is to "denuclearize" all American and Soviet forces which operate beyond superpower home territory, including those in the Pacific.[5] Nuclear weapons, however, are deeply integrated with conventional weapons in both U.S. and Soviet forward-deployed forces. Proposals to excise nuclear weapons while leaving intact conventional offensive forces and military alliances are simply unrealistic. Furthermore, "denuclearization" might enhance the likelihood of a superpower *conventional* war, which carries the risk of escalation to nuclear attack launched with home-based nuclear forces.[6]

Rather than putative attempts at nuclear excision, the control of integrated conventional and nuclear forces requires shrinking the geographical space in which they operate. Only by physically separating superpower forces where they now confront each other "eyeball to eyeball" can the threat of nuclear war in the Pacific be lessened. Only by establishing areas which are off-limits to Soviet and U.S. military intervention can the possibility of superpower combat over Third World interests be eliminated.

This approach to regional disarmament and demilitarization has three components. The first is the creation of zones free of all nuclear-*capable* and offensive conventional forces. Such a nuclear-free zone is most urgent in the Northwest Pacific, where the risk of nuclear war is greatest. But it would be buttressed by nuclear-free zones which would eventually cover the entire Pacific region.[†]

---

[*] Except for the broad, global taboo on nuclear attack which underlies a nuclear-armed peace. Warfighting doctrine and strategy, conventional and nuclear, are themselves unregulated in the Pacific nuclear frontier.

[†] The South Pacific "Nuclear-Free Zone" proposed originally by Australian Prime Minister Robert Hawke is severely flawed and would require substantial expansion in scope

The second component is the formation of non-intervention zones, in which *all* forward-deployed foreign forces would be excluded. The prime candidates for such zones are politically volatile areas where both superpowers have vital interests, such as Southeast Asia and the Middle East.

A focus on nuclear-free and non-intervention zones comprises a regional approach to defusing the nuclear threat. Pacific nations, however, are implicated not only in intermediate-range or theatre nuclear weapons but also in long-range U.S. and Soviet nuclear forces. Pacific nations host facilities which guide or test long-range nuclear weapons, making them targets as well as accomplices in escalating nuclear risk. The third component of a Pacific disarmament strategy, therefore, must aim at capping and reversing the global nuclear arms race. This would require Pacific nations to press for and participate in a freeze on the testing and deployment of intercontinental nuclear forces.

This three-pronged approach is not necessarily sequential. Indeed, popular and state initiatives – mostly at the national or sub-regional level – have been and are being undertaken on each of the components throughout the Pacific.

The success of this or any other course away from the nuclear brink in the Pacific depends on broad-based regional consensus and collective action. Regional concert by Pacific nations offers the possibility of reducing the risk of nuclear war, while preserving or enhancing regional peace and independence.

Northwest Pacific Nuclear-free Zone

The nuclear peril in the Far East is concentrated on Northeast Asia, the powder-keg of the Pacific. The outbreak of war between north and south Korea would be likely to prompt immediate U.S. nuclear attack (see Chapter 12). Nuclear war in Korea could spill over into nuclear exchanges in the Seas of Japan and Okhotsk, triggering an all-out nuclear war.

Defusing the nuclear time-bomb in Korea requires reducing tensions

---

to meaningfully contribute to this process. The Hawke Zone allows the transit of nuclear warships through a nuclear-free zone, and does not prevent signatories firing nuclear weapons into or out of the zone.[7]

in the Peninsula and eliminating the risk of U.S. nuclear attack on north Korea. Regional powers such as China and Japan have a direct interest in lessening hostilities and removing forces from the Korean Peninsula; north Korea has also called for a Korean Nuclear-free Zone. Pressed collectively by their allies and friends throughout the region, the super-powers might find a Korean Nuclear-free Zone in their interest, provided that the necessary reductions of nuclear and conventional forces occur on both sides of the Demilitarized Zone.

The pre-conditions of progress are American, Soviet and Chinese guarantees that they will not be the first to use nuclear weapons in Korea or to transfer nuclear weapons to the governments of either north or south Korea.[8] It is equally important to initiate *rapprochement* between north and south Korea. China could prod the U.S. to sponsor three-way talks between the two Koreas and the U.S.* Such talks could aim to achieve a north-south non-aggression pact, prompting great power cross-recognition of the two Koreas and setting the scene for U.S. disengagement.[10] After these steps were taken, the U.S. could then shift its nuclear-capable artillery south, beyond the range of the DMZ. This minimal adjustment to the U.S. posture could indicate good faith to all parties.

Little further progress could be made until south and north Korea replaced their offensive with truly defensive forces. The U.S. could match a phased, mutual reduction by the two Koreas with a step-by-step withdrawal of its own nuclear and conventional forces.

Intense pressure on north and south Korea would be necessary to overcome entrenched military and bureaucratic resistance to the proposal. China and the Soviet Union would probably have to pressure north Korea into disarming its offensive forces and accepting the existence of a south Korean state in exchange for prospective reductions of the American nuclear threat. By the same token, the U.S. would have to push south Korea into accepting the settlement by committing itself publicly to removing all nuclear weapons from Korea, thereby forcing political adjustments inside south Korea.†[11]

---

* The U.S. nearly launched such an initiative in Peking in May 1984 in response to north Korea's proposal for three-way talks. At the last moment, hawks in the State Department sabotaged the move.[9]

† At the same time, the U.S. would have to carefully head off any south Korean effort to substitute a home-grown Bomb for American nuclear warheads.

If political and military obstacles were overcome, north Korea, south Korea and the U.S. could phase out their offensive and nuclear forces in incremental and agreed steps. By the end of the process, the U.S. would have withdrawn *all* its nuclear-capable forces from south Korea.

Rather than a negotiated settlement, strong internal pressures for democracy and reunification in south Korea might eventually force the U.S. to withdraw all its forces hastily. At the least, success of the democratic opposition in south Korea would increase the pressure on the U.S. to seek *rapprochement* and denuclearization. While the repressive capability of the south Korean government makes it unlikely that a democratic revolution could succeed in the near future, popular sentiment for democracy and reunification runs deep.[12]

Whether prompted by external or internal pressures, the creation of a nuclear-free zone in Korea would significantly reduce the risk of nuclear war in Northeast Asia. But the threat of nuclear attack in Korea stems not only from U.S. forces on the Peninsula but also from U.S. and Soviet warships and warplanes which surround the area. The U.S. could rapidly reintroduce its medium-range nuclear forces in the Northwest Pacific into Korea. Both Soviet and U.S. theatre forces project nuclear threats from offshore which would undermine the credibility of a Korean Nuclear-Free Zone. Furthermore, Soviet and American forces directly confront each other, heightening the risk of accidental nuclear war.

To retreat from the nuclear brink in Northeast Asia, it will be necessary to withdraw from the region *all* U.S. and Soviet nuclear-capable forces which can hit targets in the region. As a first step, Soviet and U.S. naval-nuclear forces would need to disengage from the area adjacent to the Korean and Soviet coastlines. Since it depends on substantial progress in Korea, a naval-nuclear disengagement zone would have to be negotiated after or at the same time as a Korean Nuclear-free Zone.

Crucial to a broader Nuclear-free Zone in the Northwest Pacific, a naval-nuclear disengagement zone could initially incorporate the Yellow Sea and the Sea of Japan (see Map 16.2). Except for specified transit between naval bases and the Pacific Ocean, both Soviet and U.S. surface fleets could be banned from sailing these seas.*[13] Intimidating military exercises in the area by either side could also stop.

---

* Soviet use of the Sea of Okhotsk for ballistic missile submarines is probably non-negotiable and would be likely to continue under a limited naval-nuclear disengagement zone.

Even after pulling back from Korea, the Yellow Sea and the Sea of Japan, U.S. aircraft carriers, Tomahawk-armed warships, and F-16 and B-52 bombers could still hit the Soviet Far East from bases throughout the region and all the way out to 2,500 km into the Pacific. Likewise, Soviet SS-20s and Backfire bombers could hit U.S. bases in Japan, Korea, Guam, and Alaska, and aircraft carriers and warships at sea. Eventually, therefore, the naval-nuclear disengagement zone should extend 2,500 km out from the Soviet coastline; and Soviet SS-20 missiles and Backfire bombers should be dismantled or withdrawn to central Siberia, beyond range of Korea, Japan, Guam, and Alaska. Further-more, American F-16s based in Japan and Korea and B-52s based in Guam and Alaska would have to be withdrawn.*

Defusing the regional threat, in short, will require reductions not only in forward-based but also home-based nuclear forces of both the U.S. and Soviet Union. The Soviets have already conceded the possibility that Soviet territory may be included in regional nuclear-free zones in Europe.[14] The U.S. would have to concede the same principle if a Northwest Pacific Nuclear-free Zone were to be created. To avoid *de facto* reintroduction of nuclear weapons, naval bases would be closed to transit for nuclear-capable warships, as would the ocean covered by the zone.

Since Soviet SS-20 missiles and Backfire bombers in Siberia and the Far East are aimed at China as much as at U.S. forces, Soviet compliance with the nuclear-free zone proposal would require the reduction of tensions along the Sino-Soviet border. The Northeastern border is the area of greatest tension, where the military forces of both sides threaten each other's most valuable territorial assets.[15] Major breakthroughs in Sino–Soviet relations would have to occur before a U.S.–Soviet disengagement could be completed.

A Sino–Soviet *rapprochement* could emerge, however, if U.S. withdrawal from Korea were linked to Soviet withdrawal from Afghanistan, clearing the way for a battlefield nuclear-free zone along the Sino–Soviet border. A Northwest Pacific Nuclear-free Zone focused on Korea and naval-nuclear disengagement could thereby substantially reduce the risk not only of U.S.–Soviet but also of Sino–Soviet nuclear war.

---

* Anti-submarine forces in the Northwest Pacific could also be partially disengaged at this phase of the zone.

Non-intervention Zones

The risk of nuclear war in the Pacific stems not only from the integrated nuclear and conventional offensive forces which the superpowers aim directly at each other. It also arises from the possibility that Soviet and American military interventions in the same country or region will overlap, triggering a clash between the superpowers and escalation to nuclear war.[16] To reduce the nuclear peril, both superpowers must eschew military intervention in the Third World and withdraw all forward-deployed forces.*

A global "non-intervention regime" would buttress nuclear-free zones, such as the one proposed for the Northwest Pacific, improving the climate for negotiations on such zones. Furthermore, a global regime would ensure that superpower interventionary forces based in distant areas such as the Indian Ocean or even at home could not threaten the area of nuclear disengagement. This potential would undermine the credibility of nuclear-free zones in the Pacific, just as it would the zones proposed for Europe.[17] To eliminate the threat of renewed and nuclear-armed intervention, even home-based interventionary forces would eventually have to be dismantled.

Even before the superpowers have embraced the general principle of non-intervention, states in Asia and the Pacific can move in this direction by establishing regional non-intervention zones. Because of their strategic importance to the superpowers, Southeast Asia and the Indian Ocean stand out as prime candidates for such zones.[18] Both superpowers are already involved in interventions in both areas – the Soviet Union in Vietnam and Afghanistan; the U.S. in the Philippines and Diego Garcia.† Both superpowers also have an intrinsic interest in demilitarizing the sea lanes of trade, especially for oil.

In both areas, moreover, there are already strong regional sentiments in favor of non-intervention. Southeast Asian nations are committed, on paper at least, to a regional zone of peace and security. In the Indian Ocean, coastal states and even the superpowers have long pro-

---

* An exception might be made for small, multinational peace-keeping forces accountable to the United Nations General Assembly.

† The U.S. also has de facto bases in Oman and along the African coast.

posed naval disengagement. By gradual extension, Indian Ocean and Southeast Asian non-intervention zones could eventually abut each other as well as a Northwest Pacific Nuclear-free Zone, creating a continuous buffer zone between the superpowers.

Pacific allies and non-aligned nations can play a pivotal role in pressing the superpowers to respect non-intervention zones. The heavy logistical demands of intervention mean that the superpowers must rely on their allies and friends in the region to host airfields, visiting warships, and communication sites. The allies could make superpower access to these facilities contingent upon commitment to respect non-intervention zones. Alternatively, the allies could simply withdraw their support, making intervention not only in the zones but beyond much more difficult and unlikely.

The short-term prospects are poor, however, for achieving broad regional consensus to regulate superpower intervention. Many Pacific elites seek domestic or regional advantage from superpower forward deployment. By entering regional conflicts, the superpowers and their local allies strive for marginal political or military advantage over their adversaries.

Nonetheless, there is strong nationalist sentiment throughout the Pacific. To expand their efforts to insulate the region from superpower intervention, Pacific states could create and strengthen regional institutions to mediate and resolve regional conflicts. The newly created South Asian Association for Regional Cooperation, for example, is likely to move in this direction.*[19] And there have been efforts by Southeast Asian governments to settle the conflict in Indochina. Besides keeping direct superpower intervention at bay, regional resolution of conflicts would ward off *indirect* intervention – the use of local states as surrogates for external powers.

Another route to the creation of non-intervention zones is through broad superpower negotiation. As part of negotiations toward a Northwest Pacific Nuclear-free Zone, for example, the superpowers could undertake non-intervention commitments elsewhere in Asia–Pacific. This package would entail U.S. and Soviet withdrawal from existing interventionary springboards in Southeast Asia and the Indian Ocean.

---

* Members include India, Pakistan, Bangladesh, Sri Lanka, the Maldives, Bhutan, and Nepal.

Nuclear Freeze in the Pacific

The creation of a Northwest Pacific Nuclear-free Zone and non-intervention zones in Southeast Asia and the Indian Ocean would substantially eliminate the possibility that the superpowers might clash and escalate to nuclear war in the Pacific. While such steps could enhance the confidence necessary for a global disarmament regime, they would not exclude the region from an all-out nuclear war begun elsewhere in the world, most likely in Europe or the Middle East.

Should war erupt between the superpowers, it is likely that both the U.S. and Soviet Union would move rapidly to reintroduce intermediate-range nuclear weapons into the Far East. Until they are dismantled, bombers and aircraft carriers can always be sent back. Furthermore, not even the farthest corners of the Pacific could escape the devastation of radiation and nuclear winter which would result from a superpower nuclear war. Removing the threat of nuclear war from the Pacific requires simultaneous initiatives in regional and global dimensions of nuclear deployment.

Tackling the *global* aspects of nuclear war will require – as a first step – a superpower freeze on the production, testing, and deployment of new long-range nuclear weapons, including delivery systems.[20] A freeze would directly affect the Pacific. It would end U.S. and Soviet long-range ballistic missile tests into the Pacific. It would halt Star Wars and anti-satellite tests from Hawaii and Kwajalein. It would block deployment of ground or air-launched cruise missiles, Pershing II or Trident II ballistic missiles, and neutron bombs. It would disallow any additions to existing nuclear capability such as Soviet SS-18 and SS-20 missiles, or American Trident I or Tomahawk missiles.

Pacific states cannot directly veto production, testing, or deployment of long-range nuclear weapons.* Nonetheless, the region has some leverage over U.S. and Soviet long-range nuclear policies. U.S. allies host nuclear communications bases for submarines and B-52 bombers. They also supply airfields and joint naval operations for anti-submarine warfare. Australia and Japan for the U.S. side and, to a lesser extent,

---

* Pro-independence forces in French Polynesia have claimed repeatedly that they would shut down France's nuclear testing station in the islands, bringing to an end French nuclear tests in the region.[21]

Vietnam for the Soviets also host important intelligence facilities which acquire targeting information useful to nuclear attacks.

Most of these facilities support nuclear weapons which are inherently pre-emptive. Shutting them down would marginally reduce the incentive to strike first in a nuclear crisis. Faced with the serious possibility of eviction, the U.S. might find a freeze more interesting than in the past.

Once they have agreed to a freeze, the superpowers could begin to cut their nuclear arsenals. They could start with land-based missiles, the most pre-emptive and vulnerable delivery systems.[22] Anti-submarine forces – which are nearly as provocative as land-based missiles – could be cut back, and the remaining capability only operated in coastal waters adjacent to the superpowers. If a Northwest Pacific Nuclear-free Zone had not already removed them, the B-52 bombers in Guam and Backfire bombers in the Far East could be moth-balled. As the forces were dismantled, communications and intelligence facilities supporting nuclear war and intervention could be removed.*

Regional Concert

Left to their own devices, the Cold Warriors in Washington and Moscow are unlikely to cede an inch of their nuclear deployments or spheres of influence. "What should we give up?" asked U.S. Defense Secretary Caspar Weinberger in 1984. "Should we give up NATO? Korea? Japan? The Mid-east with its oil fields? The Caribbean? Defense of the continental United States? We can't give any of it up." [23] The Soviets similarly see important strategic advantages flowing from their forward deployment.[24]

The superpowers are likely to find mutual Pacific disarmament in their interest only when pressed by a regional concert of allies and non-aligned Pacific states. Indeed, collective regional action by Pacific states is probably the surest way to superpower disarmament in the Pacific.

---

* Intelligence monitoring of compliance with arms agreements may facilitate radical cuts. Special exceptions which are equitable to both superpowers and acceptable to the region acting collectively could be made to retain such facilities.

Prompted by broad-based popular movements, regional concert complements political pressures within the U.S. and Soviet Union to pull their nuclear forces and military forward-deployment back from the brink.[25]

Besides giving a voice to the smaller nations of the region *vis-à-vis* the superpowers, regional concert could help to establish a non-proliferation regime in the Pacific. Such a regime would inhibit the development of nuclear weapons by "near nuclear" nations such as Japan, south Korea, Taiwan, Indonesia, Pakistan, and Australia.[26] It could also help to prevent China or any other regional nuclear power from supplanting the U.S. and Soviet Union with their own power projection capability.

By definition, a regional concert would be organized by and composed of state leaders with diverse interests and varying levels of political power. China and Japan are the only states in the region with enough political clout individually to affect superpower decisions on long- and medium-range nuclear arms. Both states also have powerful security incentives to explore regional concert for reduction of the nuclear peril. To successfully complete its program of "socialist modernization", China needs at least twenty to thirty years of peace. Furthermore, China is apprehensive of the threat posed to its fledgling nuclear force by the nuclear arms race and Soviet deployments of SS-20 missiles and Backfire bombers in Asia.[27] China has long pressed for a Western Pacific Nuclear-free Zone and a no-first-use guarantee.[28]

Japan is well placed, in principle, to sponsor a regional concert for superpower disengagement and non-intervention, especially if it entailed Soviet withdrawal from Vietnam and Afghanistan.[29] Although Prime Minister Nakasone and the hawks behind Japan's current rearmament are unlikely to promote regional arms control initiatives, this very trend could encourage China to pursue regional arms control initiatives as a means of containing Japan's power in the region. There are also powerful neutralist and anti-militarist sentiments in Japan, even in the ruling Liberal Democratic Party. Even among Japan's military forces, there is awareness that a nuclear attack on Japan would be devastating because of the proximity of U.S. bases to Japanese cities. It is at least possible that Japan would not want to be seen as blocking arms control initiatives by countries in the region with which Japan has extensive economic ties.

The other allies and non-aligned states have little direct leverage on the superpowers, especially in creating a Korean Nuclear-free Zone. They could, however, directly veto the use of their territory to prepare for naval-nuclear war in the Pacific and Indian Oceans. The U.S. and, to a lesser extent, the Soviet Union depend on regional states for airfields for maritime strike aircraft, especially anti-submarine warfare planes. The allies also host communications and intelligence bases essential to fighting a nuclear war at sea.

The initiatives of individual nations to disengage from the nuclear peril lay the foundation for collective strategy. Rather than China or Japan, less powerful nations have taken the lead. Indeed, it has been at the edges, rather than at the strategic center, that the Cold War blocs have started to melt. New Zealand and Vanuatu, for example, have broken from nuclear alliances, established national nuclear-free zones, and promoted a far-reaching South Pacific Nuclear-free Zone. South Pacific island nations as a whole have actively supported the concept of a nuclear-free Pacific.[30] These initiatives make it possible realistically to consider diplomatic offensives aimed at bringing the region together to discuss reducing the nuclear peril in the Pacific.

New Zealand and Vanuatu have demonstrated that small nations can be politically potent in setting the stage for regional concert. If the Vanuatu experience is any indication, island states such as Belau or Kanaky (New Caledonia) which are still under a colonial thumb will adopt an active anti-nuclear foreign policy at independence. Without doubt, the revolutionary struggle in the Philippines poses the greatest immediate challenge to American forward-deployment in Pacific Command. A non-aligned Philippines supportive of a nuclear-free Pacific would enormously boost the prospects for a regional concert.

The first step toward regional concert is the creation of an inclusive North and South Pacific regional consultative framework on security issues. Unlike current American and allied proposals, such a forum must include the U.S. and the U.S.S.R., but only as observers. Such a Pacific Peace and Disarmament Forum could generate proposals and discuss collective interests in reducing the nuclear peril.

The notion of regional concert to reduce the nuclear peril parallels the sentiment that growing *economic* interdependence in the Pacific requires regional cooperation.[31] Indeed, the Soviet Union, Vietnam, and north Korea could find attractive the prospect of economic development and increased trade which would result from increased economic regionalism. This incentive could induce a positive response to an overall regional security settlement.*[33]

People's Diplomacy

At the root of Pacific governmental initiatives toward disarmament – whether at the regional or national level – are broad-based domestic movements. From Japan to the Islands to Australia, these national movements are typically composed of popular peace forces, churches, trade-unionists, and anti-nuclear, independence, or social democratic political parties.[34] Loosely constituted throughout the region as the nuclear-free Pacific movement, they have pursued not only nuclear disarmament but also political independence for the remaining colonies in the region.[35]

Since the early 1970s, the nuclear-free Pacific movement has generated a powerful "people's diplomacy", bringing together activists from island and "rim" national movements in conferences and speaking tours to adopt priorities for mutual support and regional action. Working with regional organizations such as the Fiji-based Pacific Council of Churches and the Pacific Trade Union Forum, the movement has helped to evoke a regional consciousness of common interest. These concerns have crystallized into coordinated pan-Pacific campaigns against new weapons systems such as Tomahawk missiles, or into support for anti-nuclear and independence movements such as that in Belau and Kanaky.†

The growing transnational network of the nuclear-free Pacific movement is the cutting edge of regional disarmament. Intergovernmental concert in the region may eventually develop out of the regional dialogue about the nuclear peril which the movement promotes, as well as

---

* This proposal should not be confused with suggestions for the creation of a Pacific economic or security community which excludes China, north Korea, Vietnam, and the Soviet Union, and which is managed by the U.S. and Japan.[32]

† A major and so far successful campaign of the nuclear-free Pacific movement was aimed at curtailing Japanese plans to dump low-level nuclear waste into the North Pacific near the Marianas Islands. As a result of the transnational campaign, all of the island states, including Guam, caused Japan to abandon its dumping proposal.[36]

the installation of anti-nuclear governments. Crucial elements of the power of the non-governmental forces to change the *status quo* are the nascent networks which reach into both Koreas, China, and the Soviet Union, cutting across East–West and North–South lines.

Anti-nuclear states and the nuclear-free Pacific movement face stiff American and Soviet opposition to regional controls on their nuclear shadow-boxing in the Pacific. The superpowers can be expected to insist on their "rights" to traverse the high seas in warships bristling with nuclear weapons, or to appropriate the Pacific for ballistic missile tests in preparation for the final showdown. To match the superpowers will require perseverance and carefully constructed, long-term strategy.

Without doubt, popular movements and pro-disarmament governments will chart new routes to peace and security in the Pacific. They will suffer setbacks, as well as make advances. But demands for a new order will certainly persist. "It is a matter of life and death", asserted Walter Lini, Prime Minister of Vanuatu in 1983, "that our Pacific Ocean be declared a nuclear-free zone. Testing of any kind must be outlawed, as must the dumping of nuclear waste, the firing of nuclear devices, and the passage of submarine or overflying aircraft carrying them. On this crucial issue there can be no compromise or retreat. If we continue to deny ourselves any decision on this, our children of tomorrow will condemn us, and it will be a condemnation we have deserved." [37]

Demonstrators on Sydney Harbor on departure of the U.S.S. *Buchanan* and *John Young*, 8 March 1985 (Peter Moxham, Sydney *Sun*)

EPILOGUE ☆
JUST THE TWO OF US?

Industrial centres and military installations in Australia could – I repeat, could – become nuclear targets.

—Jim Killen, Minister for Defence, 1981[1]

We acknowledge that the fact that we host these joint facilities does entail possible risk in the event of nuclear conflict.

—Bob Hawke, Prime Minister, 1983[2]

Every Australian knows about the danger of bushfires. When hot winds blow, a stab of lightning – or an arsonist – can set a firestorm raging across the mountains. On Ash Wednesday, February 16, 1983, sixty-eight people died in such a fire.

Every day of the year is a Total Fire Ban Day in the world of nuclear war. Like matches scattered in the undergrowth, fifty thousand warheads are spread across the global landscape. Who would be confident that lightning will never strike? Through its military alliance with the U.S., Australia helps provide the infrastructure for nuclear weapons. Is the alliance a firebreak against a nuclear firestorm – or a magnifying glass for nuclear war?

In 1984, New Zealand closed its ports to U.S. nuclear warships. American response made it clear that non-nuclear alliance with the U.S. was impossible. In July 1985, the U.S. State Department asserted that ANZUS was gone and "It's just the two of us." [3] New Zealand's actions, however, have prompted many Australians to ask if they too should withdraw from their military alliance with the United States.

Balance Sheet of National Survival

Whether or not to remain in the alliance is a decision which must be based on an assessment of the costs and benefits to Australia. For the United States, the benefits of the nuclear alliance are clear. It has meant the ability to locate important bases and to dock visiting nuclear warships and warplanes in Australia. The American bases and warships, however, place Australians at risk, first and foremost because they make Australia a Soviet nuclear target.*

In a nuclear war, the Soviet Union might attack only the U.S. bases at Northwest Cape, Nurrungar, and Pine Gap, killing anywhere between 500 and 20,000 people. It might attack a warship visiting Cockburn Sound, or B-52 bombers in Darwin dispersing from Guam, killing up to 125,000 people.[5] More remote is the possibility of Soviet attacks on Australia's cities, killing millions of people and intended to block any hope that the U.S. could use Australian resources to recover from a nuclear attack.[6] Leaders of both major political parties have admitted that Australia is exposed to these risks.

There are military reasons to believe that the last two types of attack are less likely than the first.† Since only the Soviets know who is on their target lists – and in a nuclear war, even *they* may lose track – it is prudent to assume that any of the possible targets in Australia could be attacked and destroyed.

---

* There is also the possible but incalculable risk of a major nuclear weapon accident aboard a visiting American warship or warplane, in peacetime or war.[4]

† The Soviets have fewer accurate, promptly deliverable nuclear warheads than they have hard or urgent military targets in the U.S. Their targeting doctrine also concentrates on military targets rather than cities, suggesting that they would not "waste" warheads on Australian cities. Conversely, as two American analysts write, "Undoubtedly there is a place in Soviet planning for destroying elements of the enemy's economic system that might enhance his strategic stature in post[nuclear]war global affairs."[7] The Soviets do have a large stockpile of obsolete "surplus" nuclear missiles which could be used against

For Australia to make a rational decision to stay in the nuclear alliance, the benefits must be commensurate with the enormous risks to national survival. Short-term commercial or military advantages such as selling more beef or gaining access to advanced defense technology hardly count. Furthermore, some of these "spin-offs" are available whether or not Australia is in the nuclear alliance.

To date, most discussions of the alliance – pro and con – have focused on the military impact of the bases on nuclear deterrence and warfighting. The argument revolves around whether the bases reduce or enhance the probability of global nuclear war. For the only conceivable benefit to Australia great enough to justify the risks which the bases pose is that they reduce the likelihood of global nuclear war. Australia's social and political life would be severely degraded by such a war, even if it escaped direct attack. If a nuclear winter were to sweep over the equator, Australia itself could be destroyed. In short, one can virtually equate Australia's national survival with avoiding global nuclear war.

Supporters of the alliance argue that Australia's military ties with the U.S. reduce the likelihood of global nuclear war, more than offsetting the risk to Australia of a direct attack should a nuclear war erupt.[9] Opponents believe that the nuclear alliance itself enhances the probability of global nuclear war, placing Australia in double jeopardy. Can either of these arguments be sustained?

---

urban–industrial targets. We do not know if Soviet economic targeting extends to Australia; nor, we are sure, does the Australian government. It is unwise, however, to discount the possibility that Australia's cities could be hit in a nuclear war. There is little analysis in the open literature of American incentives or plans to rely on allied economies for post nuclear war recovery, or the role such considerations might play in Soviet anti-recovery targeting. American strategic thinkers such as George Quester have argued that "Our planning for World War III is . . . hardly complete unless we incorporate considerations of how best to dissuade the U.S.S.R. from attacking the centers of key resources in other countries, of how best to keep the U.S.S.R. after the attack from attempting to coerce and blackmail the outside world into the delivery of such resources [in the aftermath of nuclear war], and how best to get such resources delivered as needed to the United States," so we can expect similar thinking to occur in the Kremlin.[8] It is fair to assume that there are Soviet strategists worrying about whether they should block American recovery using allied resources by nuclear devastation or post nuclear war coercive diplomacy.

Nuclear Firebreak?

Alliance supporters have argued over the years that the alliance is fundamental to Australia's defence because it deters both nuclear attack and invasion. The alliance protects Australia from invasion, they claim, because the strategic services which the bases provide are so valuable to the U.S. that it would defend them against any external threat.

Apart from the fact that Australia faces no credible threat of invasion, it is evident that American forces are vastly overextended and unlikely to rush to Australia's defense.[10] Indeed, it is much more likely that Australians would die to defend the U.S. bases, with only incidental American help. Australian defense planning already proceeds largely on the assumption that Australia must defend itself.[11] Any costs or benefits arising from nuclear alliance are extrinsic to this fundamental fact.

Nuclear alliance is not only a poor antidote to conventional invasion. It also fails to shield Australia from nuclear threats or attacks.* No less an authority than Admiral Noel Gayler, former Commander-in-Chief Pacific (CINCPAC), underscored the point in 1984: "Anyone who thinks that the Americans are going to start a nuclear war in defense of them is deluded." [12]

More recently, supporters of the *status quo* have argued that the alliance is a firebreak against the threat of global superpower nuclear war. According to Foreign Minister Bill Hayden in 1985, the bases are an "essential ingredient" of nuclear deterrence.[13] In this view, the bases – which act as the eyes, ears, and mouth of the U.S. – vitally contribute to stabilizing superpower nuclear relations by aiding the operation of U.S. deterrence forces, as well as by monitoring Soviet compliance with arms control agreements.

The base at Northwest Cape, for example, transmits nuclear fire orders and other directives to American nuclear submarines, the ultimate retaliatory force upon which "stable" nuclear deterrence depends. The Pine Gap and Nurrungar bases relay to the U.S. information collected by American spy satellites on Soviet and Chinese

---

* It does not serve as a credible shield against China, for example, from which some Australians feared nuclear attacks in the 1960s.

nuclear forces. This intelligence includes missile tests, nuclear explosions, missile launches, radars, and communications.

Nurrungar's satellite allows the U.S. to recognize and terminate false alarms by cross-checking earth-based radar warnings of Soviet nuclear missile attack. At the same time, the satellite provides warning of attack fifteen minutes earlier than the radar. It thereby gives more time for American commanders to communicate with the Soviets and to make better decisions, reducing the itch in American trigger fingers to launch a pre-emptive strike.*[14]

Since a pre-emptive strike brings enormous advantages to the side which launches it, the pre-emptive urge, as Thomas Schelling and Morton Halperin wrote a quarter of a century ago, "converts a possibility of war into an anticipation of war, precipitating war." [15]

Nurrungar and Pine Gap also play a role in arms control, helping to make the U.S. confident that the Soviets are observing the ground rules for the nuclear arms race as outlined in the SALT I and II agreements. And the bases verify compliance with the Nuclear Non-proliferation and Partial Test Ban Treaties.

Alliance supporters argue, in short, that if American commanders can transmit more nuclear information faster and with greater reliability, both superpowers will be less likely to launch a pre-emptive strike, thereby reducing the risk of nuclear war.

Force Multiplier

Every now and then, as most farmers know, a firefighter turns out to be an arsonist. Critics argue that, far from being a firebreak, the alliance increases the overall risk of nuclear war.

Like a telescopic lens on a rifle, the communication and intelligence systems based in Australia enhance the *offensive* capability of the U.S. nuclear arsenal. They allow more missiles to fire earlier, accurately pinpoint more targets, and assess damage from the initial attack. Indeed, according to one American general, systems such as those in

---

* A pre-emptive strike is an attack aimed at limiting the attacker's damage from a perceived imminent enemy attack, that is, a "defensive first-strike." It is not the same as a surprise, "bolt out of the blue" first-strike aimed at disarming the other side, the "offensive first-strike" often discounted by Australian officials who defend the U.S. bases.

Australia are "one of the most significant force multipliers" in the American nuclear arsenal.[16] Alliance critics argue that radical changes in the nuclear offensive and defensive forces have increased the pre-emptive urge. The U.S. bases in Australia, they assert, are coupled with these forces in a way which surpasses their stabilizing role, making nuclear war more rather than less probable.[17]

In this vein, three potential destabilizing effects are said to offset Nurrungar's stabilizing effects on the nuclear brink. First, Nurrungar's very early warning of Soviet missile launch could prompt the U.S. to fire a pre-emptive strike without waiting for radar to cross-check the information.* This heightens the risk of inadvertent U.S. nuclear attack. Second, the same sensors that detect nuclear explosions to verify arms control treaties can be used to assess the damage caused by American pre-emption in Soviet missile fields, serving nuclear warfighting capabilities.†[19] Third, information collected by Nurrungar's satellite may already be used in Star Wars research. By the 1990s, satellites may support an anti-ballistic missile system, dooming the Anti-Ballistic Missile Treaty.‡[21]

Northwest Cape offers another example of the dual nature of the bases. Northwest Cape may deter an all-out Soviet surprise attack by increasing U.S. capability to retaliate with submarine-launched missiles.§ Assured of a second-strike capability, the U.S. would also be less likely to launch its own pre-emptive first strike.

But Northwest Cape also serves a highly offensive part of the American arsenal: reportedly, it is used to communicate with American attack-submarines under the Guam-based commander of U.S. naval

---

* If the Soviets fire a "small" salvo of nuclear missiles in reply to a similar American "shot across the bow" or before any American strike, American commanders could "launch under warning." [18]

† NAVSTAR satellites will take over this role in 1988.

‡ Nurrungar may be relegated to a backup communications link for the satellites when satellite-to-satellite crosslinks become operative. Even as a redundant backup, however, Nurrungar would still contribute to these destabilizing effects.[20]

§ Northwest Cape would probably be a primary communications station for Ohio submarines operating in the Northwest Pacific or Indian Oceans. Should the submarines operate close to the U.S. West Coast, Northwest Cape would probably be a backup to a similar facility on the U.S. West Coast.

forces in the West Pacific who commands Northwest Cape.[22] According to U.S. Secretary of the Navy John Lehman, these submarines will attack Soviet missile-firing submarines in the North Pacific in the first five minutes of a conventional or nuclear war.[23] In January 1986, Admiral James Watkins confirmed officially that such an attack against the Soviet Union's crucial retaliatory force was the official deployment doctrine of the Navy.[24] By undermining Soviet confidence that they could ride out and retaliate to any American first-strike, this public proclamation of Navy doctrine may have increased the risk of nuclear war – and Northwest Cape's contribution to such a risk – without any consultation with Australia.*

Even the CIA's intelligence base at Pine Gap can be viewed as enhancing the risk of nuclear war. While some in Washington may indeed rely on Pine Gap's information to put a brake on the arms race, Pentagon lobbyists are equally likely to use it to shoot down arms control agreements.[25] This is possible because the significance of electronic intelligence processed at Pine Gap is not clear-cut; its interpretation is often a matter of judgement on non-technical grounds.[26]

Hawks in the influential Committee on the Present Danger, for example, used the Pentagon's accuracy estimates for the Soviet SS-19 missile to vilify the SALT arms control agreement.[27] They portrayed the U.S. as vulnerable to a disarming Soviet first-strike, creating a climate of distrust inimical to superpower negotiations. In 1985, using the same information, the CIA contended that the Pentagon had over-stated the accuracy of the SS-19, and reduced the estimated Soviet arsenal of first-strike warheads by 40 per cent! But by then the political damage was done.[28]

Besides its use in sabotaging arms control, information from Pine Gap could put the final touches to a U.S. nuclear attack plan. In the unlikely event that Pine Gap survived the start of the war, it could also help to reconstitute and retarget American nuclear forces and guide

---

* A broadcast of "go" orders to implement such plans is likely to be sent over many media, including satellites, and low and very low frequency stations in the West Pacific including Northwest Cape. Some American attack submarines, however, would already be "on station", trailing Soviet ballistic missile submarines in waters already subject to Soviet anti-submarine forces. These attack submarines would probably rely on very low frequency radio to avoid the risk of Soviet detection arising from satellite or low frequency communications.

U.S. long-range bombers around Soviet air defense radars for the last lick at a first-strike.

One might argue that Pine Gap will be needed to verify arms control agreements when the political pendulum swings back to detente. However, the best form of arms control – a freeze on missile tests and nuclear tests, and radical cuts in nuclear forces – would not require verification by Pine Gap. Soviet compliance with a freeze which banned missile tests could be adequately monitored by early-warning satellites and radar.* Such an approach has been advocated not only by popular peace movements but by retired senior military commanders such as Admiral Noel Gayler.[29]

In short, alliance critics argue that far from reducing the risk of nuclear war, the bases destabilize the nuclear brink and should be evicted immediately.

Balance Sheet Revisited

The balance sheet of national survival lists the contribution of the bases to arms control and deterrence on the one side; and their negative effects on Soviet *and* American propensity to launch a first-strike on the other side.[30] Unfortunately, there is no objective way to produce a nett measure of these contradictory effects. No one in Washington or Moscow, let alone Canberra, can determine to what extent additional information improves or degrades nuclear decisions. No one can predict whether the bases and forces together increase or decrease Soviet and American reciprocal fear of surprise attack. No one knows how to relate information flows to nuclear performance attributes such as accuracy, firepower, lethality, range, recallability, etc. Even worse, they have no method to determine how the coupling of decision-makers to forces via communication and intelligence systems in the American

---

* By 1988, the NAVSTAR satellite will be available for such monitoring, relegating the Nurrungar satellite system to a backup. Navstar can also detect missile launches, providing verification of compliance with a missile test ban, making Pine Gap superfluous for substantive arms control.

nuclear arsenal interacts with its Soviet counterpart, each element of which differs from its American counterpart.*

In short, neither supporters nor critics of the alliance can sustain an argument built on the premise that the bases stabilize or destabilize the nuclear brink. No one in a position of authority can determine whether more nuclear communication and intelligence in a crisis will accelerate American or Soviet first-strikes or brake the momentum.

Not only are these effects incalculable, they are also unlikely to significantly or even marginally influence nuclear war decisions. Compressed in time, such decisions are likely to be based as much on gut-fear as on a rational calculation of nuclear deterrence.[31]

In the final moments of truth, therefore, the bases in Australia would be irrelevant. If the world topples over the nuclear brink, it will be because of poor decisions, terrifying weapons deployed in aggressive fashion, organizations running amok, and misunderstandings.[32] It will not be saved – or destroyed – by more or less communication and intelligence hardware. Trying to ascertain whether the bases increase or decrease the risk of nuclear war is like asking how many warheads can crowd onto the head of a missile – it is simply the wrong question.[33]

Willing Accomplice?

Since it is not possible to determine what direct impact the bases have on the risk of nuclear war, we must find alternative criteria to decide whether the alliance enhances or reduces the likelihood of a global nuclear war. Instead of gauging the military impact of the bases, we could ascertain whether the alliance represents potential Australian political leverage over American nuclear-related decisions. For even if it could be proven that the nuclear alliance reduces the risk of nuclear war, it is possible that an alternative approach might reduce the risk even more.

We believe that there are three possible paths open to Australia. Each

---

* Indeed, our Freedom of Information Act requests and informal enquiries in Washington, D.C., indicate that the Pentagon has not even considered the problem.

approach aims to affect the political perceptions and attitudes which ultimately determine the risk of launching a nuclear war.*

As an ally and willing accomplice, Australia might influence American behavior well before the brink, reducing the probability of a crisis. This outcome would result from American fear of pre- or post-crisis allied response to its escalatory tactics, inducing conservative behavior on the part of the U.S. leadership.† Of course, fear of Australia's reaction *after* a nuclear war is unlikely to endow it with any influence in Washington just before a nuclear war.

There is little evidence, however, to demonstrate that junior allies such as Australia have affected American decisions early in budding crises at the lower levels of the escalation ladder. In 1958, the U.S. came to the very brink of attacking China with the bomb over Taiwan. Then CINCPAC Admiral Harry Felt dismissed 1958 ANZUS meetings held at the height of the crisis as "talk talk." [35]

In the Cuban Missile Crisis, Secretary of State Dean Rusk advised Kennedy that "if we take a strong action the allies and Latin America will turn against us." [36] He recommended that the U.S. proceed unilaterally to wipe out the Soviet missile sites in Cuba "after informing MacMillan, De Gaulle, Adenauer, and possibly Turkey and a few Latin Americans." [37] Rusk felt at the time, "If we don't do this we go down with a whimper. Maybe its better to go down with a bang." [38] Allies such as Australia were not even to be warned in advance, let alone consulted on the best way to go down.

In response to crisis in the Middle East in 1973, the U.S. did not even

---

* There is no historical "frequency" of nuclear war with which to estimate nuclear "risk", nor a formal, deductive method to predict it. Indeed, if a global nuclear war can occur only once, its probability is indeterminate. The term "risk" collapses into a subjective, consensual judgment.[34]

† A variant of this argument runs as follows: indeed, the bases and alliance may be destabilizing, but eviction will lead the U.S. to relocate the same facilities to U.S.-controlled territory (Diego Garcia, Guam, satellites), leaving the risk unchanged. As an active partner, Australia could influence American behavior, and the bases should therefore be kept as a means to this end. This argument, however, suffers from two irremediable flaws. First, the evidence cited above is cause for skepticism that such influence can be exercised. Second, if such influence could be shown to exist, proponents of this argument must also admit that Australian support for America's nuclear modernization and escalatory tactics could also "egg on" the U.S., offsetting any stabilizing effects.

inform, let alone consult with Australia, when it signalled a global nuclear alert through Northwest Cape. Prime Minister Gough Whitlam noted angrily at the time that the alert was "a good example of how a foreign base on Australian soil might be used to launch World War III without Australia's consent or knowledge." [39]

Nor can it be said that a willing accomplice has much impact on U.S. arms racing. Senior Pentagon official Frank Gaffney, for example, stated in 1986 that the Complete Test Ban Treaty is "frivolous". Yet the proposed Treaty, which Gaffney rejected as "neither strategically acceptable nor conducive to effective, verifiable arms control," is the centerpiece of Australia's arms control diplomacy. [40]

Honest Broker?

Australia might be able to do more to reduce the risk of nuclear war as an honest broker than as a willing accomplice. Australia could use the bases and its regional influence to affect directly the political relationships which determine whether nuclear war is *felt* to be more or less likely, and therefore *is* more or less likely.

To this end, Australia would continue in the alliance but use Pine Gap and Nurrungar as bargaining chips with the U.S. To protest against provocative U.S. attack submarine strategy and pending Trident II missile deployments, Australia would immediately evict Northwest Cape. This move would communicate to the United States that Australia is serious about reducing the nuclear peril. If the U.S. did not make a good-faith effort to achieve meaningful nuclear arms control and reductions within five years, Australia would evict Pine Gap and Nurrungar. This policy would place the onus to produce tangible results where it belongs, on the U.S. To pressure the Soviets to participate, Australia could also make the eviction contingent upon Soviet nuclear arms control and reductions.

The U.S. might, of course, pick up its marbles and go home. By so doing, however, it would admit that Pine Gap and Nurrungar are not very important in avoiding or fighting a nuclear war – at least, that they are less valuable than keeping an ally subordinate and compliant. But given a "fair go", the U.S. could not complain that Australian demands were unfair or unfriendly.

Go it Alone?

Instead of waltzing on with Uncle Sam, Australia could go-it-alone at the outset, recognizing the futility of trying to dictate terms to a super-power as a dependent ally. It could energetically promote collective constraints and sanctions by Pacific states on both American and Soviet nuclear deployments in the Pacific. Pursuing a regional concert for arms control could be more productive than remaining a willing accomplice or giving the U.S. a "fair go".

Australia would first evict all the bases and put up a "not welcome" sign to all nuclear warships and warplanes. Out of self-interest, Australia would support the creation of non-intervention zones in the region, aimed equally at the forward-deployed forces of both super-powers. It would demilitarize its relations with regional states and adjust its military posture to a strictly territorial defense by phasing out long-range strike forces.[41]

With its own house in order, no axes to grind and none to wield in Asia or the Pacific, Australia would see the political credibility of its anti-nuclear diplomacy increase substantially, presenting a more potent political challenge to the regional nuclear arms race.[42] Since Australia would not support the American nuclear arsenal or its interventionary power projection, this policy should eliminate the risk that the Soviets would make Australia a target in any circumstance – assuming that Soviet military bureaucrats ever revise their target lists.

Historical precedents give credence to the idea that an independent course maximizes Australia's influence. Independent diplomatic initiatives pursued by Australia in the 1945–1950 period forced the U.S. to adjust its foreign policy on key issues.[43]

By itself, Australia's ability to overcome the regional inertia in the face of the nuclear peril facing the Pacific would be severely limited. But combined with the voices of New Zealand and island states, the call would echo to even distant corners of the region. Even a small shift toward regional concert for nuclear arms control could greatly exceed the impact of a willing accomplice or an honest broker.

Whichever way Australia chooses, it is imperative that she address the real political issues which constitute the risk of nuclear war. Instead of engaging in fruitless debates about the role of the bases and the efficacy of nuclear deterrence, Australia could force the U.S. to choose whether it is committed to arms control or to nuclear superiority. Australia could demand that the Soviets choose between non-nuclear friendship and nuclear intimidation in the Pacific.

Rather than preparing to abdicate all responsibility at the moment of greatest threat to national survival – the brink of a nuclear war – Australia could take itself out of the line-of-fire and off the nuclear frontline. Rather than remaining a junior partner of the U.S., Australia could join New Zealand as a strong regional voice for a truly peaceful order in the Pacific.

Marshall Islanders set up protest camp next to radar screen in Kwajalein
in "Operation Homecoming", Fall 1982
(Julian Riklon)

APPENDIXES

Appendix A:
Reference Tables

Appendix A1:
CINCPAC Defense Representatives in Pacific Command

Australia	US Air Force Liaison Officer to Australia
Burma	US Defense Attache
China	US Defense Attache
Hong Kong	US Defense Liaison Office Representative
India	US Defense Attache
Indian Ocean	Commander, Middle East Force (as of 1979)
Indonesia	US Defense Attache
Japan	Commander, US Forces, Japan
South Korea	Commander, US Forces, Korea
Madagascar	US Defense Attache
Malaysia	US Defense Attache
Nepal	US Defense Attache
New Zealand	US Defense Attache
Philippines	Commander, US Naval Forces, Philippines
Singapore	US Defense Attache
Southwest Pacific Island Area	CINCPAC REP Southwest Pacific
Sri Lanka	US Defense Attache
Thailand	Commander, US Military Advisory Group, Thailand

Note: The CINCPAC-appointed Defense Representatives are instructed to "take local initiative to improve the interface between non-combat DOD [US Department of Defense] elements, the U.S. Ambassador, and the host government defense establishment". (Instruction 5400.20 D, p. 2). CINCPAC REP Southwest Pacific is based in Fiji. CINCPAC also has representatives to Strategic Air Command at Anderson Air Force Base in Guam and at the Joint Strategic Target Planning Staff at the Offut Air Force Base, Omaha, Nebraska, and at the Naval Station at Adak in the the Aleutians.

Sources: CINCPAC, "U.S. Defense Representatives in Foreign Countries", Effective Instruction 5400.20D, January 12, 1984, pp. 3–4. Department of the Navy, *Environmental Impact Statement, Military Use of Kaho'olawe Training Area*, Honolulu, 1979, pp. 1–4. N. Foster, personal communication, December 26, 1984.

Appendix A2:
U.S Command Posts in Pacific Command

Site	Command	Service
Hawaii	Commander-in-Chief, Pacific, Camp H.M. Smith[a]	U
	Commander-in-Chief, Pacific Fleet, Makalapa	N
	Commander, 3rd Fleet	N
	Commander, Submarine Force, Pacific	N
	Commanding General Fleet Marine Force, Pacific Camp H.M. Smith	N
	Naval Logistics Command, Pacific	N
	Commander, Intelligence Center, Pacific	U
	Commander, Middle East Force, Persian Gulf[b]	N
	Army Western Command, Fort Shafter	AR
	Commander, Pacific Air Forces, Hickam AFB	AF
San Diego	Commander, Naval Air Force, Pacific	N
	Commander, Training, Pacific	N
	Commander, Naval Surface Force, Pacific	N
	Commander, Anti-Submarine Wing, Pacific	N
Guam	Commander, Naval Forces, Marianas, Nimitz Hill	N
	Command Post, SAC 8th Air Force, Anderson AFB	AF
Okinawa	Command Post, III Marine Amphibious Force, Camp Courtney	N
	Command Post, 18th Tactical Fighter Wing, Kadena AB 3 AWAC (Airborne Warning & Control) Aircraft, Kadena AB	AF
Japan	Commander, 7th Fleet, Yokosuka	N
	Commander, Naval Forces, Yokosuka	N
	Command Post, U.S. Air Force U.S. Fifth AF, Yokota	AF
	Commander, U.S. Army, Camp Zama	AR
Alaska	Command Post, Alaska Air Command, Elmendorf AB[c]	AF
Korea (south)	Commander, UN Command, U.S. 8th Army U.S. Forces, Seoul, Yong San AB	AR
	Command Post, 314th Air Division of 5th AF, Osan AB	AF

Appendix A2: (continued)

Site	Command	Service
Philippines	Command, U.S. Naval Forces, Subic Bay	N
	Command Post, 3rd Tactical Air Wing, Clark AB	AF
Diego Garcia	Commander, Middle East Forces in Persian Gulf[d]	N

Key: N = Navy, AF = Air Force, AR = Army, U = Unified

Notes: a. Alternate Command Post underground at Camp H.M. Smith; another alternate Command Post at Kunia; Blue Eagle PACOM Airborne Command Post at Hickam AFB. CINCPAC also maintains a rapidly deployable mobile command post.

b. Operational control only of forces deployed by Commander, U.S. Naval Forces, Europe, London.

c. CINCPAC does not control Alaskan-based forces, only the Aleutians.

d. CENTCOM regional commander afloat in region, operating out of Diego Garcia.

Sources: J. Laurance, "U.S. Pacific Fleet Organization", *Signal*, February 1984, p. 71; Office of Assistant Secretary of Defense (Manpower, Reserve Affairs, and Logistics), *Base Structure Annex to Manpower Requirements, Report for FY 1982*, January 1981; U.S. House of Representatives, Committee on Appropriations, Subcommittee on the Department of Defense, *Department of Defense Appropriations for 1985* (Hearings), Part 1, U.S. GPO, Washington, D.C., 1984, pp. 785, 789, 839, 843; N. Weatherbie, "C and S in Japan: Coordination and Change", *Signal*, February 1984, pp. 42–43; C. Weinberger, *Annual Report to Congress, FY 1985*, U.S. Department of Defense, Washington, D.C., 1984, p. 197; O. Wilkes, Foreign Military Bases Project files, SIPRI, Stockholm, 1983.

Appendix A3:
U.S. Navy General Purpose Forces, Strength and Disposition, 1958–1984

Ship Types	1958	1968	1978	1984
Aircraft Carriers				
Attack	9	9	6	6
Anti-submarine[a]	5	4	—	—
Surface Combatants				
Battleship	—	1	—	1
Cruiser	9	13	16	17
Destroyer	104	240	30	29
Escort/Frigate	37	59	33	43
Patrol	—	—	1	—
Attack Submarines	43	115	36	48
Amphibious Warfare Vessels	86	157	32	32
Mine Warfare Vessels	43	86	—	—
Auxiliaries	124	247	52	55
Pacific Fleet Totals				
(General Purpose Forces)	463	503	206	231
Navy Totals				
(General Purpose Forces)	901	932	418	465

Notes: 1984 excludes mobilization forces assigned to Pacific Fleet.
a. Anti-submarine warfare aircraft carriers phased out in mid-1970s, and ASW functions transferred to attack carriers.
Sources: R. Weinland, *The U.S. Navy in the Pacific: Past, Present, and Glimpses of the Future,* Center for Naval Analyses, Professional Paper 264, Virginia, 1979, p. 7; J. Collins, *U.S./Soviet Military Balance, Statistical Trends, 1970–1982,* Congressional Research Service Report 83–153S, Washington, D.C., August 1, 1983, pp. 116; 130. U.S. Navy, Office of Public Affairs, February 1, 1984.

Appendix A4:
U.S. Marine Forces and Bases in the Pacific

Forces	Bases
Okinawa	
10,000 Personnel	6 Marine Corps Bases
III MAF	3 Ranges (exercise or gunnery)
3rd Marine Wing	Air Wing at Futema Air Station
1st Marine Wing	and Kadena Air Base
3rd Force Service Support Group	
1st MAB	
Philippines	
About 2,000 Personnel	Use of Philippines sites for
1st MAU	bombing exercises
Japan	
Foreign Transiting Tankers	Marine Corps Air Station at
Marine Fighter Aircraft and	Iwakuni; Marine Air Wing, Misawa.
Helicopters	Use of Sasebo and Yokosuka
Logistics/Naval Support	naval bases
—2 squadrons/24 F-14 fighters	
—1 squadron/19 A-4 fighters	
—1 squadron/10 A-6 fighters	
—1 detachment/6 AV-8 fighters	
Hawaii	
24 F-4 fighters	Marine Corps Air Station,
	Kaneohe, Oahu

Notes: MAF = Marine Amphibious Force, normally constitutes 32,600 troops plus tanks, aircraft, and artillery; MAB = Marine Amphibious Brigade, normally constitutes 15,500 troops plus tanks, aircraft, and artillery; MAU = Marine Amphibious Unit, normally constitutes 2,500 troops plus tanks, aircraft, and artillery.

Sources: U.S. House of Representatives, Committee on Appropriations, Subcommittee on the Department of Defense, *Department of Defense Appropriations for 1985* (Hearings), Part 1, U.S. GPO, Washington, D.C., 1984, pp. 807, 859, 862; R. Halloran, "18-Month Survey Finds U.S. Forces Lacking Readiness," *New York Times*, July 22, 1984, p. 14; O. Wilkes, Foreign Military Bases Project, SIPRI, 1983; J. Collins, *U.S./Soviet Military Balance, Concepts and Capabilities*, McGraw Hill, New York, 1980, p. 347; J. Collins, *U.S./Soviet Military Balance, Statistical Trends, 1970–1982*, Congressional Research Service Report 83–153S, Washington, D.C., August 1, 1983, pp. 127–130.

Appendix A5:
U.S. Army Bases in the Pacific

Forces	Bases
South Korea	
8th U.S. Army	Camp Casey
2nd Infantry Division	Taegu
19th Support Command	*Totals:*
	24 camps/barracks
	11 training/gunnery sites
	4 armistice sites (Panmunjom)
	4 supply, maintenance, administrative only
Japan	
Camp Zama	HQ U.S. Army, Japan
Army logistics/repair depot	Sagamihara
Exercise	Camp Fuji
Okinawa	
Army Logistics Depots	4 Sites
Philippines	
Logistic Support Unit	Manila
Guam	
Army Civic Action Team Base	Camp Covington
Hawaii	
25th Infantry Division	Schofield Barracks, Oahu

Sources: U.S. House of Representatives, Committee on Appropriations, Subcommittee on the Department of Defense, *Department of Defense Appropriations for 1985* (Hearings), Part I, U.S. GPO, Washington, D.C., 1984, Appendix A2, Part 1, pp. 785-787; O. Wilkes, Foreign Military Bases Project, SIPRI, 1983.

Appendix A6:
U.S. Central Command Forces

Army
1 Airborne Division
1 Airmobile/Air Assault Division
1 Mechanized Infantry Division
1 Light Infantry Division
1 Air Cavalry Brigade

Air Force
7 Tactical Fighter Wings
2 Strategic Bomber Squadrons

Navy
3 Carrier Battle Groups
1 Surface Action Group
5 Maritime Patrol Air Squadrons

Marine Corps
1 1/3 Marine Amphibious
Forces

Source: C. Weinberger, *Annual Report to Congress, FY 1985*, Department of Defense, Washington, D.C., 1984, p. 197.

Appendix A7:
Major U.S. Logistics and Storage Bases in PACOM

Forces	Base
Okinawa	
U.S. Air Force	Kadena AB, MAC terminal, air refuelling squadron, logistics for SAC B52s.
U.S. Army	Sundry port, fuel, munitions, supply depots.
U.S. Marine Corps	Air and amphibious equipment logistics; Naval Hospital.
Guam	
U.S. Air Force	MAC terminal, squadron 6 KC 135 air refuellers.
U.S. Navy	Fuel and nuclear weapons storage; munitions, magazine, supply depots.
Hawaii	
U.S. Navy	Lualualei, naval numbers storage including nuclear weapons; Red Hill, Naval supply center, especially fuel. Seven other logistics sites, especially Pearl Harbor Naval Shipyard for repairs.
Johnston Island	
?	Storage of obsolete chemical weapons.
Alaska	
U.S. Air Force	Elmendorf, MAC refuelling point, logistics.

Appendix A7: (continued)

Forces	Base
Japan	
U.S. Navy	Naval medical Center, Yokosuka. Fuel and munitions at Tsurumi, Koshiba, and Yokohawa.
U.S. Army	Fuel and munitions depot at Yokohama, Akizuki, Kawakami, Kure, Hiro and Sagamihara. Twelve logistics sites operated for U.S. by Japan.
Philippines	
U.S. Air Force	Clark, MAC terminal, fuel and munitions storage.
U.S. Navy	Cubi Point, fuel and munitions storage. Subic Bay, major ship repair facility, fuel and munitions storage, naval medical center.
Singapore	
U.S. Air Force	Changi, Lockheed repair facility contracts to USAF.
U.S. Navy	Sembawang, USN office contract ship repair.
Australia	
U.S. Air Force	Learmonth, Pearce, Richmond, MAC depots.
New Zealand	
U.S. Air Force	MAC Terminal, Christchurch.
U.S. Navy	Support for *Operation Deepfreeze* in Antarctica.
Diego Garcia	
U.S. Air Force	MAC alternative airfield en route to Middle East.
U.S. Navy	Naval logistics, especially fuel and munitions storage. Near Term Prepositioned Force for CENTCOM.

Source: O. Wilkes, Foreign Military Bases Project, SIPRI, 1983.

APPENDIX A8:
Ship Visits in Pacific Command, 1983 (Ship-Days in Port)

	Ship Type[b]											
	CVN	CV	CGN	CG	DDG	DD	FFG	FF	SSN	SS	AMP	Totals
Northwest Pacific/East Asia[a]												
Guam	5	10		2		1	55	43	144		27	272
Hong Kong			5	34	27	26	22	61	24		128	342
Japan	143	18	9	433	251	79	63	678	197		384	2255
Okinawa					2			1			56	59
Saipan											2	2
south Korea	4	10	4	17	28	17	15	92	18		29	234
East Pacific												
Alaska											12	12
Canada		4	1	1		4	10	6	13		4	47
Hawaii	1		1	110	1012	18	32	1884	3805	407	168	7442
Mexico	1					4	6		3		11	24
Southwest Pacific												
American Samoa			3									3
Australia	12		27	6	15	18	6	61	58		48	251
Fiji					4							4
New Caledonia				1								1
New Zealand			11		8				5			24
Papua New Guinea					2							2
Tonga			3		3							6
Southeast Asia												
Indonesia											3	3

Location											Total
Malaysia					4			3			3	10
Philippines	32	34	16	186	156	231	149	359	226	397	600	2386
Singapore		8		13	8	17	12	43	4		64	169
Thailand				8	19	7		36	24	34	34	162
Indian Ocean												
Diego Garcia		15		19	7	1	18	67	77			204
Maldives							5	5				10
Seychelles						3						3
East Africa												
Djibouti					1	1		4				6
Kenya	6			5	11	15		10	9		9	65
Somalia						2			2		2	6
Middle East												
Bahrain				27	66	43		41				177
Oman			5	18	12			21				56
United Arab Emirates				3		5						8
Saudi Arabia						11						11
South Asia												
Pakistan				3		7	4	16	8			34
Sri Lanka				5		5			8			31
Totals incl. Hawaii	197	95	94	847	1620	558	490	3425	4607	805	1584	14,321
excl. Hawaii	196	91	93	737	608	540	458	1541	802	339	1416	6,879

Key: CV = aircraft carrier; CG = Guided Missile Cruiser; DDG = Guided Missile Destroyer; DD = Destroyer; FF = Frigate; FFG = Guided Missile Frigate; SS = Attack Submarine; AMP = all classes of amphibious and supply warships (LST, LHA, LKA, LPD, LPH, LCC etc); N = nuclear powered class.

Notes: a. No visits to Taiwan listed. China visit cancelled 1985. b. No battleship port visits listed for 1983 for *New Jersey*.

Source: U.S. Navy, Office of Information, Washington DC, computer printout, 1984.

Appendix A9:
Major Signals Intelligence (SIGINT^a) Bases
in PACOM

Japan
Misawa: Major SIGINT station in NE Asia; AF 6290th Electronic Security Group; Naval Security Group; Army Security Group, and Marines Personnel. Covers Seas of Japan, Okhotsk, Kurile Islands, Soviet Far East and Siberia.
Karii Seya: Major naval HF SIGINT "Operations Complex".
Hakata: Army Security Agency SIGINT station.
Atsugi: Air Base, EP-3E and SIGINT aircraft.
Camp Fuchinobe: National Security Agency Pacific representative and base.

Okinawa
Torii: Army Security Agency upper and lower spectrum SIGINT site.
Hansa: Sobe, Naval, Security Army, Air Force, National Security Agency SIGINT site.
Onna Pt.: National Security Agency COMINT relay center.

South Korea
Yonchon, Sinsan-ni, Kangwha: Army Security Agency Sites.

Guam
Agana NAS: 2 squadrons SIGINT EP3s; SR-71 strategic reconnaissance aircraft.
Finegayan: Naval Security Group SIGINT site (Classic Wizard).

Philippines
San Miguel: Naval Security Group, SIGINT site.

Hong Kong
Kittiwake: joint U.S.-U.K.-Australia SIGINT station aimed at PRC.

Australia
Pine Gap: Satellite Ground Station for upper spectrum COMINT satellites over Soviet Union; COMINT in Australia region.
NW Cape: Naval Security Group SIGINT site.
Shoal Bay: Australia SIGINT station, provides SIGINT to U.S.

New Zealand
Tangimoana: HF Radio Direction Finding Facility.

Diego Garcia
Ocean Surveillance SIGINT site (Classic Wizard).

Alaska
Shemya AB: USAF aerial surveillance squadron 'Cobra Ball' for monitoring Soviet test missiles over Pacific; also SAC RC-135 airborne spy planes; ground ELINT site for 'Cobra Dane' radar for monitoring Soviet missile tests plus probable SIGINT site; ship-borne 'Cobra Judy' missile test monitoring radar off Aleutians in NW Pacific.

Adak: Naval Security Group SIGINT site. *Gambell, NE Cape* (both St. Lawrence Is.), *Kenai, Attu*, probable SIGINT sites, possibly NSA.

Hawaii
Kunia: National Security Agency SIGINT analysis site in underground bunker.
Wahiawa: Naval Security Group, SIGINT site. *Helemano*: Army Security Agency, SIGINT site.
Pearl Harbor: Fleet Intelligence Center, Navy.
Camp H.M. Smith: Intelligence Command, Pacific; National Security Agency Operations Group, Chief of NSA Pacific, NSAPAC representative to CINCPAC.

Canada
Massett AB: Queen Charlotte Island, Canadian SIGINT feeding to U.S. HF Direction Finding Stations.
Whitehouse: Canadian SIGINT site feeding data to Alaska, Elmendorf AB SIGINT site.

China
Leninsk and Sang Shagan: N.W. China, two Chinese SIGINT stations with U.S. equipment, data shared with U.S. on Soviet missile tests.

Taiwan
Shu Lin Kou: SIGINT Station for National Security Agency.

Pakistan
Bada Beir (Peshawar): SIGINT site on Soviet and Chinese nuclear and missile tests, possibly reactivated?

Key: HF = high frequency radio; LF = low frequency radio.
Notes: National Security Agency is administered and funded as a U.S. defense agency.
a. SIGINT: SIGINT is composed of Communications Intelligence (COMINT), Electronic Intelligence (ELINT) Signals Intelligence, comprises COMINT, ELINT, foreign instrumentation SIGINT, non-imagery infrared and light signals. COMINT: Communications Intelligence, the interception/processing of foreign communications passed by radio, wire, or other electromagnetic means, and processing of foreign encrypted communications. ELINT: Electronics Intelligence; the observation, recording and processing for intelligence information from foreign, non-communications, electro-magnetic radiations (not from atomic detonations or radiation). PHOTINT: Photographic Intelligence.
b. Extensive SIGINT facilities constructed by U.S. in Thailand during Vietnam War may be available again to U.S.
Sources: P. Bamford, *The Puzzle Palace, A Report on NSA, America's Most Secret Agency*, Houghton Mifflin, Boston, 1982, pp. 165–166, 438–441; P. Chapman, *Canada and the Movement for a Nuclear-Free Pacific*, Project Ploughshares, Working Paper 84–2, Conrad Grebel College, Waterloo, Canada, 1984; *National Times* (Sydney) May 6, 1983, p. 6; O. Wilkes, Foreign Military Bases Project, SIPRI, 1983.

Appendix A10:
Pacific Missile Range Bases

Site	Function
Vandenberg, California	Launch ballistic missiles.
Pt. Mugu, California	Launch ballistic missiles.
Submarine launch site off California coast	Submarine-launched ballistic missiles.
Kwajalein Atoll	Instrumented terminal impact area for incoming re-entry vehicles from test missiles; Pacific Barrier Radar.
Guam	Pacific Barrier Radar.
Hawaii	
Kaena Pt.	Mid-range missile tracking radar (AF).
Kokee (Kauai)	Mid-range missile tracking radar (Navy).
Halaeakala (Maui)	ARPA Optical site infrared and optical missile tracking and identification techniques.
South Pt. (Hawaii)	Missile launch site for ARPA tests.
Midway Island	Missile impact locating system.
Wake Island	Missile impact locating system.
Saipan Island	Missile tracking radar and telemetry system.
Oeno Island	Missile impact locating system.*
Broad Ocean Areas	
600 km NW Guam	Oceanic splashdown for re-entry vehicles.
"North of Kwajalein" t	Oceanic splashdown for re-entry vehicles.
"Wake"	Oceanic splashdown for re-entry vehicles.
"Oeno"	Designated for future Trident tests.
Tasman Sea SE of Sydney	Designated for future MX tests.

Note: Former sites which might be reactivated include Easter Island, Enderbury, San Nicholas, Johnston, and Eniwetok Islands.
* Oeno Island was used for satellite observation in 1969–70 by the U.S. Air Force.
t Sites in quotation marks are Air Force designations.
Sources: O. Wilkes, Foreign Military Bases Project files; SIPRI, 1983; Ballistic Missile Defense Systems Command, *SSTSS*, 1981; Air Force, Navy Offices of Public Affairs, November 1984; Space and Missile Tracking Organization, *SAMTO Test and Evaluation Support Resource Plan (FY 1982–1989)*, Vandenberg Air Force Base, California, 1982, p. III-1–3.

Appendix A11:
Tomahawk-capable U.S. Pacific Fleet Warships

Tomahawk-capable Naval Units Assigned to the Pacific Fleet: Class and Type[a]	U.S. Navy Vessel Registration Numbers	Number of Tomahawk SLCMs per Naval Unit[b]	Number and Type of Nuclear Warheads per Tomahawk
Attack Submarines			
9 Sturgeon SSN:	639, 648, 652, 660, 662,† 665,* 672, 682, 684	8 [12][c]	1 W80
8 Los Angeles:	688,* 692,† 969 697, 698, 701,* 711,* 713,* 715,* 716,* 718*	8 [12][c]	1 W80
Cruisers[f]			
2 Virginia CGN:	39,† 41	16	1 W80
1 Long Beach CGN:	9	16	1 W80
[Ticonderoga CGs][e]	all	24	1 W80
Destroyers[g]			
5 Spruance DDG:	964, 973, 976,* 984, 985, 992	8 [16 VLS][d]	1 W80
Battleships			
2 Iowa BB:	62,* 63	32	1 W80

Note: SCLMs may be nuclear or conventionally armed.

a. Jane's, *Fighting Ships, 1983–1984*, London, 1984, pp. 633, 636, 659, 660, 664, 674; T. Cochran *et al.*, *U.S. Nuclear Forces and Capabilities*, Ballinger, Cambridge, 1984 p. 172-173, 258. Note that these numbers will increase by the time SLCMs are widely deployed on the surface fleet.

b. T. Cochran *et al.*, *ibid.*, p. 186.

c. Present torpedo tube launching allows for carriage of 8 SLCMs. VLS will allow twelve tubes for Tomahawk. *Ibid.*, p. 186.

d. Two unknown units of the Spruance-class will have 16 VLS for Tomahawk. It is assumed that the remainder will have a minimum of eight SLCMs.

e. Ticonderoga is a new class of guided missile cruisers not yet deployed in the Pacific.

f. No CG-37 California-class Tomahawk-capable currently assigned to Pacific Fleet.

g. First Tomahawk-capable DDG-51 Burke-class not launched until 1989.

* Known to be fitted with land-attack Tomahawk missile capability as of March 1, 1985.

† To be fitted with land-attack Tomahawk missile capability by December 1986.

Sources: As above.

Appendix B:
Command Structure: Pacific Command

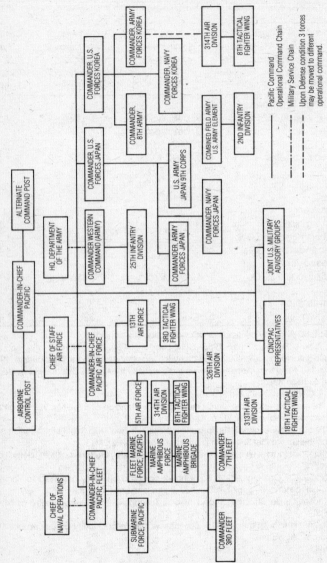

Source: W. Simons, "Command and Control in the Pacific," *Journal of Defense and Diplomacy*, Volume 3, no. 1, January 1985, p. 19.

APPENDIX C:
Satellite Tracking and Ground Control, and Early Warning Bases in Pacific Command

C1. Satellite Tracking/Ground Control

Japan
Dodaira, Baker-Nunn camera operated by Japan feeding to U.S. Defense Mapping Agency eventually.

South Korea
Pulmosan (Taegu), ground-based electro-optical satellite tracking system (GEODSS) to track high altitude satellites.

Marshall Islands
Kwajalein, Missile and satellite tracking radar, part of Pacific Radar Barrier to monitor Soviet satellite and ASAT launches and maritime reconnaissance satellites on first orbit; DSCS ground station. NAVSTAR navigation system monitoring site and antenna.

Guam
Northwest Field, Satellite Control Facility for EW, reconnaissance, weather satellites control and data acquisition. Pacific Radar Barrier satellite tracking radar planned.

Davidan, Satellite tracking and telemetry station.

Philippines
San Miguel, Pacific Radar Barrier satellite tracking site.

Australia
Orroral Valley, NASA satellite tracking/data acquisition antenna serving DOD scientific, geodetic weather satellites.

NW Cape, Ground station CIA/NSA Ryolite upper spectrum SIGINT; also satellite control facility.

Hawaii
Kaena Point, Oahu, Major Satellite Control Facility, NAVSTAR navigation satellite system monitoring station.

Haleakala, Maui, electro-optical satellite tracking system (GEODSS).

Kokee, Kauai, NASA space tracking, data acquisition station.

Diego Garcia
GEODSS electro-optical deep space surveillance system.

NAVSTAR navigation satellite system monitoring site and antenna.

Mauritius
Port Louis, U.S. operates tracking/telemetry at British naval base.

Seychelles
Mahe, Satellite tracking/telemetry station; DCS satellites.

C2. Satellite Photographic Intelligence Launch and Recovery in the Pacific

U.S.
Vandenberg AFB, California, Launch site for many intelligence satellites.
Midway Islands
Naval AF for C-130 aircraft for mid-air recovery of spy satellite film capsules.
Okinawa
Kadena AB, MAC film recovery HC-130s.
Hawaii
Hickam AFB, YC-130 aircraft, HH-53 helicopters.
Australia
Pine Gap, Satellite Ground Station for photographic satellites, radio data dump.

C3. Satellite Intelligence Systems in PACOM

Photographic Reconnaissance: "Big Bird" Project 467 satellites with variable area and close look capabilities, film capsules plus radio-photo transmission, lifetime greater than one year, inclination placed in high orbits in low earth orbit.
Electronic Intelligence: either large area 300–400 km orbit to monitor high frequency, short-range air defense radars to aid U.S. bomber design of electronic counter-measures, lifetime 1–2 years; or low altitude, concentrated focus ferret satellites in polar orbit.
Ocean Surveillance: use infrared, radio altimeter, and ELINT to locate and track vessels.

C4. Tactical Early Warning: (EW) Ground Station and Assets in PACOM

Air Surveillance Radar
Japan: 28 air surveillance radar sites run by Japan, provides WE to USAF; integrated into similar system in south Korea.
Okinawa: 4 air surveillance radar sites and control center, Kadena AB, run by Japan, provides EW to USAF. 3 AWAC (Airborne Warning and Control) aircraft, Kadena AB.
South Korea: 14 air defense radar/missile sites across south Korea, integrated with AWACs, naval E-2Cs, Japan/Okinawa systems; controlled from Osan AB. OV-10 observation aircraft, Osan AFB.
Philippines: Air surveillance radar site operated by U.S. or Philippine AF.
Alaska, Canada, see Table 12.1. *FIX*

Hawaii: 2 air surveillance radar sites.
Note: Extensive air surveillance radars in Thailand may be available to the U.S. again. U.S. may also have access to 3 EW radars in Singapore and Malaysia. Integrated Air Defense System of the Five Power Defense Agreement through ANZUS.

C5. Fixed Sub-Surface Oceanic Intelligence

Japan
Kami Seya: Naval Ocean Surveillance Information System Center analyzing data collected by Orion aircraft and underwater hydrophone nets (SOSUS), ASW Center.
Tsushima Sts, SOSUS chain across seabed between Kyushu and south Korea.
Tsugaru Sts: SOSUS chain across seabed between Honshu and Hokkaido.
Misawa, ASW Center.
Kuriles
SOSUS in Kuriles trench alleged by Soviets.
Okinawa
Kadena, ASW Operation Center.
Guam
Agana, Guam, ASW Center. SOSUS Station and network.
Philippines
Cubi Pt, ASW Center, SOSUS offshore.
Alaska
Adak, SOSUS station, ASW Center for SOSUS off Aleutians.
Hawaii
Ford Island, Pearl Harbor, probably Fleet Ocean Surveillance Information Center, Pacific.
Pearl Harbor, SOSUS Evaluation Center.
Barber Pt, Oahu; SOSUS system; ASW Center.
North of Hawaii, deep ocean Sea Spider SOSUS network.
Diego Garcia
Probably SOSUS site.
Christmas Island
Hydrophone array related to Diego Garcia SOSUS, possibly dismantled.

C6. Mobile Subsurface Ocean Intelligence:

Attack submarines, surface fleet fixed and towed sonar and helicopter dipping sonar.

C7. Aerial Maritime Reconnaissance

Alaska
Adak, Naval AF, P3C Orions.
Japan
Iwakuni AB, Misawa AB, Kami Seya, P3C Orions
Guam
Agana, Naval Air Station, 1 squadron P3C Orions, Anderson AFB, B-52s used for VP role in Indian Ocean, South China Sea, Northwest Pacific since early 1980s.
Hawaii
Barber's Pt, Naval Air Station, P3C Orions.
Midway Island
P3C Orions.
Philippines
Langley Pt, Naval Air Station, *Cubi Pt, Subic Bay*, P3C Orions for South China Sea.
Singapore
Tengah AB, aircraft staging to Diego Garcia.
Thailand
Takhli AB, Orions staging to Diego Garcia.
Cocos Island
Australian AF, used by U.S. P3C Orions staging to Diego Garcia.
Diego Garcia
AF for 3–5 P3C Orions. Plus Oceanic Reconnaissance Satellites ground stations, see above.

Key: AB = Air Base; AF = Airfield; ANZUS = Australia, New Zealand, U.S. alliance; ASAT = Anti-Satellite; ASW = Anti-Submarine Warfare; AWAC = Airborne Warning and Control; CIA = Central Intelligence Agency; DCS = Defense Communications System; DOD = Department of Defense; MAC = Military Airlift Command; NASA = National Aeronautics and Space Administration; NSA = National Security Agency; NUDET = Nuclear detonation at 100 km altitude.

Sources: B. Jasani, *Outer Space – Battlefield of the Future?* Taylor and Francis, London, 1978; Office of the Assistant Secretary of Defense (Manpower, Reserve Affairs and Logistics), *Base Structure Annex to Manpower Requirements Report for Fiscal Year 1982*, U.S. Department of Defense, Washington, D.C., 1981; O. Wilkes, SIPRI Foreign Military Bases Project, Stockholm, 1983;

APPENDIX D:
Major Radio Communication Systems in Pacific Command

A. Very Low Frequency (VLF)

Description: frequency: 30–300 Hz; wave length: 1000–100 km (surface); signal range: thousands of kilometres, depending on radiating power, greater than 4,800 kilometres.
Characteristics: NUDET effect: phase shift up to hours; reliable; jam resistant, penetrates water to 6–9 m; needs very large antenna, high power requirement (200 KWe, plus).
Uses: Sonar, navigation, slow submarine communication, one way (to launch platforms) only.

Fixed Bases for Submerged Submarine Communication
Australia, NW Cape Naval CS, fleet broadcast, strategic submarines.
Hawaii, Wahiawa NCS.
Japan, Yosami Naval CS.

Mobile VLF Transmitters for Communication TACAMO EC130s (to be replaced with E6 aircraft), trails a 4 km vertical wire antenna. Airfields for continuously airborne VLF communications with Trident; Hickam AFB Hawaii, with Agana AFB Guam as backup.

Omega VLF (Navigation)
Australia, Darriman, Victoria.
Japan, Tsushima.
Mafete (operated by French for US)
Reunion (Indian Ocean)

B. Low Frequency

Description: frequency: 30–300 KHz; wavelength: 10–1 km. (surface); signal range: thousands of kilometres, depending on radiating power.
Characteristics: NUDET effect: absorption for minutes to hours; penetrates water to 0.5 m, requires large antennae.
Uses: LORAN-C navigation, fleet/submarine communication

Fixed Bases (LORAN A or C)
Canada, Williams Lake
Guam
Japan, Iwo-Jima
Johnston Island (U.S.)
Marcus (U.S.)

Micronesia, Yap, Eniwetok, Kwajalein, West Fayu, Saipan Islands
Okinawa, Gesashi, Mikayo, Jima, Hokkaido
Wake Island

Mobile Bases:
Aircraft for navigation, blind bombing.
Surface and Submarine Fleet Short Range only.

C. Medium Frequency (MF)

Description: frequency: 300 KHz-3 MHz; wavelength: 1000–100 m
(groundwave in lower MF, skywave); signal range: depends on radiating
power, antenna directivity, local terrain.
Characteristics: Dependable in lower MF, decreasingly so in higher MF.
Uses: Ships, aircraft, troops for tactical communications.

D. High Frequency (HF)

Description: frequency: 3–30 MHz; wavelength: 100–10 m; signal range:
short, medium, long range up to 3000–4000 km depending on ionospheric
conditions (skywave, surface wave).
Characteristics: varying reliability, NUDET effect: ionospheric absorption;
multipath fading for hours; unreliable at high altitudes due to auroras,
especially in N-S direction. New frequency-hopping HF is jam resistant.
Uses: Tactical Air Fleet, submarine communications; teletype; voice;
OTH-B radar; positive control SAC bombers, GIANT/TALK SCOPE SIGNAL.

Fixed Bases
Alaska: Adak NCS, HF for North Pacific Fleet, Elmendorf AFS, HF SAC Signal
Scope
Australia: NW Cape: powerful HF station
Diego Garcia: HF tactical and broadcast transmitter
Guam: Barrigada, Naval HF station to West Pacific
Hawaii: Bellows AF Station, SAC; Wahiawa NCS
Japan: Yokosuka NCS, major naval HF station; Yokota AFS, SAC Scope
Signal III HF; relocating to Owada and Tokorozawa; Fuchu (USAF), where
Japanese C3 integrated into U.S. C3; Fuyaka, Negishi, Nagai, Atsugi;
Camp Asaka, Sagami, Sofu, all AFS.
Okinawa: Senaha, AFS
Philippines: Dau (Clark AFB), SAC HF Scope Signal III HF site; grounder
terminal for PACOM's Airborne Command Post; AF HF site; Camp
O'Donnell, AF site; San Miguel, naval HF receiver site; Tarlac, naval HF
transmissions
South Korea: Seoul, 3 sites for Voice of UN Command.

New Zealand: Christchurch, naval communications, especially for Antarctica.

Mobile Bases:
Most mobile weapon systems in PACOM, workhorse of fleet communications.

E. Very High Frequency/Ultra High Frequency (VHF/UHF)

Description: frequency: 30–300 MHz (VHF), 300 MHz-3 GHz (UHF); wavelength: 10–1 m (VHF), 100–10 cm (UHF), both direct or ground wave; signal range: to horizon, 16–48 km, UHF, less than 480 km, airborne line-of-sight, or relay aircraft needed.
Characteristics: line-of-sight (LOS) transmission, high data rates; relatively secure but ionosphere can propagate; blocked by local terrain; NUDET effect: absorption for minutes, scintillation for hours.
Uses: Short-range tactical communications, troposcatter relay networks (UHF), radar, strategic communications; teletype, LOS satellite broadcast.

Fixed Bases
Alaska: Green Pine SAC, UHF stations, Aleutians/Alaska; Navstar UHF ground station
Diego Garcia: NAVSTAR UHF Ground Station
Guam: NAVSTAR UHF ground station: SCF at Finegayin NCS (UHF)
Hawaii: SCF at Wahiawa (UHF)
Japan: Kwajalein, NAVSTAR UHF ground station, 10 troposcatter relay (UHF) sites
Okinawa: Yaedake, troposcatter relay site to Japan
Taiwan: Juzan, troposcatter relay site between Japan and Philippines

Mobile Bases:
SHF/UHF installed on EC-135 aircraft, AFSATCOM
UHF from Airborne Command Posts
UHF on all AF tactical aircraft, AFSATCOM
UHF on Minuteman Missile launched Emergency Rocket Communications System

F. Super High Frequency (SHF)

Description: frequency, 3–30 GHz; wavelength: 10–1 cm; direct; signal range, short range.
Characteristics: Not reflected far by skywave, high data rates; NUDET effect: absorption for minutes, scintillation for hours.
Uses: Line-of-sight communications, relay networks, satellites.

Fixed Bases
Australia: NW Cape, Satellite Control Facility, DSCS terminal (SHF), Nurrungar, DSCS Terminal, Pine Gap, Satellite Control Facility
Diego Garcia: DSCS Satellite Terminal (SHF)
Guam: Finegayan, Naval Communications area Master Station, West Pacific; DSCS Satellite ground station (SHF)
Hawaii: Wahiawa, DSCS Terminal
Japan: Camp Zama, Main Entry, DSCS Terminal for Japan (SHF)
Okinawa: Fort Buckner, DSCS Terminal (SHF)
Seychelles: AFS, Satellite Control Station
South Korea: DSCS Ground Stations (SHF) at Yongsam AB; Song So

Mobile Bases:
Mobile Ground Terminals, "austere backup"
FLTSATCOM Terminals on surface and submarine fleet, naval air, e.g., P3C Orions (UHF)
AFSATCOM aircraft-terminals (UHF)

G. Extremely High Frequency (EHF)

Description: frequency: 30–300 GHz; wavelength: 1–0.1 cm, direct; signal range: short.
Characteristics: Projected straight up, reflected back, less vulnerable to nuclear explosion effects; experimental.
Uses: line-of-sight (LOS) radio, satellites, e.g., MILSTAR, interim FLTSATCOM 7, submarines, radar.

Fixed Bases
Widely dispersed ground stations for MILSTAR; Satellite Control Facilities above.

Mobile Bases
AF E4B Airborne Command Posts, B-52s, P3s, C-130, TACAMO
Mobile Receivers
Naval C-130, TACAMO, P-35, ASW helicopters, surface and submarine fleet
Army mobile vehicular terminals

Telephone Submarine Cables are not listed here.

H. Switching Devices:

Guam: Finegayan NCS – AV
Hawaii: Wahiawa NCS – AV, AD, AS
Japan: Fuchu AFS – AV

Camp Drake – AD
Okinawa: Fort Buckner – AS
Philippines: Clark AFS – AV
South Korea: Taegu – AD, AS
Taiwan: U.S. AR, Juzon – AS

Key: AD = AUTODIN; AFS = Air Force Station; AS = AUTOSEVCOM (manual or automatic); AV = AUTOVON; LORAN = Long Range Aid to Navigation; LOS = Line of sight; NCS = Naval Communication Station; NUDET = Nuclear detonation at 100 km altitude; OTH = Over-the-horizon; SCF = Satellite Control Facility

Sources: W. Arkin and R. Fieldhouse, "Nuclear Weapon Command, Control and Communications," in *SIPRI Yearbook, 1984*, Taylor and Francis, London, 1984, p. 458; *Aviation Week and Space Technology*, May 22, 1978, p. 24; D. Ball, *Can Nuclear War Be Controlled?* Adelphi Paper 169, London, 1981; D. Brick and F. Ellersick, "Challenges and Opportunities Face USAF's Tactical Communications," *Defense Electronics*, March 1981, pp. 45–55; J. Bussert, "Computers Add New Effectiveness to SOSUS/CAESAR," *Defense Electronics*, October 1979, pp. 59–64; Chief of Naval Operations, *Naval Operational Planning*, NWP-11 (Rev C), Washington, D.C., 1978, pp. C-5 to C-18; R. Denaro, "Navstar, the All-Purpose Satellite," *IEEE Spectrum*, May 1981, p. 35; H. Higgins, "The Rediscovery of HF for Command and Control," *Signal*, March 1981, p. 57; M. King and P. Fleming, "An Overview of the Effects of Nuclear Weapons in Communications Capabilities," *Signal*, January 1980, p. 65; T. Laney, "Overview of Strategic Command, Control, Communications, and Intelligence," in Program on Information Resources Policy, Seminar on *Command, Control, Communications and Intelligence*, Harvard University, Cambridge, 1980, p. 77; J. Laurance, "U.S. Pacific Fleet Organization," *Signal*, February 1984, pp. 71–72; J. Moreau, "The Coast Guard in the Central and Western Pacific," *Proceedings/Naval Review*, May 1983, p. 274; J. Schultz, "Milstar to Close Dangerous C3I Gap," *Defense Electronics*, March 1983, pp. 46–59; J. Schultz, "Inside the Blue Cube, USAF Modernizes Satellite Tracking Network," *Defense Electronics*, April 1983, pp. 52–59; U.S. Senate, Committee on Armed Services, *Department of Defense Authorization for Appropriations for Fiscal Year 1984* (Hearings), Part 5, Washington, D.C., 1983, p. 2469; U.S. Congressional Budget Office, *Strategic Command and Control and Communications: Alternative Approaches to Modernization*, Washington, D.C., 1981, p. 30; U.S. House of Representatives, Committee on Appropriations, *Department of Defense Appropriations for 1985* (Hearings), Part 5, p. 437.

APPENDIX E:
U.S. and Soviet Forces in East Asia and the Pacific, January 1, 1983; January 1, 1985

	United States			U.S.S.R.[a]
	West Pac	East Pac	Total	
A. Ground Forces				
Divisions				
Army	1	1	2	45 (53)
Marine	0.67	1.33	2	0 (1)
Total	1.67	2.33	4	45 (54)
Naval Infantry[b]	0	0	0	4[a]
Regiments				
Medium Tanks				
Army	155	13	168	13,000 (14,900)
Marine/Naval Infantry[a]	34 (39)	123 (118)	157	20 (120)
Total	189 (194)	136 (131)	325	13,020 (15,020)
B. Air Forces				
Bombers [c,d]				
Air Force				
Strike				
Heavy	14	0	14	60 (15)
Medium	0	0	0	115 (100)
Total	14	0	14	175 (115)
Support				
Heavy	0	0	0	15 (2)
Medium	0	0	0	60 (60)
Total	0	0	0	75 (62)

	United States			U.S.S.R.[a]
	West Pac	East Pac	Total	
Navy				
Strike				
Heavy	0	0	0	0 (100)
Medium	0	0	0	125 (100)
Total	0	0	0	125
Support				
Heavy	0	0	0	20 (50)
Medium	0	0	0	40 (70)
Total	0	0	0	60
Grand Total	14	0	14	435 (347)
Interceptors[e,f]	0	0	0	750 (150)
Fighter/Attack Aircraft				
Air Force[g]	216 (240)	0 (133)	216 (240)	800 (1,690)
Marine	59 (53)	127	186	0
Navy[h]	174	174 (232)	348 (406)	15 (70)
Total	449 (467)	301 (365)	750 (832)	815 (1,760)
C. Naval Forces				
ASW				
Navy (P-3 Orion)	36	72 (81)	108 (117)	50 (70)
Naval Ships				
Aircraft Carriers				
Multipurpose	3 (2)	3 (4)	6	0 (2)
Helicopter	1	5	6	1 (1)

	United States			U.S.S.R.[a]
	West Pac	East Pac	Total	
Battleships	0	0 (1)	0 (1)	0
Cruisers[i,j]	5	9 (12)	14 (17)	13 (14)
Destroyers[k]	13 (8)	18 (21)	31 (29)	20
Frigates[l,m]	17 (7)	24 (43)	41 (50)	50 (51)
Total	39 (23)	59 (86)	98 (109)	84 (87)
Submarines				
Strategic[n]	0	1 (5)	1 (5)	31
Attack[o]	13 (8)	33 (36)	46 (44)	91
Total	13 (8)	34 (41)	47 (49)	122 (134)
Amphibious[p]	7 (5)	24 (20)	31 (25)	12 (19)

Notes: Numbers in ( ) are for January 1, 1985, where different from January 1, 1983.

a. All Soviet figures are confined to forces in the Transbaikal and Far East Military Districts.

b. The four Soviet navy infantry regiments reportedly are subordinate to a "marine" division headquarters, but no coordinated exercises have yet occurred.

c. U.S. Bomber figures exclude anti-submarine warfare (ASW) aircraft, such as P-3s. B-52 bombers based in Guam belong to Strategic Air Command.

d. Soviet heavy "bombers" are Bear variants. Medium bombers are Badger variants, with Backfire variants added in 1985. Those for strike purposes carry gravity bombs and/or cruise missiles. Support types carry out tanker, reconnaissance, electronic warfare, and other tasks. About 115 fixed- and rotary-wing ASW aircraft are excluded from 1984 figures (100 in 1985).

e. U.S. fighter/attack figures indicate squadrons/primary aircraft authorization aircraft.

f. Soviet fighter/attack aircraft exclude reconnaissance types assigned to Frontal Aviation.

g. Soviet interceptors assigned to Air Defense Forces for homeland defense could supplement Frontal Aviation in some circumstances.

h. The U.S. aircraft carrier undergoing overhaul is not included, but its airwing is. It could fly combat missions from land bases.

i. Three of PACOM's 14 cruisers in 1984 were nuclear-powered; in 1985, the number was 6 out of 17.

j. Cruisers with the Soviet Pacific Fleet include 3 Kara, 2 Kresta I, 3 Kresta II, 2 Kyndas, and 3 Sverdlov Class.

k. Destroyers with the Soviet Pacific Fleet include 3 Kanin, 4 Kashin, 1 Kilden, and 2 Kotlin DDGs, plus 10 Kilden/Kotlin/Skory DDs. In 1985, 14 out of PACOM's 29 destroyers are DDGs.

l. Thirty FFs and 11 FFGs comprise the 1984 PACOM frigate mix and 19 out of 47 in 1985. FFs in 1984 include 2 from the U.S. Naval Reserve, excluded in 1985 figures.

m. The 50 Soviet frigates are a mix of Kola, Koni, Krivak, and Riga Class FFs, along with Grisha, Mirka, and Petya Class FFLs. Grisha heretofore has been considered a coastal combatant, but U.S. naval intelligence now carries that class with frigates. Krivak, once called a destroyer, is now considered a guided missile frigate. Seven are included in the Far East total.

n. Note that 2 Ohio submarines out of 3 in the U.S. Pacific Fleet were deployed as of October 1984. Note that the Ohio submarines are controlled by JCS through Pacific Command, but are not assigned to the 7th or the 3rd Fleet. Tritten estimates that there were 22 strategic submarines in the Soviet Pacific Fleet (5 Delta III, 1 Delta II, 6 Delta I, 1 Yankee II, 9 Yankee I) in 1983, plus 9 theater ballistic missile submarines (2 Hotel II, 7 Golf II).

o. Sixty-one of PACOM's 86 escorts and 22 out of 46 attack submarines were armed with Harpoon cruise missiles on January 1, 1983. That figure is increasing rapidly. Two diesel-powered attack submarines are found in East Pac. Two are in West Pac. All the rest are nuclear-powered.

p. West Pac included an amphibious squadron of 1 LPH, 2 LSTs, 2 LPDs, and 2 LSDs on December 31, 1982. That figure fluctuates. In 1985, U.S. amphibious ships included 7 LPDs, 3 LKAs, 5 LSDs, 9 LSTs, and 1 LCC, plus the 6 LHA and LPH helicopter carriers listed separately.

q. The separate category naval infantry abolished for 1985 accounting in source report and apparently shifted to Medium Tanks. Source states that 3 or 4 Soviet naval infantry regiments and 1 tank regiment are subordinate to a "marine" division.

Key:

ASW	= Anti-submarine Warfare	LHA	= Amphibious Assault Ship
DD	= Destroyer	LKA	= Amphibious Cargo Ship
DDG	= Guided Missile Destroyer	LPD	= Amphibious Transport Dock
FF	= Frigate	LPH	= Landing Platform Helicopter
FFG	= Guided Missile Destroyer	LSD	= Landing Ship, Dock
FFL	= Light Frigate	LST	= Landing Ship, Tank
LCC	= Amphibious Command Ship	PACOM	= Pacific Command

Sources: J. Collins, U.S./Soviet Military Balance, Statistical Trends, 1970–1982, Congressional Research Service Report 83–153S, Washington, D.C., 1983, pp. 127–130; J. Collins, U.S.-Soviet Military Balance, 1980–1985, Tables 43, 44, forthcoming, Pergamon, New York, 1985; J. Tritten, Soviet Navy Data Base: 1982–1983, RAND P-6859, 1983, p. 14, 15.

List of Acronyms and Abbreviations

ADM	Atomic demolition mine
ALCM	Air-launched cruise missile
ANZUS	Australia, New Zealand, & United States Treaty
ASEAN	Association of Southeast Asian Nations
ASW	Anti-submarine warfare
AWAC	Airborne Warning and Control Aircraft
C^3I	Command/control, communications/intelligence
CENTCOM	Central Command
CEP	Circular error probable
CIA	Central Intelligence Agency
CINCFE	Commander-in-Chief, Far East
CINCPAC	Commander-in-Chief, Pacific Command
CINCPACFLT	Commander-in-Chief, U.S. Pacific Fleet
CINCSAC	Commander-in-Chief, Strategic Air Command
CONUS	Continental United States
DCA	Defense Communications Agency
DEFCON	Defense Condition
DMZ	Demilitarized Zone
DNA	Defense Nuclear Agency
DSCS	Defense Satellite Communication System
ELINT	Electronic intelligence
FEC	Far East Command
FMS	Foreign Military Sales
FOIA	Freedom of Information Act
FSM	Federated States of Micronesia
HF	High frequency
ICBM	Intercontinental ballistic missile
IPAC	Intelligence Center, Pacific
JCS	Joint Chiefs of Staff
JMSDF	Japanese Maritime Self-Defense Force
JSSC	Joint Strategic Survey Committee
JUSMAG	Joint U.S. Military Advisory Group
km	Kilometer, 0.6 miles
kt	Kiloton, 1,000 tons of TNT equivalent, a measure of nuclear firepower
KPR	Korean People's Republic
LF	Low frequency
m	meter
MAAG	Military Advisory Assistance Group
MAC	Military Airlift Command
MAD	Mutual assured destruction

MAF	Marine Amphibious Force
MARV	Maneuverable re-entry vehicle
MIRV	Multiple independently targetable re-entry vehicle
MSC	Military Sealift Command
MSG	Mobile Support Group
Mt	Megaton, 1,000 kilotons (see kt)
NATO	North Atlantic Treaty Organization
NBCWRS	Nuclear Biological and Chemical Warning and Reporting System
NORAD	North American Air Defense
NSC	National Security Council
NUDET	Nuclear detonation
NUTS	"Nuclear Use" theories or theorists
Nuwax	Nuclear weapons accident exercise
OPLANS	Operational Plans
OPREP	Operational report
PACAF	Pacific Air Force
PACOM	Pacific Command
Pentagon	U.S. Department of Defense
PHOTINT	Photographic intelligence
PMR	Pacific Missile Range
PRC	People's Republic of China
PSYOP	Psychological operation
RDF	Rapid Deployment Force
ROK	Republic of Korea
SAC	Strategic Air Command
SAG	Surface Action Group
SALT	Strategic Arms Limitation Treaty
SDF	Self Defense Force (Japan)
SEATO	Southeast Asia Treaty Organization
SHAPE	Supreme Headquarters, Allied Powers Europe
SHF	Super high frequency
SIGINT	Signals intelligence
SIOP	*Single Integrated Operational Plan*
SLBM	Sea-launched ballistic missile
SLCM	Sea-launched cruise missile
SLOC	Sea Lanes of Communication
SOP	*Standard Operating Procedure for Atomic Warfare*
SOSUS	Sound Surveillance System
SRAM	Short-range attack missile
SRF	Strategic Rocket Force (Soviet)
SSBN	Ballistic missile nuclear-powered submarine
SSN	Nuclear attack submarine

TJOC	Theater Joint Operations Command (Tokyo)
UHF	Ultra high frequency
URG	Underway Replenishment Group
USAF	United States Air Force
U.S.S.R.	Union of Soviet Socialist Republics
VHF	Very high frequency
VLF	Very low frequency
WESTCOM	Western Command (Army)

REFERENCES

We have omitted an alphabetical bibliography to save space. The first time each reference is cited by a superscripted number in the text, it is given in full in the references for that chapter. The term "note" is used throughout whenever subsequent reference is made to a source already cited in full in that chapter.

Introduction: Nuclear Peril in the Pacific

1. In *U.S. News and World Report*, August 20, 1984, pp. 45–48.

2. In H. Martin, "Our Nation's Future Does Indeed Lie in the Pacific", *Defense Systems Review*, Volume 3, no. 4, June 14, 1985, p. 6.

3. J. Lehman, "Rebirth of a U.S. Naval Strategy", *Strategic Review*, Summer, 1981, p. 10.

4. R. Randolph, "The Pacific Basin, Why the Region is Getting Special Attention from U.S.", *San Francisco Chronicle*, April 17, 1985, p. F1.

5. R. Timpson, "Opportunities and Challenges for American Business in the Asian/Pacific Region", in G. Mitchell *et al.* edited, *Asian/Pacific Dynamics – Economic, Political, Security*, World Affairs Council of Pittsburgh, 1985, p. 28.

6. A. Bennett, "U.S. Firms Rush Through China's Open Door", *Wall Street Journal*, May 8, 1985, p. 22.

7. B. Blechman, "A Pacific Century", *National Defense*, January 1985, pp. 48–50.

8. W. Kennedy and S. de Gyurky, "An Alternative Strategy for the '80s", *National Defense*, July/August 1983, pp. 39, 47-54.

9. R. Nairn, "Should the U.S. Pull Out of NATO?" *Wall Street Journal*, December 15, 1981.

10. A. Albrecht, "America's Economic Interests in the Asian/Pacific Region", in G. Mitchell, note 5, p. 25.

11. R. Randolph, note 4.

12. B. Schemmer, "An Exclusive AFJ Interview with Admiral William J. Crowe, Commander-in-Chief, U.S. Pacific Command", *Armed Forces Journal*, April 1984, p. 47.

13. U.S. Air Force, "United States Pacific Command", Fact Sheet 81-39, Washington, D.C.

14. R. Armitage, "The United States' Role in the Pacific", paper to National Defense University, Pacific Symposium, Honolulu, February 22, 1985, p. 3.

15. E. Ravenal, "Defense Budget: Where's the Bottom Line?" *Oakland Tribune*, April 16, 1984, p. B-6.

16. For country data see Deadline Data on World Affairs, ABC· Clio Corporation, Santa Barbara, California, 1985.

17. See U.S. Bureau of the Census, *Statistical Abstract of the United States, 1984*, U.S Government Printing Office, Washington D.C., 1985, p. 812.

18. J. Conant, "An Officer and Intellectual", *Newsweek*, July 22, 1985, p. 29.

19. CINCPAC, "SecDef Quarterly Report", cable O 100602Z, April 25, 1984, p. 8; released under F.O.I.A. request.

20. J. Lehman, note 3, p. 13.

21. By comparison with the instability induced by the MX missile. T. Postol, "The Trident and Strategic Stability", *Oceanus*, Summer 1985, p. 52.

22. Interview, "A Common-Sense Soldier Discusses 'The Price of Peace' ", *Sea Power*, May 1984, pp. 13–22.

23. "The Pacific Basin", *Proceedings*, August 1985, p. 32.

24. T. Carrington, "Expanding Navy Is On a Collision Course with Budget Politics", *Wall Street Journal*, August 29, 1985, p. 1.

25. F. West *et al.*, "Toward the Year 1985: The Relationship Between U.S. Policy and Naval Forces in the Pacific", Appendix C, in Institute for Foreign Policy Analysis, *Environments for U.S. Naval Strategy in the Pacific Ocean–Indian Ocean Area, 1985–1995* (mimeo), Conference Report for Center for Advanced Research, U.S. Naval War College, Cambridge, Massachusetts, June 1977, p. 318.

26. In W. Mossberg, "Nuclear Attack Sub Shows Its Capabilities in Long, Silent Patrols", *Wall Street Journal*, May 19, 1983, p. 1.

27. S. Canby, "American Strategy – The Ends-Means Mismatch: A Performance Gap", *RUSI Journal*, September 1985, p. 20.

28. *The Press*, (Christchurch), "Hint of Fatal Flaw in ANZUS Alliance", May 11, 1985.

Chapter 1: The New Order in the Pacific

1. In G. Herken, *The Winning Weapon, the Atomic Bomb in the Cold War, 1945–1950*, Knopf, New York, 1980, p. 112.

2. G. Weller, *Bases Overseas, An American Trusteeship in Power*, Harcourt Brace, New York, 1944, p. 388.

3. H. Willmott, *Empires in Balance, Japanese and Allied Pacific Strategies to April 1942*, Orbis, London, 1982, Chapter 1–3, *passim*.

4. J. Masland, "Public Opinion and American Pacific Naval Policy", *Proceedings*, July 1941, p. 990.

5. H. Willmott, note 3, p. 141.

6. *Ibid.*, p. 139.

7. R. Love, "Fighting a Global War, 1941–1945", in K. Hagan, edited, *In Peace and War, Interpretations of American Naval History, 1775–1978*, Greenwood Press, Connecticut, 1978, pp. 271–273.

8. R. Dingman, "American Policy and Strategy in East Asia, 1898–1950: Creation of a Commitment", in U.S. Air Force Academy, *The American Military and the Far East*, Proceedings of the 9th Military History Symposium, U.S. GPO, Washington, D.C., 1980, pp. 32–33.

9. Saburo Ienaga, *The Pacific War, 1931–1945*, Pantheon, New York, 1978, pp. 198–199.

10. In J. Mountcastle, *The Holocaust: American Incendiary Bombs of World War II*, Masters Thesis, U.S. Army Command and General Staff College, Fort Leavenworth, 1977, p. 50.

11. In W. Burchett, *Shadows of Hiroshima*, Verso, London, 1983, p. 12.

12. G. Anders, *Burning Conscience*, Monthly Review, New York, 1961.

13. In U.S. Air Force, *Air Power and Warfare*, Proceedings of the 8th Military History Symposium, U.S. GPO, Washington, D.C., 1978, p. 200.

14. U.S. Bureau of Yards and Docks, *Building the Navy's Bases in World War II*, Volume 1, U.S. GPO, Washington, D.C., 1947, p. 347.

15. *Ibid.*, pp. 349–358.

16. *Ibid.*, p. iii.

17. E. Converse, *United States Plans for a Postwar Overseas Military Base System, 1942–1948*, Ph.D. Dissertation, Department of History, Princeton University Press, Princeton, New Jersey, 1984, p. 10.

18. *Ibid.*, p. 49.

19. R. Payne, *The Marshall Story*, Prentice Hall, New York, 1951, p. 251.

20. E. Converse, note 17, p. 154.

21. *Ibid.*, p. 176.

22. U.S. Congress, Committee of Naval Affairs and Merchant Marine and Fisheries Committee, "No. 67: Survey of Pacific Areas", Report to Chairman, May 29, 1946, p. 2.

23. E. Converse, note 17, p. 96.

24. *Ibid.*, p. 92.

25. Cited in *ibid.*, p. 160.

26. *Ibid.*

27. U.S. Joint Chiefs of Staff, "Overall Effect of Atomic Bomb on Warfare and Military Organization", JCS 1477/1, Washington, D.C., October 30, 1945, p. 6.

28. U.S. Joint Chiefs of Staff, Joint Strategic Survey Committee, "Effect of Atomic Weapons on National Security and Post-War Military Plans", JCS 1477/4, Washington, D.C., January 12, 1946, p. 3.

29. J. Dower, "Occupied Japan and the American Lake", in E. Friedman and M. Selden, edited, *America's Asia: Dissenting Essays on Asian-American Relations*, Random House, New York, 1971, p. 169.

30. *Ibid.*, p. 165.

31. J. Greenwood, "The Emergence of the Postwar Strategic Air Force, 1945–1953", in U.S. Air Force, note 13, p. 226.

32. U.S. Joint Chiefs of Staff, Joint Strategic Survey Committee, "U.S. Requirements for Post-War Air Bases", JCS 570, Modern Military Branch, U.S. National Archives, Washington, D.C., November 8, 1943, p. A101057.

33. J. Schnabel, *The History of the Joint Chiefs of Staff, The Joint Chiefs of Staff and National Policy*, Volume 1, Glazier, Delaware, 1979, p. 333.

34. Cited in E. Converse, note 17, p. 155.

35. U.S. Joint Chiefs of Staff, note 32, p. A101063.

36. R. Pruessen, *John Foster Dulles: The Road to Power*, Free Press, New York, p. 472.

37. General Albert Wedemeyer, cited in M. Schaller, *The U.S. Crusade in China, 1938–1945*, Columbia University Press, New York, 1979, p. 265.

38. B. Cumings, *The Origins of the Korean War, Liberation and the Emergence of Separate Regimes, 1945–1947*, Princeton University Press, Princeton, New Jersey, 1981, p. 91.

39. *Ibid.*, p. 130.

40. G. Kennan, "The Sources of Soviet Conduct", *Foreign Affairs*, July 1947, in T. Etzold and J. Gaddis, edited, *Containment: Documents on American Policy and Strategy*, Columbia University Press, New York, 1978, p. 87.

41. F. Siegel, *Troubled Journey: From Pearl Harbor to Ronald Reagan*, Hill and Wang, New York, 1984, p. 35.

42. U.S. National Security Council, "The Positions of the United States in Asia", NSC 48, December 23, 1949, in T. Etzold and J. Gaddis, edited, note 40, p. 264.

43. T. Etzold, "The Far East in American Strategy", in T. Etzold, edited, *Aspects of Sino-American Relations Since 1784*, New Viewpoints, New York, 1978, p.110.

44. Cited in J. Spanier, *The Truman-MacArthur Controversy and the Korean War*, Harvard University Press, Cambridge, 1959, p. 17.

45. U.S. Department of State, Policy Planning Staff, "Conversation between General of the Army MacArthur and Mr. George Kennan", PPS 28/2, March 5, 1948, in T. Etzold and J. Gaddis, edited, note 40, p. 229.

46. U.S. Department of State, Policy Planning Staff, "Review of Current Trends: U.S. Foreign Policy, Far East", PPS 23, February 24, 1948, in T. Etzold and J. Gaddis, edited, note 40, pp. 227–228.

47. National Security Council, in T. Etzold and J. Gaddis, edited, note 40, pp. 261, 264.

48. Cited in W. Manchester, *American Caesar: Douglas MacArthur*, Little Brown, Boston, 1978, p. 573.

49. U.S. Department of State, note 46, p. 228.

50. *Ibid.*

Chapter 2: The Korean Watershed

1. In T. Etzold and J. Gaddis, edited, *Containment: Documents on American Policy and Strategy*, Columbia University Press, New York, 1978, p. 442.

2. Joint Strategic Survey Committee Report to Joint Chiefs of Staff Evaluation Board for Operation "Crossroads" (mimeo), Enclosure A of JCS 1803/19, June 9, 1950, p. 103.

3. G. Kennan, "The Sources of Soviet Conduct", in T. Etzold and J. Gaddis, edited, note 1, p. 87; J. Gaddis, *Strategies of Containment*, Oxford University Press, 1982, pp. 57–61.

4. U.S. Department of State, Policy Planning Staff, "Review of Current Trends: U.S. Foreign Policy", in T. Etzold and J. Gaddis, note 1, p. 227.

5. D. Yergin, *Shattered Peace: The Origins of the Cold War and the National Security State*, Houghton Mifflin Co., Boston, 1977, pp. 42–68.

6. V. Davis, *Postwar Defense Policy and the U.S. Navy, 1943–1946*, University of North Carolina Press, 1966, pp. 10–11.

7. F. West *et al.*, "Toward the Year 1985: The Relationship Between U.S. Policy and Naval Forces in the Pacific", Appendix C, in Institute for Foreign Policy Analysis, *Environments for U.S. Naval Strategy in the Pacific Ocean–Indian Ocean Area, 1985–1995*, (mimeo,) Conference Report for Center for Advanced Research, U.S. Naval War College, Cambridge, Massachusetts, June 1977, p. 391.

8. V. Davis, note 6, p. 180; F. West, note 7, p. 404.

9. In A. Rogow, *James Forrestal, A Study of Personality, Politics, and Policy*, MacMillan, New York, 1963, p. 152.

10. *Ibid.*, p. 175-176.

11. A. Rogow, note 9, p. 6.

12. D. Yergin, note 5, p. 81.

13. J. Schnabel, *The History of the Joint Chiefs of Staff, The Joint Chiefs of Staff and National Policy*, Volume I, 1945-1947, Glazier, Delaware, 1979, p. 103.

14. In N. Graebner, "The United States and East Asia, 1945-1960: The Evolution of a Commitment", in U.S. Air Force Academy, *The American Military and the Far East*, Proceedings of the 9th Military History Symposium, U.S. GPO, Washington, D.C., 1980, p. 54.

15. In W. Poole, *The History of the Joint Chiefs of Staff, The Joint Chiefs of Staff and National Policy*, Volume IV, 1950-1952, Glazier, Delaware, 1979, p. 379.

16. U.S. National Security Council, United States Objectives and Programs for National Security", NSC 68, April 14, 1950, in T. Etzold and J. Gaddis, edited, note 1, p. 441.

17. In G. Kennan, *The Nuclear Delusion, Soviet-American Relations in the Atomic Age*, Pantheon, New York, 1982, pp. 4-5.

18. In T. Etzold and J. Gaddis, note 1, pp. 426, 433.

19. Cited in R. Donovan, *Tumultuous Years: The Presidency of Harry S. Truman, 1949-1953*, Norton, New York, 1982, p. 83.

20. U.S. Joint Chiefs of Staff, "United States Assistance to Other Countries from the Standpoint of National Security", JCS 1769/1, in T. Etzold and J. Gaddis, edited, note 1, p. 78.

21. J. Spanier, *The Truman-MacArthur Controversy*, Harvard University Press, Cambridge, 1959, cited in W. Manchester, *American Caesar: Douglas MacArthur*, Little Brown, Boston, 1978, pp. 539-540.

22. W. Manchester, *American Caesar: Douglas MacArthur*, Little Brown, Boston, 1978, p. 541.

23. B. Cumings, *The Origins of the Korean War*, Princeton University Press, Princeton, New Jersey, 1981, pp. 439-440.

24. U.S. National Security Council, note 16, pp. 414-415.

25. N. Graebner, note 14, p. 59.

26. B. Cumings, *The Origins of the Korean War*, Princeton University Press, Princeton, New Jersey, 1981, p. 439.

27. U.S. National Security Council, note 16, p. 393.

28. D. MacArthur, *Reminiscences*, McGraw-Hill, New York, 1964, p. 411.

29. In R. Watson and J. Schnabel, *The History of the Joint Chiefs of Staff, The Joint Chiefs of Staff and National Policy*, Volume III, Glazier, Delaware, 1979, p. 400.

30. W. Manchester, note 22, pp. 692-693.

31. J. Sanders, *Peddlers of Crisis: The Committee on the Present Danger and the Politics of Containment*, Pluto Press, London, 1983, p. 97.

32. G. Kennan, in note 3, p. 87.

33. T. Hoopes, *The Devil and John Foster Dulles*, Little Brown, Boston, 1973, p. 117.

34. J. Schlight, "The Impact of the Orient on Airpower", in U.S. Air Force Academy, note 14, p. 167.

35. J. Halliday, *A Political History of Japanese Capitalism*, Pantheon, New York, pp. 199-200.

36. Cited in *ibid.*, p. 201.

37. W. Borden, *The Pacific Alliance, United States Foreign Economic Policy and Japanese Trade Recovery, 1947–1955*, University of Wisconsin Press, 1984, pp. 150–151.

38. *Ibid.*, pp. 86, 211.

39. C. Wolf, *Foreign Aid: Theory and Practice in Southern Asia*, Princeton University Press, 1960, p. 158, 210.

40. D. Spencer, "Military Transfer of Technology, International Techno-Economic Transfers Via Military By-Products and Initiative Based on Cases from Japan and other Pacific Countries" (mimeo), Howard University report to U.S. Department of Defense, Washington D.C., March 1967, p. 54. This little known but essential reference is available from the U.S. National Technical Information Service.

41. In W. Borden, note 37, p. 168.

42. Takafusa Nakamura, *The Postwar Japanese Economy, Its Development and Structure*, University of Tokyo Press, 1980, pp. 41–42.

43. D. Spencer, note 40, pp. 86–88.

44. *Ibid.*, p. 92.

45. *Ibid.*, p. 81.

46. C. Johnson, *MITI, and the Japanese Miracle, The Growth of Industrial Policy*, Stanford University Press, 1982, p. 236.

47. D. Spencer, note 40, p. 88.

48. W. Borden, note 41, p. 159.

49. M. Armitage and R. Mason, *Air Power in the Nuclear Age*, University of Illinois Press, Urbana, 1983, p. 23.

50. See G. Kerr, *Okinawa: THe History of an Island People*, Charles Tuttle Co., Rutland, Vermont, pp. 6, 7, 16.

51. W. Berry, *American Military Bases in the Philippines, Base Negotiations, and Philippine-American Relations*, Ph.D. Dissertation, Cornell University, New York, 1981, p. 198.

52. D. Rosenberg, "American Postwar Air Doctrine and Organization: The Navy Experience", in U.S. Air Force Academy, note 14, p. 264.

53. *Ibid.*

54. *Ibid.*

55. In K. Condit, *The History of the Joint Chiefs of Staff, The Joint Chiefs of Staff and National Policy*, Volume II, Glazier, Delaware, 1979, p. 117.

56. F. West *et al.*, note 7, p. 416.

57. *Ibid.*, p. 421.

Chapter 3: New Look at the Nuclear Brink

1. D. Rosenberg, "The Origins of Overkill: Nuclear Weapons and American Strategy, 1945-1960", *International Security*, Volume 7, no. 4, Spring 1983, p. 71.

2. T. Hoopes, *The Devil and John Foster Dulles*, Little Brown, Boston, 1973, p. 131.

3. D. Eisenhower, *Mandate for Change, 1953-1956*, Doubleday, New York, 1961, p. 181.

4. L. Rumbaugh *et al.*, *Tactical Employment of Atomic Weapons*, Operations Research Group, Johns Hopkins University report to Operations Research Office, Far East Command, report ORO- R-2 (FEC), Tokyo, March 1, 1951; declassified 1983, available at the library, Army War College, Carlisle Barracks, Pennsylvania.

5. *Ibid.*, p. 275.

6. Memorandum, Far East Command, July 20, 1951, attached to L. Rumbaugh *et al.*, note 4.

7. L. Rumbaugh *et al.*, note 4, pp. 152-153.

8. *Ibid.*, p. 384.

9. *Ibid.*, p. 230.

10. *Ibid.*, p. 208.

11. *Ibid.*, p. 344.

12. *Ibid.*, p. 261.

13. *Ibid.*, pp. 257, 351.

14. *Ibid.*, p. 269.

15. *Ibid.*, p. 258.

16. *Ibid.*, p. 169.

17. *Ibid.*, p. 252.

18. Emphasis in original, *ibid.*, p. 241.

19. *Ibid.*, pp. 241-242.

20. R. Watson and J. Schnabel, *The History of the Joint Chiefs of Staff, The Joint Chiefs of Staff and National Policy*, Volume III, The Korean War, Part 2, Glazier, Delaware, 1979, p. 613.

21. Strategic Air Command, *The Development of Strategic Air Command, 1946-1981*, Office of the Historian, Omaha, Nebraska, July 1982, p. 44.

22. W. Pincus, "In '40s and '50s, Nuclear Arms Still Seen Usable", *Washington Post*, July 22, 1985, p. A-1.

23. *New York Times*, "For Eisenhower, 2 Goals If Bomb Was to Be Used", June 8, 1984, p. A-7.

24. D. MacArthur, *Reminiscences*, McGraw Hill, New York, 1967, p. 411.

25. R. Donovan, *Tumultuous Years*, Norton, New York, 1982, pp. 308-310.

26. *New York Times*, note 23.

27. In C. Alexander, *Holding the Line: The Eisenhower Era, 1952–1961*, Indiana University Press, Bloomington, Indiana, 1976, pp. 68–69.

28. *Ibid.*, p. 68.

29. *Ibid.*, pp. 67–68.

30. M. Taylor, *An Uncertain Trumpet*, Harper and Row, New York, 1959, pp. 39–40.

31. C. Alexander, note 27, pp. 67–68.

32. T. Hoopes, note 2, pp. 196–197.

33. F. West *et al.*, "Toward the Year 1985: The Relationship Between U.S. Policy and Naval Forces in the Pacific", Appendix C, in Institute for Foreign Policy Analysis, *Environments for U.S. Naval Strategy in the Pacific Ocean–Indian Ocean Area, 1985–1995* (mimeo), Conference Report for Center for Advanced Research, U.S. Naval War College, Cambridge, Massachusetts, June 1977, p. 417.

34. L. Gelb and R. Betts, *The Irony of Vietnam: The System Worked*, The Brookings Institution, Washington, D.C., 1979, pp. 56–57.

35. Quote is from N. Polmar, *Strategic Weapons: An Introduction*, Crane Russak, New York, 1982, p. 3; French reactions to *Operation Vulture* were reported in *Washington Post*, August 31, 1971, p. A-6.

36. A. Radford, "Studies With Respect to Possible U.S. Action Regarding Indochina", Memorandum for Secretary of Defense, May 26, 1954, in *Pentagon Papers*, Volume 1, Beacon, Boston, (no date, about 1971), pp. 511–515.

37. F. West, note 33, p. 418.

38. J. Staaveren, "Air Operations in the Taiwan Crisis of 1958" (mimeo), U.S. Air Force Historical Division Liaison Office, Washington, D.C., 1962, declassified, 1984.

39. C. Alexander, note 27, p. 89.

40. Strategic Air Command, note 21, p. 72.

41. J. Staaveren, note 38, pp. 10–11.

42. *Ibid.*, p. 11.

43. *Ibid.*

44. M. Halperin, *The 1958 Taiwan Straits Crisis, A Documented History*, Rand RM-4900-ISA, 1966 (declassified 1975), p. 145.

45. J. Staaveren, note 38, pp. 15–16.

46. *Ibid.*, p. 16.

47. Our emphasis, in *Reminiscences of Admiral Harry Donald Felt*, U.S. Naval Institute Press, Volume 2, Annapolis, Maryland, 1974, p. 396.

48. M. Halperin, note 44, p. 127.

49. Confidential interview with authors, former CINCPAC, July 22, 1985.

50. J. Staaveren, note 38, pp. 22–26.

51. In *Reminiscences*, note 47, p. 491.

52. Our emphasis, J. Staaveren, note 38, p. 28.

53. In *Reminiscences*, note 47, p. 396.

54. J. Staaveren, note 38, p. 41.

55. M. Halperin, note 44, pp. 99, 109.

56. Our emphasis, in *ibid.*, p. 113.

57. *Ibid.*, p. 268.

58. *Ibid.*, pp. 285–286.

59. J. Staaveren, note 38, pp. 29, 35.

60. *Ibid.*, p. 52.

61. In J. Gaddis, *Strategies of Containment*, Oxford University Press, 1982, p. 194.

62. See T. Hoopes, note 2, p. 451.

63. August 23, 1958 memo, in M. Halperin, note 44, p. 102.

64. L. Rumbaugh *et al.*, note 4, p. 383.

65. In T. Hoopes, note 2, p. 450.

66. J. Staaveren, note 38, p. 16.

67. *Ibid.*, Appendix 2.

68. *Ibid.*, p. 16.

69. M. Halperin, note 44, pp. 251–252.

70. Interview with authors, July 19, 1985.

Chapter 4: Nuclear Overkill

1. In U.S. Dept. of State, *Foreign Relations of the United States*, 1948, I (Part 2), p. 631.

2. U.S. Joint Chiefs of Staff, "Statement of the Views of the Joint Chiefs of Staff on Department of Defense Interest in the Use of Atomic Weapons", Washington, D.C., December 11, 1951, p. 1.

3. R. Dingman, "Strategic Planning and the Policy Process: American Plans for War in East Asia, 1945–1950", *Naval War College Review*, November-December, 1979, p. 16.

4. In H. Borowski, *A Hollow Threat, Strategic Air Power and Containment Before Korea*, Greenwood Press, Westport, Connecticut, 1982, p. 76.

5. Strategic Air Command, *The Strategic Air Command, 1947*, Volume 1, Historical Section, June 1949, p. 105; declassified under F.O.I.A. request.

6. Strategic Air Command, *The Strategic Air Command 1948*, Volume 1, Narrative, undated, p. 192; declassified under F.O.I.A. request.

7. *Ibid*, p. 151.

8. H. Borowski, note 4, pp. 103, 106.

9. Strategic Air Command, note 6, pp. 185–186.

10. *Ibid.*, p. 186.

11. R. Dingman, note 3, p. 14.

12. G. Herken, *The Winning Weapon, The Atomic Bomb in the Cold War, 1945–1950*, Knopf, New York, 1980, pp. 248–253.

13. J. Greenwood, "The Emergence of the Postwar Strategic Air Force, 1945–1953", in U.S. Air Force Academy, *Air Power and Warfare*, Proceedings of the 8th Military History Symposium, U.S. GPO, Washington, D.C., 1978, p. 229.

14. R. Watson and J. Schnabel, *The History of the Joint Chiefs of Staff, the Joint Chiefs of Staff and National Policy*, Volume III, The Korean War, Part 2, Glazier, Delaware, 1979, pp. 151, 158.

15. *Ibid.*, p. 170.

16. Strategic Air Command, *History, Strategic Air Command, July–December 1950*, Volume 1, p. 28 of Chapter 1 (unpaginated), circa 1950–early 1951; declassified under F.O.I.A. request.

17. Strategic Air Command, *The Development of the Strategic Air Command, 1946–1981*, Office of the Historian, Omaha, Nebraska, July 1982, p. 22.

18. Cited in I.F. Stone, *The Hidden History of the Korean War*, Monthly Review, New York, 1969, p. 312.

19. T. Hoopes, "Overseas Bases in American Strategy", *Foreign Affairs*, Volume 37, no. 1, October 1958, p. 70.

20. *Ibid.*

21. See *ibid, passim.*

22. D. Ball, *Targeting for Strategic Deterrence*, Adelphi Paper 185, London, 1983, p. 8.

23. F. Schurmann, *The Logic of World Power*, Pantheon, New York, 1974, p. 271.

24. C. Sorrels, *U.S. Cruise Missile Program: Development, Deployment and Implications for Arms Control*, McGraw Hill, New York, 1983, p. 3.

25. R. Huisken, *The Origins of the Strategic Cruise Missile*, Praeger, New York, 1981, pp. 23–24.

26. P. Bracken, *The Command and Control of Nuclear Forces*, Yale University Press, New Haven, Connecticut, 1983, p. 160.

27. Initial Operating Capability was 1954, T. Cochran *et al.*, *Nuclear Weapons Data Book, U.S. Nuclear Forces and Capabilities*, Ballinger, Cambridge, Massachusetts, 1983, p. 282; Far East Command, *Standard Operating Procedure No. 1 for Atomic Operations in the Far East Command* (mimeo), Far East Command, Tokyo, November 1, 1956, p. A-10 refers to use of Honest John missiles in Korea.

28. In D. Rosenberg, "American Postwar Air Doctrine and Organization: The Navy Experience", in U.S. Air Force Academy, note 13, 1978, p. 253.

29. V. Davis, *Postwar Defense Policy and the U.S. Navy, 1943–1946*, University of North Carolina Press, 1966, p. 245.

30. D. Rosenberg, note 28, pp. 264–265.

31. J. Field, *History of U.S. Naval Operations, Korea*, U.S. GPO, Washington, D.C., 1962, p. 363.

32. N. Polmar, *Strategic Weapons*, Crane Russak, New York, 1982, p. 20.

33. *Ibid.*

34. F. West, *et al.*, "Toward the Year 1985: The Relationship Between U.S. Policy and Naval Forces in the Pacific", Appendix C, in Institute for Foreign Policy Analysis, *Environment for U.S. Naval Strategy in the Pacific Ocean–Indian Ocean Area, 1985–1995*, Conference Report for Center for Advanced Research, U.S. Naval War College, Cambridge, Massachusetts, June 1977, p. 433; M. Leitenberg, "Background information on Tactical Nuclear Weapons", in SIPRI, *Tactical Perspectives*, Taylor and Francis, London, 1978, p. 120.

35. W. Pincus, "In '40s and '50s, Nuclear Arms Still Seen Usable", *Washington Post*, 22 July 1985, p. A-1.

36. Interview with authors, August 1, 1985.

37. F. Kennedy, Jr., "The Creation of the Cold War Navy, 1953–1962", in K. Hagan, edited, *In Peace and War; Interpretations of American Naval History, 1775–1978*, Greenwood Press, Westport, Connecticut, 1978, p. 307.

38. U.S. Senate, Armed Services Committee, Subcommittee on the Air Force, *Study of Airpower* (Hearings), U.S. GPO, Washington, D.C., 1956, p. 169.

39. *Ibid.*, pp. 968, 1012.

40. Reference to overbombing, from D. Ellsberg, memoranda dictated for the record, 1971, p. 78. Reference to ground bursts, from D. Ellsberg, 1959 notes on CINCPAC Atomic Annex E of the *General Emergency Operational Plan*, promulgated in 1958, p. 14. See note 60, Chapter 5.

41. In D. Rosenberg, "The Origins of Overkill, Nuclear Weapons and American Strategy, 1945–1960", *International Security*, Volume 7, no. 4, Spring 1983, p. 7.

42. N. Polmar, note 32, p. 17.

43. R. Huisken, note 25, p. 20; Foreign Broadcast Information Service, Asia-Pacific, Annex, February 27, 1984.

44. F. West, *et al.*, note 34, p. 427.

45. *Ibid.*, p. 433.

46. In U.S. Senate, Armed Services Committee, note 38, p. 1442.

Chapter 5: Nuclear War by the Book

1. In D. Ball, *Politics and Force Levels, The Strategic Missile Program of the Kennedy Administration*, University of California Press, Berkeley, California, 1980, p. 12.

2. H. Kissinger, *Nuclear Weapons and Foreign Policy*, Norton, New York, 1969, p. 166.

3. See memorandum, Lt. Gen. J. Hull to Chief of Staff, U.S. Army, "Location of Proving Ground for Atomic Weapons", no date, (circa May 1948), in JSC 471-6 series, Modern Military Branch, National Archives, Washington, D.C., pp. 1-2.

4. Far East Command, *FEC SOP no. 1, Standard Operating Procedure No. 1 for Atomic Operations in the Far East Command* (mimeo), Far East Command, Tokyo, June 2, 1955; revised version, November 1, 1956, declassified, in the archives, Military History Institute, Carlisle Barracks, Pennsylvania. Hereafter, referred to as FEC.

5. D. Fitzgerald, "Okinawa and U.S.-Japan Relations", Masters Thesis, School of Government, University of Massachusetts, Amherst, Massachusetts, 1970, p. 62.

6. J. Schnabel, *The History of the Joint Chiefs of Staff, The Joint Chiefs of Staff and National Policy*, Volume 1, Glazier, Delaware, 1979, pp. 172-180.

7. F. West *et al.*, "Toward the Year 1985: The Relationship Between U.S. Policy and Naval Forces in the Pacific", Appendix C, in Institute for Foreign Policy Analysis, *Environments for U.S. Naval Strategy in the Pacific Ocean–Indian Ocean Area, 1985–1995* (mimeo), Conference Report for Center for Advanced Research, U.S. Naval War College, Cambridge, Massachusetts, June 1977, pp. 401-402.

8. H. Borowski, *A Hollow Threat, Strategic Air Power and Containment before Korea*, Greenwood, Connecticut, 1982, pp. 73-74, 165.

9. Strategic Air Command, *The Development of the Strategic Air Command, 1946–1981*, Office of the Historian, Omaha, Nebraska, July 1982, p. p. 47.

10. *Ibid.*, p. 49.

11. W. Poole, *The History of the Joint Chiefs of Staff, the Joint Chiefs of Staff and National Policy*, Volume IV, 1950–1952, Glazier, Delaware, 1979, p. 407.

12. F. West, note 7, p. 428.

13. FEC, note 4, 1955, p. 4.

14. Our emphasis, L. Rumbaugh *et al.*, *Tactical Employment of Atomic Weapons*, Operations Research Group, Johns Hopkins University report to Operations Research Office, Far East Command, report ORO-R-2 (FEC), Tokyo, March 1, 1951, p. 235.

15. *Ibid.*, pp. 252.

16. J. Hull, note 3, p. 1.

17. FEC, note 4, 1955, p. 1.

18. *Ibid.*, p. 4.

19. FEC, note 4, 1955, p. 8; and 1956, p. 3.

20. FEC, note 4, 1956, p. 6.

21. *Ibid.*, pp. D3-D7.

22. FEC, note 4, 1955, p. 4; and 1956, pp. 2, 12, E-2.

23. FEC, note 4, 1956, p. 2.

24. FEC, note 4, 1955, p. 6; and 1956, p. 5.

25. In the 1956 *SOP* only, FEC, note 4, p. 9.

26. FEC, note 4, 1956, p. E-4.

27. FEC, note 4, 1955, p. 4.

28. *Ibid.*, pp. 8–11.

29. FEC, note 4, 1956, pp. B-1, E-2.

30. *Ibid.*, p. 5; and 1955, pp. 5–6.

31. FEC, note 4, 1956, p. E-2.

32. D. Rosenberg, "The Origins of Overkill: Nuclear Weapons and American Strategy, 1945–1960", *International Security*, Volume 7, no. 4, Spring 1983, p. 61.

33. *Ibid.*

34. FEC, note 4, 1956, pp. 4–8.

35. FEC, note 4, 1955, pp. H-1, 8; and 1956, p. C-1.

36. FEC, note 4, 1956, p. C-1.

37. Our emphasis, *ibid.*, p. A-22.

38. Our emphasis, *ibid.*, p. 8.

39. Our emphasis, *ibid.*, p. 8a. Original reads "insure", and is marked "Change No. 2", March 1957.

40. Our emphasis, *ibid.*, p. 11.

41. L. Rumbaugh *et al.*, note 14, p. 170.

42. *Ibid.*, p. 162.

43. Strategic Air Command, *The Strategic Air Command, 1947*, Volume 1, Historical Section, June 1949, p. 107.

44. Our emphasis, FEC, note 4, 1955, p. A-2.

45. Our emphasis, FEC, note 4, 1956, p. 9, marked "Change No. 2", March 1957.

46. A. Wohlstetter, *Selection and Use of Strategic Air Bases*, Rand 2-266 (declassified), report to U.S. Air Force, Santa Monica, California, April 1954, p. 236.

47. FEC, note 4, 1955, p. 4.

48. See Notes below, note 60, p. 3.

49. R. Watson and J. Schnabel, *The History of the Joint Chiefs of Staff, The Joint Chiefs of Staff and National Policy*, Volume III, The Korean War, part 2, 1979, p. 158.

50. FEC, note 4, 1956, p. D-8.

51. Our emphasis, FEC, note 4, 1956, p. D-1,2.

52. In CINCPAC message to JCS No. 4335, DTG 192243Z (top secret), August 1958, attached to "Note by the Secretaries to the Joint Chiefs of Staff on Security Treaty-Japan", JCS 2180/119, August 21, 1958, p. 10.

53. *Ibid.*

54. FEC, note 4, 1956, p. A-13.

55. *Ibid.*, p. A-17.

56. *Ibid.*, p. 11.

57. *Ibid.*, p. A-19.

58. *Ibid.*, p. A-11.

59. J. Staaveren, "Air Operations in the Taiwan Crisis of 1958" (mimeo), U.S. Air Force Historical Division Liaison Office, Washington, D.C., 1962, pp. 28, 30, 53; declassified 1984.

60. These and all subsequent references to the CINCPAC 1958 Nuclear Annex to the *General Emergency Operational Plan* are taken from Daniel Ellsberg's 1959 unpublished notes, kindly provided to authors by Ellsberg. These unpaginated notes were typed in 1959 and 1960 by Ellsberg in the top secret documents room of CINCPAC in Hawaii while studying the CINCPAC command and control system as a consultant to then-CINCPAC Admiral Felt. Hereafter, these notes are referred to as "Notes", and pagination refers to our own pagination for convenience. Copies are available from the authors. The veracity of these notes, aside from Ellsberg's own credibility, rests on their close correspondence with Felt's concerns about the nuclear command and control, and communications problems documented in the Staaveren study cited above. The Notes are sometimes abbreviated paraphrases of the *Operational Plan*, which we cite as typed by Ellsberg. We have filed a Freedom of Information Act request on the original documents, with no response as this manuscript goes to press. The "Notes" are to be distinguished from D. Ellsberg's 1971 dictated memos of record of his 1959–1961 experiences in the Pacific, hereafter referred to as "Memos", also paginated and available from the authors. Daniel Ellsberg is preparing a complete personal *memoire* of these years for publication, which promises to be an important addition to our knowledge of the nuclear peril and U.S. interventions in Asia in the 1950s and 1960s. We are indebted to Daniel Ellsberg for generously giving us access to these personal records when he is about to draw on them for his own work. This textual reference is to p. 7 of Notes.

61. Notes, note 60, p. 3.

62. *Ibid.*

63. *Ibid.*

64. *Ibid.*

65. Memos, note 60, p. 78.

66. Notes, note 60, p. 3.

67. *Ibid.*

68. W. Lang *et al.*, "Review of United States Overseas Military Bases" (mimeo), U.S. Department of Defense Report to the President, Washington, D.C., 1960, declassified, p. 12.

69. Interview with authors, July 22, 1985.

70. Our emphasis, Notes, note 60, p. 14.

71. *Ibid.*

72. J. Staaveren, note 59, p. 34.

73. *Ibid.*, p. 55.

74. *Ibid.*, p. 31.

75. Memos, note 60, p. 45.

76. Our emphasis, Notes, note 60, p. 1.

77. *Ibid.*, p. 2.

78. Memos, note 60, p. 34.

79. Emphasis in original, *ibid.*, p. 36.

80. *Ibid.*, p. 22.

81. *Ibid.*, pp. 56–60.

82. Notes, note 60, p. 5.

83. *Ibid.*

84. D. Ellsberg, in K. Pope edited, *Year of Disobedience*, privately published, Boulder, Colorado, 1979, p. 10.

85. Notes, note 60, p. 5.

86. *Ibid.*, p. 16.

87. *Ibid.*, p. 14.

88. *Ibid.*, p. 11.

89. *Ibid.*, p. 15.

90. *Ibid.*, p. 3.

91. Emphasis in original, Memos, note 60, p. 67.

92. *Ibid.*

93. *Ibid.*, p. 15.

94. *Ibid.*, pp. 68–70.

95. *Ibid.*, p. 72.

96. Emphasis in original, *ibid.*, p. 73.

97. Notes, note 60, p. 6.

98. D. Morrison, "Japanese Principles, U.S. Policies", *Bulletin of the Atomic Scientists*, June/July 1985, p. 23.

99. Memos, note 60, pp. 80–87.

100. Interview with authors, note 69.

101. R. Halloran, "Ex-Envoy Says He Protested Atom Bombs Off Japan", *New York Times*, May 23, 1981, p. 3.

102. Interview with authors, note 69.

Chapter 6: Losing the War, Winning the Peace

1. In S. Hersh, *The Price of Power, Kissinger in the Nixon White House*, Summit, New York, 1980, p. 406.

2. In *ibid.*, p. 568.

3. In J. Sanders, *Peddlers of Crisis, The Committee on the Present Danger and the Politics of Containment*, South End, Boston, 1983, p. 151.

4. M. Taylor, *The Uncertain Trumpet*, Harper and Row, New York, 1959, pp. 39–40.

5. R. Hilsman, "Orchestrating the Instrumentalities: The Case of Southeast Asia", in R. Hilsman and R. Good, edited, *Foreign Policy in the Sixties*, Johns Hopkins University Press, Baltimore, 1965, p. 201.

6. F. Schurmann, *The Logic of World Power*, Pantheon, New York, 1974, p. 439.

7. C. Dunn, *Base Development in South Vietnam, 1965–1970*, U.S. Department of the Army, Washington, D.C. 1972, pp. 50–71.

8. L. Grinter, *The Philippine Bases: Continuing Utility in a Changing Strategic Context*, National Defense University, Washington, D.C., February 1980, p. 8.

9. Strategic Air Command, *The Development of the Strategic Air Command*, Office of the Historian, Strategic Air Command, 1982, p. 175.

10. S. Hersh, note 1, pp. 53, 120, 124–129, 369.

11. W. Feeney, "The Pacific Basing System and U.S. Security", in W. Tow and W. Feeney, editors, *U.S. Foreign Policy and Asian-Pacific Security*, Westview Books, Boulder, Colorado, 1982, p. 203.

12. G. Kennan, *Cloud of Danger*, Little, Brown, Boston, 1977, pp. 97–98.

13. S. Hersh, note 1, p. 352.

14. H. Kissinger, *Years of Upheaval*, Little, Brown, Boston, 1982, p. 238.

15. J. Sanders, note 3, p. 160.

16. This sentence and the following paragraphs draw on F. Schurmann's forthcoming *The Grand Design, A Study of the Foreign Policies and Politics of Richard Nixon*, especially Chapter 4.

17. *Ibid.*, pp. 42, 89, 136.

18. *Ibid.*, p. 277.

19. H. Kissinger, note 14, p. 531.

20. J. Sanders, "Breaking Out of the Containment Syndrome", *World Policy Journal*, Volume 1, no. 1, Fall 1983, p. 113.

21. *Ibid.*

22. S. Bowles *et al.*, *Beyond the Wasteland, A Democratic Alternative to Economic Decline*, Anchor, Doubleday, New York, 1983, pp. 99–103.

23. On Hyundai, for example, see L. Jones and Il Sakong, *Government, Business, and Entrepreneurship in Economic Development: The Korean Case*, Harvard University Press, 1980, p. 357.

24. D. Spencer, "Military Transfer of Technology, International Techno-Economic Transfers Via Military By-Products and Initiative, Based on Cases from Japan and other Pacific Countries" (mimeo), Howard University, Washington, D.C., March 1967, p. 125–126. This is an invaluable and neglected source for economic historians of the period.

25. U.S. Senate, Committee on Foreign Relations, *Security Agreements and Commitments Abroad* (Hearings), Part 4, U.S. GPO, Washington, D.C., 1970, p. 1544.

26. E. Benoit, "Impacts of the End of Vietnam Hostilities and the Reduction of British Military Presence in Malaysia and Singapore", in Asian Development Bank, *Southeast Asia's Economy in the 1970s*, Longman, London 1971, pp. 635–646.

27. D. Spencer, note 24, p. 169.

28. See D. Gisselquist, *Oil Prices and Trade Deficits: U.S. Conflict with Japan and West Germany*, Praeger, New York, 1979; and R. Parboni, *The Dollar and Its Rivals*, Verso, London, 1981.

29. In U.S. House of Representatives, Committee on Armed Services, Investigations Subcommittee, *Reorganization Proposals for the Joint Chiefs of Staff* (Hearings), HR 6828, 6954, U.S. GPO, Washington, D.C., 1982, p. 828. "Insure" in the original.

30. See L. Krause and L. Sekiguchi, editors, *Economic Interaction in the Pacific Basin*, The Brookings Institution, 1980; J. Crawford, *Pacific Economic Cooperation, Suggestions for Action*, Heinemann Educational Books (Asia), 1981; G. Boyd, *Region Building in the Pacific*, Pergamon, 1982.

31. In J. Crawford, edited, note 30, p. 229.

32. R. Holbrooke, "U.S. Position in the Pacific in 1980", *Current Policy Series*, U.S. State Department, no. 154, March 27, 1980, p. 1.

33. H. Brown, *Thinking About National Security: Defense and Foreign Policy in a Dangerous World*, Westview Books, Boulder, Colorado, 1983, p. 113.

Chapter 7: Resurgent Rollback

1. In C. Tyroler, edited, *Alerting America, The Papers of the Committee on the Present Danger*, Pergamon, New York, 1984, p. 174.

2. R. Solomon, "American Defense Planning and Asian Security: Policy Choices for Time of Transition", in R. Solomon, edited, *Asian Security in the 1980s: Problems and Policies of a Time of Transition*, Rand Corporation, Santa Monica, California, 1979, p. 19.

3. W. LeHardy, "Where the Dawn Comes Up Like Thunder: The Army's Future in the Pacific", *Parameters*, Volume 8, no. 4, December 1978, p. 40.

4. J. Hessman, "Sea Power and the Central Front", *Air Force Magazine*, July 1983, p. 52.

5. D. Yergin, *Shattered Peace: The Origins of the Cold War and the National Security State*, Houghton Mifflin Co., Boston, 1977, p. 339.

6. F. West *et al.*, "Toward the Year 1985: The Relationship Between U.S. Policy and

Naval Forces in the Pacific", Appendix C, in Institute for Foreign Policy Analysis, *Environments for U.S. Naval Strategy in the Pacific Ocean–Indian Ocean Area, 1985–1995* (mimeo), Conference Report for Center for Advanced Research, U.S. Naval War College, Cambridge, Massachusetts, June 1977, pp. 448–449.

7. R. Hanks, *The Pacific Far East: Endangered American Strategic Position*, Institute for Foreign Policy Analysis, Washington, D.C., 1981, p. 2.

8. In "Foreword" to W. Thompson, *Power Projection: A Net Assessment of U.S. and Soviet Capabilities*, National Strategy Information Center, New York, 1979, p. 3.

9. R. Tucker, *The Purposes of American Power*, Praeger, 1981, pp. 7–8.

Chapter 8: New Militarism

1. "New CINCPAC Says Allies in Pacific America's Best", *Honolulu Advertiser*, January 4, 1984, p. A-4.

2. S. Foley, speech to Current Strategy Forum, Naval War College, Newport, Rhode Island, June 23, 1983, p. 11.

3. R. Armitage, "The United States' Role in the Pacific", speech at Pacific Symposium, Honolulu, February 22, 1985, U.S. Department of Defense News Release 87-85, p. 2.

4. R. Pipes, "How to Cope with the Soviet Threat, a Long-Term Strategy for the West", *Commentary*, August 1984, p. 14, his emphasis.

5. R. Burt, "U.S. Strategy Focus Shifting from Europe to Pacific", *New York Times*, May 5, 1980, p. I-3.

6. *Ibid.*

7. F. West *et al.*, "Toward the Year 1985: The Relationship Between U.S. Policy and Naval Forces in the Pacific", Appendix C, in Institute for Foreign Policy Analysis, *Environments for U.S. Naval Strategy in the Pacific Ocean–Indian Ocean Area, 1985–1995* (mimeo), Conference Report for Center for Advanced Research, U.S. Naval War College, Cambridge, Massachusetts, June 1977, p. 340–344.

8. W. Beeman, "Transforming the RDF – U.S. Quietly Builds New 500,000-Man Army for Mideast", Pacific News Service, February 9, 1983.

9. In S. Sloan, "NATO Nuclear Forces: Modernization and Arms Control", Congressional Research Service, Washington, D.C., October 1983, p. 35.

10. U.S. Senate, Committee on Armed Services, *Department of Defense Authorization for Appropriations for FY 1983* (Hearings), Part 6, U.S. GPO, Washington, D.C., 1982, p. 3724.

11. In F. Hiatt, "Limited Soviet War Held 'Almost Inevitable,'" *Washington Post*, June 22, 1984, p. 15.

12. T. Connors, "Global War Games 1983, Testing New National Strategies", *All Hands*, January-February 1984, p. 34.

13. F. West, note 7, p. 435.

14. R. Halloran, "Pentagon Draws Up First Strategy for Fighting a Long Nuclear War", *New York Times*, May 30, 1982, p. 1.

15. In "President Disputes General on War Probability", *Washington Post*, June 23, 1984, p. 1.

16. C. Weinberger, *Annual Report to the Congress for FY 1983, Department of Defense*, U.S. GPO, Washington, D.C., 1982, p. I-15.

17. *Ibid*, p. I-16.

18. R. Halloran, note 14, p. 1.

19. J. Hessman, "Sea Power and the Central Front", *Air Force Magazine*, July 1983, p. 57.

20. U.S. Senate, Committee on Armed Services, note 10, p. 3275.

21. G. Wilson, "Readiness Is Improving, Top Navy Officer Insists", *Washington Post*, August 4, 1984, p. 14.

22. K. McGruther, *The Evolving Soviet Navy*, Naval War College Press, Newport, Rhode Island, 1978, p. 16.

23. U.S. Senate, Committee on Armed Services, *Department of Defense Authorization for Appropriations for FY 1985* (Hearings), Part 2, U.S. GPO, Washington, D.C., 1984, p. 922.

24. U.S. Senate, Committee on Armed Services, note 10, p. 3724.

25. F. Hiatt, "Military Priorities Hit by Critics of Readiness", *Washington Post*, July 30, 1984, p. 1.

26. C. Weinberger, note 16.

27. *Ibid*.

28. For one of the best expositions of modern day implications of Mackinder's views, see Colin Gray, *The Geopolitics of the Nuclear Era: Heartland, Rimlands, and the Technological Revolution*, National Strategy Information Center, New York, 1977.

29. J. Roherty, *Decisions of Robert McNamara*, University of Miami Press, Florida, 1970, pp. 147–148.

30. C. Hood, "The Face That Launched 600 Ships", *Defense and Foreign Affairs*, December 1983, p. 11; T. Rosenberg, "Fool of Ships", *New Republic*, June 3, 1985, pp. 20–23.

31. R. Komer, "Maritime Strategy Versus Coalition Defense", *Foreign Affairs*, Volume 60, no. 5, Summer 1982, pp. 1124–1144.

32. J. Lehman, speech to Naval War College, June 21, 1984; declassified under F.O.I.A. request.

33. W. Biddle, "Could the Navy Keep 600 Ships Afloat?" *New York Times*, July 7, 1985.

34. C. Corddry, "Pentagon Officials Warned to Curb Feud", *Baltimore Sun*, October 12, 1983, p. 8.

35. J. Lehman, note 32.

36. R. Komer, "Carrier-Heavy Navy is Waste-Heavy", *Los Angeles Times*, May 16, 1984, p. B-5.

37. J. Lehman, "Rebirth of a U.S. Naval Strategy", *Strategic Review*, Summer 1981, p. 13.

38. *Ibid.*

39. *Ibid.*

40. J. Lehman, cited in *U.S. Defense Policy*, Congressional Quarterly, Washington, D.C., 1983, p. 140.

41. F. West, note 7, pp. 333, 337.

42. *Ibid*, p. 337.

43. In C. Hood, note 30.

44. J. Roherty, note 29, p. 148.

45. J. Lehman, *Aircraft Carriers: The Real Choices*, Washington Paper #52, Center for Strategic and International Studies, Georgetown University, 1978, pp. 32–44.

46. *Ibid.*, p. 32.

47. In T. Donlan, "Everything Shipshape? Just Ask the Navy's Top Skipper", *Barron's*, June 11, 1984, p. 16.

48. Statement in "The Today Show", NBC Network, September 9, 1983.

49. C. Wright, "U.S. Naval Operations in 1983", *Proceedings/Naval Review*, May 1984, pp. 52, 295.

50. S. Foley, note 2, p. 10.

51. United Press International, "Fleet Reports Soviet Air Surveillance, Two U.S. Carrier Groups Maneuver Off Vladivostok", *Washington Post*, December 20, 1984, p. A-26.

52. In CINCPAC, "SecDef Quarterly Report Oct-Dec 84", cable to U.S. Secretary of Defense, January 9, 1985, paragraph 3; declassified under F.O.I.A. request.

53. *U.S. News and World Report*, May 18, 1981, p. 30.

54. U.S. Senate, Committee on Armed Services, *Department of Defense Authorization for Appropriations for FY 1984*, Part 1, U.S. GPO, Washington, D.C., 1983, p. 457.

55. In *Defense Week*, April 30, 1984, p. 16.

56. In CINCPAC, note 52, paragraph 8.

57. *Korea Annual*, Yonhap Publishing News Agency, Seoul, 1984, p. 393.

58. J. Anderson, *Seattle Post-Intelligencer*, March 2, 1983.

59. H. Albinski, *The Australian-American Security Relationship*, St. Martins Press, New York, 1982, p. 75.

60. CINCPAC, "Amplified Logistics Planning Guideline", Effective Instruction 4000 IL, CH-1, May 11, 1982, p. VI-1; released under F.O.I.A. request.

61. S. Talbott, *Deadly Gambits, The Reagan Administration and the Stalemate in Nuclear Arms Control*, Knopf, New York, 1984, p. 14.

62. For ship estimates, see John Collins, "U.S.-Soviet Military Balance", Washington, D.C., Congressional Research Service, August 1, 1983, pp. 127–128; for personnel estimates, see U.S. House of Representatives, Committee on Appropriations, Subcommittee on the Department of Defense, *Department of Defense Appropriations for 1985* (Hearings), Part 1, U.S. GPO, Washington, D.C., 1984, p. 267.

63. U.S. Senate, Committee on Armed Services, note 23, p. 1246.

64. W. Crowe, 1984, "The Pacific Area" (mimeo), testifying before the Senate Armed Services Committee, February 23, 1984, p. 14.

65. In J. Lehman, "Beyond SALT II, The Soviet Strategic Nuclear Advantage and How to Eliminate It", in J. Lehman and S. Weiss edited, *Beyond the SALT II Failure*, Praeger, New York, 1981, p. 143.

66. S. Talbott, note 61, p. 16.

67. T. Carrington, "Newest Trident Touches Off Feud Over Arms Control", *Asian Wall Street Journal*, June 23, 1985, p. 64.

68. B. Trainor, speech to Naval War College, June 21, 1984, declassified under F.O.I.A.

69. L. Gelb, "Weinberger's War Guide: Follow the Direct Route", *New York Times*, December 2, 1984, p. E-25; R. Halloran, "Shultz and Weinberger: Disputing the Use of Force", *New York Times*, November 30, 1984, p. B-6. The media has confused this struggle for foreign policy control with the "moral" issues involved in exercising superpower.

70. D. Baucom, *Air University Review*, September-October 1984, p. 2.

71. J. Gaddis, "The Rise and Fall and Future of Detente", *Foreign Affairs*, Winter, 1983/84, pp. 354–377.

72. R. Komer, *Maritime Strategy or Coalition Defense*, Abt Books, Cambridge, Massachusetts, 1984.

73. J. Record, "Jousting with Unreality, Reagan's Military Strategy", *International Security*, Winter, 1983–1984, p. 18.

74. R. Halloran, "Navy Trains to Battle Soviet Submarine in Arctic", *New York Times*, May 19, 1983, p. 17.

75. L. Brooks, "Escalation and Naval Strategy", *Proceedings*, August 1984, p. 37.

76. B. Trainor, note 68.

77. *Ibid.*

78. S. Turner, "A Strategy for the 90s", *New York Times Magazine*, May 6, 1984, p. 40.

79. B. Trainor, note 68.

80. J. Record, "Limitless War, Limited Means", *Baltimore Sun*, August 3, 1984, p. 13

81. F. Hiatt, "Military Game Finds Even a Small War Would Sap Supplies", *Washington Post*, August 3, 1984, p. 1.

82. R. Halloran, "18 Month Survey Finds U.S. Forces Lacking Readiness", *New York Times*, July 22, 1984, p. 12.

83. U.S. Senate, Committee on Armed Services, note 23, Part 2, p. 1221.

84. U.S. House of Representatives, Committee on Appropriations, Subcommittee on the Department of Defense, note 62, Part 2, p. 579.

85. T. Etzold, "From Far East to Middle East: Overextension in American Strategy Since World War II, *Proceedings/Naval Review*, May 1981, p. 77.

86. J. Record, note 80.

87. F. Halliday, *The Making of the Second Cold War*, Verso, London, 1983, p. 89.

88. In U.S. Senate, Committee on Armed Services, note 23, Part 2, 1984, p. 919.

89. See R. Smoke, "Extended Deterrence: Some Observations", *Naval War College Review*, September-October 1983, pp. 37–49.

90. U.S. Congressional Budget Office, *Planning U.S. General Purpose Forces Related to Asia*, U.S. GPO, Washington, D.C., 1977, p. 55.

91. In U.S. House of Representatives, Committee on International Relations, Subcommittee on International Security and Scientific Affairs, *First Use of Nuclear Weapons: Preserving Responsible Control* (Hearings), U.S. GPO, Washington, D.C., 1976, p. 64.

92. U.S. House of Representatives, Committee on Appropriations, Subcommittee on the Department of Defense, note 62, p. 117.

93. K. Dunn and W. Staudenmaier, "Strategy for Survival", *Foreign Policy*, no. 52, Fall 1983, p. 38.

94. B. Trainor, note 68.

Chapter 9: Deadly Connection

1. In S. Hersh, *The Price of Power, Kissinger in the Nixon White House*, Simon and Schuster, 1983, p. 52.

2. See L. Freedman, *The Evolution of Nuclear Strategy*, St. Martin's, New York, 1983, p. 118.

3. P. Nitze, 1978, in J. Sanders, *Peddlers of Crisis, The Committee on the Present Danger*, Pluto, London, 1983, p. 256.

4. F. Kaplan, *The Wizards of Armageddon*, Simon and Schuster, New York, 1983, p. 370.

5. N. Gayler, (former CINCPAC), "A Commander-in-Chief's Perspective on Nuclear Weapons", in G. Prins, edited, *The Nuclear Crisis Reader*, Vintage, New York, 1983, pp. 234–243.

6. S. Deitchman, *Military Power and the Advance of Technology*, Westview, Boulder, Colorado, 1983, p. 22.

7. J. Van Staaveren, "Air Operations in the Taiwan Crises of 1958", U.S. Air Force Historical Division Liaison Office, November 1962, p. 51.

8. S. Kaplan, *Diplomacy of Power, Soviet Armed Forces as a Political Instrument*, The Brookings Institution, Washington, 1981, p. 370.

9. P. Wolfowitz, "Security Treaty Between Australia, New Zealand, and the United States", (mimeo), testimony before the House Subcommittee on Asia and Pacific Affairs, Washington, D.C., March 18, 1985.

10. See M. Klare, "Securing the Firebreak", *World Policy Journal*, Spring 1985, p. 231.

11. *Ibid.*, p. 231.

12. J. Gaddis, *Strategies of Containment, A Critical Appraisal of Postwar American National Security Policy*, Oxford University Press, 1982, p. 149.

13. Cited in J. Rose, *The Evolution of U.S. Army Nuclear Doctrine*, Westview, Colorado, 1980, pp. 88–89.

14. Answer to author's question, National Defense University, "Pacific Seminar", Honolulu, February 21, 1985.

15. S. Hersh, note 1, p. 124.

16. B. Blechman and S. Kaplan, *Force Without War, U.S. Armed Forces as a Political Instrument*, The Brookings Institution, Washington, D.C., 1978. pp. 47–49.

17. In interview with authors, April 24, 1984, Washington D.C., his emphasis.

18. *Ibid.*

19. CINCPAC, "Logistics Planning", Effective Instruction C4000.1L, March 20, 1981, p. I-4; released under F.O.I.A. request.

20. C. Simpson, *Inside the Green Berets, The First Thirty Years*, Presidio Press, Novato, California, 1983. p. 22.

Chapter 10: Pacific Command

1. In E. Pomeroy, *Pacific Outpost, American Strategy in Guam and Micronesia*, Stanford University Press, 1951, p. 169.

2 U.S. Chief of Naval Operations, *Strategic Concepts of the U.S. Navy*, NWP 1 (Rev. A), 1978, p. I-3-2.

3. U.S. Air Force, "United States Pacific Command", Fact Sheet 81–39, Washington, D.C.

4. B. Schemmer, "Admiral William J. Crowe, Jr.", *Armed Forces Journal International*, April 1984, p. 44.

5. Interview, Lieutenant-Colonel Ralph Cossa, Stanford, January 8, 1985.

6. F. Schurmann, *The Logic of World Power, An Enquiry Into the Origins, Currents and Contradictions of World Politics*, Pantheon, New York, 1974, p. 272.

7. *Ibid.*

8. M. Weisner, "Pacific Command: A Unique C4 Challenge", *Signal*, February 1978, p. 8.

9. T. Milton, "A Time of Transition in the Pacific", *Air Force*, October 1978, p. 54.

10. J. Collins, *U.S./Soviet Military Balance, Concepts and Capabilities*, McGraw-Hill, New York, 1980, pp. 607, 610.

11. Telephone conversation with authors, J. Berg, U.S. Air Force Office of Public Information and P. Johnson, U.S. Navy Office of Public Affairs, November 6, 1984.

12. CINCPAC, Public Affairs Office, "The U.S. Pacific Command", Camp Smith, Honolulu, 1985, p. 6.

13. U.S. House of Representatives, Committee on Appropriations, Subcommittee on the Department of Defense, *Department of Defense Appropriations for 1985*, (Hearings), Part 1, U.S. GPO, Washington D.C., 1984, pp. 785, 788, 839; W. Simons, "Command and Control in the Pacific", *Journal of Defense and Diplomacy*, Volume 3, no. 1, January 1985, pp. 19–20.

14. R. Hart, *The Great White Fleet*, Little Brown, Boston, 1965, pp. 189–264.

15. H. Willmott, *Empires in the Balance, Japanese and Allied Pacific Strategies to April 1942*, Orbis, London, 1982, p. 33.

16. Telephone communication with authors, Office of Information, U.S. Navy, March 15, 1984.

17. C. Wright, "U.S. Naval Operations in 1982", *Proceedings/Naval Review*, May 1983. p. 57.

18. R. Weinland, *The Navy in the Pacific: Past, Present, and Glimpses of the Future*, Center for Naval Analyses, Professional Paper 264, Virginia, 1979, p. 6; U.S. Navy, Office of Public Affairs, February 1, 1984.

19. S. Roberts, *The U.S. Navy in the 1980s*, Center for Naval Analyses, Professional Paper 313, Virginia, 1981, pp. 13–14.

20. G. Steele, "The Seventh Fleet", *Proceedings*, January 1976, p. 30.

21. S. Deitchman, "Designing the Fleet and Its Air Arm", *Astronautics and Aeronautics*, Volume 16, no. 1, November 1978, p. 21.

22. J. Lehman, testimony to U.S. House of Representatives, Armed Services Committee, on FY 1986 Military Posture of the Navy and Marine Corps (mimeo), Washington, D.C., February 7, 1985, p. 15.

23. *All Hands*, "Harpoon Goes With the Fleet", September 1983, p. 41.

24. U.S. Senate, Committee on Armed Services, *Department of Defense Authorization for Appropriations for FY 1985*, Part 8, U.S. GPO, Washington, D.C., 1984, p. 3879.

25. Calculated from S. Deitchman, note 21, pp. 21–22.

26. Calculated from Conways, *All the World's Fighting Ships 1947–1982*, Part 1, Naval Institute Press, Annapolis, Maryland, 1983, pp. 203–206.

27. In U.S. Senate, Committee on Armed Services, *Department of Defense Authorization for FY 1983*, Part 6, U.S. GPO, Washington D.C., 1982, p. 3724.

28. U.S. Chief of Naval Operations, *Naval Operational Planning*, NWP 11 (Rev. C), Washington D.C., 1978, Appendix F, p. F-12.

29. See E. Simmons, "Commentary: Marines in East Asia", in U.S. Air Force Academy, *The American Military and the Far East*, U.S. GPO, Washington D.C., 1980, pp. 172–173.

30. In U.S. Senate, Committee on Armed Services, *Department of Defense Authorization for Appropriations for Fiscal Year 1985* (Hearings), Part 2, U.S. GPO, Washington D.C., 1984, p. 922.

31. U.S. House of Representatives, Committee on Appropriations, note 13, Part 1, p. 807.

32. A. Millett, *Semper Fidelis, The History of The United States Marine Corps*, MacMillan, New York, 1980, pp. 395, 427.

33. Office of the Assistant Secretary of Defense, (Manpower, Reserve Affairs and Logistics), *Base Structure Annex to Manpower Requirements, Report for FY 1982*, U.S. Department of Defense, Washington D.C., January 1981, p. 169.

34. Testimony of General P. Kelley to U.S. House of Representatives, Committee on Armed Services on Marine Corps FY 1986, Posture, Plans, and Programs (mimeo), Washington, D.C., February 7, 1985, p. 38.

35. Briefing, Intelligence Center Pacific, February 20, 1985.

36. C. Wright, "U.S. Naval Operations in 1983", *Proceedings/Naval Review*, May 1984, pp. 293–294.

37. *Ibid.*

38. U.S. House of Representatives, Committee on Appropriations, note 13, Part 1, pp. 1005, 1011.

39. *Ibid.*, p. 841.

40. J. Collins, *U.S./Soviet Military Balance, Statistical Trends 1970–1982*, Congressional Research Service Report 83–153S, Washington D.C., 1983, p. 130; Office of Assistant Secretary of Defense, note 33, p. 170.

41. A. Millett, note 32, p. 434.

42. R. Mahoney, *U.S. Navy Responses to International Incidents and Crises*, CRC 332, Volume 1, Center for Naval Analyses, Virginia, 1977, p. 17.

43. J. Schlight, "The Impact of the Orient on Airpower", in U.S. Air Force Academy, note 29, p. 163.

44. B. and F. Brodie, *From Crossbow to H-Bomb, The Evolution of Weapons and Tactics of Warfare*, Indiana University Press, Bloomington, 1973, p. 282.

45. C. Sorrels, *U.S. Cruise Missile Program: Development, Deployment, and Implications for Arms Control*, McGraw-Hill, New York, 1983, pp. 112–116.

46. B. Cooper, *Maritime Roles for Land-Based Aviation*, Congressional Research Service Report 83–151 F, Washington D.C., 1983, p. 35.

47. Calculated from Strategic Air Command, *Development of the Strategic Air Command, 1946–1981*, Office of the Historian, Offut AFB, Omaha, Nebraska, 1982, p. 41.

48. J. Wooten, *Regional Support Facilities for the Rapid Deployment Force*, Congressional Research Service Report 82053 F, Washington D.C., 1982, p. 32.

49. R. Littauer and N. Uphoff, *The Air War in Indochina*, Beacon, Boston, 1971, pp. 31–69.

50. Strategic Air Command, note 47, p. 129.

51. R. Littauer and N. Uphoff, note 49, p. 277.

52. U.S. House of Representatives, Committee on Appropriations, note 13, Part 6, p. 608; B. Cooper, note 46, p. 47.

53. B. Cooper, note 46, p. 47.

54. Strategic Air Command, "SAC Support to Theatre Commands", Fact Sheet 84–35, Offut AFB, Omaha, Nebraska, 1984, p. 1.

55. R. Flint, "The United States Army and the Pacific Frontier", in U.S. Air Force Academy, note 29, 1980, p. 146.

56. U.S. House of Representatives, Committee on Appropriations, note 13, Part 1, p. 786.

57. CINCPAC, note 12, p. 4.

58. D. Meyer, "Does the U.S. Need to Modernize Its Army in the Pacific?" *Armed Forces Journal International*, May 1985, p. 100.

59. B. Cumings, *The Origins of the Korean War*, Princeton University Press, New Jersey, 1981, pp. 267–426.

60. C. Haberman, "U.S. and North Korea Trade Charges on DMZ Clash", *New York Times*, November 25, 1984, p. 3.

61. V. Marchetti and J. Marks, *The CIA and the Cult of Intelligence*, Dell, New York, 1974, p. 127.

62. P. DeSilva, *Sub Rosa, The CIA And The Uses of Intelligence*, Times Books, New York, 1983, pp. 151–152.

63. U.S. Department of Defense, *The Pentagon Papers*, Volume 2, Beacon Press, Boston, 1972, p. 648.

64. *Ibid.*, p. 649.

65. *Ibid.*, p. 648.

66. J. Kelly, "Cover to Cover: Rewald's CIA Story", *Counterspy*, June-August, 1984, p. 16.

67. R. Shultz, "Strategy Lessons from an Unconventional War: The U.S. Experience in Vietnam", in S. Sarkesian, editor, *Non-Nuclear Conflicts in the Nuclear Age*, Praeger, 1980, pp. 140–143.

68. E. Lansdale, *In the Midst of Wars, An American's Mission to Southeast Asia*, Harper and Row, New York, 1972, p. 73.

69. U.S. Senate, Committee on Foreign Relations, *United States Security Agreements and Commitments* (Hearings), U.S. GPO, Washington, D.C., 1970, Part 5, p. 1315.

70. Takashi Matsuo, "The U.S. Forces and Bases in Japan", in Gensuikyo, *Okinawa International Conference Against Miliary Bases*, Naha, 1981, p. 85.

71. Jane's, *All the World's Aircraft, 1983–84*, New York, 1984, p. 421.

72. U.S. House of Representatives, Committee on Appropriations, note 13, Part 8, p. 800.

73. CINCPAC, "Quarterly Report to SecDef", July-September 1983, cable P 062230Z, October 1983, p. 3; released under F.O.I.A. request.

74. CINCPAC, "Quarterly Report to SecDef", April-June 1984, cable P 100545Z, July 1984, Honolulu, p. 2; released under F.O.I.A. request.

75. In D. Meyer, note 58, p. 100.

76. V. Daniels and J. Erdheim, *Game Warden*, Operations Evaluation Group, Center for Naval Analyses, Virginia, January 1976, p. 18–19.

77. U.S. Senate, Committee on Foreign Relations, note 69, Part 5, p. 1353.

78. U.S. Chief of Naval Operations, note 28, pp. 23–1, 23–2.

79. U.S. Senate, Committee on Foreign Relations, note 69, Part 5, p. 1360.

80. M. Johnson, *The Military as an Instrument of U.S. Policy in Southwest Asia, The Rapid Development Joint Task Force, 1979–1982*, Westview, Colorado, 1983, pp. 5–12.

81. *Ibid.*, p. 102; U.S. House of Representatives, Committee on Appropriations, note 13, Part 1, p. 196.

82. M. Johnson, note 80, p. 106.

83. J. Heiser, *Logistic Support*, Vietnam Studies, U.S. Army, Washington D.C., 1972, p. 7.

84. *Ibid.*, pp. 62–64.

85. C. Mohr, "Marines Prepare for Duty in Asia", *New York Times*, April 10, 1985.

86. U.S. Chief of Naval Operations, note 28, p. 6–5.

87. J. Heiser, note 83, p. 73, 124.

88. U.S. House of Representatives, Committee on Appropriations, note 13, Part 1, p. 942.

89. C. Mohr, note 85.

Chapter 11: The Invisible Arsenal

1. In Program on Resources Policy, *Seminar on Command, Control, Communications, and Intelligence*, Incidental Paper, Center for Information Policy Research, Harvard University Press, Cambridge, Massachusetts, Spring 1981, p. 157.

2. In Mitre Corporation, *Worldwide Deployment of Tactical Forces and the C^3I Connection*, Mitre M82–64, Bedford, Massachusetts, 1982, p. 53.

3. V. Lang, "Inter-Operability – The Key to C^3 Systems in Support of U.S. PACOM", *Signal*, February 1984, pp. 26–28.

4. T. Sargent, "DCA Pacific Area: Tying the Pacific Defense Structure Together", *Signal*, February 1984, pp. 35–37.

5. B. Blair, *Strategic Command and Control, Redefining the Nuclear Threat*, The Brookings Institution, Washington, D.C., 1985, p. 53.

6. *Ibid.*, p. 55.

7. C. Williams, "Pacific Command: Command, Control, Communications, and Computers", *Signal*, March 1975, p. 63.

8. B. Katz, "Korean War Prompted Expansion of U.S. Naval Communications with Japan", *Signal*, May 1973, p. 37–38.

9. R. Adams, *Command and Control Systems Evolution and Management in Department of Defense*, Army War College, Carlisle Barracks, Pennsylvania, 1974, pp. 18–22; T. Rienzi, *Communications Electronics*, Vietnam Studies, U.S. Army, Washington, D.C., 1972.

10. M. Van Orden, "Satellite Communications in the Navy", *Proceedings/Naval Review*, May 1967, p. 144.

11. C. Williams, note 7, p. 63.

12. V. Lang, note 3, p. 27.

13. B. Jasani, *Outer Space – Battlefield of the Future?*, Taylor and Francis, London, 1978, pp. 97–101.

14. U.S. House of Representatives, Committee on Appropriations, Subcommittee on the Department of Defense, *Department of Defense Appropriations for 1985* (Hearings), Part 5, U.S. GPO, Washington, D.C., 1984, p. 437.

15. T. Sargent, note 4, p. 36.

16. J. Lee, "U.S. AWESTCOM: Reaching for Excellence", *Signal*, February 1984, p. 20.

17. D. Ball, "The U.S. Fleet Satellite Communications (FLTSATCOM) System: The Australian Connection", *Pacific Defense Reporter*, February, 1982, p. 30.

18. R. Denaro, "Navstar: the All-Purpose Satellite", *IEEE Spectrum*, May 1981, p. 40.

19. F. Klotz, *The U.S. President and the Control of Strategic Nuclear Weapons*, Dissertation, Oxford University, 1980, p. 39.

20. See R. Watson and J. Schnabel, *The History of the Joint Chiefs of Staff, the Joint Chiefs of Staff and National Policy*, Volume III, part 2, Glazier, Delaware, 1979.

21. D. Zagoria and J. Zagoria, "Crises on the Korean Peninsula", in S. Kaplan, edited, *Diplomacy of Power, Soviet Armed Forces as a Political Instrument*, The Brookings Institution, 1981, p. 398.

22. In Program on Resources Policy, note 1, p. 140.

23. CINCPAC, "Mission and Functions of the Intelligence Center, Pacific", Effective Instruction 5400.21D, July 14, 1982, p. 3; released under F.O.I.A. request.

24. J. Richelson, *The U.S. Intelligence Community*, Ballinger, Cambridge, 1985, p. 258.

25. *Ibid.*, p. 81.

26. CINCPAC, note 23, p. 4.

27. B. Jasani, "Military Space Technology and Its Implications", in B. Jasani, editor, *Outer Space – A New Dimension of the Arms Race*, Taylor and Francis, London, 1982, pp. 45–49.

28. P. Bamford, *The Puzzle Palace, A Report on NSA, America's Most Secret Agency*, Houghton Mifflin, Boston, 1982, p. 186.

29. J. Richelson, note 24, p. 90.

30. A. Cockburn, *The Threat: Inside the Soviet Military Machine*, Vintage, New York, 1984, p. 370.

31. See D. Pearson, "KAL007, What the U.S. Knew and When We Knew It", *The Nation*, New York, August 18–25, 1984.

32. T. Bernard and T. Eskelson, "U.S. Spy Plane Capable of Interceding in Attack on Korean Jet", *Denver Post*, September 13, 1983.

33. J. Richelson, note 24, p. 87.

34. *Ibid.*

35. *Ibid.*, p. 141.

36. *Ibid.*, p. 88.

37. J. Waterford, "U.S. Navy Still Receiving New Zealand South Pacific Intelligence", *Canberra Times*, May 17, 1985, p. 3.

38. R. Herrick, *Soviet Naval Mission Assignments*, Ketron Inc., report to Assistant Director, Net Assessment, Navy Program Planning Office, Volume 2, 1980, p. 111–209.

39. J. Bussert, "Computers Add New Effectiveness to SOSUS/CAESAR", *Defense Electronics*, October 1979, p. 64.

40. Institute of Naval Studies, *The Navy's Role in the Exploration of the Ocean (Project Blue Water)*, phase 1, Study 19, Center for Naval Analyses, University of Rochester, report to Chief of Naval Operations, 1968, p. 1–84.

41. K. Tsipis, *Arsenal, Understanding Weapons in the Nuclear Age*, Simon and Schuster, New York, 1983, p. 232.

42. See O. Wilkes, "Strategic Antisubmarine Warfare and its Implications for a Counterforce First Strike", in *SIPRI Yearbook, 1979*, Taylor and Francis, London, pp. 427–452.

43. B. Jasani, note 27, p. 54.

Chapter 12: The Means of Annihilation

1. In G. Quester, "Presidential Authority and Nuclear Weapons", U.S. House of Representatives, Committee on International Relations, Subcommittee on International Sec-

urity and Scientific Affairs, *First Use of Nuclear Weapons, Preserving Responsible Control* (Hearing), U.S. GPO, Washington, D.C., 1976, p. 218.

2. See for example, T. Cochran *et al.*, *Nuclear Weapons Data Book: U.S. Nuclear Forces and Capabilities*, Ballinger, Cambridge, Massachusetts, 1984; K. Tsipis, *Arsenal, Understanding Weapons in the Nuclear Age*, Simon and Schuster, New York, 1983; R. Aldridge, *First Strike!*, South End, Boston, 1983; annual *SIPRI Yearbooks*; Jane's *Weapon Systems*; and W. Arkin and R. Fieldhouse, *Nuclear Battlefields, Global Links in the Arms Race*, Ballinger, Cambridge, Massachusetts, 1985.

3. J. Collins, *U.S./Soviet Military Balance*, McGraw Hill, New York, 1980, p. 122.

4. D. Ball, *Targeting for Strategic Deterrence*, Adelphi Paper 185, London, 1983.

5. Office of Technology Assessment, *The Effects of Nuclear War*, U.S. GPO, Washington, D.C., 1980, pp. 63–106.

6. Jane's *Fighting Ships 1983–1984*, London, 1984, p. 635.

7. General Dynamics, *The World's Missile Systems*, Pomona, California, 1982, p. 175.

8. Stanford Research Institute International, *Strategic Systems Test Support Study*, report to U.S. Ballistic Missile Defense Systems Command, Alabama, 1981, Volume II, p. 165; released under F.O.I.A. request.

9. Jane's, note 6, p. 634.

10. R. Steer, "Understanding Anti-Submarine Warfare Technology", in K. Tsipis, P. Janeway, editors, *Review of U.S. Military Research and Development 1984*, Pergamon, 1984, p. 215.

11. T. Woolfe, "Journalists Get Rare Defense Closeup in Tour Aboard Trident Sub Jackson", *Hartford Courant*, October 6, 1984, p. B-1.

12. P. Pringle and W. Arkin, *S.I.O.P., The Secret U.S. Plan for Nuclear War*, Norton, New York, p. 161.

13. C. Wright, "U.S. Naval Operations in 1982", *Proceedings/Naval Review*, May 1983, p. 230.

14. T. Cochran *et al.*, note 2, p. 139.

15. See R. Jones, "Ballistic Missile Submarines and Arms Control in the Indian Ocean", *Asian Survey*, Volume 20, no. 3, March 1980, p. 271; O. Wilkes, personal communication, July 16, 1983.

16. O. Wilkes, *ibid.*

17. R. Aldridge, "Background Paper on Trident and the Militarization of the Indian Ocean" (mimeo), February 15, 1983.

18. United Press International, "Ice Broken by Soviet Submarine", *Philadelphia Inquirer*, December 17, 1984, p. 13.

19. G. Wilson, "The Navy is Preparing for Submarine Warfare Beneath Coastal Ice", *Washington Post*, May 19, 1983, p. 5; R. Halloran, "Navy Trains to Battle Soviet Submarines in Arctic", *New York Times*, May 19, 1983, p. 17.

20. Telephone communication with authors, Public Affairs Office, Air Force, November 20, 1984.

21. R. Halloran, "Joint Chiefs' Head Urges New Bomber", New York Times, January 29, 1981.

22. K. Tsipis, note 2, p. 160.

23. Calculated from T. Cochran et al., note 2, p. 149.

24. K. Tsipis, note 2, p. 233.

25. C. Wright, note 13, p. 230.

26. N. Friedman, Submarine Design and Development, Naval Institute Press, Annapolis, Maryland, 1984, p. 178.

27. D. Kaplan, The Nuclear Navy, Fund for Constitutional Government Report, Washington, D.C., 1983, Tables, p. 8.

28. W. West, "Maritime Strategy and NATO Deterrence", Naval War College Review, September/October 1985, p. 5.

29. W. Arkin and R. Fieldhouse, "Nuclear Weapons Command, Control, and Communications", in SIPRI Yearbook, 1984, Taylor and Francis, London, 1984, pp. 455–516; F. Klotz, The U.S. President and the Control of Nuclear Weapons, Ph.D. Dissertation, Oxford University, 1980, p. 429.

30. W. Simons "Command and Control in the Pacific", Journal of Defense and Diplomacy, Volume 3, no. 1, January 1985, p. 22.

31. U.S. Department of the Army, "Safeguarding of the Single Integrated Operational Plan (SIOP)", Western Command memorandum no. 380–4, Fort Shafter Hawaii, August 29, 1983, p. 4, released under F.O.I.A. request to P. Wills.

32. Personal communication, Rear Admiral G. Edwards, Commander Maritime Forces Pacific (Canada) to P. Chapman, Project Ploughshares, Canada, December 29, 1983 and attached map.

33. F. Schurmann, The Logic of World Power, Pantheon, New York, 1974, p. 542; and B. Palmer, The 25-Year War, America's Military Role in Vietnam, University Press of Kentucky, 1984, p. 126.

34. J. Lehman, in D. Hoffman, "President Disputes General on War Probability", Washington Post, June 23, 1984, p. 11.

35. Briefing to authors, Intelligence Center, Pacific, February 20, 1985.

36. P. Bracken, The Command and Control of Nuclear Forces, Yale University Press, 1983, p. 46.

37. U.S. Senate, Committee on Armed Service, Recent False Alarms from the Nation's Missile Attack Warning System, U.S. GPO, Washington, D.C., 1980, pp. 6, 9–10.

38. Ibid., p. 5.

39. Cited in M. Leitenberg, "Background Information on Tactical Nuclear Weapons", in SIPRI Tactical Nuclear Weapons: European Perspectives Taylor and Francis, London 1978 p. 9.

40. CINCPAC, "HQ U.S. CINCPAC Airborne Command Post Contingency Backup Support for U.S. CINCPAC", Effective Instruction 3120.27B, 1983, December 29, 1983; released under F.O.I.A. request.

41. In Program on Information Resources Policy, *Seminar on Command, Control, Communications and Intelligence*, Harvard University Press, Cambridge, Massachusetts, 1980, p. 15.

42. P. Bracken, note 36, p. 128.

43. M. Leitenberg, note 39, p. 8.

44. T. Cochran *et al.*, note 2, p. 92.

45. See Chief of Naval Operations, *Loading and Underway Replenishment of Nuclear Weapons*, NWP 14 (Rev. C), 1983.

46. CINCPAC, "Pacific Command (PACOM) Targeting Program", Effective Instruction C3810.26E, Honolulu, October 25, 1983; released under F.O.I.A. request.

47. Commander-in-Chief, U.S. Pacific Fleet, "Mission and Function of Fleet Intelligence Center Pacific", Pearl Harbor, Hawaii, CINCPACFLT Instruction 5450.1M, July 7, 1984, p. 1; released under F.O.I.A. request to P. Wills.

48. CINCPAC, "Residual Capability Assessment Reporting", Effective Instruction 3401.5B, February 19, 1981, p. I-1; released under F.O.I.A. request.

49. CINCPAC, "Pacific Command Nuclear Biological Chemical Warning and Reporting System (Short Title: PACOM NBCWRS)", Effective Instruction 3401.3J, February 6, 1981, p. I-7; released under F.O.I.A. request.

50. U.S. House of Representatives, Committee on Armed Services, Subcommittee on Investigations, *Review of the Department of Defense, Command, Control, and Communications Systems and Facilities*, U.S. GPO, Washington, D.C., 1977, pp. 7–8.

51. J. McCartney, "U.S. Test Could Start New Phase of Arms Race", *Philadelphia Enquirer*, October 6, 1984, p. 1.

52. M. King and P. Fleming, "An Overview of the Effects of Nuclear Weapons in Communications Capabilities", *Signal*, January 1980, p. 64.

53. U.S. House of Representatives, Committee on Appropriations, *Department of Defense Appropriations for 1985* (Hearings), Part 1, U.S. GPO, Washington, D.C., 1984, p. 519.

54. Cited in J. Rose, *The Evolution of U.S. Army Nuclear Doctrine, 1945–1980*, Westview, Colorado, 1980, p. 171.

55. See Appendix in Nautilus, *Warships and Warheads, U.S.–Pacific Connections*, Box 309, Leverett, Massachusetts, December 1984.

56. U.S. Army Field Manual 100–5, July 1976, in H. Tromp and G. La Rocque, *Nuclear War in Europe*, Groningen University Press, 1982, p. 259.

57. W. Arkin and R. Fieldhouse, note 2, p. 231.

58. U.S. Department of the Army, Western Command, "Tactical Training for Nuclear-Capable Units", WESTCOM Regulation no. 350–10, Fort Shafter, Hawaii, June 14, 1984, p. 1; released under F.O.I.A. request to P. Wills.

59. J. Anderson, "Little Weapons with a Big Bang", *Washington Post,* June 3, 1984.

60. W. Stowe, "Atomic Demolition Munitions", *National Defense*, May-June 1975, p. 467.

61. U.S. Department of the Army, Western Command, "Organization and Training for Nuclear, Biological, and Chemical Defense", WESTCOM Supplement 1 to Army Regulation 220–58, Fort Shafter, Hawaii, December 21, 1979, p. 4, released under F.O.I.A. request to P. Wills.

62. *Ibid.*, pp. 1–2.

63. U.S. Department of the Army, Western Command, note 58, p. 2.

64. *Ibid*, pp. 2–4.

65. *Korea Herald*, "Long War Theory Applies to Korea", January 23, 1983.

66. R. Stilwell, "Why They Should Stay", *Asian Wall Street Journal*, June 13, 1977.

67. U.S. House of Representatives, Committee on International Relations, Subcommittee on International Security and Scientific Affairs, *First Use of Nuclear Weapons: Preserving Responsible Control* (Hearings), U.S. GPO, Washington, D.C., 1976, p. 93.

68. W. Overholt, "A U.S. Nuclear Posture for Asia", in W. Overholt, editor, *Asia's Nuclear Future*, Westview, Colorado, 1977, p. 236.

69. Interview with authors, Washington, D.C., April 24, 1984.

70. P. Nitze *et al.*, *Securing the Seas, The Soviet Naval Challenge and Western Alliance Options*, Westview, Colorado, 1977, p. 13.

71. W. Pincus, "U.S. Military Seeking Small Nuclear Weapons", *Washington Post,* June 27, 1985, p. 33.

72. U.S. Joint Chiefs of Staff, *United States Military Posture for FY 1983*, in U.S. Senate, Committee on Armed Services, *Department of Defense Authorization for Appropriations for Fiscal Year 1984* (Hearings), Part 1, Washington, D.C., 1984, p. 460.

73. In *Defense Week*, February 14, 1984, p. 16.

74. In U.S. Senate, Committee on Armed Service, *Department of Defense Authorization for Appropriations for FY 1984* (Hearings), Part 5, U.S. GPO, Washington, D.C., 1983, p. 2463.

75. *Ibid.*

76. W. Crowe, "The Pacific Area" (mimeo), statement before the U.S. Senate, February 23, 1984.

77. U.S. House of Representatives, Committee on Appropriations, note 53, Part 5, pp. 170–171.

78. *Ibid.*, Part 5, p. 550.

79. *Ibid.*, p. 557.

80. Our emphasis, *ibid.*

81. U.S. Senate, Committee on Armed Services, note 74, Part 5, p. 2458.

Chapter 13: Pacific Missile Test Laboratory

1. Statement (mimeo), Ebeye, June 21, 1984.

2. In R. Hallow, "Short Leash for Micronesia Imperils 'Star Wars' Defense", *Washington Times*, June 26, 1985, p. 1.

3. See G. Johnson, *Collision Course at Kwajalein, Marshall Islanders in the Shadow of the Bomb*, 1984, p. 11, from Pacific Concerns Resource Center, P.O. Box 27692, Honolulu, Hawaii, 96827, U.S.A.

4. G. Seaborg, *Kennedy, Kruschev and the Test Ban*, University of California Press, 1981, p. 150–158.

5. O. Wilkes, "Kwajalein Atoll and the Nuclear Arms Race" (mimeo), 1978, p. 4.

6. G. Seaborg, note 4, p. 156.

7. *Ibid.*

8. Strategic Air Command, *The Development of Strategic Air Command, 1946–1981*, Office of the Historian, Offut Air Force Base, Omaha, Nebraska, 1982, p. 85.

9. Stanford Research Institute International (hereafter, SRI), *Strategic Systems Test Support Study, (SSTSS)*, report to U.S. Ballistic Missile Defense Systems Command, Alabama, November 1981, Volume 1, pp. 15–22; released under F.O.I.A. request.

10. G. Johnson, note 3, p. 19.

11. H. Barry, "The Marshall Islands", in F. King, edited, *Oceania and Beyond*, Greenwood Press, Connecticut, 1976, p. 54.

12. SRI, note 9, Volume II, pp. 221–223.

13. *Ibid.*, p. 224.

14. Authors' interview with Warren Nelson, nuclear weapons specialist, Senate Armed Services Committee, November 8th, 1984.

15. In U.S. Senate, Committee on Armed Services, *Fiscal Year 1978 Authorization for Military Procurement* (Hearings), Part 10, U.S. GPO, Washington, D.C., 1977, p. 6539.

16. Interview, note 14.

17. SRI, note 9, Volume II, p. 79.

18. W. Bello, P. Hayes, L. Zarsky, "Missile Planners Take Aim at South Pacific", *National Times*, November 23–29, 1984, p. 19.

19. SRI, note 9, Volume I, p. 8.

20. Telephone interview with authors, Lieutenant R. Still, U.S. Navy Office of Public Affairs, October 29, 1984.

21. U.S. Senate, Committee on Armed Services, note 15.

22. Telephone interview with authors, Bob Lake, Pacific Missile Test Center, October 29, 1984.

23. "No Missile Tests in NZ, Says PM", *New Zealand Herald*, November 13, 1984, p. 3.

24. B. Toohey, "Sydney Role in U.S. Missile Tests", *National Times* (Sydney), February 1, 1985, p. 3.

25. P. Kelly, "Hawke Leaves a Way Out of Dilemma", *Australian*, February 4, 1985.

26. SRI, note 9, Volume II, p. 188.

27. B. Toohey, note 24; M. Grattan, "PM Backs Down on MX", *The Age* (Melbourne), February 6, 1985, p. 1.

28. See articles in *Melbourne Age, Australian, Sydney Morning Herald*, and *National Times* for the weeks of February 1–15, 1985.

29. U.S. General Accounting Office, *Status of the Peacekeeper (MX) Weapon System*, GAO/NSIAD-84-112, Washington, D.C., May 1984, pp. 10–11.

30. Confidential interview with authors.

31. Stockholm International Peace Research Institute, *Arms Control: A Survey and Appraisal of Multilateral Agreements*, Taylor and Francis, London, 1978, p. 91.

32. Space and Missile Test Organization, *SAMTO Test and Evaluation Support Resource Plan (FY 82–89)*, Vandenberg Air Force Base, California, 1982, p. i; released under F.O.I.A. request.

33. *Ibid.*, p. 111-3-13.

34. SRI, note 9, Volume II, p. 174.

Chapter 14: Tomahawk: Missile in Search of a Mission

1. S. Hostettler, "Statement before the Procurement and Military Nuclear Systems Subcommittee of the House Armed Services Committee on Tomahawk Weapon System" (mimeo), March 14, 1984, pp. 8–9.

2. In D. Wettern, "U.S. Naval Strategy, Problems with Allies and Enemies", *Navy International*, August 1984, p. 478.

3. C. Wright, "U.S. Naval Operations in 1983", *Proceedings, Naval Review*, May 1984, p. 290.

4. Communication with authors, J. Berg, U.S. Air Force Office of Public Affairs, November 20, 1984.

5. C. Corddry, "Nuclear Cruise Missiles Said to Be on Subs", *Baltimore Sun*, June 27, 1984; W. Pincus, "Cruise Missiles Deployed on Attack Submarines", *Washington Post*, June 28, 1984.

6. Junko Yamaka, "Japan's Anti-Tomahawk Movement", *The Freeze*, October 1984, p. 15; *Washington Times*, "Sturgeon Class Sub Visits Japan", August 6, 1984, p. 6.

7. R. Huisken, *The Origins of the Strategic Cruise Missile*, Praeger, N.Y., 1981, pp. 96, 186.

8. U.S. Congress, Arms Control and Foreign Policy Caucus, "Fact Sheet – Nuclear Armed Sea-Launched Cruise Missiles: An Overlooked Weapon with Underestimated Implications", *Congressional Record* (House), May 31, 1984, p. H5051.

9. R. Smith, "Missile Deployments Roil Europe", *Science*, January 27, 1984, pp. 371–376.

10. C. Sorrels, *U.S. Cruise Missile Program: Development, Deployment, and Implications for Arms Control*, McGraw Hill, N.Y., 1983, p. 184. This is the best available reference work on cruise missiles.

11. M. Libbey, "Tomahawk", *Proceedings/Naval Review*, May 1984, p. 155.

12. *Ibid*, p. 156.

13. G. MacDonald *et al.*, in R. Betts, *Cruise Missiles, Technology, Strategy, Politics*, The Brookings Institution, Washington, D.C., 1981, p. 56.

14. U.S. Congress, Arms Control and Foreign Policy Caucus, note 8.

15. F. Hiatt, "Admiral Sees Sustainability", *Washington Post*, July 31, 1984, p. 12.

16. J. Cassity, "Managing Air Force E & I: The Engineering Installation Center does it all", *Signal*, September 1983.

17. Science Applications, Inc., *Ground Launched Anti-Ship System (GLASS)*, Report to Defense Nuclear Agency, 29 July, 1983; released under a F.O.I.A. request.

18. S. Hostettler, note 1, p. 3.

19. P. Rogers, "ALCM in its Second Operational Year", *Air Force Magazine*, February 1984, p. 47.

20. K. Tsipis, *Arsenal, Understanding Weapons in the Nuclear Age*, Simon and Schuster, N.Y., 1983, p. 161.

21. M. Libbey, note 11, p. 155.

22. *Ibid.*, p. 160.

23. S. Hostettler, note 1, pp. 23–24.

24. C. Sorrels, note 10.

25. *Ibid.*, p. 222.

26. *Ibid.*, p. 38.

27. Emphasis in original, S. Lodgaard and F. Blackaby, "Nuclear Weapons", *World Armaments and Disarmament, SIPRI Yearbook, 1984*, Taylor and Francis, London, 1984, p. 37.

28. D. Ball, *Can Nuclear War Be Controlled?* Adelphi Paper #169, London, 1981.

29. C. Sorrels, note 10, p. 145.

30. For example: "The purpose of the Tomahawk is to attack SS-20 or Backfire bomber bases or the bases of the strategic nuclear-powered submarine at one stroke and thereby disarm the U.S.S.R." in Sakamoto Kuniaki, "Opposing the Deployment of the Tomahawk Missile", *Gensuiken News*, #108, 1984, p. 13.

31. C. Sorrels, note 10, pp. 39–40.

32. R. Aldridge, "Last Lick in a First Strike", *Asahi Evening News*, March 7, 1984.

33. U.S. Congress, Arms Control and Foreign Policy Caucus, note 8, p. H-5053.

34. M. Libbey, note 11, p. 162.

35. Personal communication with authors, D. Keller, Defense Nuclear Agency, January 2, 1985.

36. S. Hostettler, note 1, p. 6.

37. C. Sorrels, note 10, p. 133.

38. U.S. Senate, *Department of Defense Authorization for Appropriations for FY 1985* (Hearings), Part 8, U.S. GPO, Washington, D.C., 1984, p. 3874.

39. *Ibid.*, p. 3875.

40. *Ibid.*, p. 3900.

41. *Ibid.*, p. 3893.

42. *Ibid.*, p. 3872.

43. D. Ball, *Nuclear War at Sea*, Center for Strategic and Defense Studies, Reference paper 9, Australian National University, Canberra, 1985, p. 18.

44. Cited in B. Knickerbocker, "New Nuclear-Armed Cruise Missile Raises Deterrence Questions", *Christian Science Monitor*, February 27, 1984.

45. J. Sokolsky, "First Use at Sea, Maritime Forces and Nuclear Escalation", paper to Canadian Political Science Association, Montreal, June 1985, p. 7.

46. Press release, Campaign Against Deployment of Sea-Launched Cruise Missiles, Honolulu, March 1, 1985.

47. Interview with authors, January 5, 1985.

48. R. Hibbs, "An Uncontrollable Tomahawk?" *Proceedings*, January 1985, p. 70.

Chapter 15: Exercise of Power

1. In D. Rosenberg, "American Postwar Air Doctrine and Organization: The Navy Experience", in U.S. Air Force, *Air Power and Warfare*, Proceedings of the 8th Military History Symposium, U.S. GPO, Washington, D.C., 1978, pp. 268.

2. J. Kelly, "Security Treaty Between Australia, New Zealand, and the United States" (mimeo), statement to U.S. House of Representatives, Committee on Asian and Pacific Affairs, March 18, 1985, p. 3.

3. G. Shultz, "On Alliance Responsibility", address before the East-West Center and the Pacific and Asian Affairs Council, Honolulu, Hawaii, July 17, 1985, pp. 4–5.

4. J. Lehman, testimony to U.S. House of Representatives, Committee on Armed Services, *FY 1986 Military Posture of U.S. Navy and Marine Corps* (mimeo), February 7, 1985, p. 21.

5. T. Diebel and R. Dougherty, "The Atlantic and Pacific Alliances", in U. Johnson edited, *China Policy for the Next Decade*, Oelgeschlager, Gunn, and Hain, Boston, Massachusetts, 1984, p. 330.

6. W. Tow and W. Feeney, "Introduction", and W. Tow, "U.S. Alliance Policies and Asian-Pacific Security: A Transregional Approach", in W. Tow and W. Feeney, edited, *U.S. Foreign Policy and Asian-Pacific Security*, Westview, Boulder, Colorado, 1982, pp. 3, 34.

7. U. Johnson *et al.*, "The Policy Paper: China Policy for the Next Decade", U. Johnson edited, note 5, p. 8.

8. See M. Klare, *American Arms Supermarket*, University of Texas Press, 1984, pp. 29–33.

9. Quote in *ibid*, p. 30. For military sales data see U.S. Department of Defense, *Foreign Military Sales, Foreign Military Construction Sales and Military Assistance, Facts*, September 30, 1984.

10. R. Grimmett, *Trends in Conventional Arms Transfers to the Third World by Major Suppliers, 1978–1983*, U.S. Congressional Research Service Report 84–82 F, Washington, D.C., May 1984, p. 21.

11. *Ibid*, p. 2.

12. *Ibid*, p. 25.

13. *Ibid*, p. 27.

14. J. Lee, "U.S. AWESTCOM: Reaching for Excellence", *Signal*, February 1984, p. 20–21.

15. W. Nelson, "When Friendship May Spell Trouble" (mimeo), Honolulu, 1983, p. 3.

16. H. Martin, "Our Nation's Future Does Indeed Lie in the Pacific", *Defense Systems Review*, Volume 2, no. 4, June 14, 1985, p. 6.

17. Briefing, Intelligence Center, Pacific, Hawaii, February 20, 1985.

18. CINCPAC, "FY '83 Exercise Program Analysis", declassified telex to JCS, #R.2921442, October 1983, p. 2; released under F.O.I.A. request.

19. W. Crowe, "The Pacific Area" (mimeo), statement before the Senate Armed Services Committee, February 1984, p. 5.

20. CINCPAC, "Code Words, Nicknames, Reconnaissance Nicknames, and Exercise Terms", Instruction 5510.1H, October 20, 1983, p. 5; released under F.O.I.A. request.

21. J. Christensen, "Allies Together", *Surface Warfare*, July–August 1983, p. 12.

22. CINCPAC, Public Affairs Office, News Release #83–39, December 28, 1983; *Newsweek*, April 2, 1984, pp. 40–41.

23. W. Andrews, "U.S. and 4 Friendly Navies Start Largest-Ever RIMPAC Exercise", *Washington Times*, May 15, 1984, p. 3.

24. C. Wright, "U.S. Naval Operations in 1983", *Proceedings/Naval Review*, May 1984, p. 293; Wright is the best public source on naval exercises; and S. MacDonald, "Tangent Flash", *Surface Warfare*, November-December 1983, p. 12.

25. W. Scott, "Realistic Training, Unity Boosts Combat", *Aviation Week and Space Technology*, February 7, 1983, p. 58.

26. R. Roferewski, "Special Report: U.S. Pacific Air Forces Modernization", *Aviation Week Space Technology*, February 7, 1983, p. 46.

27. W. Scott, note 25, p. 60.

28. *Ibid.*, p. 62.

29. O. Wilkes, Foreign Military Bases Project files, SIPRI, Stockholm, 1983.

30. N. Weatherbie, "C^3 in Japan, Coordination and Change", *Signal*, February, 1984, p. 40.

31. U.S. Senate, Committee on Foreign Relations, *U.S. Security Agreements and Commitments Abroad* (Hearings), Part 5, U.S. GPO, 1970, pp. 723, 1518, 1358.

32. D. Alves, *The ANZUS Partners*, Center for Strategic and International Studies, Georgetown University, Washington, D.C., 1984, p. 80.

33. G. Murray, "Under Soviet Eyes, U.S. and Japan Hold Sea Exercises", *Christian Science Monitor*, September 22, 1983, p. 6.

34. *Ibid.*

35. In M. Sayle, "The Siberian Cruise of the USS *Enterprise*", *Far Eastern Economic Review*, June 16, 1983, p. 72; see also, S. Foley, "Address to Current Strategy Forum" (mimeo), U.S. Naval War College, Rhode Island, June 23, 1983, p. 10; and U.S. Navy, "FLEETEX '83, Off the Aleutians, Going in Cold", *Surface Warfare*, July/August 1983, p. 13.

36. S. Foley, Remarks to Dallas Rotary Club, Dallas, Texas, October 12, 1983, p. 3.

37. In U.S. Senate, Committee on Armed Services, *Department of Defense Authorization for Appropriations for Fiscal Year 1985* (Hearings), Part 2, U.S. GPO, 1984, p. 877.

38. J. Clad, "A Whistlestop for Warships No Longer", *Far Eastern Economic Review*, August 30, 1984, p. 30.

39. The exercises heightened popular opposition in New Zealand. See O. Wilkes, "Stop the Spectre of Militarism from Romping Around New Zealand! Oppose Triad-84 ANZUS Exercises This October" (mimeo), Peace Movement, Wellington, September 1984.

40. Strategic Air Command, *The Development of Strategic Air Command, 1946–1981*, Office of the Historian, Offut AFB, Omaha, Nebraska, 1982, pp. 222–236.

41. CINCPAC, "Battle damage scripting procedures for nuclear, biological, chemical, and special situations exercises", Instruction 3500.9A, August 14, 1981, p. III-6; released under F.O.I.A. request.

42. *Ibid*, p. A-16-1.

43. CINCPAC, "Port Visits in PACOM", Instruction 3128.3B.313, October 14, 1983, p. 1-1; released under F.O.I.A. request.

44. *Ibid.*, p. 2–1.

45. U.S. Navy, Office of Information, Washington, D.C., computer printouts, 1976 to 1984.

46. See L. Moselina, "Olongapo's R & R Industry: A Sociological Study of Institution-alized Prostitution", *Makatao* (Philippines), January-June 1981.

47. *Stars and Stripes*, "And for the Nighttime Action, Korea's It . . .", July 3, 1977.

48. *Baltimore Sun*, "Australia Assails 'Insensitivity' of American Sailors to Women", July 19, 1984, p. 4.

49. *Ibid.*

50. *Philadelphia Enquirer*, "U.S. Sailors Hose Protestors Painting Slogan on Ship's Hull", October 22, 1984, p. 12.

51. U.S. Navy, note 45.

52. See D. Kaplan, *The Nuclear Navy*, Fund for Constitutional Government Report, Washington, D.C., July 1983.

53. CINCPAC, "Release of Information on Nuclear Weapons", Instruction 5720.2D, January 20, 1982, p. I-2; released under F.O.I.A. request.

54. See Appendix, Nautilus, *Warships and Warheads, U.S.–Pacific Connections*, Box 309, Leverett, Massachusetts, 1984.

55. Chief of Naval Operations, *Loading and Underway Replenishment of Nuclear Weapons*, NWP 14–1 (Rev. C), 1983, p. 3–1; released under F.O.I.A. request.

56. W. Biddle, "A Pentagon Study Described '60 Fire at Mcguire Air Base", *New York Times*, July 10, 1985.

57. See U.S. Department of Defense, "Nuclear Weapons Accidents: 1950–1980", in Center for Defense Information, *The Defense Monitor*, Volume 10, no. 5, 1981.

58. U.S. Defense Nuclear Agency, *Nuclear Weapon Accident Response Procedures Manual*, DNA 5100.1, Washington, D.C., 1984, p. 44; released under F.O.I.A. request.

59. U.S. Defense Nuclear Agency, *Joint DOD/DOE Nuclear Weapons Accident Exercise (NUWAX-79), After Action Report*, Kirtland Air Force Base, New Mexico, Volume 1, p. 11. Reports of the same title were issued in 1981 and 1983. All were released under F.O.I.A. request.

60. U.S. Defense Nuclear Agency, NUWAX-81 report, note 59, Volume 1, pp. 10, 42; see also the same report series for U.S. Defense Nuclear Agency, NUWAX-83, pp. 9, 13; and M. Wilkinson, "After the Big Blast, The Disturbing Reality of Nuclear 'Accidents' ", *National Times* (Sydney), March 22, 1985, p. 11.

61. U.S. Defense Nuclear Agency, note 58, p. 99.

62. *Ibid.*, p. 98.

63. Background briefing, Washington, D.C., March 15, 1985.

64. CINCPAC, *Organization and Functions Manual, FY84*, CINCPAC Instruction 5400.6K, December 15, 1983, p. 77, released under F.O.I.A. to P. Wills.

65. Our emphasis, see U.S. Defense Nuclear Agency, NUWAX-81 report, note 59, Volume 1, p. 14.

66. See, for example, T. Szulc, *The Bombs of Palomares*, Viking Press, New York, 1967.

67. U.S. Defense Nuclear Agency, note 58, p. 71.

68. *Ibid.*, p. 106.

69. *Ibid.*, p. 101.

70. U.S. Defense Nuclear Agency, NUWAX-83 report, note 59, Volume 1, p. 34.

71. *Ibid.*, NUWAX-81 report, Volume 2, p. 26.

72. U.S. Defense Nuclear Agency, note 58, p. 123.

73. *Ibid.*, p. 33.

74. *Ibid.*, p. 81.

75. Navy data from I. Lind, "Summary of Navy Nuclear Weapon Accidents and Incidents, 1965–1977" (mimeo), press release, Honolulu, January 16, 1986. Commander-in-Chief, U.S. Pacific Fleet, "Medical Department Responsibility and Procedures in the Event of a Nuclear Weapons Incident/Accident", CINCPACFLT Instruction 6470.2C, November 6, 1981, pp. 1–2. Released under F.O.I.A. request to P. Wills.

76. D. Knibb, "An Ally's Nuclear Ship Ban Tests Shultz's Skill", *Wall Street Journal*, September 24, 1984, p. 33.

77. P. Wolfowitz, "The ANZUS Relationship: Alliance Management", *Current Policy*, No. 592, U.S. Department of State, Washington, D.C., June 24, 1984, p. 5.

78. In CINCPAC, "Secretary of Defense Quarterly Report", telex, July 10, 1984; released under F.O.I.A. request.

79. L. Gelb, "U.S. Tries to Fight Allied Resistance to Nuclear Arms", *New York Times*, February 14, 1985.

Chapter 16: The Soviet "Threat"

1. In U.S. Senate, Committee on Armed Services, *Study on Airpower* (Hearings), Washington, D.C., 1956, p. 1467.

2. Admiral W.J. Crowe, statement before the U.S. Senate, Committee on Armed Services (mimeo), February 27, 1985, p. 8.

3. In R. Scheer, *With Enough Shovels, Reagan, Bush, and Nuclear War*, Random, New York, 1982, p. 234.

4. G. Shultz, Department of State Press Release #169, Wellington, New Zealand, July 16, 1984.

5. C. Gray, *The Geopolitics of the Nuclear Era*, Crane, Russak, New York, 1982, pp. 64–65.

6. In F. Hiatt, "Limited Soviet War Held 'Almost Inevitable,'" *Washington Post*, June 22, 1984, p. 15.

7. P. Langer, "Soviet Military Power in Asia", in D. Zagoria, editor, *Soviet Policy in East Asia*, Yale University Press, New Haven, 1982, p. 268.

8. M. MccGwire, "Soviet Military Objectives" (draft mimeo), The Brookings Institution, Washington, D.C., 1984, unpaginated.

9. W. Crowe, "Remarks to San Diego Council of the Navy League" (mimeo), January 24, 1985, p. 16.

10. M. MccGwire, note 8.

11. A. Cockburn, *The Threat, Inside the Soviet Military Machine*, Vintage, New York, 1984, pp. 238, 359.

12. G. MacDonald *et al.*, "Soviet Strategic Air Defenses", in R. Betts, editor, *Cruise Missiles, Technology, Strategy, Politics*, Brookings, Washington, D.C., 1981, pp. 568–571.

13. In M. Sayle, "KE007, A Conspiracy of Circumstance", *New York Review of Books*, April 25, 1985, p. 53.

14. *Aviation Week and Space Technology*, March 12, 1984, p. 83.

15. J. Collins, *U.S.-Soviet Military Balance, Concepts and Capabilities, 1960–1980*, McGraw Hill, New York, pp. 355–357.

16. Naotoshi Sakonjo, "The Military Balance in East Asia and Western Pacific" (mimeo), paper for CORE Study Group Meeting, Pacific Forum on Pacific-Asian Security Policies, private workshop, Oahu, 1982, p. 18.

17. In N. Polmar, *Guide to the Soviet Navy*, Naval Institute Press, Annapolis, Maryland, 1983, p. 21.

18. B. Blechman and R. Berman, *Guide to Far Eastern Navies*, U.S. Naval Institute, Annapolis, 1978, p. 40.

19. M. MccGwire, note 8, 1984, p. 13.

20. J. Lehman, "Things That Go Bump in the Night", *Washington Post*, April 3, 1984.

21. D. Meyer, "Exclusive AFJ Interview with Admiral William J. Crowe, Jr.", *Armed Forces Journal International*, May 1985, p. 106.

22. P. Nitze, *Securing the Seas, The Soviet Naval Challenge and Western Alliance Options*, Westview, Colorado, 1977, p. 114.

23. Naotoshi Sakonjo, note 16, p. 7.

24. N. Polmar, note 17, p. 126; P. Nitze, footnote 22, p. 261.

25. J. Lehman, *Aircraft Carriers, The Real Choices*, CSIS Washington Paper 52, Georgetown University, Washington, D.C., 1978, pp. 75–76.

26. R. Toth, "Soviet Pacific Fleet Buildup Poses Threat", *Los Angeles Times*, July 29, 1985, p. 1; J. Collins, note 15, p. 357.

27. C. Wright, "U.S. Naval Operations in 1983", *Proceedings/Naval Review*, May 1984, p. 53.

28. Interview with authors, January 5, 1985.

29. D. Dalgleish and L. Schweikart, *Trident*, Southern Illinois University Press, Carbondale, 1984, p. 210.

30. See A. Cockburn, note 11, p. 425; U.S. House of Representatives, Committee on Appropriations, *Department of Defense Appropriations for 1985* (Hearings), Part 2, U.S. GPO, Washington, D.C., 1984, p. 678.

31. T. McKearney, "Their Carrier Battle Group", *Proceedings*, December 1982, p. 78.

32. P. Murphy, "Trends in Soviet Naval Force Structure", in P. Murphy editor, *Naval Power In Soviet Policy*, Studies in Communist Affairs, Volume 2, U.S. Air Force, Washington, D.C., 1978, p. 125.

33. T. McKearney, note 31, p. 76.

34. N. Friedman "U.S. vs. Soviet Style in Fleet Design", in P. Murphy, edited, note 32, p. 206.

35. C. Sorrels, *U.S. Cruise Missile Program: Development, Deployment, and Implication for Arms Control*, McGraw Hill, New York, 1983, pp. 132–133, 184.

36. *Ibid.*; A. Cockburn, note 11, p. 423.

37. S. Deitchman, *Military Power and the Advance of Technology*, Westview, Boulder, Colorado, 1983, p. 212.

38. In P. Murphy, note 32, p. 208.

39. W. Crowe, "The View From the Top, Admiral Crowe on Defending the Pacific", *Pacific Defense Reporter*, November 1983, p. 22; and *New York Times*, "20 Soviet Bombers Fly Close to Japan", September 24, 1984, p. 5.

40. W. O'Neil, "Backfire: Long Shadow on the Sealanes", *Proceedings*, March 1977, pp. 28–35.

41. C. Sorrels, note 35, p. 132–133.

42. See R. Herrick, *Soviet Naval Strategy, Fifty Years of Theory and Practice*, U.S. Naval Institute Press, Annapolis, 1968, p. 104; P. Murphy, note 32, p. 125; S. Kaplan, *Diplomacy of Power, Soviet Armed Forces as a Political Instrument*, The Brookings Institution, Washington, D.C., 1982, p. 164; J. Collins, *U.S./Soviet Military Balance, Statistical Trends, 1970–1982*, Congressional Research Service Report 83–153S, Washington, D.C., 1983, pp. 127–128; M. Urban states that there are 5,000 Soviet marines in the Far East, in "Power Projection by Sea, The Threat of Soviet Naval Infantry", *Asia-Pacific Defense Forum*, Spring 1985, p. 16.

43. *The Japan Times*, "Soviet Threat Exaggerated: Institute", September 15, 1981.

44. F. West *et al.*, "Toward the Year 1985: The Relationship Between U.S. Policy and Naval Forces in the Pacific", Appendix C, in Institute for Foreign Policy Analysis, *Environments for U.S. Naval Strategy in the Pacific Ocean–Indian Ocean Area, 1985–1995* (mimeo), Conference Report for Center for Advanced Research, U.S. Naval War College, Cambridge, Massachusetts, June 1977, p. 318.

45. M. McGwire, note 8.

46. M. Sadykiewicz, "Soviet Far East High Command", in Jae Kyu Park and J. Ha, *The Soviet Union and East Asia in the 1980s*, Westview, Colorado, 1983, p. 200.

47. In A. Cockburn, note 11, p. 282.

48. H. Kurtz, "Reagan Bombing Joke is Said to Cause Partial Soviet Alert", *Washington Post*, October 12, 1984, p. 10.

49. B. Jasani, *Outer Space – Battlefield of the Future?* Taylor and Francis, London, 1978, p. 179; see also W. Arkin and R. Fieldhouse, "Nuclear Weapon Command, Control, and Communications", in *SIPRI Yearbook 1984*, Taylor and Francis, London, 1984, pp. 493–499.

50. D. Ball, *Soviet Strategic Planning and the Control of Nuclear War*, Center for Strategic and Defense Studies Paper 109, p. 20.

51. S. Meyer, "The U.S.S.R. Use of Space", in *Space, National Security and C^3I*, Mitre Corporation Report 85-3, Bedford, Massachusetts, 1985, p. 22.

52. Interview with R. Cossa, former CINCPAC intelligence officer, January 5, 1985.

53. J. Richelson, "Strategic Reconnaissance and National Style" (mimeo), School of Government and Public Administration, The American University, Washington, D.C., 1985, pp. 30–32.

54. See J. Westwood, "The Soviet Union and the Southern Sea Route", *Naval War College Review*, January-February 1982, pp. 54–67. This is the best available reference on the subject.

55. In 1976, the east–west railway moved about 130,000 tonnes of cargo in both directions, which is to rise eventually to an estimated million tonnes. In wartime, the flow from west to east would be greater than *vice versa*. Between 500,000 but less than a million tonnes, in other words, is the maximum theoretical wartime *annual* eastward flow. Assuming that 70 per cent is the maximum eastward flow, theoretical overland lift is 700,000 tonnes annually, or a maximum of 2,000 tonnes per day. Conservatively attributing the national domestic *coastal sealift* in 1976 on an average *per capita* basis to the Far Eastern population, 7 million tonnes of cargo flowed through Far Eastern ports in the early 1980s. If fifty per cent or 3.5 million tonnes of these flows are imports, domestic maritime imports in the Far East are at least five times greater than the maximum overland lift. This estimate ignores maritime international trade with the Far East. Airlift would contribute only marginally to these east-west flows. See W. Carr, "The Soviet Merchant Fleet: Its Economic Role and Its Impact on Western Shipowners", in U.S. Congress, Joint Economic Committee, *The Soviet Economy in the 1980s: Problems and Prospects*, Volume 2, October 1979, p. 668; R. Campbell, "Prospects for Siberian Economic Development", in D. Zagoria, editor, note 7, p. 25! The Center for Naval Analysis also investigates this topic although nothing is published. CINCPAC refused to release to the authors intelligence analyses of Soviet Far Eastern logistics.

56. Jane's "Soviet Far East Bases", *Defense Weekly*, April 14, 1984, p. 560.

57. At a daily 1 1kg of fuel oil per shaft horsepower (shp) x Soviet Pacific Fleet 6.5 million shp in 1978 x estimated 1.4 increase in shp by 1985 x 0.8 Fleet underway rate, at low speeds = about 7,000 tonnes per day, assuming no attrition. This would at least double at higher speeds. Shp estimate from B. Blechman and R. Berman, "The Naval Balance in the Western Pacific", in B. Blechman and R. Berman, note 18, p. 52; oil usage rate calculated from Jane's *Fighting Ships, 1983–1984*, Jane's, London, 1984, pp. 506, 510, 515.

58. J. Westwood, note 54, p. 63.

59. M. Hellner, "Sea Power and the Struggle for Asia", *Proceedings/Naval Review*, April, 1956, pp. 357–358.

60. N. Gayler, "Security Implications of the Soviet Military Presence in Asia", in *Asian Security in the 1980s*, Rand Report R-2492-ISA, November 1979, p. 65.

61. In U.S. Senate, Committee on Armed Services, *Department of Defense Authorization for Appropriations for Fiscal Year 1985* (Hearings), Part 8, U.S. GPO, Washington, D.C., 1984, p. 3890.

62. A. Cordesman, "The Western Naval Threat to Soviet Military Dominance: A Soviet Assessment", *Armed Forces Journal*, April 1983, p. 67.

63. Naotoshi Sakonjo, note 16, p. 10.

64. A. Cordesman, note 62, pp. 76, 80.

65. J. Hessman, "Sea Power and the Central Front", *Air Force Magazine*, July 1983, p. 56.

66. J. Herzog, "Perspectives on Soviet Naval Development: A Navy to Match National Purposes", in P. Murphy, note 32, pp. 51–52.

67. Chief of Naval Operations, *Naval Operational Planning*, NWP 11 (Rev. C), Washington, D.C., 1978, pp. 2–14, 2–15.

68. U.S. Senate, Committee on Armed Services, note 61, Part 2, p. 892.

69. J. Lehman, note 25, p. 76.

70. U.S. House of Representatives, Committee on Appropriations, note 30, Part 5, p. 204.

71. Our emphasis, in U.S. Senate, Committee on Armed Services, note 61, Part 2, p. 932.

72. J. Watkins, Statement before the Subcommittee on Preparedness of the Senate Armed Services Committee (mimeo), 1982, p. 3.

73. *Ibid.*, p. 4.

74. P. Karsten, *The Naval Aristocracy*, Free Press, New York, 1972, p. 394.

75. Chief of Naval Operations, note 67, Appendix F, "Sample Solution of an Operation Problem", pp. F-1 to F-40.

76. *Ibid.*

77. A. Cordesman, note 62, p. 76.

78. P. Nitze, note 22, p. 231.

79. B. Blechman and R. Berman, note 18, p. 52.

80. J. Barron, *MiG Pilot*, McGraw Hill, New York, 1980, pp. 177–185.

81. R. Barnett, *Beyond War, Japan's Comprehensive National Security*, Pergamon, New York, 1984, p. 18.

82. R. Solomon, "Coalition Building or Condominium? The Soviet Presence in Asia and American Policy Alternatives", in D. Zagoria, note 7, p. 307.

83. B. Garrett, *Soviet Perceptions of China and Sino-American Military Ties: Implications for the Strategic Balance and Arms Control*, Rosenbaum Inc. report for SALT/Arms Control Support Group, Office of Assistant Secretary of Defense (Atomic Energy), Pentagon, Washington, D.C., June 1981, p. 25.

84. W. Crowe, note 39.

85. W. Crowe, "The Pacific Area" (mimeo), statement before U.S. Senate, Committee on Armed Services, February 1984, p. 11.

86. B. Schemmer, "An Exclusive AFJ Interview with Admiral William J. Crowe, Jr., Commander-in-Chief, U.S. Pacific Command", *Armed Forces Journal International*, April 1984, p. 47.

87. See B. Cumings, "North Korea: Security in the Crucible of Great Power Confrontations", in R. Thomas, edited, *The Great Power Triangle and Asian Security*, Lexington Books, Massachusetts, 1983, pp. 155–158; and L. Rosenberger, "The Soviet–Vietnamese Alliance and Kampuchea", *Survey*, Volume 27, no. 118/119, 1983, pp. 207–231. These are the best studies of stress and hostility in Soviet alliances in Asia.

88. R. Solomon, note 82, p. 296–297.

89. J. Makinson, "Japan Scales a New Peak", *Financial Times*, August 20, 1985, p. 12.

90. K. McGruther, *The Evolving Soviet Navy*, Naval War College Press, Newport, Rhode Island, 1978, p. 6.

91. W. Crowe, "Pacific is Unsung Success Story for the U.S.", *U.S. News and World Report*, October 22, 1984, p. 78.

92. Interview with authors, January 5, 1985.

93. For details, see J. Steele, *Soviet Power, The Kremlin's Foreign Policy – Brezhnev to Andropov*, Simon and Schuster, New York, 1983, pp. 154–155; and S. Goldman, *Soviet Policy Toward Japan and the Strategic Balance in Northeast Asia*, Congressional Research Service Report 84–64 F, Washington, D.C., February 1984, p. 23.

94. Kensuke Ebata, "Cam Rahn Bay – Forward Base of the Soviet Pacific Fleet", *Defense Weekly*, Volume 2, no. 2, July 1984, p. 66.

95. J. Davis, "Soviet Strategy in Asia: An American Perspective" (mimeo), CORE Study Group Meeting, note 16, p. 11.

96. Authors' communication with Office of Public Affairs, CINCPAC, Honolulu, July 25, 1985.

97. Interview with authors, January 5, 1985.

98. M. Samuels, *Contest for the South China Sea*, Methuen, New York, 1982, p. 142.

99. A. Rubinstein, "Air Support in the Arab East", in S. Kaplan, note 42, p. 486.

100. R. Feinberg, *The Intemperate Zone, the Third World Challenge to U.S. Foreign Policy*, Norton, New York, 1984, pp. 175, 158.

101. In S. Kaplan, note 42, p. 13.

102. K. McGruther, note 90, p. 37.

103. F. West, note 44, p. 359; B. Blechman and R. Berman, note 18, p. 43; P. Murphy, note 32, p. 131.

104. K. Weiss, "The Naval Dimension of the Sino–Soviet Rivalry", *Naval War College Review*, January-February 1985, p. 43.

105. U.S. Senate, Committee on Armed Services, *Department of Defense Authorization for Appropriations for Fiscal Year 1984* (Hearings), Part 6, U.S. GPO, Washington, D.C., 1983, p. 2975.

106. S. Kaplan, note 42, pp. 44–89.

107. A. Cordesman, *The Gulf and the Search for Strategic Stability*, Westview, Boulder, Colorado, 1984, pp. 838–863.

108. S. Kaplan, note 42, pp. 668–673.

109. *Ibid.*, pp. 148–201, 668–673.

110. *Ibid.*, p. 670.

111. *Ibid.*, p. 345.

112. *Ibid.*, p. 181.

113. M. MccGwire, "The Military Dimension of Soviet Policy in the Third World" (mimeo), The Brookings Institution, Washington, D.C., 1984, p. 9.

114. A. Horelick, *Soviet Policy Dilemmas in Asia*, Rand P-5774, Santa Monica, California, 1976, p. 15.

115. C. Gray, note 5, p. 37.

116. H. Gelman, *The Soviet Far East Buildup and Soviet Risk-Taking Against China*, Rand P-2943, 1982, pp. 3, 7.

117. S. Goldman, note 93, p. v.

118. A. Horelick, note 114, p. 1.

119. J. Steele, note 93, p. 160; A. Whiting, *Siberian Development and East Asia*, Stanford University Press, 1981, pp. 112–159; R. Campbell, "Prospects for Siberian Economic Development", in D. Zagoria, edited, note 7, pp. 229–254.

120. In U.S. Senate, Committee on Armed Services, note 1, p. 1532.

121. M. MccGwire, note 8, Chapter 7, p. 3.

122. H. Brown, *Thinking About National Security, Defense, and Foreign Policy in a Dangerous World*, Westview, Colorado, 1983, p. 138.

Chapter 17: "Socialist Bomb"

1. In L. Freedman, *The Evolution of Nuclear Strategy*, St. Martins Press, New York, 1981, p. 366.

2. In S. Meyer, *Soviet Theatre Nuclear Forces*, Part I, Adelphi Paper 187, 1983, p. 31.

3. See Appendix, Nautilus, *Warships and Warheads, U.S.-Pacific Connections*, Leverett, Massachusetts, 1984, for details of calculations.

4. J. Tritten, *Soviet Navy Data Base: 1982–1983*, Rand P-6859, Santa Monica, California, 1983, Table 10; General Dynamics, *The World's Missile Systems*, Pomona, California, 1982, pp. 213–215.

5. R. Herrick, *Soviet Naval Mission Assignments*, Ketron Inc. report to Assistant Director of Net Assessment, Office of Program Planning, U.S. Navy, 1979, Volumes 2 and 3; released under F.O.I.A. request.

6. See J. Tritten's estimates, note 4, pp. 36–41; and F. West *et al.*, "Toward the Year 1985: The Relationship Between U.S. Policy and Naval Forces in the Pacific", Appendix C, in Institute for Foreign Policy Analysis, *Environment for U.S. Naval Strategy in the Pacific Ocean–Indian Ocean Area, 1985–1995*, Conference Report for Center for Advanced Research, U.S. Naval War College, Cambridge, Massachusetts, June 1977, pp. 320–321.

7. *Time*, "Sub Flub, Nuclear Mystery Near Japan", Oct. 1, 1984, p. 40.

8. D. Kaplan, "When Incidents Are Accidents", *Oceanus*, July 1983, p. 30.

9. R. Herrick, *Soviet Naval Strategy, Fifty Years of Theory and Practice*, U.S. Naval Institute Press, Annapolis, Maryland, 1968, pp. 64–67.

10. J. Tritten, note 4, pp. 31, 40; C. Sorrels, *U.S. Cruise Missile Program: Development, Deployment, and Implications for Arms Control*, McGraw Hill, New York, 1983, pp. 125–127.

11. United Press International, "Soviet Nuclear Sub with Missiles Sinks", *Bulletin Today* (Manila), August 12, 1983.

12. U.S. Congress, Arms Control and Foreign Policy Caucus, "Fact Sheet - Nuclear-Armed, Sea-Launched Cruise Missiles: An Overlooked Weapon with Underestimated Implications", in *Congressional Record*, (House), May 31, 1984, p. H5052.

13. G. McCormick and M. Miller, "American Seapower at Risk, Nuclear Weapons in Soviet Naval Planning", *Orbis*, Summer 1981, Volume 2, no. 25, pp. 356–357.

14. L. Hodgden, "Satellites at Sea, Space and Naval Warfare", in W. Durch edited, *National Interests and the Military Use of Space*, Ballinger, Cambridge, 1984, p. 124; and S. Meyer, "Soviet Military Programmes and the 'New High Ground,'" *Survival*, Volume 25, no. 5, September–October 1983, pp. 207–209.

15. See U.S. Senate, Committee on Armed Services, *Department of Defense Authorization for*

Appropriations for Fiscal Year 1984 (Hearings), Part 5, U.S. GPO, Washington, D.C., 1984, p. 2454.

16. Communication with authors, Office of Public Affairs of the Office of the U.S. Secretary of Defense, Washington, D.C., May 10, 1985.

17. Communication with authors, Office of Public Affairs, Space and Missile Tracking Organization, California, May 15, 1985.

18. Office of Public Affairs of the Office of the U.S. Secretary of Defense, note 16.

19. R. Berman and J. Baker, *Soviet Strategic Forces: Requirements and Responses*, The Brookings Institution, Washington, D.C., 1982, p. 111.

20. S. Sagan, "Nuclear Alerts and Crisis Management", *International Security*, Volume 9, no. 4, 1985, pp. 99-139.

21. Cited in H. Gelman, *The Soviet Far East Buildup and Soviet Risk-Taking Against China*, Rand 2943, 1982, p. 37.

22. S. Meyer, *Soviet Theatre Nuclear Forces, Part II, Capabilities and Implications*, Adelphi Paper 188, 1984, p. 21.

23. R. Berman and J. Baker, note 19, p. 12.

24. *Ibid.*, pp. 102, 111.

25. E. Warner, "Soviet Strategic Force Posture: Some Alternative Explanations", in F. Horton *et al.*, *Comparative Defense Policy*, Johns Hopkins University Press, 1974, p. 316.

26. S. Kaplan, *Diplomacy of Power, Soviet Armed Forces as a Political Instrument*, The Brookings Institution, Washington, D.C., 1981, p. 669.

27. K. Spielmann, *The Political Utility of Strategic Superiority, A Preliminary Investigation into the Soviet View*, Institute for Defense Analyses, IDA P-1349, May 1979, pp. 47-48; H. Gelman, note 21, p. 42.

28. S. Lodgaard, "Long Range Theatre Nuclear Forces", in *SIPRI Yearbook 1983*, Taylor and Francis, London, 1983, p. 7.

29. S. Meyer, note 22, 1984, p. 26; S. Talbott, *Endgame, The Inside Story of SALT II*, Harper and Row, 1979, p. 71.

30. Pentagon estimates provided in General Dynamics, *The World's Missile Systems*, Pomona, California, 1982, p. 287.

31. A. Cockburn, *The Threat, Inside the Soviet Military Machine*, Vintage, New York, 1984, p. 322.

32. In D. Ball, "Management of the Superpower Balance", in T. Millar, edited, *International Security in the Southeast Asian and Southwest Pacific Region*, University of Queensland Press, 1983, p. 229.

33. R. Smith, "Missile Deployments Roil Europe", *Science*, February 9, 1984, p. 372.

34. T. Wolfe, *The SALT Experience*, Ballinger, Cambridge, Massachusetts, 1979, p. 104.

35. R. Garthoff, "The Soviet SS-20 Decision", *Survival*, Volume 25, no. 3, May-June 1983, p. 112.

36. R. Smith, note 33; D. Johnstone, *The Politics of Euromissiles, Europe's Role in America's World*, Verso, London, p. 7.

37. S. Talbott, *Deadly Gambits, The Reagan Administration and the Stalemate in Nuclear Arms Control*, Knopf, New York, 1984, p. 68.

38. Confidential source.

39. R. Toth, "Soviet Pacific Fleet Buildup", in *Los Angeles Times*, July 29, 1985, p. 7.

40. United Press International, "Soviet and Japanese Officials Argue About Missiles in Asia", *New York Times*, April 13, 1983.

41. R. Armitage, "Japan's Growing Commitment to Self-Defense", *Asia Pacific Defense Forum*, Spring, 1985, p. 40.

42. S. Lodgaard and F. Blackaby, "Nuclear Weapons", *SIPRI Yearbook, 1984*, Taylor and Francis, London, 1984, p. 29.

43. *New York Times*, "New Soviet Missile Sites Reported", April 23, 1985, p. A-3.

44. W. Crowe, "The Pacific Area" (mimeo), Statement before U.S. Senate, Committee on Armed Services, Washington, D.C., February 1984, p. 9.

45. See J. Kahan, *Security in the Nuclear Age*, The Brookings Institution, 1975, pp. 27, 32, 73, 99-131; E. Warner, note 25, for dispassionate accounts of U.S. over-reactions to Soviet nuclear deployments.

46. Our emphasis, V.M. Kulish *et al.*, cited in K. Spielmann, note 27, p. 29.

47. F. Halliday, "The Conjuncture of the Seventies and After: A Reply to Ougaard", *New Left Review*, no. 147, September 1984, p. 78.

48. Our emphasis, R. Jervis, "Why Nuclear Superiority Does Not Matter", *Political Science Quarterly*, Volume 94, no. 4, 1979-1980, p. 619.

49. See G. Allison, *Essence of Decision, Explaining the Cuban Missile Crisis*, Little Brown, Boston, 1971, pp. 102-117, and R. Garthoff, *Intelligence Assessment and Policy Making*, The Brookings Institution, Washington, D.C., 1984, pp. 40-62.

50. S. Sagan, note 20, p. 111.

51. *Ibid.*, p. 129.

52. B. Blechman and D. Hart, "The Political Utility of Nuclear Weapons, the 1973 Middle East Crisis", *International Security*, Volume 7, no. 1, 1982, p. 137.

53. *Ibid.*, pp. 136-138.

54. B. Blechman and S. Kaplan, *Force Without War, U.S. Armed Forces as a Political Instrument*, The Brookings Institution, Washington, D.C., 1978, pp. 47-49, 127-129.

55. Our emphasis; K. Spielmann, note 27, p. 57.

56. S. Meyer, note 22, p. 20.

57. J. Richelson, "The Dilemmas of Counterpower Targeting", *Comparative Strategy*,

Volume 2, no. 3, 1980, p. 230; T. Postol, "The Trident and Strategic Stability", *Oceanus*, July 26, 1985, p. 48.

Chapter 18: States of Terror

1. H. Kahn, *Thinking About the Unthinkable in the 1980s*, Simon and Schuster, New York, 1984, p. 92.

2. In D. Holloway, *The Soviet Union and the Arms Race*, Yale University Press, New Haven, 1983, pp. 165–166.

3. J. Herz, *International Politics in the Atomic Age*, Columbia University Press, New York, 1959, p. 168.

4. L. Freedman, *The Evolution of Nuclear Strategy*, MacMillan, New York, 1982, p. 24.

5. G. Herken, *The Winning Weapon, The Atomic Bomb in the Cold War, 1945–1950*, Knopf, New York, 1980, p. 260.

6. In *ibid.*, p. 49.

7. S. Kaplan, *Diplomacy of Power, Soviet Armed Forces as a Political Instrument*, The Brookings Institution, 1981, pp. 3–4.

8. R. Smoke, "Extended Deterrence, Some Observations", *Naval War College Review*, September-October, 1983, p. 37.

9. J. Kahan, *Security in the Nuclear Age*, The Brookings Institution, Washington, D.C., 1975, p. 17.

10. *Ibid.*

11. E. Warner, "Soviet Strategic Force Posture: Some Alternative Explanations", in F. Horton *et al.*, edited, *Comparative Defense Policy*, Johns Hopkins, 1974, p. 320.

12. J. Kahan, note 9, pp. 20–24.

13. D. Kaplan, *The Wizards of Armageddon*, Simon and Schuster, New York, 1983, p. 319.

14. In L. Freedman, note 4, p. 246.

15. On the upgrade, see B. Blair, *Strategic Command and Control, Re-Defining the Nuclear Threat*, The Brookings Institution, Washington, D.C., 1985, p. 54.

16. T. Cochran *et al.*, *U.S. Forces and Capabilities*, Ballinger, 1984, p. 107; S. Weiner, "Systems and Technology", in A. Carter *et al.*, *Ballistic Missile Defense*, The Brookings Institution, 1984, p. 52.

17. J. Edwards, *Superweapon, The Making of the MX*, Norton, New York, 1982, p. 199; G. Herken, note 5, p. 99.

18. J. Edwards, note 17, p. 89.

19. J. Kahan, note 9, pp. 105–110.

20. R. Garthoff, *Intelligence assessment and Policymaking: A Decision Point in the Kennedy Administration*, The Brookings Institution, Washington, D.C., 1984, pp. 3–4, 13.

21. S. Hersh, *The Price of Power*, Simon and Schuster, New York, 1983, pp. 147–167.

22. Our emphasis, in J. Kahan, note 9, p. 163.

23. D. Holloway, note 2, p. 43, 54.

24. "Report of the Special Inter-Departmental Committee on Implications of NIE 11-8-62 and Related Intelligence", in R. Garthoff, note 20, pp. 37, 40.

25. S. Keeny and W. Panofsky, "MAD versus NUTS: Can Doctrine or Weaponry Remedy the Mutual Hostage Relationship", in C. Kegley & E. Wittkopf, edited, *The Nuclear Reader*, St. Martin's Press, New York, 1985, pp. 38–42.

26. C. Gray, "Nuclear Strategy: The Case for a Theory of Victory", *International Security*, Volume 4, no. 1, Summer, 1979, p. 82.

27. J. Kahan, note 9, pp. 144–146.

28. In *ibid.*, p. 148.

29. In *ibid.*, p. 162.

30. *Ibid.*, pp. 166–169.

31. L. Freedman, note 4, pp. 377–395; G. Herken, *Counsels of War*, Knopf, New York, p. 260–264.

32. D. Ball, *Targeting for Strategic Deterrence*, Adelphi Paper 185, London, 1983, p. 24.

33. R. Halloran, "Pentagon Draws Up First Strategy for Fighting a Long Nuclear War", *New York Times*, May 30, 1982.

34. Testimony D. Latham, in U.S. Senate, Committee on Armed Services, *Department of Defense Authorizations for FY 1984* (Hearings), Part 5, U.S. GPO, Washington, D.C., 1983, p. 2492.

35. R. Halloran, note 33.

36. U.S. Senate, Committee on Armed Services, *Department of Defense Authorizations for FY 1985*, Part 7, U.S. GPO, Washington, D.C., 1984, p. 3515.

37. Emphasis in original, *ibid.*, p. 3502.

38. *Ibid.*, p. 3504.

39. *New York Times*, March 24, 1983, p. 20.

40. Union of Concerned Scientists, *The Fallacy of Star Wars*, Random House, 1985.

41. L. Dye, "An Upside Down 'Star Wars' Test of Shuttle Fails", *Los Angeles Times*, June 20, 1985, p. 4.

42. In *Newsweek*, "The Star Warriors", June 17, 1985, p. 34.

43. D. Ball, *Can Nuclear War Be Controlled?* Adelphi Paper 169, London, 1981, pp. 7, 34–37.

44. The term comes from C. Zraket, *The Impact of Command, Control, Communications and Intelligence on Deterrence*, MITRE Corporation, Bedford, Massachusetts, November 1983, p. 8.

45. Office of Technology Assessment, *The Effects of Nuclear War*, Allenheld and Osmun, New Jersey, 1980, pp. 81–95.

46. In *Pravda*, July 25, 1981.

47. G. Snyder, *The Soviet Strategic Culture, Implications for Limited Nuclear Operations*, Rand R-2154-AF, Santa Monica, California, 1977, p. 39.

48. S. Meyer, *Soviet Theater Nuclear Forces, Part II, Capabilities and Implications*, Adelphi Paper 188, 1984, p. 35.

49. S. Meyer, *Soviet Theater Nuclear Forces, Part I, Development of Doctrine and Objectives*, Adelphi Paper 187, 1983, p. 32.

50. *Ibid.*, p. 25.

51. I. Clark, *Limited Nuclear War*, Princeton University Press, New Jersey, 1982, pp. 207, 225.

52. In D. Ford, "U.S. Command and Control", *The New Yorker*, April 8, 1985, p. 53.

53. In U.S. House of Representatives, Committee on Appropriations, *Department of Defense Appropriations for 1985* (Hearings), Part 1, U.S. GPO, Washington, D.C., 1984, p. 484.

54. J. Richelson, "PD-59, NSC-13 and the Reagan Strategic Modernization Program", *Journal of Strategic Studies*, Volume 6, no. 2, June 1983, pp. 133–135.

55. *Ibid.*, pp. 135–136.

56. W. Arkin, "Sleight of Hand with Trident II", *Bulletin of the Atomic Scientists*, December 1984, pp. 5–6.

57. R. Berman and J. Baker, *Soviet Strategic Forces: Requirements and Responses*, The Brookings Institution, Washington, D.C., 1982, p. 137.

58. Our emphasis, "Report of the Special Inter-Departmental Committee", in R. Garthoff, note 20, pp. 11, 44, 45.

59. D. Ford, note 52, p. 84; B. Schneider, "Soviet Uncertainties in Targeting Peacekeeper", in C. Gray *et al.*, edited, *Missiles for the Nineties*, Westview, Boulder, Colorado, 1984, p. 118.

60. In U.S. Senate, Committee on Armed Services, *Fiscal Year 1978 Authorization for Military Procurement* (Hearing), Part 10, U.S. GPO, Washington, D.C., 1977, p. 6538.

61. In B. Schneider, note 59, p. 117.

62. D. Sanger, "Chip Testing Problems Abound, Pentagon Says", *New York Times*, April 16, 1985, p. D-1.

63. K. Tsipis, "The Operational Characteristics of Ballistic Missiles", *SIPRI Yearbook, 1984*, Taylor and Francis, London, 1984, pp. 416–417.

64. In B. Schneider, note 59, p. 122.

65. L. Freedman, note 4, pp. 164–166; S. Lunn and J. Seabright, "Intercontinental Nuclear Weapons", *SIPRI Yearbook, 1983*, Taylor and Francis, London, 1983, p. 47.

66. F. Barnaby, "Strategic Nuclear Weapons", *SIPRI Yearbook, 1982*, Taylor and Francis, London, 1982, pp. 266–267; S. Lunn and J. Seabright, note 65, pp. 46–49.

67. D. Ball, "Management of the Superpower Balance", in T. Miller, edited, *International Security in the Southeast Asian and Southwest Pacific Region*, University of Queensland Press, St. Lucia, 1983, pp. 218–223.

68. J. Richelson, "Evaluating the Strategic Balance", *American Journal of Political Science*, Volume 24, no. 24, November 1980, pp. 797–800; T. Brown, "Missile Accuracy and Strategic Lethality", *Survival*, Volume 18, no. 2, March-April, 1976, pp. 52–59.

69. In U.S. Senate, Committee on Foreign Relations, *U.S. Security Agreements and Commitments Abroad* (Hearings), Part 5, U.S. GPO, Washington, D.C., 1970, p. 1233.

70. R. Sutter, *Chinese Nuclear Weapons and American Interests – Conflicting Policy Choices*, U.S. Congressional Research Service Report 83–187 F, U.S. GPO, Washington, D.C., September 1983, pp. 1–20.

71. R. Laird, "French Nuclear Forces in the 1980s and 1990s", *Comparative Strategy*, Volume 4, no. 4, 1984, pp. 387–412.

72. Based on B. Schneider, note 59, p. 112.

73. K. Payne and B. Schneider, "The New Missiles: Putting the Debate into Proper Perspective", in C. Gray *et al.*, edited, note 59, p. 5.

74. H. Kahn, note 1, p. 120.

75. Committee on the Present Danger, "Is America Becoming Number 2?" in C. Tyroler, edited, *Alerting America*, Pergamon-Brassey, McLean, Virginia, 1984, p. 63.

76. A. Horelick and M. Bush, *Strategic Power and Soviet Foreign Policy*, University of Chicago Press, 1966, p. 165.

77. E. Luttwak, *The Missing Dimension of U.S. Defense Policy: Force, Perceptions and Power*, Essex Corporation Report to U.S. Defense Advanced Research Projects Agency, 1976, pp. 22, 37.

78. In G. Herken, note 5, p. 266.

Chapter 19: Nuclear Epitaph?

1. In D. Frei, *Risks of Unintentional Nuclear War*, Rowman and Allanheld, New Jersey, 1983, p. 101.

2. A. Allison *et al.*, *Hawks, Doves and Owls, An Agenda for Avoiding Nuclear War*, Norton, New York, 1985, pp. 6–19.

3. Associated Press, "Afghan Guerrillas [sic] Report Major Setback", *New York Times*, June 2, 1985, p. 3.

4. See T. Ali, *Can Pakistan Survive? The Death of a State*, Penguin, 1983, pp. 115–148.

5. L. Spector, *Nuclear Proliferation Today*, Ballinger, Cambridge, 1984, p. 178.

6. R. Tempest, "Pakistani Peninsula Conjures Up Visions of Naval Base", *Los Angeles Times*, December 1, 1985, p. 17.

7. R. Halloran, "New Soviet Afghan Bases Seen as Peril to Gulf", *New York Times*, November 14, 1982, p. 21.

8. T. Ali, note 4, p. 97.

9. B. Gwertzman, "U.S. Expresses 'Serious Concern' Over Firing of North Korea Missile", *New York Times*, August 28, 1984.

10. P. Grose, "U.S. is Continuing Military Buildup in *Pueblo* Crisis", *New York Times*, January 29, 1968, p. 3.

11. S. Sagan, "Nuclear Alerts and Crisis Management", *International Security*, Volume 9, no. 4, Spring 1985, p. 134.

12. R. Feinberg, *The Intemperate Zone*, Norton, New York, 1983, p. 46.

13. D. Frei, note 1, p. 118.

14. In N. Polmar, "The Navy of the Democratic People's Republic of Korea", in B. Blechman and R. Berman, edited, *Guide to Far Eastern Navies*, Naval Institute Press, Annapolis, Maryland, 1978, p. 325.

15. F. West *et al.*, "Toward the Year 1985: The Relationship Between U.S. Policy and Naval Forces in the Pacific", Appendix C, in Institute for Foreign Policy Analysis, *Environments for U.S. Naval Strategy in the Pacific Ocean–Indian Ocean Area, 1985–1995* (mimeo), Conference Report for Center for Advanced Research, U.S. Naval War College, Cambridge, Massachusetts, June 1977, p. 327.

16. R. Lebow, *Between Peace and War, The Nature of International Crisis*, Johns Hopkins University Press, 1981, p. 334.

17. In U.S. Senate, Committee on Armed Services, *Department of Defense Authorization for Fiscal Year 1985* (Hearings), Part 8, 1984, U.S. GPO, Washington, D.C., p. 3890.

18. G. Sick, *All Fall Down, America's Tragic Encounter With Iran*, Random House, New York, pp. 154–155.

19. D. Oberdorfer, *Tet!* Doubleday, New York, pp. 7–33, 140.

20. T. Rienzi, *Communications-Electronics, 1962–1970*, U.S. Department of the Army, 1973, pp. 106–111.

21. U.S. House of Representatives,, Committee on Appropriations, *Department of Defense Appropriations for 1985* (Hearings), Part 1, 1984, U.S. GPO, Washington, D.C., p. 961.

22. In F. A'Hearn, *The Informational Arsenal, A C^3I Profile*, Center for Information Policy Research, Harvard University Press, 1983, p. 88.

23. J. Dickenson, "Can't the Army Talk to the Navy?" *Washington Post*, September 13, 1985, p. B-5.

24. B. Keller, "U.S. Plans Were Made on Open Line", *New York Times*, October 15, 1985, p. 10; *Newsweek*, "The Pentagon Under Siege", October 28, 1985, p. 38.

25. J. Finney, "A U.S. Destroyer in Far East Bumped by Soviet Warship", *New York Times*, May 11, 1967, p. 2.

26. J. Finney, "A Soviet Warship Bumps U.S. Vessel 2d Time in Two Days", *New York Times*, May 12, 1967, p. 4.

27. M. Weisskopf, "U.S.–Soviet Naval Meeting Cancelled", *Washington Post*, June 20, 1985, p. 28.

28. *Ibid.*

29. In U.S. Senate, Committee on Armed Services, *Department of Defense Authorization for Appropriations for Fiscal Year 1985*, Part 8, U.S. GPO, Washington, D.C., 1984, p. 3892.

30. N. Polmar, note 14, pp. 321, 327.

31. C. Wright, "U.S. Naval Operations in 1984", *Proceedings/Naval Review*, May 1985, p. 304.

32. W. O'Neil, "Backfire: Long Shadow on the Sea Lanes", *Proceedings*, March 1977, p. 32; B. Knickerbocker, "Why Soviets are Sensitive about Northern Pacific Coast", *Christian Science Monitor*, September 6, 1983, p. 3.

33. In M. Healy, "Lehman: We'll Sink Their Subs", *Defense Week*, May 13, 1985, p. 18.

34. In U.S. Senate, Committee on Armed Services, note 29, pp. 3878, 3888.

35. J. Collins, *U.S.–Soviet Military Balance, 1980–1985*, McGraw Hill, New York, 1985, p. 144.

36. In R. Lebow, note 16, p. 264.

37. J. Steinbruner, "An Assessment of Nuclear Crises", in E. Griffith's and J. Polyani, edited, *The Dangers of Nuclear War*, University of Toronto Press, 1979, p. 38; S. Sagan, note 11, pp. 112–118.

38. D. Campbell, "Nuclear War, America's Base Motives", *The New Statesman*, December 17, 1982, p. 13.

39. J. Fialka, "Nuclear Reaction: U.S. Tests Response to an Atomic Attack", *Wall Street Journal*, March 26, 1983, p. 1.

40. See P. Grose, note 10.

41. M. Halperin, *Limited War in the Nuclear Age*, John Wiley, New York, 1963, p. 37.

42. R. Lebow, note 16, pp. 117–118.

43. U.S. Senate, Committee on Armed Services, *Recent False Alerts From the Nation's Missile Attack Warning System*, U.S. GPO, Washington, D.C., 1980, pp. 6–8.

44. CINCPAC, "Pacific Command Nuclear, Biological, Chemical Warning and Reporting System", Effective Instruction 3480.6F, April 14, 1982, pp. 1-C-2, 1-C-3; released under F.O.I.A. request.

45. S. Sagan, note 11, p. 118.

46. In D. Ford, "U.S. Command and Control", *New Yorker*, April 1, 1985, p. 79; see also L. Gelb, "The Mind of the President", *New York Times Magazine*, October 6, 1985, p. 112.

47. In R. Scheer, *With Enough Shovels, Reagan, Bush, and Nuclear War*, Random, New York, 1982, pp. 240–241.

48. CINCPAC "Battle Damage Scripting Procedures for Nuclear, Biological, Chemical and Special Situation Exercises", Effective Instruction 3500.0A, August 1981, pp. 11–2, 11–10; released under F.O.I.A. request.

49. In R. Scheer, note 47, p. 17.

50. Mizoe Shogo, *Asahi Journal*, June 26, 1981.

51. CINCPAC, "Pacific Command Nuclear Biological, Chemical Warning and Reporting System", Effective Instruction 3401.3J, February 6, 1981, p. II-2; released under F.O.I.A. request.

52. D. Ball, "Limiting Damage from Nuclear Attack", in D. Ball and J. Langtry, *Civil Defense and Australia's Security in the Nuclear Age*, Allen and Unwin, Sydney, 1983, pp. 163–164.

53. B. Blechman and D. Hart, "The Utility of Nuclear Weapons, The 1973 Middle East Crisis", *International Security*, Volume 7, no. 1, 1982, p. 140.

54. U.S. Joint Chiefs of Staff, Evaluation Board for Operations Crossroads, "The Evaluation of the Atomic Bomb as a Military Weapon" (mimeo), JCS 1691/7, Enclosure D, June 30, 1946, Modern Military Branch, U.S. National Archives, pp. 84–85.

55. R. Turco *et al.*, "Nuclear Winter: Global Consequences of Multiple Nuclear Explosions", and P. Ehrlich *et al.*, "Long-Term Biological Consequences of Nuclear War", *Science*, Volume 222, no. 4630, December 23, 1983, pp. 1283–1300.

56. U.S. Department of Defense, "The Potential Effects of Nuclear War on the Climate", (mimeo), report to U.S. Congress, Washington, D.C., March 1, 1985.

Chapter 20: Charting a New Pacific

1. In W. Bodde, "The South Pacific: Myths and Realities" (mimeo), Pacific Islands Luncheon, Hilton Hotel, February 11, 1982, p. 5; J. Borg, "Anti-Nuke Faction 'Biggest Threat' to U.S.–Pacific Ties", *Honolulu Advertiser*, February 11, 1982, p. B-11.

2. Quoted in M. Hamel-Green, "A Future for the South Pacific – Nuclear Free", *Peace Dossier 8*, Victorian Association for Peace Studies, December 1983, p. 4.

3. H. Schandler, "U.S. Interests and Arms Control Issues in Northeast Asia", paper to National Defense University Pacific Symposium, Honolulu, February 1985, pp. 14–23.

4. A. Arbatov, "Arms Limitation and the Situation in the Asian–Pacific and Indian Ocean Regions", *Asian Survey*, Volume 24, no. 11, November 1984, p. 1111.

5. M. Halperin, "Reshaping U.S. Nuclear Doctrine" (mimeo), Avoiding Nuclear War Project, Harvard University, 1985, pp. 130–132.

6. R. Forsberg, "The Freeze and Beyond", paper to Conference on Future of Arms

Control, Centre for Strategic and Defence Studies, Australian National University, August 1985, p. 9.

7. Nuclear Free and Independent Pacific Campaign, "The Case for a Comprehensive Nuclear Free Zone in the South Pacific" (mimeo), submission to South Pacific Forum States, Melbourne, 1985.

8. M. Weinstein, "Korea and Arms Control II", in J. Barton, edited, *Arms Control II*, Oelgeschlager Hain and Gunn, Boston, 1981, p. 176.

9. *Washington Post*, "U.S. to Consider 3-Way Korean Talks", February 1, 1984, p. 8; *Newsweek*, "Administration Infighting Over Korea", May 14, 1984, p. 19.

10. B. Cumings, "Ending the Cold War in Korea", *World Policy Journal*, Summer 1984, pp. 784, 788.

11. M. Weinstein, note 8, p. 176.

12. Young Whan Kihl, *Politics and Policies in Divided Korea, Regimes in Contest*, Westview Press, Boulder, Colorado, 1984, p. 205.

13. M. MccGwire, "Soviet–American Naval Arms Control", in G. Quester, edited, *Navies and Arms Control*, Praeger, New York, 1980, p. 84.

14. S. Lodgaard, "Nuclear Disengagement", in S. Lodgaard and M. Thee, edited, *Nuclear Disengagements in Europe*, Taylor and Francis, London, 1983, p. 38.

15. W. Kennedy, *Military Geography of the Sino-Soviet Border*, 434th Military Intelligence Detachment (Strategic), Strategic Studies Institute, U.S. Army War College, ACN 81047, Pennsylvania, 1981, pp. 6–7, 20.

16. R. Forsberg, "Confining the Military to Defense as a Route to Disarmament", *World Policy Journal*, Volume 1, no. 2, Winter 1984, p. 303. See also J. Gerson, *The Deadly Connection, Nuclear War and U.S. Intervention*, New Society Publishers, Philadelphia, Pennsylvania, 1986.

17. R. Forsberg, "Parallel Cuts in Nuclear and Conventional Forces", *Bulletin of the Atomic Scientists*, August 1985, p. 155.

18. R. Tanter, "Nuclear-Free Zones as a Demilitarization Strategy in Asia and the Pacific", paper to United Nations University Conference on Regional Peace and Security in Asia and Pacific, Tashkent, 1985, pp. 30–36, 41–44.

19. *Christian Science Monitor*, "South Asia Links", editorial, December 16, 1985.

20. R. Forsberg, "A Bilateral Nuclear-Weapon Freeze", *Scientific American*, Volume 247, no. 5, November 1982, pp. 52–61.

21. See D. Robie, "For and Against N-tests", *Star Weekender* (New Zealand), October 27, 1979; and M. Mataoa, "Tahitian Independence", in Pacific Concerns Resource Center, *Nuclear Free and Independent Pacific Conference 1983*, Honolulu, Hawaii, 1983, p. 44.

22. A. Karkoszka, *Strategic Disarmament Verification and National Security*, Taylor and Francis, London, 1977, pp. 81–86.

23. In H. Kurtz, "Higher Military Spending is Vital, Weinberger Tells U.S. Mayors", *Washington Post*, January 28, 1984, p. 2.

24. H. Gelman, "Soviet Policy Towards China", *Survey*, Volume 27, no. 118/119, pp. 166–169.

25. M. Klare and F. Schurmann, "Time to Rethink: What Does National Security Mean?" *Oakland Tribune*, April 27, 1984; J. Hull, "Cracks Are Forming in Business's Support of Defense Spending", *Wall Street Journal*, August 17, 1984, p. 1; S. Cohen, "Friends and Foes of Change", *Rethinking the Soviet Experience*, Oxford University Press, 1985, pp. 128–157.

26. L. Dunn and H. Kahn, *Trends in Nuclear Proliferation, 1975–1995*, report to U.S. Arms Control and Disarmament Agency, ACDA/PAB-264, Hudson Institute, Croton-on-Hudson, New York, 1976, pp. 51–55; and L. Dunn, *U.S. Defense Planning For a More Proliferated World*, report HI-2956/2-RR to Assistant Secretary of Defense, Program Analysis and Evaluation, U.S. Department of Defense, Hudson Institute, Croton-on-Hudson, New York, April 1979, pp. 218–248.

27. H. Schandler, note 3, p. 11.

28. J. Wolf, "Arms Control", in U. Johnson *et al.*, *China Policy for the Next Decade*, Oelgeschlager Gunn and Hain, Boston, 1984, pp. 406–408.

29. Yoshikazu Sakamoto, "Major Power Relations in East Asia", *Bulletin of the Atomic Scientists*, February 1984, p. 24.

30. R. Kiste and R. Herr, "The Potential for Soviet Penetration of the South Pacific Islands: An Assessment", paper prepared for U.S. Department of State, December 1984, p. 58.

31. G. Boyd, *Regionalism and Global Security*, Lexington Books, Lexington, Massachusetts, 1984, pp. 89–102.

32. B. Dickson edited, *The Emerging Pacific Community Concept: An American Perspective*, Center for Strategic and International Studies, Georgetown University, Washington, D.C., 1983.

33. R. Campbell, "Prospects for Siberian Economic Development", in D. Zagoria, edited, *Soviet Policy in the Far East*, Yale University Press, New Haven, 1982, p. 254; M. Weinstein, edited, *The Security of Korea, U.S. and Japanese Perspectives*, Westview Press, Boulder, Colorado, 1980, p. 163; D. Scheffer, "Normalization: Time for a U.S. Initiative", *World Policy Journal*, Spring, 1986, p. 104.

34. Pacific Concerns Resource Center, note 21, pp. 88–89; J. Falk, "The Labour Movement and Nuclear Technology in the South Pacific", in P. Davis edited, *Social Democracy in the Pacific*, Ross Publications, Auckland, 1983, pp. 148–163.

35. See Pacific Concerns Resource Center, note 21, and Pacific Concerns Resource Center, *Nuclear Free Pacific Conference 1980*, Honolulu, Hawaii.

36. See B. Shimabukuro, "All Nuke Waste Storage Opposed", *Pacific Daily News*, Sep-

tember 4, 1982; and F. Quimby, "Protests Mount Against Dumping", *Pacific Daily News*, July 1, 1980.

37. In Nuclear Free and Independent Pacific Campaign, note 7, p. 11.

Epilogue: Just the Two of Us?

1. In Joint Committee on Foreign Affairs and Defence, *Threats to Australia's Security – Their Nature and Probability*, Australian Government Publishing Service, Canberra, 1981, p. 18.

2. R. Bernstein, "Australia Assures U.S. on Use of Joint Bases", *New York Times*, June 19, 1983, p. 15.

3. In G. Moffett, "Shultz Heads East to Reinforce U.S. Ties with Pacific Basin Allies", *Christian Science Monitor*, July 5, 1985, p. 5.

4. P. Hayes, *et al.*, "Catastrophic Dimensions of Nuclear Weapons in Australia, A Latent Political Time-Bomb" (mimeo), background information supplied to Australian Senate Standing Committee on Foreign Affairs and Defence, November 1985.

5. D. Ball, "Limiting Damage from Nuclear Attack", in D. Ball and J. Langtry edited, *Civil Defence and Australia's Security in the Nuclear Age*, Allen and Unwin, Sydney, 1983, pp. 158–168.

6. For analysis of Soviet targeting, see D. Ball, *Soviet Strategic Planning and the Control of Nuclear War*, Reference Paper no. 109, Strategic and Defence Studies Centre, Australian National University, Canberra, 1983, pp. 7–9; J. Douglass and A. Hoeber, *Soviet Strategy for Nuclear War*, Hoover Institution Press, Stanford, California, 1979, pp. 72–88.

7. B. Lambeth and K. Lewis, "Economic Targeting in Nuclear War: U.S. and Soviet Approaches", *Orbis*, Spring 1983, p. 145.

8. In G. Quester, *New Alternatives for Targeting the Soviet Union*, Analytical Assessments Corporation, report to Defense Nuclear Agency, DNA 001-79-C-0061, Marina del Rey, California, 1979, p. 27.

9. D. Ball, note 5, p. 175.

10. Joint Committee On Foreign Affairs and Defence, note 1, pp. 25, 31–37.

11. R. Babbage, "Australian Defence Planning, Force Structure and Equipment: The American Effect", *Australian Outlook*, Volume 38, no. 3, December 1984, pp. 165–168.

12. N. Gayler, interview with authors, April 24, 1984, Washington, D.C.

13. W. Hayden, "The ANZUS Treaty", speech to Fabian Society, Lorne, Victoria, May 5, 1985, p. 6.

14. A. Mack, "Arms Control and the Joint Facilities: The Case of Nurrungar" (mimeo), paper to the Future of Arms Control Conference, Centre for Strategic and Defence Studies, Australian National University, August 1985, pp. 6–8, 11.

15. T. Schelling and M. Halperin, *Strategy and Arms Control*, Pergamon-Braissey, New Jersey, 1985, pp. 10–11.

16. Lieutenant General Robert Bazley in 1982, in F. A'Hearn, *The Informational Arsenal, A C^3I Profile*, Center for Information Policy Research, Harvard University, November 1983, p. 108.

17. J. Falk, *Taking Australia Off the Map, Facing the Threat of Nuclear War*, Penguin Books, Melbourne, 1983, pp. 169–173.

18. T. Karas, "Military Satellites and War-Fighting Doctrines", and D. Shapley, "Strategic Doctrine, The Militarization and 'Semi-Militarization' of Space", in B. Jasani, edited, *Space Weapons, The Arms Control Dilemma*, Taylor and Francis, London, 1984, pp. 48, 61–63.

19. A. Mack, note 14, pp. 14–18.

20. *Ibid.*, p. 35.

21. *Ibid.*, 24–25.

22. Commander, Naval Telecommunications Command, "U.S. Naval Communication Station Harold E. Holt; Mission and Function Of", NAVTELCOM Instruction 5450.25C, TelCom-01, February 2, 1983, enclosure 1, p. 1, released under F.O.I.A. request; D. Ball, *A Suitable Piece of Real Estate, American Installations in Australia*, Hale and Iremonger, Sydney, 1980, p. 52.

23. In M. Hedy, "Lehman: We'll Sink Their Subs", *Defense Week*, May 13, 1985, p. 18; T. Stefanik, *Strategic Antisubmarine Warfare and Naval Strategy*, forthcoming, Lexington Books, Massachusetts, 1986.

24. J. Watkins, "The Maritime Strategy", *Proceedings*, January 1986, p. 11.

25. M. Krepon, "The Political Dynamics of Verification and Compliance Debates", in W. Potter edited, *Verification and Arms Control*, Lexington Books, Massachusetts, 1985, pp. 144–150; A. Krass "The Politics of Verification", *World Policy Journal*, Fall 1985, pp. 744–745.

26. B. Keller, "Imperfect Science, Important Conclusions", *New York Times*, July 28, 1985, p. 4E.

27. P. Nitze, "Considerations Bearing on the Merits of the SALT II Agreement as Signed at Vienna", in C. Tyroler, edited, *Alerting America, The Papers of the Committee on the Present Danger*, Pergamon-Braissey, New Jersey, 1984, pp. 143–158.

28. M. Gordon, "CIA Downgrades Estimate of Soviet SS-19 . . . Says Missile Too Inaccurate for First Strikes", *National Journal*, July 20, 1985, p. 1692.

29. N. Gayler, "A Commander-in-Chief's Perspective On Nuclear Weapons" and "The Way Out: A General Nuclear Settlement", in G. Prins, edited, *The Nuclear Crisis Reader*, Vintage, New York, 1984, pp. 15–28 and pp. 234–244.

30. D. Ball, note 22, pp. 130–138.

31. P. Morgan, *Deterrence, A Conceptual Analysis*, Sage Publications, Beverly Hills, California, 1983, pp. 116–118.

32. P. Bracken, *The Command and Control of Nuclear Forces*, Yale University Press, New Haven, 1983, p. 220.

33. See A. Rapoport, *Strategy and Conscience*, Schocken, New York, 1969, pp. 25–26.

34. *Ibid.*, p. 25.

35. Telephone interview with authors, August 1, 1985.

36. In G. Allison, *Essence of Decision, Explaining the Cuban Missile Crisis*, Little Brown, Boston, 1971, p. 199.

37. *Ibid.*, p. 200.

38. *Ibid.*

39. In J. Siracusa and G. Barclay, "The Historical Influence of the United States on Australian Strategic Thinking", *Australian Outlook*, Volume 38, no. 3, December 1984, p. 155.

40. In P. Cole-Adams, "U.S. Hardline on Soviets Breeds Nuclear Aversion", *Age* (Melbourne), February 15, 1986.

41. R. Babbage, *Rethinking Australia's Defence*, Queensland University Press, St. Lucia, 1980, pp. 165–168; D. Martin, *Armed Neutrality for Australia*, Dove Communications, Melbourne, 1984, pp. 133–197.

42. J. Camilleri, "A Peace Strategy for Australia", *Bowyang* (Melbourne), no. 8, 1983, pp. 55–57.

43. See A. Renouf, *Let Justice Be Done, The Foreign Policy of Dr. H.V. Evatt*, University of Queensland Press, St. Lucia, 1983; R. Bell, *Unequal Allies, Australian-American Relations and the Pacific War*, Melbourne University Press, 1977, pp. 145–225.

Sunrise over the U.S. Electronic Security Group's antenna installation,
Misawa, Japan, August 1983
(U.S. Air Force)

LIST OF TABLES, ☆
MAPS AND FIGURES

Tables

Maps

Figures

INDEX ☆

FOR THE BEST IN PAPERBACKS, LOOK FOR THE

In every corner of the world, on every subject under the sun, Penguins represent quality and variety – the very best in publishing today.

For complete information about books available from Penguin and how to order them, write to us at the appropriate address below. Please note that for copyright reasons the selection of books varies from country to country.

In the United Kingdom: For a complete list of books available from Penguin in the U.K., please write to *Dept EP, Penguin Books Ltd, Harmondsworth, Middlesex, UB7 0DA*

In the United States: For a complete list of books available from Penguin in the U.S., please write to *Dept BA, Viking Penguin, 299 Murray Hill Parkway, East Rutherford, New Jersey 07073*

In Canada: For a complete list of books available from Penguin in Canada, please write to *Penguin Books Canada Limited, 2801 John Street, Markham, Ontario L3R 1B4*

In Australia: For a complete list of books available from Penguin in Australia, please write to the *Marketing Department, Penguin Books Australia Ltd, P.O. Box 257, Ringwood, Victoria 3134*

In New Zealand: For a complete list of books available from Penguin in New Zealand, please write to the *Marketing Department, Penguin Books (N.Z.) Ltd, Private Bag, Takapuna, Auckland 9*

In India: For a complete list of books available from Penguin in India, please write to *Penguin Overseas Ltd, 706 Eros Apartments, 56 Nehru Place, New Delhi 110019*

FOR THE BEST IN PAPERBACKS, LOOK FOR THE

A CHOICE OF PENGUINS AND PELICANS

A Question of Economics   Peter Donaldson

Twenty key issues – the City, trade unions, 'free market forces' and many others – are presented clearly and fully in this major book based on a television series.

The Economist Economics   Rupert Pennant-Rea and Clive Crook

Based on a series of 'briefs' published in the *Economist* in 1984, this important new book makes the key issues of contemporary economic thinking accessible to the general reader.

The Tyranny of the Status Quo   Milton and Rose Friedman

Despite the rhetoric, big government has actually *grown* under Reagan and Thatcher. The Friedmans consider why this is – and what we can do now to change it.

Business Wargames   Barrie G. James

Successful companies use military strategy to win. Barrie James shows how – and draws some vital lessons for today's manager.

Atlas of Management Thinking   Edward de Bono

This fascinating book provides a vital repertoire of non-verbal images – to help activate the right side of any manager's brain.

The Winning Streak   Walter Goldsmith and David Clutterbuck

A brilliant analysis of what Britain's best-run and successful companies have in common – a must for all managers.

Lateral Thinking for Management Edward de Bono

Creativity and lateral thinking can work together for managers in developing new products or ideas; Edward de Bono shows how.

Understanding Organizations Charles B. Handy

Of practical as well as theoretical interest, this book shows how general concepts can help solve specific organizational problems.

The Art of Japanese Management Richard Tanner Pascale and Anthony G. Athos With an Introduction by Sir Peter Parker

Japanese industrial success owes much to Japanese management techniques, which we in the West neglect at our peril. The lessons are set out in this important book.

My Years with General Motors Alfred P. Sloan With an Introduction by John Egan

A business classic by the man who took General Motors to the top – and kept them there for decades.

Introducing Management Ken Elliott and Peter Lawrence (eds.)

An important and comprehensive collection of texts on modern management which draw some provocative conclusions.

English Culture and the Decline of the Industrial Spirit Martin J. Wiener

A major analysis of why the 'world's first industrial nation has never been comfortable with industrialism'. 'Very persuasive' – Anthony Sampson in the *Observer*

A CHOICE OF PENGUINS AND PELICANS

Dinosaur and Co Tom Lloyd

A lively and optimistic survey of a new breed of businessmen who are breaking away from huge companies to form dynamic enterprises in microelectronics, biotechnology and other developing areas.

The Money Machine: How the City Works Philip Coggan

How are the big deals made? Which are the institutions that *really* matter? What causes the pound to rise or interest rates to fall? This book provides clear and concise answers to these and many other money-related questions.

Parkinson's Law C. Northcote Parkinson

'Work expands so as to fill the time available for its completion': that law underlies this 'extraordinarily funny and witty book' (Stephen Potter in the *Sunday Times*) which also makes some painfully serious points for those in business or the Civil Service.

Debt and Danger Harold Lever and Christopher Huhne

The international debt crisis was brought about by Western bankers in search of quick profit and is now one of our most pressing problems. This book looks at the background and shows what we must do to avoid disaster.

Lloyd's Bank Tax Guide 1986/7

Cut through the complexities! Work the system in *your* favour! Don't pay a penny more than you have to! Written for anyone who has to deal with personal tax, this up-to-date and concise new handbook includes all the important changes in this year's budget.

The Spirit of Enterprise George Gilder

A lucidly written and excitingly argued defence of capitalism and the role of the entrepreneur within it.

FOR THE BEST IN PAPERBACKS, LOOK FOR THE

A CHOICE OF PENGUINS AND PELICANS

Metamagical Themas   Douglas R. Hofstadter

A new mind-bending bestseller by the author of *Gödel, Escher, Bach*.

The Body   Anthony Smith

A completely updated edition of the well-known book by the author of *The Mind*. The clear and comprehensive text deals with everything from sex to the skeleton, sleep to the senses.

Why Big Fierce Animals are Rare   Paul Colinvaux

'A vivid picture of how the natural world works' – *Nature*

How to Lie with Statistics   Darrell Huff

A classic introduction to the ways statistics can be used to prove *anything*, the book is both informative and 'wildly funny' – *Evening News*

The Penguin Dictionary of Computers   Anthony Chandor and others

An invaluable glossary of over 300 words, from 'aberration' to 'zoom' by way of 'crippled lead-frog tests' and 'output bus drivers'.

The Cosmic Code   Heinz R. Pagels

Tracing the historical development of quantum physics, the author describes the baffling and seemingly lawless world of leptons, hadrons, gluons and quarks and provides a lucid and exciting guide for the layman to the world of infinitesimal particles.

A CHOICE OF PENGUINS AND PELICANS

Setting Genes to Work   Stephanie Yanchinski

Combining informativeness and accuracy with readability, Stephanie Yanchinski explores the hopes, fears and, more importantly, the realities of biotechnology – the science of using micro-organisms to manufacture chemicals, drugs, fuel and food.

Brighter than a Thousand Suns   Robert Jungk

'By far the most interesting historical work on the atomic bomb I know of' – C. P. Snow

Turing's Man   J. David Bolter

We live today in a computer age, which has meant some startling changes in the ways we understand freedom, creativity and language. This major book looks at the implications.

Einstein's Universe   Nigel Calder

'A valuable contribution to the de-mystification of relativity' – *Nature*

The Creative Computer   Donald R. Michie and Rory Johnston

Computers *can* create the new knowledge we need to solve some of our most pressing human problems; this path-breaking book shows how.

Only One Earth   Barbara Ward and Rene Dubos

An extraordinary document which explains with eloquence and passion how we should go about 'the care and maintenance of a small planet'.

A CHOICE OF PENGUINS AND PELICANS

The Second World War (6 volumes)   Winston S. Churchill

The definitive history of the cataclysm which swept the world for the second time in thirty years.

1917: The Russian Revolutions and the Origins of Present-Day Communism
Leonard Schapiro

A superb narrative history of one of the greatest episodes in modern history by one of our greatest historians.

Imperial Spain 1496–1716   J. H. Elliot

A brilliant modern study of the sudden rise of a barren and isolated country to be the greatest power on earth, and of its equally sudden decline. 'Outstandingly good' – *Daily Telegraph*

Joan of Arc: The Image of Female Heroism   Marina Warner

'A profound book, about human history in general and the place of women in it' – Christopher Hill

Man and the Natural World: Changing Attitudes in England 1500–1800
Keith Thomas

'A delight to read and a pleasure to own' – Auberon Waugh in the *Sunday Telegraph*

The Making of the English Working Class   E. P. Thompson

Probably the most imaginative – and the most famous – post-war work of English social history.

A CHOICE OF PENGUINS AND PELICANS

The French Revolution   Christopher Hibbert

'One of the best accounts of the Revolution that I know . . . Mr Hibbert is outstanding' – J. H. Plumb in the *Sunday Telegraph*

The Germans   Gordon A. Craig

An intimate study of a complex and fascinating nation by 'one of the ablest and most distinguished American historians of modern Germany' – Hugh Trevor-Roper

Ireland: A Positive Proposal   Kevin Boyle and Tom Hadden

A timely and realistic book on Northern Ireland which explains the historical context – and offers a practical and coherent set of proposals which could actually work.

A History of Venice   John Julius Norwich

'Lord Norwich has loved and understood Venice as well as any other Englishman has ever done' – Peter Levi in the *Sunday Times*

Montaillou: Cathars and Catholics in a French Village 1294–1324
Emmanuel Le Roy Ladurie

'A classic adventure in eavesdropping across time' – Michael Ratcliffe in *The Times*

Star Wars   E. P. Thompson and others

Is Star Wars a serious defence strategy or just a science fiction fantasy? This major book sets out all the arguments and makes an unanswerable case *against* Star Wars.

The Apartheid Handbook   Roger Omond

This book provides the essential hard information about how apartheid actually works from day to day and fills in the details behind the headlines.

The World Turned Upside Down   Christopher Hill

This classic study of radical ideas during the English Revolution 'will stand as a notable monument to . . . one of the finest historians of the present age' – *The Times Literary Supplement*

Islam in the World   Malise Ruthven

'His exposition of "the Qurenic world view" is the most convincing, and the most appealing, that I have read' – Edward Mortimer in *The Times*

The Knight, the Lady and the Priest   Georges Duby

'A very fine book' (Philippe Aries) that traces back to its medieval origin one of our most important institutions, modern marriage.

A Social History of England   New Edition   Asa Briggs

'A treasure house of scholarly knowledge . . . beautifully written and full of the author's love of his country, its people and its landscape' – John Keegan in the *Sunday Times*, Books of the Year

The Second World War   A. J. P. Taylor

A brilliant and detailed illustrated history, enlivened by all Professor Taylor's customary iconoclasm and wit.

A CHOICE OF PENGUINS AND PELICANS

Adieux Simone de Beauvoir

This 'farewell to Sartre' by his life-long companion is a 'true labour of love' (the *Listener*) and 'an extraordinary achievement' (*New Statesman*).

British Society 1914–45 John Stevenson

A major contribution to the Pelican Social History of Britain, which 'will undoubtedly be the standard work for students of modern Britain for many years to come' – *The Times Educational Supplement*

The Pelican History of Greek Literature Peter Levi

A remarkable survey covering all the major writers from Homer to Plutarch, with brilliant translations by the author, one of the leading poets of today.

Art and Literature Sigmund Freud

Volume 14 of the Pelican Freud Library contains Freud's major essays on Leonardo, Michelangelo and Dostoevsky, plus shorter pieces on Shakespeare, the nature of creativity and much more.

A History of the Crusades Sir Steven Runciman

This three-volume history of the events which transferred world power to Western Europe – and founded Modern History – has been universally acclaimed as a masterpiece.

A Night to Remember Walter Lord

The classic account of the sinking of the *Titanic*. 'A stunning book, incomparably the best on its subject and one of the most exciting books of this or any year' – *The New York Times*

FOR THE BEST IN PAPERBACKS, LOOK FOR THE 🐧

PENGUIN REFERENCE BOOKS

The Penguin English Dictionary

Over 1,000 pages long and with over 68,000 definitions, this cheap, compact and totally up-to-date book is ideal for today's needs. It includes many technical and colloquial terms, guides to pronunciation and common abbreviations.

The Penguin Reference Dictionary

The ideal comprehensive guide to written and spoken English the world over, with detailed etymologies and a wide selection of colloquial and idiomatic usage. There are over 100,000 entries and thousands of examples of how words are actually used – all clear, precise and up-to-date.

The Penguin English Thesaurus

This unique volume will increase anyone's command of the English language and build up your word power. Fully cross-referenced, it includes synonyms of every kind (formal or colloquial, idiomatic and figurative) for almost 900 headings. It is a must for writers and utterly fascinating for any English speaker.

The Penguin Dictionary of Quotations

A treasure-trove of over 12,000 new gems and old favourites, from Aesop and Matthew Arnold to Xenophon and Zola.

FOR THE BEST IN PAPERBACKS, LOOK FOR THE

PENGUIN REFERENCE BOOKS

The Penguin Guide to the Law

This acclaimed reference book is designed for everyday use, and forms the most comprehensive handbook ever published on the law as it affects the individual.

The Penguin Medical Encyclopedia

Covers the body and mind in sickness and in health, including drugs, surgery, history, institutions, medical vocabulary and many other aspects. 'Highly commendable' – *Journal of the Institute of Health Education*

The Penguin French Dictionary

This invaluable French-English, English-French dictionary includes both the literary and dated vocabulary needed by students, and the up-to-date slang and specialized vocabulary (scientific, legal, sporting, etc) needed in everyday life. As a passport to the French language, it is second to none.

A Dictionary of Literary Terms

Defines over 2,000 literary terms (including lesser known, foreign language and technical terms) explained with illustrations from literature past and present.

The Penguin Map of Europe

Covers all land eastwards to the Urals, southwards to North Africa and up to Syria, Iraq and Iran. Scale – 1:5,500,000, 4-colour artwork. Features main roads, railways, oil and gas pipelines, plus extra information including national flags, currencies and populations.

The Penguin Dictionary of Troublesome Words

A witty, straightforward guide to the pitfalls and hotly disputed issues in standard written English, illustrated with examples and including a glossary of grammatical terms and an appendix on punctuation.